WINTE

'C. J. Sansom has earned a genre-transcending reputation with his first two novels, the 16th-century crime thrillers, *Dissolution* and *Dark Fire* . . . *Winter in Madrid* is a departure . . . There are shades of Julian Mitchell's *Another Country* in the portrayal of public-school ideological rebellion, and throughout Sansom offers an intriguing and equivocal vision of a country in ideological turmoil, to which the three Rookwood men are drawn by separate but equally powerful motives . . . This is a novel about systems of authority and ideology: always, in the end, corrupting and corruptible, both beyond and beneath the scope of individual heroism' *Sunday Telegraph*

'Sansom cannot easily be pigeonholed. [*Winter in Madrid*] subtly mixes elements of different genres: part thriller, part romance, and part historical drama . . . Post-civil war Madrid is finely and minutely observed, giving the entire novel a remarkable sense of place . . . Together with the book's intricate and tightly structured plotting, Sansom spins the reader through to its bloody conclusion . . . Compelling and well-written, [this is] a well-crafted and entertaining piece of fiction' *Sunday Express*

'Sansom's action-packed thriller is a classic tale of old loyalties pitched against new ideologies. Its portrait of murderous corruption, ranging from the Monarchists and Falangists in the government to the diplomats at the British Embassy, shows Franco's Madrid to have been even murkier than Harry Lime's Vienna' *Daily Mail*

'The reality of Madrid of 1940 is recreated in authentic and believable detail. Sansom evokes the sights and sounds of a city [where] fear, hatred and desolation are palpable. There are some powerful set pieces in the novel . . . As a portrait of a traumatized city, wrapped in silence because speech was dangerous, *Winter in Madrid* is a remarkable achievement'

Times Literary Supplement

'It is a bold author who, having found acclaim with two historical novels firmly grounded in a particular period, sets his third novel in an entirely different place some 500 years later – but that is what C. J. Sansom has done, and he has pulled it off magnificently . . . *Winter in Madrid* shares with [his first two novels] the author's enviable ability to land his readers in an alien world, yet make them feel entirely at home . . . In Sansom's capable hands, story, characters and that indefinable spirit of place meld and twist into a narrative that grips the reader throughout its 500-plus pages . . . weaving together hard facts with romantic fiction – his bleak winter thriller chills to the bone' *Literary Review*

'*Winter in Madrid* may surprise fans of Sansom's usual medieval crime novels. It finds him dispensing with his quill and fast-forwarding five centuries to 1940s Spain . . . If post-civil war Madrid isn't natural territory for Sansom, you wouldn't know it – the sorry state of the city is evoked in all its blood, dust and melancholy, while the story itself never becomes bogged down in polemic . . . The climax is tremendously exciting and skilfully played out, and the characters, while tending towards stereotypes, are so convincing that it's tempting to cast the actors who will play them in the inevitable big-screen adaptation' *Time Out*

'A compelling tale of game-playing, memories and the impact of impossible choices. If you like Sebastian Faulks and Carlos Ruiz Zafón, you'll love this' *Daily Express*

'Sansom adroitly draws the disparate strands of his ambitious saga together. His non-pareil evocations of time and place anchor his characters with satisfying precision . . . There are touches of Graham Greene; Hemingway's here too . . . But Sansom transfigures his sources into a moral universe very much his own. The sexual and moral equivocation is handled with cool assurance' *Independent*

C. J. SANSOM was educated at Birmingham University, where he took a BA and then a PhD in history. After working in a variety of jobs, he retrained as a solicitor and practised in Sussex, until becoming a full-time writer. As well as *Winter in Madrid*, C. J. Sansom has written three novels in his historical crime series featuring lawyer Matthew Shardlake. He lives in Sussex.

Also by C. J. Sansom

The Shardlake series

DISSOLUTION

DARK FIRE

SOVEREIGN

C. J. SANSOM

WINTER IN MADRID

PAN BOOKS

First published 2006 by Macmillan

This paperback edition published 2006 by Pan Books
an imprint of Pan Macmillan Ltd
Pan Macmillan, 20 New Wharf Road, London N1 9RR
Basingstoke and Oxford
Associated companies throughout the world
www.panmacmillan.com

ISBN-13: 978-0-330-44263-3
ISBN-10: 0-330-44263-5

3 5 7 9 8 6 4 2

A CIP catalogue record for this book is available from the British Library.

Typeset by SetSystems Ltd, Saffron Walden, Essex
Printed and bound in Great Britain by
Mackays of Chatham plc, Chatham, Kent

To the memory of

the thousands of children of Republican parents

who disappeared into the orphanages of

Franco's Spain

Prologue

The Jarama Valley, Spain, February 1937

BERNIE HAD LAIN at the foot of the knoll for hours, half conscious.

The British Battalion had been brought up to the front two days before, rattling across the bare Castilian plain in an ancient locomotive; they had marched by night to the front line. The Battalion had a few older men, veterans of the Great War, but most of the soldiers were working-class boys without even the Officer Training Corps experience that Bernie and the smattering of other public-school men possessed. Even here in their own war the working class stood at a disadvantage.

The Republic had held a strong position, on top of a hill that sloped down steeply to the Jarama river valley, dotted with little knolls and planted with olive trees. In the far distance the grey smudge of Madrid was visible, the city that had withstood the Fascists since the generals' uprising last summer. Madrid, where Barbara was.

Franco's army had already crossed the river. There were Moroccan colonial troops down there, experts at using every fold in the ground as cover. The Battalion was ordered into position to defend the hill. Their rifles were old, there was a shortage of ammunition and many did not fire properly. They had been issued with French steel helmets from the Great War that the old soldiers said weren't bullet-proof.

Despite the Battalion's ragged fire, the Moors slipped gradually up the hill as the morning advanced, hundreds of silent deadly bundles in their grey ponchos, appearing and disappearing again among the olive trees, coming ever closer. Shelling from the Fascist positions began, the yellow earth around the Battalion positions exploding in huge fountains to the terror of the raw troops. Then in the afternoon the order to retreat came. Everything turned to chaos. As they ran, Bernie saw the ground between the olive trees was strewn with books the soldiers had thrown from their packs to lighten them – poetry and Marxist primers and pornography from the Madrid street markets.

That night the Battalion survivors crouched exhausted in an old sunken road on the *meseta*. There was no news of how the battle had gone elsewhere along the line. Bernie slept from sheer exhaustion.

In the morning the Russian staff commander ordered the remnants of the Battalion to advance again. Bernie saw Captain Wintringham arguing with him, their heads outlined against a cold sky turning from purple-pink to blue as the sun rose. The Battalion was exhausted, outnumbered; the Moors were dug in now and had brought up machine guns. But the Russian was adamant, his face set.

The men were ordered to line up, huddling against the lip of the sunken road. The Fascists had begun firing again with the dawn and the noise was already tremendous, loud rifle cracks and the stutter of the machine guns. Standing waiting for the order to go over, Bernie was too tired to think. The phrase 'fucking done for, fucking done for' went round and round in his head, like a metronome. Many of the men were too exhausted to do anything but stare blindly ahead; others shook with fear.

Wintringham led the charge himself and went down almost at once with a bullet to the leg. Bernie winced and jerked as bullets cracked around him, watching the men he had trained with collapse with howls or sad little sighs as they were hit. A hundred yards out the desperate urge to fall and hug the ground became too strong and Bernie threw himself behind the shelter of a thick old olive tree.

He lay against the gnarled trunk for a long time, bullets whining and cracking around him, looking at the bodies of his comrades, blood turning the pale earth black as it soaked in. He twisted his body, trying to burrow as deep as he could into the ground.

Late in the morning the firing ceased, though Bernie could hear it continuing further up the line. To his right he saw a high, steep knoll covered with scrubby grass. He decided to make a dash for it. He got up and ran, crouched over almost double, and had almost reached cover when there was a crack and he felt a stinging blow in his right thigh. He spun over and hit the earth. He could feel blood trickling down his trousers but dared not look round. Using his elbows and his good leg he crawled frantically towards the shelter of the knoll, his old arm injury sending pain lancing into his shoulder. Another bullet made earth spit up around him but he made it to the knoll. He threw himself into the lee of the little hill and passed out.

When he came to it was afternoon; he was lying in a long shadow and the warmth of the day was receding. He had fallen against the incline of the hill and could see only a few feet of earth and stones ahead of him. He was conscious of a raging thirst. Everything was quiet and still; he could hear a bird singing in one of the olive trees but also a murmur of distant voices somewhere. They were talking Spanish so it must be the Fascists, unless the Spanish troops further north had made a breakthrough, which he couldn't believe after what had happened to his section. He lay still, his head cushioned in the dusty earth, conscious that his right leg was numb.

He drifted in and out of consciousness; still he could hear the murmuring voices, ahead and to the left somewhere. Some time later he woke properly, his head suddenly clear, his thirst agonizing. There was no sound of voices now, just the bird singing; surely not the same one.

Bernie had thought Spain would be hot; the memories of his visit with Harry six years ago were all of dry heat, hard as a hammer. But in February, although the days were warm enough, it grew cold at dusk, and he wasn't sure he could get through a night out here. He could feel the lice crawling in the thick down on his stomach. They had infested the base camp and Bernie hated their crawling itch. Pain was a strange thing: his leg was bearable but the urge to scratch his stomach was desperate. For all he knew, though, he could be surrounded by Fascist soldiers who had taken his still form for a corpse, and would open fire at any sign of movement.

He raised his head a little, gritting his teeth, dreading the impact of a bullet. Nothing. Above him only the bare hillside. Stiffly, he turned over. Pain shot through his leg like a knife and he had to clench his jaw shut against a scream. He pulled himself up on his elbows and looked down. Half his trouser leg was torn away and his thigh was covered with dark, clotted blood. It wasn't bleeding now, the bullet must have missed the artery, but if he moved too much it might start again.

To the left he saw two bodies in Brigade uniforms. Both had fallen on their faces and one was too far off to see but the other was McKie, the young Scots miner. Fearfully, trying not to move his leg, he swivelled on his elbows again and looked upwards, to the top of the knoll.

Forty feet above him, projecting over the lip of the hill, was a tank. One of the German ones Hitler had given Franco. An arm protruded limply from the gun turret. The Fascists must have brought up tanks and this one had been stopped just before it lurched down the knoll. It was precariously balanced, the front protruding almost halfway over; from where he lay Bernie could see the pipes and bolts of the underside, the heavy plated tracks. It could topple over on him at any moment; he had to move.

He began crawling slowly away. Pain stabbed through his leg and after a couple of yards he had to stop, sweating and gasping. He could see McKie now. One arm had been shot off and lay a few yards away. Untidy brown hair was ruffled slightly by the breeze, in death as it had been in life, though the face beneath was already white. McKie's eyes were closed, the pleasantly ugly face looked peaceful. Poor devil, Bernie thought, and felt tears pricking the corners of his eyes.

When he had first seen dead bodies, the men brought back from the fighting in Madrid and laid out in rows in the street, Bernie had felt sick with horror. Yet when they had gone into battle yesterday his squeamishness had vanished. It had to when you were under fire, Pa had told him on one of the rare occasions he spoke about the Somme, every sense had to be tuned to survival. You didn't see, you *watched*, as an animal watches. You didn't hear, you *listened*, as an animal listens. You became as focused and heartless as an animal. But Pa had long spells of depression, evenings spent sitting in his little office behind the shop, head bowed under the weak yellow light as he fought to forget the trenches.

Bernie remembered McKie's jokes about how Scotland would be independent under socialism, laughing as he looked forward to its being free of the useless Sassenachs. He licked his dry lips. Would this moment, McKie's hair ruffling in the breeze, come to him in dreams if he got out of it alive, even if they succeeded and created a new, free world?

He heard a creak, a small, metallic sound. He looked up; the tank was swaying slightly, the long gun barrel outlined against the darkening sky moving slowly up and down. Surely his movements at the bottom of the knoll couldn't have been enough to shift it, but it was moving.

Bernie tried to rise but pain stabbed through his injured leg. He began crawling again, past McKie's body. His leg hurt more now and he could feel blood oozing down it. His head was swimming; he had a horror of fainting and of the tank falling down the hill and crashing down onto his prone body. He must stay conscious.

Directly ahead of him was a puddle of dirty water. Despite the danger, his thirst was so great that he buried his head in it and took a deep drink. It tasted of earth and made him want to retch. He lifted his head and jerked back in surprise as he caught the reflection of his face: every line was filled with dirt above a straggly beard and his eyes looked mad. He suddenly heard Barbara's voice in his head, remembered soft hands on his neck. 'You're so beautiful,' she had said once. 'Too beautiful for me.' What would she say now?

There was another creak, louder this time, and he looked up to see the tank inching slowly forwards. A little stream of earth and stones pattered down the side of the knoll. 'Oh Christ,' he breathed. 'Oh Christ.' He heaved himself forward.

There was a creaking noise and the tank went over. It rolled slowly down the hill with a clanking grinding noise, missing Bernie's feet by inches. At the bottom the long gun buried itself in the earth and the tank came to a halt, shuddering like a huge felled beast. The observer was thrown from his turret and landed face down, spread-eagled in the trench. His hair was whitish-blond: a German. Bernie closed his eyes, gasping with relief.

Another noise made him turn and look upwards. Five men stood in a row at the top of the knoll, drawn by the noise. Their faces were as dirty and weary as Bernie's. They were Fascists; they wore the olive-green battledress of Franco's troops. They raised their rifles, covering him. One of the soldiers pulled a pistol from his holster. There was a click as he slipped the safety catch. He stepped forward and descended the knoll.

Bernie leaned on one hand and raised the other in weary supplication.

The Fascist came to a halt three feet away. He was a tall, thin man with a little moustache like the Generalísimo's. His face was hard and angry.

'*Me entrego*,' Bernie said. 'I surrender.' It was all there was left to do.

'*¡Cabrón comunista!*' The man had a heavy southern accent. Bernie was still trying to make out the words as the Fascist brought up his pistol and aimed at his head.

Part One

☆

AUTUMN

Chapter One

London, September 1940

A BOMB HAD FALLEN in Victoria Street. It had gouged a wide crater in the road and taken down the fronts of several shops. The street was roped off; ARP men and volunteers had formed a chain and were carefully moving rubble from one of the ruined buildings. Harry realized there must be someone under there. The efforts of the rescuers, old men and boys caked with the dust that hung round them in a pall, seemed pitiful against the huge piles of brick and plaster. He put down his suitcase.

Coming into Victoria on the train, he had seen other craters and shattered buildings. He had felt oddly distanced from the destruction, as he had since the big raids began ten days before. Down in Surrey, Uncle James had almost given himself a stroke looking at the photographs in the *Telegraph*. Harry had scarcely responded as his uncle snarled red-faced over this new example of German frightfulness. His mind had retreated from the fury.

It could not retreat, though, from the crater in Westminster suddenly and immediately before him. At once he was back at Dunkirk: German dive-bombers overhead, the sandy shoreline exploding. He clenched his hands, digging the nails into his palms as he took deep breaths. His heart began pounding but he didn't start shaking; he could control his reactions now.

An ARP warden strode across to him, a hard-faced man in his fifties with a grey pencil moustache and ramrod back, his black uniform streaked with dust.

'You can't come up 'ere,' he snapped briskly. 'Road's closed. Can't you see we've 'ad a bomb?' He looked suspicious, disapproving, wondering no doubt why an apparently fit man in his early thirties was not in uniform.

'I'm sorry,' Harry said. 'I'm just up from the country. I hadn't realized it was so bad.'

Most Cockneys confronted with Harry's public school accent would have adopted a servile tone, but not this man. 'There's no escape anywhere,' he rasped. 'Not this time. Not in the tahn, not in the country either for long, if yer ask me.' The warden looked Harry over coldly. 'You on leave?'

'Invalided out,' Harry said abruptly. 'Look, I have to get to Queen Anne's Gate. Official business.'

The warden's manner changed at once. He took Harry's arm and steered him round. 'Go up through Petty France. There was only the one bomb round here.'

'Thank you.'

'That's all right, sir.' The warden leaned in close. 'Were you at Dunkirk?'

'Yes.'

'There's blood and ruin down the Isle of Dogs. I was in the trenches last time, I knew it'd come again and this time everyone'd be in it, not just soldiering men. You'll get the chance to fight again, you wait and see. Bayonet into Jerry's guts, twist and then out again, eh?' He gave a strange smile, then stepped back and saluted, pale eyes glittering.

'Thank you.' Harry saluted and turned away, crossing into Gillingham Street. He frowned; the man's words had filled him with disgust.

AT VICTORIA it had been as busy as a normal Monday; it seemed the reports that London was carrying on as usual were true. As he walked on through the broad Georgian streets everything was quiet in the autumn sunlight. But for the white crosses of tape over the windows to protect against blast, you could have been back before the war. An occasional businessman in a bowler hat walked by, there were still nannies wheeling prams. People's expressions were normal, even cheerful. Many had left their gas masks at home, though Harry had his slung over his shoulder in its square box. He knew the defiant good humour most people had adopted hid the fear of invasion, but he preferred the pretence that things were normal to reminders that they now lived in a world where the wreck of the British army milled in chaos on a French beach, and deranged trench veterans stood in the streets happily forecasting Armageddon.

His mind went back to Rookwood, as it often did these days. The old quadrangle on a summer's day, masters in gowns and mortar-boards walking under the great elms, boys strolling by in dark blue blazers or cricket whites. It was an escape to the other side of the looking glass, away from the madness. But sooner or later the heavy painful thought would always intrude: how the hell had it all changed from that to this?

ST ERMIN'S hotel had once been grand but the elegance was faded now; the chandelier in the entrance hall was dusty and there was a smell of cabbage and polish. Watercolours of stags and Highland lochs covered the oak-panelled walls. Somewhere a grandfather clock ticked somnolently.

There was nobody at the reception desk. Harry rang the bell and a bald, heavily built man in a commissionaire's uniform appeared. 'Good morning, sir,' he said in the relaxed, unctuous voice of a lifetime in service. 'I hope I haven't kept you waiting.'

'I've an appointment at two thirty with a Miss Maxse. Lieutenant Brett.' Harry pronounced the woman's name 'Macksie' as the caller from the Foreign Office had instructed.

The man nodded. 'If you would follow me, sir.' His footsteps soundless on the thick dusty carpet, he led Harry to a lounge full of easy chairs and coffee tables. It was empty apart from a man and woman sitting in a bay window.

'Lieutenant Brett, madam.' The receptionist bowed and left.

The two rose to their feet. The woman extended a hand. She was in her fifties, small and fine-boned, smartly dressed in a blue two-piece suit. She had tightly curled grey hair and a sharp, intelligent face. Keen grey eyes met Harry's.

'How do you do, so nice to meet you.' Her confident contralto made Harry think of a girls' school headmistress. 'Marjorie Maxse. I've been hearing all about you.'

'Nothing too bad, I hope.'

'Oh, quite the contrary. Let me introduce Roger Jebb.' The man took Harry's hand in a hard grip. He was about Miss Maxse's age, with a long tanned face and thinning black hair.

'What about some tea?' Miss Maxse asked.

'Thank you.'

A silver teapot and china cups had been laid out on a table. There was a plate of scones too, pots of jam and what looked like real cream. Miss Maxse began pouring tea. 'Any trouble getting here? I gather one or two came down round here last night.'

'Victoria Street's closed off.'

'It *is* a nuisance. And it's going to go on for some time.' She spoke as though it were a spell of rain. She smiled. 'We prefer to meet new people here, for the first interview. The manager's an old friend of ours, so we won't be disturbed. Sugar?' she continued in the same conversational tone. 'Do have a scone, they're awfully good.'

'Thanks.' Harry scooped up jam and cream. He looked up to see Miss Maxse studying him closely; she gave him a sympathetic smile, unembarrassed.

'How are you getting on now? You were invalided out, weren't you? After Dunkirk?'

'Yes. A bomb landed twenty feet away. Threw up a lot of sand. I was lucky; it shielded me from the worst of the blast.' He saw Jebb studying him too, from flinty grey eyes.

'You had a bit of shell shock, I believe,' he said abruptly.

'It was very minor,' Harry said. 'I'm all right now.'

'Your face went blank there, just for a second,' Jebb said.

'It used to be a lot more than a second,' he replied quietly. 'And both hands used to tremble all the time. You might as well know.'

'And your hearing suffered, too, I believe?' Miss Maxse asked the question very quietly, but Harry caught it.

'That's almost back to normal as well. Just a little deafness in the left one.'

'Lucky, that,' Jebb observed. 'Hearing loss from blast, that's often permanent.' He produced a paperclip from his pocket and began absent-mindedly bending it open as he continued looking at Harry.

'The doctor said I was lucky.'

'The hearing damage means the end of active service, of course,'

Miss Maxse went on. 'Even if it is minor. That must be a blow. You joined up straight away last September, didn't you?' She leaned forward, teacup enfolded in her hands.

'Yes. Yes, I did. Excuse me, Miss Maxse, but I'm a bit in the dark . . .'

She smiled again. 'Of course. What did the Foreign Office tell you when they rang?'

'Only that some people there thought there might be some work I could do.'

'Well, we're separate from the FO.' Miss Maxse smiled brightly. 'We're Intelligence.' She gave a tinkling laugh, as though overcome by the strangeness of it all.

'Oh,' Harry said.

Her voice became serious. 'Our work is crucial now, quite crucial. With France gone, the whole Continent is either allied to the Nazis or dependent on them. There aren't any normal diplomatic relationships any more.'

'We're the front line now,' Jebb added. 'Smoke?'

'No, thanks. I don't.'

'Your uncle's Colonel James Brett, isn't he?'

'Yes, sir, that's right.'

'Served with me in India. Back in 1910, believe it or not!' Jebb gave a harsh bark of laughter. 'How is he?'

'Retired now.' But judging by that tan you stayed on, Harry thought. Indian police, perhaps.

Miss Maxse put down her cup and clasped her hands together. 'How would you feel about working for us?' she asked.

Harry felt the old shrinking weariness again; but something else too, a spark of interest.

'I still want to help the war effort, of course.'

'D'you think you're fit to cope with demanding work?' Jebb asked. 'Honestly, now. If you're not you should say. It's nothing to be ashamed of,' he added gruffly. Miss Maxse smiled encouragingly.

'I think so,' Harry said carefully. 'I'm almost back to normal.'

'We're recruiting a lot of people, Harry,' Miss Maxse said. 'I may call you Harry, mayn't I? Some because we think they'd be suited to the kind of work we do, others because they can offer us something particular. Now, you were a modern languages specialist before you joined up. Good degree at Cambridge, then a fellowship at King's till the war came.'

'Yes, that's right.' They knew a lot about him.

'How's your Spanish? Fluent?'

It was a surprising question. 'I'd say so.'

'French literature's your subject, isn't it?'

Harry frowned. 'Yes, but I keep my Spanish up. I'm a member of a Spanish Circle in Cambridge.'

Jebb nodded. 'Academics mainly, is it? Spanish plays and so on.'

'Yes.'

'Any exiles from the Civil War?'

'One or two.' He met Jebb's gaze. 'But the Circle's not political. We have a sort of unspoken agreement to avoid politics.'

Jebb laid the paperclip, tortured now into fantastic curls, on the table, and opened his briefcase. He pulled out a cardboard file with a diagonal red cross on the front.

'I'd like to take you back to 1931,' he said. 'Your second year at Cambridge. You went to Spain that summer, didn't you? With a friend from your school, Rookwood.'

Harry frowned again. How could they know all this? 'Yes.'

Jebb opened the file. 'One Bernard Piper, later of the British Communist Party. Went on to fight in the Spanish Civil War. Reported missing believed killed at the Battle of the Jarama, 1937.' He took out a photograph and laid it on the table. A row of men in untidy military uniforms stood on a bare hillside. Bernie stood in the middle, taller than the others, his blond hair cut short, smiling boyishly into the camera.

Harry looked up at Jebb. 'Was that taken in Spain?'

'Yes.' The hard little eyes narrowed. 'And you went out to try and find him.'

'At his family's request, as I spoke Spanish.'

'But no luck.'

'There were ten thousand dead at the Jarama,' Harry said bleakly. 'They weren't all accounted for. Bernie's probably in a mass grave somewhere outside Madrid. Sir, might I ask where you got this information? I think I've a right—'

'You haven't actually. But since you ask, we keep files on all Communist Party members. Just as well, now Stalin's helped Hitler butcher Poland.'

Miss Maxse smiled placatingly. 'No one's associating you with them.'

'I should hope not,' Harry said stiffly.

'Would you say you had any politics?'

It wasn't the sort of question you expected in England. Their knowledge of his life, of Bernie's history, disturbed him. He hesitated before answering.

'I suppose I'm a sort of liberal Tory if anything.'

'You weren't tempted to go and fight for the Spanish Republic, like Piper?' Jebb asked. 'The crusade against fascism?'

'So far as I'm concerned, Spain before the Civil War was rotten with chaos, and the Fascists and Communists both took advantage. I came across some Russians in '37. They were swine.'

'That must have been quite an adventure,' Miss Maxse said brightly. 'Going to Madrid in the middle of the Civil War.'

'I went to try and find my friend. For his family, as I said.'

'You were close friends at school, weren't you?' Jebb asked.

'You've been asking questions at Rookwood?' The thought angered him.

'Yes.' Jebb nodded, unapologetic.

Harry's eyes widened suddenly. 'Is this about Bernie? Is he alive?'

'Our file on Bernard Piper's closed,' Jebb said, his tone unexpectedly gentle. 'So far as we know he died at the Jarama.'

Miss Maxse sat upright. 'You must understand, Harry, if we're to trust you to work for us, we do need to know all about you. But I think we're happy.' Jebb nodded, and she went on. 'I think it's time we got down to brass tacks. We wouldn't normally dive straight in like this but it's a question of time, you see. Urgency. We need information about someone. We think you can help us. It could be very important.'

Jebb leaned forward. 'Everything we tell you from now on is strictly confidential, is that understood? In fact, I have to warn you that if you discuss any of it outside this room, you'll be in serious trouble.'

Harry met his eyes. 'All right.'

'This isn't about Bernard Piper. It's another old schoolfriend of yours, who's also developed some interesting political connections.' Jebb delved in his case again and laid another photograph on the table.

It was not a face Harry had ever expected to see again. Sandy Forsyth would be thirty-one now, a few months older than Harry, but he looked almost middle-aged. He had a Clark Gable moustache and heavily oiled hair, already starting to recede, swept back from his brow. His face had filled out and acquired new lines but the keen eyes, the Roman nose and wide thin-lipped mouth were the same. It was a posed photograph; Sandy was smiling at the camera with a film star's smile, half enigmatic and half inviting. He wasn't a handsome man but the photograph made him appear so. Harry looked up again.

'I wouldn't have called him a close friend,' he said quietly.

'You were friendly for a time, Harry,' Miss Maxse said. 'The year before he was expelled. After that business involving Mr Taylor. We've spoken to him, you see.'

'Mr Taylor.' Harry hesitated a moment. 'How is he?'

'He's all right these days,' Jebb said. 'No thanks to Forsyth. Now, when he was expelled, did you part on good terms?' He jabbed the paperclip at Harry. 'This is important.'

'Yes. I was Forsyth's only friend at Rookwood, really.'

'I wouldn't have thought you had an awful lot in common,' Miss Maxse said with a smile.

'We didn't, in a lot of ways.'

'Bit of a bad hat wasn't he, Forsyth? Didn't fit in. But you were always a steady chap.'

Harry sighed. 'Sandy had a good side too. Though . . .' He paused. Miss Maxse smiled encouragingly.

'I sometimes wondered why he wanted to be friends with me. When a lot of the people he mixed with were – well, bad hats, to use your phrase.'

'Anything sexual in it, Harry, d'you think?' Her tone was light and casual, as when she spoke of the bombs. Harry stared at her in astonishment for a moment, then gave an embarrassed laugh.

'Certainly not.'

'Sorry to embarrass you, but these things happen at public schools. You know, crushes.'

'There was nothing like that.'

'After Forsyth left,' Jebb said, 'did you keep in touch?'

'We exchanged letters for a couple of years. Less and less as time went on. We hadn't much in common once Sandy left Rookwood.' He sighed. 'In fact, I'm not sure why he went on writing for so long. Maybe to impress – he wrote about clubs and girls and that sort of thing.' Jebb nodded encouragingly. 'In his last letter he said he was working for some bookie in London. He wrote about doping horses and fake bets as though it was all a joke.' But now Harry was remembering Sandy's other side: the walks over the Downs in search of fossils, the long talks. What did these people want?

'You still believe in traditional values, don't you?' Miss Maxse asked with a smile. 'The things Rookwood stands for.'

'I suppose so. Though . . .'

'Yes?'

'I wonder how the country got to this.' He met her eyes. 'We weren't ready for what happened in France. Defeat.'

'The jelly-backed French let us down.' Jebb grunted.

'We were forced to retreat too, sir,' Harry said. 'I was there.'

'You're right. We weren't properly prepared.' Miss Maxse spoke with sudden feeling. 'Perhaps we behaved too honourably at Munich. After the Great War we couldn't believe anyone would *want* war again. But we know now Hitler always did. He won't be happy till all of Europe's under his heel. The New Dark Age, as Winston calls it.'

There was a moment's silence, then Jebb coughed. 'OK, Harry. I want to talk about Spain. When France fell last June and Mussolini declared war on us, we expected Franco to follow. Hitler had won his Civil War for him, and of course Franco wants Gibraltar. With German help he could take it from the landward side and that'd be the Mediterranean choked off to us.'

'Spain's in ruins now,' Harry said. 'Franco couldn't fight another war.'

'But he could let Hitler in. There are Wehrmacht divisions waiting on the Franco-Spanish border. The Spanish Fascist Party wants to enter the war.' He inclined his head. 'On the other hand, most of the Royalist generals distrust the Falange and they're scared of a popular uprising if the Germans come in. They're not Fascists, they just wanted to beat the Reds. It's a fluid situation, Franco could declare war any day. Our embassy people in Madrid are living on their nerves.'

'Franco's cautious,' Harry ventured. 'A lot of people think he could have won the Civil War earlier if he'd been bolder.'

Jebb grunted. 'I hope you're right. Sir Samuel Hoare's gone out there as ambassador to try and keep them out of the war.'

'I heard.'

'Their economy's in ruins, as you say. That weakness is our trump card, because the Royal Navy can still control what goes in and out.'

'The blockade.'

'Fortunately the Americans aren't challenging it. We're letting in just enough oil to keep Spain going, a bit less actually. And they've had another bad harvest. They're trying to import wheat and raise loans abroad to pay for it. Our reports say people are collapsing from hunger in the Barcelona factories.'

'It sounds as bad as during the Civil War.' Harry shook his head. 'What they've been through.'

'There are all sorts of rumours coming out of Spain now. Franco's exploring any number of schemes to gain economic self-sufficiency, some of them pretty crackpot. Last year an Austrian scientist claimed to have found a way of manufacturing synthetic oil from plant extracts and got money out of him to develop it. It was all a fraud, of course.' Jebb gave his bark of a laugh again. 'Then they claimed to have found huge gold reserves down at Badajoz. Another mare's nest. But now we hear they really *have* found gold deposits, in the sierras not far from Madrid. There's a geologist with South African experience working for them, one Alberto Otero. And they're keeping it quiet, which makes us more inclined to think there's something in it. The boffins say that geologically it's a possibility.'

'And that would make Spain less dependent on us?'

'They've no gold reserves to back the currency. Stalin made the Republic send the gold reserve to Moscow during the Civil War. And kept it, of course. That makes buying anything on the open market very difficult for them. At the moment they're trying to get export credits from us and the Yanks.'

'So if the rumours are true – they'd be less dependent on us?'

'Exactly. And therefore more inclined to enter the war. Anything could tip the balance.'

'We're trying to perform a high-wire act out there,' Miss Maxse added. 'How much of a stick to wave, how many carrots to offer. How much wheat to allow through, how much oil.'

Jebb nodded. 'The point is, Brett, the man who introduced Otero to the regime was Sandy Forsyth.'

'He's in Spain?' Harry's eyes widened.

'Yes. I don't know if you saw the adverts in the newspapers a couple of years ago, tours of the Civil War battlefields?'

'I remember. The Nationalists ran the tours for English people. A propaganda stunt.'

'Somehow Forsyth got involved. Went to Spain as a tour guide. Franco's people paid him quite well. Then he stayed on, got involved in various business schemes, some of them pretty shady I would imagine. He's a clever businessman apparently, of the flashy sort.' Jebb's mouth crinkled with distaste, then he stared keenly at Harry. 'He has some important contacts now.'

Harry took a deep breath. 'May I ask how you know all this?

Jebb shrugged. 'Sneaky beakies working out of our embassy. They pay minor functionaries for information. Madrid's full of spies. But no one's got near Forsyth himself. We've no agents in the Falange and it's the Falangist faction in the government that Forsyth's with. And word is he's clever, likely to smell a rat if a stranger appeared and started asking questions.'

'Yes.' Harry nodded. 'Sandy's clever.'

'But if *you* were to turn up in Madrid,' Miss Maxse said. 'As a translator attached to the embassy say, and run across him in a cafe? The way people do. Renew an old friendship.'

'We want you to find out what he's doing,' Jebb said bluntly. 'Perhaps get him on our side.'

So that was it. They wanted him to spy on Sandy, like Mr Taylor had all those years ago at Rookwood. Harry looked out of the window at the blue sky, where the barrage balloons floated like huge grey whales.

'How'd you feel about that?' Miss Maxse's voice was gentle.

'Sandy Forsyth working with the Falange.' Harry shook his head. 'It's not as if he needed to make money – his father's a bishop.'

'Sometimes it's the excitement as much as the politics, Harry. Sometimes the two go together.'

'Yes.' He remembered Sandy coming breathless into the study from one of his forbidden betting trips, opening his hand to show a five-pound note, white and crinkled. 'Look what I got from a nice gee-gee.'

'Working with the Falange,' Harry said reflectively. 'I suppose he was always a black sheep, but sometimes – a man can do something against the rules and get a bad name and that can make him worse.'

'We've nothing against black sheep,' Jebb said. 'Black sheep can make the best agents.' He laughed knowingly. Another memory of Sandy returned to Harry: staring angrily across the study table, his voice a bitter whisper. 'You see what they're like, how they control us, what they do if we try to break away.'

'I think you're someone who likes to play the game,' Miss Maxse said. 'That's what we expected. But we can't win this war playing a straight bat.' She shook her head sadly, the short curls bobbing. 'Not against this enemy. It means killing, you know that already, and it means deception too, I'm afraid.' She smiled apologetically.

Harry felt opposing emotions churn inside him, panic beginning to stir. The thought of going back to Spain both excited and appalled him. He had heard things were very bad from the Spanish exiles at Cambridge. In the newsreels he had seen Franco addressing ecstatic crowds who responded with Fascist salutes, but behind that, they said, was a world of denunciations and midnight arrests. And Sandy Forsyth in the middle of it all? He looked at the photo again. 'I'm not sure,' he said slowly. 'I mean, I'm not sure I could carry it off.'

'We'd give you training,' Jebb said. 'Bit of a crash course because the powers that be want an answer to this one ASAP.' He looked at Harry. 'People at the highest level.'

Part of Harry wanted to retreat now, go back to Surrey, forget it all. But he had spent the last three months fighting that panicky urge to hide.

'What sort of training?' he asked. 'I'm not sure I'd be any good at deception.'

'It's easier than you think,' Miss Maxse replied. 'If you believe in the cause you're lying for. And you would be lying, deceiving, let's not mince words. But we'd teach you all the black arts.'

Harry bit his lip. There was silence in the room for a long moment.

Miss Maxse said, 'We wouldn't expect you just to go in cold.'

'All right,' he said at length. 'Perhaps I could bring Sandy round. I can't believe he's a Fascist.'

'The hard part will be early on,' Jebb said. 'Working your way into his confidence. That's when it'll feel strange, difficult, and that's when you'll most need to pass it off.'

'Yes. Sandy's got the sort of mind that can see round corners.'

'So we gather.' Miss Maxse turned to Jebb. He hesitated a moment, then nodded.

'Good,' Miss Maxse said briskly.

'We'll need to move quickly,' Jebb said. 'Make some arrangements, put things in place for you. You'll need to be vetted properly, of course. Are you staying up tonight?'

'Yes, I'm going to my cousin's.'

He looked at Harry sharply again. 'No ties here, apart from your family?'

'No.' He shook his head.

Jebb took out a little notebook. 'Number?' Harry gave it to him.

'Someone will ring you tomorrow. Don't go out, please.'

'Yes, sir.'

They rose from their chairs. Miss Maxse shook Harry's hand warmly. 'Thank you, Harry,' she said.

Jebb gave Harry a tight little smile. 'Be ready for the siren tonight. We're expecting more raids.' He threw the twisted paperclip into a wastepaper basket.

'Dear me,' Miss Maxse said. 'That was government property. You are a squanderbug, Roger.' She smiled at Harry again, a smile of dismissal. 'We're grateful, Harry. This could be very important.'

Outside the lounge Harry paused a moment. A sad heavy feeling settled on his stomach. Black arts: what the hell did that mean? The term made him shudder. He realized that half consciously he was listening, as Sandy used to do at masters' doors, his good ear turned towards the door to catch what Jebb and Miss Maxse might be saying. But he could hear nothing. He turned to find the receptionist had appeared, his steps unheard on the dusty carpet. Harry smiled nervously and allowed himself to be led outside. Was he falling already into the habits of a – what? Sneak, spy, betrayer?

Chapter Two

THE JOURNEY TO Will's house in Harrow normally lasted under an hour, but today it took half the afternoon, the tube continually stopping and starting. In the underground stations little knots of people sat on the platforms, huddled together, whey-faced. Harry had heard some of the bombed-out east-enders had taken up residence in the tubes.

He thought of *spying* on Sandy Forsyth and a sick, incredulous feeling lurched through him. He scanned the pale tired faces of his fellow passengers. He supposed any one of them might be a spy – what could you tell from people's looks? The photo kept coming back to his mind: Sandy's confident smile, the Clark Gable moustache. The train lurched slowly on through the tunnels.

IT HAD BEEN Rookwood that gave Harry his identity. His father, a barrister, had been blown to pieces on the Somme when Harry was six years old, and his mother had died in the influenza epidemic the winter the First War – as people were starting to call the last war – ended. Harry still had their wedding photograph and often looked at it. His father, standing outside the church in a morning suit, looked very like him: dark and solid and dependable-looking. His arm was round Harry's mother, who was fair like Cousin Will, curly tresses falling round her shoulders under a wide-brimmed Edwardian hat. They were smiling happily into the camera. The picture had been taken in bright sunlight and was slightly overexposed, making haloes of light around their figures. Harry had little memory of them; like the world of the photograph they were a vanished dream.

After his mother died, Harry had gone to live with Uncle James, his father's elder brother, a professional army officer wounded in the first battles of 1914. It had been a stomach wound, nothing you could see, but Uncle James's innards troubled him constantly. His discomfort worsened an already peppery disposition and was a constant source of worry to Aunt Emily, his nervous, anxious wife. When Harry came to their house in the pretty Surrey village they were only in their forties, but they seemed much older already, like a pair of anxious, fussy pensioners.

They were kind to him, but Harry had always felt unwanted. They were childless and never seemed quite to know what to do with him. Uncle James would clap him on the shoulder, almost knocking him over, and ask heartily what he was playing at today, while his aunt worried endlessly about what he should eat.

Occasionally he went to stay with Aunt Jenny, his mother's sister and Will's mother. She had been devoted to his mother and found it difficult to be reminded of her, although she showered him, guiltily perhaps, with food parcels and postal orders when he went to school.

As a child Harry had been taught by a tutor, a retired teacher his uncle knew. He spent much of his free time roaming the lanes and woods around the village. There he met the local boys, sons of farmers and farriers, but though he played cowboys and Indians and hunted rabbits with them he was always apart: Harry the Toff. 'Say "awful", Harry,' they would goad him. '*Or*-ful, *or*-ful.'

One summer day when Harry came home from the fields, Uncle James called him into his study. He was just twelve. There was another man there, standing by the window, the sun directly behind him so that at first he was just a tall shadow framed by dust motes. 'I'd like you to meet Mr Taylor,' Uncle James said. 'He teaches at my old school. My *alma mater*. That's the Latin right, eh?' And to Harry's surprise he laughed nervously, like a child.

The man moved forward and took Harry's hand in a firm grip. He was tall and thin and wore a dark suit. Black hair receded from a widow's peak on his high forehead and keen grey eyes studied him from behind a pair of pince-nez.

'How do you do, Harry.' The voice was sharp. 'You're a bit of a ragamuffin, aren't you?'

'He's been running a little wild,' Uncle James said apologetically.

'We'll soon tidy you up if you come to Rookwood. Would you like to go to Public School, Harry?'

'I don't know, sir.'

'Your tutor's report is good. Do you like rugger?'

'I've never played, sir. I play football with the boys in the village.'

'Rugger's much better. A gentleman's game.'

'Rookwood was your father's old school as well as mine,' Uncle James said.

Harry looked up. 'Father's?'

'Yes. Your *pater*, as they say at Rookwood.'

'Do you know what *pater* means, Harry?' Mr Taylor asked.

'It's Latin for father, sir.'

'Very good.' Mr Taylor smiled. 'The boy might just do, Brett.'

He asked more questions. He was friendly enough but had an air of authority, of expecting obedience, which made Harry cautious. After a while he was sent from the room while Mr Taylor talked with his uncle. When Uncle James called him back Mr Taylor had gone. His uncle asked him to sit down and looked at him seriously, stroking his greying moustache.

'Your aunt and I think it's time you went away to school, Harry. Better than staying here with a couple of old fogeys like us. And you should be mixing with boys from your own class, not the village lads.'

Harry had no idea what a Public School was like. Into his head came a picture of a big building full of light, bright like the light in his parents' photograph, welcoming him.

'What do you think, Harry, would you like to go?'

'Yes, Uncle. Yes, I would.'

WILL LIVED IN a quiet street of mock-Tudor villas. A new air-raid shelter, a long low concrete building, stood incongruously by the grass verge.

His cousin was home already and answered the doorbell. He had changed into a brightly patterned jumper and beamed at Harry through his glasses.

'Hello, Harry! Made it all right, then?'

'Fine, thanks.' Harry clasped his hand. 'How are you, Will?'

'Oh, bearing up, like everyone. How are the old ears?'

'Just about back to normal. A bit deaf on one side.'

Will led Harry into the hall. A tall, thin woman with mousy hair and a long disapproving face came out of the kitchen, drying her hands on a tea towel.

'Muriel.' Harry made himself smile warmly. 'How are you?'

'Oh, struggling on. I won't shake hands, I've been cooking. I thought we might skip high tea, go straight on to dinner.'

'We've got a nice steak for dinner, though. Got an arrangement with the butcher. Now, come on up, you'll want a wash.'

Harry had stayed in the back bedroom before. There was a big double bed and little ornaments on doilies on the dressing table. 'I'll leave you to it,' Will said. 'Have a wash, then come down.'

Harry washed his face at the little sink, studying it in the mirror as he dried himself. He was putting on weight, his stocky frame starting to become fat through recent lack of exercise, the square jaw rounding out. People told him it was an attractive face, though he always thought the regular features under his curly brown hair a little too broad to be handsome. There were new lines around the eyes these days. He tried to make his face as expressionless as he could. Would Sandy be able to read his thoughts behind such a mask? It had been the done thing at school to hide your feelings – you showed them only through a set mouth, a raised eyebrow. People looked for little signs. Now he must learn to show nothing, or untrue things. He lay on the bed, remembering school and Sandy Forsyth.

HARRY HAD LOVED the school from the start. Set in an eighteenth-century mansion deep in the Sussex countryside, Rookwood had originally been founded by a group of London businessmen trading overseas to educate the sons of their ships' officers. The House names reflected its naval past: Raleigh and Drake and Hawkins. Now the sons of civil servants and minor aristocrats went there, with a leavening of scholarship boys funded by bequests.

The school and its orderly routines had given Harry a sense of belonging and purpose. The discipline could be harsh but he had no desire to break the rules and seldom got lines, let alone the cane. He did well in most classes, especially French and Latin – languages came easily to him. He enjoyed games too, rugger and especially cricket with its measured pace; in his last year he had been captain of the junior team.

Sometimes he would walk on his own round Big Hall, where the photos of each year's sixth forms hung. He would stand looking at the photograph for 1902, where his father's boyish face stared out from a double row of stiffly posed prefects in tasselled caps. Then he would turn to the tablet behind the stage to the Great War fallen, the names picked out in gold. Seeing his father's name there as well set tears pricking in his eyes, quickly brushed away lest someone see.

The year Sandy Forsyth came, in 1925, Harry entered the fourth form. Although the boys still slept in a big communal dormitory, they had had studies since the previous year, two or three each to a little room with antiquated armchairs and scarred tables. Harry's friends were mostly the quieter, more serious boys, and he had been glad to share a study with Bernie Piper, one of the scholarship boys. Piper came in as he was unpacking.

''Ello, Brett,' he said. 'I see I've got to put up wiv the smell of your socks for the next year.' Bernie's father was an East End grocer and he had spoken broad cockney when he arrived at Rookwood. It had gradually mutated into the upper-class drawl of the others, but the London twang always reasserted itself for a while when he came back from the hols.

''Ave a good summer?'

'Bit boring. Uncle James was ill a lot of the time. Glad to be back.'

'You ought t'ave spent it serving in my dad's shop. Then you'd know wot boring is.'

Another face appeared in the doorway, a heavily built boy with black hair. He put down an expensive-looking suitcase and leaned against the doorpost with an air of supercilious detachment. 'Harry Brett?' he asked.

'Yes.'

'I'm Sandy Forsyth. New boy. I'm in this study.' He hauled in the suitcase and stood looking at them. His large brown eyes were keen and there was something hard in his face.

'Where have you come from?' Bernie asked.

'Braildon. Up in Hertfordshire. Heard of it?'

'Yes,' Harry said. 'Supposed to be a good school.'

'Yeah. So they say.'

'It's not bad here.'

'No? I hear they're quite hot on discipline.'

'Cane you as soon as look at you,' Bernie agreed.

'Where are you from?' Forsyth asked.

'Wapping,' Bernie said proudly. 'I'm one of the proles the ruling class allow in.' Bernie had declared himself a socialist the term before, to general disapproval. Forsyth raised his eyebrows.

'I bet you got in more easily than I did.'

'What d'you mean?'

'I'm a bit of a bad lad.' The new boy took a packet of Gold Flake from his pocket and pulled out a cigarette. Bernie and Harry glanced at the open door. 'You can't smoke in the studies,' Harry said quickly.

'We can shut the door. Want one?'

Bernie laughed. 'You get caned for smoking here. It's not worth it.'

'OK.' He gave Bernie a sudden broad grin, showing large white teeth. 'You a red, then?'

'I'm a socialist, if that's what you mean.'

The new boy shrugged. 'We had a debating society at Braildon, last year one of the Fifth spoke for Communism. It got pretty rowdy.' He laughed. Bernie grunted, giving him a look of dislike.

'I wanted to lead a debate in favour of atheism,' Forsyth went on. 'But they wouldn't let me. Because my dad's a bishop. Where do people go here if they want a smoke?'

'Behind the gym,' Bernie answered coldly.

'Right-ho then. See you later.' Forsyth got up and sauntered out.

'Arsehole,' Bernie said as he disappeared.

AND THEN, later that day, Harry was asked to spy on Sandy for the first time. He was in the study alone when a fag appeared with a message Mr Taylor wanted to see him.

Taylor was their form master that year. He had a reputation as a disciplinarian and the junior boys held him in awe. Seeing his tall, thin figure striding across the quad, the habitual severe expression on his face, Harry would think back to the day he had come to Uncle James's house; they had scarcely spoken since.

Mr Taylor was in his study, a comfortable room with carpets and portraits of old headmasters on the wall; he was devoted to school history. A large desk was strewn with papers for marking. The master stood in his black gown, sorting through papers.

'Ah Brett.' His tone was cordial as he waved a long arm to beckon Harry in. Harry stood in front of the desk, hands behind his back in the approved manner. Taylor's hair was receding fast, the widow's peak now a separate black tuft beneath a balding crown.

'Did you have good holidays? Aunt and Uncle OK?'

'Yes, sir.'

The master nodded. 'You're in my form this year. I've had good reports of you, I shall expect great things.'

'Thank you, sir.'

The master nodded. 'I wanted to talk to you about the studies. We've put the new boy in with you in place of Piper. Forsyth. Have you met him yet?'

'Yes, sir. I don't think Piper knows.'

'He'll be told. How are you getting on with Forsyth?'

'All right, sir,' Harry said neutrally.

'You may have heard of his father, the bishop?'

'Forsyth mentioned him.'

'Forsyth comes to us from Braildon. His parents felt Rookwood, with its reputation for – ah – order, was better suited to him.' Taylor smiled benignly, making deep creases appear in his thin cheeks. 'I'm telling you in confidence. You're a steady boy, Brett; we think you could be prefect material one day. Keep an eye on Forsyth, will you?' He paused. 'Keep him on the straight and narrow.'

Harry gave the master a quick look. It was an odd remark; one of the studied ambiguities the masters spoke in more and more as the boys got older. You were expected to understand. Officially it was frowned on for boys to sneak on one another, but Harry knew many masters had particular pupils whom they used as sources of information. Was this what Taylor was asking him to do? He knew instinctively he didn't want to; the whole idea made him uneasy.

'I'll certainly help show him around, sir,' he said carefully.

Taylor eyed him keenly. 'And let me know if there are any problems. Just a quiet word. We want to help Forsyth develop in the right direction. It's important to his father.'

That was clear enough. Harry said nothing. Mr Taylor frowned a little.

Then an extraordinary thing happened. Something tiny moved on the master's desk, among the papers; Harry saw it out of the corner of his eye. Taylor gave a sudden shout and jumped away. To Harry's amazement he stood almost cringing, eyes averted from a fat house spider scuttling across his blotter. It stopped on top of a Latin textbook, standing quite still.

Taylor turned to Harry, his face bright red. His eyes strayed momentarily to the desk and he looked away with a shudder.

'Brett, get rid of that thing for me. Please.' There was a pleading note in the master's voice.

Wonderingly, Harry took out his handkerchief and reached for the spider. He picked it up and held it gently.

'Ah – thank you, Brett.' Taylor swallowed. 'I – ah – we shouldn't have such – er – arachnids in the studies. Spread disease. Kill it, please kill it,' he added rapidly.

Harry hesitated, then squeezed it between finger and thumb. It made a faint pop, making him wince.

'Get rid of it.' For a moment, Taylor's eyes seemed almost wild behind the gold-rimmed pince-nez. 'And don't tell anyone about this. Do you understand? You may go,' he added brusquely.

At Will's house the soup at dinner was tinned, heavy with watery vegetables. Muriel apologized as she passed it round.

'I hadn't time to make any, I'm sorry. Of course, I've no woman to help now. I have to deal with the cooking, looking after the children, the ration books, *everything*.' She pushed back a stray hair and gave Harry a challenging stare. Will and Muriel's children, a thin dark boy of nine and a little girl of six, sat watching Harry with interest.

'It must be difficult,' he replied solemnly. 'But the soup's fine.'

'It's scrumptious!' Ronald called loudly. His mother sighed. Harry didn't know why Muriel had had children; he supposed because it was the done thing.

'How's work?' he asked his cousin to break the silence. Will worked in the Foreign Office, at the Middle East desk.

'There could be problems in Persia.' The eyes behind the thick glasses were troubled. 'The Shah's leaning towards Hitler. How was your meeting?' he asked with exaggerated casualness. He had phoned Harry a few days before to tell him some people connected with the Foreign Office had spoken to him and would be in touch but had said he didn't know what it was about. From his manner now, Harry thought he had guessed who the 'people' were. He wondered whether Will had talked about him in the office, mentioned a cousin who had been to Rookwood and spoke Spanish, and someone had passed the information on to Jebb's people. Or was there some huge filing system about citizens somewhere, which the spies had consulted?

He nearly answered, they want me to go to Madrid, but remembered he mustn't. 'Looks like they've got something for me. Means going abroad. A bit hush-hush.'

'Careless talk costs lives,' the little girl said solemnly.

'Be quiet, Prue,' Muriel snapped. 'Drink your soup.'

Harry smiled reassuringly. 'It's nothing dangerous. Not like France.'

'Did you kill many Germans in France?' Ronnie piped up.

Muriel set her spoon in her plate with a clang. 'I told you not to ask questions like that.'

'No, Ronnie, I didn't,' Harry said. 'They killed a lot of our men, though.'

'We'll get them back for it, though, won't we? And for the bombing?'

Muriel sighed deeply. Will turned to his son.

'Did I ever tell you I met Ribbentrop, Ronnie?'

'Wow! You met him? You should have *killed* him!'

'We weren't at war then, Ronnie. He was just the German ambassador. He was always saying the wrong thing. Brickendrop, we used to call him.'

'What was he like?'

'A silly man. His son was at Eton and once Ribbentrop went to the school to meet him. Ribbentrop stood in the quad with his arm raised and shouted, "*Heil Hitler!*"'

'Crumbs!' Ronnie said. 'He wouldn't have got away with that at Rookwood. I'm hoping to go to Rookwood next year, did you know that, cousin Harry?'

'If we can afford the fees, Ronnie, maybe.'

'And if it's still there,' Muriel said suddenly. 'If it's not been requisitioned or blown up.' Harry and Will stared at her. She wiped her mouth with her napkin and rose.

'I'm going to get the steaks. They'll be dry, they've been under the grill.' She looked at her husband. 'What are we going to do tonight?'

'We won't go to the shelter unless the siren goes,' he replied. Muriel left the room. Prue had gone tense. Harry noticed that she had a teddy bear on her lap and was clutching it tightly. Will sighed.

'When these raids began we started going up to the shelter after dinner. But some of the people there – well, they're a bit common, Muriel doesn't like them, and it's pretty uncomfortable. Prue gets frightened. We stay at home unless Wailing Winnie starts.' He sighed again, staring out of the French windows across the back garden. Dusk was deepening into night and a clear full moon was rising. 'It's a bomber's moon. You go over, if you like.'

'It's all right,' Harry said. 'I'll stay with you.'

His uncle's village was on the 'bomber's run' from the Channel up to London; the sirens often went as the planes passed overhead, but they ignored them. Harry hated Wailing Winnie's swirling howl. It reminded him of the sound dive-bombers made: when he first came home after Dunkirk he would clench his teeth and clench his hands till they turned white every time the sirens went off.

'If it goes in the night, we'll get up and make for the shelter,' Will said. 'It's just over the road.'

'Yes, I saw it.'

'It's been bad. Ten days of it leaves you so bloody tired, and God knows how long it's going to go on for. Muriel's thinking of taking the children to the country.' Will got up and drew the heavy black-out curtains. There was a sound of breaking glass from the kitchen, followed by an angry cry. He hurried out. 'Better go and help Muriel.'

THE SIRENS STARTED at one a.m. They began in Westminster and, as other boroughs followed, the wailing moan rippled outwards to the suburbs. Harry woke from a dream, in which he was running through Madrid, darting in and out of shops and bars, asking if anyone had seen his friend Bernie. But he was speaking in English, not Spanish, and nobody understood. He rose and dressed in moments, as he had learned to do in the army. His mind was clear and focused, no panic. He wondered why he had been asking for Bernie, not Sandy. Someone had phoned from the Foreign Office at ten, asking him to go to an address in Surrey tomorrow.

He twitched the curtain open a crack. In the moonlight shadowy figures were running across the road, making for the shelter. Huge searchlight beams stabbed the sky as far as the eye could see.

He went out into the hall. The light was on and Ronnie stood there in pyjamas and dressing gown. 'Prue's upset,' he said. 'She won't come.' He looked at the open door of his parents' bedroom. A loud, terrified child's sobbing could be heard.

Even now, with the siren wailing in his ears, Harry felt reluctant to invade Will and Muriel's bedroom, but he made himself go in. They were both in dressing gowns too. Muriel sat on the bed, her hair in curlers. She nursed her sobbing daughter in her arms, making soothing noises. Harry wouldn't have thought her capable of such gentleness. One of the little girl's arms hung down, still clutching the teddy bear. Will stood looking at them uncertainly; with his thin hair sticking up and his glasses askew he seemed the most vulnerable of them all. The sound went on; Harry felt his legs begin to tremble.

'We should go,' he said brusquely.

Muriel looked up. 'Who the bloody hell asked you?'

'Prue won't go to the shelter,' Will explained quietly.

'It's dark,' the little girl wailed. 'It's so dark there, please let me stay at home!'

Harry stepped forward and grasped Muriel's bony elbow. This was what the corporal had done on the beach after the bomb fell, picked him up and led him gently to the boat. Muriel gave him an astonished look.

'We have to go. The bombers are coming. Will, we have to get them up.' His cousin took Muriel's other arm and they raised her gently. Prue had buried her head in her mother's breast, still sobbing and holding the teddy bear tightly by its arm. Its glass eyes stared up at Harry.

'All right, all right, I can walk by myself,' Muriel snapped. They released her. Ronnie clattered down the stairs and the others followed. The boy switched off the light and opened the front door.

It was strange to be in a night-time London without streetlamps. There was no one outside now, but the dark shape of the shelter was visible in the moonlight across the road. There was a distant sound of ack-ack fire and something else, a low heavy drone from the south.

'Hell,' Will said. 'They're coming this way!' He looked suddenly confused. 'But it's the docks they go for, the docks.'

'Maybe they're lost.' Or want to hit civilian morale, Harry thought. His legs had stopped shaking. He had to take charge. 'Come on,' he said. 'Let's get over the road.'

They began running but Muriel was slowed by the little girl. In the middle of the road Will turned to help her and slipped. He went down with a crash and a yell. Ronnie, ahead, paused and looked back.

'Will, get up!' Muriel's cry was hysterical. Will tried to lift himself but fell back. Prue, the teddy bear still dangling from her arm, began screaming. Harry knelt by Will's side.

'I've twisted my ankle.' Will's face was full of pain and fear. 'Leave me, get the others into the shelter.' Behind him Muriel held the keening Prue tightly. Muriel was swearing, over and over again, language Harry wouldn't have thought she knew.

'Bloody fucking bastard Hitler oh God Christ!'

Still the siren wailed. The planes were almost overhead. Harry heard the whine of bombs falling, growing louder and ending in a sudden loud crump. There was a flash of light from a few streets away, a momentary tug of hot air at his dressing gown. It was so like Dunkirk. His legs were shaking again and there was a dry acid taste at the back of his mouth but his mind was very clear. He had to get Will up.

There was another whine and crump, closer, and the ground shook with the impacts. Muriel stopped swearing and stood stock still, eyes and mouth wide open. She bent her thin dressing-gowned body over to protect her still weeping daughter. Harry took her arm and looked into her terrified eyes. He spoke to her slowly and clearly.

'You have to take Prue into the shelter, Muriel. Now. See, there's

Ronnie; he doesn't know what to do. You have to get them in. I'll bring Will.'

Life came back into her eyes. She turned wordlessly and began walking rapidly towards the shelter, stretching out her other hand for Ronnie to take. Harry bent and took Will's hand. 'Come on, old chap, get up. Put your good leg down, take the weight.'

He hauled his cousin to his feet as another great crash sounded, no more than a street away. There was a brief yellow flash and a wave of blast almost toppled them over but Harry had his arm round Will and managed to keep him steady. There was a feeling of pressure and a whining noise in Harry's bad ear. Will leaned into him and hopped on his good leg, smiling through gritted teeth.

'Don't get blown up,' he said. 'The sneaky beakies will be furious!' So he *had* guessed who wanted me, Harry thought. More bombs fell, yellow flashes lighting the road, but they seemed more distant now.

Someone had been watching from the shelter, holding the door open a crack. Arms reached out, taking hold of Will, and they fell together into the crowded darkness. Harry was guided to a seat. He found himself next to Muriel. He could just make out her thin form, still bent over Prue. The little girl was still sobbing. Ronnie was huddled against her as well.

'I'm sorry, Harry,' Muriel said quietly. 'I just couldn't bear any more. My children, every day I think about what could happen to them. All the time, all the time.'

'It's all right,' he said. 'It's OK.'

'I'm sorry I went to pieces. You got us through.' She raised an arm to touch Harry's, but let it fall, as though the effort were too much.

Harry leaned his throbbing head against the gritty concrete wall. He had helped them, taken control, he hadn't fallen apart. He would have a few months ago.

He remembered his first sight of the beach at Dunkirk, walking over a sand dune then seeing the endless black columns of men snaking into a sea dotted with boats. They were all sizes – he saw a pleasure steamer next to a minesweeper. There were smoking wrecks too, and German dive-bombers buzzing overhead, shrieking down and dropping their bombs on the boats and the men. The retreat had been so fast, so chaotic, the horror and shame of it had been almost too much to take in. Harry was ordered to help line the men up on the beach for evacuation. Sitting in the shelter, he felt again the numb shame that came then, the realization of total defeat.

Muriel muttered something. She was on his deaf side and he turned to her. 'What?'

'Are you all right? You're shaking all over.' There was a tremble in her voice. He opened his eyes. The gloom was spotted with the red pinpoints of cigarette ends. The shelterers were quiet, trying to hear what was happening outside.

'Yes. It just – brought everything back. The evacuation.'

'I know,' she muttered.

'I think they've gone now,' someone said. The door opened a crack and someone peered out. A draught of fresh air cut through the odour of sweat and urine.

'It's dreadful, the smell in here,' Muriel said. 'That's why I don't like to come over, I can't stand it.'

'Sometimes people can't help it – they lose control when they're frightened.'

'I suppose so.' Her voice softened. Harry wished he could make out her face.

'Is everyone all right?' he asked.

'Fine,' Will answered from Muriel's other side. 'Good work there, Harry. Thanks, old man.'

'Did the soldiers – lose control?' Muriel asked. 'In France? It must all have been so frightening.'

'Yes. Sometimes.' Harry remembered the smell as he approached the line of men on the beach. They hadn't washed for days. Sergeant Tomlinson's voice came back to him.

'We're lucky – things are going faster now the little boats are coming over. Some poor sods have been standing here three days.' He was a big, fair-haired man, his face grey with exhaustion. He nodded towards the sea, shaking his head. 'Look at those stupid buggers, they'll capsize that boat.'

Harry followed his gaze to the head of the queue. Men stood shoulder deep in the cold Channel. At the head of the line men were piling into a fishing smack, their weight already tipping it over at an angle.

'We'd better go down,' Harry said. Tomlinson had nodded, and they began marching to the shore. Harry could see the fishermen remonstrating with the men still piling in.

'I suppose it's lucky discipline hasn't broken down completely,' Harry had said. Tomlinson turned to him, but his reply was lost in the scream of a dive-bomber, right above them, drowning the fainter whine of the falling bombs. Then there was a roar that felt as though it would burst Harry's head as he was lifted off his feet in a cloud of red-stained sand.

'Then he wasn't there,' Harry said aloud. 'Just bits. Pieces.'

'Sorry?' Muriel asked, puzzled.

Harry squeezed his eyes closed, trying to shut out the images. 'Nothing, Muriel. It's OK, sorry.'

He felt her hand find his and clutch it. It felt work-roughened, hard, dry. He blinked back tears.

'We made it tonight, eh?' he said.

'Yes, thanks to you.'

The warble of the all-clear was audible. The entire shelter seemed to exhale and relax. The door opened fully and the leader stood silhouetted against a starry sky lit with the glow of fires.

'They've gone, folks,' he said. 'We can go home again.'

Chapter Three

THE PLANE LEFT CROYDON at dawn. Harry had been driven there straight from the SIS training centre. He had never flown before. It was an ordinary civil flight and the other passengers were English and Spanish businessmen. They chatted easily among themselves, mostly about the difficulties the war had made for trade, as they flew out over the Atlantic before turning south, avoiding German-occupied France. Harry felt a moment's fear as the plane took off and he realized the railway lines he could see far below, smaller than Ronnie's train set, were real. That passed quickly, though, as they flew into a bank of cloud, grey like thick fog against the windowpane. The cloud and the steady drone of the engines grew monotonous and Harry leaned back in his seat. He thought of his training, the three weeks' coaching and preparation they had given him before, this morning, they put him in a car to the airport.

The morning after the bombing Harry had been driven from London to a mansion in the Surrey countryside, where he had spent the entire three weeks. He never knew its name or even where it was exactly. It was a Victorian redbrick pile; something about the layout of the rooms, the uncarpeted floors and a faint, indefinable smell, made him think it had once been a school.

The people who trained him were mostly young. There was something eager and adventurous about them, a quickness of reaction and an energy that made them seize your attention, hold your eye, take charge of the conversation. Sometimes they reminded Harry oddly of eager salesmen. They taught him the general business of spying: letterdrops, how to tell if you were being watched, how to get a message out if you were on the run. Not that that would happen to Harry, they reassured him – he had diplomatic protection, a useful by-product of his cover.

From the general they moved to the specific: how to deal with Sandy Forsyth. They made him do what they called role-plays, a former policeman from Kenya playing Sandy. A suspicious Sandy, doubting his story; a drunk and hostile Sandy asking what the fuck Brett was doing here, he had always hated him; a Sandy who was himself a spy, a secret Fascist.

'You don't know how he'll react to you, you have to be prepared for every possible eventuality,' the policeman said. 'You have to adapt yourself to his moods, reflect what he's thinking and feeling.'

Harry had to be absolutely consistent in his own story, they said, it had to be watertight. That was easy enough. He could be absolutely truthful about his life up to the day Will had received the telephone call from the Foreign Office. In the cover story they had rung looking for a translator to replace a man in Madrid who had to leave suddenly. Harry soon had it pat, but they told him there was still a problem. Not with his face, but with his voice; there was an uncertainty, almost a reluctance, when he told his story. A sharp operator, as Forsyth appeared to be, might pick up that he was lying. Harry worked at it and satisfied them after a while. 'Of course,' the policeman said, 'any oddness in tone could be put down to your little bit of deafness, that can affect the voice. Play that up, and tell him about the panics you had after Dunkirk as well.'

Harry was surprised. 'But those have gone, I don't get them any more.'

'You feel them coming still, don't you? You manage to suppress them but you feel them coming?' He glanced at the file on his knees; Harry had his own buff file with a red cross and 'secret' on it now. 'Well, play up to that – a moment's confusion, like pausing to ask him to repeat something, can play to your advantage. Gives you time to think and fixes you in his mind as an invalid, not someone to be afraid of.'

The information about his panics had come, Harry knew, from the odd woman who had interviewed him one day. She never said who she was but Harry guessed she was some sort of psychiatrist. She had something of the busy eagerness of the spies about her. The gaze from her blue eyes was so penetrating that Harry recoiled for a second.

She shook his hand and cheerfully asked him to sit down at the little table.

'Need to ask a few personal questions, Harry. I may call you Harry?'

'Yes – er . . .'

'Miss Crane, call me Miss Crane. You seem to have led a pretty straightforward life, Harry. Not like some of the rum 'uns we get here, I can tell you.' She laughed.

'I suppose I have. An ordinary life.'

'Losing both parents when you were so young, though, that can't have been easy. Passed around between uncles and aunts and your boarding school.'

That made him suddenly angry. 'My aunt and uncle have always been kind. And I was happy at school. And Rookwood's a public school, not a boarding school.'

Miss Crane eyed him quizzically. 'Is there a difference?'

'Yes, there is.' The heat that came into his voice surprised Harry. 'A boarding school makes it sound like a place where you're just left, to mark time. Rookwood – a public school, you're part of a community, it becomes part of you, shapes you.'

She still smiled but her reply was brutal. 'Not the same as having parents who love you, is it?'

Harry felt his anger being replaced by heavy weariness. He lowered his gaze. 'You have to deal with things as they are, make the best of things. Soldier on.'

'On your own? There isn't a girlfriend, is there? Anyone?'

He frowned, wondering if she was going to start making suggestions about his sex life, like Miss Maxse had. 'There isn't now. There was someone at Cambridge, but it didn't work out.'

'Why was that?'

'Laura and I got bored with each other, Miss Crane. Nothing dramatic.'

She changed the subject. 'And after Dunkirk? The shell shock, when you found you were having panic attacks, were frightened of loud noises. Did you decide to soldier on then, too?'

'Yes, not that I was a soldier any more. I won't be again.'

'Does that make you angry?'

He looked at her. 'Wouldn't you be?'

She inclined her head reprovingly. 'It's you we're here to talk about, Harry.'

He sighed. 'Yes, I decided to soldier on.'

'Were you tempted not to? To retreat into – being an invalid?'

He looked at her again. God, she was sharp. 'Yes, yes, I suppose I was. But I didn't. I started by going into the hospital grounds, then crossing the road, then walking into town. It got easier. I wasn't as badly affected as some poor sods.'

'Must have taken courage, guts. Like helping your cousin's family in the bombing the night before you came here.'

'You go on or go under. That's life these days, isn't it?' he replied sharply. 'Even when you've seen everything you took for granted, believed in, smashed to pieces.' He gave a long sigh. 'I think the sight of everyone retreating on that beach, the chaos, all that affected me as much as the shell that nearly hit me.'

'But soldiering on, it must be very lonely.'

Her voice was suddenly gentle. Harry found his eyes filling with tears. He said, without intending to, 'That night in the shelter, it was so strange. Muriel, Will's wife, she took my hand. We've never got on, I always felt she resented me, but she took my hand. Yet . . .'

'Yes?'

'It felt so dry. So cold. I felt – sad.'

'Perhaps it wasn't Muriel's hand you wanted.'

He looked at her. 'No, you're right,' he said in surprise. But I don't know whose I did want.'

'We all need someone's hand.'

'Do we?' Harry laughed uneasily. 'This is a long way from my mission.'

She nodded. 'Just getting to know you, Harry, just getting to know you.'

Harry was jerked out of his reverie as the plane tilted. He clutched at the arms of his seat and looked out of the window, then leaned forward and stared out. They had come out into sunshine again, they were over land. Spain. Harry looked down at the Castilian landscape, a sea of yellow and brown dotted with patchwork fields.

As the plane circled lower he made out white empty roads, red-tiled houses, here and there a jumble of ruins from the Civil War. Then the pilot said they were about to land at Barajas airport and a few minutes later they were down on the runway, the engines stopped and he was here, in Spain. He felt a mixture of excitement and fear; he could still hardly believe he was actually back in Madrid.

Looking out of the window he saw half a dozen civil guards standing outside the terminal building, staring over the runway. Harry recognized their dark green uniforms, the yellow holsters clipped to their belts. They still wore their sinister, archaic leather hats, round with two little wings at the back, black and shiny like a beetle's carapace. When he first came to Spain in 1931 the *civiles*, old supporters of the right, had been under threat from the Republic and you could see the fear and anger in their hard faces. When he returned in 1937, during the Civil War, they were gone. Now they had returned and Harry felt a dryness in his mouth as he looked at their faces, their cold, still expressions.

He joined the passengers heading for the exit. Dry heat enveloped him as he descended the steps and joined the crocodile crossing the tarmac. The airport building was no more than a low concrete warehouse, the paint flaking away. One of the *civiles* came across and stood by them. '*Por allí, por allí*,' he snapped officiously, pointing to a door marked '*Inmigración*'.

Harry had a diplomatic passport and was waved quickly through, his bags chalked without a glance. He looked round the empty entrance hall. There was a whiff of disinfectant, the sickly smelling stuff they had always used in Spain.

A solitary figure leaning against a pillar reading a newspaper waved and came across.

'Harry Brett? Simon Tolhurst, from the embassy. How was the flight?'

He was about Harry's age, tall and fair, with an eager friendly manner. He was built like Harry, solidity turning to fat, although with the embassy man the process had gone further.

'Fine. Cloudy most of the way, but not too bumpy.' Harry noticed Tolhurst wore an Eton tie, the bright colours clashing with his white linen jacket.

'I'll drive you to the embassy, take about an hour. We don't use Spanish drivers; they're all government spies.' He laughed and lowered his voice, though there was no one around. 'The way they bend their ears back to listen, you'd think they're going to meet in the middle. Very obvious.'

Tolhurst led him out into the sun and helped put his case in the back of a highly polished old Ford. The airport was out in the country, fields all around. Harry stood looking over the harsh brown landscape. In a field across the road he saw a peasant leading a couple of skinny oxen, ploughing the stubble in with a wooden plough as his ancestors had in Roman times. In the distance the jumbled peaks of the Guadarrama mountains stood out against the harsh blue sky, shimmering in heat haze. Harry felt sweat prickling at his brow.

'Hot for October,' he said.

'Been a bloody hot summer. They've had a dreadful harvest; they're very worried about the food situation. That may help us, though – makes them less likely to enter the war. We'd better get on. You've got an appointment with the ambassador.'

Tolhurst eased out onto a long deserted road flanked by dusty poplars, the leaves yellowing at the tips like giant torches.

'How long have you been in Spain?' Harry asked.

'Four months. Came when they expanded the embassy, sent Sir Sam over. Did a spell in Cuba before. Lot more relaxed. Fun.' He shook his head. 'This is one awful country, I'm afraid. You've been before, haven't you?'

'Before the Civil War, then briefly during it. To Madrid both times.'

Tolhurst shook his head again. 'It's a pretty grim place now.'

As they drove over the stony, potholed road they talked about the Blitz, agreeing Hitler had abandoned his invasion plans for now. Tolhurst asked Harry where he had gone to school.

'Rookwood, eh? Good place, I believe. Those were the days, eh?' he added wistfully.

Harry smiled sadly. 'Yes.'

He looked out at the countryside. There was a new emptiness to the landscape. Only the occasional peasant driving a donkey and cart passed them, and once an army truck going north, a group of tired-looking young soldiers staring vacantly from the back. The villages were empty too. It was siesta time, but in the old days there would have been a few people about. Now even the once ubiquitous skinny dogs had gone and only a few chickens were left foraging round closed doorways. One village square had huge posters of Franco all over the cracked, unpainted walls, his arms folded confidently as his jowly face smiled into the distance. *¡HASTA EL FUTURO!* Towards the future. Harry took a deep breath. The posters, Harry saw, covered older ones whose tattered edges were visible beneath. He recognized the bottom half of the old slogan, *¡NO PASARAN!* They shall not pass. But they had.

Then they were in the rich northern suburbs. From the look of the elegant houses the Civil War might never have happened. 'Does the ambassador live out here?' Harry asked.

'No, Sir Sam lives in the Castellana.' Tolhurst laughed. 'It's a bit embarrassing, actually. He's next door to the German ambassador.'

Harry turned, open-mouthed. 'But we're at war!'

'Spain's "non-belligerent". But it's crawling with Germans, the scum are all over the place. The German embassy here's the largest in the world. We don't speak to them, of course.'

'How did the ambassador end up next door to the Germans?'

'Only big house available. He makes a joke of glaring at von Stohrer over the garden wall.'

They drove on into the town centre. Most of the buildings were unpainted and even more dilapidated than Harry remembered, though once many must have been grand. There were posters everywhere, Franco and the yoke-and-arrows symbol of the Falange. Most people were shabbily dressed, even more than he remembered, many looking thin and tired. Men in overalls with scrawny weather-beaten faces walked by, and women in black shawls, patched and mended. Even the barefoot skinny children playing in the dusty gutters had pinched watchful faces. Harry had half expected to see military parades and Falangist rallies like in the newsreels, but the city was quieter than he had known it, as well as dingier. He saw priests and nuns among the passers-by; they were back, too, like the *civiles*. The few wealthier-looking men wore jackets and hats despite the heat.

Harry turned to Tolhurst. 'When I was here in '37 wearing a jacket and hat on a hot day was illegal. Bourgeois affectation.'

'You're not allowed to go out *without* a jacket now, not if you're wearing a shirt. Point to remember.'

The trams were running but there were few cars and they weaved their way among donkey carts and bicycles. Harry jerked round in amazement as a familiar shape caught his eye, a hooked black cross.

'Did you see that? The bloody swastika's flying beside the Spanish flag on that building!'

Tolhurst nodded. 'Have to get used to that. It's not just swastikas – the Germans run the police and the press. Franco makes no secret he wants the Nazis to win. Now, look over there.'

They had stopped at an intersection. Harry noticed a trio of colourfully dressed girls wearing thick make-up. They caught his glance and smiled, turning their heads provocatively.

'There are tarts everywhere. You have to be very careful, most of them have the clap and some are government spies. Embassy staff aren't allowed near them.'

A pith-helmeted traffic policeman waved them on. 'Do you think Franco will come into the war?' Harry asked.

Tolhurst ran a hand through his yellow hair, making it stick up. 'God knows. It's a terrible atmosphere; the newspapers and radio are wildly pro-German. Himmler's coming on a state visit next week. But you just have to carry on as normal, as much as you can.' He blew out his cheeks and smiled ruefully. 'But most people keep a suitcase packed, in case we have to get out in a hurry. Oh, I say, there's a gasogene!'

He pointed to where a big old Renault was puttering along, slower than the donkey carts. Fixed to the back was what looked like a large squat boiler, clouds of smoke pouring from a little chimney. Pipes led under the car from the thing. The driver, a middle-aged bourgeois, ignored stares from the pavement as people stopped to look. A tram clattered by hooting and he swerved wildly to avoid it, the unwieldy vehicle almost teetering over.

'What the hell was that?' Harry asked.

'Spain's revolutionary answer to the petrol shortage. Uses coal or wood instead of petrol. OK unless you want to go uphill. The French have them too, I hear. Not much chance of the Germans being after that design.'

Harry studied the crowd. A few people were smiling at the bizarre vehicle, but it struck Harry that none were laughing or calling out, as Madrileños would have done before at such a thing. Again he thought how silent they were, the background buzz of conversation he remembered gone.

They drove into Opera district, catching glimpses of the Royal Palace in the distance. It stood out brightly amid the general shabbiness, the sun reflected from its white walls.

'Does Franco live there?' Harry asked.

'He receives people there but he's established himself in the Pardo Palace, outside Madrid. He's terrified of assassination. Drives everywhere in a bullet-proof Mercedes Hitler sent him.'

'There's still opposition then?'

'The *civiles* have security sewn up in the towns. But you never know. After all, Madrid was only taken eighteen months ago. In a way, it's an occupied city as much as Paris. There's still resistance in the north, from what we hear, and Republican bands hiding out in the countryside. The *vagabundos*, they call them.'

'God,' Harry said. 'What this country's been through.'

'It might not be over yet,' Tolhurst observed grimly.

They drove into a street of large nineteenth-century houses, outside one of which a Union Jack hung from a flagpole, blessedly familiar. Harry remembered coming to the embassy in 1937, to ask for Bernie after he was reported missing. The officials had been unhelpful, disapproving of the International Brigades.

A couple of *civiles* were posted at the door. Cars were drawn up outside the entrance so Tolhurst stopped a little way up the road.

'Let's get your bag,' he said.

Harry looked warily at the *civiles* as he climbed out. Then he felt his leg tugged from behind. He looked round to see a thin boy of ten, dressed in the rags of an army tunic, sitting on a kind of wheeled wooden sled.

'Señor, por favor, diez pesetas.'

Harry saw the child had no legs. The boy clung to his turn-ups. '*Por el amor de Dios*,' he pleaded, thrusting out his other hand. One of the *civiles* marched sharply down the street, clapping his hands. '*¡Vete! ¡Vete!*' At his shout the little boy slapped his hands on the cobbles, rolling his cart backwards into a side street. Tolhurst took Harry's elbow.

'You'll have to be quicker than that, old boy. Beggars don't usually get as far out as this, but they're thick as pigeons round the Centro. Not that there are any pigeons left, they've eaten them all.'

The *civil* who had chased the boy away escorted them to the embassy door. '*Gracias por su asistencia*,' Tolhurst said formally. The man nodded, but Harry saw a look of contempt in his eyes.

'It's a bit of a shock at first, the children,' Tolhurst said as he turned the handle of the big wooden door. 'But you have to get used to it. Now, time to meet your reception committee. The big guns are waiting for you.' He sounded jealous, Harry thought, as Tolhurst led the way into the hot, gloomy interior.

THE AMBASSADOR sat behind an enormous desk in an imposing room cooled by quietly whirring fans. There were eighteenth-century prints on the wall, thick rugs on the tiled floor. Another man, in the uniform of a naval captain, sat to one side of the desk. A window looked on to an interior courtyard full of potted plants, where a little group of men in shirtsleeves sat talking on a bench.

Harry recognized Sir Samuel Hoare from the newsreels. He had been a minister under Chamberlain, an appeaser dismissed when Churchill took over. A small man with delicately pointed, severe features and thin white hair, he wore a morning coat with a blue flower in the buttonhole. He stood and leaned across the desk, thrusting out a hand.

'Welcome, Brett, welcome.' The handshake was surprisingly strong. Cold, pale blue eyes stared into Harry's for a moment, then the ambassador waved at the other man. 'Captain Alan Hillgarth, our naval attaché. He has overall responsibility for Special Services.' Hoare pronounced the final words with a touch of distaste.

Hillgarth was in his forties, tall and darkly handsome with large brown eyes. They were hard but there was something mischievous, almost childlike, about them and about the wide sensual mouth. Harry remembered Sandy reading adventure stories at Rookwood by a man called Hillgarth. They were about spies, adventures in dark backwaters of Europe. Sandy Forsyth had liked them but Harry had found them rather garbled.

The captain shook his hand warmly. 'Hello, Brett. You'll be directly responsible to me, through Tolhurst here.'

'Sit, please; sit, all.' Hoare waved Harry to a chair.

'We're glad to see you,' Hillgarth said. 'We've had reports of your training. You seemed to pick up everything reasonably well.'

'Thank you, sir.'

'Ready to spin your yarn to Forsyth?'

'Yes, sir.'

'We've got you a flat, Tolhurst here will take you round afterwards. Now, you know the drill? The cover story?'

'Yes, sir. I've been seconded as an interpreter, after the illness of the previous man.'

'Poor old Greene,' Hillgarth said with a sudden laugh. 'Still doesn't know why he was rushed off home.'

'Good interpreter,' Hoare interjected. 'Knew his job. Brett, you'll have to be very careful what you say. As well as your – ah – other work, you'll be interpreting for some senior people, and things are delicate here. Very delicate.' Hoare looked at him sharply and Harry felt suddenly intimidated. He still couldn't get used to the fact that he was talking to a man he had seen on the newsreels. He took a deep breath.

'I understand, sir. They briefed me in England. I translate everything into the most diplomatic language possible, never add comments of my own.'

Hillgarth nodded. 'He's doing a session with the junior trade minister and me on Thursday. I'll keep him in order.'

'Maestre, yes.' Hoare grunted. 'We don't want to upset *him*.'

Hillgarth produced a gold cigarette case and offered it to Harry. 'Smoke?'

'I don't, thanks.'

Hillgarth lit up and blew out a cloud of smoke. 'We don't want you to meet Forsyth straight away, Brett. Take a few days to get yourself known on the circuit, settle in. And get used to being watched and followed – the government put spies on all embassy staff. Most of them are pretty hopeless, you can spot them a mile off, though a few Gestapo-trained men are coming through now. Watch out for anyone on your tail, and report to Tolhurst.' He smiled as though it were all an adventure, in a way that reminded Harry of the people at the training school.

'I will, sir.'

'Now,' Hillgarth went on. 'Forsyth. You knew him well for a time at school, but you haven't seen him since. Correct?'

'Yes, sir.'

'But you think he might be well disposed towards you?'

'I hope so, sir. But I don't really know what he's been up to since we stopped writing. That was ten years ago.' Harry glanced out at the courtyard. One of the men there was looking in at them.

'Those bloody airmen!' Hoare snapped. 'I'm fed up of them peering in here!' He waved a hand imperiously and the men got up and walked off, disappearing through a side door. Harry saw Hillgarth gave Hoare a quick look of dislike before turning back to him.

'Those are pilots who had to bale out over France,' Hillgarth said pointedly. 'Some of them have walked here.'

'Yes, yes, yes,' Hoare said pettishly. 'We must get on.'

'Of course, ambassador,' Hillgarth said with heavy formality. He turned back to Harry. 'Now, we first heard about Forsyth two months ago. I've an agent in the Industry Ministry here, a junior clerk. He let us know they were all very excited there about something that was going on out in the country, about fifty miles from Madrid. Our man can't get to the papers but he overheard a couple of conversations. Gold deposits. Large ones, geologically verified. We know they're sending mining equipment out, and mercury and other chemicals; scarce resources.'

'Sandy was always interested in geology,' Harry said. 'At school he had a thing about fossils, he used to go off and try to find dinosaur bones.'

'Did he now?' Hillgarth said. 'Didn't know that. He never got himself any formal qualifications that we know of, but he's working with a man who has. Alberto Otero.'

'The man with experience in South Africa?'

'Just so.' Hillgarth nodded approvingly. 'Mining engineer. They gave you some reading up on gold mining back home, I believe.'

'Yes, sir.' It had been odd, grappling with the heavy textbooks in the evening in his little room.

'So far as Forsyth's concerned, of course, you know nothing about gold. Babe in arms on the subject.'

'Yes, sir.' Harry paused. 'Do you know how Forsyth and this Otero came together?'

'No. There are a lot of gaps. We only know that while he was working as a tour guide Forsyth got in with the Auxilio Social, the Falange organization that handles what passes for social welfare here.' He raised his eyebrows. 'It's corrupt as hell. Rich pickings, with supplies so short.'

'Does Forsyth still keep in touch with his family?'

Hillgarth shook his head. 'His father hasn't heard from him in years.'

Harry remembered the one time he had seen the bishop; he had come down to the school after Sandy's disgrace to plead for his son. Looking from the classroom Harry had seen him in the quadrangle, recognized him by the red episcopal shirt under his suit. He looked solid and patrician, nothing like Sandy.

'Forsyth supported the Nationalists, then?' Harry asked.

'I think it was the rich pickings he supported,' Hillgarth replied.

'You weren't a Republican supporter, were you?' Hoare gave Harry a searching look.

'I didn't support either side, sir.'

Hoare grunted. 'I thought that was the great dividing line before the War, who supported the Reds in Spain and who the Nats. I'm surprised at a Hispanicist supporting neither side.'

'Well I didn't, sir. A plague on both their houses was what I thought.' He's a tetchy little bully, Harry thought.

'I could never understand how anyone could think a Red Spain could be less than a disaster.'

Hillgarth looked irritated by the interruption. He leaned forward. 'Forsyth wouldn't have known any Spanish before coming out here, would he?'

'No, but he would have picked it up quickly. He's smart. That was one reason the masters hated him at school; he was bright but he wouldn't work.'

Hillgarth raised his eyebrows. 'Hated? That's a strong word.'

'It got to that, I think.'

'Well, according to our man he's got in with the state mining agency. Does wheeler-dealing for them; negotiating supplies and so on.' He paused. 'The Falange faction dominates the Ministry of Mines. They'd love Spain to be able to pay for food imports, instead of begging us and the Americans for loans. Trouble is, we've no hard intelligence in there. If you could get directly to Forsyth it could be of incalculable help. We must find out if there's anything in these gold stories.'

'Yes, sir.'

There was a moment's silence, the oily swishing of the ceiling fan suddenly loud, then Hillgarth went on. 'Forsyth works through a company he's set up. Nuevas Iniciativas. It's listed on the Madrid Stock Exchange as a supply procurement company. The shares have been going up, Ministry of Mines officials have been buying in. The firm has a little office near Calle Toledo; Forsyth's there most days. Our man hasn't been able to get his home address, which is a blasted nuisance – we just know he lives out in Vigo district with some tart. Most days at siesta time he goes for coffee to a local cafe. That's where we want you to make contact with him.'

'Does he go by himself?'

'Apart from him there's just a secretary at the office. He always takes that half-hour by himself in the afternoon.'

Harry nodded. 'He used to like going off alone at school.'

'We've had him watched. It's bloody nerve-racking – I worry Forsyth might spot our man.' He passed Harry a couple of photos from a file on the desk. 'He took these.'

The first photograph showed Sandy, well dressed and tanned, walking down a street talking to an army officer. Sandy had bent to catch his words, his face solemnly attentive. The second showed him striding carelessly along, jacket unbuttoned, smoking. There was a confident, knowing smile on his face.

'He looks prosperous.'

Hillgarth nodded. 'Oh, he's not short of money.' He turned back to the file. 'The flat we've got you is a couple of streets from his office. It's on the fringe of a poor area, but with the housing shortage it'll be credible to house a junior diplomat there.'

'Yes, sir.'

'Your flat's actually not bad, I'm told. Used to belong to some Communist functionary under the Republic. Probably been shot by now. Settle in there, but don't go to the cafe yet.'

'What's it called, sir?'

'Café Rocinante.'

Harry smiled wryly. 'The name of Don Quijote's horse.'

Hillgarth nodded, then looked steadily at Harry. 'Word of advice,' he said with a smile, his tone friendly though his eyes were hard. 'You look too serious, like you had the weight of the world on your shoulders. Cheer up a bit, smile. Look on it as an adventure.'

Harry blinked. An adventure. Spying on an old friend who was working with fascists.

The ambassador gave a sudden harsh laugh. 'Adventure! Dear God preserve us. There are too many adventurers in this damn country if you ask me.' He turned to Harry, his face animated. 'Listen, Brett. You sound like you've got your head screwed on, but be damned careful. I agreed to your coming because it's important we find out what's going on, but I don't want you upsetting any applecarts.'

'I'm not sure I understand, sir.'

'This regime is divided in two. Most of the generals who won the Civil War are solid sensible people who admire England and want Spain kept out of the war. It's my job to build bridges and strengthen their hand with Franco. I don't want it getting to the Generalísimo that we've got spies nosing round one of his pet projects.'

Hillgarth nodded.

'I understand,' said Harry. Hoare doesn't want me here at all, he thought. I'm in the middle of some bloody piece of politics.

Hillgarth rose. 'Well, I've got this ceremony for the Naval Heroes of Spain. Better show the flag, eh, ambassador?'

Hoare nodded and Hillgarth rose, Harry and Tolhurst following. Hillgarth picked up the file and handed it to Harry. It had a red cross on the front.

'Tolly will take you to your flat. Take Forsyth's dossier, have a good look, but bring it back tomorrow. Tolly will show you where to sign it out.'

As they left, Harry turned to look at Hoare. He was staring out of the window, frowning at the airmen who had started to drift back into the yard.

Chapter Four

OUTSIDE THE AMBASSADOR'S ROOM Tolhurst smiled apologetically. 'Sorry about Sam,' he said in a low voice. 'He wouldn't normally be in at a briefing for a new agent, but he's nervous about this job. He's got a rule: intelligence gathering is allowed, but no espionage, no antagonizing the regime. Some socialists came a few weeks ago to try and get help for the guerrillas fighting against Franco. Bloody dangerous for them. He sent them packing.'

Harry hadn't liked Hoare, but was still slightly shocked by Tolhurst calling him Sam. 'Because he wants good relations with the Monarchists?' he asked.

'Exactly. After the Civil War they hate the Reds, you can imagine.' Tolhurst fell silent as they stepped into the street, the *civiles* saluting as they passed. He opened the door of the Ford, wincing at the heat of the handle.

He renewed the conversation as they drove away. 'They say Churchill sent Sam here to get him out of the way,' he confided cheerfully. 'Can't stand him, doesn't trust him either. That's why he put the captain in charge of Intelligence; he's an old friend of Winston's. From his days out of government.'

'Aren't we all supposed to be on the same side?'

'There's a lot of internal politics.'

'You can say that again.'

Tolhurst smiled sardonically. 'Sam's a bitter man. He wanted to be Viceroy of India.'

'The in-fighting can't make anyone's job easier.'

'Way things are, old boy.' Tolhurst looked at him seriously. 'Best you should know the score.'

Harry changed the subject. 'When I was at school I remember some adventure books by an Alan Hillgarth. Not the same man, I suppose?'

Tolhurst nodded. 'The very same. Not bad, are they? Ever read the one set in Spanish Morocco? *The War Maker*. Franco comes into it. Fictionalized, of course. The captain admired him, you can tell.'

'I haven't read it. I know Sandy Forsyth liked them.'

'Did he now?' Tolhurst said with interest. 'I'll tell the captain. That'll amuse him.'

They drove through the centre into a maze of narrow streets of four-storey tenements. It was late afternoon and the heat was starting to lift, long shadows falling across the road as Tolhurst steered carefully over the cobbles. The tenements had had no attention for years, plaster was falling from the brickwork like flesh from skeletons. There were several bombsites, heaps of stone overgrown with weeds. There were no other cars around and passers-by glanced at the car curiously. A donkey pulling a cart shied away into the pavement as they passed, nearly unseating its rider. Harry watched as the man steadied himself, mouthing a curse.

'I was wondering,' he said, 'how I was recruited.' He kept his tone casual. 'Just interest. Never mind if you can't tell me.'

'Oh, that's no secret. They were hunting up Forsyth's old contacts and a master at Rookwood mentioned you.'

'Mr Taylor?'

'Don't know the name. When they found you knew Spain they were in seventh heaven. That's where the interpreter idea came from.'

'I see.'

'Real piece of luck.' Tolhurst skirted a crack in the road by a bombsite. 'Did you know, the embassy here was the first piece of British soil to be hit by a German bomb?'

'What? Oh, during the Civil War?'

'Hit the garden by accident when the Germans were bombing Madrid. Sam's had it put back in order. He has his good points. He's a first-class organizer, the embassy runs like clockwork. You have to give the pink rat his due.'

'The what?'

Tolhurst smiled confidentially. 'It's his nickname. He gets these fits of panic, thinks Spain's about to come into the war and he'll be shot, has to be persuaded not to run off to Portugal. D'you know, the other evening a bat flew into his study and he hid under the table, screaming for someone to take it away. You can imagine what Hillgarth thinks. But when he's on form Sam's a bloody good diplomat. Loves strutting about as the King-Emperor's representative; the Monarchists all go soppy at anything to do with royalty, of course. Ah, here we are.'

Tolhurst had pulled up in a dusty square. There was a statue of a soldier in eighteenth-century dress on a pedestal in the middle, one arm missing, and a few fly-blown shops with half-empty windows. Tenements ringed the square, the windows behind the rusty iron balconies shuttered against the afternoon heat. The place must have had style once. Harry studied them through the window. He remembered a picture he had bought in a back-street shop in 1931: a crumbling tenement building like this, a girl leaning out of a window, smiling as a gipsy serenaded her underneath. He had it in his room at Cambridge. There was something romantic about decaying buildings; the Victorians had loved them, of course. But it was different if you had to live in them.

Tolhurst pointed to a narrow street leading north, where the buildings looked even more down at heel.

'Wouldn't go down there if I were you. That's La Latina. Bad area, leads across the river to Carabanchel.'

'I know,' Harry replied. 'There was a family we used to visit in Carabanchel when I came in 1931.'

Tolhurst looked at him curiously.

'The Nationalists shelled it badly during the Siege, didn't they?' Harry asked.

'Yes, and they've left it to rot since the Civil War. See the place as full of their enemies. There are people starving down there, I'm told, and packs of wild dogs living in the ruined buildings. People have been bitten and got rabies.'

Harry looked down the long empty street.

'What else is there you should know?' Tolhurst asked. 'English people aren't very popular generally. It's the propaganda. It's never more than dirty looks, though.'

'How do we deal with Germans if we meet them?'

'Oh, just cut the bastards dead. Be careful about greeting people who look English on the streets,' he added as he opened the car door. 'They're just as likely to be Gestapo.'

Outside the air was full of dust, a breeze lifting little whorls of it from the street. They took Harry's case from the car. A thin old woman in black crossed the square, a huge bag of clothes on her head supported by one hand. Harry wondered which side she had supported during the Civil War, or whether she had been one of the thousands without politics, caught in the middle. Her face was deeply lined, her expression tired but stoical; one of those who endured – somehow, only just.

Tolhurst handed Harry a brown card. 'Your rations. The embassy gets diplomatic rations and we distribute them. Better than we get at home. A lot better than the rations they get here.' His eyes followed the old woman. 'They say people are digging up vegetable roots for food. You can buy stuff on the black market, of course, but it's expensive.'

'Thanks.' Harry pocketed the card. Tolhurst went over to one of the tenements, producing a key, and they entered a dark vestibule with cracked flaking paint. Water dripped somewhere and there was a smell of stale urine. They climbed stone steps to the second floor, where the doors of three flats faced them. Two little girls were playing with battered dolls in the hallway. '*Buenas tardes*,' Harry said, but they looked away. Tolhurst unlocked one of the doors.

It was a three-bedroomed flat, such as Harry remembered would often house a family of ten in crowded squalor. It had been cleaned and there was a smell of polish. It was furnished like a middle-class home, full of heavy old sofas and cabinets. There were no pictures on the mustard-yellow walls, only blank squares where they had hung. Dust motes danced in a beam of sunlight.

'It's big,' said Harry.

'Yes, better than the shoebox where I live. Just the one Communist Party official used to live here. Disgrace when you see how most people are crowded together. Left empty for a year after he was taken away. Then the authorities remembered they had it and put it up for rent.'

Harry ran a finger along the film of dust on the table. 'By the way, what's this about Himmler coming here?'

Tolhurst looked serious. 'It's all over the Fascist press. State visit next week.' He shook his head. 'You never get used to the idea that we might have to run. There have been so many false alarms.'

Harry nodded. He's not really brave, he thought, no more than I am. 'So you report directly to Hillgarth?' he asked.

'That's right.' Tolhurst tapped the leg of an ornate bureau with his foot. 'I don't get to do any actual secret work, though. I'm the admin man.' He gave a self-deprecating laugh. 'Simon Tolhurst, general dogsbody. Flats found, reports typed, expenses checked.' He paused. 'By the way, make sure you keep a careful note of everything you spend. London's red-hot on expenses.' Tolhurst looked out of the window at the central courtyard where patched washing flapped on lines strung between the balconies, then turned back to Harry. 'Tell me,' he asked curiously, 'does Madrid look much different to when you were here under the Republic?'

'Yes. It was bad enough then but it looks worse now. Even poorer.'

'Maybe things'll get better. I suppose at least now there's strong government.'

'Maybe.'

'Did you hear what Dalí said – Spain's a nation of peasants who need a firm hand? Cuba was the same, they just can't handle democracy. Everything goes to pot.' Tolhurst shook his head, as though it was all beyond him. Harry felt a spurt of anger at his naiveté, then reflected that it was beyond him too, the tragedy that had happened here. Bernie was the one who had had all the answers but his side had lost and Bernie was dead.

'Coffee?' he asked Tolhurst. 'If there is any.'

'Oh yes, place is stocked. And there's a phone, but be careful what you say, it'll be tapped as you're Dip Corps. Same with letters home, they're censored. So take care if you're writing to family, or a girlfriend. Got anyone back home?' he added diffidently.

Harry shook his head. 'No. You?'

'No. They don't let me out of the embassy much.' Tolhurst looked at him curiously. 'What took you to Carabanchel, when you were here before?'

'I came with Bernie Piper. My Communist schoolfriend.' Harry smiled wryly. 'I'm sure it's in my file.'

'Ah. Yes.' Tolhurst reddened slightly.

'He got friendly with a family down there. They were good people; Christ knows what's happened to them now.' He sighed. 'I'll get that coffee.'

Tolhurst looked at his watch. 'Actually, I'd better not. Got to check some damned expenses. Come to the embassy at nine tomorrow, we'll show you the ropes for the translators.'

'Will the other translators know I'm working for Hillgarth?'

Tolhurst shook his head. 'Lord, no. They're all regular Dip Corps, just performers in Sam's circus.' He laughed and extended a damp hand to Harry. 'It's all right, we'll run through it all tomorrow.'

Harry took off his collar and tie, feeling a welcome current of air playing on the damp ring around his neck. He sat in a leather armchair and looked through Forsyth's file. There wasn't much there: some more photographs, details of his work with Auxilio Social, his contacts in the Falange. Sandy was living in a big house, paying liberally for black market goods.

Outside he heard a woman's voice, harsh, calling her children in. He put down the file and walked over to the window, looking through the washing to the shadowy courtyard, where children were playing. He opened the windows, the old familiar smell of cooking mingled with rot striking his nostrils. He could see the woman leaning out, she was young and pretty but wore a widow's black. She called her children again and they ran indoors.

Harry turned back to the room. It was poorly lit and seemed full of gloomy corners, the places where pictures or posters had been removed standing out as ghostly squares. He wondered what had hung there. Pictures of Lenin and Stalin? There was something oppressive about the still, quiet atmosphere. The Communist would have been taken after Franco occupied Madrid, hauled away and shot in a cellar probably. Harry switched on the light but nothing happened. The light in the hall was the same; probably a power cut.

He had been uneasy about spying on Sandy but now he felt a growing anger. Sandy was working with Falangists, people who wanted to make war against England. 'Why, Sandy?' he asked aloud. His voice in the silence startled him. He felt suddenly alone. He was in a hostile country, working for an embassy that seemed to be a hotbed of rivalries. Tolhurst couldn't have been friendlier but Harry guessed he would be reporting his impressions of him to Hillgarth, taking pleasure in being in the know. He thought of Hillgarth telling him to treat this as an adventure, and wondered, as he had wondered from time to time during his training, if he was the right man for this job, if he was up to it. He had said nothing about his doubts: it was an important job and they needed him to do it. For a second, though, he felt panic clutch at the corners of his mind.

This won't do, he told himself. There was a radio on a table in the corner and he switched it on. The glass panel in the centre lit up; the power must be back on. He remembered when he was at his uncle's, on holiday from Rookwood, playing with the radio in the sitting room in the evening. Twiddling the dial, he would hear voices from far-off countries: Italy, Russia, Hitler's harsh screech from Germany. He had wished he could understand the voices that came and went, so far away, interrupted by swishes and crackles. His interest in languages had begun there. Now he twiddled the dial, looking for the BBC, but could find only a Spanish station playing martial music.

He wandered through to the bedroom. The bed had been freshly made up and he lay down, suddenly tired; it had been a long day. Now the playing children had gone he was struck again by the silence outside, it was as though Madrid lay under a shroud. An occupied city, Tolhurst had said. He could hear the blood hissing in his ears. It seemed louder in his bad one. He thought of unpacking, but let his mind drift back, to 1931, his first visit to Madrid. He and Bernie, twenty years old, arriving at Atocha station on a July day, rucksacks on their backs. He remembered emerging from the soot-smelling station into blazing sunlight, and there was the red-yellow-purple flag of the Republic flying over the Agriculture Ministry opposite, outlined against a cobalt-blue sky so bright he had to screw up his eyes.

AFTER SANDY FORSYTH left Rookwood in disgrace, Bernie returned to the study and his friendship with Harry resumed: two quiet, studious boys working for their Cambridge entrance. Bernie tended to keep his political views to himself in those days. He made the rugby XV in his last year and enjoyed the rough, speedy brutality of the field. Harry preferred cricket; when he made the first eleven it was one of the high points of his life.

Seven people from that year's sixth form sat the Cambridge entrance. Harry came second and Bernie first, winning the £50 prize donated by an Old Boy. Bernie said it was more money than he had ever imagined seeing, let alone owning. In the autumn they went to Cambridge together but to different colleges and their paths diverged, Harry mixing with a serious, studious set and Bernie off with the socialist groups, bored with his studies. They still met for a drink now and then but less often as time passed. Harry hadn't seen Bernie for over a month when he breezed into his rooms one summer morning at the end of their second year.

'What're you doing these hols?' he asked once Harry had made tea.

'I'm going to France. It's been decided. I'm going to spend the summer travelling around, trying to get fluent. My cousin Will and his wife were going to come to start with, for their holidays, but she's expecting.' He sighed; it had been a disappointment and he was nervous of travelling alone. 'Are you going to work in the shop again?'

'No. I'm going to Spain for a month. They're doing some great things there.' Harry was reading Spanish as a second language; he knew the monarchy had fallen that April. A Republic had been declared, with a government of liberals and socialists dedicated, they said, to bringing reform and progress to one of Europe's most backward countries.

'I want to see it,' Bernie said. His face shone with enthusiasm. 'This new constitution's a people's constitution, it's the end for the landlords and the church.' He looked at Harry thoughtfully. 'But I don't really want to go to Spain alone, either. I wondered if you'd like to come. After all, you speak the language, why not go and see Spain too, see it first hand instead of reading dusty old Spanish playwrights? I could come to France first if you don't want to be on your own,' Bernie added. 'I'd like to see it. Then we could go on to Spain.' He smiled. Bernie was always persuasive.

'Spain's pretty primitive, though, isn't it? How will we find our way around?'

Bernie pulled a battered Labour Party card from his pocket. 'This'll help us. I'll introduce you to the international socialist brotherhood.'

Harry smiled. 'Can I charge an interpreter's fee?' He realized that was why Bernie wanted him to come and felt an unexpected sadness.

THEY TOOK the ferry to France in July. They spent ten days in Paris then travelled slowly south by train, spending their nights in cheap hostels along the way. It was a pleasant, lazy time, and to Harry's pleasure their easy companionship from Rookwood returned. Bernie pored over a Spanish grammar, he wanted to be able to speak to the people. Some of his enthusiasm for what he called the new Spain rubbed off on Harry and they were both staring eagerly out of the window as the train pulled into Atocha that hot summer morning.

Madrid was exciting, extraordinary. Walking round the Centro they saw buildings decorated with socialist and anarchist flags, posters for rallies and strike meetings covering the peeling walls of the old buildings. Here and there they saw burned-out churches, which made Harry shudder but Bernie smile with grim pleasure.

'Not much of a workers' paradise,' Harry said, wiping a sheen of sweat from his brow. The heat was baking, a heat such as neither of the English boys had imagined could exist. They were standing in the Puerta del Sol, hot and dusty. Pedlars with donkey carts threaded their way between the trams and ragged shoeshine boys slumped against the walls in the shade. Old women in black shawls shuffled by like dusty, smelly birds.

'Christ, Harry, they've had centuries of oppression,' Bernie said. 'Not least from the church. Most of those burned-out churches were full of gold and silver. It's going to take a long time.'

They got a room on the second floor of a crumbling *hostal* in a narrow street off the Puerta del Sol. On the balcony opposite theirs a couple of prostitutes often sat resting. They would call bawdy remarks across the street, laughing. Harry would redden and turn away, but Bernie shouted back at them, saying they'd no money for such luxuries.

The heat continued; during the hottest part of the day they stayed in the *hostal*, lying on their beds with their shirts open, reading or dozing, savouring every tiny breeze that wafted through the window. Then in the late afternoon they would walk in the city before spending the evenings in the bars.

One evening they went to a bar in La Latina called El Toro where flamenco dancing was advertised. Bernie had seen it in *El Socialista*, the socialist newspaper, full of optimism and hope, which he got Harry to translate for him. When they got there the bulls' heads round the walls startled them. The other customers were working men and eyed Harry and Bernie curiously, giving one another amused nudges. The boys ordered a greasy *cocido* and sat at a bench under a banner advertising a strike meeting, next to a burly brown-faced man with a drooping moustache. The buzz of conversation died as two men in narrow jackets and round black hats walked into the centre of the room, carrying guitars. They were followed by a woman in wide red and black skirts and a low bodice, a black mantilla covering her head. All had narrow faces and skin so dark they reminded Harry of Singh, Rookwood's Indian boy. The men began to play and the woman sang, with a fierce intensity that kept his attention even though he couldn't follow the words. They performed three songs, each one greeted with applause, then one of the men came round with a hat. '*Muy bien*,' Harry said, '*muchas gracias*.' He put a peseta in the cap.

The big man next to them said something to them in Spanish. 'What was that?' Bernie whispered to Harry.

'He says they're singing about oppression by the landlords.'

The workman was studying them with amused interest. 'That is good,' Bernie said in halting Spanish.

The big man nodded approvingly. He extended a hand to Bernie and Harry. It was hard and callused.

'Pedro Mera García,' the man said. 'Where are you from?'

'*Inglaterra*.' Bernie pulled his party card from his pocket. '*Partido Laborista Inglés*.' Pedro smiled broadly. '*Bienvenidos, compadres*.'

SO BERNIE'S FRIENDSHIP with the Mera family began. They regarded him as a comrade, and the apolitical Harry as his slightly retarded cousin. There was an evening in early September, shortly before they were due to return to England, that Harry particularly remembered. It was cooler in the evenings now and Bernie sat on the balcony with Pedro, his wife Inés and their elder son Antonio, who was Harry and Bernie's age and like his father a union activist in the brickworks. Inside the *salón* Harry had been teaching three-year-old Carmela some English words. Her ten-year-old brother, Francisco, thin and tubercular, sat watching with large, tired eyes as Carmela sat on the arm of Harry's chair, repeating the strange words with fascinated solemnity.

At last she got bored and went to play with her dolls. Harry went onto the tiny balcony and looked out across the square, where a welcome breeze stirred up the dust. The sound of voices came up from below. A beer seller called his trade in a high sharp voice. Doves circled in the darkening sky, flashes of white against the red-tiled roofs.

'Help me, Harry,' Bernie said. 'I want to ask Pedro if the government will win the vote of confidence tomorrow.'

Harry asked and Pedro nodded. 'He should. But the President's looking for any excuse to get Azaña out. He agrees with the Monarchists that even the miserable reforms the government's trying to put through are an attack on their rights.'

Antonio laughed bitterly. 'What will they do if we ever really challenge them?' He shook his head. 'This proposal for an agrarian reform act has no funds to back it because Azaña won't raise taxes. People feel let down and angry.'

'Now that you've got the Republic,' Bernie said, 'Spain must never go back.'

Pedro nodded. 'I think the Socialists should leave the government, have an election, win a proper majority. Then we'll see.'

'But would the ruling classes let you govern? Won't they bring out the army?'

Pedro passed Bernie a cigarette. Bernie had started smoking since he came to Spain. 'Let them try that,' Pedro said. 'Let them try and see what we will give them.'

Next day Harry and Bernie went to see the vote of confidence in the Cortes. There were crowds round the parliament building but they had managed to get passes through Pedro. An attendant led them up echoing marble stairs to a gallery above the chamber. The blue benches were packed with deputies in suits and frock coats. The left-liberal leader Azaña was speaking in a strong, impassioned voice, one short arm beating at the air. Depending on their politics the newspapers portrayed him either as a frog-faced monster or as the father of the Republic, but Harry thought how ordinary he looked. He spoke fiercely, passionately. He made a point and turned to the deputies behind him, who clapped and shouted their approval. Azaña ran a hand through his wispy white hair and went on, listing the Republic's achievements. Harry scanned the faces below, recognizing the socialist politicians whose faces he had seen in newspapers: round fat Prieto; Largo Caballero, surprisingly bourgeois-looking with his square face and white moustache. For once Harry felt caught up in the excitement.

'Lively lot, aren't they?' he whispered to Bernie. But Bernie's face when he turned was angry, contemptuous.

'It's a bloody theatre,' Bernie said angrily. 'Look at them. Millions of Spaniards want a decent life and they get this – circus. He surveyed the rustling sea of heads below him. 'Something stronger than this is needed if we're to have socialism. Come on, let's get out of here.'

That night they went to a bar in the Centro. Bernie was in an angry, cynical mood.

'Democracy,' he said angrily. 'It just swallows people up into a corrupt bourgeois system. It's the same in England.'

'But it'll take years to make Spain a modern country,' Harry said. 'And what's the alternative? Revolution and bloodshed, like in Russia?'

'The workers have to take things into their own hands.' He looked at Harry, then sighed. 'Oh come on,' he said. 'Let's go back to the *hostal*. It's late.'

They stumbled up the road in silence, both a little drunk. Their room was stuffy and Bernie pulled off his shirt and went onto the balcony. The two whores sat drinking opposite, wearing colourful dressing gowns. They called across.

'¡Ay, *inglés! ¿Por que no juegues con nosotros?*'

'I can't come and play!' Bernie called back cheerfully. 'I've no money!'

'We don't want money! We keep saying, if only the handsome

blond would come and play!' The women laughed. Bernie laughed too and turned to Harry. Harry felt uneasy, a little shocked.

'Fancy it?' Bernie asked. They had joked about going with a Spanish prostitute for weeks but it had been bravado, they had done nothing about it.

'No. God, Bernie, you could catch something.'

Bernie grinned at him. 'Scared?' He ran a hand through his thick blond hair, his big bicep flexing.

Harry blushed. 'I don't want to do it with a couple of drunk whores. Besides, it's you they want, not me.' Jealousy flickered inside him as it sometimes did. Bernie had something he lacked: an energy, a daring, a lust for life. It wasn't just his looks.

'They'd've asked you too if you'd been at the balcony.'

'Don't go,' Harry said. 'You could catch something.'

Bernie's eyes were alive with excitement. 'I'm going. Come on. Last chance.' Bernie chuckled, then smiled at him. 'You've got to learn to live, Harry, boy. Learn to live.'

Two days later they left Madrid. Antonio Mera helped them carry their bags to the station.

They changed trams at the Puerta de Toledo. It was mid-afternoon, siesta time, the sunny streets empty. A lorry rolled slowly by, its canvas cover gaily painted, the words 'La Barraca' on its side.

'Lorca's new theatre for the people,' Antonio said. He was a tall dark youth, broad like his father. His lip curled slightly. 'Off to bring Calderón to the peasants.'

'That's a good thing, isn't it?' Harry said. 'I thought education was one thing the Republic had reformed.'

Antonio shrugged. 'They've closed the Jesuit schools, but there aren't enough new ones. The old story, the bourgeois parties won't tax the rich to pay for them.'

A little way off there was a crack, like a car backfiring. The sound was repeated twice, closer. A youth no older than Bernie and Harry ran out of a side street. He wore flannels and a dark shirt, expensive clothes for Carabanchel. His face was terrified, wide-eyed, gleaming with sweat. He tore away down the street, disappearing into an alley.

'Who's that?' Harry asked.

Antonio took a deep breath. 'I wonder. That could be one of Redondo's fascists.'

Two more young men appeared, in vests and workmen's trousers. One held something small and dark in his hand. Harry stared open-mouthed as he realized it was a gun.

'Down there!' Antonio called, pointing to where the youth had fled. 'He went down there!'

'*¡Gracias, compadre!*' The boy raised his gun in salute and the two sped away. Harry waited breathlessly for more shots but none came.

'They were going to kill him,' he said in a shocked whisper.

Antonio looked guilty for a moment, then frowned. 'He was from the JONS. We have to stop the Fascists taking root.'

'Who were the others?'

'Communists. They've sworn to stop them. Good luck to them, I say.'

'They're right,' Bernie agreed. 'Fascists are vermin, the lowest of the low.'

'He was just a boy running,' Harry protested. 'He didn't have a gun.'

Antonio laughed bitterly. 'They've got guns all right. But the Spanish workers won't go down like the Italians.'

The tram arrived, the ordinary everyday jingling tram, and they got aboard. Harry studied Antonio. He looked tired; he had another shift at the brickworks tonight. He thought sadly, Bernie's got more in common with him than with me.

HARRY LAY ON the bed, tears pricking at the corners of his eyes. He remembered how, on the train back, Bernie said he wasn't going back to Cambridge. He'd had enough of living cut off from the real world and was going back to London, where the class struggle was. Harry thought he would change his mind, but he didn't; he didn't return to Cambridge in the autumn. They exchanged letters for a while but Bernie's letters talking about strikes and anti-fascist demonstrations were as alien in their way as Sandy Forsyth's about the dogtracks had been, and after a while that correspondence too petered out.

Harry got up. He felt restless now. He needed to get out of the flat, the silence was getting on his nerves. He washed, changed his shirt, then descended the dank staircase.

The square was still quiet. There was a faint smell he remembered, urine from malfunctioning drains. He thought of the picture on his wall, the romantic veneer it gave to poverty and want. He had been young and naive in 1931, but his attachment to the picture had stayed over the years, the young girl smiling at the gipsy. In 1931 he had thought the scene in the picture would soon be in the past; like Bernie, he had hoped Spain would progress. Yet the Republic had collapsed into chaos, then civil war, and now fascism. Harry circled, pausing at a baker's shop. There was little on display, only a few *barras de pan*, none of the little sticky cakes the Spaniards loved. Bernie had eaten five one afternoon then had a *paella* in the evening and been spectacularly sick.

A couple of workmen passed Harry, giving him quick hostile glances. He was conscious of his well-cut jacket, his tie. He noticed a church at the corner of the square; it had been burned out, probably in 1936. The ornate facade still stood but there was no roof; the sky was visible through weed-encrusted windows. A big notice in bright crayon declared that Mass was said at the priest's house next door, and confessions heard. *¡Arriba España!*, the notice concluded.

Harry had his bearings now. If he headed uphill he should reach the Plaza Mayor. On the way was El Toro, the bar where he and Bernie had met Pedro. A Socialist haunt once. He walked on, his footsteps echoing in the narrow street, a welcome evening breeze cooling him. He was glad he had come out.

El Toro was still there, the sign of a bull's head swinging outside. Harry hesitated a moment then walked in. It had not changed in nine years: bulls' heads mounted on the walls, old black-and-white posters yellow with nicotine and age advertising ancient bullfights. The Socialists had disapproved of bullfighting but the landlord's wine was good and he was a supporter so they had indulged him.

There were only a few patrons, old men in berets. They gave Harry unfriendly stares. The young, energetic landlord Harry remembered, darting to and fro behind his crowded bar, was gone. In his place stood a stocky middle-aged man with a heavy square face. He tipped his head interrogatively. '*¿Señor?*'

Harry ordered a glass of red wine, fishing in his pockets for the unfamiliar coins embossed, like everything else, with the Falangist yoke and arrows. The barman set his drink before him.

'*¿Alemán?*' he asked. German?

'*No. Inglés.*'

The barman raised his eyebrows and turned away. Harry went and sat at a bench. He picked up a discarded copy of *Arriba*, the Falange newspaper, the thin paper crinkling. On the front page a Spanish border guard shook hands with a German officer on a Pyrenean road. The article spoke of eternal friendship, how the Führer and the Caudillo would decide the future of the Western Mediterranean together. Harry took a sip of the wine; it was harsh as vinegar.

He studied the picture, the breathless celebration of the New Order. He remembered telling Bernie once that he stood for Rookwood values. He had probably sounded pompous. Bernie had laughed impatiently and said Rookwood was a training ground for the capitalist elite. Maybe it was, Harry thought, but it was a better elite than Hitler's. Despite everything, that was still true. He remembered the newsreels he had seen of the things that happened in Germany, elderly Jews cleaning the streets with toothbrushes amidst laughing crowds.

He looked up. The barman was talking quietly to a couple of the old men. They kept glancing at him. Harry forced himself to drain his glass and got up. He called '*Adiós*,' but there was no reply.

There were more people about now: well-dressed, middle-class office workers making their way home. He passed under an archway and stood in the Plaza Mayor, the centre of old Madrid, of festivals and *pronunciamientos*. The two big fountains were dry but there were still cafes round the broad square, little tables outside where a scattering of office workers sat with coffees or brandies. Even here, though, the shop windows were half empty, paint flaking from the ancient buildings. Beggars huddled in some of the ornate doorways. A pair of *civiles* circled.

Harry stood irresolutely, wondering whether to have a coffee. The street lights were starting to come on, weak and white. Harry remembered how easy it was to get lost in the narrow streets, or trip in a pothole. A couple of the beggars had risen and were walking towards him. He turned away.

As he left the square he noticed that a woman walking ahead of him had stopped dead, her back to him: a woman in an expensive-looking white dress, red hair covered with a little hat. He stopped too, astonished. Surely it was Barbara. That was her hair, her walk. The woman began walking again, turning rapidly down a side street, moving quickly, her figure fading to a white blur in the dusk.

Harry ran after her, then stood irresolute at the corner, unsure whether to follow. It couldn't be Barbara, she couldn't still be here. And Barbara would never have worn clothes like that.

Chapter Five

THAT MORNING BARBARA had woken as usual when the church clock across the road struck seven. She rose from sleep to the heat of Sandy's body beside her, her face resting on his shoulder. She stirred and he made a gentle grunting noise, like a child. Then she remembered and guilt stabbed through her. Today she was meeting Markby's contact; the culmination of all the lies she had told him.

He turned and smiled, eyes heavy with sleep. 'Morning, sweetie-pie.'

'Hello, Sandy.' She brushed a hand gently across his cheek, spiny with stubble.

He sighed. 'Better get up. I've got a meeting at nine.'

'Have a proper breakfast, Sandy. Get Pilar to make you something.'

He rubbed his eyes. 'It's OK, I'll get a coffee on the way.' He leaned over, smiling mischievously. 'I'll leave you to your English breakfast. You can eat all the cornflakes.' He kissed her, his moustache tickling her upper lip, then got up and opened the wardrobe next to his bed. As he stood selecting clothes, Barbara watched the play of muscles in his broad chest and flat, ridged stomach. Sandy did no exercise and ate carelessly; it was a mystery how he kept his figure, but he did. He saw her studying him and smiled, that Clark Gable curl of the mouth to one side.

'Want me to come back to bed?'

'You've got to get off. What is it this morning, the Jews' committee?'

'Yes. There's five new families arrived. With nothing but what they could carry from France.'

'Be careful, Sandy. Don't upset the régime.'

'Franco doesn't mean the anti-Jewish propaganda. He has to keep in with Hitler.'

'I wish you'd let me help. I've so much experience dealing with refugees.'

'It's diplomatic stuff. Not a job for a woman; you know what the Spaniards are like about that.'

She looked at him seriously; felt guilt again. 'It's good work, Sandy. What you're doing.'

He smiled. 'Making up for all my sins. I'll be back late, I've a meeting at the Ministry of Mines all afternoon.' He moved away to his dressing table. At that distance, without her glasses, Sandy's face began to blur. He laid the suit he had chosen over the back of a chair and padded off to the bathroom. She reached for a cigarette and lay smoking, as he splashed about. Sandy returned, shaved and dressed. He came back to the bed and bent to kiss her, his cheeks smooth now.

'All right for some,' he said.

'It's you that taught me to be lazy, Sandy.' Barbara gave a sad half-smile.

'What are you doing today?'

'Nothing much. Thought I might go to the Prado later.' She wondered whether Sandy might notice the slight tremor that came to her voice with the lie, but he only brushed her cheek with his hand before going to the door, his form turning to a blur again.

She had met Markby at a dinner they had given three weeks before. Most of the guests were government officials and their wives; when the women left the tables there would be deal-making among the men, perhaps a Falangist song. But there was a journalist as well, Terry Markby, a *Daily Express* reporter Sandy had met in one of the bars the Falange people frequented. He was a mousy, middle-aged man, his dinner jacket too large for him. He looked ill at ease and Barbara felt sorry for him. She asked what he was working on and he leaned close to her, lowering his voice. He had a heavy Bristol accent.

'Trying to find out about these concentration camps for Republican prisoners. Beaverbrook wouldn't have taken stories like that during the Civil War, but it's different now.'

'I've heard rumours,' she replied guardedly. 'But if anything like that was going on I'm sure the Red Cross would have sniffed it out. I used to work for them, you see. In the Civil War.'

'Did you?' Markby looked at her with surprise. Barbara knew she had been even more gauche and clumsy than usual that evening, had heard the mistakes in her Spanish. When she went to the kitchen to check on Pilar her glasses had misted up and on coming out she had unthinkingly wiped them on her hem, catching a cross look from Sandy.

'Yes, I did,' she replied a little sharply. 'And if a lot of people were missing they'd know.'

'Which side of the lines were you on?'

'Both, at different times.'

'It was a bloody business.'

'It was a civil war, Spaniard against Spaniard. You have to understand that to understand the things that happened here.'

The journalist spoke quietly. On his other side Inés Vilar Cuesta was leading a loud demand from the ladies for nylon stockings.

'A lot of people have been arrested *since* Franco won. Their families assumed they'd been shot, but a lot were taken to the camps. And there were a lot of prisoners taken in the war, people posted missing believed killed. Franco's using them as forced labour.'

Barbara frowned. She had tried for so long to tell herself that now Franco had won he should be supported in the task of rebuilding Spain. But she found it increasingly hard to shut her eyes to the things that went on; she knew that what the journalist said could have some truth in it.

'Have you evidence?' she asked. 'Who told you?'

He shook his head. 'I'm sorry, I can't say. Can't reveal my sources.' He cast a weary eye round the company. 'Especially not here.'

She hesitated, then lowered her voice to a whisper.

'I knew someone who was listed missing believed killed. Nineteen thirty-seven, at the Jarama. A British International Brigader.'

'Republican side?' Markby raised thin pale eyebrows.

'I never shared his politics. I'm not political. But he's dead,' she added flatly. 'They just never found his body. The Jarama was terrible, thousands dead. Thousands.' Even now, after three years, she felt a sinking in her stomach at the thought of it.

Markby put his head on one side, considering. 'Most foreign prisoners were sent home, I know. But I hear some slipped through the net. If you could give me his name and rank I might be able to find something out. The prisoners of war are kept in a separate camp, out near Cuenca.'

Barbara looked over her guests. The women had rounded on a senior official in the Supply Ministry, insisting he get them nylons. Tonight she was seeing the New Spain at its worst, greedy and corrupt. Sandy, at the head of the table, was smiling at them all, indulgently and sarcastically. That was the confidence public school gave you. It struck her that though he was only thirty-one, in his wing-collared shirt, with his oiled swept-back hair and his moustache, Sandy could have been ten years older. It was a look he cultivated. She turned back to Markby, taking a deep breath.

'There's no point. Bernie's dead.'

'Yes, if he was at the Jarama it's very unlikely he'd have survived. Still, you never know. Do no harm to try.' He smiled at her. He was right, Barbara thought, even the faintest chance.

'His name was Bernard Piper,' she said quickly. 'He was a private. But don't—'

'What?'

'Raise false hopes.'

He studied her, a journalist's searching look. 'I wouldn't want to do that, Mrs Forsyth. It's only the slimmest chance. But worth a look.'

She nodded. Markby surveyed the company, the dinner jackets and couturier dresses interspersed with military uniforms, then turned that keen evaluating gaze back to Barbara. 'You're moving in different circles now.'

'I was sent to work in the Nationalist zone after Bernie – after he disappeared. I met Sandy there.'

Markby nodded at the company. 'Your husband's friends might not like you sniffing after a prisoner of war.'

She hesitated. 'No.'

Markby smiled reassuringly. 'Leave it with me. I'll see if I can find anything out. *Entre nous*.'

She held his eyes. 'I doubt you'll get a story out of this.'

He shrugged. 'Any chance to help a fellow Englishman.' He

smiled, a sweet, strangely innocent smile, although of course he wasn't innocent at all. If he did find Bernie, Barbara thought, and the story came out, it would be the end of everything here for her. She was shocked to realize that if only Bernie was alive, she wouldn't care about the rest.

SHE GOT UP and put on the silk dressing gown Sandy had got her last Christmas. She opened the window; it was another hot day, the garden bright with flowers. Strange to think that in six weeks winter would be here with its mist and frosts.

She stumbled against a chair, swore and took her glasses from the dressing-table drawer. She looked in the mirror. Sandy urged her to do without them whenever she could, memorize the layout of the house properly so she didn't bump into things. 'Wouldn't it be fun, darling,' he had said. 'Walking around confidently greeting people and no one knowing you're a bit short-sighted.' He had developed a thing about those glasses, he hated her wearing them, but although she had always hated them too she still wore them when she was on her own. She needed them. 'Bloody idiotic nonsense,' she muttered as she took out her curlers and ran the comb through her thick auburn hair. It flowed in waves. That stylist was good, her hair never looked unkempt now. She applied her make-up carefully, eyeshadow that highlighted her clear green eyes, powder to emphasize her cheekbones. Sandy had taught her all this. 'You can decide how you look, you know,' he had said. 'Make people see you as you want to be seen. If you want to.' She had been reluctant to believe him but he had persisted and he was right: for the first time in her life she had begun, very nervously, to question her belief that she was an ugly woman. Even with Bernie she had found it hard to think what he could see in her, despite his endless loving reassurance. Tears came to her eyes. She blinked them quickly away. She needed to be strong today, clear-headed.

She wasn't meeting Markby's contact till late afternoon. She would go to the Prado first; she couldn't bear being cooped up all day in the house, waiting. She put on her best outdoor dress, the white one with the rose pattern. There was a knock at the door and Pilar appeared. The girl had a round surly face and curly black hair struggling to escape from beneath her maid's cap. Barbara addressed her in Spanish.

'Pilar, please prepare breakfast. A good one today, toast and orange juice and eggs, please.'

'There is no juice, *señora*, there was none in the shops yesterday.'

'Never mind. Ask the daily to go out later and try to find some, would you?'

The girl left. Barbara wished she would smile occasionally. But perhaps she had lost people in the Civil War; nearly everyone had. Barbara thought she caught a faint note of contempt sometimes when Pilar called her '*señora*', as though she knew she and Sandy weren't really married. She told herself it was imagination. She had no experience of servants and when she first came to the house had been uneasy around Pilar, nervous and eager to please. Sandy had told her she must be clear and precise in her orders, keep a distance. 'It's what they prefer, lovey.' She remembered Maria Herreira telling her never to trust servants, they were all peasants and half of them had been Reds. Yet Maria was a kind woman who did voluntary work with old people for the church. She lit another cigarette and made her way downstairs to breakfast, to the cornflakes that Sandy was able to get in rationed, half-starved Madrid as though by magic.

When the Spanish Civil War broke out in 1936, Barbara had been working at the Red Cross headquarters in Geneva for three years. She worked in the Displaced Persons section, tracing missing members of families in Eastern Europe torn apart by the Great War and still missing. She matched names and records, wrote letters to Interior Ministries from Riga to Budapest. She managed to put enough people in touch with their families to make it worthwhile. Even where their relatives were all dead, at least the families knew for certain.

She had been excited by the job at first, it was a change from nursing in Birmingham. She had got it partly because of her years of work for the British Red Cross. After four years, though, she was bored. She was twenty-six; soon she would be thirty and she began to fear she was fossilizing among the order of her files, the stolid dullness of the Swiss. She went for an interview with a Swiss official in a neat office overlooking the still blue lake.

'It's bad in Spain,' he told her. 'There're thousands who've found themselves on one side of the lines and their relatives on the other. We're sending medical supplies and trying to arrange exchanges. But it's a savage war. The Russians and Germans are getting involved.' He looked at her over his half-moon glasses with tired eyes. All the hopes of 1919, that the Great War had truly been the war to end war, were disintegrating. First Mussolini in Abyssinia, now this.

'I'd like to get out in the field, sir,' Barbara said firmly.

SHE ARRIVED in an unbearably hot Madrid in September 1936. Franco was advancing from the south; the Moroccan colonial army, airlifted across the Straits of Gibraltar by Hitler, was now only seventy miles away. The city was full of refugees, ragged lost-looking families from the *pueblos* dragging enormous bundles through the streets or crowded together on donkey carts. Now she saw the chaos of war at first hand. She never forgot the old man with shocked eyes who passed her that first day, carrying all he had left: a dirty mattress slung over his shoulder and a canary in a wooden cage. He symbolized all the refugees, the displaced persons, all those caught in the middle of war.

Red militiamen hurtled by in lorries and buses on their way to the front line – ordinary Madrileños, their only uniform the dark blue boiler suits all workers wore and red neckerchiefs. They would wave their ancient-looking weapons as they passed, calling out the Republic's shout of defiance. '*¡No pasarán!*' Barbara, who believed in peace more than anything, wanted to weep for them all. She wanted to weep for herself too at first, because she was frightened: by the chaos, by the stories of nightmare atrocities on both sides, by the Fascist aeroplanes that had begun to appear in the skies, making people pause, look up, sometimes run for the safety of the metro. Once she saw a stick of bombs fall, a pall of smoke rising from the west of the city. The bombing of cities was what Europe had feared for years; now it was happening.

The Red Cross mission was based in a little office in the city centre, an oasis of sanity where half a dozen men and women, mostly Swiss, laboured to distribute medical supplies and arrange exchanges of refugee children. Although she spoke no Spanish, Barbara's French was good and it was a relief to be able to make herself understood.

'We need help with the refugee exchanges,' Director Doumergue told her on her second day. 'There are hundreds of children separated from their families. There's a whole group from Burgos who were at a summer camp in the Guadarramas – we want to exchange them for some Madrid children caught in Sevilla.' The director was another calm, serious Swiss, a young man with a plump, tired face. Barbara knew she'd been flapping, panicking, and that wasn't like her. Babs we all depend on, they used to call her in Birmingham. She'd have to pull herself together. She brushed a stray tangle of red hair from her brow. 'Of course,' she said. 'What do you need me to do?

That afternoon she went to visit the children in the convent where they had been lodged, to take their details. Monique, the office interpreter, came with her. She was a small, pretty woman, wearing a neat dress and freshly ironed blouse. They walked through the Puerta del Sol, past huge posters of President Azaña, Lenin and Stalin. Monique nodded at Stalin's poster. 'That's the way things are going now,' she said. 'Only Russia will aid the Republic. God help them.'

The square was full of loudspeakers, a woman's voice rising and falling, punctuated by tinny squeaks from the speaker. Barbara asked what they were saying.

'That's Dolores Ibárruri. *La Pasionaria*. She's telling housewives that if the Fascists come they must boil their olive oil and pour it from the balconies onto their heads.'

Barbara shuddered. 'If only both sides could see everything will be destroyed.'

'Too late for that,' Monique answered heavily.

They entered the convent through a stout wooden gate in a high wall designed to shield the sisters from the outside world. It had been thrown open and across the little yard a militiaman kept guard by the door, a rifle slung over his shoulder. The building had been burned out; there was no glass at the windows and black trails of soot rose up the walls. There was a sickly smell of smoke.

Barbara stood in the yard. 'What's happened? I thought the children were with the nuns . . .'

'The nuns have all fled. And the priests. Those that got away. Most of the convents and churches were burned by the mob in July.' Monique gave her a searching look. 'Are you a Catholic?'

'No, no, I'm nothing really. It's just a bit of a shock.'

'It's not so bad at the back. The nuns ran a hospital, there are beds.'

The entrance hall had been burned and vandalized, sheets of paper torn from breviaries lay about among the broken statues.

'What must it have been like for those nuns?' Barbara asked. 'Shut away in here, then a mob runs in and burns the place down.'

Monique shrugged. 'The Church supports the Nationalists. And they've lived off the backs of the people for centuries. Once it was the same in France.'

Monique led the way down a narrow echoing corridor and opened a door. On the other side was a hospital ward with about twenty beds. The walls were bare, lighter patches in the shape of crosses showing where religious symbols had been removed. About thirty ten-year-olds sat on the beds, dirty and frightened-looking. A tall Frenchwoman in a nurse's uniform hurried over to them.

'Ah, Monique, you have come. Is there any news of getting the children home?'

'Not yet, Anna. We'll take their details, then go to the ministry. Has the doctor been?'

'Yes.' The nurse sighed. 'They are all well enough. Just frightened. They come from religious homes – they were scared when they saw the convent had been burned.'

Barbara looked over the sad little faces, most of them smeared with the tracks of tears. 'If any are ill, I'm a nurse—'

'No,' said Monique. 'Anna is here. Getting them transferred back, that's the best thing we can do for them.'

They spent the next hour taking details; some of the children were terrified, the nurse had to persuade them to talk. At last they were done. Barbara coughed from the smell of smoke.

'Could they not be taken somewhere else?' she asked Monique. 'This smoke, it's bad for them.'

Monique shook her head. 'There are thousands of refugees in this city, more every day. We're lucky some official took time to find anywhere for these children.'

It was a relief to be back outside, even in the boiling sunlight. Monique waved at the militiaman. '*Salud*,' he called. Monique offered Barbara a cigarette and looked at her keenly.

'This is what it's like everywhere,' she said.

'I can take it. I was a nurse before I went to Geneva.' Barbara blew out a cloud of smoke. 'It's just – those children, will they ever be the same again, if they get home?'

'Nobody in Spain will ever be the same again,' Monique answered, in sudden angry despair.

By November 1936 Franco had reached the outskirts of Madrid. But his forces were held in the Casa de Campo, the old royal park just west of the city. There were Russian aircraft in the skies now, protecting the city, and fewer bombs fell. Hoardings had been erected to cover the bombed houses, displaying more portraits of Lenin and Stalin. Banners spanned the streets. '*¡NO PASARAN!*' The determination to resist was even greater than in the summer and Barbara admired it even as she wondered how it could survive the cold of winter. With only one road to the city still open, supplies were already becoming short. She half hoped Franco would take Madrid so the war could end, though there were terrible stories of Nationalist atrocities. There had been plenty on the Republican side too, but Franco's sounded even worse, coldly systematic.

After two months she had adjusted, so far as anyone could. She had had successes, had helped get dozens of refugees exchanged; now the Red Cross was trying to negotiate prisoner exchanges between the Republican and Nationalist zones. She was proud of how quickly she was picking up Spanish. But the children were still in the convent – their case had fallen into some bureaucratic abyss. Sister Anna had not been paid for weeks, though she stayed on. At least the children would not run away; they were terrified of the Red hordes beyond the convent walls.

One day Barbara and Monique had spent an afternoon at the Interior Ministry, trying again to get the children exchanged. Each time they saw a different official, and today's man was even less helpful than the others. He wore the black leather jacket that marked him out as a Communist. It looked odd on him; he was plump and middle-aged and looked like a bank clerk. He smoked cigarettes constantly without offering them any.

'There is no heating at the convent, Comrade,' Barbara said. 'With the cold weather coming the children will become ill.'

The man grunted. He reached forward and took a tattered file from a pile on his desk. He read it, puffing at his cigarette, then looked at the women.

'These are children of rich Catholic families. If they go back they will be asked about military dispositions here.'

'They've hardly been out of the building. They're afraid to.' Barbara was surprised how easily her Spanish came now when she was roused. The official smiled grimly.

'Yes, because they are frightened of us Reds. I am not happy with sending them back. Security is everything.' He put the file back on the pile. 'Everything.'

As they left the ministry, Monique shook her head in despair. 'Security. Always the excuse for the worst things.'

'We'll have to try another tack. Perhaps if Geneva could get on to the minister?'

'I doubt it.'

Barbara sighed. 'We have to try. I'll have to organize some more supplies for them. Oh God, I'm tired. Do you want to come for a drink?'

'No, I have some washing to do. I'll see you tomorrow.'

Barbara watched Monique walk away. A tide of loneliness washed over her. She was conscious of how separate she was from the closeness, the solidarity of the city's inhabitants. She decided to go to a bar off the Puerta del Sol where English people sometimes gathered, Red Cross staff and journalists and diplomats.

The bar was almost empty, no one there that she knew. She ordered a glass of wine and went to sit at a corner table. She didn't like sitting in bars on her own but perhaps someone she knew would come in.

After a while she heard a man's voice speaking English, with the long lazy vowels of a public-school education. She looked up; she could see his face in the mirror behind the bar. She thought he was the most attractive man she had ever seen.

She watched him covertly. The stranger was standing alone at the bar, talking to the barman in halting Spanish. He wore a cheap shirt and a boiler suit; one arm was in a white sling. He was in his twenties and had broad shoulders and dark blond hair. His face was long and oval, with large eyes and a full, strong mouth. He seemed ill at ease standing there alone. His eyes met Barbara's in the mirror and she looked away, then jumped as the white-aproned waiter appeared at her elbow, asking if she wanted another *vino*. He was carrying the bottle and her elbow jogged his, making him drop it. It landed on the table with a crash, wine pumping out over the waiter's trousers.

'Oh, I'm so sorry. That was me, I'm sorry.'

The man looked annoyed; it might be the only pair of trousers he had. He began dabbing at them.

'I'm so sorry. Listen, I'll pay for them to be cleaned, I—' Barbara stumbled over her words, forgetting her Spanish. Then she heard that drawling voice at her elbow.

'Excuse me, are you English? May I help?'

'Oh no – no, it's all right.'

The waiter recovered himself. She offered to pay for the spilt bottle as well as his trousers and he went off, mollified, to fetch another glass. Barbara smiled nervously at the Englishman.

'How stupid of me. I've always been so clumsy.'

'These things happen.' He held out a hand. He had brown slender fingers, the wrist covered in a fair down that caught the light and shone like gold. She saw his other arm was encased in plaster from above the elbow to the wrist. His large eyes were dark olive, like a Spaniard's. 'Bernie Piper,' he said, studying her curiously. 'You're a long way from home.'

'Barbara Clare. Yes, afraid so. I'm here with the Red Cross.'

'Mind if I join you? Only I haven't spoken English to anyone for weeks.'

'Well, I – no, please do.'

And so it began.

Someone from the Madrid office of the *Daily Express* had telephoned Barbara three days previously and told her there was a man who might be able to help her. His name was Luis and he could meet her in a bar in the old town on Monday afternoon. She had asked to speak to Markby but he was away. As Barbara put the phone down she wondered if it was tapped; Sandy said it wasn't but she had heard they tapped all the foreigners' telephones.

After breakfast she went back to her room. Her mirrored bureau was an eighteenth-century antique she and Sandy had picked up in the Rastro market in the spring. It had probably been looted from some wealthy house in Madrid at the start of the Civil War. You saw families there on Sundays, hunting for their stolen heirlooms. They went cheap, it was food and petrol that were valuable now.

The bureau had come with a key and Barbara used it to store personal, precious things. Bernie's photograph was in there. It had been taken just before he went to the front, in a photographer's studio with chaises longues and potted palms. He stood in his uniform, arms folded, smiling at the camera.

He had been so beautiful. It was a word people used about women but Bernie had been the beautiful one. She hadn't looked at the photograph for a long time; seeing it still hurt her, she mourned Bernie as deeply as ever. Guiltily, because Sandy had rescued her and set her on her feet, but what she had with Bernie had been different. She sighed. She mustn't hope too much, she mustn't.

It still amazed her that Bernie had been interested in her, she must have looked a fright in that bar, her hair all frizzy and wearing that tatty old jumper. She took off her glasses. She told herself that without them, yes, she could be called quite attractive. She put the glasses on again. As so often, even amid her preoccupation with Bernie, just thinking she was attractive triggered a memory, one of the bad ones. Usually she tried to push them away but she let this one come, even though it left her feeling she was standing on the edge of a precipice. Millie Howard and her gang of eleven-year-olds, forming a circle round her in the quadrangle of the grammar school, chanting. 'Speccy frizzy-hair, speccy frizzy-hair.' If she hadn't had the glasses to mark her out as different, if she hadn't responded with blushing and tears, would it ever have happened, the tormenting that had gone on for so long? She closed her eyes. Now she saw her older sister, radiant Carol who had inherited their mother's blonde hair and heart-shaped face, walking through the lounge of the little house in Erdington, off to meet another boy. She swirled past, leaving a rich smell of perfume. 'Doesn't she look lovely?' her mother had asked her father, while Barbara's heart burned with jealousy and sadness. A little while before she had broken down and told her mother how the girls taunted her at school. 'Looks aren't everything, darling,' her mother had said. 'You're much cleverer than Carol.'

She lit a cigarette with a shaking hand. Mum and Dad, Carol and her good-looking accountant husband were under the air-raids now. The Blitz had moved beyond London; in the week-old, censored edition of the *Daily Mail* she bought at the station, she had read of the first raids on Birmingham. And here she was, sitting in a fine house, still picking at those old wounds while her family were running for the air-raid shelters. It was so petty, she felt ashamed. Sometimes she wondered if there was something wrong with her mind, whether she was a little crazy. She got up and put on her jacket and hat. She would kill some time in the Prado. Then she would see what this man knew. The thought gave her a welcome sense of purpose.

The Prado art gallery was full of blank walls; most of the pictures had been taken down for safe keeping during the Civil War and so far only a few had been returned. It was cold and damp. She had a bad lunch in the little café, then sat smoking till it was time to leave.

Sandy had noticed something was up with her; yesterday he had asked her if she was all right. She replied she was bored; it was true, now they were established in the house there were long hours when she had nothing to do. He had asked if she would like to do some voluntary work, he might be able to fix something up. She had agreed, to put him off the scent. He had nodded, apparently satisfied, and gone off to his study to do some more work.

Sandy had been working on what he called his 'Min of Mines project' for six months now. He was often out late, and often worked at home, worked harder than Barbara had ever seen. Sometimes his eyes gleamed with excitement and he smiled as though he had some wonderful secret. Barbara didn't like that little secret smile. At other times he seemed preoccupied, worried. He said the project was confidential, he wasn't allowed to talk about it. Sometimes he made mysterious trips out to the countryside. There was a geologist involved, a man called Otero who had visited the house a couple of times. Barbara didn't like him either; he gave her the creeps. She worried that they might be involved in something illegal; half of Spain seemed to be working the *estraperlo*, the black market. Sandy was scarcely more open about the committee to aid Jewish refugees from France he worked for. Barbara wondered if Sandy felt his voluntary work detracted from the picture he liked to paint of himself as a hard, successful businessman, though it was that better side of him, the side that liked to help those in trouble, that had drawn her to him.

At four she left the Prado and headed into the centre. Shops were opening again after the siesta as she walked through the narrow streets, hot and dusty and smelling of dung. Her sensible shoes rang on the cobbles. Turning a corner, she saw an old man in a tattered shirt trying to manoeuvre a cart filled with cans of olive oil up onto the pavement. He held the cart by its shafts, trying to haul it on to the high kerb. Behind him was a newly painted building, a big banner with the yoke and arrows over the door. As Barbara watched, a pair of blue-shirted young men appeared in the doorway. They bowed, apologizing for blocking her way, and asked the old man if they could help. He relinquished the shafts gratefully and they pulled the cart up onto the pavement for him. 'My donkey is dead,' he told them. 'I have no money for another.'

'Soon everyone in Spain will have a horse. Just give us time, *señor*.'

'I had him twenty years. I ate him when he died. Poor Hector, his meat was stringy. Thank you, *compadres*.'

'*De nada*.' The Falangists clapped the old man on the back and went back inside. Barbara stepped off the pavement to let him pass. She wondered if things really would get better now. She didn't know; after four years in Spain she still felt like an alien, there was so much she didn't understand.

She knew there were idealists in the Falange, people who genuinely wanted to improve Spaniards' lives, but she knew there were many more who had joined to take advantage of the chance of a corrupt profit. She looked again at the yoke and arrows. Like the blue shirts they reminded her the Falange were fascists, blood-brothers to the Nazis. She saw one of the Falangists looking at her from the window and hurried on.

THE BAR WAS a dark, run-down place. The mandatory portrait of Franco, spotted with grease, hung behind the bar, where a couple of young men lounged. A big grey-haired woman in black was washing glasses at the sink. One of the men carried a crutch; he had lost half a leg, the trouser end crudely sewn up. They all looked at Barbara curiously. Usually only whores came into bars alone, not foreign women wearing expensive dresses and little round hats.

A young man sitting at a table at the back raised his hand. As she walked across he rose and bowed, taking her hand in a strong, dry grip.

'Señora Forsyth?'

'Yes.' She replied in Spanish, trying to keep her voice confident. 'Are you Luis?'

'Yes. Please sit. Allow me to get you a coffee.'

She studied him as he went to the bar. He was tall and thin, in his early thirties with black hair and a long sad face. He wore threadbare trousers and an old, stained jacket. His cheeks were stubbly, like those of the other men in the cafe; there was a shortage of razor blades in the city. He walked like a soldier. He came back with two coffees and a plate of tapas. She took a sip and grimaced. He smiled wryly.

'It is not very good, I am afraid.'

'It's all right.' She looked at the tapas, little brown meatballs with tiny delicate bones sticking out. 'What are they?'

'They call it pigeon but I think it is something else. I am not sure what. I would not recommend it.'

She watched as Luis ate, picking the minute bones from his mouth. She had decided not to say anything; leave him to begin. He shifted nervously in his seat, studied her face with large dark eyes.

'I understand from Mr Markby that you are trying to trace a man who went missing at the Jarama. An Englishman.' He spoke very quietly.

'Yes I am, that's right.'

He nodded. 'A Communist.' His eyes still scanned her face. Barbara wondered with a flicker of fear if he was police, if Markby had betrayed her or been betrayed himself. She forced herself to stay calm.

'My interest is personal, not political. He was – he was my – my boyfriend, before I met my husband. I believed he was dead.'

Luis shifted in his seat again. He coughed. 'You live in National Spain, I am told you are married to a man with friends in the government. Yet you are looking for a Communist from the war. Forgive me, but this seems strange.'

'I worked for the Red Cross, we were a neutral organization.'

He gave a quick bitter smile. 'You were fortunate. No Spaniard has been able to be neutral for a long time.' He studied her. 'So, you are not an opponent of the New Spain.'

'No. General Franco won and that's that. Britain isn't at war with Spain.' Not yet, anyway, she thought.

'Forgive me.' Luis spread his hands, suddenly apologetic. 'Only I have to protect my own position, I have to be careful. Your husband knows nothing of your – search?'

'No.'

'Please keep it so, *señora.* If your enquiries became known, they could bring trouble.'

'I know.' Her heart was starting to thump with excitement. If he had no information he wouldn't be this wary, this careful. But what did he know? Where had Markby found him?

Luis eyed her intently again. 'Say you were to find this man, Señora Forsyth. What would you wish to do?'

'I'd want to see him repatriated. As he was a prisoner of war he should be returned home. That's what the Geneva Conventions say.'

He shrugged. 'That is not how the Generalísimo sees things. He would not like the suggestion that a man who came to our country to make war on Spaniards should simply be sent home. And if it were to be publicly suggested there were still foreign prisoners of war in Spain, such prisoners might disappear. You understand?'

She looked at him, meeting his eyes. Deep-set, unreadable. 'What do you know?' she asked.

He leaned forward. A harsh meaty smell came from his mouth. Barbara forced herself not to recoil.

'My family is from Sevilla,' he said. 'When Franco's rebels took the city my brother and I were conscripted and spent three years fighting the Reds. After the victory, part of the army was disbanded, but some of us had to stay on and Agustín and I were assigned to guard duties at a camp near Cuenca. You know where that is?'

'Markby mentioned it. Out towards Aragón, isn't it?'

Luis nodded. 'That's right. Where the famous "hanging houses" are.'

'The what?'

'There are ancient houses built right on the edge of the gorge that runs beside the city, so that they seem to hang over it. Some find them beautiful.' He sighed. 'Cuenca is high on the *meseta* – you boil in summer and freeze in winter. This is the only time of year it is bearable, frost and snow will come soon. I had two winters up there and, believe me, that was enough.'

'What is it like? The camp?'

He shifted uneasily again, lowered his voice to a whisper. 'A labour camp. One of the camps that does not officially exist. This one was for Republican prisoners of war. About eight kilometres from Cuenca, up in the Tierra Muerta. The dead land.'

'The what?'

'An area of bare hills below the Valdemeca mountains. That is what it is called.'

'How many prisoners?'

He shrugged. 'Five hundred or so.'

'Foreigners?'

'A few. Poles, Germans, people whose countries do not want them back.'

She met his gaze firmly. 'How did Señor Markby find you? When did you tell him this?'

Luis hesitated, scratched his stubbly cheeks. 'I am sorry, *señora*, I cannot tell you. Only that we unemployed veterans have our meeting places, and some people have contacts the government would not like them to have.'

'With foreign journalists? Selling stories?'

'I can say no more.' He looked genuinely sorry, very young again.

She nodded, took a deep breath, felt a catch in her throat. 'What were conditions like in the camp?'

He shook his head. 'Not good. Wooden huts surrounded by barbed wire. You have to understand; these people will never be freed. They work the stone quarries and repair the roads. There is not much food. A lot die. The government wants them to die.'

She made herself stay calm. She must treat this as though Luis was a foreign official talking about a refugee camp she needed information on. She produced a pack of cigarettes and offered it to him.

'English cigarettes?' Luis lit one and savoured the smoke, closing his eyes. When he looked at her again his face expression was hard, serious.

'Was your *brigadista* strong, Señora Forsyth?'

'Yes, he was. A strong man.'

'Only the strong ones survive.'

She felt tears coming, blinked them away. This was the sort of thing he would say if he was deceiving her, trying to appeal to her emotions. Yet his story seemed to have the ring of truth. She fumbled in her handbag and slid Bernie's photograph across the table. Luis studied it a moment, then shook his head.

'I do not remember that face, but he would not look like that now. We were not supposed to talk with the prisoners, apart from giving them orders. They thought their ideas might contaminate us.' He gave her a long stare. 'But we used to admire them, we soldiers, the way they kept going somehow.'

There was silence for a moment. The smoke from their cigarettes curled up, wreathing round an ancient fan that hung from the ceiling, broken and unmoving.

'You don't remember the name Bernie Piper?'

He shook his head, looked again at the photograph. 'I remember a fair-haired foreigner who was one of the Communists. Most of the English prisoners were returned – your government tried to get them back. But a few who were listed as missing ended up in Cuenca.' He pushed the picture back across the table. 'I was given my discharge this spring, but my brother stayed on.' He looked at her meaningfully. 'He can get information if I ask. I would need to visit him, letters are censored.' He paused.

She asked him straight out. 'How much will it take?'

Luis smiled sadly. 'You are direct, *señora*. I think for three hundred pesetas Agustín could say whether this man was a prisoner at the camp or not.'

Three hundred. Barbara swallowed, but allowed nothing to show on her face. 'How long would it take? I need to know soon. If Spain comes into the war, I'll have to leave.'

He nodded, suddenly business-like. 'Give me a week. I will visit Agustín next weekend. But I will need some money now, an advance.' She raised her eyebrows and Luis reddened suddenly, looking embarrassed. 'I have no money for the train.'

'Oh. I see.'

'I will need fifty pesetas. No, don't take your purse out here, give it to me outside.'

Barbara glanced across to the bar. The crippled man and his friend were deep in conversation, the landlady serving a new customer, but she sensed that all of them were aware of her presence. She took a deep breath.

'If Bernie is there, what then? You couldn't get him out.'

Luis shrugged. 'That might be possible. But very difficult.' He paused. 'Very expensive.'

So here it was. Barbara stared back at him, realizing he might know nothing, might have told Markby what he wanted to hear and be telling the same to this rich Englishwoman.

'How much?' she asked.

He shook his head. 'One step at a time, *señora*. Let us try and see if it is him first.'

She nodded. 'It is about money for you, yes? We should know where we are.'

Luis frowned a little. 'You are not poor,' he observed.

'I can get money. Some.'

'I *am* poor. Like everyone in Spain now. Do you know how old I was when I was conscripted? Eighteen. I lost my best years.' He spoke with bitterness, then sighed and looked down at the table for a moment before meeting her gaze again. 'I have had no work since I left the army in the spring, a bit of labour on the roads that pays nothing. My mother in Sevilla is ill and I can do nothing to help her. If I am to help you, *señora*, find information it is dangerous to find, then – ' He set his lips hard, looked at her defiantly.

'All right,' she said quickly, her tone conciliatory. 'If you can find what Agustín knows, I'll give you what you ask. I'll get it somehow.' She could probably get three hundred easily, but it was better not to let him know that.

Luis nodded. His eyes roved round the bar, through the window to the darkening street. He leaned forward again. 'I will go to Cuenca this weekend. I will meet you here in a week's time, at five.' He got up, bowing slightly to her. Barbara saw his jacket had a big hole at the elbow.

Outside he shook her hand again and she passed him fifty pesetas. Walking away, she fingered Bernie's photo. But she mustn't hope for too much, she must be careful. Her mind went round and round. For Bernie to have survived while thousands died and for Markby to have found a clue to him would be a big coincidence. Yet if Markby had ferreted out that all the foreigners went to Cuenca, and then looked for a guard from there . . . all that would need was money and contacts among the thousands of discharged soldiers in Madrid. She must contact Markby again, question him. And if Luis said Bernie was alive, she could go and make a stink at the embassy. Or could she? They said the embassy was desperate to keep Franco out of the war. She remembered what Luis had said about prisoners disappearing if there were unwelcome enquiries.

She crossed the Plaza Mayor, walking quickly to reach the Centro before dark. Then she stopped dead. The Civil War had ended in April 1939. If Luis had left the army this spring, 1940, he could not possibly have passed two winters in the camp.

Chapter Six

IT HAD BEEN RAINING solidly for twenty-four hours, a heavy soaking rain that fell vertically from a windless sky, swishing and gurgling on the cobbles. It was colder, too; Harry had found a winter eiderdown at the flat and spread it out over the big double bed.

That morning he was due to visit the Trade Ministry with Hillgarth, his first outing in his interpreter's role. He was glad to be doing something at last.

They had integrated him into embassy life. The head of the translation section, Weaver, had tested his Spanish in his office. He was very tall, thin, with a patrician air. 'All righty,' he said in languid tones after talking with Harry for half an hour. 'You'll do.'

'Thank you, sir,' Harry said tonelessly. Weaver's haughty effeteness annoyed him.

Weaver sighed. 'The ambassador doesn't really like Hillgarth's people getting involved with the regular work, but there we are.' He looked at Harry as though he were some strange exotic animal.

'Yes, sir,' Harry replied.

'I'll show you to your room. There are some press releases come in that you can start working on.'

He had taken Harry to a little office. A battered desk took up most of the space, press releases in Spanish stacked on the blotter. They came in regularly and for the next three days Harry was busy. He saw nothing of Hillgarth, though Tolhurst dropped in occasionally to see how he was doing.

He liked Tolhurst, his self-deprecation and his ironic comments, but he hadn't taken to most of the embassy staff. They affected a contempt for the Spaniards; the bleak poverty Harry had seen had depressed him but it seemed to amuse some of the embassy people. Most food shops in Madrid had '*No hay . . .*' signs outside. 'We have no . . . potatoes, lettuce, apples . . .' Yesterday in the canteen Harry had overheard two of the cultural attaché's staff laughing about there still being no hay for the poor donkeys and had felt an unexpected anger. Under the callousness, though, Harry sensed the fear that Franco would join the war. Each day everyone scoured the papers. At the moment Himmler's visit was the focus of everyone's anxiety: was he coming just to discuss security issues, as the press said, or was it something more?

Hillgarth picked him up from his flat at ten in a big American car, a Packard, driven by an English chauffeur, a thickset Cockney. Harry had put on his morning suit, the trousers carefully screwed into the press overnight; Hillgarth wore his captain's uniform again.

'We're going to see the junior trade minister, General Maestre,' Hillgarth said, squinting into the rain. 'I'm confirming which oil ships the navy's allowing in. And I want to ask him about Carceller, the new minister.' He drummed his fingers on the armrest for a moment, looking thoughtful. The day before, a series of cabinet changes had been announced; Harry had translated the press releases. The changes favoured the Falange; Franco's brother-in-law Serrano Suñer had been made Foreign Minister.

'Maestre's all right,' Hillgarth continued. 'One of the old school. Cousin of a duke.'

Harry looked through the window. People walked by, hunched against the rain, workmen in their overalls and women in the ubiquitous black, shawls drawn over their heads. They did not hurry; they were soaked already. Umbrellas, Tolhurst had told him, were impossible to get even on the black market. As they passed a baker's shop, Harry saw a crowd of black-shawled women standing in the rain. Many had thin children with them and Harry saw, here and there through the smears of rain, the bloated gas-filled stomachs of malnutrition. The women crowded round the door, banging and shouting at someone within.

Hillgarth grunted. 'There've been rumours of potatoes coming in. He's probably got some, saving them for the black market. The supply agency's offering the potato farmers so little they won't sell. That's so the Junta de Abastos can take their cut before they sell on.'

'And Franco allows it?'

'He can't stop it. The *junta*'s a Falange organization. It's a bloody disaster; it's rotten with corruption. They'll have a famine on their hands if they're not careful. But that's what happens with revolutions, the scum always rises to the top.'

They passed the parliament building, shuttered and empty, and turned into the Trade Ministry courtyard. A *civil* waved them through the gate. 'Is this a revolution?' Harry asked. 'It seems more like – I don't know – decay.'

'Oh, it's a revolution all right, for the Falangists anyway. They want a state like Hitler's. You should see some of the people we have to deal with. Make your hair stand on end. Make the books I used to write seem tame.'

In a wood-panelled office under a huge portrait of Franco, a man in a general's uniform, the creases immaculate, stood waiting for them. He was in his early fifties, tall and fit-looking. He had a tanned face from which clear brown eyes shone. Thinning black hair was brushed carefully across the crown of his head to hide his baldness. A younger man in morning dress stood beside him, his face expressionless.

The officer smiled and shook Hillgarth's hand warmly. He spoke to him in Spanish, in a clear rich voice. His younger colleague translated.

'My dear captain, a pleasure to see you.'

'And you, general. I think we can give you the certificates today.' Hillgarth glanced at Harry, who repeated his words in Spanish.

'Very good. The matter should be settled.' Maestre gave Harry a courtly smile. 'You have a new translator, I see. Senor Greene is not incapacitated, I hope.'

'Had to go home. Family problems, compassionate leave.'

General Maestre nodded. 'Oh, I am sorry to hear it. I hope his family have not been bombed.'

'No. Private problems.'

They took their places round the desk. Hillgarth opened his briefcase and produced the certificates that would allow specified oil tankers to be escorted in by the Royal Navy. Hillgarth and Maestre went through them, checking dates and routes and tonnage. Harry translated Hillgarth's words into Spanish and the young Spaniard translated Maestre's replies into English. Harry was unsure of one or two technical terms, but Maestre's manner was friendly and polite. Maestre wasn't what Harry had expected one of Franco's ministers to be like.

At length Maestre gathered the papers together, sighing theatrically.

'Ah, captain. If you knew how angry it makes some of my colleagues, Spain having to ask permission from the Royal Navy to import necessities. It insults our pride, you know.'

'England's at war, sir; we have to be sure anything imported by a neutral is not sold on to Germany.'

The general held the certificates out to his translator. 'Fernando, have these taken across to the Navy Ministry.' The young man seemed to hesitate a moment, but Maestre raised his eyebrows at him and he bowed and left the room. The general relaxed at once, producing a cigarette case and offering it round.

'That's got rid of him,' he said in perfect English. Harry's eyes widened. The general smiled. 'Oh yes, Mr Brett, I speak English. I studied at Cambridge. That young man is there to see I don't say anything I shouldn't. One of Serrano Suñer's men. The captain knows what I mean.'

'All too well, Minister. Brett here studied at Cambridge too.'

'Did you?' Maestre looked at him with interest, then smiled reflectively. 'During the Civil War, when we were fighting the Reds on the *meseta*, amidst the heat and flies I would often think of my days at Cambridge: the cool river, the magnificent gardens, everything so peaceful and stately. You need such things in war to keep you sane. What college were you at?'

'King's, sir.'

Maestre nodded. 'I had a year at Peterhouse. Wonderful, as I say.' He pulled out a gold cigarette case. 'Will you smoke?'

'Thanks, I don't.'

'Any news?' Hillgarth asked. 'About the new minister?'

Maestre leaned back and blew out a cloud of smoke. 'Don't worry about Carceller. He's got a lot of Falangist notions – ' he curled his lip disdainfully – 'but he's a realist at heart.'

'Sir Sam will be pleased.'

The general nodded slowly. Then he turned to Harry with an urbane smile.

'Well, young man, how do you find Spain?'

Harry hesitated. 'Full of unexpected things.'

'We passed a big queue of women outside a baker's,' Hillgarth said. 'They'd heard he'd got potatoes.'

Maestre shook his head sadly. 'Those Falangists could cause a famine in the Garden of Eden. Have you heard the new joke, Alan? Hitler meets Franco and asks how he can starve Britain into surrender, the U-boats are not enough. Franco replies, "Mein führer, I will send them my Junta de Abastos. In three weeks they will be desperate to sign."' Hillgarth and Maestre laughed, Harry joining in uncertainly. Maestre smiled at him, bowing his head a little.

'Forgive me, *señor*, we Spaniards have a dark sense of humour, it is how we cope with our problems. But I should not joke about England's troubles.'

'Oh, we're coping,' Hillgarth said.

'I hear when the Queen was asked if the royal children would leave London because of the bombing she said – what was it? – they won't leave without me, I won't leave without the King, and the King won't go.'

'Yes, that's right.'

'What a fine woman.' He smiled at Harry. 'What style. She has *duende*.'

'Thank you.'

'And now the Italians are being beaten in Greece. The tide will turn. Juan March knows.' The general raised his eyebrows at Hillgarth, then rose and turned again to Harry.

'Mr Brett, I am giving a party in ten days, for my daughter who will be eighteen. My only child. There are so few suitable young men in Madrid these days, perhaps you would like to come? It would be good for Milagros to meet a young man from England.' He smiled with sudden tenderness at the mention of his daughter's name.

'Thank you, sir. If – er – embassy commitments allow—'

'Excellent! I am sure Sir Sam can spare you for one evening. I will have an invitation sent. And, captain, the Knights of St George, we shall discuss that later.'

Hillgarth glanced quickly at Harry, then gave Maestre a barely perceptible shake of the head. 'Yes. Later.'

The general hesitated, then nodded sharply. He shook Harry's hand. 'I must leave you now, I am afraid. It was a great pleasure to meet you. There is a ceremony at the palace, the Italian ambassador is pinning a new medal on the chest of the Generalísimo.' He laughed. 'So many honours, Il Duce weighs him down with them.'

THE RAIN HAD STOPPED. Walking through the car park Hillgarth looked thoughtful. 'That name Maestre mentioned in there. Juan March. Know it?'

'He's a Spanish businessman, isn't he? Helped finance Franco during the Civil War. A crook, I heard.'

'Well, forget you heard his name, all right? And the Knights of St George, forget that too. Something private the embassy's engaged on. Maestre thought you knew more than you do since you were with me. All right?'

'I won't say anything, sir.'

'Good man.' Hillgarth's tone lightened. 'You should go to that party. Relax a bit. Chance to meet some *señoritas*. God knows there's little enough social life in Madrid. The Maestres are a good family. Connected to the Astors.'

'Thank you, sir, I might.' Harry wondered what the party would be like.

The chauffeur was waiting in the car, reading a week-old *Daily Mail*. As they got in, Harry glanced at the cover. The German raids were moving out of London now, Birmingham had been badly hit. Barbara's home city. Harry remembered the woman he had seen a few nights ago. It couldn't possibly have been her. She must be back home now; he hoped she was safe.

'Maestre's daughter's quite attractive,' Hillgarth continued as they drove back to the embassy. 'Real little Spanish pomegranate— Jesus Christ!' They both fell back against their seats as the car braked sharply. They were turning into Calle Fernando del Santo, where the embassy was. The normally quiet street was filled with people, a roaring, shouting mob. The driver was startled out of his calm.

'What the hell?'

They were Falangists, young men mostly in bright blue shirts and red berets. There were about a hundred of them. They stood facing the embassy, shouting, their arms stretched out in the Fascist salute. They waved banners reading, '*¡Gibraltar español!*' The usual *civiles* in front of the embassy were absent.

'*¡Abajo Inglaterra!*' the crowd yelled. '*¡Viva Hitler, viva Mussolini, viva Franco!*'

'Oh, God,' Hillgarth said wearily. 'Not another demonstration.'

Someone in the crowd pointed at the car and the nearest Falangists turned and yelled their slogans at them, shouting, faces distorted, arms stretching in and out like metronomes. A stone bounced off the bonnet.

'Drive on, Potter,' Hillgarth said steadily.

'Are you sure, sir? They look nasty.'

'It's all show. Get on, man.'

The chauffeur proceeded at a snail's pace, forcing a passage between the demonstrators and the embassy wall. Half of them were teenagers, their Falange Youth uniform a copy of the Hitler Youth with blue shirts instead of brown, the girls in wide skirts and the boys in shorts. One boy had a drum and began banging it dramatically. It seemed to inflame the crowd and some of the boys reached out and began rocking the big car. Others followed and Harry and Hillgarth bounced around inside as the car inched slowly on. Harry felt disgust; they were scarcely more than children.

'Give them a hoot,' Hillgarth said. The horn sounded and an older Falangist elbowed his way out of the crowd, motioning the youngsters away from the car.

'See,' Hillgarth said, 'they were just getting carried away.'

A tall, broadly built youth of around seventeen, worked up into a paroxysm of rage, pushed through the crowd and walked alongside the car, screaming insults in English through the window. 'Death to King George! Death to the fat Jew pig Churchill!' Hillgarth laughed, but Harry flinched away, the ridiculousness of the catcalls somehow making them even nastier.

'Where are the *civiles?*' he asked.

'Tipped the wink to go for a walk, I'd guess. These are Serrano Suñer's people. OK, Potter, pull up opposite the door. When we get out, Brett, chin up. Ignore them.'

Harry followed Hillgarth out on to the pavement. The shrieking was louder and he felt exposed and suddenly afraid. His heart began to pound. The Falangists shouted at them from the other side of the car, the enraged youth still howling in English. 'Sink the English ships! Kill the Bolshevist Jews!' Another stone sailed across the road and cracked the glass in the embassy door. Harry flinched and had to fight the urge to crouch down.

Hillgarth grasped the handle. 'Hell, it's locked.' He rattled it. A figure moved in the shadowy interior and Tolhurst appeared, running in a crouch to the door. He fumbled with the catch.

'Come on, Tolly!' Hillgarth shouted. 'Stand up for Christ's sake, they're only a bunch of hooligans!'

Then the chauffeur shouted, 'Look out!' and Harry caught a glimpse of something hurtling through the air. He felt a hard blow on his neck and staggered. He and Hillgarth threw up their arms as something white swirled round their heads, half choking them. There was a joyous yell from the crowd. For a second Harry saw red sand flying.

The door opened and Hillgarth ducked inside. Tolhurst reached out and grabbed Harry's arm, pulling him inside with surprising strength. He locked the door again and turned to them, mouth open. Harry ran his hands over his neck and shoulders but there were no wounds, no redness, only white powder. He leaned against a desk, taking deep whooping breaths. Hillgarth sniffed his sleeve and laughed.

'Flour! It's bloody flour!'

'Cheeky bastards,' Tolhurst said.

'Does Sam know about all this?' Hillgarth's face was alive with excitement.

'He's phoning the Interior Ministry now, sir. Are you both all right?'

'Yes. Come on, Brett, we need to clean up.' Chuckling again, Hillgarth made for an inner door. Outside the mob was laughing at what they had done, though the demented youth still raved on. Tolhurst looked at Harry. 'You all right?'

He was still trembling. 'Yes – yes, sorry.'

Tolhurst took his arm. 'Come on, I'll take you to my room, I've a clothes brush there.'

Harry allowed himself to be led away.

TOLHURST'S OFFICE was even smaller than Harry's. He produced a clothes brush from his desk.

'I've a spare suit here. It'll be a bit wide for you but it should do.'

'Thanks.' Harry brushed off the worst of the flour. He felt much better, calm again, even though he could still hear the shouting from outside. Tolhurst looked out of the window.

'The police'll come along and clear them in a minute. Serrano Suñer's made his point. And Sir Sam's chewed his ear over the phone.'

'The demonstration didn't send him into a funk?'

Tolhurst shook his head. 'No, he's on form today, no sign of the pink rat. You never know how he's going to react.'

'I had a touch of the pink rat myself when that flour landed,' Harry said self-consciously. 'I didn't know what it was. I was back at Dunkirk for a moment. I'm sorry, it must have seemed like I was yellow.'

Tolhurst looked uncomfortable. 'No. Not at all. I know about shell shock, my father had it in the last lot.' He hesitated. 'They wouldn't let embassy staff join up last year, you know. I was quite relieved, I'm afraid.' He lit a cigarette. 'I'm not one of the world's heroes. Happier behind a desk, if truth be told. Don't know how I'd have coped with what you went through.'

'You don't know what you can do till you get out there.'

'I suppose not.'

'Captain Hillgarth seems pretty fearless.'

'Yes. I think he enjoys danger. You have to admire that sort of courage, don't you?'

'That was a minor panic I had then, compared to what I was like a couple of months ago.'

Tolhurst nodded. 'Good. That's good.' He turned back to the window. 'Come and look at them. They've no bread yet they can throw flour. Bet it came from the Auxilio Social stores, the Falange are responsible for feeding the poor.'

Harry joined him, looking at the unruly sea of blue.

'Lucky *no hay* potatoes then, eh?'

'D'you know, we sent some of the bread they get on the ration to London for analysis. The boffins said it wasn't fit for human consumption; the flour was adulterated with bloody sawdust. Yet they can afford to throw good white flour at us.'

'The Falangist bigwigs won't have to eat the sawdust.'

'Too bloody right they won't.'

'They were shouting anti-Jewish slogans. I didn't think the Falange went in for that.'

'They do now. Same as Mussolini, to please the Nazis.'

'Bastards,' Harry said with sudden fierceness. 'After Dunkirk I sometimes used to wonder, what's the point of going on, fighting, but then you see things like this. Fascism. Turning teenaged thugs on to innocent people. Then it's bombing civilians, machine-gunning retreating soldiers. Christ, I hate them.'

Tolhurst nodded. 'Yes. But we have to deal with them here. Unfortunately.' He pointed a finger. 'Look at that idiot.'

The boy who had yelled in English had taken hold of a 'Gibraltar español' banner and was marching up and down in front of the embassy with a military swagger, the crowd cheering him on. Harry wondered where he had learned English. He was a tall, well-set-up lad, probably from a middle-class home.

The door opened and the ambassador's wiry form darted in. He looked furious.

'You all right, Brett?'

'Yes, sir, thank you. It was only flour.'

'I won't have my staff attacked!' Hoare's thin voice was shaking with anger.

'I'm all right, sir, honestly.'

'Yes, yes, yes, but it's the principle.' He took a deep breath. 'I think Stokes is looking for you, Tolhurst.' He nodded at the door.

'Yes, sir.' Tolhurst melted away. The ambassador glanced out of the window, snorted, then turned back to Harry. His pale eyes were calculating.

'Hillgarth told me about your meeting this morning. Maestre's a blabbermouth. The things he mentioned, Juan March and the Knights of St George; you're not to discuss them with anyone. There are lots of angles to what we're doing here. Need-to-know basis, do you understand?'

'Yes, sir. I told the captain I'd say nothing.'

'Good man. Glad you're all right.' Hoare clapped Harry on the shoulder, then looked with distaste at the flour on his hand. He turned to the door. 'Tell Tolhurst to get that cleaned up.'

Left alone, Harry sat down. He felt terribly weary and there was a humming in his ears, a pressure. It took him back again to Dunkirk, after the shell landed next to him. He had tried to sit up. He was covered with sand that was wet and warm. He couldn't think properly, bring his thoughts together. Then a touch on his shoulder, and he opened his eyes. A small, wiry corporal was leaning over him.

'Are you all right, sir?' Harry could hardly hear the man, there was something wrong with his ears. He sat up. His uniform was covered in bloody sand and there were lumps of red scattered around. Tomlinson, he realized.

He let the corporal drag him down to the beach, into the sea. The water was chilly and he began trembling from head to foot, he couldn't move. 'Tomlinson,' he said. He could hardly hear his own voice. 'Such little pieces.'

The corporal grasped his shoulders, turned him round, looked into his eyes. 'Come on, sir, come on, into the boat.'

The corporal led him deeper into the water. Other men in khaki were splashing all around. Then Harry was looking up at the brown wooden hull of the boat. It seemed so high. Two men reached down and took his arms. He felt himself being lifted into the air again, then passed out.

He became aware that voices were still calling outside. He got up and went back to the window. The youth was standing to attention now, banner at his side, yelling up at the embassy. Harry caught the words. 'Death to the enemies of Spain! Death to the English! Death to the Jews!'

The boy stopped in mid-flow. His mouth dropped open and his face reddened. Harry saw a tiny black circle appear at the crotch of his grey shorts. It grew larger and larger, then something ran glistening down his thigh. He had worked himself into such a state he had wet himself. The boy stood rigid, his face blank with horror. Someone called, '*¡Lucas! ¡Lucas, continua!*' but he dared not move, he was the one trapped by the crowd now. Harry looked down. 'Serve you right, you little bastard,' he said aloud.

Chapter Seven

THE FALANGISTS DISPERSED shortly afterwards. The boy who had wet himself had to turn round eventually, slinking back to his comrades. They stared at his soaked shorts then quickly looked away again. The fire had gone out of them, anyway, they were getting tired; they put away their drums and banners and marched off. Harry turned away, shaking his head. He sat at Tolhurst's desk, grateful for the quiet. Tolhurst had been decent. He had been surprised by the strength of his grip when he pulled him inside; there must be some muscle under that fat.

He looked round the office. A battered desk, an ancient filing cabinet and a cupboard. Dust in the corners. The King's portrait on the wall but no personal photographs. He thought of his own parents' picture, which stood in the flat now. Did Tolhurst have parents living, he wondered, or had they been scythed down too in the Great War? He closed his eyes and for a moment saw the beach again, thrusting it away with his mind. He had done well today; not long ago an incident like that would have had him crouching in terror under a table, another pink rat.

He remembered his time in hospital in Dover, the disillusion and despair. He was partly deaf, the nurses had to shout to make him hear. A doctor came and gave him tests. He seemed pleased with him. He leaned in close to the bed.

'Your hearing should come back, there's no real damage to the eardrums. You've got to rest, you understand, lie here and rest.'

'I've no choice,' Harry shouted, then remembered it was he, not the doctor, who was deaf, and lowered his voice. 'If I get out of bed I start shaking.'

'It's shock. That'll get better too.'

And so it had, with the determination that took him out of bed, then out of the ward, then into the grounds. But neither his recovery nor the Air Force's victory in the Battle of Britain could heal his sense of angry shame at the retreat from France. For the first time Harry had found himself questioning the things he had been taught at Rookwood, that the rules there were good and right, England a country destined to lead the world. It was the Fascists who were winning now, everywhere. He had always hated them, as he had always hated the cheats and bullies at school. That gave him something to hold on to. If they invaded he would fight if he could, even for this broken, fractured England. It was for that he had answered the spies' unwelcome call, come here to Spain. He jumped as the door opened and Tolhurst reappeared, a pile of papers under his arm. 'Still here, Brett?'

'Yes. I was watching the fireworks. One of them pissed himself.'

'Serve the little bastard right. Are you all right now?'

'Yes, I'm fine. Just needed a minute to pull myself together.' Harry stood up. He looked at his morning suit, from which specks of flour still drifted to the floor. 'I ought to change.'

Tolhurst opened the cupboard and took out a crumpled dark suit and trilby hat. Harry changed into it. The suit was baggy and smelt of old sweat.

'I keep meaning to take it home and press it,' Tolhurst said apologetically.

'It's fine. Thanks. I think I'll go home unless they want me for something else. I've no work left downstairs.'

Tolhurst nodded. 'All right. By the way, there's a drinks party for some of the younger embassy staff next week. At the Ritz. It's a Nazi haunt these days; we're showing the flag. Why don't you come?'

'Thanks. I'd like to. Thanks, Tolhurst.'

'Oh, call me Tolly. Everyone does.'

'Then call me Harry.'

'OK. Anyway, listen, if you're going home don't take the metro, there's a power cut again.'

'All right. The walk'll do me good.'

'I'll arrange for your jacket to be cleaned.'

'Thanks again, er, Tolly.'

Harry left Tolhurst to his work. Outside it was still dry but a cold sharp wind had started to blow from the mountains. He put on the trilby, shuddering a little at the cloying damp of old Brylcreem. He walked to the city centre. In the Puerta del Sol a group of gipsy beggars sat huddled together in a doorway. 'Alms,' they called after him. 'Alms. In the name of God.' There had always been beggars in Spain but now they were everywhere. If you met their eyes they would get up and follow; you developed the trick of seeing them only with your peripheral vision. They had talked about peripheral vision during Harry's training: use it to find out whether you're being followed, it's amazing how much you can train yourself to see without eye movement so people don't know you've seen them.

In Calle Toledo one of the restaurants had put out its rubbish for collection. The bins had been tipped over on the street, spilling out across the pavement. A family were hunting among the rubbish for food. There was an old woman, a younger one who looked like she was her daughter, and two pot-bellied children. The young woman might have been pretty once but her black hair was greasy and dishevelled and she had the red patches of consumption in her pale cheeks. A little girl picked out a piece of orange peel and rammed it to her mouth, sucking desperately. The old woman grabbed a chicken bone and pocketed it. Passers-by turned to avoid them; across the road, a couple of *civiles* stood watching from a shop doorway. A priest in a neat black suit walked swiftly by, averting his gaze.

The young woman was bending over, poking among the slops, when a sudden gust of wind caught her thin black dress, blowing it over her head. She cried out and stood up, arms clawing at it. She had no underclothes and her thin body was suddenly exposed, startlingly pale with prominent ribs and sagging breasts. The old woman ran over and tried to disentangle the dress.

The *civiles* sprang to life. They darted across the road, grabbing at the woman. One jerked at the dress, there was a ripping tear but it dropped again, covering her. She put her arms across her breasts, shivering violently.

'What are you doing?' one of the guards shouted in her face. 'Whore!' He was a tall middle-aged man with a black moustache. His expression was furious, outraged.

'It was an accident.' The old woman wrung her hands together. 'You saw it, the wind, please, it was an accident.'

'You should not allow such accidents!' he yelled in her face. 'A priest went by not two minutes ago.' He yanked at the young woman's arm. 'You are under arrest for offending public morals!'

She buried her head in her hands and wept, her cries turning to coughs. The older woman stood beseechingly in front of the *civil*, hands still clasped together as though in prayer. 'My daughter,' she pleaded. 'My daughter!'

The younger *civil* looked uncomfortable but the older one was still furious. He pushed the old woman away. 'The rest of you, away from there! Those bins are private property! Why don't you find work? *¡Vete!*'

The old woman gathered the children and stood trembling as her daughter was led away, sagging between the *civiles*. Sickened, Harry watched as they took her down the street, between the high stone buildings of a modern European city.

Then he saw the man. A short, thin man with black hair, in a dark jacket and white collarless shirt, who ducked into a shop doorway as he caught Harry's eye. Harry turned and walked on, pretending he hadn't seen him.

Ahead a white-helmeted, white-clad traffic policeman stood in the middle of the road; pedestrians were supposed to wait until signalled to cross but many darted over when his head was turned, risking the traffic and the two-peseta fine. Harry stopped and looked right and left. The man was close, ten paces behind. He had a square pale face, surprisingly delicate-looking features. As he saw Harry looking in his direction he floundered for a moment then walked quickly past him, head bowed.

Harry ran across the road, between a donkey cart and an ancient Ford. Whoever the man was, he wasn't very good at this. He felt a cold whisper of uneasiness, but reminded himself he had been warned to expect someone to tail him, that it happened to all the embassy people. He was junior staff so perhaps the spy was junior too.

He didn't look round again until he reached the doorway of the flats, though it was an effort. He felt angry now as much as scared.

When he turned at last his follower had disappeared. He climbed the stairs and unlocked the door, then jumped violently as a voice called from within.

'Harry, is that you?'

Tolhurst was sitting on the settee in the *salón*. 'Sorry to barge in, old chap, did I startle you? Only I've got a message from Hillgarth, he wanted you to have it at once. It came right after you left so I drove over.'

'All right.' Harry crossed to the window and looked down at the street. 'God, I don't believe it, he's there. I'm being tailed, come and look.'

'OK. Don't twitch the curtain, old man.' Tolhurst joined him and they stood looking down at the young man. He was walking up and down the road, looking at the house numbers, scratching his head. Tolhurst laughed.

'Some of these people are just hopeless.'

'A spy for a spy,' Harry said quietly.

'It's the way it works.' Tolhurst looked at him seriously. 'Listen, there's been a change of plan. Captain Hillgarth wants you to move on Forsyth now, call in at the Café Rocinante tomorrow afternoon and see if you can make contact. Come for a briefing at the embassy at nine tomorrow.' Tolhurst looked at him keenly. 'OK?'

Harry took a deep breath. 'Yes.' He smiled wryly. 'It's what I came for, isn't it.'

'OK.' Tolhurst jerked his head towards the window. 'Make sure you lose chummy.'

'Why the change of plan?'

'Hitler's visiting France, big meeting with Pétain. There's word he's coming on here afterwards. This is all very hush hush, by the way.'

Harry looked at him seriously. 'So Franco could be about to enter the war.'

Tolhurst nodded. 'Moving in that direction, at least. We need to know as much as we can, about everything.'

'Yes.' Harry nodded grimly. 'I can see.'

'I'd better get back, tell Hillgarth I've caught you.' He glanced round the bare walls. 'You ought to cover up those blank spaces.

We've loads of pictures at the embassy if you want some.' He raised his eyebrows. 'Let's be optimistic, and assume we're not all going to be kicked out, or worse.'

After Tolhurst left, Harry returned to the window. It was raining again, little spots tapping the glass. The man had disappeared; probably he was hanging around somewhere waiting for him to emerge. He thought about the poor woman who had been arrested. Where would they put her? In some stinking cell probably. The incident seemed to crystallize everything he had seen these last few days. Harry realized he wasn't neutral any more; he hated what Franco was doing here.

His mind went back to Sandy and tomorrow's meeting. He thought of German tanks rolling south over the Pyrenees, war in Spain again. He wondered how the embassy had got that information. Perhaps it was something to do with what Hillgarth and Maestre had been talking about. Juan March, the crooked millionaire, had financed Franco during the Civil War but he could still be pro-English, like Maestre. He wondered what the Knights of St George were, some sort of code. Hoare had told him to put it out of his mind but why had he and Hillgarth been so obviously worried that he knew? He shrugged. Well, he had better start preparing himself mentally for his task, prepare to meet Sandy, Sandy who was making a profit out of the Spanish Hell.

What would he be like now? He thought back to the year at Rookwood when he had shared a study with Sandy, that strange year.

The incident with the spider in Taylor's study had been the start of a difficult time. Things felt unsettled, uncomfortable. Bernie had been moved to a different study, but he remained friendly with Harry. Bernie and Sandy loathed each other. It wasn't anything particular; it was visceral, instinctive. The school was full of feuds and rivalries between boys, but this was more unsettling because it was expressed not in rows and fights but cold glances and sarcastic comments. Yet Sandy and Bernie were in some ways alike. They shared a contempt for Rookwood, its beliefs and the system, which Harry found painful.

Bernie kept his socialism mainly to himself because he knew most of the boys would have found his ideas not just distasteful but incomprehensible. He carried on doing well in class; he was clever, as scholarship boys had to be to get to Rookwood at all. He played rugger aggressively, making the junior team. But occasionally his feelings about Rookwood showed through and he would talk about it to Harry with cold, hard disdain.

'They're preparing us to be part of the ruling class,' he said to Harry one afternoon. It was wet and they were all in Harry's study, Harry and Bernie at the table, Sandy sitting reading by the fire. 'To rule the workers here and the natives in the colonies.'

'Well, someone's got to rule them,' Harry replied. 'I've thought of applying to the Colonial Office myself when I leave. My cousin might be able to help.'

'Oh God!' Bernie laughed harshly.

'Being a district commissioner's bloody hard work. My uncle's got a friend who was in Uganda for years, only white man for miles. He came back with malaria. Some of them die out there.'

'And others make a packet,' Bernie replied contemptuously. 'You should listen to yourself, Harry. "My cousin might be able to help. My uncle's friend." None of the people I know at home have cousins or uncles to help them rule huge chunks of Africa.'

'And the socialists can run things better, can they? Those idiots MacDonald and Snowden?'

'They've sold out. They're weak. We need a stronger type of socialism, like they've got in Russia.'

Sandy looked up then and laughed. 'D'you think Russia's any better than here? It's probably like this place, only worse.'

Harry frowned. 'How can Rookwood be like Russia?'

Sandy shrugged. 'A system built on bloody lies. They say they're educating you, but they're trying to drill you full of things they want you to know, just like the Russians with all their propaganda. They tell us when to go to bed, when to get up, how to talk, how to think. People like you don't mind, Harry, but Piper and me are different.' He looked at Bernie, his brown eyes alive with malicious humour.

'You do talk a lot of shit, Forsyth,' Bernie replied. 'You think sneaking out late to go drinking with Piers Knight and his mates is being different. I want freedom for my *class*. And our day's coming.'

'And I suppose I'll be on the way to the guillotine.'

'Maybe you will.'

Sandy had fallen in with a crowd of fourth- and fifth-formers who went to the local town to drink and, they said, meet girls. Bernie said they were all wastrels and Harry agreed although, after Taylor's attempts to recruit him as a spy, he could see things a little from Sandy's side: the black sheep, the boy who had to be kept an eye on; it wasn't a status he envied. Sandy did as little work as possible; his attitude to the masters and his schoolwork one of barely veiled contempt.

That term, Harry took to going for walks on his own. It cleared his head to go ranging for miles over chalky Sussex woodlands. One damp November afternoon he turned a corner and was astonished to see Sandy Forsyth crouched on his haunches in the lane, turning a dark round stone over and over in his hands. He looked up.

'Hello, Brett.'

'What're you doing? You've got chalk all over your blazer.'

'Never mind that. Look here.' He stood up and passed Harry the stone. At first it looked like a dark flinty rock but then he saw it was full of concentric circles, spiralling inwards.

'What is it?'

Sandy smiled, not cynically as usual but broadly, a happy smile. 'It's an ammonite. A fossilized sea creature. Once all this was a sea and it was full of these, swimming about. When it died it sank to the bottom and over years its shell turned to rock. You can't imagine how many years. Millions.'

'I didn't know fossils were like this. I thought they were big, dinosaurs.'

'Oh, there were dinosaurs here too. The first dinosaur fossils were found near here a century ago, by a man called Mantell.' Sandy's smile turned sardonic. 'Wasn't popular in some circles. Fossils were a challenge to the Church's idea the earth was only a few thousand years old. My dad still thinks God put the fossils in himself, to test men's faith. He's a very *traditional* Anglican.'

Harry had never seen Forsyth like this before. His face was alive with excited interest, his uniform streaked with chalk and his thick black hair, normally neatly combed, stood up in little tufts. He smiled. 'I often come out fossil hunting. This is a good one. I don't tell people – they'd think I was a swot.'

Harry studied the stone, cleaning mud from the whorls of the shell with his fingers. 'It's amazing.' He thought it was beautiful, but you didn't use words like that at Rookwood.

'Come out with me some time if you like,' Sandy said diffidently. 'I'm building a collection. I've got a rock with a fly in it, three hundred million years old. Insects and spiders are as old as the dinosaurs, much older than us.' He paused, reddening slightly at his display of enthusiasm.

'Are they?'

'Oh, yes.' He looked out over the Downs. 'They'll be here when we've gone.'

'Taylor's frightened of spiders.'

Sandy laughed. 'What?'

'I found out once.' Harry reddened, he wished he hadn't said that.

'Stupid old bugger. I'm going to go in for hunting fossils when I leave this dump, go on expeditions to places like Mongolia.' He grinned. 'I want to have adventures, far away from here.'

And so they became friends of a sort. They went on long walks hunting fossils and Harry learned about the life that had heaved and rolled in the ancient seas that had flowed where they stood. Sandy knew a lot. Once he found the tooth of a dinosaur, an iguanodon, buried in the side of a quarry. 'They're rare,' he said gleefully. 'And they're worth money. I'll take it up to the Natural History Museum in the hols.'

Money was important to Sandy. His father made him a generous allowance, but he wanted more. 'It means you can do what you want in life,' he said. 'When I'm older I'm going to make a packet.'

'Hunting dinosaur bones?' Harry asked. They were exploring one of the old iron workings dotted around the woods. Sandy studied the horizon, the bare brown trees. It was an early winter's day, still and cold.

'I'll make my fortune first.'

'I suppose I don't think much about money.'

'Piper would say that's because you've got plenty. We all have here. But it's our families' money. I want to make my own.'

'My money was left me by my father. I wish I'd known him, he was killed in the war.'

Sandy's eyes went back to the horizon. 'My dad was a padre on the Western Front. Telling all those soldiers God was with them before they went over the top. My brother Peter is following in his footsteps, he's at theological college now and then he's going to join the army. He was Head Boy at Braildon, Head of Games, Greek Prize, all that.' Sandy's face darkened. 'But he's stupid, as stupid with his religion as Piper is with his socialism. It's all nonsense.' He turned and looked at Harry and there was something strange, fierce, in his eyes. 'My mother left when I was ten, you know. They don't talk about it but I think it was because she couldn't stand all the rubbish. She used to say she wanted some fun in life. I remember feeling sorry for her, I knew she didn't have any.'

Harry felt uncomfortable. 'Where is she now?' he asked.

He shrugged. 'They don't know. Or won't say.' He grinned broadly, showing square white teeth. 'You need some fun in life, she was right. Why don't you come out with me and my crowd? There's some girls we meet in the town.' He raised his eyebrows.

Harry hesitated. 'What do you do?' he asked diffidently. 'When you're with them?'

'Everything.'

'Everything? Really?'

Sandy laughed. He jumped off the rock he'd been sitting on and slapped Harry on the arm. 'No, not really. But we will, one day. I want to be the first.'

Harry kicked a stone. 'I don't want to get into trouble, it's not worth it.'

'Come on.' Harry felt the force of Sandy's personality bearing down on him. 'I plan it all, make sure we always leave when there's no one around, never go anywhere the masters might come – or if they did, would be more worried than us about being seen.' He laughed.

'Some dive? I'm not sure I fancy that.'

'We won't get caught. I got caught breaking the rules at Braildon,

I'm more careful now. It's fun, knowing they're out to get you and you've got them fooled.'

'What did you get sacked for? At Braildon?'

'I was in the town and this master caught me coming out of a pub. He reported me and I got all the usual stuff, why couldn't I be like my brother, how much better than me he was.' The hard angry look came into Sandy's eyes again. 'I got him back, though.'

'What did you do?'

Sandy sat down again and folded his arms. 'This master, Dacre, he was young. He had this little red car. He thought he was the bee's knees, driving about in it. I know how to drive; I sneaked out one night and took it out of the masters' garage. There's a steep hill near the school. I drove the car right to the edge, jumped out, and over it went.' Sandy smiled, his happy smile, all white teeth. 'It was amazing watching it go down the hill, smashing up bushes. It hit a tree and the front caved in like cardboard.'

'God! That was dangerous.'

'Not really. Not if you know how. But when I jumped out of the car I cut my face on a branch. They saw that and put two and two together. But it was worth it, and it got me out of Braildon. I didn't think anywhere else would take me, but my father pulled strings and got me in here. Worse luck.'

Harry dug at the ground with his foot. 'I think that's going a bit far. Destroying someone's car.'

Sandy gave him an even stare. 'Do unto others as they would do to you.'

'That's not what the Bible says.'

'It's what I say.' He shrugged. 'Come on, we'd better get back, we don't want to miss roll-call or we'll be in trouble, won't we? With our kind teachers.'

They said little as they walked back. The winter sun set slowly, turning the puddles in the brown muddy paths pink. When they reached the road the high walls of the school came into view. Sandy turned to Harry. 'D'you know where the money came from that started the school, and that funded the scholarships for people like Piper?'

'Some merchants a couple of hundred years ago, wasn't it?'

'Yes. But d'you know what their main trade was?'

'Silks and peppers and stuff?'

'Slavery. They were slavers, capturing niggers in Africa and shipping them to America. I found a book in the library.' He turned to Harry. 'It's amazing what you can find out if you look. Things people want to keep hidden that might come in useful.' And he smiled again, a secret smile.

The trouble began a few weeks later, in class with Taylor. The form had had a Latin translation to prepare and Sandy had skimped it. He was called on to read and produced a succession of nonsensical howlers that made the class laugh. Some boys would have been humiliated, but Sandy sat with a smirk on his face, laughing along with the class. Taylor was furious. He stood above Sandy, his face red.

'You didn't even try to do that translation, Forsyth. You've as good a brain as anyone here, but you just don't bother.'

'Oh no, sir,' Sandy said seriously. 'I found it difficult, sir.'

Taylor got even redder. 'You think you can get away with that dumb insolence, don't you? There's a lot you think you can get away with, but we're watching you.'

'Thank you, sir,' Sandy replied coolly. The class laughed again, but Harry could see Forsyth had gone too far. You didn't provoke Taylor.

The master crossed to his desk and picked up his cane. 'That's sheer insolence, Forsyth. Come out here!'

Sandy set his lips. You could see he hadn't expected that. Canings in front of the class were rare. 'I don't think that's fair, sir,' he said.

'I'll give you fair,' Taylor marched up to Sandy and hauled him out of his place by the collar. Sandy wasn't tall but he was stocky and Harry wondered for a moment if he might resist, but he allowed himself to be led to the front of the room. His eyes were blazing, though, with a fierce anger Harry had never seen before, as he bent over the master's desk and Taylor brought the cane down, again and again, lips tight with anger.

After class, Harry went up to the studies. Sandy was leaning on the table. He was pale and breathing heavily.

'You all right?' he asked.

'I will be.' There was a moment's silence. He squirmed and winced. 'You see, Harry? You see how they control us?'

'You shouldn't have provoked him.'

'I'll get my own back,' Sandy muttered.

'Don't be stupid: How can you get back at him?'

'I'll find a way.'

THE SCHOOL ate their meals at long tables in the dining room, the form master sitting at the end. One evening, a week later, Harry saw that Sandy and Taylor were both missing. Sandy wasn't seen again that night and another master took the class next morning. He announced that Alexander Forsyth would not be returning; he had been expelled for an assault on Mr Taylor, who would be having a period of sick leave. The boys plied him with questions but the master said it was too unpleasant to talk about, a spasm of disgust crossing his face. It was that morning, through the classroom window, that Harry saw Bishop Forsyth walking in the quadrangle. His face was stern and drawn. Bernie, next to him, whispered, 'I wonder what Forsyth did. Good riddance to bad rubbish, anyway. I wonder if they'll let me back in the study.'

At lunchtime the boys were full of excitement, wondering what had happened. Harry skipped the meal and went up to the dormitory. Sandy was there, packing his fossil collection carefully into a suitcase. He gave Harry a cynical half-smile.

'Hello, Brett. Heard what happened?'

'I heard you were going. What did you do? They won't say.'

Sandy sat on the bed, still smiling. 'Best revenge I've ever had. It was you put the idea into my mind, actually. Spiders.'

'What?'

'Remember that day we were out fossil hunting and I told you insects and spiders were as old as the dinosaurs.'

Harry felt his heart sink. He remembered Taylor asking him to spy on Sandy, though he had kept that to himself. Taylor had been distant with him ever since.

Sandy smiled. 'Ever been up in the attics? They're full of cobwebs.' He smiled broadly. 'And where there are cobwebs there are spiders. I collected a biscuit tin full, I went for the big ones. Then yesterday I went to Taylor's study when he was in the common room.' He laughed. 'I put them everywhere. In the drawers, in the cigarette box on his desk, even in his cheesy old slippers. Then I went into the study next door; you know it's been empty since old Henderson retired at Christmas. I sat there to wait. I knew Taylor would be along at four to do his marking. I wanted to hear him scream.'

Harry clenched his hands. Sandy had used what he had told him, this was partly his fault. 'Did he?' he asked.

Sandy shrugged. 'No. It went wrong. I heard him come up the corridor and shut the door but there was no sound, just silence. I thought, come on, you bastard, you must have found them by now. Then I heard his door open and footsteps like somebody drunk and then a thud. Then there was a funny whimpering noise, like a cat mewing. It got louder, it turned into a sort of screech and some of the other masters came out of their rooms. I heard Jevons say, "What's the matter?" and then Taylor's voice. "In my room," he said, "it's full of them." Then Williams went into his room and called out that it was full of spiders."

'Hell, Sandy, what did you do it for?'

Sandy met his gaze evenly. "Revenge, of course. I said I'd get him. Anyway, then I hear Taylor's voice, saying he was going to be sick. Williams said to get him into the empty room and next thing the door was open and they were all staring at me.' He smiled. 'It was almost worth it to see Taylor's face. He'd been sick, his face was all white and there was vomit down his gown. Then Williams grabs me and says, "Got you, you little swine."'

Sandy shut his case and stood up. 'The head said Taylor was in the war, it affected him, he saw some spiders on a body or something. How was I to know?' He shrugged again. 'Anyway, that's that, I'm off home. Dad tried pleading with them but it didn't work. It's all right, Harry, there's no need to look angry. I didn't say you'd told me about the spiders. I refused to say how I knew.'

'It's not that. It was a rotten thing to do. And it was me that made it possible.'

'I didn't know he was going to go potty. Anyway, he's ended up being sent off to some sanatorium and I've got the sack. That's life. I knew something like this would happen sooner or later.' He gave

Harry an odd look. Harry saw tears in his face for a moment. 'It's my fate, you see, my fate to be the bad lad. Couldn't avoid it if I tried.'

HARRY SAT UP with a jerk; he had fallen asleep sitting on the sofa. He had been dreaming, something about being trapped in his study; a storm had been raging outside and Sandy and Bernie and a load of other boys were banging at the window, crying out to him to let them in. He shivered; it was cold now, and almost dark. He got up and went to draw the curtains. The buildings, the streets, were so silent it unnerved him. He looked out at the empty square, the one-armed statue a dim shape in the weak white light of the streetlamp. There was nothing moving, not even a cat. Harry realized he hadn't seen a cat since he came here, perhaps like the pigeons they had all been eaten. No sign of his watcher; maybe they let him go home in the evenings.

He wondered suddenly if they knew, at Rookwood, what had happened to Bernie. If they did, they probably weren't surprised, or sorry. And Sandy's fate, or whatever it was that drove him, had washed him up here. Where, tomorrow, he would be spying on him, after all. Harry remembered Jebb telling him it was Mr Taylor who had given them his name, and smiled grimly at the irony. The way the wheels came round, perhaps there was something in those notions of fate after all.

Chapter Eight

THE SAME AFTERNOON Barbara went for a long walk. She felt restless and worried, as she had since her meeting with Luis. The weather was fine after the rain but still cool and for the first time since the spring she wore her coat.

She went to the Retiro park; it had been refurbished since the end of the Civil War, new trees planted to replace those cut down for fuel during the Siege. Once again it was a meeting place for the respectable women of Madrid.

Now it was getting colder only the hardier or lonelier women gathered on the benches to gossip. Barbara recognized the wife of one of Sandy's friends and nodded to her, but walked on to the zoo at the rear of the park; she wanted to be on her own.

The zoo was almost deserted. She took a seat by the sealions' pit, lit a cigarette and sat watching them. She had heard the animals had suffered terribly during the Siege; many had died of starvation, but there was a new elephant now, donated by the Generalísimo himself. Sandy was a bullfight aficionado but no matter how many times he argued with her about the skill and courage involved, Barbara couldn't stomach it, the big strong animal tormented and killed, horses gored and dying, kicking in the sand. She had been to the *corrida* twice then refused to go again. Sandy had laughed and told her not to mention it in front of his Spanish friends; they would think her the worst sort of English sentimentalist.

She twisted the handle of her crocodile-skin handbag. Critical thoughts about Sandy kept coming into her head these days. It wasn't fair; he was the one being placed in danger by her deceit, it could destroy his career if what she was doing came out. She oscillated between guilt over that and anger at the stifled life she led now, the way Sandy always wanted to run everything.

The day after meeting Luis she had gone to the *Express* office in the Puerta del Sol and asked for Markby. They told her he was away in the north, reporting on the German troops coming over the frontier from France and buying everything up.

She might have to tackle Luis herself. Why had he said he had been in Cuenca through two winters? Was he just deceiving her, and Markby, for money? He had seemed nervous and uneasy throughout their interview, but had been very firm about the money he wanted.

A woman in a fur coat appeared, a little boy of eight marching at her side. He wore the uniform of a little *flecha*, the youngest section of the Falange Youth. Seeing the sealions he left his mother's side and ran over to the pen, aiming his wooden rifle at them. 'Bang! Bang!' he shouted. 'Die, Reds, die!' Barbara shuddered. Sandy said the Falange Youth were just Spanish boy scouts, but sometimes she wondered.

Seeing her, the little boy ran over and stretched out his arm in the Fascist salute. 'Good morning, *señora*! *¡Viva Franco!* Can I help you at all today?'

Barbara gave a tired smile. 'No, I'm fine, thank you.'

The child's mother came over, taking his hand. 'Come, Manolito, the elephant is this way.' She shook her head at Barbara. 'Children are tiring, no?'

Barbara smiled hesitantly.

'But they are our gift from God.'

'Come on, Mama, the elephants, the elephants!'

Barbara watched them go. Sandy didn't want children; she was thirty now and she would probably never have any. Once she had longed to have Bernie's child. Her mind went back to those other autumn days, with him in Red Madrid. Only four years ago, but it was like another age.

THAT FIRST NIGHT in the bar, Bernie had seemed an extraordinary, exotic creature to her. It wasn't just his beauty: the incongruity between his public-school accent and his grubby private's uniform added to her sense of unreality.

'How did you hurt your arm?' she asked.

'Got winged by a sniper in the Casa de Campo. It's healing well, just nicked the bone. I'm on sick leave, staying with friends in Carabanchel.'

'Isn't that the suburb the Nationalists are shelling? I heard there was fighting there.'

'Yes. In the part furthest from the city. But the people living further in won't go.' He smiled. 'They're magnificent, so strong. I met the family when I came over on a visit five years ago. The eldest son's with the militia in the Casa de Campo. His mother takes hot food out there every day.'

'You don't want to go home?'

A hardness came into his face. 'I'm here till this is finished. Till we've made Madrid the grave of fascism.'

'There seems to be more Russian equipment coming now.'

'Yes. We're going to throw Franco back. What about you, what are you doing here?'

'I'm with the Red Cross. Helping find missing people, arranging exchanges. Children mostly.'

'They got some Red Cross medical equipment when I was in hospital. God knows they needed it.' He fixed her with those big olive eyes. 'But you supply the Fascists too, don't you?'

'We have to. We have to be neutral.'

'Don't forget which side it was that rose up to destroy an elected government.'

She changed the subject. 'Where on the arm were you hit?'

'Above the elbow. They say it'll soon be good as new. Then I'm going back to the front.'

'A bit higher and you could've got it in the shoulder. That can be nasty.'

'Are you a medic?'

'A nurse. Though I haven't done nursing for years. I'm a bureaucrat now.' She gave a self-deprecating laugh.

'Don't knock it, the world needs organization.'

She laughed again. 'I don't think I've ever heard anyone say that. It doesn't matter how useful the work you do is, the word bureaucracy always stinks.'

'How long have you been with the Red Cross?'

'Four years. I don't go back to England much now.'

'Family there?'

'Yes, but I haven't seen them for a couple of years. We don't have much in common. What do you do? Back home?'

'Well, before I left I was a sculptor's model.'

She almost spilled her wine. 'A what?'

'I modelled for some sculptors in London. Don't worry, nothing improper. It's a job.'

She struggled for something to say. 'That must get awfully cold.'

'Yes. There're statues with goose pimples all over London.'

The doors banged open and a large group of boiler-suited militia came in, girls from the Women's Battalion among them. They crowded round the bar, shouting and jostling. Bernie looked serious.

'New recruits, off to the front tomorrow. D'you want to go somewhere else? We could go to the Café Gijón. Might see Hemingway.'

'Isn't that near the telephone exchange the Nationalists keep trying to shell?'

'The Gijón's safe enough, it's some way down Gran Vía.'

A militiawoman, no more than eighteen, came up and put her arm round Bernie.

'*¡Compadre! ¡Salud!*' She tightened her grip and shouted something at her comrades in Spanish, making them laugh and cheer. Barbara didn't understand but Bernie reddened.

'My friend and I have to go,' he said apologetically. The militiawoman pouted. Bernie took Barbara's arm with his good hand and steered her through the crowd.

OUTSIDE IN the Puerta del Sol he kept hold of her arm. Barbara's heart beat faster. The setting autumn sun cast a red glow over the posters of Lenin and Stalin. Trams clanked through the square.

'Did you understand what they were saying?' Bernie asked.

'No. My Spanish isn't up to much.'

'Probably just as well. The militia are pretty uninhibited.' He gave an embarrassed laugh. 'How d'you manage in your work, if you don't speak the lingo?'

'Oh, we have interpreters. And my Spanish is coming on. We're a bit of a Tower of Babel in our office, I'm afraid. French and Swiss mostly. I can speak French.'

They turned into Calle Montero. A crippled beggar in a doorway stretched out a hand. '*Por solidaridad*,' he called. Bernie gave him a ten-centimo coin.

'For solidarity.' He smiled grimly. 'That's replaced "for the love of God". When we've won this war, there won't be any more beggars. Or priests.'

As they crossed into Gran Vía there was a deep rumble overhead. People tensed and looked up. Some turned and ran. Barbara looked around nervously.

'Shouldn't we find an air-raid shelter?'

'It's all right. It's only a reconnaissance plane. Come on.'

The Café Gijón, haunt of bohemian radicals before the war, was ostentatiously modern, with art deco fittings. The walls were mostly mirrors. The bar was full of officers.

'No Hemingway,' she said with a smile.

'Never mind. What will you have?'

She asked for a white wine and sat at a table while Bernie went to the bar. She moved her seat around, looking for a position where there were no mirrors, but the wretched things were everywhere. She hated catching sight of herself. Bernie came back, holding two glasses on a tray with his good arm.

'Take this, would you?'

'Oh, yes, sorry.'

'Are you all right?'

'Yes.' She fiddled with her glasses. 'I just don't like mirrors much.'

'Why ever not?'

She looked away. 'I just don't, that's all. Are you a Hemingway fan?'

'Not really. Do you read much?'

'Yes, I get a lot of time in the evenings. I don't like Hemingway either. I think he enjoys war. I hate it.' She looked up, wondering if she had been too vehement, but he smiled encouragingly and offered her a cigarette.

'It's been a bad couple of years if you work in the Red Cross,' she went on. 'First Abyssinia, now this.'

'There won't be an end to war until fascism's defeated.'

'Till Madrid's become its grave?'

'Yes.'

'There'll be a lot of other graves too.'

'We cannot escape history,' he quoted.

'Are you a Communist?' Barbara asked suddenly.

He smiled, raising his glass. 'Central London branch.' His eyes were bright with mischief. 'Shocked?'

She laughed. 'After two months here? I'm past being shocked.'

TWO DAYS LATER they went for a walk in the Retiro. A banner had been placed over the front gate: *NO PASARAN*. The fighting was growing fiercer, Franco's troops had broken through to the university in the north of the city but were being held there. More Russian arms were arriving; she had seen a line of tanks driving down Gran Vía, tearing up cobbles, cheered by the people. At night the streets were unlit to hinder night bombers but there were constant white flashes of artillery from the Casa de Campo, endless rumbles and thumps; like thunder, an endless storm.

'I always hated the idea of war, ever since I was a little girl,' Barbara told Bernie. 'I lost an uncle on the Somme.'

'My father was there too. He's never been the same since.'

'When I was little I used to meet people who'd, you know, been through it. They carried on as normal, but you could see they were marked.'

Bernie put his head on one side. 'That's a lot of gloomy thinking for a little girl.'

'Oh, I was always thinking.' She gave a self-deprecating laugh. 'I spent a lot of time on my own.'

'Are you an only child like me?'

'No, I've a sister four years older. She's married, lives a quiet life in Birmingham.'

'You've still got a trace of the accent.'

'Oh God, don't say that.'

'It's nice. *Noice*,' he said, imitating her. 'My parents are working-class Londoners. It's hard being the only kid. I had a lot of expectations put on me, 'specially when I got the scholarship to Rookwood.'

'Nobody ever had any expectations of me.'

He looked at her curiously, then winced suddenly, cradling his wounded arm in the other.

'Does it hurt?'

'A bit. D'you mind if we sit down?'

She helped him to a bench. Through the rough material of his greatcoat his body was hard and firm. It excited her.

They lit cigarettes. They were sitting in front of the lake; it had been drained, the water shining in the moonlight at night was a guide for bombers. A faint smell of rot came from the mud left at the bottom. A tree had been felled nearby and some men were cutting it up with axes; the weather was cold now and there was no fuel. Across the lake bed the statue of Alfonso XII still stood in its great marble arch; the snout of a big anti-aircraft gun nearby, thrusting up from the trees, made a weird contrast.

'If you hate war,' he said, coming back to their discussion, 'you must be an anti-fascist.'

'I hate all this nationalist master-race rubbish. But communism's crazy too – people don't want to hold everything in common, it's not natural. My dad owns a shop. But he's not rich, and he doesn't exploit anybody.'

'My dad runs a shop too, but he doesn't own it. That makes the difference. The party isn't against shopkeepers and other small businesses; we recognize there'll be a long transition to communism. That's why we stopped what the ultra-revolutionaries were doing here. It's the big capitalists we oppose, the ones who support fascism. People like Juan March.'

'Who's he?'

'Franco's biggest backer. A crooked businessman from Majorca who's made millions out of other people's sweat. Corrupt as hell.'

Barbara stubbed out her cigarette. 'You can't say all the bad's on one side in this war. What about all the people who go missing, get picked up at night by the Seguridad and never get seen again? And don't say it doesn't happen. We get frantic women turning up at our offices all the time saying their husbands have disappeared. They can't get any answer about where they are.'

Bernie's gaze was even. 'Innocent people get caught up in war.'

'Exactly. Thousands and thousands of them.' Barbara turned her head away. She didn't want to quarrel with him, it was the last thing she wanted. She felt a warm hand laid on hers.

'Don't let's fight,' he said.

His touch was like an electric charge but she pulled her hand away and put it in her pocket. She hadn't expected that; she believed he'd asked her out a second time because he was lonely and didn't know any other English people. Now she thought, perhaps he wants a woman, an Englishwoman, otherwise why would he look at me? Her heart began to pound.

'Barbara?' He leaned across, trying to get her to meet his eyes. Unexpectedly he pulled a face, crossed his eyes and stuck out his tongue. She laughed and pushed him away.

'I didn't mean to upset you,' he said. 'I'm sorry.'

'No – it's just – don't take my hand. I'll be your friend but don't do that.'

'All right. I'm sorry.'

'Perhaps we shouldn't talk about politics. You think I'm stupid, don't you?'

He shook his head. 'No. This is the first proper talk with a girl I've had for ages.'

'You won't convert me, you know.'

He smiled again, challengingly. 'Give me time.'

After a while they got up and walked on. He told her about the family he was staying with, the Meras.

'Pedro, the father, he's a foreman on a building site. Earns ten pesetas a day. They've got three kids and live in a two-bedroom flat. But the welcome they gave my friend Harry and I when we came here in '31, we'd never seen anything like it. Inés, Señora Mera, she looked after me when I came out of hospital, wouldn't hear of me going anywhere else. She's indomitable, one of those tiny Spanish women made of fire.' He looked at her with those huge eyes. 'I could take you to meet them if you like.' He smiled. 'They'd be interested to meet you.'

'Do you know, I've never met an ordinary Spanish family.' She sighed. 'The way people look at me in the street sometimes, I think there's something disapproving. I don't know what. Maybe I'm getting paranoid.'

'You're too well dressed.'

She looked down at her old coat in disbelief. 'Me?'

'Yes. That's a good heavy coat, with a brooch.'

'This old thing. It's just coloured glass. I picked it up in Geneva.'

'Even so, anything like that's seen as ostentation. The people here are going through hell. Solidarity's everything now, it has to be.'

Barbara took off her brooch. 'There, is that better?'

He smiled. 'That's fine. One of the people.'

'Of course you'll always get the best, being in uniform.'

'I'm a soldier.' He looked offended. 'I wear the uniform to show solidarity.'

'I'm sorry.' She cursed herself for putting her foot in it again. Why on earth did he bother with her? 'Tell me about your public school.'

Bernie shrugged. 'Rookwood's what made me a communist. I fell for it all at first. Sons of the empire, cricket a game for gentlemen, the dear old school song. But I soon saw through it.'

'Were you unhappy there?'

'I learned to hide what I felt about it. That's one thing they teach you. When I left and came back to London it was like a – a liberation.'

'You haven't any London accent left.'

'No, that's one thing Rookwood took away for good. If I try to speak cockney now, it just sounds stupid.'

'You must have had friends, though?' She couldn't imagine him not having friends.

'There was Harry, who came here with me five years ago. He was all right. His heart's in the right place. We've lost touch now,' he added sadly. 'Moved into different worlds.' He stopped and leaned against a tree. 'So many good people like Harry fall for bourgeois ideology.'

'I suppose I'm bourgeois, in your eyes.'

'You're something different.' He winked.

NOVEMBER TURNED to December and sharp cold rains drove down from the Guadarramas. The Fascists were held in the Casa de Campo.

They tried to break through from the north but were held there as well. The shelling went on but the desperate crisis was over. There were Russian fighters in the sky now, fast snub-nosed monoplanes, and if German raiders came over they were chased away. Sometimes there were dogfights over the city. People said the Russians had taken over everything and were running the Republic from behind the scenes. The government officials were even unfriendlier now and sometimes they had a frightened air. The children in the orphanage were moved overnight to a state camp somewhere outside Madrid; the Red Cross weren't consulted.

Bernie kept seeking Barbara out. She spent half her evenings with him in the Gijón or one of the bars in the Centro. At weekends they would walk through the safe eastern part of the city and sometimes out to the countryside beyond. They shared an ironic sense of humour and laughed as they talked about books and politics and their childhoods, lonely in their different ways.

'My dad's shop's one of five the owner has,' Bernie told her one day. They were sitting on a field wall just outside town, enjoying the sun on a rare warm day. Clouds chased each other, their shadows skimming over the brown fields. It was hard to believe the front line was only a few miles away. 'Mr Willis lives in a big house in Richmond, pays my dad a pittance. He knows Dad would never get another job, the war affected him; my mum does most of the work with a girl assistant.'

'I suppose I was well off in comparison. My dad has a bike repair shop in Erdington. It's always done well.' She felt the sadness that always came on her when she spoke of her childhood; she almost never talked of it but found herself telling Bernie. 'After my sister was born he hoped for a boy to take over the shop one day, but he got me. Then my mother couldn't have any more.' She lit a cigarette.

'Are you close to your sister? I often wished I had one.'

'No.' Barbara turned her face away. 'Carol's very beautiful. She's always loved showing herself off. Especially to me.' She glanced at Bernie; he smiled encouragingly. 'I had the brains though, I was the bright one, the one who got into the grammar school.' She bit her lip at the memories those words brought back. She glanced at him again. Oh hell, she thought, in for a penny. Though it wrenched her heart she told him how she had been bullied from the day she went to the grammar school until she left at fourteen.

'They called me speccy and frizzy-hair on my first day and I burst into tears. That's where it all started, I can see that now. I suppose it marked me down as someone who could be tormented, made to cry. Then everywhere I went I had girls calling out about my hair, my glasses.' She gave a long shuddering sigh. 'Girls can be very cruel.'

She felt dreadful now, she wished she hadn't blurted all this out, it had been a stupid thing to do. Bernie lifted his hand as though to take hers, then let it fall again. 'It was the same at Rookwood. If you had something a bit different about you and wouldn't fight back, you got picked on. They started on me when I came because of my accent, called me a pleb. I thumped a few of them and that put paid to that. Funny, I thought it was just public schools where those things happened.' He shook his head. 'Girls too, eh?'

'Yes. I wish I'd hit them, but I was too well brought up.' She threw away her cigarette. 'All that bloody misery, just because I've got glasses and look a bit odd.' She stood up abruptly and walked a few paces away, gazing at the town, a distant smudge. On the far side of it she could see tiny flashes, like pinpoints, where the Fascists were shelling.

Bernie came over and stood beside her. He gave her another cigarette.

'You don't.'

'Don't what?'

'Look odd. Don't be silly. And I like those glasses.'

She felt angry as she always did when people paid her compliments. Just trying to make her feel better about how she was. She shrugged. 'Well, I got away,' she said. 'They wanted me to stay in that hell hole, go on to university, but I wouldn't. I left when I was fourteen. Worked as a typist till I was old enough to start nursing.'

He was silent a moment. Barbara wished he would stop looking at her. 'How did you get involved with the Red Cross?' he asked.

'The school used to have people to give talks on Wednesday afternoons. This woman came and told us about the work the Red Cross did, trying to help refugees in Europe. Miss Forbes.' She smiled. 'She was stout and middle-aged and had grey hair spilling out from under this silly flowery hat but she seemed so kind, she tried so hard to get across how important the work was. I joined them as a junior volunteer at first. I'd just about lost faith in the human race by then; they gave it back to me. Some.' She felt tears pricking at her eyes and moved back towards the wall.

'And you ended up in Geneva?'

'Yes. I needed to get away from home too.' She blew out a long cloud of smoke and looked at him. 'What did your parents think about you volunteering for the International Brigades?'

'Just another disappointment. Like my leaving university.' He shrugged. 'I feel guilty sometimes, about leaving them.'

To work for the party, Barbara thought. And be a sculptor's model. She imagined him without clothes for a second, and dropped her eyes.

'They didn't want me to come here of course,' he said, 'they didn't understand.' Bernie gave her that hard direct look again. 'But I had to come out here. When I saw the newsreels, the refugee columns. We have to destroy fascism, we have to.'

HE TOOK HER to see the Mera family, but the visit was not a success: Barbara didn't understand the family's accents, and though they were kind to her she felt uneasy in the crowded muddle of their flat. They greeted Bernie as a hero and she gathered he had done something brave in the Casa de Campo. He shared a room in the tenement flat with one of the sons, a thin boy of fifteen with the pale hollow face of a consumptive. On the way home Barbara said it could be dangerous for Bernie to share a room with him. He replied with one of his occasional bursts of anger.

'I'm not going to treat Francisco like a leper. With good food and the right medicine you can cure TB.'

'I know.' She felt ashamed of herself.

'The Spanish working class is the best in the world. They know what it's like to fight oppression and they're not afraid to. They practise real solidarity with each other and they're internationalists, they believe in socialism and they *work* for it. They're not greedy materialists like most British trade unionists. They're the best of Spain.'

'I'm sorry. I just – oh, I couldn't understand what they said, and –

oh, I'm being bourgeois, aren't I?' She looked at him nervously but his anger had evaporated.

'At least you're starting to see it. It's more than most people can.'

Barbara could have understood if Bernie had just wanted her as a friend. But he was always trying to take her hand in his and twice he had tried to kiss her. Why, she asked, why did he want her when he could have had anybody? She could only think it was because she was English, that despite all his internationalism he wanted an Englishwoman. She dreaded that his telling her earlier there was nothing wrong with her appearance had been a ploy to get her into bed. She knew men weren't fussy; she had been caught that way once and that was the worst memory, one that filled her mind with shame. Her longings and confusion ate her up.

Bernie's arm was healing, out of plaster though still in a sling. He reported to military headquarters every week. When he was fit, he said, they were going to transfer him to a new training camp for English volunteers in the south. She dreaded the day.

'I offered to help with new fighters who've come across from England,' he told her. 'But they say that's all taken care of.' He frowned. 'I think they're worried my damned public-school accent might put off the working-class boys who are coming over.'

'Poor Bernie,' she said. 'Caught between two classes.'

'I've never been caught,' he said bitterly. 'I know where my class loyalties are.'

ONE SATURDAY early in December they went for a walk to the northern suburbs. The district was full of the houses of the rich, big villas set in their own gardens. It was very cold; there had been a light dusting of snow the night before. Most of it had melted, leaving the air chill and damp, but there were still white patches on the broad roofs of the houses.

Many of the suburb's inhabitants had fled to the Nationalist zone or been imprisoned and some of the houses were shut up. Others had been occupied by squatters, the gardens left to run wild or planted with vegetables; chickens and pigs roamed in some of them. The mess offended Barbara's sense of tidiness but she was beginning now to see things with Bernie's eyes: these people needed homes and food.

They paused before the gates of a big house where washing hung from the windows. A girl of fifteen or so was milking a cow tied to a tree in the middle of a lawn speckled with cowpats. When the girl saw Bernie's military greatcoat, she looked up and gave the clenched-fist salute.

'They'll have had their houses shot up by Franco's artillery, or been bombed out,' Bernie said.

'I wonder where the original owners went.'

'They've gone, that's what matters.'

A sound made them look up at the sky. A big German bomber was ploughing along, accompanied by a couple of small fighters. Three red-nosed Russian planes circled them, the manoeuvres leaving trails of white vapour stretching across the blue sky. Barbara craned her neck to look. The display seemed beautiful until you realized what was happening up there.

A church stood at the end of the street, a heavy nineteenth-century Gothic building. The doors were open and a banner hung outside. *Establo de la revolución*. Revolution stables.

'Come on,' Bernie said. 'Let's take a look.'

The interior had been wrecked, most of the pews removed and the stained-glass windows broken. Statues had been pulled from their niches and flung to the floor; bales of straw were stacked in a corner. The back of the church had been railed off and a flock of sheep penned in. They were closely packed together and as Bernie and Barbara approached they shuffled away in fear, bleating and jostling, their eyes with the strange sideways-pointing pupils wide. Bernie made soothing noises, trying to calm them.

Barbara approached the heap of broken statues. A plaster head of the Virgin, eyes full of painted tears, looked up reproachfully from the floor, reminding her of the convent where the children had been billeted. She felt Bernie at her elbow.

'Tears of the Virgin,' she said with an awkward laugh.

'The Church has always supported the oppressors. They call Franco's rebellion a crusade, bless the fascist soldiers. You can't blame the people for being angry.'

'I've never understood religion, all that dogma. But it's sad.'

She felt his good arm circle her body and pull her round. She was so surprised she had no time to react as he leant forward. She felt the warmth of his cheek and then a hot moistness as he kissed her. She pulled away, staggering back.

'What the hell d'you think you're doing?'

He stood looking shamefaced, a lick of blond hair falling across his brow.

'You wanted it,' he said. 'I know you did. Barbara, I'll be at this training camp in a few weeks. I might never see you again.'

'So what d'you want, a bit of sex with an Englishwoman? Well not with me!' Her voice rose, ringing around the church. The sheep, frightened, bleated plaintively.

He stepped towards her, shouting back now. 'You know it's not like that! You know how I feel, you must, are you blind?'

'Blind with my stupid glasses, is that it?'

'Can't you see I love you!' he shouted.

'Liar!'

She ran out of the church and down the path. As she went through the gate she skidded on a patch of wet snow and collapsed sobbing against the stone wall. She heard Bernie come up behind her. He laid a hand on her shoulder.

'Why should I be a liar? Why? I do love you. You feel the same, I've seen it, why won't you believe me?'

She turned to face him. 'Because I'm ugly and clumsy and . . . No!' She buried her face in her hands, sobbing wildly. A small boy walking by, barefoot and carrying a piglet, stopped and stared at them.

'Why do you hate yourself so?' Bernie asked gently.

She wanted to scream. She wiped her eyes, pushed him away, and began walking down the street. Then the little boy shouted, 'Look! Look!' Barbara turned; he had put the squealing piglet under one arm and was pointing excitedly upwards with the other. High in the sky one of the German fighters had been hit and was plunging to earth. There was a loud crump from some way off and the boy cheered. After a quick upward glance, Bernie hurried towards her.

'Barbara, wait.' He stepped in front of her. 'Please, listen. Never mind sex, I don't care about that, but I love you, I do love you.'

She shook her head.

'Tell me you don't feel the same and I'll walk away now.'

Into Barbara's head had come a picture of a dozen little girls, calling after her in the playground. 'Speccy four-eyes, frizzy carrot hair!'

'I'm sorry, it's no use, I can't – no.'

'You don't understand, you don't see . . .'

Barbara turned to face him and her heart lurched at the pain and sadness in his face. Then she jumped, hearing a screaming noise from above. She looked up. The second German fighter had been hit and was falling towards them. Already it was terrifyingly close, flames pouring from its side in a long red-yellow trail. It fell like a stone; she saw the propellers, still turning, shiny as insects' wings. Bernie was staring upward too. Barbara pushed him away and as he staggered back the air was filled with a giant roar and she saw the high wall of the house they were passing leap outwards at her. Something hit her head with a terrible smashing pain.

She was only unconscious for a moment. When she came round she was aware of the pain in her head, she tried frantically to remember what had happened, where she was. She opened her eyes and saw Bernie leaning over her, dimly because her glasses were gone. There were bricks and dust all around. He was leaning over her and he was crying, she had never seen a man cry. 'Barbara, Barbara, are you all right, oh God, I thought you were dead. I love you, I love you!'

She let him lift her up. She buried her face in his chest and started weeping; they were both sitting crying in the street. She heard footsteps, people crowding round from the houses.

'Are you safe?' someone called. 'My God, look!'

'I'm all right,' Barbara said. 'My glasses, where are my glasses?'

'They're here,' Bernie said softly. He handed them to her and she put them on. She saw the garden wall had fallen down, only just missing them, showering the road with bricks. One of them must have hit her. Flames and black smoke poured from every window of the villa, and the tail of the plane was sticking out of the collapsed roof. Barbara saw a black swastika; it had been painted over in yellow but it showed through. She lifted her hand to her head. It came away covered with blood. An old black-shawled woman put her arm round her. 'It is only a cut, *señorita*. Ay, that was a miracle.'

Barbara reached a hand out to Bernie. He was nursing his injured arm, his face pale. Both their coats were white with dust.

'Are you all right?' she asked him.

'The blast knocked me over. I hurt the arm a bit. But, oh God, I thought you were dead. I love you, please believe me, you have to believe me now!' He began crying again.

'Yes,' she said. 'I do. I'm so sorry, I'm so sorry.'

They hugged each other. The little crowd of Spaniards, refugees who perhaps three months ago had never left their pueblos, stood beside them, looking at the wreckage of the aeroplane sticking out of the burning villa.

SITTING ON THE BENCH watching the sealions, Barbara remembered the warmth of Bernie's grasp again. His injured arm, how it must have hurt him to hold her. She looked at her watch, the tiny Dior watch Sandy had given her. She had resolved nothing in her mind, just gone all emotional about the past. It was time to go home, Sandy would be waiting.

He was back by the time she returned, his car in the drive. She took off her coat. Pilar trotted up from the basement and stood quietly in the hall, hands folded in front of her as she always did when Barbara came in.

'I don't need anything, Pilar. Thanks.'

'*Muy bien, señora.*' The girl curtsied and went back downstairs to the kitchen. Barbara kicked off her shoes; her feet were sore after walking all afternoon.

She went up to Sandy's study. He often worked for hours up there, studying paperwork and making telephone calls. The room was at the back of the house, with a small window that caught little light. He had filled it with ornaments and works of art he had picked up. An Expressionist painting of a distorted figure leading a donkey through a fantastic desert landscape dominated the room, lit by a wall-lamp.

He was sitting at his desk now, surrounded by a mass of papers, running a pencil down the margin of a column of figures. He hadn't heard her and his face wore the look it sometimes had when he thought no one could see: intense, calculating, somehow predatory. In his free hand he held a cigarette, a long trail of ash threatening to fall from the end.

She studied him with a newly critical gaze. His hair was still slicked back with Brylcreem, so thickly you could see the lines of the comb running through. The Brylcreemed hair, like the little straight moustache, was the fashion in Falange circles. He saw her and smiled.

'Hello, darling. Good day?'

'All right. I went to the Retiro this afternoon. It's starting to get cold.'

'You've got your glasses on.'

'Oh, Sandy, I can't go out in the street without them. I'd get run over. I have to wear them, it's just silly not to.'

He stared at her for a moment then smiled again. 'Oh well. The wind's got into your cheeks. Roses.'

'What about you? Working hard?'

'Just some more figures for my Min of Mines project.' He moved the papers away, out of her line of vision, then took her hand. 'I've got some good news. You know you were talking about voluntary work. I spoke to a man at the Jews' Committee today, whose sister's big in Auxilio Social. They're looking for nurses. How d'you fancy working with children?'

'I don't know. It'd be – something to do.' Something to take her mind off Bernie, the camp in Cuenca, Luis.

'The woman we need to speak to's a *marquesa*.' Sandy raised his eyebrows. He pretended to despise the snobbish worship of the aristocracy upper-class Spaniards engaged in as much as the English, but she knew he enjoyed mixing with them. 'Alicia, Marquesa de Segovia. She's going to be at this concert at the Opera House on Saturday; I've got tickets for us.' He smiled and pulled out a couple of gold-embossed cards.

Guilt filled her. 'Oh, Sandy, you always think of me.'

'I don't know what this new guitar concerto thing will be like, but there's some Beethoven too.'

'Oh, thanks, Sandy.' His generosity made her feel ashamed. She felt tears coming and got up hastily. 'I'd better get Pilar started on dinner.'

'All right, lovey. I need another hour on this.'

She went down to the kitchen, slipping on her shoes on the way. It wouldn't do to let Pilar see her walking barefoot.

In the kitchen the paint was an ugly mustard colour, not white like the rest of the house. The maid sat at a table beside the immense old kitchen range. She was looking at a photograph. As she shoved it down the front of her dress and stood up, Barbara caught a glimpse of a young man in Republican uniform. It was dangerous to carry that photograph; if she was asked for her papers and a *civil* found it, questions would be asked. Barbara pretended she hadn't seen it.

'Pilar, could you start the dinner? *Pollo al ajillo* tonight, wasn't it?'

'Yes, madam.'

'Have you everything you need?'

'Yes, madam, thank you.' There was a coldness in the girl's eyes. Barbara wanted to explain, tell her she knew what it was like, she had lost someone too. But that was impossible. She nodded and went upstairs to dress for dinner.

Chapter Nine

THE CAFÉ ROCINANTE was in a narrow street off Calle Toledo. When Harry left the embassy he saw the pale-faced young Spaniard following him again. He cursed – he would have liked to turn round and shout at the man, hit him. He doubled round a couple of streets and managed to lose him. He walked on with a feeling of satisfaction, but when he saw the cafe and crossed over to it his heart began to pound. He took long, deep breaths as he opened the door. He went over the preparation they had done in Surrey for this first meeting. Expect him to be suspicious, they had said; be friendly, naive, a newcomer to Madrid. Be receptive, a listener.

The cafe was gloomy, the daylight coming through the small dusty window barely augmented by fifteen-watt bulbs round the walls. The patrons were mainly middle-class men, shopkeepers and small businessmen. They sat at the little round tables drinking coffee or chocolate, mostly talking business. A thin boy of ten circulated, selling cigarettes from a tray tied round his neck with string. Harry felt uncomfortable, looking round the place while trying not to attract attention. So this was what being a spy was like. There was a faint hissing and churning in his bad ear.

Apart from a couple of middle-aged matrons sitting talking about how expensive things were on the black market, there was only one other woman, smoking alone with an empty coffee cup in front of her. She was in her thirties, thin and anxious-looking, wearing a faded dress. She watched the other customers constantly, her eyes darting from table to table. Harry wondered whether she might be some sort of informer; she was a bit obvious, but then so was his 'tail'.

He saw Sandy at once, sitting alone at a table reading a copy of *ABC*. There was a coffee on the table and a big cigar in the ashtray. If he hadn't seen the photographs he wouldn't have recognized him.

In his well-cut suit, with his moustache and slicked-back hair, there was hardly anything of the schoolboy Harry remembered. He was heavier, though with muscle not fat, and there were already lines on his face. He was only a few months older than Harry, but he looked forty. How had he come to look so old?

He approached the table. Sandy didn't look up and Harry stood there a moment, feeling foolish. He coughed and Sandy lowered the newspaper and stared at him enquiringly.

'Sandy Forsyth?' Harry pretended surprise. 'Is it? It's me. Harry Brett.'

Sandy looked blank for a moment, then recognition dawned. His whole face lit up and he gave the wide smile Harry remembered, showing large square white teeth.

'Harry Brett! It *is* you. I don't believe it! After all these years! God, what are you doing here?' He got up and grasped Harry's hand firmly. Harry took a deep breath.

'I'm working as an interpreter at the embassy.'

'Good Lord! Yes, of course, you did languages at Cambridge, didn't you? What a turn up!' He leaned across and clapped him on the shoulder. 'Jesus, you haven't changed much. Sit down, d'you want a coffee? What're you doing in the Rocinante?'

'I'm billeted near here, just round the corner. Thought I'd try it out.' A momentary catch in his throat as he told his first actual lie, but looking at the simple happy surprise on Sandy's face, Harry saw he had taken him in. He felt a stab of guilt, then relief that Sandy was so pleased to see him, though this would not make things easier.

Sandy clicked his fingers and an elderly waiter in a greasy white jacket came across. Harry ordered a hot chocolate. Cigar smoke wreathed from Sandy's mouth as he studied Harry. 'Well, damn me.' He shook his head. 'It's been – what – fifteen years. I'm surprised you recognized me.'

'Well, you've certainly changed. I wasn't sure for a minute . . .'

'I thought you'd have forgotten me years ago.'

'Never forget those days.'

'Rookwood, eh?' Sandy shook his head. 'You've put on a bit of weight.'

'I guess so. You look fit.'

'Work keeps me on my toes. Remember those afternoons hunting for fossils?' Sandy smiled again, looked suddenly younger. 'They were the best times for me at Rookwood. The best times.'

He sighed and his face seemed to close up as he leaned back in his chair. He was still smiling but something wary had come into his eyes.

'How did you end up working for HMG?'

'Got shot up at Dunkirk.'

'God, yes, the war.' He spoke as though it was something he had forgotten, nothing to do with him. 'Nothing bad, I hope.'

'No, I'm all right now. Little bit of a hearing problem. Anyway, I didn't want to go back to Cambridge afterwards. The Foreign Office were looking for interpreters and they took me on.'

'Cambridge, eh? So you didn't go into the Colonial Office after all?' He laughed. 'Boys' dreams, eh? Remember you were going to be a district officer in Bongoland, and I was going to be a dinosaur hunter?' Sandy's expression was open again, amused. He reached for his cigar and took a long draw.

'Yes. Funny how things turn out.' Harry tried to make his voice sound casual. 'What are you doing out here? It gave me a shock when I saw you. I thought, I know him, who is he? Then I realized.' The lies were flowing smoothly now.

Sandy took another puff of his cigar, blowing out more acrid smoke. 'Fetched up here three years ago. Lot of business opportunities. Doing my bit to help get Spain back on its feet. Though I might move on in a while.'

The old waiter came over and laid a little cup of chocolate in front of Harry. Sandy nodded at the urchin, who was selling Lucky Strikes to the thin woman. 'Want a cigar? Make Roberto's day. He's got a couple of Havanas tucked away there. A bit dry but they're OK.'

'Thanks, I don't smoke.' Harry glanced at the woman. She wasn't even pretending to do anything but watch the customers. There was a clerkly look about her pinched face.

'Never took it up, eh? I remember you never used to join us bad lads behind the gym.'

Harry laughed. 'I just never enjoyed it. The couple of times I tried I felt sick.' He reached for his chocolate. His hand was steady.

'Oh come on, Brett, you disapproved.' There was a light sardonic edge to Sandy's voice now. 'You were always a Rookwood man to your fingertips. Always followed the rules.'

'Maybe. Listen, call me Harry.'

Sandy smiled. 'Like the old days, eh?' Sandy smiled again, with genuine warmth.

'Anyway, Sandy, you were still in London last I heard.'

'I needed to get out. Some racing people had decided they didn't like me. Rough business, racing.' He looked at Harry. 'That was when we lost touch, wasn't it? I was sorry, I used to like getting your letters.' He sighed. 'Had a good scheme going, but it annoyed some big fish. Still, it taught me some lessons. Then a chap I knew at Newmarket told me Franco's people were looking for guides for tours of the battlefields. People with the right background, to get a little foreign exchange and drum up some support for the Nationalists in Britain. So I spent a year showing old colonels from Torquay round the northern battle sites. Then I got involved in a couple of business ventures.' He spread his arms. 'Somehow I just stayed. Came to Madrid last year, followed the Generalísimo in.'

'I see.' Better not press too closely, Harry thought. Too soon. 'Are you still in touch with your father?' he asked.

Sandy's face went cold. 'I've lost touch with him now. It was for the best, we could never see eye to eye.' He was silent a moment, then smiled again. 'Anyway. How long have you been in Madrid?'

'Only a few days.'

'But you were here before, weren't you? You came with Piper after school.'

Harry stared at him, astonished. Sandy chuckled and pointed his cigar butt at him. 'You didn't know I knew that, did you?'

Harry's heart beat fast. How *could* he know?

'Yes, we did. In the Republic's time. But how—'

'You came again later, too, didn't you?' Harry was pleased to see that Sandy's face was full of mischief, which it wouldn't have been had he known Harry's real purpose here. 'Came to try and find him after he went missing at the Jarama and met his girlfriend. Barbara.' He laughed now. 'Don't look so amazed. I'm sorry. Only I met Barbara in Burgos when I was doing the tours, the Red Cross sent her there after Piper went west. She told me all about it.'

So that was it. Harry took a deep breath, leaned back in his chair. 'I wrote to her via the Red Cross office in Madrid, but never heard back. The letters mustn't have got sent on.'

'Probably not. It was pretty chaotic in the Republic by then.'

'How on earth did you two meet? What a coincidence.'

'Not really. There weren't many English people in Burgos in '37. Coincidence we were both in the Nationalist Zone I suppose. We met at a party Texas Oil threw for expatriates.' He smiled broadly. 'In fact, we got together. She's with me now, we've a house out in Vigo. You wouldn't recognize her these days.'

'I thought I saw her the other day, crossing the Plaza Mayor.'

'Did you? What was she doing there? Looking for a shop with something worth buying, maybe.' He smiled.

This is a complication, Harry thought. Barbara. How on earth had she got involved with him?

'Is she still working for the Red Cross?' he asked.

'No, she's a housewife now. She was pretty cut up over Piper, but she's OK now. I'm trying to persuade her to do a bit of voluntary work.'

'It devastated her, Bernie being killed. We never found where his body was.'

Sandy shrugged. 'The Reds didn't care what happened to their men. All those failed offensives the Russians ordered. God knows how many there are buried in the sierras. But Barbara's fine now. I'm sure she'd love to see you. We're having a couple of people round on Tuesday, why don't you join us?'

It was the entrée Harry had been told to angle for, offered on a plate.

'Will that be all right – for Barbara? I wouldn't want to bring back, well, bad memories.'

'She'd be delighted to see you.' Sandy lowered his voice. 'By the way, we tell people we're married, though we're not actually. Makes it easier, the government are a puritan lot.'

Harry saw him watching for his reaction. He smiled and nodded. 'Understood,' he said awkwardly.

'Everyone was living over the brush during the Civil War, of course, you never knew how long you'd got.' He smiled. 'I know Barbara was very grateful for all the help you gave her.'

'Was she? I wished I could have done more. But thanks, I'd love to come.'

Sandy leaned forward, clapped him on the shoulder again. 'Now, more about *you*. How are that old aunt and uncle of yours?'

'Oh, same as ever. They don't change.'

'You're not married?'

'No. There was someone, but it didn't work out.'

'Plenty of nice *señoritas* here.'

'As a matter of fact I've been invited to a party next week, by one of the junior ministers I did some interpreting for. His daughter's eighteenth.'

'Oh, who's that?' Sandy looked interested.

'General Maestre.'

Sandy's eyes narrowed. 'Maestre, eh? You are moving in exalted circles. What's he like?'

'Very courteous. You know him?'

'I met him briefly once. He had a pretty brutal reputation during the Civil War, you know.' He paused reflectively. 'I expect you'll get to meet a lot of government people, in your line.'

'I suppose so. I just go where they want me to.'

'I've met Maestre's new boss, Carceller. Dealt with quite a few people in the government. Met the Generalísimo himself as a matter of fact,' Sandy added proudly. 'At a reception for foreign businessmen.' He's trying to impress, Harry thought.

'What's he like?'

Sandy leaned forward and spoke quietly again. 'Not what you'd think when you see him strutting about on the newsreels. Looks more like a bank manager than a general. But he's crafty, a real Galician. He'll still be here when people like Maestre are long gone. And they say he's the hardest man that ever lived. Signs death warrants over coffee in the evenings.'

'What if we win the war? Franco'll be out then, surely, even if he doesn't come in with Hitler.' They had told him to steer clear of politics at first, but Sandy had started on the topic. It was a chance to find out what he thought of the regime.

Sandy shook his head confidently. 'He won't come in. Too scared of the naval blockade. The regime's not that strong; if the Germans marched into Spain, the Reds would start coming out of their holes. And if we win – ' Sandy shrugged – 'Franco has his uses. There's no one more anti-communist.' He smiled ironically. 'Don't worry. I'm not helping an enemy of England.'

'You're very sure.'

'I am.'

'Things seem pretty desperate here. The poverty. There's a really grim atmosphere.'

Sandy shrugged. 'That's Spain. It's what it's always been like, always will be. They need order.'

Harry inclined his head. 'I wouldn't have thought you'd like the idea of being ordered about by a dictatorship, Sandy.'

He laughed. 'This isn't a real dictatorship. It's too chaotic for that. There's lots of opportunities for business if you keep your wits about you. Not that I'll stay here for ever.'

'You might move on.'

Sandy shrugged. 'Next year perhaps.'

'People here look as though they're on the verge of starvation.'

Sandy looked at Harry seriously. 'The last two harvests have been disastrous because of drought. And half the infrastructure was wrecked in the war. Britain's not helping, frankly. There's hardly enough oil being allowed in to keep transport going. Have you seen those gasogene things?'

'Yes.'

'The place is a bureaucratic nightmare, of course, but the market will win out. People like me are showing the way.' He looked into Harry's eyes. 'That will help them, you know. I do want to help them.'

The woman was staring at them again. Harry leaned across, whispering. 'See her, at that table? She's been looking at us ever since I arrived. I can't help worrying she might be an informer.'

Sandy looked blank for a moment, then threw his head back

and roared with laughter. The other customers turned and stared at them.

'Oh, Harry, Harry, you are priceless!'

'What? What do you mean?'

'She's a tart, Harry. She's always here, she's looking for business.'

'What?'

'You keep looking over, meeting her eyes and turning away again, the poor girl won't know what's going on.' Sandy grinned at the woman. She didn't understand his words but reddened at his mocking look.

'All right, I didn't know. She doesn't *look* like a tart.'

'A lot don't now. She's probably the widow of some Republican. A lot of them have gone on the game to make ends meet.'

The woman got up. Fumbling with her handbag, she dropped some coins on the table and walked out. Sandy watched her go, still grinning at her embarrassment. 'You do have to look out, though,' Sandy continued. 'I thought someone was following me recently.'

'Were they?'

'Not sure. They seem to have disappeared, anyway.' Sandy looked at his watch. 'Well, I must get back to the office. Let me get these.'

'Thanks.'

Sandy laughed again, shook his head. 'It *is* good to see you again.' There was genuine affection in his voice. 'Wait till I tell Barbara. Can I get you at the embassy about Tuesday?'

'Yes. Ask for the translation section.'

Out in the street Sandy shook Harry's hand. He looked at him seriously. 'England's lost the war, you know. I was right – all the Rookwood ideas, empire and noblesse oblige and playing the game, it's all nonsense. One knock and it's all fallen down. People who create opportunities for themselves, who make themselves up, they're the future.' He shook his head. 'Oh, well.' He sounded almost regretful.

'It's not over yet.'

'Not quite yet. But almost.' Sandy smiled commiseratingly, then turned and walked away.

Chapter Ten

THE DOORS OF THE Opera House stood open, light from the chandeliers shining out over Plaza Isabel II. The October evening was cold, and around the square *civiles* cradled their guns in the shadows. A red carpet trailed down the steps to the kerb in anticipation of the Generalísimo's arrival. The bright lights made Barbara blink as she approached, her arm in Sandy's.

The evening before she had taken her deception of Sandy a stage further. She had savings in England and had written to her bank asking them to send her money to Spain. She had tried the *Express* office again too, asked them to send a telegram to Markby saying she needed to talk to him, but they didn't know where he was.

She waited in the *salón* for Sandy to come home. She had told Pilar to make up a fire and the room was cosy and welcoming, a bottle of his favourite whisky and a glass on a little table by his chair. She sat there reading, waiting, as she did most nights.

He arrived at seven. Barbara had taken her glasses off when she heard his footsteps but she could see he was excited about something. He kissed her warmly.

'Mmm. I do like that dress. Shows off your white skin. Listen, you'll never guess who I met today in the Rocinante. Never in a million years. Is this Glenfiddich? Marvellous. You'll *never* guess.' He sounded like a schoolboy in his eagerness.

'I won't know if you don't tell me.'

'Harry Brett.'

She was so astonished she had to sit down.

Sandy nodded. 'I couldn't believe it myself. Walked in large as life. He's an interpreter at the embassy. He was wounded at Dunkirk, then sent out here.'

'Good God. Is he all right?'

'Seems to be. His hand was shaking a little. But he's the same old Harry. Formal, very serious. He doesn't know what to make of Spain.' He smiled and shook his head indulgently. Barbara looked at him. Harry. Bernie's friend. She forced her face into a smile.

'You were good friends at school, weren't you?'

'Yes. He's a good chap.'

'You know, he's the only person from England you ever speak of with affection.'

Sandy shrugged. 'I've invited him round for Tuesday night. Sebastian's bringing that awful Jenny with him, I'm afraid. Are you all right?'

She had come out in a scarlet flush. 'Yes, it was just a surprise.' She swallowed.

'I can put him off if you'd rather. If it brings things back. '

'No. No, it would be marvellous to see him.'

'Well, I must go up and change.' He left the room. Barbara closed her eyes, remembering those terrible days after Bernie went missing. Harry had helped her then, but it had been Sandy who had saved her. She felt ashamed again.

THE HALL WAS nearly full, a buzz of excited chatter. Barbara looked round. Everyone was in their best clothes, even the numerous women in full mourning wore dresses of black silk and some had lacy mantillas hanging over their foreheads. The men were in evening dress or military or Falange uniforms. There was a sprinkling of clerics in black or red robes. Barbara had changed into a white evening dress with a green brooch that set off her eyes, and a white fur stole.

The hall had been refurbished for its first performance since the Civil War. The walls and white fluted pillars were freshly painted, the seats covered with new red plush. Sandy was in his element, smiling at acquaintances. He nodded to a colonel as he passed with his wife. 'They can put on a show when they want to,' he whispered.

'I suppose it's a sign of things getting back to normal.'

Sandy read from the programme. '"El concierto de Aranjuez. To celebrate Señor Rodrigo's return from exile, his new work is a reflection on past glories amid the peaceful gardens of the Palace of

Aranjuez." We'll have to drive down one weekend and see the palace, lovey.'

'That would be nice.'

The hall was filling up. The orchestra was practising, shafts of music piercing the air. People glanced up at the empty royal box.

'The Generalísimo's not here yet,' Sandy whispered.

There was a flurry of activity as two soldiers led a couple in evening dress to their seats in a neighbouring box. Both were very tall, the woman statuesque with long blonde hair, the man with a bald head and an eagle-like nose. There was a swastika armband on his evening jacket. Barbara recognized his face from the newspapers. Von Stohrer, the German ambassador.

Sandy nudged her arm. 'Don't stare, lovey.'

'I hate seeing that – emblem.'

'Spain's neutral, lovey. Just ignore them. He took her arm and indicated a tall middle-aged woman in black sitting nearby, talking quietly to a female companion. 'There's the *marquesa*. Let's go and introduce ourselves.' He steered her down the aisle. 'Don't mention her husband, by the way,' he whispered. 'The peasants on one of his estates fed him to his pigs in '36. Very nasty.' Barbara shuddered slightly. He often spoke lightly of the horrors people had suffered in the Civil War.

Sandy bowed to the *marquesa*. Barbara wasn't sure how to greet her so she curtsied, receiving a little smile in return. The *marquesa* was about fifty, with a kindly face that must once have been pretty but was now seamed into wrinkled sadness.

'Your grace,' Sandy began. 'Allow me to introduce myself. Alexander Forsyth. This is my wife, Señora Barbara. Forgive this intrusion, but Señor Cana told me you are seeking volunteers for your orphanage.'

'Yes, he spoke to me. I understand you are a nurse, *señora*.'

'I haven't done any nursing for years, I'm afraid.'

The *marquesa* smiled gravely. 'Those skills are never forgotten. Many of the children in our orphanage are ill, or were injured in the war. So many orphans in Madrid.' She shook her head sadly. 'No parents or homes or schooling, some of them begging in the streets.'

'Where is the orphanage, your grace?'

'Near Atocha, in a building the church gave us. The nuns help with the teaching, but we need more medical help. The nursing orders have so many calls upon them still.'

'Of course.'

'Do you think you could help us, *señora*?'

Barbara thought of the barefoot wild-faced urchins she saw roaming the streets. 'Yes. I'd like to.'

The *marquesa* put a finger to her chin. 'Forgive me asking, *señora*, but you are English. Are you a Catholic?'

'No. No, I'm afraid not. I was baptized an Anglican.' Barbara laughed awkwardly. Her parents had never gone to church. And what would the *marquesa* think if she knew she and Sandy weren't even married?

'The church authorities may need persuading. But we need nurses, Señora Forsyth. I can speak to the bishop, perhaps telephone you?'

Sandy spread his hands. 'We quite understand.'

'I will see what can be done. It would be so good if you could help us.' She inclined her head, indicating the interview was over. Barbara curtsied again and followed Sandy down the aisle.

'She'll do it,' Sandy said. 'The *marquesa* has got a lot of clout.'

'I don't see why my religion should be a problem. The Church of England's nothing to be ashamed of.'

He rounded on her, suddenly angry. 'You weren't bloody brought up in the heart of it,' he snapped. 'You didn't have to live with those hypocrites day in day out. At least with the Catholics, you know where you are.'

She had forgotten the Church was such a raw nerve. Like mention of his family, it could make Sandy turn suddenly.

'All right, all right. I'm sorry.'

Sandy had turned away; he was looking at a tall balding man in a general's uniform standing nearby. The soldier was staring back disapprovingly. He raised his eyebrows slightly and walked away. Sandy turned to Barbara, a trapped, angry look on his face.

'Now see what you've done,' he muttered. 'Made me look a fool in front of Maestre. He heard.'

'What do you mean? Who's Maestre?'

'An opponent of the Min of Mines project. It doesn't matter.

Sorry. Look, lovey, you know not to get me started on the Church, eh? Come on, they want us to sit down.'

Flunkeys in eighteenth-century dress were moving through the crowd urging people to their seats. The hall was full now. Sandy led them to their row, near the middle, next to a man in Falange uniform. Barbara recognized him: Otero, one of Sandy's business associates. He was some sort of mining engineer. He had a round clerkly face, but the olive eyes above the starched blue shirt were keen and hard. She didn't like him.

'Alberto.' Sandy laid his hand on the man's shoulder.

'*Hola, amigo*. Señora.'

There was a susurrating murmur from the crowd. At the far end of the hall a door opened and a bevy of flunkeys bowed in a middle-aged couple. Barbara had heard that Franco was a small man but was surprised how tiny, even delicate, he looked. He wore a general's uniform with a broad red sash round his paunchy middle. He held his arms stiffly at his sides, moving them back and forth as though leading a parade. His balding head gleamed under the lights. Doña Carmen, walking behind, was slightly taller than her husband, a tiara in her jet back hair. Her long haughty face was made for the regal expression it wore. There seemed something posed, though, about the stoniness of the Generalísimo's face, the little mouth set hard under the wispy moustache, and the surprisingly large eyes staring ahead as he marched past the stage

The Falangists in the audience sprang to their feet, stretching out their arms in the Fascist salute. '*¡Jefe!*' they called out. The rest of the audience and the orchestra followed. Sandy nudged Barbara. She stared at him, she hadn't expected to have to do this but he nodded urgently. She rose reluctantly and stood with arm extended although she could not bring herself to join the shouting. Making the gesture felt awful, shameful.

'*¡Je-fe! ¡Je-fe! ¡Fran-co! ¡Fran-co!*' The Generalísimo did not acknowledge the salutes, marching on like an automaton until he reached a door at the other end. The flunkeys opened it and the pair disappeared through. The shouts went on, people turning their heads and outstretched arms to the royal box as Franco and Doña Carmen reappeared above them. The couple stood a moment, looking down.

Doña Carmen was smiling now but Franco's face stayed coldly expressionless. He raised a hand briefly and at once the noise ceased. The crowd sat down. The conductor stood, bowing to the royal box.

Barbara liked classical music. When she had lived at home, she had preferred it to the jazz her sister liked and would sometimes sit listening to concerts with her parents. She had never heard anything like this concerto but she liked it. The guitar began the allegro on a liquid flowing note and then the strings joined in, the tempo slowly rising. It was cheerful and gentle and around her Barbara saw people relax, smiling and nodding.

The allegro moved to a climax and the adagio began. The music was slower now, the guitar alternating with wind instruments, and the sound was pure flowing sadness. All over the hall people began to weep, first one or two, then more and more, women and a few men too. She could hear half-suppressed sobs everywhere. Most of the people here would have lost someone in the Civil War. Barbara glanced at Sandy; he gave her a tense, embarrassed smile.

She looked up at the royal box. Carmen Franco's face was composed and still. The Generalísimo's wore a slight frown. Then she noticed a quivering movement of the muscles round his mouth. She thought he was going to weep too but then his features settled again and she realized he had been stifling a yawn. She turned away, with a sudden, violent revulsion.

The horn playing made Barbara think of a bare empty plain. She knew the man Luis was most likely a liar, but there was still a possibility Bernie was out there somewhere, imprisoned while she sat here. She clenched a fist tightly round her stole, fingers digging into the soft fur.

The guitar notes quickened and then the violins took over, bringing the music to a wrenching climax. Barbara felt something break and well up inside her and then she was crying too, tears flowing down her cheeks. Sandy looked at her curiously, then took her hand and squeezed it diffidently.

When the music ended there was a long moment of silence before the audience broke into thunderous applause. It went on as the blind composer Rodrigo was led to the front of the stage. Tear tracks glistened on his face too as he shook the conductor's hand and spoke with the soloist, the clapping going on and on. Sandy turned to Barbara. 'Are you all right?'

'Yes. Sorry.'

He sighed. 'I shouldn't have snapped earlier. But you should know how some things get me.' She caught an undertone of irritation behind his reassurance.

'It's not that. It's just – oh, everyone's lost so much. Everyone.'

'I know. Come on, dry your eyes. It's the interval. D'you want to stay here? I'll get you a brandy at the bar if you like.'

'No, I'm all right. I'll come.' She glanced round and saw Otero looking at her curiously. He caught her eye and smiled, quickly and insincerely.

'Good girl,' Sandy said. 'Come on, then.'

In the bar Sandy got her a gin and tonic. It was strong, she needed it. She felt her face flush as she drank. Otero joined them with his wife, who was surprisingly young and pretty.

'Wasn't it sad?' she asked Barbara.

'Yes. But very beautiful.'

Otero straightened his tie. 'A great composer. He must be very proud, his *concierto* played for the first time before the Generalísimo.'

'Yes, did you see him?' Otero's wife asked Barbara eagerly. 'I've always wanted to. Every inch the soldier.'

Barbara smiled stiffly. 'Yes.' She caught a whisper from Otero to Sandy.

'Any word on the latest Jews?'

'Yes. They'll do anything to escape being sent back to Vichy.'

'Good. We need something more to show. I can make it look good.' Otero noticed Barbara listening and gave her another of his sharp looks.

'Well, Señora Forsyth,' he said. 'I wonder if Don Rodrigo will get to meet the Generalísimo?

'I'm sure he will have loved the music,' she replied neutrally.

A man pushed through the crowd towards them. It was the general whose gaze had upset Sandy earlier. Otero's mouth tightened and his sharp eyes flickered around but Sandy bowed and gave the soldier a friendly smile.

'General Maestre.'

The general stared coldly into his eyes. 'Señor Forsyth. And my old friend Captain Otero – that is your Falange rank, I think.'

'Yes, sir.'

Maestre nodded. 'I hear your project is proceeding well. Building materials requisitioned here, chemicals there.'

'We only ask for what we need, sir.' There was a note of defiance in Otero's voice. 'The Generalísimo himself has—'

'Approved. Yes, I know. A project to help Spain in its path back to prosperity. And make money for you, of course.'

'I'm a businessman, sir,' Sandy said with a smile.

'Yes. You help us and become rich at the same time.'

'I hope so.'

Maestre nodded twice, slowly. He studied Barbara a moment with narrowed eyes, then bowed abruptly and walked away. As he turned, Barbara heard him mutter the word '*sinvergüenza*'. It meant shameless, without morals.

Otero looked at Sandy; Barbara could see the Falangist was scared. 'It's all right,' Sandy said. 'Everything's under control. Look, we'll talk tomorrow.'

Otero hesitated a moment. '*Algo va mal*,' he muttered. 'Come on,' he said sharply to his wife. They joined the trickle of people heading for the exit. Sandy leaned against the bar, twirling the stem of his empty glass, his expression thoughtful.

'What was that all about?' Barbara asked. 'What did he mean, all is not well?'

Sandy stroked his moustache. 'He's an old woman, for all the Falange regalia.'

'What have you done to annoy that general? You don't annoy generals here.'

His eyes were pensive, half-closed. 'Maestre's on the supply committee for our Min of Mines project. He's a Monarchist.' He shrugged. 'It's just politics. Jockeying for position.'

'The general doesn't like your project because it's got Falange support?'

'Exactly. But at the end of the day Maestre won't count, because we've got Franco's blessing.' He got up, adjusting his lapels.

'What was Otero saying about the Jews?'

Sandy shrugged again. 'That's confidential too. We have to keep the committee's work quiet, Barbara. If the Germans found out there'd be a fuss.'

'I hate seeing the Nazis being feted.'

'They're enjoying their bit of flattery. But that's all it is. Diplomatic games.' His voice was impatient now. He placed a hand in the small of her back. 'Come on, it's Beethoven next. Try to forget the war. It's far away.'

Chapter Eleven

THE DAY THE GERMAN PLANE crashed into the house in Vigo, Barbara and Bernie took a tram back to Barbara's neat little flat off the Calle Mayor, sitting with their arms round each other, covered in dust. When they got home they sat side by side on her bed, holding hands.

'Are you sure you're all right?' Bernie asked. 'You're white as a sheet.'

'It's just a cut. The dust makes it look worse than it is. I should have a bath.'

'Go and get one. I'll make us something to eat.' He gave her hand a squeeze.

By the time she had bathed he had prepared a meal. They ate chorizo and chickpeas at the little table. They were silent, both still shocked. Halfway through he reached across the table and took her hand.

'I love you,' he said. 'I do love you. I meant it.'

'I love you too.' She took a deep breath. 'I – I couldn't believe you. When I was young – it's so hard to explain . . .'

'The bullying?'

'It sounds a silly thing, but when it just goes on for years, that endless putting you down – why do children pick on people, why do they need someone to hate? They used to spit at me sometimes. For no reason, just because I was me.'

He squeezed her hand. 'Why do you take their word for what you are? Why won't you take mine instead?'

She burst out weeping. He came round the table and knelt beside her and held her tightly. She felt a sense of release.

'I've only been with a man once,' she said quietly.

'You don't have to now. I'd never want to do anything you didn't. Ever.'

She looked into his eyes, deep dark olive. The past seemed to recede, washing away down a corridor in her mind. She knew it would return but for now it was far away. She took a deep breath.

'I do want to. I have since the day I met you. Stay with me, don't go back to Carabanchel tonight.'

'Are you sure you don't need to sleep now?'

'No.' She took off her glasses. He smiled and took them from her gently.

'I like those,' he said gently. 'They make you look clever.'

She smiled. 'So you didn't just pick me out to convert to communism.'

He shook his head, his smile broadening.

SHE WOKE in the middle of the night to feel his fingers caressing her neck. It was dark, she could only make out the outline of his head but she felt his body against her.

'I can't believe this is happening,' she whispered. 'Not with you.'

'I loved you the first day I met you,' Bernie said. 'I've never met anyone like you.'

She laughed nervously. 'Like me? What does that mean?'

'Alive, compassionate, sensual though you pretend not to be.'

Tears welled up in her eyes. 'I thought you were too beautiful for me. You're the most beautiful man I've ever seen.' She whispered, 'I thought, if we were ever naked together I'd feel ashamed.'

'You silly girl. Silly girl.' He held her close again.

IT FELT WRONG to be so happy in the besieged city. The fighting to the north continued; Franco's forces were still being held. The government had fled to Valencia, and Madrid was run by committees that people said the Communists controlled. The loudspeakers in the city centre called on citizens to be wary of traitors in their midst.

Barbara worked on, dealing with exchanges of prisoners and enquiries about missing persons, but side by side with her sense of helplessness in the face of murderous chaos was an inner warmth, a lightness. 'I love him,' she would tell herself, and then, wonderingly, 'And he loves me.'

He waited for her every day outside the office and they would go to her flat or the cinema or a cafe. The doctors said Bernie's arm was healing well. In a month or so he would be fit for service again. He had asked again to help the party with new recruits to the International Brigades but they said they had enough people.

'If only you didn't have to go back,' she said to him one evening. It was a few days before Christmas; they were sitting in a bar in the Centro after visiting the cinema. They had seen a Soviet film about the modernization of Central Asia, then a gangster movie with Jimmy Cagney. It was the topsy-turvy world they lived in now. Some nights the Nationalists in the Casa de Campo fired artillery down Gran Vía at the time the cinemas emptied, but not that night.

'I'm an enlisted soldier in the Republican Army,' Bernie said. 'I have to go back when they tell me. Otherwise I could be shot.'

'I wish we could just go home. Away from this. It's what we've feared for years in the Red Cross. A war where there's no difference between soldiers and civilians. A city full of people caught in the middle.' She sighed. 'I saw an old man in the street today, he looked like he'd been a professional of some sort, he had a thick coat on but it was old and dusty and he was looking in the bins for something to eat, peering in while pretending not to. He caught my eye and he looked so ashamed.'

'I doubt he's suffering any more than the poor. He'll get the same rations. Why should it be worse for him, just because he's middle class? This war's got to be fought. It's got to be.'

She took his hand across the table, looked him in the eye. 'If you were allowed to go home now, with me, would you?'

He dropped his eyes. 'I have to stay. It's my duty.'

'To the party?'

'To mankind.'

'I wish I had your faith sometimes. Then I mightn't feel so bad.'

'It's not faith. I wish you'd try to understand Marxism, it exposes the bones of reality. Oh, Barbara, I wish you could see things clearly.'

She gave a tired laugh. 'No, I've never been any good at that. Please don't go back, Bernie. If you go now I'm not sure I could bear it. Not now. Please, please, let's go back to England.' She reached out and clasped his hand. 'You've a British passport, you could get out. You could go into the embassy.'

He was silent for a moment. Then Barbara heard his name called out, in a voice with a strong Scottish accent. She turned and saw a fair-haired young man waving at him from the bar where he stood with a group of tired-looking men in uniform.

'Piper!' The Scotsman raised his glass. 'How's the arm?'

'All right, McNeil. Getting better! I'll be back soon.'

'*¡No pasarán!*' The soldier and Bernie exchanged the clenched-fist salute. Bernie turned back to Barbara, lowering his voice. 'I can't do it, Barbara. I love you but I can't. And I don't have a passport, I had to surrender it to the army. And . . .' He sighed.

'What?'

'I'd be ashamed for the rest of my life.' He nodded at the soldiers at the bar. 'I can't leave them. I know it's hard for a woman to understand, but I can't. I have to go back, though I don't want to.'

'Don't you?'

'No. But I'm a soldier. What I want doesn't matter.'

THE FIGHTING in the Casa de Campo ground into stalemate, trench warfare like the Western Front in the Great War. But everyone said Franco would renew his offensive in the spring, probably somewhere in the open country south of the city. There were still casualties enough; Barbara saw wounded men brought back from the front every day, lying pale-faced in carts or trucks. The mood among the populace was changing, the fiery combativeness of the autumn giving way to depression. There were shortages too; people were looking ill, getting boils and chilblains. Barbara felt guilty about the better Red Cross food she shared with Bernie. Her happiness alternated with the fear of losing him, and anger too that he could come into her life and transform it and then just march away. Sometimes the anger turned to a desperate fearful weariness.

Two days later they were walking from Barbara's flat to her office. It was bright and cold, the sun just up, frost on the pavements. The queues for the daily ration began at seven; already a long line of black-clad women waited outside the government offices in Calle Mayor.

The women stopped talking suddenly and stared along the street. Barbara saw a couple of horse-drawn carts coming towards them.

Chapter Twelve

ITZ DINING ROOM was lit by sparkling chandeliers. Harry
s seat at the long dining table reserved for the embassy staff.
st sat next to him; on his other side, Goach, the old man who
structed him in protocol, settled carefully into his chair. He
d, with a drooping white moustache and a soft voice, and wore
cle on a long black thread. The collar of his dinner jacket was
with dandruff.

rry's wing collar chafed at his neck as he looked round the
wo dozen embassy staff had come to show the flag. At the head
able Hoare sat with his wife, Lady Maud, a large plain woman.
th was on Hoare's other side, his naval uniform bright with

rry had reported back to Hillgarth after his meeting with
Tolhurst had been there too. Hillgarth had been pleased with
gress, especially with the invitation to dinner, and intrigued to
out Barbara.

if you can get him to talk more about his business,' Hillgarth
. 'You don't know who the other guests are going to be?'

I didn't ask. Didn't want to press too closely.'

garth nodded. 'Quite right. What about his girly, could she be
plans?'

n't know.' Harry frowned.

were just friends?' Hillgarth interjected sharply.

sir. It's just, I don't want to involve her unless I have to. But
ight be necessary,' he added. 'It's odd, their getting together
didn't get on with Bernie.'

der if he went after the girly because she was his enemy's
?' Tolhurst mused.

't know.' Harry shook his head. 'When I knew Sandy he

As they passed she smelt the fresh tarry paint and saw that they contained little white coffins, for children whose souls had not yet been soiled, the Catholic practice living on. The women stared at them, bleakly and silently. One made the sign of the cross, then began to weep.

'People are at the end of their tether,' Barbara said. 'They can't take much more. All the death!' She burst out crying too, there in the street. Bernie put his arm round her but she shrugged him off. 'I see you in a coffin! You!'

He held her at arm's length and looked into her eyes. 'If Franco takes Madrid there'll be a massacre. I won't abandon them. I won't!'

CHRISTMAS DAY CAME. They ate a greasy mutton stew in Barbara's flat, then went upstairs to bed. They lay in each other's arms and talked.

'This isn't the Christmas I expected,' Barbara said. 'I thought I'd be in Birmingham, going with Mum and Dad to visit my sister and her family. I always get restless after a couple of days, I want to get away.'

He held her tight. 'How did they make you think so badly of yourself?'

'I don't know. It just happened.'

'You should be angry.'

'They could never understand why I went to work for the Red Cross.' She ran a finger over his chest. 'They'd have liked to see me married with children, like Carol.'

'Would you like children?'

'Only when there are no wars any more.'

Bernie lit cigarettes for them, fumbling in the dark. His face was serious in the red glow. 'I'm a disappointment to my parents. They think I've thrown away everything Rookwood offered. I wish I'd never won that bloody scholarship.'

'Didn't you get anything out of school?'

He laughed bitterly. 'Like Caliban said, they taught me language, so I know how to swear.'

She found his heart and laid her hand there, feeling the soft thump-thump.

'Perhaps that's what drew us together. Two disappointments.' She paused. 'You believe in fate, Bernie, don't you?'

'No. Historical destiny.'

'What's the difference?'

'You can influence destiny, you can hamper it or hurry it forward. You can't do anything to change fate.'

'I wish my destiny could be with you.'

She felt his chest rise and fall sharply as he took a deep breath. 'Barbara.'

'What?'

'You know I'm nearly fit again. In a couple of weeks they're sending me to the new training camp at Albacete. They told me yesterday.'

'Oh God.' Her heart sank.

'I'm sorry. I was waiting for the right moment but there isn't one, is there?'

'No.'

'I don't think I really cared if I lived before, but I do now. Now that I'm going back.'

FOR TWO WEEKS after he left she had no news. She went to work and stumbled through the day, but when she returned to the flat and he wasn't there the silence seemed to echo as though he was dead already.

In the first week of February news came of a Fascist offensive to the south of Madrid. They were aiming to sweep round and cut the capital off completely, but they were held at the Jarama river. The radio and newspapers spoke of a heroic defence, Franco's advance checked before it had really begun. The International Brigades were prominent in the fighting. They said there were heavy casualties.

Every morning before work Barbara went to army headquarters in the Puerta del Sol. At first the staff were suspicious, but when she came a second day and a third they were kind to her. She had let herself go, she was losing weight and there were dark rings under her eyes, her pain visible to all.

The headquarters was chaotic, uniformed clerks running around clutching papers, telephones ringing everywhere. Barbara wondered

whether some of those phone lines connected
might be a connection between one of those
place where Bernie was now. She did that al
connections in her head: the same sun shines
same moon, I hold a book that he held, put a
he put in his . . .

There was serious fighting in the secon
February, but still she had no news. She had
but they told her communications were difficul
February the fighting lessened, turned into anot
hoped news might start coming through now.

She heard on the last day of February, a cold
had come to HQ before work as usual and this ti
asked her to wait in a side room. She knew at
She sat in a shabby little office with a desk
portrait of Stalin on the wall. She thought, irrel
keep that big moustache in order?

The door opened and a man in captain's un
was a paper in his hand and his face was sombr
run through her, as though she had fallen throug
She didn't get up to shake hands, just sat there.

'Miss Clare. Good afternoon. I hear you h
times.'

'Yes. For news.' She gulped. 'He's dead, isn'

The officer raised a hand. 'We do not kno
But he is on the list of those missing belie
Battalion was in heavy fighting on the thirtee

'Missing believed killed,' she said flatly. 'I
You just haven't found a body.'

He didn't answer, just inclined his head.

'They fought magnificently. They held
on their own for two days.' He paused. 'Man

Barbara felt herself fall from the ch
the floor she started weeping uncontrollabl
floorboards because under them was the ea
was buried now.

THE
took
Tolhu
had i
was b
a mor
spotte
H
table;
of the
Hillga
medal
H
Sandy
his pro
learn a
'Se
had saic
'No
Hill
in on hi
'I do
'You
'Yes,
I see it m
– Sandy
'Won
girlfriend
'I dor

was still a boy, really. He's changed. Everything about him seemed contrived, showy. Except for his being pleased to see me, that was real.' He frowned again.

'Use that.' Hillgarth looked at Harry seriously. 'What you're doing is important. This gold business fits into a bigger picture, the question of how we handle the regime. It matters a lot.'

Harry met Hillgarth's gaze. 'I know, sir.'

THE WAITER laid a menu before him, large and white. The choices could have come from before the war. Harry wondered if they still had food as good as this at the London Ritz. He had had a letter from Will that morning. He was being transferred to a new post out in the countryside, somewhere in the Midlands; Muriel was delighted to get away from the bombs, though worried the house might be burgled. The news from home had filled Harry with almost unbearable nostalgia. He looked up from the menu with a sigh, his eyes widened at the sight of four officers in grey uniforms who were taking seats at a table a little way off, among the well-dressed Madrileños. The officers' harsh, clipped voices were instantly recognizable.

'There's Jerry,' Tolhurst said quietly. 'Military advisers. The Gestapo people wear civvies.'

One of the Germans caught Harry's stare, raised an eyebrow and turned away.

'The Ritz is such a German and Italian haunt now,' Tolhurst continued. 'That's why Sir Sam likes to fly the flag now and then.'

'Ready for tomorrow?' Tolhurst asked quietly. 'The dinner with our friend?'

'Yes.'

'Wonder if that girly knows anything?' Tolhurst's eyes were alight with curiosity.

'I don't know, Tolly.' Harry looked down the table. Tonight's dinner, too, had its hidden agenda: they were all under instructions to be cheerful, relaxed, show they weren't worried by the cabinet changes. Everyone was drinking hard, joking and guffawing. It was like a rugby club dinner. The embassy secretaries, brought along to make up the numbers, looked ill at ease.

Waiters in starched white coats brought food and wine. The food was superb, the best Harry had eaten since his arrival. 'The old standards are coming back,' said Goach at his elbow. Harry wondered how old he was; they said he had been at the embassy since the Spanish-American War forty years ago. No one, apparently, knew more about Spanish protocol.

'They are at the Ritz, at least, judging by the food,' said Harry.

'Oh, in other places too. They're reopening the theatres, the Opera House. I remember the old King spoke to me there once. He was very charming. Put one at ease.' He sighed. 'I think the Generalísimo would like to invite him back, but the Falange won't have it. Wretched shower. They threw flour at you on Thursday, I heard?'

'Yes, they did.'

'Filthy rabble. He had the Hapsburg jaw, you know. Protruding.'

'What?'

'King Alfonso. Only slightly. The burdens of royalty. The Duke of Windsor passed through Madrid, you know, back in June. When he escaped from France.' Goach shook his head. 'They just rushed him through the embassy and out to Lisbon. No formal reception or anything. I mean, he *was* the King once.' He shook his head again, sadly.

Harry looked round the table again. He wondered what Bernie would have made of this.

'Penny for 'em,' Tolhurst said. Harry turned to him.

'Sometimes I feel like I'm in Wonderland,' he said quietly. 'I wouldn't be surprised to see a white rabbit in a suit pop up.'

Tolhurst looked puzzled. 'What d'you mean?'

Harry laughed. 'They haven't a clue what life's like out there.' He nodded towards the window. 'Doesn't it ever get to you, Simon, all the sheer bloody misery you see in this city?'

Tolhurst frowned thoughtfully. Through the chatter Harry caught the ambassador's sharp tones. 'This Special Operations nonsense is mad. I hear they're using Spanish Republican exiles to train British soldiers in political warfare. Bloody Communists.'

'Set Europe ablaze,' Hillgarth replied.

'Oh yes, that's a typical Winston phrase. Purple prose.' Hoare's sharp voice was raised. 'I *know* what the Reds are like, I was in Russia when the Tsar fell.'

Hillgarth lowered his voice but Harry heard him. 'All right, Sam. I agree with you. It's not the time for that.'

Tolhurst came out of his brown study. 'I suppose I'm used to it. The poverty. Cuba's just the same.'

'I can't get used to it,' Harry said.

Tolhurst thought a moment. 'Ever been to a bullfight?'

'I went once, in '31. Didn't like it. Why?'

'The first time I went it made me feel sick, all the blood when they spear the bull, the terrified expression still on the bloody thing's face when they brought its head to the restaurant afterwards. But I had to go; it was part of the diplomatic life. The second time it wasn't so bad. I thought, dammit, it's only an animal, then the third time I started appreciating the skill, the matadors' bravery. You have to shut your eyes to the bad side of a country if you're a diplomat, d'you see?'

Or a spy, Harry thought. He traced a line in the white tablecloth with his fork. 'Isn't that how it always starts, though? We deaden ourselves for protection, stop seeing the cruelty and suffering.'

'I suppose if we let ourselves think about all the gruesome things we start imagining them happening to us. I know I do sometimes.' Tolhurst laughed uneasily. Harry looked up and down the table, saw the forced quality of the smiles, the harsh undertone to the laughter.

'I don't think you're alone,' he said.

Someone on Tolhurst's other side grabbed his arm and began whispering to him about two clerks who had been caught together in a stationery cupboard. Tolhurst turned away with relief to the gossip.

'Julian, a pansy? I don't believe it.'

Harry turned back to Goach. 'Nice salmon.'

'Very good.'

'What?' Harry hadn't caught the old man's reply. Among a crowd, his deafness could still be a problem. For a moment he felt disorientated.

'I said it's very good,' Goach said. 'Very good.'

Harry leaned forward. 'You've been in the diplomatic service a long time, sir. I heard a phrase the other day, the Knights of St George. Any idea what it might mean? I wondered if it might be embassy slang of some sort.'

Goach adjusted his monocle, frowned. 'Don't think so, Brett, never heard that one before. Where d'you hear it?'

'Oh, round the embassy somewhere. It just struck me as odd.'

Goach shook his head again. 'Sorry, no idea.' He glanced at Hoare for a moment, then said, 'He's a good man, the ambassador. For all the faults he may have, he'll keep Spain out of the war.'

'I hope so,' Harry said, then added, 'If Spain does stay out, and we win, what happens to the country afterwards?'

Goach gave a little laugh. 'Let's win the war first.' He thought a moment. 'Though if Franco stays out, keeps the Fascist element in the government under control, well, we'd have reason to be grateful to him, wouldn't we?'

'You think he's a Monarchist at heart?'

'Oh, I'm sure of it. If you analyse his speeches carefully, you can see he cares everything about Spain's traditions, its old values.'

'What about its people?'

Goach shrugged. 'They've always needed a firm hand.'

'They've got that all right.'

Goach inclined his head, then lowered it to his plate. There was a shout of laughter from the other end of the table, matched by a guffaw from the Germans, as they tried to be louder.

Chapter Thirteen

ON TUESDAY, Barbara went to meet Luis again. It was a fine day, still and quiet, leaves fluttering down from the trees. Barbara walked because the Castellana was closed to traffic; Reichsführer Himmler would be driven down it later on his way to meet the Generalísimo at the Royal Palace.

She had to cross the Castellana. Swastika flags hung from every building and were strung across the road, the scarlet banners with the hooked cross gaudy against the grey buildings. *Civiles* stood at intervals along the road, some cradling sub-machine guns. Nearby a parade of Falange Youth was lined up on the kerb, holding little swastika flags. Barbara hurried across and disappeared into the maze of streets leading to the Centro.

As she neared the cafe her heart was beating fast. Luis was already there, she saw him through the window. He was at the same table, nursing a coffee. His expression was gloomy. Barbara noticed again how down at heel he looked; he wore the same threadbare jacket, cheap rope-soled *alpargatas* on his feet. She took a deep breath and went in. The landlady nodded to her from beneath Franco's portrait. She wished she could get away from the Generalísimo's cold stare; it was everywhere, even on the stamps now.

Luis stood up with a relieved smile. '*Señora. Buenos días*. I thought you might not come!'

'I'm sorry,' she said without an answering smile. 'I had to walk and it took longer than I thought. Himmler's visit.'

'It does not matter. A coffee?'

She let him fetch her a cup of the filthy coffee. She lit a cigarette but this time did not offer him one. She took a deep breath and looked him in the eye. 'Señor Luis, before we discuss this further there is something I must ask.'

'Of course.'

'Last time you told me you left the army in the spring.'

'That is correct, yes.' He looked puzzled.

'But you also told me you spent *two* winters out there. How could that be? Cuenca was in Red hands until the surrender last year.'

Luis swallowed hard. Then a sad smile settled over his face. '*Señora*, I said I had spent two winters up on the *meseta*, not at Cuenca. The previous winter I was in another part of it. A posting at Teruel. You remember that name?'

'Yes, of course.' It had been one of the war's most savage battles. Barbara tried to remember exactly what words he had used.

'Teruel is over a hundred kilometres from Cuenca, but it is still the *meseta*. High and cold. During the battle there men with frostbite had to be taken out of the trenches to have their feet amputated.' He sounded almost angry now.

She took a deep breath. 'I see.'

'You were afraid I was not telling you the truth,' he said bluntly.

'I have to be sure, Señor Luis. I'm risking a lot. I have to be sure of everything.'

He nodded slowly. 'All right. I understand. Yes. It is good you are careful.' He spread his arms. 'You must ask me anything at any time.'

'Thank you.' She lit another cigarette.

'I went to Cuenca last weekend,' he said. 'As I promised.'

Barbara nodded. She looked into his eyes again. They were unreadable.

'I stayed in the town and Agustín came to see me. He confirmed there is a prisoner in the camp called Bernard Piper. He has been there since it opened.'

Barbara lowered her head so Luis would not see how affected she was by the mention of Bernie's name. She must keep calm, in control. She knew from her refugee work how desperate people would seize on any hope.

She looked up, gave him a firm stare. 'You understand, *señor*, I will need proof. I need you to get your brother to tell you more about him. Things I haven't told you or Markby, things you couldn't know. Not that he's fair-haired, for example, you could see that from the photograph.'

Luis sat back. He pursed his lips.

'It's not unreasonable,' Barbara said. 'Thousands of International Brigaders died in the war, you know how slim the chances are of his having survived. I need proof before anything else happens.'

'And I am poor and could be making up a story.' He nodded again. 'No, *señora*, it is not unreasonable. What a world we live in.' He thought a moment. 'If I were to ask Agustín to tell me everything about this man, then, and give the details to you?'

'Yes.'

'Have you spoken with Señor Markby again?'

'No.' She had tried, but he was still away.

Luis leaned forward. 'I will go to Cuenca again, though I cannot go too often to visit my brother or people may get suspicious.' He looked strained now. He rubbed his brow with his hand. 'I suppose I could say our mother has got worse. She is not well.' He looked up. 'But time may be important, Señora Clare. If you wish us to do something. You know the rumours. If Spain were to come into the war, you would have to leave. And your Brigader, if he was a Communist he could find himself handed over to the Germans. That is what has happened in France.'

It was true, but she wondered if he was trying to frighten her, hurry her.

'If you were to do something,' she repeated. 'You mean – ' she lowered her voice – 'escape?' Her heart began thudding, hard.

Luis nodded. 'Agustín thinks it can be done. But it will be dangerous.'

'How?' she asked. 'How could it be done?'

He leaned forward and lowered his voice. 'Let me explain how the camp works. It is surrounded by barbed wire. There are watchtowers with machine guns.' She shuddered involuntarily. 'I am sorry, *señora*, but I must explain how it is.'

'I know. Go on.'

'It is impossible for someone inside the camp to get out. But labour details go out every day – to repair roads, lay pipes, and to work in a quarry up in the hills. Piper has been on the quarry detail for some time. If Agustín can get himself a place as a guard on that work detail, perhaps he could help your friend to escape. Perhaps he could make some excuse to escort Piper away somewhere; then Piper could pretend to assault Agustín and get away.' He frowned. 'That is as far as we have been able to plan as yet.'

Barbara nodded. It sounded possible, at least.

'That is the only way we can think of. But when the escape is discovered, Agustín will be questioned. If the truth is found out, he will be shot. He will do it only for money.' Luis looked at her seriously. 'Let us be frank now.'

She nodded, trying to take deep breaths to still her heart without letting Luis see.

'Agustín's term of service ends in the spring and he does not want to have to renew it. There are some there who like that work but Agustín does not. He does it only to support our mother in Sevilla.'

'How much, then?'

'Two thousand pesetas.'

'That's a lot,' she said, though it was less than she had feared.

'Agustín has to risk his life.'

'If I were to agree, I'd have to get the money from England. It wouldn't be easy, with the exchange restrictions.' She took a deep breath. 'But if you can convince me Bernie is at that camp, then we'll see.'

'The money should be agreed, *señora*.'

'No. I need the proof first.' She drew on her cigarette, staring at him through the cloud of smoke. 'One more visit to Cuenca won't be risky. I'll give you the money for the fare.' And then, she thought, will I see you again?

He hesitated a moment, then nodded. Barbara thanked God for her years of negotiating with corrupt officials. Luis leaned back, looking tired. Barbara thought, he's less used to this sort of thing than I am.

'Did Agustín say anything about him – about Bernie, how he is?' Her voice stumbled over his name.

'He is well. But the winters are hard for the prisoners.' He looked at her seriously. 'If we do this, I think you will have to come out to Cuenca, get him away to Madrid, to the British Embassy. You have a car?'

'Yes. Yes, I can do that.'

He studied her speculatively. 'Your husband, he knows nothing?'

'No.' She raised her head. 'I just want to rescue Bernie, get him to the British Embassy so they can send him home.'

'Very well.' He sighed wearily. Barbara lit another cigarette and gave him one.

'Shall we meet here again then?' she asked. 'Next week?'

'The same time.' He looked awkward. 'I shall have to have the fare now.'

Again they went outside to pass over the money. When she handed the envelope to him he gave a bitter little laugh.

'Spaniards were a proud people once. The things we do now.' He turned and walked quickly away, his thin shabby form disappearing up the road.

There were more road closures on the way home and she had to walk down Calle Fernando el Santo, past the British Embassy. She glanced at the building. Harry Brett was probably in there; she would see him tonight. Harry, Bernie's friend.

At the bottom of the street *civiles* were turning pedestrians back from the Castellana.

'I am sorry, *señora*,' one said. 'No one may cross for the next hour. Security.'

She nodded and stepped back. A little crowd had gathered. Somewhere up the road youthful voices cheered and then a black Mercedes, flanked by soldiers on motorcycles, drove slowly past. There was a swastika pennant on the bonnet. In the back Barbara saw a pale, puffy face, its owner's black uniform and cap making it appear disembodied. There was a quick glint of sunlight on spectacles, and it seemed to Barbara that Heinrich Himmler turned and looked at her for a second. Then the car was gone in a swirl of autumn leaves. More cheers sounded from the Falange Youth ahead. Barbara shivered and turned away.

Chapter Fourteen

HARRY WALKED ALONG the Castellana, the Nazi flags on the buildings looming up through the mist that had descended on the city. He wore his hat and coat; it was late October now and the evenings were getting chilly. He was on his way to take the tram out to Vigo district, for dinner with Sandy and Barbara.

He and Tolhurst had talked some more about Barbara that afternoon.

'Bit of a turn-up, that,' Tolhurst had said. 'Never knew where he lived, you see. Our source said he was with a girly, but we thought it was some Spanish tart.'

'I wish I understood how she ended up with Sandy.' Harry shook his head. 'Though she was in a bad way when I met her in '37. I wrote afterwards but she never replied, or didn't get the letters.'

'She wasn't political, was she? The Red boyfriend's ideas didn't rub off?'

'No. She was Red Cross, a practical, commonsense type. I don't know what she'll make of the regime now.'

He would find out tonight. Walking along Harry felt a sudden weariness at the thought of the task before him. But he was committed, he had to go on.

He became conscious of footsteps behind him, a faint sound through the mist. Hell, his follower again. He hadn't seen the man over the weekend but it sounded as though he was back. He quickly took a left turn, then a right. The doorway to a block of flats stood open, the concierge away somewhere. They were middle-class flats, well maintained, the air smelling of cleaning fluid. Harry stepped inside, stood behind the door, and peered out. He heard footsteps, a pit-pat and the crunching of dead leaves. A moment later the young man who had followed him before appeared. He stood in the centre of the empty road, looking up and down, a frown on his pale delicate features. Harry quickly withdrew his head. He heard the footsteps recede, back the way they had come. He waited a few minutes, then stepped outside. The street was clear, save for a woman in a fur coat walking a dog; she gave him a suspicious look. He went back the way he had come. He shook his head. The man really wasn't much good.

The spy hadn't frightened him but he did feel a clutch of fear, that momentary light-headedness that came on him sometimes, as he walked up Sandy's drive half an hour later. He hadn't told Sandy about his panics after Dunkirk, despite the spies saying it could do no harm. Pride had stopped him, he supposed. The house was a big villa standing in a large garden. Harry stood on the step for a moment, collecting himself, then took a deep breath and rang the bell.

A young maid answered the door, pretty but rather glum-looking. She took him through a hall where Chinese porcelain stood on little tables into a large salon where a fire burned. Everything was comfortable, expensive.

Sandy came forward, taking his hand in a firm grasp. His dinner jacket was immaculate, his hair sleek with oil. 'Harry, marvellous you could come. 'Now then, Barbara you know, of course.'

She was standing smoking by the mantelpiece, a glass of wine in her hand. She looked utterly different, the old cardigans and untidy hair replaced by an expensive silk dress that set off her fine skin and figure, her face thinner, and carefully made up to emphasize her high cheekbones and bright green eyes, her long, styled hair curled at the ends. Only the glasses were the same. Despite the changes she looked tired and strained but her smile was warm as she took his hand.

'Harry, how are you?'

'I'm all right. You've changed a lot.'

'I've never forgotten how kind you were three years ago. I was in such a state back then.'

'Just did what I could. It was a rough time.'

'Sandy says you tried to write to me. I'm so sorry, I never got the letters. The Red Cross moved me to Burgos. I needed to get away from Madrid, after—' She made a gesture with one hand.

'Yes. I wrote to you in Madrid. I guess letters weren't forwarded across the lines.'

'My fault,' Barbara said. 'I should have tried to keep in touch.'

'I often wondered how you were. I hear you don't work for the Red Cross any more?'

'No, I gave that up after I met Sandy. Had to really, I wasn't in a fit state to work. But I might be doing some voluntary work soon with war orphans.'

Harry shook his head, smiling. 'And you met up with Sandy. How extraordinary.'

'Yes. He helped put me back together.'

Sandy came over to her, putting an arm round her shoulders, squeezing protectively. It seemed to Harry that Barbara flinched a little.

'And you, Harry,' she asked. 'Are you all right? Sandy said you were at Dunkirk.'

'Yes. I'm fine now. Just a spot of deafness.'

'How are things at home? I get letters from my family but they don't give me much idea how people are bearing up. The Spanish papers say it's pretty bad.'

'People are coping well. The Battle of Britain was a boost.'

'That's good. One's so far away, I didn't worry too much during the phoney war, but since the bombing – I expect you hear all about how things are at the embassy. All the papers are censored here.'

Sandy laughed. 'Yes, they even censor the fashion shows in the *Daily Mail*. If they think the dresses are too low-cut they put a black band across them.'

'Well, things are tough, but not as bad as the papers here make them out. There's an amazing spirit, Churchill's rallied everyone.'

'Have some wine,' Sandy said. 'We're having some food later, once the others arrive. Look, why don't you two meet up one afternoon, have a longer chat about home? It'd do Barbara good.'

'Yes, yes we could.' She nodded agreement, but Harry sensed reluctance in her voice.

'That would be good.' Harry turned to Sandy. 'And what exactly are you up to now? You didn't really say the other day.'

He smiled broadly. 'Oh, I've fingers in a number of pies.'

Harry smiled at Barbara. 'Sandy's come up in the world.'

'Yes, he has.' She seemed bored by this mention of business. Harry felt glad. If she didn't know anything she wouldn't have anything to tell.

'I'm involved mainly with a government-backed project just now,' Sandy said. 'Mineral extraction. All very dull, just exploratory stuff. Takes some organizing, though.'

'Mining, eh?' Harry asked. This had to be the gold. His luck was continuing. His heart pounded. Steady, he thought, take it carefully. 'I remember at school you wanted to be a palaeontologist. The secrets of the earth, you used to say.'

Sandy laughed. 'Oh, it's not dinosaurs now.' The doorbell rang. 'Excuse me. Must go and welcome Sebastian and Jenny.'

He went out. Barbara was silent a moment, then smiled uncertainly.

'It's good to see you again.'

'And you. You've a fine house here.'

'Yes. I've landed on my feet, I suppose.' She paused, then asked quickly, 'Do you think Franco will come into the war?'

'Nobody knows. There are all sorts of rumours. If it happens it'll be sudden.'

They fell silent as Sandy reappeared, accompanied by a well-dressed couple. The man was in his thirties, small and slim, handsome in a dark, southern Spanish way. He wore the Falange uniform, dark military dress with a blue shirt. The woman was younger, attractive, too, with blonde hair and smooth round features. Her expression was haughty.

'Harry,' Sandy said in Spanish. 'Let me introduce Sebastian de Salas, a colleague of mine. Sebastian, this is Harry Brett.'

The Spaniard pressed Harry's hand. 'I am delighted, *señor*. There are so few Englishmen in Madrid.' He turned to his companion. 'Jenny sees so few of her compatriots.'

'Hello there!' The woman's voice was cut-glass, her eyes hard and appraising. She turned to give Barbara a cold, formal smile. 'Hello there, Babs, what a nice dress.'

'Would you like some wine?' Barbara's tone was equally cool.

'I'd rather have a G and T. Been out at the golf club all afternoon.'

'Come on everyone,' Sandy said cheerfully. 'Take the weight off your feet.'

They sat down in the comfortable armchairs. 'What do you do then, Harry?' Jenny asked brusquely.

'I'm a translator at the embassy.'

'Met anyone interesting?'

'Just a junior minister.'

'Jenny's an Hon, Harry,' Sandy said. 'Sebastian's an aristocrat too.'

The Spaniard laughed self-deprecatingly. 'A small one. We have a little castle in Extremadura, but it is falling down.'

'Don't knock it, Sebastian,' Jenny said. 'I'm a cousin of Lord Redesdale. Know him?'

'No.' Harry wanted to laugh, she was ridiculous. Jenny took the glass Barbara handed to her.

'I say, thanks. Mmm, lovely.' She leaned back against de Salas.

'How long have you been in Madrid, Señor Brett?' de Salas asked.

'A little over a week.'

'And how do you find Spain?'

'The Civil War seems to have caused a lot of – dislocation.'

'Yes.' De Salas nodded sadly. 'The war did much damage and now we have the bad harvests. People are suffering. But we are working to improve things. It is a hard road, but we have made a start.'

'Sebastian's in the Falange, as you can see.' Sandy's tone was neutral but his look at Harry was keen, mischievous. De Salas smiled and Harry smiled neutrally back. Sandy put his hand on Barbara's arm.

'Babs, see how Pilar's getting on, would you?'

She nodded and went out. The obedient housewife, Harry thought. The idea pained him for some reason.

'Señor Brett,' de Salas said when she had left. 'May I ask something? Only, I fear many Englishman do not understand the Falange.'

'It's often hard to understand foreign countries' politics,' Harry replied carefully. He remembered the screaming horde around the car, the boy who had wet himself.

'In England you have democracy, yes? That is what you are fighting for, your system.'

'Yes.' God, Harry thought, he's gone straight to the point.

De Salas smiled. 'Please understand I mean no offence.'

'No, of course.'

'Democracy has worked well in England and America, but it does not work everywhere. In Spain under the Republic, democracy brought chaos and bloodshed.' He smiled sadly. 'Not all countries are suited to its freedoms, they tear themselves apart. Sometimes in the end the authoritarian way is the only one.'

Harry nodded, remembering he should avoid politics if he could. 'I can see that. Only I suppose one might ask, who holds the rulers to account?'

De Salas laughed and spread his hands. 'Oh, *señor*, the whole *nation* holds them to account. The whole nation represented by one party. That is the beauty of our system. Listen, do you know why the Falange wear blue shirts?'

'Don't say it's because all the other colours were taken,' Sandy interjected with a laugh.

'Because blue is the colour of workmen's overalls. We represent everyone in Spain. The Falange is a middle way between socialism and capitalism. It has worked in Italy. We know how hard life is in Spain now, but we will do justice to everyone. Just give us time.' He smiled earnestly.

'I hope so,' Harry said. He studied de Salas. His expression was open, sincere. He means it, Harry thought.

Barbara returned. 'We can go through,' she said.

Sandy got up and stood between Harry and de Salas, a hand on each of their shoulders. 'We should renew this talk another time. But let's change the subject now, eh, out of deference to the ladies.' He gave them a fatherly smile and Harry wondered again, how did he come to seem so middle-aged, so much older than he was? He had felt sorry for Sandy before but now he struck him as faintly repulsive.

A cold buffet had been laid in the dining room. They filled their plates and took them to the oak table. Sandy opened a fresh bottle of wine. Jenny had brought the gin bottle with her.

'Sandy,' de Salas said, 'you should have invited a *señorita* for *Señor* Brett.'

'Yes, Sandy, we're one short,' Jenny agreed. 'Bad form.'

'There wasn't time.'

'It's all right,' Harry said. 'I should meet plenty of *señoritas* on Thursday. I'm going to my first Spanish party.'

'And where is that?' de Salas asked.

'General Maestre's house. It's his daughter's eighteenth.'

De Salas looked at Harry with new interest. 'Maestre, eh?'

'Yes. I translated at a meeting between him and one of our diplomats.'

Sandy's voice was suddenly sharp. '*No*, Sebastian, no business tonight.'

De Salas nodded and turned to Barbara. 'How are your plans going, *señora*, to work with the orphans? The *marquesa* was helpful?'

'Yes, thanks. She's hoping to fix something up.'

'I am glad. Will you enjoy going back to nursing?'

'I'd like to do something to help. I feel I ought to, really.'

'Jenny is a nurse too, like Barbara,' de Salas told Harry. 'I met her when she came out to help during the war.'

'What?' Jenny lifted her head, her face flushed. Harry realized she was drunk. 'I didn't catch that. Why am I like Barbara?'

'I was saying you were a nurse.'

'Oh yes! Yes!' She laughed. 'I'm not a proper nurse, though. I never trained. But when I came out, they put me straight into helping at operations. After the Jarama battle. Just as well I'm not squeamish.'

Barbara bowed her head to her plate. Sandy gave her a solicitous glance.

'Harry,' he said, 'do have some of this marvellous red. I had to pay the earth for it. Scandalous.'

De Salas smiled at Harry. 'I expect the embassy has its own supplies.'

'We get rations. They're not too bad.'

De Salas nodded. 'Is it true there is much hardship in England? Food is rationed?'

'Yes. But everyone gets enough.'

'Do they? It is not what we read here.' He leaned forward, genuinely interested. 'But tell me, please, I am interested, why do you go on with the war? You were beaten in France, why not surrender now?'

He wouldn't let it go. Harry glanced at Barbara. 'It's what all the Spaniards think,' she told him.

'Hitler has offered you peace. And I have seen so many killed in Spain, I wish the killing could stop in Europe.'

Sandy leaned forward. 'He's got a point, you know. England should surrender now, while good terms are on the table. I'm not being unpatriotic, Harry, I only want what's in my country's best interests. I've been away nearly four years, and sometimes you see things more clearly from a distance. And England can't win.'

'People are determined.'

'To defend democracy, eh?' de Salas smiled sadly.

'Yes.'

'Perhaps Hitler would let us keep democracy?' Sandy suggested. 'In return for leaving the war.'

'He hasn't a very good record in that department.' Harry felt sudden anger. He had actually fought the Germans, while Sandy was sitting here making money. Sandy may have taken people round former battlefields, but Harry had been on a real one.

'There isn't much democracy left in England, from what I hear,' Jenny interjected loudly. 'Oswald Mosley was locked up just for leading the wrong party.'

Barbara shot her a look of venom. De Salas coughed.

'I think perhaps we are getting a little heated,' he said awkwardly.

The party didn't last long. Soon de Salas said they must go and led a stumbling Jenny away.

'Don't invite her again, Sandy, please,' Barbara said when they had left.

Sandy raised his eyebrows at Harry as he lit a cigar. 'Jenny spent the whole of the Civil War nursing out here. She was pretty wild before, ran away from Roedean apparently. Can't seem to cope with peace, just gets drunk all the time. Sebastian's thinking of giving her the heave-ho.'

'She's foul,' Barbara said. She turned to Harry. 'I'm sorry, I wasn't very sociable tonight.'

'Don Sebastian seems civilized enough,' Harry said. 'In his way.'

'Yes.' Sandy nodded. 'Spanish fascism's not like Nazism, Harry, you have to remember that. They're much more like the Italians. I'm doing some charitable work with refugee Jews, for example. Have to keep it a bit quiet because they're terrified of annoying the Germans, but the authorities wink at it.' He smiled. 'Don't mind what I was saying earlier about Britain surrendering. It was just – conversation. It's the big topic here, as you might imagine. They'd be happy if the war ended, they've had enough bloodshed, as Sebastian was saying.'

Barbara lit a cigarette. 'I agree they haven't got the Nazi ideas about racial purity here. But they're still a brutal lot.'

Sandy raised his eyebrows. 'I thought you agreed Franco had brought some order at last.'

Barbara shrugged. 'Maybe. I'll get Pilar to clean up, Sandy, then I'm going up. I'll leave you to your drinks. Sorry, Harry, I'm not feeling too bright. Got a bad headache.' She gave him a wan smile. 'I'll ring you and we can meet up.'

'Yes, do. A call to the embassy will usually get me. Later this week, perhaps.'

'Perhaps.' He sensed the reluctance in her voice again. Why, he wondered.

When they were alone, Sandy poured them a whisky and lit a cigar. He seemed to have a tremendous capacity. Harry had been drinking slowly to keep his head clear.

'Is Barbara all right?' he asked.

Sandy waved a hand dismissively. 'Oh yes. Just tired and worried about home. The bombing and everything. Listen, when she rings you, take her out for a nice lunch somewhere. She's on her own here too much.'

'OK.'

'It's a funny old place, Spain, but there are lots of business opportunities.' He laughed. 'Might be as well not to mention you know me, when you go to the ball for Maestre's girly. The government's a nest of rivalries, and the faction I'm working with and Maestre's don't get on.'

'Oh?' Harry paused, then asked innocently. 'Maestre's a Monarchist, isn't he?'

Sandy's eyes through the cigar smoke were hooded, calculating. 'Yes, that's right. Hidebound lot.' He looked at Harry seriously. 'By the way, you remember what I was saying in the cafe, about maybe getting out of Spain?'

'Yes.'

'Don't tell Barbara, would you? If I do decide to go it won't be for a while. I'll tell her when the time's right.'

'Of course. Understood.'

'Still got business to finish here. Money to make.' He smiled. 'I expect all your funds are invested in safe things?'

Harry hesitated. That calculating look was back in Sandy's face. 'Yes. My parents left some money, and my uncle put it in safe securities. I've left everything where he put it. Too safe, I sometimes think.' He laughed uncertainly. In fact, he didn't think money could ever be kept too safe, but he wanted to see where Sandy was leading.

'Money can always make more money, if you know where to put it.'

'Yes, I suppose so.'

To Harry's disappointment, Sandy stood up. 'Anyway, I want to show you something. Come upstairs.'

He led Harry upstairs to a small comfortable study, full of objets d'art. 'My sanctum. I come up here to work in peace.' Harry's eyes flickered over the desk; there were cardboard folders and papers but he couldn't see what they were.

'Look at this.' Sandy switched on the little light above the figure of the man sprawled over the distorted horse, limping across the desert.

'I think it's a Dalí,' he said. 'Isn't it amazing?'

'Disturbing,' Harry said. Most of the objects displayed in the room had an unsettling quality: a woman's hand in a lace sleeve exquisitely sculpted in silver; a Japanese vase showing a bloody battle scene, the colours extraordinary.

'You can pick up the most astonishing things in the Rastro,' Sandy said. 'Stuff the Reds looted from rich people's houses during the war. Here, this is what I want to show you.' He opened a drawer in the desk and lifted out a tray. It was full of fossils, stones with the bones of strange creatures embedded inside.

'My collection. The best bits, anyway.' He pointed to a dark stone. 'Remember that?'

'God, yes. The ammonite.'

'I used to enjoy our fossil hunts – like I said the other day, they're the only good thing I remember about Rookwood.' He smiled awkwardly. Harry felt oddly touched, suddenly guilty for what he was doing.

'Now,' Sandy said. 'Have a look at this.' He knelt and lifted the lid from a long, flat wooden box that lay by his desk. Inside was a large, flat white stone.

'Found that down towards Extremadura a few months ago.'

Embedded in the stone were the bones of a long foot, the three toes ending in curved claws. One claw was much bigger than the other two, the length of a man's hand.

'Beautiful, isn't he? Early Cretaceous, over a hundred million years old.' His face was alight with genuine wonder; for a moment he looked like a schoolboy again.

'What species is it?'

'That's the interesting bit. I think it may be something new. I'm going to take it to the Natural History Museum when I go home. If it's still there.'

Sandy looked down at the fossil. 'By the way, another thing when you see Barbara. I've told her I wasn't friendly with Piper, but I didn't tell her we didn't get on at all. Thought it better not to.'

'I understand.'

'Thanks.' Sandy gave an awkward smile. 'I hated that school so much.'

'I know. You've done OK now, though.' Harry laughed. 'Do you remember when you left, you told me you thought you were fated always to be the bad lad, the loser?'

Sandy laughed. 'Yes. I was letting the bastards get me down. I got a better education on the racetracks. I learned there you can make your own future, be what you want to be.'

'I sometimes wonder myself.'

'What?'

'Oh – whether Rookwood did give you a distorted picture of the world. A complacent one.'

Sandy nodded. 'Like I said in the cafe, the future belongs to people who can reach out and seize life. We should never let the past hold us back. And there's no such thing as fate.'

He looked at Harry intently. Harry looked down at the dinosaur's limb. He noticed the claws were curled, as though the creature had been about to strike when it died.

Chapter Fifteen

Harry was debriefed by Hillgarth the next morning. He was delighted with his progress. He told him to see Sandy again as soon as possible, try to lead him on to talk about the gold, and push Barbara for information too when he met her.

It was almost lunchtime when he returned to his office. He had been translating a new speech from the governor of Barcelona but found that it had been taken from his desk. He went to see Weaver.

'Had to give it to Carne,' Weaver said languidly. 'Didn't know how long you'd be with the sneaky beakies, and it needed to be done.' He sighed. 'You might as well take the rest of the day off now.'

Harry left the building and walked home. The two other translators, he knew, were annoyed that he kept leaving his work, a frostiness was growing up between them. Blow them, Harry thought. They were affected foreign-office types and he couldn't be bothered with them. He was becoming more and more conscious, though, of loneliness; apart from Tolhurst, he had no friends at the embassy.

At home he ate a cold lunch and then, not wanting to stay in the flat on his own all afternoon, changed into casual clothes and went out for a walk. The weather was still cold and dank, a faint mist obscuring the end of the street. He stood in the square, wondering where to go, then turned down the street that led into La Latina, with Carabanchel beyond, what Tolhurst had called a bad area that first afternoon. He remembered Bernie's friends, the Meras. He wondered if they might still be down there somewhere.

As he walked through La Latina he thought about Barbara. He didn't relish the task before him, asking prying questions about Sandy's work without seeming too obvious. She had changed out of all recognition. But she wasn't happy, he could see. He had told Hillgarth that, then felt guilty.

He walked down to the Puerta de Toledo. Beyond lay Carabanchel. He hesitated for a few moments, then crossed the bridge and walked into the warren of tall tenements.

On this damp cold afternoon, the *barrio* was almost deserted, only a few people walking by. He thought, how Bernie and I must have stood out here in '31, pale and English in our white shirts. Some of the houses looked about to fall down and were supported by wooden beams; the streets were full of potholes and broken slabs and there was the occasional bombsite, half-demolished walls standing among piles of rubble like broken teeth. Harry flinched as a large rat ran from a bombed house and streaked along the gutter ahead of him.

Then he heard steady footsteps behind. He swore quietly. His spy again, he must have been waiting near the flat. In his preoccupation he had forgotten to watch out for him; bad tradecraft. He backed into the doorway of the nearest tenement. The door was closed and he reached for the handle, slipping into a dark hallway. Water dripped somewhere and there was a strong smell of urine. He pushed the door to, leaving just a crack to peer round.

He saw the pale young man plod past, hunched into his coat. Harry waited a few minutes, then emerged and turned down a side street. The area seemed familiar. A little group of middle-aged men eyed him coldly as he passed the corner where they stood talking. He remembered with a stab of sadness how welcoming the people had been nine years before.

He turned into a square. Two sides had been shelled into rubble, all the houses down, a chaos of broken walls rising from a sea of shattered bricks and sodden rags of bedding. Weeds had grown up between the stones, tall scabrous dark-green things. Square holes in the ground half filled with green scummy water marked where cellars had stood. The square was deserted and the houses that had been left standing looked derelict, their windows all broken.

Harry had never seen destruction on such a scale; the bombsites in London were small by comparison. He stepped closer, looking over the devastation. The square must have been intensively shelled. Every day there was news of more raids on England – did London look like this now?

Then he saw a sign on a corner, Plaza General Blanco, and felt a dreadful lurch in his stomach. This was the square where the Mera family had lived. He looked round again, trying to fix his bearings, and realized that the tenement block where the family had lived was gone, rubble. He stood there, his mouth falling open.

There was a flash of movement and Harry started as a dog jumped on to the remains of a wall and stood looking at him. It was a little tan mongrel with a curly tail; once it had been someone's pet but now it was half starved, ribs showing through a coat half eaten away by mange.

It barked twice, sharply, and a dozen shapes slipped from behind walls and through the weeds, thin mangy dogs of all shapes and sizes. Some were no bigger than the mongrel, but there were three or four large ones including an Alsatian. They gathered together, watching him. Harry stepped back, remembering what Tolhurst had said on his first day about feral dogs, rabies. He looked round frantically but apart from the dogs there was no sign of life in the misty shattered square. His heart began thumping and a hissing noise sounded in his bad ear.

The dogs padded over the rubble towards him, fanning out slowly and carefully, unnervingly quiet. The Alsatian, evidently the leader, stepped ahead and bared its teeth. How easily that lift of the lip could transform a dog into a wild animal.

You mustn't show fear. That was what they said about dogs. '*¡Vete!*' he shouted. 'Go away!' To his relief they paused, stopping ten yards from him. The Alsatian bared its teeth again.

Harry stepped back, keeping his eyes on them. He almost stumbled on a half brick and flailed his arms to keep his balance. Staring into the Alsatian's eyes, he bent and picked the half brick up. The dogs tensed.

He hurled it at the Alsatian with a shout. It caught the animal on a scabby haunch and it yelped, twisting away. '*¡Vete!*' Harry yelled again. For a second the dogs hesitated, then they turned and ran after their leader.

The pack stopped just out of range and stood watching him. Harry's legs were shaking. He picked up another piece of brick, then slowly retreated. The dogs stayed where they were. He stopped at the far side of the square, his back pressed against a wall. A tattered

Republican poster still hung from it, steel-helmeted soldiers leaping into gunfire.

He retraced his steps slowly, keeping against the walls, watching for movement from the bombsite. The dogs had disappeared among the rubbish but he felt their eyes on him and did not turn his back till he was in the street that led to the square. He leaned against a wall, taking deep breaths.

Then he heard the scream, a yell of pure terror. Another followed, even louder. Harry hesitated a moment, then ran back.

The spy was standing at the edge of the bombsite. The dogs had him surrounded, jumping up at him. A big mongrel had him by the shin, worrying it, trying to bring him down as he screamed again. His trouser leg and the dog's muzzle were red with blood. As Harry watched one of the smaller dogs leapt up and seized the man's arm, making him stumble. He went down on the ground with another yell. The Alsatian leaped for his neck. The man managed to throw his arm across his throat but the Alsatian seized the arm. The dogs gave low growls of excitement as he almost disappeared under them.

Harry picked up another piece of brick and threw it. It landed among the dogs and they jumped back, baring their teeth and snarling. He ran across the square in a half crouch, picking up stones and pieces of rubble and hurling them with both hands, yelling at the dogs. Again he aimed mostly for the leader, the Alsatian. The dogs hesitated and Harry thought they were about to go for him too but the Alsatian jumped back and ran off. It was limping; the brick he had thrown earlier must have done some damage. The others followed, disappearing once more among the weeds.

The man lay spreadeagled on the broken cobbles, holding his arm over his throat. He stared at Harry open-mouthed, breathing in loud gasps. His trouser leg was torn and covered with blood.

'Can you get up?' Harry asked. The man stared up at him, his eyes wide with shock. 'We've got to get away,' Harry said gently. 'They could come back, they've tasted blood now. Come on, I'll help you.'

He took the man under the arms and helped him to his feet. He was light, no more than skin and bone. He stood on one leg, put the other to the ground then lifted it again, wincing. The Alsatian reappeared, watching them from the top of a pile of rubble. Harry shouted and it retreated again. He helped the man from the square, glancing back every few seconds. Once they were a couple of streets away he lowered him to the front step of a tenement. A woman looked out of a window at them, then closed her shutters.

'Thank you,' the spy said breathlessly. 'Thank you, *señor*.' His leg was still bleeding, there was blood on Harry's trousers. He thought of rabies – if the dogs had it, the spy would die.

'I thought I'd shaken you off,' Harry said.

The spy looked terrified. 'You know?' His eyes widened. He was even younger than Harry had thought, little more than a boy. His pale face was quite white now, from shock and fear.

'I've known for a while. I thought I'd got rid of you.'

The man looked at him sadly. 'I am always losing you. I lost you when you went out this morning. Then later I saw you near your flat, but I lost you again before the square.' He gave Harry a weak grin. 'You are better at this than me.'

'What's your name?'

'Enrique. Enrique Roque Casas. You speak good Spanish, *señor*.'

'I'm a translator. But you know that, I expect.'

He looked shamefaced. 'You have saved my life. Believe me, *señor*, I did not want this job, but we need the money. Now I am ashamed.' He laid his hand on his leg and drew it away covered in blood. His teeth began to chatter.

'Come on, I'll help you home. Where do you live?' The reply was a mumble Harry couldn't catch, there was a faint hissing in his bad ear. He bent his good ear towards him and asked again.

'Only a few streets away, near the river. *Madre de Dios* – I had heard about those dogs, but I forgot. I did not want to have to report I had lost you again. They are not happy with me as it is.' Enrique was shivering now, shock setting in.

'Come on,' Harry said. 'Take my coat.' He took it off and wrapped it round the thin shoulders. Supporting him, Harry followed Enrique's directions through the narrow streets, ignoring the stares of passers-by. He thought, this is ridiculous, but he couldn't just leave the wretched man; he was in shock and that leg needed seeing to.

'So who do you work for?' he asked brusquely.

'The Foreign Ministry, *señor*. Our block leader got me the job. They said they wanted me to follow a British diplomat, tell them everywhere you went.'

'I see.'

'All the diplomats are followed, except the Germans. Even the Italians. They said you were a translator, *señor*, you would probably only go to the embassy and the good restaurants in town, but I was to record it all.'

'And they might get something useful. If I went to a brothel, say, I could be blackmailed.'

Enrique nodded. 'You know how the business works, *señor*.'

Only too well, Harry thought.

They stopped before a broken-down tenement. 'This house, *señor*,' Enrique said.

Harry pushed the door open and entered a dank gloomy hall. 'We are on the first floor,' Enrique said. 'If you could help me.'

Harry helped him up a flight of stairs. Enrique produced a key and opened a door with a shaking hand. It led into a small, gloomy hall. There was a close, fusty smell. Enrique opened another door and limped into a small *salón*. Harry followed, taking off his hat. A *brasero* burned under a table but the room was still chilly. A couple of scuffed wooden chairs were drawn up to a table where a small thin boy of about eight sat, scrawling dark shapes over and over again with a crayon on a copy of *Arriba*. At the sight of Harry he jumped up and ran to a sagging single bed in one corner. Curtains had been rigged round it but they were open. An old woman lay there, propped up against pillows, thin grey hair spilling round a wrinkled face that had one side twisted into a leering grimace, the eye half shut. The boy jumped on to the bed, wriggling against the old woman's side. Harry was shocked by the fear and anger in his look.

The old woman heaved herself up on one arm. 'Enrique, what has happened, who is this?' She spoke slowly, her voice slurred, and Harry realized that she had had a stroke.

Enrique seemed to regain control of himself. He went over and kissed her cheek, patting the boy's head. 'It is all right, Mama. An accident, some dogs, this man helped me home. Please, *señor*.' He pulled out one of the rickety wooden chairs and Harry sat down. It creaked under his weight. Enrique limped back to the old woman. He sat on the bed and took her hand. 'Don't worry, Mama, it's all right. Where's Sofia?'

'Gone to the shops.' The old woman leaned over to pat the boy. He had burrowed against her left arm, which was white and shrivelled. He sat up and pointed at Enrique's leg.

'*¡Sangre!*' he shouted shrilly. '*¡Sangre!*' Blood!

'It's all right, Paquito, it's only a cut, it's nothing,' Enrique said reassuringly. The old woman stroked the child's head. '*No es nada, niño*. It's all right, it's nothing.

She looked at Harry. 'Foreigner?' she said in a loud whisper to her son. 'Is he German?'

'I'm English, *señora*.' She looked at him anxiously, and Harry guessed she knew what her son did for a living. He looked at Enrique's tattered, blood-spotted trousers.

'You should get that leg washed.'

The old woman nodded. 'Water, Enrique, get water.'

'*Sí*, Mama.' Enrique nodded and limped to the door. Harry rose to help but Enrique waved him back.

'No. No, stay here, *señor*, please. You have done enough.' He picked up a bucket from the corner and went out, leaving Harry standing awkwardly. He supposed he could leave but he didn't want to be rude. He remembered the Alsatian tearing at the spy's arm, trying to reach his throat, and shivered.

The pair on the bed stared at him. It was hard to read any expression on the old woman's face, but the boy's was angry and afraid. Harry smiled awkwardly. He looked round the room. It was clean. If the old woman was here all the time it was probably impossible to avoid that fusty smell. There were dried flowers in vases and cheap pictures of country scenes on the walls, an effort had been made to make the room look cheerful, but Harry saw that the wall under the window was covered with black streaks of fungus where water dripped from a rotten windowsill on to a folded blanket. He looked away. There were photographs too, he saw, pinned to the wall. The old woman pointed at one of them. 'My wedding,' she croaked. 'With my brother.'

Harry nodded politely and got up to look, the child tensing as he crossed the room. The photograph showed a young couple standing in the doorway of a church, a smiling young priest next to them. From the clothes it seemed to have been taken around the same time as his parents' wedding. The woman smiled with the half of her face that could still move. '*Dias mas felices*,' she whispered. Happier days.

'*Sí, mas felices, señora.*'

'Please, *señor*, sit down.'

Harry took his chair again. The old woman stroked the boy's hair. He stared at Harry with frightened eyes.

The door opened and a girl in a heavy coat came in, carrying a shopping bag. She was in her early twenties, small and dark-haired, with a heart-shaped face and large brown eyes. When she saw Harry she stopped dead. He stood up.

'What has happened?' she asked sharply. 'Who are you?'

'It's all right,' the old woman said. 'Some dogs attacked Enrique. This man helped him home. Your brother has gone to get some water.'

She lowered her bag to the floor, still frowning anxiously.

'I'm sorry if I startled you,' Harry said.

'Where are you from?'

'I'm English. My name's Harry Brett. I work at the embassy.'

Her eyes widened. 'Then – you are the one who he—'

'Er, yes.' So the girl knew what her brother did for a living too.

'What has he done now?' She gave Harry a long hard look, then turned and left the room.

'My daughter,' the old woman said. She smiled. '*Mi Sofia. Corazón de mi vida.*' Heart of my life.

There were voices on the stairs, the girl's angry, Enrique's an apologetic mumble. He limped in, followed by the girl who was carrying the bucket of water. Enrique sat in a chair opposite Harry, and the girl took a pair of scissors from a drawer. She looked over at the boy.

'Paquito, go into the kitchen. Go on. Light the oven for heat.'

Obediently the boy got up from the bed and left the room, with a last scared glance at Harry.

'I think his leg's the worst,' Harry said. 'But they got his arm too. Can I help?'

She shook her head. 'I am all right.' She turned to her brother. 'You're going to have to find some new trousers from somewhere.' She began cutting his trouser leg, Enrique biting his lip to stifle cries of pain. The leg was a mess, full of puncture marks, lengthened into tears in the flesh where the dogs had torn at it. Sofia took off his jacket and cut his shirtsleeve, revealing more bites. She produced a bottle of iodine from the drawer. 'This will sting badly, Enrique, but otherwise these wounds will become infected.'

'Is there any sign of rabies?' Enrique asked tremulously.

'You cannot tell,' she replied quietly. 'Were any of the dogs behaving wildly, staggering or blinking?'

'One staggered, the Alsatian,' he replied anxiously. 'Is that not right, *señor*?'

Sofia looked at Harry, her face sharp with fear.

'I hit it with a stone when it went for me earlier. That was why. None of the dogs seemed ill.'

'Then that is hopeful,' Sofia said.

'Those dogs are a danger,' Harry said. 'They should be destroyed.'

'That will be the day, when the government does something for us.' Sofia went on bathing her brother's leg. Harry watched, surprised by her steady cool professionalism.

'Sofia was to be a doctor,' the old woman croaked from the bed.

Harry turned to her. 'Really?' he asked awkwardly.

Sofia did not look up. 'The war put a stop to my training.' She began cutting cloth into strips.

'Oughtn't your brother see a doctor?'

'We cannot afford one,' she replied brusquely. 'I will see the wounds are kept clean.'

Harry hesitated. 'I could pay. After all, I rescued him, I ought to see it through.'

She looked at him. 'There is something else you could do for us, *señor*, something that would cost no money.'

'Whatever I can.'

'Say nothing. My brother told me on the stairs you have known for some time he was following you. He only did it because we need the money.'

Harry looked at Enrique; sitting there in his cloth bandages he looked weary, a scared boy.

'The block leader, the Falange official for this tenement, he knew we were struggling and said he could get Enrique work. We were not happy when we learned what it was but we need the money.'

'I know,' Harry said. 'Your brother told me.'

Her eyes narrowed. 'So you asked him about what he did.'

'Wouldn't you?'

The girl pursed her lips. 'Perhaps.' She went on looking at him. Her face was serious, but it wasn't pleading; he sensed she wasn't someone who would plead.

'Thank God Ramón was not around downstairs,' Enrique said.

'Yes, that gives us a chance. We can say Enrique was attacked by dogs but not that you were there; they might even pay him till he is better.'

'And when I am better, *señor*, you will not have to worry about who is following if you know it is only me,' Enrique added. 'I will say you just walk the streets for fresh air, which is all I have seen you do anyway.'

Harry laughed and shook his head. Enrique laughed too, nervously. Sofia frowned.

'I'm sorry,' Harry said. 'I'm sorry, only the whole thing is so strange.'

'It's the world we live in all the time,' she replied sharply.

'I didn't bring this situation about, you know,' Harry replied. 'All right, I'll say nothing.'

'Thank you.' Sofia exhaled with relief. She produced a packet of cheap cigarettes and passed one to Enrique before offering one to Harry.

'No, thanks. I don't.'

Enrique took a deep draw. There was a harsh snore from the bed; the old woman had fallen asleep.

'Is she all right?' Harry asked.

The girl looked at her tenderly. 'She sleeps all the time. She had a stroke when Papa was killed fighting for the militia.'

Harry nodded. 'And Paquito is your little brother?'

'No. He lived in the flat opposite with his parents.' She looked at him with that unflinching stare. 'They were union activists. One day last year I came home and found the door of his flat open, blood smeared on the walls. They had taken his parents and left him behind. We took him in, so the nuns would not get him.'

'He has not been as he should in the head since then,' Enrique added.

'I'm sorry.'

'Sofia has work in a dairy,' Enrique continued. 'But it is not enough to keep four of us, *señor*, that is why I took that job.'

Harry took a deep breath. 'I won't say anything. I promise. It's all right.'

'Only please, *señor*,' Enrique said with another attempt at humour. 'Do not lead me into that square again.'

Harry smiled. 'I won't.' He felt an odd sense of kinship with Enrique; someone else forced by circumstances to be a reluctant spy.

'That was a strange place for a diplomat to go walking,' Sofia said, her eyes keen.

'There was a family I knew there once. Years ago, before the Civil War. They lived in the square where the dogs were. Their block had been bombed.' He sighed. 'I don't know what became of them.'

'No one is left there now,' Sofia said. She looked at him curiously. 'So you knew Spain before – this?'

'Yes.'

She nodded but said no more. Harry got up.

'I won't say anything about Enrique. And please, you must let me pay for a doctor.'

Sofia stubbed out her cigarette. 'No. Thank you, you have done enough.'

'Please. Send the bill to me.' He took out a piece of paper and wrote his address down, handing it to her. She got up and took it. He realized that of course Enrique knew where he lived anyway.

'We will see you,' she said noncommittally. 'Thank you, *Señor* – Brett, is that how you say it?' she asked, rolling her 'r's.

'Yes.'

'Brett.' She stood and nodded gravely. 'And I am Sofia.' She extended a small, shapely hand. It was warm and delicate. 'We are in your debt, *señor*. Goodbye.'

It was a dismissal. To his surprise, Harry realized he didn't want to leave. He wanted to stay, learn more about their lives. But he rose, picking up his hat.

'*Adios*.'

He left the flat and descended the dark staircase to the street. As he walked back to the Puerta de Toledo he found his legs were shaking a little and the buzzing was back in his ears. The ruined square came back to him, the dogs. Were the Mera family all dead, he wondered. Like Bernie?

Chapter Sixteen

IT WAS BECAUSE OF Bernie's parents that Harry had met Barbara. He had spent Easter 1937 with his aunt and uncle. He was in the first year of his fellowship then. Since going up to Cambridge four years before he had seen little of them; strangely, that seemed to make them miss him and on his rare visits they greeted him with affection, eager to hear his news.

One afternoon at the end of April the telephone rang in the hall of the big old house. Uncle James came into the lounge where Harry was reading the *Telegraph* He looked worried.

'That was your friend Bernie Piper's mother on the phone,' he said. 'The boy you went to Spain with.'

Harry hadn't heard from Bernie in five years. 'Has something happened?'

'It was hard to follow her, she was gabbling so, I don't think she's used to the telephone. Apparently he went out to fight in the war in Spain. For the Reds,' Uncle James added with distaste. 'They've had a letter saying he's missing in action. She wants to know if you can help. Sounds like a can of worms to me. I told her you weren't in, actually.'

Harry felt a chill settle on his stomach. He remembered Bernie's mother, a nervous, birdlike woman. Bernie had taken him to see her in London just before they went to Spain in 1931; he wanted Harry to convince her they would be safe. She had believed his reassurances, if not her son's; perhaps he represented the respectable solidity of Rookwood that Bernie had rejected.

'I ought to talk to her. I'll phone back.'

'They don't have a phone. She asked if you could go and see her. Bit of a cheek.' He paused. 'Still, poor woman must be desperate.'

Harry took the train to London the next day. He remembered the way to the little grocer's shop on the Isle of Dogs, among the little streets where shabby unemployed men walked. The shop was the same, vegetables in open boxes on the floor, cheap canned goods on the shelves. Bernie's father sat behind the counter. He was as tall and strongly built as Bernie and must once have been as good-looking, but now he was faded, stooped, with sad dead eyes.

'It's you,' he said. 'Hello. Mother's in there.' He jerked his head to a glassed door behind the counter. He didn't follow Harry in.

Edna Piper was sitting at the table in the little parlour. Her narrow face under its untidy hair lit up when Harry appeared. She stood and took his hand in a bony grip.

''Arry, 'Arry. How are you?'

'I'm all right thanks, Mrs Piper.'

'I was so sorry Bernie lost touch with you, wasting his time with those people in Chelsea—' she broke off. 'Did you know he'd gone to fight in Spain?'

'No. I'm afraid I haven't heard from Bernie for years. We lost touch.'

She sighed. 'It's as though he'd never been to the school, apart from the way he speaks. Sit down, I'm sorry, would you like some tea?'

'No. No, thanks. What – what's happened? My uncle wasn't very clear, I'm afraid.'

'We had a letter a month ago from the British Embassy. It said there was some battle in February and that Bernie was missing in action. It was so short and curt.' Her eyes filled with tears. 'His pa says that means he's dead, they just never found a body.'

Harry sat opposite her. There was an envelope on the table with a bright Spanish stamp. Mrs Piper picked it up, turning it over and over.

'Bernie just breezed in here one day last October and said he was going out to fight the Fascists. Looked at me all defiant because he knew I'd argue. But it was his father it affected most. Bernie didn't think of that, but I saw how he slumped like all the air was sucked out of him when he told us. This'll finish him.' She looked bleakly at Harry. 'Sometimes children crucify their parents, you know.'

'I'm sorry.'

'You lost both yours, didn't you?'

'Yes.'

'Pete won't come in, he's certain Bernie's dead.' She held up the letter. 'Would you look at this? It's from an English girl Bernie knew out there.'

Harry pulled out the letter and read it. It was dated three weeks before:

'Dear Mr and Mrs Piper,

You don't know me but Bernie and I were very close and I wanted to write to you. I know the embassy has written saying Bernie is missing believed killed. I work for the Red Cross out here and I wanted you to know I am working hard to try and find out more, whether he could possibly still be alive. It is difficult to get information here but I will go on trying. Bernie was always such a wonderful person.

Yours truly,

Barbara Clare'

'I don't know what she means,' Mrs Piper said. 'She says he may still be alive, then that he was a wonderful person, like he was dead.'

'It sounds like she's hoping against hope,' Harry said. His heart seemed to fall; for the first time it sunk in that Bernie was gone. He put the letter down.

'He wrote to us about her, you know, back at Christmas. Said he'd met an English girl out there. She must be in a dreadful state. I don't like to think of her there alone.'

'Have you written back?'

'Straight away, but there's been no reply.' She took a deep breath. 'I don't think letters always get through. I wondered – you speak Spanish, don't you, you know the country?'

'I've not been to Spain since 1931,' Harry said hesitantly.

'Which side do you support?' she asked suddenly.

He shook his head. 'Neither. I just think the whole thing's a tragedy.'

'I've had the Spanish Dependants' Aid round, but I don't want money, I just want Bernie.' Mrs Piper looked him in the eye. 'Would you go there? Try to find this girl, find what happened?' She leaned forward and grasped his hand in both of hers. 'It's a lot to ask but you were such good friends. If you could find out for sure, find out if there's *any* hope.'

TWO DAYS AFTER his visit to Mrs Piper, Harry took the train for Madrid. He had managed to book a hotel room. The travel agent said it would be full of journalists; they were the only people travelling to Spain now.

From the train window Harry saw slogans everywhere proclaiming the workers' war. It was a warm, fresh Castilian spring but people looked grim, embattled. When he arrived in Madrid he was astonished how different everything looked from the time of his first visit: the huge posters, the soldiers and militia everywhere, the people with the strained worried faces despite the propaganda booming from the loudspeakers around the Centro. The newspapers were full of an attempted coup in Barcelona by 'Trotsky-Fascist' traitors.

He checked into the hotel, it was near the Castellana. He had Barbara's address but wanted to orient himself first. That afternoon he went for a walk through La Latina to Carabanchel. He remembered walking down here with Bernie in 1931 to visit the Meras, the heat of that summer, how carefree they had been.

The further south he walked the fewer people there were. Soldiers eyed him suspiciously. There were barricades across many of the streets, crude structures built with cobblestones, a small gap for pedestrians; the streets without their cobbles were seas of mud. The sound of artillery became audible, occasional whistles and crumps in the distance. Harry turned back. He wondered, feeling sick to his stomach, whether the Meras were still down in Carabanchel.

In his hotel that evening he met a journalist, a cynical scholarly looking man called Phillips. He asked him what had happened in Barcelona.

'The Russians asserting control.' He laughed. 'Trotskyists my arse. There aren't any.'

'So it's true? The Russians have taken over the Republic?'

'Oh it's true all right. They run everything now; they've got their own torture chambers in a basement in the Puerta del Sol. They've got the trump card, you see. If the government challenges them, Stalin can say all right, we'll stop the arms shipments. He's even got them to ship the Bank of Spain's gold to Moscow. They won't see that again in a hurry.'

Harry shook his head. 'I'm glad we're following non-intervention.'

Phillips laughed again. 'Non-intervention my fanny. If Baldwin had let the French give the Republic arms last year, they wouldn't have touched the Russians with a barge pole. This is our fault. The Republic will lose in the end; the Germans and Italians are pouring in arms and men.'

'And then what?'

Phillips stretched out an arm in the Fascist salute. '*Sieg heil*, old boy. Another Fascist power. Well, I must toddle off to bed. Got to do a report from the Casa de Campo tomorrow, worse luck. Wish I'd brought my tin hat.'

HARRY WENT TO Red Cross HQ next day and asked for Miss Clare. He was shown into an office where a harassed-looking Swiss man sat behind a trestle table stacked with papers. They spoke in French. The official looked at him seriously.

'Do you know Miss Clare personally?'

'No, it was her friend I knew. His parents asked me to contact her.'

'She has taken it badly. We have given her a period of sick leave but we wonder if she might be better off returning to England.'

'I see.'

'It would be a great shame, she has been a tower of strength in the office. But she won't go, not till she knows for sure about her boyfriend, she says. But she may never know for sure.' He paused. 'I have had a complaint from the authorities, I am afraid. She is becoming a nuisance. We need to keep good relations with them. If you could help her see things in some sort of perspective . . .'

'I'll do what I can.' He sighed. 'Perspective seems in short supply here.'

'It is. Very short.'

THE ADDRESS was a block of flats. He knocked at her door and heard shuffling footsteps within. He wondered if he had got the wrong flat, they sounded like an old lady's footsteps, but it was a tall young woman with disordered red hair and a strained puffy face who opened the door. There were bags under the startlingly green eyes half hidden by smeared glasses.

'*¿Sí?*' she asked without interest.

'Miss Clare? You don't know me. My name's Brett, Harry Brett.' She looked at him uncomprehendingly. 'I'm a friend of Bernie's.'

At his name she came to life. 'Is there news?' she asked eagerly. 'Have you news?'

'I'm afraid not. Bernie's parents had your letter, they asked me to come out and see what could be done.'

'Oh.' She was downcast again at once, but held the door open. 'Come in.'

The flat was cluttered and untidy, the air thick with cigarette smoke. She frowned, a puzzled look. 'I know your name from somewhere.'

'Rookwood. I was there with Bernie.'

She smiled, her face suddenly warm. 'Of course. Harry. Bernie talked about you.'

'Did he?'

'He said you were his best friend at school.' She paused. 'He hated that school, though.'

'Still?'

She sighed. 'It was all tied up with his politics. Looks like it's done for him in the end, his bloody politics. Sorry, my manners are awful.' She swept a pile of clothes from an armchair. 'Sit down. Coffee? It's pretty dire, I'm afraid.'

'Thanks. That would be nice.'

She made him a coffee and sat opposite him. The life seemed to have gone out of her again. She slumped in her chair, smoking strong Spanish cigarettes.

'Did you go to the Red Cross?' she asked.

'Yes. They said you were on sick leave.'

'Nearly two months now, it's been.' She shook her head. 'They want me to go back to England, they say Bernie's bound to be dead. I believed that at first but now I'm not sure, I can't be sure till someone tells me where the body is.'

'Have you made any progress?'

'No. They're getting fed up of me, they've told me not to come again. They've even complained to old Doumergue.' She lit another cigarette. 'There was a commissar Bernie knew from the fighting in the Casa de Campo, a Communist who worked at army HQ. Captain Duro. He was kind; he was trying to find out what he could but he left suddenly, last week, transferred or something. There have been a lot of changes recently. I asked if I could go out there, to the lines, but of course they said no.'

'Maybe it would be better to go home.'

'Nothing to go home for.' Her eyes went blank, inward-looking; she seemed to forget he was there. Harry felt desperately sorry for her. 'Come for lunch at my hotel,' he said.

She gave him a quick, sad smile and nodded.

He spent most of the next couple of days with her. She wanted to hear all he could tell her about Bernie. It seemed to lift her out of herself for a while, though she kept slipping back into that withdrawn, glassy-eyed sadness. She wore old skirts and unironed blouses and no make-up; she didn't seem to care how she looked.

On the second day he visited the British Embassy but they said what everyone else had: that 'missing believed killed' meant they hadn't found an identifiable body. He walked back to Barbara's flat. He wasn't looking forward to telling her what they had said. He had promised to visit army HQ the next day, perhaps they would take more notice of a man; after that he didn't see what else he could do. He was sure Bernie was dead.

He rang her bell and heard the dragging footsteps again. She opened the door and leaned against it, staring at him. She was drunk. 'Come in,' she said.

There was a half-empty bottle of wine on the table and another in the wastepaper basket. She slumped into a chair beside the table.

'Have a drink,' she said. 'Drink with me, Harry.'

'Don't you think you've had enough?' he asked gently.

'No. Take a cup and have one.'

He let her pour him a drink. She raised her cup. 'Here's to the bloody revolution.'

'The bloody revolution.'

He told her what the embassy had said. She put down her glass. The inward look came over her face again. 'He was so full of life, always. So funny. So beautiful.' She looked up. 'He said some of the boys at school got crushes on him. He didn't like it.'

'No. No, he didn't.'

'Did you have a crush on him?'

'No.' Harry smiled sadly. He remembered the night Bernie had gone to the prostitutes. 'I was jealous of his looks sometimes.'

'Have you a girlfriend back in England?'

'Yes.' He hesitated. 'A nice girl.' He had been going out with Laura for some months; he was surprised to realize he had hardly thought of her since coming to Madrid.

'They say there's someone for everyone, and there is, but they don't tell you sometimes they're just taken away from you again. Gone. Vanished.' She clenched a fist against her forehead and began to cry, harsh wracking sobs. 'I've just been deluding myself, haven't I? He's gone.'

'I'm afraid it looks that way,' Harry replied quietly.

'Visit army HQ for me tomorrow, though, will you? Speak to Captain Duro. But if they've no more news. I'll – I'll give up. I'll have to accept it.'

'I will. I promise.'

She shook her head. 'I don't usually get like this. I've shocked you, haven't I?'

He leaned across the table and took her hand. 'I'm sorry,' he said gently. 'I'm so, so sorry.'

She clasped his hand and leaned her head against it and wept and wept.

The soldier at the entrance to military headquarters was reluctant to let Harry in but he explained what he wanted in Spanish and that helped. Inside he told a sergeant he had come to see what he could find out about a soldier missing on the Jarama. He mentioned Bernie's name and the name of the Communist Barbara said had helped her. The sergeant said he would consult an officer and showed him to a little windowless office to wait. He sat down at a table. He stared at a picture of Stalin on the wall, the screwed-up little eyes and the big moustache, a smile like a grimace. There was a map of Spain, too, pencil lines marking the shrinking areas the Republic held.

A Spaniard in a captain's uniform came in, carrying a folder. He was short and swarthy and had a tired, stubbly face. There was another captain with him, a tall pale burly man. They sat opposite him. The Spaniard nodded curtly.

'I understand you are making enquiries about a certain Captain Duro.'

'No. No, I'm trying to find out about an English volunteer, Bernie Piper. His girlfriend has been here, she said Captain Duro was helping her.'

'May I see your passport, please?'

Harry handed it over. The Spaniard opened it, holding it up to the light. He grunted and slipped it into his folder.

'Could I have that back, please?' Harry said. 'I need it.'

The captain folded his arms on top of the folder and turned to his colleague. The other man nodded. 'You speak good Spanish, *señor*.' His accent was foreign, guttural.

'It's my subject. I'm a lecturer – at Cambridge.'

'Who sent you here?'

Harry frowned. 'Private Piper's parents.'

'But his woman is already here. The records say he is missing believed killed. That means dead but no body. But we have first this woman from the Red Cross coming day after day, and now you. And always you talk about Captain Duro.'

'Look, we just want to know, that's all.' Harry was getting angry now. 'Private Piper came to fight for your Republic, don't you owe us that much?'

'You support the Nationalists, *señor*?'

'No, I don't. I'm English, we're neutral.' Harry began to feel uneasy. He noticed both officers wore revolvers. The foreign officer snatched the folder brusquely from his colleague.

'Miss Barbara Clare, who has been here many times, I see she asked to visit the battlefield. That is a restricted zone. As she works for the Red Cross, she should know that. They have denied responsibility for her enquiries.'

'She wasn't asking on their behalf. Look, Bernie Piper was her – well, her lover.'

'And you, what is your connection with him?'

'We were at school together.'

The captain laughed, a harsh sound deep in his throat. 'You call that a connection?'

'Look here,' he said. 'I came here in good faith to find a missing soldier. But if you won't help me, perhaps I'd better go.' He started to rise.

'Sit down.' The foreign officer stood up and pushed him hard on the chest. Harry was taken off balance and fell over on the floorboards, landing painfully on his pelvis. The officer looked at him coldly as he stood up. 'Sit on that chair.'

Harry's heart was beating hard. He remembered what the journalist had said about torture chambers in the Puerta del Sol. The Spanish officer looked uneasy. He leaned over and whispered something in his colleague's ear. The other man shook his head impatiently, then took out a packet of cigarettes and lit one. Harry stared at the pack; there was Cyrillic writing on it.

The officer smiled. 'Yes, I am Russian. We help our Spanish comrades with matters of security. They need that help; there are Fascist and Trotskyist spies everywhere. Asking questions. Making up lies.'

Harry tried to keep his voice steady. 'I came here to make enquiries about a friend—'

'Private Piper did not come out here via established International Brigade procedures. He simply turned up in Madrid last November. That is not normal.'

'I don't know anything about that. I haven't seen Bernie for years.'

'Yet you came out here looking for him?'

'His parents asked me to.'

The Russian leaned forward. 'And who told you to ask about Captain Duro?'

Harry took a deep breath. He was in an underground room in a foreign city under martial law. There was no way out of here unless they let him go.

'Miss Clare. She said Captain Duro introduced himself when she first came here making enquiries. I told you, he met Bernie in the Casa de Campo. He tried to find out more for her. Then she was told he had been transferred. No one else would help her.'

'Now we are getting somewhere. Captain Duro was not, in fact, transferred. He was arrested as a saboteur. He was overheard saying we should have treated with the rebels in Barcelona.' He leaned back, crossing his arms. 'Treated with Trotsky-Fascist saboteurs.'

'Look, I really don't know anything about this. I've only been in the country three days.'

'This Private Piper's file shows that after he was injured in the fighting in the Casa de Campo, he offered to help with the reception of volunteers arriving from England. But it was felt he was a bourgeois, a sentimentalist, one likely to disapprove of some of the hard measures we need here. It was felt he should be allowed to recover then sent to the front. He was foot-soldier material, not one of the men of steel we need now.'

Harry stared at the Russian.

'Such people are easily seduced by Trotsky-Fascism.' The Russian turned to his colleague. The Spaniard leaned in close; Harry caught the whispered words, 'Red Cross.' The Russian frowned.

'We shall discuss this outside.' He turned to Harry. 'You, Señor Brett, you stay here.' Harry felt a shiver run down his spine, felt cold in the hot stuffy room.

The soldiers went out. Harry heard a low rumble of voices. He thought feverishly about what would happen if they took him away somewhere. Barbara was expecting him back at the flat. She had seemed calmer after her outburst yesterday; he hoped she hadn't hit the bottle again. She would look for him if he didn't return. His palms were sweating. He told himself he must stay calm.

The voices from the corridor rose. He heard the Russian shouting. 'Who is in charge here?' Footsteps retreated, then there was silence, a thick silence he could almost feel. He remembered the boys talking eagerly about types of torture at school. What the rack did, thumb-screws, new tortures with electric shocks.

The door opened and the Spanish officer entered, alone, his face set. He handed Harry his passport.

'Be thankful for your Red Cross connections,' he said coldly. 'Be grateful we need their medicines. You can go. Get out now before he changes his mind.' He stared into Harry's eyes. 'You have twenty-four hours to leave Spain.'

Back in the flat, Harry told Barbara what had happened. He had to leave Spain at once and she should go too; she must never go back to military HQ. He had thought she might not believe what had occurred, but she did.

'We know about what's happening,' she said quietly. 'In the Red Cross, I mean. The arrests and disappearances.' She shook her head. 'I'd just stopped thinking about it. I haven't thought of anything but finding out about Bernie. I've been so selfish. I'm sorry you went through that.'

'I volunteered to go. Maybe we've both been naive.'

'Less excuse for me, I've been here nine months.'

'Barbara, you should come back to England.'

'No.' She stood up, a new decisiveness about her. 'I'll go back to work, tell Doumergue what's happened. I'll see if I can get a transfer.'

'Are you sure you're up to that?'

She smiled wanly. 'I'll be better working. It'll help me pull myself together.'

Harry packed, then went back to Barbara's flat for supper. Neither of them felt like going out into the city.

'I had to have some *hope*,' she said. 'I couldn't accept Bernie was dead.'

'What will you do now?'

She smiled bravely. 'I talked Doumergue into transferring me. I'm going to help organize medical supplies in Burgos.'

'The Nationalist zone?'

'Yes.' She gave a brittle laugh. 'See the other side of the story. There's no fighting in Burgos, it's well behind the lines.'

'Will you be able to stand that? Working with the people Bernie fought against?'

'Oh, the Nationalists and the Communists are no better than each other. I know that, but I just want to do my job, help the people caught in the middle. Damn all the bloody politics. I'm past caring.'

Harry looked at her. He wondered if she was up to it.

'Can you feel Bernie's presence?' she asked suddenly. 'Here, in the flat?'

'No.' He smiled awkwardly. 'I don't get feelings like that.'

'Sometimes a sort of warmth steals over me, as though he was here. I suppose that just proves he's dead.'

'Whatever happens, you've some good memories. That'll be a comfort, in time.'

'I suppose so. What about you?'

He smiled. 'Back home to the routine.'

'It sounds a good life. Are you happy?'

'Content, I suppose. Perhaps that's as much as we should hope for.'

'I always wanted more.' Her eyes took on a faraway look for a moment. 'Oh God, I'm going to have to pull myself together to work in Burgos.' She smiled. 'Will you write to me?'

'Yes, of course.'

'Tell me all about Cambridge, while I'm up to my neck in forms.' She gave that quick, sad little smile again.

Chapter Seventeen

GENERAL MAESTRE'S HOUSE was an eighteenth-century mansion in the northern suburbs. He sent a car to pick up Harry and Tolhurst, a big American Lincoln; they drove at speed up a dark empty Castellana from which the Nazi flags had been taken down. Himmler had gone, but the previous day the newspapers had sprung even more sensational news: Hitler and Franco had met at the town of Hendaye on the French border for six hours of talks. The papers predicted that Spain would soon join the war.

'The meeting went badly, actually, that's the word from Sam,' Hillgarth had told Harry and Tolhurst that afternoon. He had summoned them to a meeting in Tolhurst's office. Dressed today in an ordinary suit, he looked tired. He sat with one leg crossed over the other, constantly jiggling his free foot. 'He's got a source in Franco's entourage. Said Franco told Hitler he'd only enter the war if Hitler guaranteed huge amounts of supplies. He knows we'd let nothing through the blockade. Well, let's hope that's right.' He picked up a copy of *ABC* from Tolhurst's narrow desk; the Generalísimo was shown leaning down from the royal train to greet Hitler, grinning broadly, eyes alight.

'Franco's besotted with Hitler, wants to be part of the New Order.' Hillgarth shook his head, then looked at them keenly. 'You're both going to that party tonight, aren't you? See if you can find out from Maestre how the new trade minister's doing. Carceller made a pro-Fascist speech the other day; Maestre may not last much longer as deputy. Then we'll have lost a friend.'

'Did you see the report from our man in Gerona, sir?' Tolhurst asked. 'Food trains heading for the French border, "For Our German Allies" painted on the side?'

Hillgarth nodded. He shifted in his chair, bringing his foot to rest. 'Time to move on with Forsyth, Brett. Find out more about this damned gold. And what about this Clare woman, where does she fit in?'

'I don't think Barbara knows anything.'

Hillgarth eyed him keenly. 'Well, find out,' he said tersely. 'You know her.'

'Not well. But we're meeting for lunch on Monday.' He had phoned yesterday; Barbara had seemed hesitant but accepted his invitation. Harry felt guilty but at the same time full of curiosity about her relationship with Sandy. Being a spy stimulates nosiness, he thought. 'I think my best bet's to follow up what Sandy said about business opportunities,' he went on. 'It may help me get a picture of what he's doing.'

'When are you seeing him again?'

'I thought I'd arrange something when I met Barbara.'

Hillgarth's foot jigged again. 'This can't wait. You should have organized something when you spoke to the woman.'

'We don't want to seem too eager,' Tolhurst interjected.

Hillgarth waved a hand impatiently. 'We need that information.' He rose abruptly. 'I've got to go. See to it.'

'Yes, sir.'

'He's worried,' Tolhurst said as the door closed. 'Better fix another meeting with Forsyth pronto.'

'All right. But Sandy's sharp.'

'We'll have to be sharper.'

The ball had a Moorish theme. A pair of Moroccan guards flanked the front door, dressed in turbans and long yellow cloaks and holding lances. Harry looked at their impassive brown faces as he passed, recalling the savage reputation the Moors had during the Civil War.

Inside, the wide hallway was decorated with Moorish tapestries; guests circulated, the men in evening dress and many of the women in wide Andalusian skirts. A partition separating the hall from the *salón* had been pushed back, creating one enormous room. It was full of people. A servant, Spanish but wearing a fez and kaftan, took their names and waved a waiter across to serve them drinks.

'Know anyone?' Harry asked.

'One or two people. Look, there's Goach.' The old protocol expert stood in a corner, talking earnestly to a tall red-robed cleric. 'He's a Catholic, you know, loves a monsignor.'

'Look at the waiters in fancy dress. They must be hot.'

Tolhurst leaned close. 'Talking of things Moroccan, look over there.'

Harry followed his gaze. In the middle of the room Maestre stood with two other men, like him in uniform. One was a lieutenant. The other, a general like Maestre, was an extraordinary figure. Elderly, thin and white-haired, he was talking animatedly, threatening to splash his companions with the drink he held in one hand. His other sleeve hung empty. His cadaverous scarred face had only one eye, a black patch screwed into an empty socket on the other side. He laughed, showing an almost toothless mouth.

'Millán Astray,' Tolhurst said. 'You can't mistake him. Founder of the Spanish Foreign Legion. Astray's pro-Fascist and mad as a hatter, but his old troops love him. Franco served under him, and so did Maestre. Chief of the bridegrooms of death.'

'The what?'

'That's what they called the legion. Make the French legion look like Sunday-school teachers.' Tolhurst leaned closer and lowered his voice. 'The captain told me a story about Maestre. Some nuns from a nursing order came out to Morocco during the tribal rebellions. Maestre and some of his men met them at Melilla docks and presented them with a huge basket of roses – with the heads of two Moroccan rebel leaders in the middle.'

'Sounds like a tall story.' Harry looked again at Maestre. Millán Astray's gestures had become even wilder and Maestre looked a little strained, but still bent his head politely to listen.

'Maestre told Captain Hillgarth himself. Nuns never batted an eyelid, apparently. The legion had a bit of a thing about heads, used to parade with them stuck on the end of their bayonets.' Tolhurst shook his head wonderingly. 'Half the government are ex-legion now. It's one thing that holds the Monarchist and Falangist factions together. A shared past.'

Millán Astray had put down his drink and was squeezing the

shoulder of Maestre's other companion as he went on talking animatedly. Even that hand, Harry saw, had fingers missing. Maestre caught Harry's eye, and muttered something to Millán Astray. The old man nodded and Maestre and the lieutenant came over to Harry and Tolhurst. On the way Maestre whispered to a small plump woman in a wide Andalusian skirt and long white gloves and she followed the others over. Maestre extended a hand to Harry with a welcoming smile.

'Ah, Señor Brett. I am so glad that you could come. And you must be Señor Tolhurst.'

'Yes, sir. Thank you for inviting me.'

'I am always glad to welcome friends from the embassy. I should be circulating but I have been reliving old times in Morocco. My wife, Elena.'

Harry and Tolhurst bowed.

'And my right-hand man from those days, Lieutenant Alfonso Gomez.'

The other man shook hands and bowed stiffly. He was short and stocky, with a stern face the colour of mahogany and keen eyes. 'You are English?' he asked.

'Yes, from the embassy.'

Señora Maestre smiled. 'I am told you were at Eton, Señor Tolhurst?'

'A fine place.' Maestre nodded approvingly. 'Where English gentlemen are bred, eh?'

'I hope so, sir.'

'And you, Señor Brett?' Señora Maestre asked.

'I went to another public school, *señora*. Rookwood.' He saw Gomez looking at him, weighing him up.

Señora Maestre nodded. 'And what do your family do?'

Harry was taken aback by her directness. 'I'm from an army background.'

She nodded happily. 'Excellent, just like us. And you are a lecturer at Cambridge?' Her eyes were keen, probing.

'Yes. In peacetime. Only a fellow, not – senior.'

Maestre nodded approvingly. 'Cambridge. How I loved my time there, as Señor Brett knows. It was there I got my love of England.'

'You must meet my daughter,' Señora Maestre said. 'She has never met an Englishman. Only Italians, and they are not a good influence.' She raised her eyebrows and gave a little shudder.

'Yes, you young men go with Elena,' Maestre added. As Harry passed him he touched his arm and spoke softly, his keen brown eyes serious. 'You are among friends tonight. No Germans here, and no blue shirts, except for Millán Astray and he is an exception. He has little to do nowadays, we invited him as a kindness.'

Harry and Tolhurst followed Señora Maestre as she cut a path through the crowd, skirts swishing. At the far end three girls stood together self-consciously, nursing tall crystal glasses of wine. Two wore flamenco dresses; the third, short and plump like her mother with olive skin and a round face with heavy features, wore an evening dress of white silk. Señora Maestre clapped her hands and they looked up. Harry remembered for an instant the flamenco singers who had danced in El Toro when he and Bernie were there nine years before. But those had been dressed in black.

'Milagros!' Señora Maestre said. 'You should talk to your guests. Señor Brett, Señor Tolhurst, my daughter Milagros and her friends, Dolores and Catalina.' She turned quickly to a man who was passing by. 'Marqués! You came!' She took the man's arm and led him away.

'Are you from London?' Milagros asked Harry with a shy smile. She seemed nervous, ill at ease.

'Near there. A place called Surrey. Simon's from London, aren't you?'

'What – oh, yes.' Tolhurst had gone red and was starting to perspire. A lock of fair hair fell over his forehead and he brushed it away, almost spilling his drink. Milagros's friends exchanged glances and giggled.

'I have seen pictures of your King and Queen,' Milagros said. 'And the princesses, how old are they now?'

'Princess Elizabeth's fourteen.'

'She is very pretty. Don't you think so?'

'Yes, yes she is.'

A waiter passed by, filling their glasses again. Harry smiled at Milagros, delving for something to say. 'So, you are eighteen today.'

'Yes, tonight I am launched on the world.' She spoke with an undertone of regret, for her childhood perhaps. She studied Harry for a moment, then smiled and seemed to relax. 'My father says you are a translator. Have you been doing that for long?'

'No. I used to be a university teacher.'

Milagros smiled again, sadly. 'I was not clever at school. But now that time is over.'

'Yes,' one of her friends said cheerfully. 'Now it is time for her to find a husband.' They giggled and Milagros flushed. Harry felt sorry for her.

'I say,' Tolhurst broke in suddenly. 'Your name, Milagros. And yours, Dolores. They sound very strange in English – Miracles and Sadness. We don't have religious names for girls.' He laughed and the girls looked at him coldly.

'There's Charity,' Harry said awkwardly.

'Are you a little hot, Señor Simon?' Dolores asked maliciously. 'Would you like a cloth for your brow?'

Tolhurst reddened even further. 'No, no, I'm all right. I—'

'Look, Dolores, there's Jorge,' Catalina said excitedly. 'Come on.' Giggling, the two girls walked off to a good-looking young man in a cadet's uniform. Milagros looked embarrassed.

'I am sorry, my friends were a little impolite.'

'It's all right,' Tolhurst said awkwardly. I'll – uh – go and get something to eat.' He walked away, head lowered.

Harry smiled ruefully. 'I don't think he's been to a big occasion like this for a while.'

The girl produced a fan and waved it gently in front of her face. 'Neither have I, there have been no parties since we came back to Madrid last year. But now things are getting back to normal a little. But it feels rather strange after so long.'

'Yes. Yes, it does. It's my first party too, for – for a while.' Since Dunkirk. Harry felt oddly apart, as though there was a glass wall between him and the partygoers. On his deaf side it was hard to make out any words in the cacophony of noise.

Milagros looked at him seriously. Harry turned his head so that his good ear was towards her. 'How I hope Spain can stay out of the war in Europe,' she said. 'What do you think, *señor*?'

'I hope so too.'

Milagros studied him again. 'Forgive me asking, but are you a soldier? My family have been soldiers for generations; we cannot help noticing when a man stands awkwardly, like your friend. But you stand like a soldier.'

'That's clever of you. I was in the army until a few months ago.'

'Papa was in Morocco when I was young. It was a terrible place. I was so glad to come home. But then the Civil War came.' She smiled, making an effort to be cheerful. 'And you, *señor*, were you in the army for long?'

'No. I only joined up when the war started.'

'They say the bombing of London is terrible.'

'Yes. It's a difficult time.' He remembered the bombs falling.

'It is so sad. And London is so beautiful, I hear. Many museums and art galleries.'

'Yes. They've taken the pictures away for the war.'

'In Madrid we have the Prado. They are putting the pictures back there now. I have never seen them, I should like to go.' She smiled at Harry, encouragingly but a little embarrassed, and he thought, she wants me to take her. He was flattered but she was so young, scarcely more than a child.

'Well, I'd like to go too, though just now I'm very busy . . .'

'That would be so nice. We have a telephone, you could ring my mother to arrange it—'

Catalina and Dolores reappeared with a group of cadets crowding round them. Milagros frowned.

'Milagros, you must meet Carlos. He has a medal already, he has been fighting the Red bandits in the north—'

'Excuse me,' Harry said. 'I'd better find Simon.' He made his escape, puffing out his cheeks with relief. She was a nice child. But just a child. He collected another glass from a passing waiter. He'd better watch how much he had. He thought of Sofia, as he had several times since the day before. She had seemed full of life, energy. He had said nothing to Hillgarth about the spy. He would keep his promise.

Tolhurst was standing in the middle of the room, talking to Goach, who was looking at him with slight distaste through his monocle. Poor old Tolly, Harry thought suddenly. With his big frame Tolhurst should have looked impressive but there was always something slouched and drooping about him.

Goach cheered up as Harry joined them. 'Evening, Brett. I say, you'd better watch out. The general and his wife are looking for a good catch for Milagros. The general's brother told me. Monsignor Maestre.' He nodded to where the priest was talking to a couple of older women. Harry could see a resemblance to Maestre in the thin face, the authoritative manner.

'You know him, sir?'

'Yes, he's quite a scholar. Expert on Spanish church liturgy during the Reconquista period.' Goach smiled and bowed as the monsignor, hearing his name, came over.

'Ah, George,' the monsignor said in Spanish. 'I have been getting some more subscriptions.' His eyes flicked over Harry and Tolhurst, quick and sharp as his brother's.

'Splendid, splendid.' Goach made introductions. 'The monsignor's head of an appeal for rebuilding all the burned-out churches in Madrid. The Vatican's been a great help but it's a huge task, needs a lot of money.'

Monsignor Maestre shook his head sorrowfully. 'Indeed it does. But we are getting there. Though nothing can replace our martyrs, our murdered priests and nuns.' He turned to Harry and Tolhurst. 'I remember, during the darkest time of our war, some English churches sent us their church plate to make up for what we had lost. It was a great comfort, made us feel we were not forgotten.'

'I'm glad,' Harry said. 'It must have been a hard time.'

'You do not know, *señor*, the things they did to us. It is as well you do not. We want to rebuild the churches in La Latina and Carabanchel.' The priest looked at Harry seriously. 'The people there need a beacon, something to cleave to.'

'There's a burned-out church near where I live, at the top of La Latina,' Harry said.

The monsignor's face hardened. 'Yes, and the people who did it need to be shown they could not destroy the authority of Christ's church. That we have returned stronger than before.'

Goach nodded. 'Quite.'

A burst of harsh laughter made Monsignor Maestre frown. 'It is a pity my brother invited Millán Astray. He is so *inculto*. And a Falangist. They are all so irreligious.' He raised his eyebrows. 'We needed them during our war, but now – well, thank God the Generalísimo is a true Christian.'

'Some of the Falangists would make him their God,' Goach said quietly.

'Indeed they would.'

Harry looked between them. They were both being very outspoken. But they were all Monarchists here, except for Millán Astray. The crippled general was holding forth to a group of cadets now; they seemed to be hanging on his every word.

The monsignor took Goach's arm. 'George, come with me, I'd like you to meet the bishop's secretary.' With a nod at Harry and Tolhurst, he led Goach away, red skirts billowing around his feet. Tolhurst took a swig of wine.

'I thought he'd never stop. How did you get on with the *señorita*?'

'She wanted me to take her to the Prado.' Harry looked over to where Milagros was talking to her friends again. She caught his eye and smiled uncertainly. He felt guilty, his sudden departure must have seemed rude.

'Lot of little cats.' Tolhurst wiped his glasses on his sleeve. 'I suppose I was a bit stupid, making fun of their names. I don't know, I can't seem to get on with girls, not socially.' He swayed slightly, more than a little drunk. 'You see, I was in Cuba so long, I got used to tarts.' He laughed. 'I like tarts, but you forget how to talk to respectable girls.' He looked at Harry. 'Señorita Maestre not your type, then?'

'No.'

'No Vera Lynn, is she?'

'She's young. Poor girl, she's scared for the future.'

'Aren't we all? Listen, there's a chap in the press office, knows this little brothel near Opera—'

Harry nudged him to be quiet. Maestre was approaching again, smiling broadly.

'Señor Brett, I hope Milagros has not abandoned you.'

'No, no. She does you credit, general.'

Maestre looked across to where the girls were deep in conversation with some more cadets. He shook his head indulgently. 'I am afraid they cannot resist a young officer. The young all live for the day now.

You must forgive them.' He must have thought Milagros left *me*, Harry thought.

Maestre took a drink, wiped his little moustache and looked at them. 'Gentlemen,' he said. 'You both know Captain Hillgarth, yes? He and I are good friends.'

'Yes, sir.' Tolhurst's face was immediately attentive.

'He should know there is a lot of annoyance in the government over Negrín. It was not a good idea for England to give asylum to the Republican prime minister. These noises in the British Parliament annoy our friends.' He shook his head. 'You English, you let vipers into your bosom sometimes, you know.'

'It's difficult, sir,' Tolhurst said seriously. 'I don't know how the Commons got wind Sir Samuel recommended Negrín be asked to leave, but it's got the Labour members hot under the collar.'

'Surely you can control your Parliament?'

'Not really,' Tolhurst said. 'It's democracy,' he added apologetically.

Maestre spread his hands, smiling in puzzlement. 'But England is not a decadent republic like France was, you have a monarchy and aristocracy, you understand the principle of authority.'

'I'll tell Captain Hillgarth,' Tolhurst said. 'By the way, sir,' he added quietly, 'the captain was asking how things are going with the new minister.'

Maestre nodded. 'Tell him there is nothing to worry about there,' he replied softly.

Señora Maestre appeared. She tapped her husband's arm with her fan. 'Santiago, are you talking politics again? This is our daughter's ball.' She shook her head. 'You must forgive him.'

Maestre smiled. 'You are right, my dear, of course.'

She smiled brightly at Harry and Tolhurst. 'I hear Juan March is in Madrid. If he has returned to stay, he is bound to be doing some entertaining.'

'I heard it was just a short visit,' Maestre replied. Harry looked at him. Juan March again. The name Hillgarth had told him to forget, along with the Knights of St George.

Señora Maestre beamed at her guests. 'He is Spain's most successful businessman. He had to leave under the Republic of course. It would be good if he returned. You cannot imagine how grey life was in the Nationalist zone during the war. It had to be that way, of course. And then when we came back—' A shadow flitted across her face.

'This house was half ruined,' Maestre said. 'Good furniture used for firewood. Everything broken or damaged. The families the Republic put in here could not even use the toilet, but the worst was our family things, photographs sold in the Rastro because they were framed in silver. You can see why Negrín being given a home in London angers people.' Maestre looked across at his daughter, his face full of tenderness for a moment. 'Milagros is a sensitive child, she found it hard to bear. She is not happy. I fear she is too delicate a plant to flourish in Spain now. I sometimes even think she might be happier abroad.' He put his arm round his wife's shoulders. 'I think we should start the dancing, my dear. I will ask the chamber orchestra to come in.' He smiled at Harry. 'Only the best for Milagros. I will tell her she must give you a dance. Excuse us.' He led his wife away.

'Hell,' Tolhurst said. 'I'm awful at dancing.'

'This Juan March,' Harry said in neutral tones. 'He's quite an important man, isn't he?'

'I'll say. He's got millions. Gigantic crook, started as a smuggler. Lives in Switzerland now, took all his money out before the Civil War started. Pro-Monarchist. Probably just come to sort out his affairs.' Tolhurst spoke lightly, but Harry saw a watchfulness come into his face. He changed the subject. 'Terrible about the Maestres' losses, all the upper- and middle-class families suffered dreadfully. One thing about this regime, at least they protect people of – you know, our class.'

'Yes, I suppose they do. Our class. You know, I was thinking. In a funny way, I think the fact we're both Rookwood old boys means more to Sandy than to me now. He still has feelings about it, even if it's only hate.'

'And you?'

'I don't know any more, Tolly.'

Four men in dinner jackets carrying musical instruments appeared with Señora Maestre, followed by a group of the kaftaned servants pushing a little wooden stage. The guests clapped and cheered. Harry saw Milagros waving her fan at him from the other side of the room. He raised his glass. Beside him, Tolhurst sighed.

'Oh lor',' he said. 'Here we go.'

Chapter Eighteen

BARBARA HADN'T WANTED to go and meet Harry. He had been kind to her three years before and it had been good to see a friendly English face, but seeing Bernie's best friend felt somehow like tempting fate. She had considered telling Harry but he seemed so friendly with Sandy. And he had changed: there was an angry unhappiness about him that had not been there three years ago. She had to keep everything secret. Harry was here now and Sandy had taken a shine to him, so she must brazen it out and deceive Harry too. A second person to deceive, and Bernie's best friend this time.

On Saturday she had heard on the BBC about a big German raid on Birmingham. Nearly two hundred people had been killed. She had sat by the radio, aghast. She hadn't told Sandy; he would have comforted her but she felt she couldn't stand that, she didn't deserve it. She worried for two days but that morning a telegram had arrived from her father, saying they were all well, the raids had been in the town centre. She had wept with relief.

She was due to meet Luis again in two days. She feared the money from her bank in England might not come in time. Doubtful of Luis's story though she had been after their first meeting, now she was more inclined to believe him. If he turned up at the cafe with proof, that would settle it. She cautioned herself that it was what she wanted to believe, she mustn't hope too much. And if it were true? Helping Bernie escape from a prison camp, getting him to the embassy? And what if Sandy found out? What would he do? Lately she had come to realize that among the complex of emotions she felt for Sandy, there was an element of fear, fear of the ruthlessness she knew was part of him.

The previous evening she had done something that only a few weeks ago she would have found inconceivable. Sandy had been out with some of his cronies and she had gone into his study to try and find out what money he had. She told herself she would never steal from him, but if her savings did not arrive in time perhaps she could get money from him with some lie. If he had enough. Like most men, Sandy didn't think money was something women should know about.

Her heart beating fast, feeling she was crossing some sort of boundary for good, Barbara had hunted for the key to Sandy's desk in his study. He kept it in the bedroom, in his sock drawer – she had seen him put it there sometimes when he came to bed after an evening's work. She found it right at the back, inside a folded sock. She looked at it, hesitated again for a moment, then went to his study.

Some of the drawers were locked, but not all. In one she found two bank books. One was an account with a local branch of a Spanish bank containing a thousand pesetas; the records showed regular payments and withdrawals that she guessed covered their expenses. To her surprise the second was with a bank in Argentina. There were several entries but no withdrawals, and the balance was nearly half a million Argentine pesos, however much that was. Of course, there was no way of getting the money out herself: the accounts were in Sandy's sole name. She felt oddly relieved.

She left the study, pausing at the door to make sure Pilar was not around. Putting the key back, she felt that something steely was entering into her, something she hadn't known was there.

She had arranged to meet Harry in a restaurant near the Royal Palace, a quiet little place that served good black-market food. She was late. The daily maid had been in a state because she had been stopped by the *civiles* on the way to work and had forgotten her papers; Barbara had to write a letter confirming she worked for her. Harry was already sitting at one of the little tables reading a newspaper. A few businessmen and well-to-do couples occupied the other tables. Harry rose to greet her.

'Barbara, how are you?' He looked pale and tired.

'Oh, not so bad.'

'It's cold.'

'Yes, winter's nearly here.'

The waiter took her coat and hat and laid menus in front of them.

'Well, how are you?' she asked brightly. 'How's the embassy?'

'A bit boring. Interpreting at meetings with officials mostly.' He seemed nervous, ill at ease.

'How are your people? All right?'

'My uncle and aunt are fine. Down in Surrey you'd hardly know there was a war on. My cousin's family had it a bit rough in London though.' He paused, looked at her seriously. 'I hear Birmingham's been hit.'

'Yes. They sent me a telegram, they're all OK.'

'I thought about you when I heard. You must have been terribly worried.'

'I was, and I expect there'll be more raids.' She sighed. 'But you've had them much longer in London, haven't you?'

'There was one when I was there last month, with my cousin Will. But he's safe in the country now, some secret work.'

'That must be a relief.'

'Yes.'

Barbara lit a cigarette. 'I think my parents are just trying to carry on, same as everyone. What else can they do? Mum and Dad don't say much in their letters.'

'How's Sandy's father? The bishop?'

'Do you know, I haven't the faintest idea. They haven't been in touch since Sandy came out here. He never talks about his father, or his brother. It's sad.' She studied Harry. He did look different, very tense. He had been quite good-looking when she met him three years ago, though not her type. Now he looked older, fleshier, with new lines around his eyes. She thought, a whole generation of men is ageing fast. She hesitated, then asked, 'How are you these days? You look a bit tired.'

'Oh, I'm OK. I had shell shock, you know,' he added suddenly. 'I used to get bad panic attacks.'

'I'm sorry.'

'But I'm much better now, haven't had one for a while.'

'At least you're doing something useful at the embassy.'

He smiled, a tense smile. 'You look very different from the last time we met,' he said.

Barbara blushed. 'Yes, all those tatty jumpers. I didn't care how I looked then, I was in such a state.' She smiled at him warmly. 'You helped me.'

He bit his lip, staring at her with his earnest blue eyes so that for a second she thought, oh God, he's guessed something. Then he said, 'What's it like, living here? Madrid seems in a terrible state. The poverty and misery, all the beggars. It's worse than during the Civil War.'

She sighed. 'The Civil War wrecked Spain, especially Madrid. The harvest's been bad again and now there's our blockade, limiting the supplies they can bring in. According to the papers anyway. Though I don't know.' She smiled sadly. 'I don't really know what to believe.'

'It's the silence I can't stand. Remember how noisy Madrid used to be? It's as though all the energy and hope has been sucked out of people.'

'That's war.'

Harry looked at her seriously. 'You know what frightens me? We stopped Hitler invading England this year, but if he tries again next year we might lose. We'd fight like hell, fight on the beaches and in the streets like Churchill said, but we could lose. I imagine Britain ending up like Spain, a wrecked, ruined country ruled by corrupt fascists. This could happen at home.'

'Could it? I know discipline's harsh, but there are people like Sebastian de Salas who really do want to rebuild the country.' She stopped, passed a hand across her brow. 'Oh God,' she said. 'I'm defending them. Everyone I know is on their side, you see.' She bit her lip. She should have known if she met Harry all her confusion and fear would come to the surface. But perhaps it was good for her to face some things. So long as they kept off the subject of Bernie.

'What does Sandy think of them?' Harry asked.

'He thinks Spain is better off than if the Reds had won.'

'Do you agree?'

'Oh, who the hell knows?' she said with sudden emotion.

Harry smiled. 'I'm sorry, I've been going on. Let's change the subject.'

'Shall we look at the menu?'

They made their choices and the waiter brought a bottle of wine. Harry tasted it and nodded.

'Very nice.'

'Most of the wine is awful, but they have a good cellar here.'

'You can get it if you can afford it, eh?'

She glanced up at the bitterness in his voice.

'I'm starting work at an orphanage soon,' she said.

'Back to nursing?'

'Yes. I wanted to do something positive. Sandy suggested it actually.'

Harry nodded, hesitated again, then said, 'He looks well. Very prosperous.'

'He is. He's so good at organization. He's a good businessman.'

There was a pause as the waiter brought their soup, then Harry said, 'Sandy always carved out his own path. Even at school. He certainly looks successful.' He looked at her. 'Working with the Ministry of Mines, didn't he say the other night?'

Barbara shrugged. 'Yes. I don't know much about it. He says it's confidential.' She smiled sadly. 'I've become the little housewife; I don't concern myself with business matters.'

Harry nodded. The restaurant door opened. Three young men in Falange uniform appeared in the doorway. A door at the rear of the restaurant opened and a little plump man in a stained frockcoat appeared, smiling nervously at the blue-shirted visitors.

'*Buenas tardes, señor*,' one of them said cheerfully. He was about Harry's age, tall and slim with the usual pencil moustache. 'A table for three, please.' The manager bowed them to an empty table.

'I hope they don't get too raucous,' Barbara whispered.

The Falangist glanced round. Then he came over to their table, smiling broadly. He extended a hand. 'Ah, foreign visitors? *Alemanes*?'

'No. *Inglés*.' Barbara smiled nervously. The Falangist dropped his hand, though the smile remained.

'So. *Ingléses*.' He nodded cheerfully. 'Unfortunately you will have to leave soon; the Generalísimo is going to join the Führer's crusade against England. Soon we shall have Gibraltar.'

Barbara glanced nervously at Harry. His face was coldly impassive. The leader gave a mock bow and went to rejoin his friends. They looked over at her and Harry and laughed mockingly. Harry was red with anger.

'Keep quiet,' she said. 'Don't antagonize them.'

'I know,' Harry muttered. 'Bastards.'

The waiter bustled over with their main course. The man looked nervously between them and the Falangists, but they had turned to the menus.

'Let's finish quickly and get out,' she said. 'Before they start drinking.'

They hurried through the rest of the meal. Harry told her about the Maestres' party, then turned the conversation back to Sandy. He seemed to want to talk about him.

'He showed me a dinosaur claw he's found.'

She smiled. 'He gets very enthusiastic about his fossils. He's like a little boy then, it's sweet.'

'He used to say at school, fossils were the key to the secrets of the earth.'

'That sounds like Sandy.' They had finished their meal, and she saw the Falangists had started on the wine – they were laughing noisily. 'We should go.'

'Of course.' Harry signalled for the bill. The waiter brought it over at once, pleased to be rid of them, no doubt, in case the Falangists started some trouble. They paid and got their coats. Outside Harry said awkwardly, 'I was wondering, would you mind if we took a look at the Royal Palace, it's just over the road? I've never seen it close up.'

'Yes, all right. Let's do that. I've plenty of time.'

They walked across. There was a hazy sun but the afternoon was cold. Barbara buttoned up her coat. They halted before the gates. They were closed, *civiles* on guard outside. Harry studied the white walls with their ornate decorations.

'No one's painted "Arriba España" on the side,' he said.

'The Falange wouldn't touch the palace. It's a symbol for the Monarchists. They hope Franco will let King Alfonso back one day.'

She paused to light a cigarette. Harry walked to the end of the road. On the other side of high railings was a sheer drop to the palace gardens. Beyond that you could see the Casa de Campo, a jumble of brownish-green landscape. She joined him.

'The battlefield,' Harry said quietly.

'Yes. The park's still a dreadful mess, apparently. But people have started going for walks there again. There are still unexploded shells but they have safe paths marked.'

Harry looked over the park. 'I'd like to go and see it. Would you mind?'

She hesitated; she didn't want be reminded of war, of the Siege.

'Rather not?' he asked gently.

Barbara took a deep breath. 'No, let's go. Perhaps I ought to see.'

IT WAS ONLY a couple of stops on the tram. They got off and walked up a short avenue. There were other visitors walking in the same direction, a young soldier with his girlfriend and two middle-aged women in black. They rounded a little hill and suddenly they were facing a wasteland of broken ground, dotted here and there with burnt-out tanks and broken rusty artillery pieces. Nearby a brick wall, pitted with bullets, was all that was left of a building. Springy grass had grown back over most of the ground but shell craters filled with water dotted the landscape and long lines of trenches cut through the earth like open wounds. Paths led across the devastated landscape, little wooden notices every so often reminding people not to leave them because of unexploded shells. In the distance the palace stood out white and clear, like a mirage.

Barbara had imagined the sight would upset her but she felt only sadness. It reminded her of pictures of the Great War. Harry seemed more affected, his face was pale. She touched his arm gently.

'Are you all right?'

He took a deep breath. 'Yes. It brought Dunkirk back, for a moment. There was abandoned artillery everywhere there as well.'

'Do you want to go back? Perhaps we shouldn't have come.'

'No. Let's go on. Here's a path.'

They walked in silence for a while. 'They say it's worse in the north,' Barbara said. 'Where the Ebro battles were. Miles of abandoned tanks. '

Over to their left the two women in black followed another path, holding each other tightly. 'So many widows.' Barbara smiled sadly. 'I was in the same boat as them, lost, till I met Sandy.'

'How did that come about?' Harry asked.

She stopped, lighting another cigarette. 'The Red Cross sent me to Burgos, of course. It was so different from Madrid. Well behind the lines, for a start. It's a gloomy city, full of big medieval buildings. The local Red Cross was full of retired generals and worthy Spanish matrons. They were kind actually, not as paranoid as the Republicans. But they could afford to be. They knew they were going to win even then.'

'It must have been strange, working with Bernie's enemies.'

It was the first time Harry had mentioned his name. She looked at him, then looked away.

'I didn't share his politics, you know that. I was a neutral. In the Red Cross that doesn't mean something negative, wishy-washy, it's *positive*, trying to be a force to ease suffering. People don't understand that. Bernie didn't.' She turned and looked him in the eye. 'Do *you* think I've done wrong?' she asked suddenly. 'Going with a man who supports the regime? I know Sandy and Bernie weren't friends at school.'

Harry smiled. 'No. No, I'm a neutral myself by nature.'

She felt a wave of relief at his answer, somehow she couldn't have borne it if he disapproved. She looked at him, she wanted to shout, *he may be alive, he may be alive*! She bit her lip.

'You remember the state I was in, Harry. I wasn't bothering about the politics, it was a struggle just to get through my work. It was like I was surrounded by a grey fog. I had to keep quiet about Bernie, of course. You couldn't expect people who were on the Nationalist side to be happy that I went out with someone they fought.'

'No.'

They crossed a couple of wooden planks laid over a trench. There were old rotten boots in the bottom, and a pile of rusty sardine tins labelled in Russian. On the lip of the trench a notice board displayed an arrow pointing in each direction. '*Nosotros*' and '*Ellos*'. Us and them. In the distance the two women walked slowly on, still clinging to each other.

'And then you met Sandy?' Harry interrupted her thoughts.

'Yes.' She looked at him seriously. 'He rescued me, you know.'

'He told me he was out there doing tours of the battlefields.'

'Yes. I was very lonely in Burgos. Then I met him at a party and he sort of – took me up. Supported me through everything.'

'Quite a coincidence, meeting another Rookwood man.'

'Yes. Though all the English people in Nationalist Spain met at one time or another. There weren't many of us.' She smiled. 'Sandy said it was fate.'

'He used to believe in fate. He told me he didn't any more.'

'I think he does, though he doesn't want to. He's a complex man.'

'Yes. He is.' They had come to another trench. 'Watch these duckboards. Give me your arm.'

He took her hand and guided her over. Again, the 'us' and 'them' signs pointing in different directions.

'He's been very good to me,' Barbara said. 'Sandy.'

'Sorry.' Harry turned to her. 'I didn't hear. I'm still a bit deaf on that side.' His expression was momentarily lost, confused.

'I said Sandy's been good to me. He's persuaded me to do this voluntary work, he knew I needed something new.' She wondered bitterly, is it guilt that makes me defend him like this?

'Good.' Harry's tone was careful, neutral. Barbara thought with sudden surprise, he doesn't like Sandy. Then why had he made friends with him again?

'He's trying to help some of the Jews who fled from France.'

'Yes. He mentioned that.'

'When the Germans invaded a lot of them fled down here with nothing but what they could carry. They try to get to Portugal and then on to America. They're terrified of the Nazis. There's a committee that tries to help them and Sandy's on it.'

'There was a Falange demonstration at the embassy recently, yelling anti-semitic slogans at the tops of their voices.'

'The regime have to toe the Nazi line, but they let Sandy's committee carry on so long as they're discreet.'

Over in the distance the two women had stopped. One was crying, the other held her close. Barbara looked at Harry again. 'Sandy and I aren't really married, did he tell you that?'

He hesitated. 'Yes.'

She reddened. 'Perhaps you think we're awful. But we – we weren't ready for that step.'

'I understand,' he said awkwardly. 'These aren't normal times.'

'Are you still with that girl, what was her name?'

'Laura. No, that ended ages ago. I'm single at the moment.' Harry looked at the Royal Palace in the distance. 'Do you think you'll stay in Spain?' he asked.

'I don't know. I don't know what the future will bring.'

He turned to her. 'I hate it,' he said with sudden passion. 'I hate what Franco's done. I used to have this idea of Spain, the romanticism of its winding streets and decayed buildings. I don't know why, perhaps because when I came here in '31 there was a spirit of hope, even among people with nothing, like the Mera family. Do you remember them?'

'Yes. But Harry, those dreams, socialism, it's all over—'

'I went to the square where they lived last week, it had been bombed or shelled. Their flat was gone. There was a man – ' he paused, then went on, his eyes bright with anger – 'a man who was attacked by some dogs that had gone wild. I helped him, took him home. He lives in a tiny damp flat with his mother, she's had a stroke but I don't think she gets any care, and a little boy who went half mad when his parents were taken away, and his sister, this bright intelligent girl who was a medical student but works in a dairy now.' He took a deep breath. 'There's the New Spain.'

She sighed. 'I know, you're right. I feel guilty at how we live, among all that. I don't tell Sandy but I do.'

He nodded. He seemed calmer again, the anger gone. Barbara studied his face. She sensed there was more to his anger and disillusion than meeting a poor family, but she didn't understand what.

He smiled suddenly. 'Sorry to go on like that. Ignore me, I'm just tired.'

'No. You're right to remind me.' She smiled. 'Doesn't look like you're still neutral, though.'

He laughed bitterly. 'No. Maybe not. Things change.'

They had arrived at the Manzanares, the little river that ran through the west of the city. Ahead was a bridge, then stairs leading up to the palace gardens.

'We can get back to the palace from here,' Barbara said.

'Yes. I'd better get back to the embassy.'

'Are you sure you're all right, Harry?' she asked suddenly. 'You seem – I don't know – preoccupied.'

'I'm fine. It's just, you know, Hendaye and everything. Everyone's jumpy at the embassy.' He smiled. 'We must have dinner again. You could come round to my flat. I'll give Sandy a ring.'

Chapter Nineteen

SANDY WAS HOME when Barbara returned to the house. He was in the *salón*, reading the paper and smoking one of the big cigars that filled the room with thick, heavy smoke.

'Just got back?' he asked.

'Yes. We went for a walk in the Casa de Campo.'

'What did you want to go there for? It's still full of unexploded bombs.'

'It's safe now. Harry wanted to go.'

'How was he?'

'A bit down. I think Dunkirk affected him more than he lets on.'

Sandy smiled through the haze of smoke. 'He needs to find himself a girl.'

'Perhaps.'

'What d'you want to do on Thursday? A dinner?'

'What?' She looked at him, puzzled.

'It's the third anniversary of the day we met. You hadn't forgotten?' He looked hurt.

'No – no, of course not. Let's have dinner somewhere, that would be good.' She smiled. 'Sandy, I'm a bit tired, I think I'll go and lie down for a bit before dinner.'

'Yes, all right.' She could tell he was annoyed that she had forgotten the anniversary. It had completely slipped her mind.

When she went out Pilar was coming up the corridor. She looked at Barbara with those dark expressionless eyes. 'Shall I make up the fire, *señora*? Only it is getting a little cold.'

'See what Mr Forsyth thinks, Pilar. He's in the lounge.'

'Very well, *señora*.' The girl raised her eyebrows a little; household matters were the mistress's province. Barbara couldn't be bothered. A heavy tiredness had descended on her on the way home from the meeting with Harry, she had to lie down. She went up and stretched out on the bed. She closed her eyes but her mind was whirling with images: Harry's visit to Madrid after Bernie disappeared, the end of hope that Bernie was still alive, then Burgos, Burgos where she had met Sandy.

SHE HAD ARRIVED in the Nationalist capital in May 1937, as summer began, bright blue sunshine falling on brown ancient buildings. Crossing the lines was impossible; she had had to travel all the way from Madrid to France, then back again across the frontier with Nationalist Spain. On the way she had read a speech by Dr Marti, the venerable Red Cross statesman, to delegates in Spain. Do not choose sides, he had said, take only a clinical point of view of how best to help. That was what she must continue to do, she told herself. Travelling to Franco's Spain wasn't a betrayal of Bernie; she was going there to do her job, as she had in the Republican zone.

They put Barbara to work in the section that tried to send messages between family members left on different sides of the lines by the war. A lot of it was familiar administrative work, light compared to dealing with the prisoners and children. She knew from their solicitous manner that her colleagues knew about Bernie. She found herself resenting being treated with gentle sympathy, she who had always been in charge, the organizer. She developed a sharp, brittle manner with them.

She never spoke about Bernie to them, and she would not have dared to mention him to the Spaniards she met, officials and the middle-class matrons and retired colonels of the Spanish Red Cross. They were always civil, with an exaggerated politeness that made her nostalgic for the informality of the Republican zone, but at the meetings and receptions she had to go to they sometimes showed an anger and contempt for what she was doing. 'I do not agree with exchanging captured soldiers,' one old soldier from the Spanish Red Cross told her one day. 'Children, yes, messages between separated families, yes, but to exchange a Spanish gentleman for Red dog – never!' He concluded with such fierceness that a spray of spittle hit her chin. She turned away, went to the toilet, and vomited.

As the summer went on she found herself getting more depressed, more withdrawn from the people around her, as though surrounded by a thin grey fog. Summer changed to autumn and cold winds began blowing through the narrow, gloomy streets where people sat hunched in cafes and trucks of grim-looking soldiers passed through endlessly. She put everything into her work, into doing something, *achieving* something positive, creeping back exhausted to her little flat in the evenings.

For a few weeks in October she shared the flat with Cordelia, a volunteer nurse from England who had come to Burgos on leave. She was an aristocratic English girl who'd been a novice nun but found she didn't have a vocation.

'So I came out here to try and do some good,' she said, a serious look on her kind ugly face.

'I suppose I did too,' Barbara replied.

'For all the people who have been persecuted for their religious beliefs.'

Barbara remembered the church she and Bernie had visited the day the plane fell, that had been converted into a stable. The frightened sheep in the corner. 'People are being persecuted for all types of belief. In both zones.'

'You were in the Red zone, weren't you? What was it like?'

'Surprisingly like here in a lot of ways.' She looked Cordelia in the eye. 'I had a boyfriend there. An English International Brigader, he was killed at the Jarama.'

Barbara had been trying to shock Cordelia, but she only nodded, looking sad. 'I'll pray for him, light a candle.'

'Don't,' Barbara said. 'Bernie would have hated that.' She paused. 'I haven't spoken his name aloud for months. Pray if you like, that can't do any harm, but don't light a candle.'

'You were fond of him.'

Barbara didn't reply.

'You should try to get out a little,' Cordelia said. 'You spend too much time here.'

'I'm too tired.'

'There's a fundraising dinner at the church I go to—'

Barbara shook her head. 'I'm not going to turn to religion, Cordelia.'

'I didn't mean that. Just that you shouldn't dwell on the past.'

'I don't dwell on it. I try not to think about him, though the feelings are always there, squashed down. The –' she looked into Cordelia's face, then shouted – 'the bloody *anger*! That he could go and leave me like that, go and get himself bloody killed, the bastard!' She began crying, her body shaking with howls and sobs. 'There, I've shocked you,' she said through her tears. 'I wanted to shock you.' She laughed, it sounded hysterical. She felt a tentative hand on her shoulder.

'Let it out,' she heard Cordelia say. 'You have to get it out somehow. I know. I've got a brother, he went to the bad, I loved him very much and I was angry with him, too, inside, furious. Don't bury yourself in it, don't.'

BARBARA LET Cordelia take her out sometimes, though she drew the line at church functions. Sometimes she felt awkward and clumsy and couldn't be bothered to talk, but occasionally she met someone who was kind or interesting to talk to and the grey fog would lift a little. On the last day of October, just before Cordelia's leave ended, they went to a party given by an official from Texas Oil, the company whose support kept Franco in fuel. She didn't enjoy it; it was a glitzy reception in the best hotel in Burgos, loud Americans standing around, happy in the deference the Spanish guests showed them. She thought of what Bernie would have said, the international capitalist conspiracy in its peacock feathers or something like that. Cordelia was talking to a Spanish priest. Barbara stood on her own, smoking and sipping bad wine, and watched her. She would be going soon, her leave over. Barbara had grown fond of her despite the fact they had nothing in common apart from a sense that they were not cut out to be ordinary wives and mothers. Looking at her she knew she would miss her, miss her undemanding kindness. She felt suddenly dowdy among all the richly dressed women and decided to slip away. She turned to go, and saw a man was standing beside her. She hadn't seen him approach. He smiled, showing large white teeth.

'Was that English I heard you and your friend talking earlier?'

Barbara smiled uncertainly. 'Yes.' She introduced herself. She thought there was something a little flashy about the man, although he had a nice smile. He told her his name was Sandy Forsyth and he was a guide for English tourists looking at the battlefields. His upper-class drawl reminded her of Bernie.

'It's all very propagandist,' he said. 'I show them the battlefields and go into the military stuff, but slip in lots about Red atrocities. It's usually old buffers with military interests. They're amazingly ignorant. One asked if it was true the Basques all had six fingers.'

Barbara laughed. Encouraged, he told her about a busload of elderly English tourists stuck by the side of the road when the bus broke down, too inhibited to relieve their bursting bladders in the bushes and standing by the bus in agonies. She laughed again; it was months since anyone had made her laugh. He smiled.

'I knew somehow that I could tell you that story and you wouldn't be shocked, though it's not really for mixed company.'

'I'm a nurse. I've been in Spain over a year, on both sides of the lines. Nothing shocks me now.'

Sandy nodded, interested. He offered her a cigarette and they stood surveying the company for a moment.

'Well,' Sandy asked. 'What do you think of the New Spain and its friends?'

'I suppose it seems very orderly after Madrid. But it's got a hard military feel. A hard place.' She looked at Cordelia, still deep in conversation with the priest. 'Maybe the Church will be a moderating influence.'

Sandy blew out a cloud of smoke. 'Don't you believe it. The Church knows what side its bread's buttered on; it'll let the regime do what it likes. They're going to win, you know, they've got the troops and the money. They know it, you can see it in their faces. It's just a matter of time.'

'You think so?'

'Oh yes.'

'Are you a Catholic?'

He laughed. 'Heavens, no.'

'My friend over there is. Yes, you're right, they're going to win.' She sighed.

'Better than the alternative.'

'Perhaps.'

'I might stay on when it's over. I'm tired of England.'

'No family ties?'

'No. You?'

'None to speak of.'

'Fancy coming out for a drink one evening? I'm between jobs. I'm looking into getting some other work but it's a bit lonesome here.'

She looked at him in surprise, she hadn't expected that.

'No strings,' Sandy added. 'Just for a drink. Bring your friend Cordelia if you like.'

'Yes, all right,' she said. 'Why not?' Though she knew, somehow, that Cordelia wouldn't approve of Sandy.

When the evening came she didn't want to go. Cordelia couldn't come, she had another church function to attend, and Barbara felt tired and depressed after work. But she had agreed to go so she did.

They met in a dark, quiet little bar near the cathedral. Sandy asked what sort of a day she had had at work. The question irritated her slightly; he had asked it as though she worked in an office or a shop.

'A bit grim, actually. They've moved me on to trying to get some children evacuated across the lines. Most of them are orphans. That's always ghastly.' She turned away, tears pricking unexpectedly at her eyes. 'I'm sorry,' she said. 'I've had a long day and this new work brings back – bad memories.'

'Do you want to talk about it?' he asked, with gentle curiosity.

She decided to tell him. Cordelia was right, it was no use just bottling it all up. 'When I was working in Madrid there was this man – an Englishman in the International Brigades, actually. We were together over last winter. Then he went to the Jarama. Missing believed killed.'

Sandy nodded. 'I'm very sorry.'

'It's only been nine months, it's hard to get over.' She sighed. 'It's a common enough story in Spain these days, I know.'

He offered her a cigarette, lit it for her. 'One of the volunteers?'

'Yes, Bernie was a Communist. Though he wasn't working class, not really; he'd got a scholarship to a public school, he spoke like you. I found out later the party thought he might be ideologically suspect because of his complicated class origins. Not enough of a man of steel.'

She looked at Sandy and was surprised to see that he had leaned back in his seat and was looking at her with an intent, frowning stare.

'Which public school did he go to?' he asked quietly.

'A place called Rookwood, in Surrey.'

'His last name wasn't Piper, by any chance?'

'Yes.' It was her turn to be shocked. 'Yes, that's right. Did you—'

'I was at Rookwood for a while. I knew Piper. Not very well, but I knew him. I don't suppose he ever mentioned me?' Sandy laughed, a strange forced bark. 'The bad hat of the form.'

'No. He didn't talk about his school much. Only that he wasn't happy there.'

'No. We had that in common, I remember.'

'Were you friends?' Barbara's heart had leapt, it was as though a part of Bernie himself had returned.

Sandy hesitated. 'Not really. Like I said, I didn't know him well.' He shook his head. 'God, this is a coincidence.'

She smiled. 'It's like fate. Meeting someone who knew him.'

The fact Sandy had known Bernie, even if they hadn't been friends, drew Barbara to him. They took to meeting every Thursday in the bar for drinks. She found herself looking forward to those nights. Cordelia had gone back to the front and these were her only nights out now. She had left one morning, giving Barbara a quick hug and refusing an offer to help carry her bags to the station. Barbara had thanked her for helping her begin to recover a little, but Cordelia had smiled and said that she would have done the same for anyone, her faith and love of God required it of her. The impersonal reply had hurt Barbara, left her feeling very alone again.

She learned that Sandy had known Harry, too, been his friend if not Bernie's. He puzzled her in some ways. He was enigmatic, saying next to nothing about himself. He had no tours on at the moment but he stayed on in Burgos, trying to set up some business, he said. He would never tell her what. He was always immaculately dressed. Barbara wondered if he had a girlfriend somewhere but he never mentioned anyone. It crossed her mind that he might be a pansy but he didn't seem to be. He was lonely too, though, you could see that.

One Thursday in December Barbara hurried to the cafe through cold relentless rain that hammered down from the darkened sky. When she arrived Sandy was already there, sitting at their usual table with a man in Falange uniform. Their heads were bent together, and although she couldn't hear what they were saying, Barbara could tell they were arguing. She hesitated, rain dripping from her coat to the floor. Sandy, seeing her, waved her over.

'Sorry, Barbara, I was just finishing some business.'

The Falangist stood up. He glanced at her. He was a middle-aged man with a stern face. He looked down at Sandy.

'Business that should be for Spaniards, *señor*,' he said. 'Spanish business, Spanish profits.' He bowed curtly to Barbara and walked away, heels clacking on the floorboards. Sandy looked after him, his face set and angry. She sat down, embarrassed. Sandy pulled himself together, gave a brittle laugh.

'Sorry about that,' he said. 'Plan I had for some work, it's fallen through. They don't seem too keen on enterprise here.' He sighed. 'Never mind. Back to the tours, I suppose.'

He got Barbara a drink and came back to the table.

'Perhaps you should think about going home,' she said. 'I've been wondering about what I'll do when the war ends. I don't think I want to go back to Geneva.'

He shook his head. 'I don't want to go back,' he said quietly. 'I've nobody there. England's stifling.'

'I know what you mean.' She raised her glass. 'To rootlessness.'

He smiled. 'To rootlessness. You know, that first night we met, I thought, there's a girl who stands apart, watching. Like me.'

'Did you?'

'Yes.'

She sighed. 'I don't like myself very much,' she said. 'That's why I stand apart.'

'Because you're angry with Bernie?'

'With Bernie? No. It's not that. He made me like myself a little. For a while.'

Sandy looked at her seriously. 'You shouldn't leave it to other people to make you like yourself. I know, I was the same once.'

'You?' She was surprised. He always seemed so confident, so sure of himself.

'Only before I was old enough to think for myself.'

She took a deep breath. 'I had a bad time at school. I was bullied.' She paused but he only nodded encouragingly. She told him the story. 'I hear their voices in my head sometimes, you know. No, not hear them, that would mean I'm mad, but I remember them. When I'm tired and make mistakes at work. Telling me I'm ugly, speccy four-eyes, no good. More since Bernie died.' She bowed her head. 'I don't talk about it. Only Bernie knew.'

'Then I am privileged you've told me.'

She didn't look up. 'I feel I can tell you things. I don't know why.'

'Look up,' he said quietly. 'Look up at me, don't be afraid.'

She raised her head, smiling bravely, blinking back tears.

'Tell them to get lost,' he said. 'When you hear them, tell them they're wrong and you'll show them all. Not out loud but in your head. That's what I did. With my parents, masters, telling me I was destined to go to the devil.'

'Did it work? Yes, it must have – you believe in yourself, don't you?'

'You have to. You have to decide what you want to be and then *go* there. Don't listen to other people's opinion of you. Everyone's looking for someone to put down. It makes them feel safe.'

'Not everyone. I'm not.'

'All right. Most people. Can I tell you something?'

'If you like.'

'You won't be offended?'

'No.'

'You don't make the best of yourself. It's as though you don't *want* to be respected. Just put a little effort into your clothes, your hair, you could be a very attractive woman.'

She lowered her head again.

'That was the other thing I thought, the night we met.' She felt the tips of his fingers touch hers. There was a moment's silence. She had a vivid memory of the church, Bernie kissing her. She pulled her hand away, looked up.

'I'm not – I'm not ready for this. After Bernie, I don't think I can ever—'

'Oh, come on, Barbara,' he said gently. 'Don't tell me you believe that romantic stuff about there only being one person for everyone.'

'I think I do, actually.' She wanted to go, the turmoil of feelings inside her made her feel sick. He raised a hand.

'All right. Forget it.'

'I just want to be friends, Sandy.'

'You need someone to look after you, Barbara.' He smiled. 'I've always wanted someone to look after.'

'No, Sandy. No. Just friends.'

He nodded. 'All right. All right. Let me look after you a bit, anyway.'

She leaned her head on her hand, hiding her face. They sat there in silence. The rain hissed down outside.

Autumn turned to winter. There were rumours of a new Nationalist offensive that would end the war. For a while Burgos was full of Italian soldiers, then they disappeared again.

Sandy kept his word; he made no more romantic overtures. She didn't feel the same towards him as she had towards Bernie, that was impossible. Yet almost despite herself, she felt thrilled and excited that another man had found her attractive. She realized that part, a small part, of her grief had been for herself, that her only chance of love had come and gone. As though his declaration had unlocked something, she began to think of him as a man, a large strong man.

In mid-December the news came that the Republicans had preempted Franco's offensive with one of their own at Teruel, far to the east. The weather was cold, there was snow on the ground in Burgos, and in the office they heard of soldiers having frostbitten feet amputated on the battlefield. The Red Cross office was busy again.

'You should give it up,' Sandy said to her when they met that Thursday evening. 'It's wearing you out.' He looked at her with concern but also with that hint of impatience she had seen recently.

Last week, for the first time, he had tried to take her hand as they left the bar. They had had more than usual to drink, he had kept ordering more wine. She had pulled it away.

She sighed. 'It's what I do. I've cancelled my Christmas leave to help.'

'I thought you were going home. To Birmingham?'

'I was. But I didn't really want to, I'm glad of the excuse.' She looked at him. 'What about you? You never talk about your family, Sandy, all I know is you have a father and a brother.'

'And a mother, somewhere, if she's still alive. I told you, I've broken with them. They belong in the past.' He looked at her. 'I am going away for a couple of weeks, though.'

'Oh?' She felt her heart sink; she had relied on him being with her over Christmas.

'Business opportunity. Importing cars from England. They don't like outsiders getting involved in their deals, I've learned that, but they'll need someone with English for this job. I'm going up to San Sebastián to look into it.'

She remembered the Falangist he had had the argument with. 'I see. It sounds a good opportunity. But it's a bad time of year to travel, and the roads will be full of soldiers, with this battle—'

'Not the roads north. I'll try and get back for Christmas Day.'

'Yes. It would be nice to celebrate it together.'

'I'll try.'

He wasn't there, though. The call to the office she had hoped for never came. It affected her more than she would have expected. On Christmas Day she went for a walk alone through the snowy streets, looking enviously into the houses with their Nativity scenes in the gardens, the families going in and out of services in Burgos's innumerable churches. She felt a sudden angry impatience with herself. Why didn't she take what Sandy had offered her? What was she waiting for? Old age? She thought of Bernie and sorrow clutched at her heart again, but Bernie was gone.

He phoned her at the office two days after Christmas. 'Sorry I took so long,' he said.

She smiled at the sound of his voice. 'How did it go?'

'Very well. You're talking to a man with an import licence signed by the trade minister himself. Listen, want to go to the bar tonight? I know it's not Thursday.'

She laughed. 'Yes, that would be nice. Usual time?'

'See you at eight. We'll have some champagne, celebrate the deal.'

She wore her new coat, the green one Sandy had picked for her that he said went well with her hair. He was there before her as usual, a large brightly coloured parcel on the table. He smiled.

'A belated Christmas present. To say sorry for being away so long.'

She opened it. Inside was a brooch in the shape of a flower. It was made of gold, little green stones glinting in the petals.

'Oh, Sandy,' she said. 'It's wonderful. Are those—'

He smiled. 'Emeralds. Just little ones.'

'You shouldn't, it must have cost the earth.'

'Not if you know where to look.'

'Thank you.' Her lip trembled. 'I'm not worth it.'

'I say you are.' He reached out and took her hand. This time she didn't withdraw.

He looked into her eyes. 'Take off your glasses,' he said. 'I want to see your face without your glasses.'

Chapter Twenty

On the Wednesday after her walk with Harry, Barbara went to meet Luis for the third time. It was a warm, sunny autumn day. As she walked down the Castellana dry leaves crunched underfoot and there was a faint tang of smoke from leaves burning somewhere. Barbara walked more and more lately; it helped her to think and she increasingly disliked being in the house.

Her money had not come from England and she was beginning to despair of it ever arriving. If Luis provided her with the proof she had asked for that Bernie was in the camp, she would have to chase it up somehow.

He was at the cafe already. He was smoking a good brand of cigarettes and she wondered if some of the money she had given him for the journey to Cuenca had gone on them; she didn't know how much the fare was. She only had his word, of course, that he had actually been anywhere.

He got up and shook her hand, formally polite as ever, then went and fetched her a cup of coffee. The cafe was quiet, the one-legged veteran with the sewn-up trouser-leg alone at the bar.

She lit a cigarette, glancing deliberately at his own packet. 'Did you get to Cuenca?' she asked.

'I did, *señora*.' He smiled. 'I met Agustín in the town again.' He leaned forward. 'Agustín managed to get a look at Bernard Piper's file, though it was not easy. He told me many details.'

She nodded. 'Yes.'

'He was born in a place called the Island of Dogs, in London. He came to fight for the Republic in 1936 and suffered a small arm wound in the battles in the Casa de Campo.'

Barbara's heart quickened. There was no way Luis, or Markby, could have known about that wound other than by looking at an official record.

'When he recovered he was sent to the Jarama, wounded and taken prisoner.'

'Wounded?' she asked sharply. 'How badly?'

'Not serious. A flesh wound in the thigh.' Luis smiled. 'He bore a charmed life, it seemed.'

'Not that charmed, Luis, if he ended up in the camp.'

'Agustín described him,' Luis continued. 'He is a tall man, broad in the shoulders, with fair hair. Probably a very handsome man, Agustín said, though now of course he has a scrubby beard and lice.' Barbara winced. 'He is known to be a difficult man, his spirit is unbowed. Agustín has told him to be careful, that better times may be coming, though no more than that for now.' Luis smiled wryly. 'He says your man has *duende*. Courage, class. He thinks he has the will to try and escape. Many in the camp have lost the will, or the energy.'

Barbara's heart was thumping wildly. She knew now it was all true, she was certain. Luis put his head on one side. 'Are you satisfied, *señora*? Satisfied that I have told you the truth?'

'Yes. Yes, I am. Thank you, Luis.' She took a deep breath. 'I haven't had the money through from my bank in England yet. It's difficult getting money out of the country now.'

He looked at her seriously. 'It is very important to get this done before the bad weather sets in. The winters are hard up there, and start early. It will be getting cold already.'

'And the diplomatic situation may change. I know. I'll chase them, I'll write again today. What if I meet you here, a week today again. I'll have the money by then, one way or another. If it comes sooner, is there any way I can get in touch with you?'

'I have no telephone, *señora*. Could I telephone you?'

She hesitated. 'Safer not. I don't want my husband learning anything, he's worried about me as it is.'

'A week, then. But we must make some arrangements then, one way or another. We will be into November soon.'

'Yes, I know.' As she spoke she thought, this doesn't leave time for me to write again. What if I asked Harry for a loan? She knew he had money. But he was a diplomat, it would be dangerous for him—

She forced her mind back to the present. 'The plan,' she asked Luis. 'It is still the same? Agustín helps him escape and I pick him up in Cuenca?'

'Yes. There may be some way that we can get him civilian clothes, so he will not be so conspicuous. Agustín is looking into that. Then it would be up to you, *señora*, to get him away and to the embassy.'

'That might not be so easy. I've walked past there, there are *civiles* outside.'

'You must resolve that one, *señora*,' Luis said with a little smile. He seemed to have lost interest now, it wouldn't be his problem once Barbara picked Bernie up.

'I'll pay you some when we have a firm plan in place, and the rest when it's all done,' Barbara said. 'It's in all our interests the whole thing goes through.'

He looked at her. 'You will make sure of that, I know.'

Barbara thought of Harry again. If she could bring Bernie into Madrid, hide him somewhere. She sighed. She became aware of Luis looking at her curiously.

'What is it?' she asked.

'Forgive me asking, *señora*, but will this matter not have consequences for you and your husband? If Señor Piper reaches the embassy the matter is likely to become public knowledge, surely. At the least, representations will be made to our government. And your husband works with the government, does he not? You said so at our first meeting.'

'Yes, Luis,' she said quietly. 'There may be consequences. I shall have to deal with them.'

He looked at her seriously. 'You are a brave woman, to put your future at risk.'

She studied him. His face was tired and strained. He wasn't much more than a boy really, made to deal with awful things too young, like half the men in the world today. 'What will you and your brother do, Luis, when this is done and your brother gets out of the army?'

He smiled sadly. 'I have a dream of us fetching my mother from Sevilla, getting somewhere to live in the country near Madrid, and perhaps growing vegetables. I have always liked growing things, and a big city needs vegetables, does it not? And we will all be together again, as a family.' His face darkened. 'Family is important to Spaniards, the war split up so many – you who come from England cannot know the pain of it. It is because of that I must do whatever I have to do to bring us together again. Can you understand that, *señora*?'

'Yes. I hope you are able to do that.'

'So do I.' He bowed his head a moment, closing his eyes, then looked up with a smile. 'Until next week, *señora*.'

'I'll have the money. One way or another.'

That evening over dinner Sandy told her he had booked a table at the Ritz for their anniversary the following night.

'Oh,' she said, surprised.

'What's wrong with that?' he asked. He still hadn't forgiven her for forgetting. 'It's the most expensive hotel in Madrid.'

'I know, Sandy. Only, it's always so full of the Germans and their Italian pals. You know I hate seeing them.'

He smiled. 'Chance to show the flag.' She wondered if he had chosen the Ritz deliberately to upset her. She looked at him, remembering his tenderness to her when they first met. Where had it gone? It was her discontent he didn't like, she realized, her discontent with the life he had chosen for her that had been growing for a long time but had only really emerged since that dinner with Markby.

'Do you remember that first Christmas after we met?' he asked her, a hard mocking expression in his eyes.

'Yes. When you went away on business, and couldn't come back till after Christmas.'

'That's right.'

He smiled. 'Only I could have. We finalized the deal before Christmas, I could have come back. But I knew that if I stayed away you'd realize how much you needed me. And I was right.'

She stared at him, she felt shocked and then furiously angry. 'So you manipulated me,' she said quietly. 'Manipulated my feelings.'

He looked at her across the table, seriously now. 'I know what people want, Barbara, I can sense it. It's a gift, very useful in business. I see below the surface. Sometimes it's easy. The Jews, for instance, they just want survival, they tremble and shake in their desperation to survive. The people I work with, what they want is usually money, though occasionally it's something else. Whatever it is I try to help oblige them. You wanted me and you wanted security, only you couldn't quite bring yourself to see it. I just helped bring that to the surface.' He inclined his head, raised his glass.

'And what about you, Sandy? What do you want?'

He smiled. 'Success, money. Knowing I can cut the mustard, make people give me what I want.'

'You're a shit sometimes, Sandy,' she said. 'You know that?'

She had never spoken to him like that before and he looked taken aback for a moment. Then his face set.

'You've been letting your appearance go lately, you know. You look a mess. I hope working at that orphanage will help you pull yourself together.'

She felt the words like a blow even as she realized he had chosen them because they would hit her where she was weakest. Something cold and hard came into her mind and she thought, don't react, the facade needs to be kept up for now. She got up, laying her napkin carefully on the table, and left the room. Her legs were shaking.

Part Two

☆

THE BEGINNING OF WINTER

Chapter Twenty-One

THE PSYCHIATRIST was a tall thin man with spectacles and silver hair. He wore a grey pinstripe suit. Bernie hadn't seen anyone wearing a suit for three and a half years, only the prisoners' boiler suits and the functional guards' uniforms, both a drab olive-green.

The doctor had been installed in the room under the *comandante*'s hut, behind a scratched table brought from the offices above. Bernie guessed he hadn't been told what the room was used for. It was just like Aranda's macabre sense of humour to put him here.

Agustín, one of the guards, had been waiting for Bernie when his work detail returned from the quarry, with orders to take him to the *comandante*. 'It is nothing to worry about, not trouble,' he whispered as they crossed the square. Bernie had nodded his thanks. Agustín was one of the better ones, an untidy young man who liked a quiet life. The sun was low and a cold wind blew down from the mountains. Bernie kept track of the days and knew this was the first of November; winter was almost here. The shepherds were starting to bring their flocks down from the high pastures. Working on the quarry detail was hard but at least you got some sense of the rhythms of the outside world. He shivered, envying Agustín the heavy poncho he wore over his uniform.

Comandante Aranda sat behind his desk. He stared up at Bernie with his hard eyes, a humorous expression on his long handsome face with its luxuriant black moustache.

'Ah, Piper,' he said. 'I have a visitor for you.'

'*¿Señor?*' Bernie stood rigidly to attention, the way Aranda expected. A spasm of pain went through his arm; his old wound hurt after a day moving rocks.

'Do you remember in San Pedro de Cardena, you were evaluated by a psychiatrist?'

'*Si, señor*.' It had been a bizarre interlude, a joke in hell. San Pedro was an abandoned medieval monastery outside Burgos. Thousands of Republican prisoners had been crammed in there after the Jarama battle. One day they had been given thick questionnaires to fill in. They were told it was for a project about the psychology of Marxist fanaticism. Two hundred questions, varying from his reaction to certain colours to his degree of patriotism.

The *comandante* lit a cigarette, studying him through a curling haze of smoke with his cold hazel eyes. Aranda had been in charge of the Tierra Muerte camp for nearly a year. He was a colonel, a veteran of the Civil War and before that the Foreign Legion. He enjoyed cruelty and even Bernie wouldn't have dared be insolent with him. As always the *comandante* was immaculately dressed, his uniform ironed into knife-edge creases. The prisoners knew every line and curve of his handsome bronzed face with its waxed moustache. If he was frowning or wore his pouting childish look, someone could be in for a beating.

This evening, though, he looked amused. He blew smoke at Bernie; at once Bernie's craving for tobacco returned and he found himself leaning forward slightly to catch another whiff.

'They are doing a follow-up study, prisoners of special interest. Dr Lorenzo is waiting for you downstairs. And Piper, be sure to cooperate with him, *¿vale?*'

'*Sí, señor comandante*.'

Bernie's heart was thumping as Agustín led him down to the basement room, opening the heavy wooden door. He had never been there but had heard the room graphically described.

The psychiatrist's face was cold. 'You may leave us,' he told Agustín.

'I shall be outside, *señor*.'

The psychiatrist waved a hand at a steel chair in front of the desk. 'Sit down.' Bernie slumped into it; he was very tired. An oil stove had been put in a corner and the room was hot. The psychiatrist ran a silver pen down the columns of a questionnaire. Bernie recognized his own writing. The lice in his beard stirred, roused by the heat.

The psychiatrist looked up. 'You are Piper, Bernard, English, age thirty-one?'

'Yes.'

'I am Dr Lorenzo. Three years ago, when you were in San Pedro, you answered a questionnaire. You recall?

'Yes, *doctor*.'

'The purpose of the study was to determine the psychological factors that cause people to embrace Marxism.' His voice was even, monotonous. 'Most Marxists are ignorant working people of low intelligence and culture. We wish to look again at the people who did not match those criteria. You, for example.' He studied Bernie keenly.

'What brings people to Marxism is simple,' Bernie said quietly. 'Poverty and oppression.'

The psychiatrist nodded. 'Yes, that is what I would expect you to say. And yet you can have been subject to none of those things; I see you attended an English public school.'

'My parents were poor. I got a place at Rookwood under a scholarship.' Bernie found his eyes straying to the corner of the room, where a tall object was covered by a tarpaulin. Lorenzo tapped the desk sharply with the silver pen.

'Pay attention, please. Tell me about your parents – what did they do?'

'They worked in a shop someone else owned.'

'And you felt sorry for them perhaps? You were close to them?'

A picture of his mother came into Bernie's head, standing in the parlour wringing her hands. 'Bernie, Bernie, why do you have to go to this awful war?' He shrugged.

'They may be dead now for all I know. I've never been allowed to write.'

'You would write if you could?'

'Yes.'

Lorenzo made another note. 'This school, this Rookwood, that would have brought you into contact with boys of a higher culture. It interests me that you rejected those values.'

Bernie laughed bitterly. 'There was no culture there. And their class was the enemy of mine.'

'Ah, yes, the Marxist metaphysic.' The psychiatrist nodded reflectively. 'Our studies show that when intelligent, privileged people are drawn to Marxism it is because of a character defect. They are unable to understand the higher values, like spirituality and patriotism. They are innately antisocial and aggressive. The *comandante* tells me, Piper, that you reject the camp's rehabilitative efforts, for example?'

Bernie laughed quietly. 'You mean the compulsory religious instruction?'

Lorenzo studied him as though he were a rat in a laboratory cage. 'Yes, you would hate Christianity. A religion of love and reconciliation. Yes, that is quite clear.'

'We get other lessons as well.'

Dr Lorenzo looked puzzled. 'What do you mean?'

'This is the torture room. That cupboard behind you will be full of rubber truncheons and pails for mock drownings.'

Lorenzo shook his head gently. 'Fantasies.'

'Then take the tarpaulin off the thing behind you,' Bernie said. 'Go on.' He realized his tone was becoming insolent and bit his lip. He did not want a complaint to Aranda.

The psychiatrist gave a little grunt of annoyance, then stood and lifted the tarpaulin. His face set as he saw the tall wooden stake with the metal seat, the restraining straps and neck collar, the heavy brass screw with its handles behind.

'The *garrote vil, doctor*. They've had six executions since I've been here. They line us up in the yard, bring out the *garrote* and make us watch. You hear the man's neck break, there's a loud crack, like a shot.'

The psychiatrist sat down again. His voice was still calm. He looked steadily at Bernie, then shook his head. 'You are an antisocial,' he said quietly. 'A psychopath.' He shook his head. 'Men such as you can never be rehabilitated; your minds are abnormal, incomplete. The *garrote* is needed, I am afraid, to keep those like you in check.' He made a note on the questionnaire, then called out to Agustín. 'Guard! I have finished with this man.'

Agustín led Bernie away. The sun had gone below the horizon and a red light bathed the wooden huts lining the earthen square. The searchlights in the watchtower above the barbed-wire fence would soon come on. Against the mess hut a large cross stood, six feet high, ropes hanging from the arms. It looked like a religious symbol, but it wasn't: they hung men from the ropes as a punishment. Bernie wished he had mentioned that to the psychiatrist.

It was time for roll-call; three hundred prisoners were shambling into lines around the little wooden platform in the middle. Agustín halted, shifting his heavy rifle on his shoulder.

'I have to fetch another five to the mad-doctor tonight,' he said. 'It will be a long evening.'

Bernie looked at him in surprise. The guards were not supposed to talk with the prisoners.

'The doctor looked displeased,' Agustín added.

Bernie looked at him, but the guard's thin face was turned away. 'Be careful,' Agustín said quietly. 'Better times may be ahead, Piper. I can say no more now. But be careful. Do not get punished now, or killed.'

BERNIE STOOD next to his friend Vicente. The lawyer's thin face, surrounded by its shock of grey hair and matted beard, looked drawn and ill. He smiled at Bernie then coughed, a liquid gurgling sound deep in his chest. Vicente had been having chest infections since the summer; he seemed to recover but then they would hit him again, worse than before. Some of the guards let him do light work in return for helping them fill in forms, but this week the sergeant in charge of the quarry detail was Ramirez, a brutal man who had had Vicente sorting rocks all day. He looked as though he could hardly stand.

'What happened to you?' he whispered to Bernie.

'They've got a psychiatrist here, he's interviewing some of the people from San Pedro. He said I was an antisocial psychopath.'

Vicente smiled wryly. 'Then that proves what I have always said, you are a good man even if you are a Bolshevik. If one of these people says you are normal, then is the time to worry. You've missed dinner.'

'I'll manage,' Bernie said. He must be sure to get a good night's sleep if he was to be fit to work tomorrow. The rice they fed the prisoners was awful, the sweepings of some Valencian storehouse mingled with gritty dust, but to be able to work you had to eat all you could.

He went over what Agustín had said. He didn't understand. Better times? Was there some political change in Spain? The *comandante* had told them Franco had met Hitler and that soon Spain would be in the war, but they knew nothing of what was actually going on outside.

Aranda stepped out of his hut. He carried his riding crop, tapping it against his leg. This evening he was smiling and all the prisoners relaxed slightly. He vaulted on to the platform and began calling out names in his clear sharp voice.

The roll-call took half an hour, the men standing rigidly to attention. Towards the end someone a few rows away fell down. The man's neighbours bent to help him.

'Leave him!' Aranda called out. 'Eyes to the front.'

At the end the *comandante* raised his arm in the Fascist salute. '*¡Arriba España!*' In the early days of Bernie's captivity, at San Pedro, many prisoners had refused to respond, but when a few were shot they had complied, and now there was a dull ragged response. Bernie had told the other prisoners about an English word that sounded almost the same as '*arriba*' and now it was '*Grieve España*' that many called back.

The prisoners were dismissed. The man who had fallen was lifted by his neighbours and they carried him back to his hut. It was one of the Poles. He stirred faintly. On the other side of the barbed-wire fence a figure, shadowy in the dusk in his long black robe, stood watching.

'Father Eduardo,' Vicente muttered. 'Come for his prey.'

They watched as the young priest came through the gate and walked towards the Pole's hut, his long *sotana* stirring up little eddies of dust from the yard. The last of the light glinted on his spectacles. 'Bastard,' Vicente muttered. 'Coming to see if he can terrify another good atheist into taking the last rites by threatening him with Hell.'

VICENTE WAS an old Left Republican, a member of Azaña's party. He had been a lawyer in Madrid, providing cheap services to the city's poor, until he joined the militia in 1936. It was a romantic gesture, he had told Bernie. 'I was too old. But even rationalist Spaniards like me are romantics at heart.' Like all his party Vicente had a visceral hatred for the Church. It was almost an obsession with the Left Republicans; a liberal-bourgeois distraction, the Communists said. Vicente despised the Communists and said they had destroyed the Republic. Establo, leader of the Communists in Bernie's hut, disapproved of Vicente and Bernie's friendship.

'In this camp you have only your convictions to keep you going,' Establo had warned Bernie once. 'If they are eaten away your strength will go too, you will give up and die.' Establo himself looked as though it was only his beliefs that kept him alive. He was in his forties but looked sixty; his skin yellow and sagging, scarred with the marks of scabies. His eyes, though, were still full of fire.

Bernie had shrugged and told Establo he would end by converting Vicente, that the lawyer had the seeds of a class perspective. He had no respect for Establo; he hadn't voted for him when the twenty Communists in the hut elected their leader. Establo was obsessed with control and couldn't bear disagreement. During the war it had been necessary to have such people but it was different here. By the end of the Civil War the parties that made up the Republic had all hated each other, but in the camp the prisoners needed to cooperate to survive. Establo, though, tried to maintain the Communists' separate identity. He told them they were still the vanguard of the working class, that one day their time would come again.

A couple of days before, Pablo, one of the other Communists, had whispered in Bernie's ear. 'Beware of mixing with the lawyer, *compadre*. Establo is making an issue of it.'

'He can go fuck himself. What's his authority, anyway?'

'Why court trouble, Bernardo? The lawyer will die soon, anyone can see that.'

THIRTY PRISONERS shuffled into their bare wooden hut and threw themselves down on the straw mattresses covering their plank beds, each with one brown army blanket. Bernie had taken the bunk next to Vicente when the last occupant died. It was partly an act of defiance against Establo, who lay on his bunk in the opposite row, staring across at him.

Vicente coughed again. His face reddened and he lay back, gasping.

'I am bad. I will have to plead sickness tomorrow.'

'You can't. Ramirez is on duty, you'll just get a beating.'

'I don't know if I can work another day.'

'Come on, if you can stick it out until Molina is back, he'll put you on easy duty.'

'I will try.'

They were silent a moment, then Bernie leaned over on his elbow, speaking quietly. 'Listen, the guard Agustín said an odd thing earlier.'

'The quiet one from Sevilla?'

'Yes.' Bernie repeated the guard's words. Vicente frowned.

'What can it mean?'

'I don't know. What if the Monarchists have toppled the Falange? We wouldn't know.'

'We'd be no better off under the Monarchists.' Vicente thought a moment. 'Better times may be ahead? For who? He might have meant just for you, not all the camp.'

'Why should they do me any favours?'

'I don't know.' Vicente lay back with a sigh that turned into a cough. He looked ill, miserable.

'Listen,' Bernie said, to distract him. 'I stood up to that bastard quack. He told me I was a degenerate because I couldn't be converted to Catholicism. I remember that scene last *Navidad*. Remember, the doll?'

Vicente gave a sound between a laugh and a groan. 'Who could forget it?'

It had been a cold day, snow on the ground. The prisoners were marched out into the yard where Father Jaime, the older of the two priests who served the camp, stood dressed in a green and yellow cope. In his regalia in the bare snowy yard he looked like a visitor from another world. Beside him young Father Eduardo, in his usual black, looked uncomfortable, his round face red with cold. Father Jaime was holding a child's doll, a baby made of wood, wrapped in a shawl. There was a silver circle painted round its brow that puzzled Bernie for a moment until he realized it was meant to be a halo.

As always Father Jaime's face was supercilious, angry, his hawk-like nose with the stiff little hairs on top lifted as though offended by more than the men's rank smell. Aranda called the prisoners into shivering lines then stood on the platform, tapping his crop against his leg.

'Today is Epiphany,' he called out, his breath making grey clouds in the freezing air. 'Today we honour the baby Jesus, who came to Earth to save us. You will offer up homage and perhaps the Lord will take pity on you and shine a light into your souls. You will each kiss the image of the Christ child Father Jaime holds. Do not worry if the person before you has tuberculosis, the Lord will not allow you to be contaminated.'

Father Jaime frowned at the levity in the *comandante*'s tone. Father Eduardo looked at his feet. Father Jaime held the doll up, threateningly, like a weapon.

One by one the men shuffled past and kissed it. A few failed to bring their lips quite to the wood and the priest called them back sharply. 'Again! Kiss the baby Jesus properly!'

It was one of the Anarchists who refused, Tomás the shipbuilder from Barcelona. He stood in front of the priest, looking him in the eyes. He was a big man and Father Jaime shrank back a little.

'I will not kiss your symbol of superstition,' he said. 'I spit on it!' And he did, leaving a trail of white spittle on the baby's wooden brow. Father Jaime cried out as though the baby were real. One of the guards landed a blow on Tomás's head that felled him to the ground. Father Eduardo looked about to step forward but a glare from Father Jaime stopped him. The older priest wiped the doll's brow with a white handkerchief.

Aranda jumped off the platform and marched over to where the big man lay. 'You insult Our Lord!' he cried. 'The Virgin in Heaven weeps as you spit on her child!'

The words were outraged but his tone was still mocking. Aranda took his crop and began methodically beating the Anarchist, starting with his legs and ending with a blow to Tomás's head that drew blood. He called a couple of guards to carry him off, then turned to Father Jaime. The priest had shrunk back, clasping the doll to his breast as though sheltering it from the scene.

Aranda bowed. 'I am sorry for that insult, sir. Please continue. We shall bring these men to religion if the effort kills us, shall we not?' Aranda nodded to the next man in line. Bernie was pleased to see a little fear as well as anger in Father Jaime's eyes as the prisoner shuffled forward and bent his head to the doll. No one else resisted.

'I remember how that doll smelled,' Bernie said to Vicente. 'Paint and saliva.'

'Those black beetles, they are all the same. Father Jaime is a brute, but that Eduardo is more cunning. He will be in the sick Pole's hut now, sniffing out whether he is about to die, whether he is weak enough to be browbeaten into taking absolution.'

Bernie shook his head. 'Eduardo's not so bad. Remember he tried to get a doctor for the camp? And the crosses for the graveyard?' He thought of the hillside, just outside the camp, where those who died were buried in unmarked graves. When Father Eduardo came in the summer he had asked for crosses to mark the dead. The *comandante* had forbidden it; those inside the camp had been sentenced to decades of imprisonment by military courts; in practice they were already dead. One day the camp would close and the huts and barbed wire would be removed, leaving no sign on the bare windswept hill that it had ever been there.

'What do crosses matter?' Vicente replied. 'More symbols of superstition. Father Eduardo's kindness is fake, it is all to an end. They're all the same, the black beetles, they'll try to get you when you're dying, at your weakest.'

It was dark outside now. Some in the hut played cards or sewed their tattered uniforms by the light of weak tallow candles. Bernie closed his eyes and tried to sleep. He thought about Tomás's beating; the Anarchist had died a few days later. He himself had trod on thin ice with the psychiatrist this afternoon. It was lucky the man seemed to see him only as a specimen. Part of Bernie wanted to make some fierce gesture like Tomás's, but he wanted to live. If they killed him that would be their final, irrevocable victory.

Eventually he slept. He had a strange dream. He came into the hut with a whole crowd of schoolboys from Rookwood, led by Mr Taylor. The boys examined the wooden pallets then stood around the table made of old packing cases in the middle. They said if this was their new dorm it was jolly rough, they didn't think much of it. 'Don't be downhearted,' Taylor said reprovingly. 'That's not the Rookwood way.'

Bernie woke with a start. The hut was completely dark, he could see nothing. He was cold; he moved the thin blanket down to cover his feet. It was the first really cold night. September and October were the easiest months: the frying heat of summer fading by a few blessed degrees each week, the temperature at night comfortable enough to allow you to sleep easily. But now winter was here.

He lay awake in the darkness, listening to the coughs and mutterings of the other men. There were creaks as some tossed uneasily on their pallets, perhaps feeling the cold too. Before long there would be frosts each morning; by Christmas people would be dying.

There was a whisper from the next bunk. 'Bernardo, are you awake?' Vicente coughed again.

'Yes.'

'Listen,' His voice was urgent. Bernie turned but he couldn't see him in the thick darkness.

'I do not think I will last through the cold weather,' Vicente said.

'Of course you will.'

'If I don't, I want you to promise me something. The black beetles will come at the end; they will try to give me absolution. Stop them. I might weaken you see, I know people weaken. It would betray everything I have lived for. Please stop them somehow.'

Bernie felt tears pricking at his eyes. 'All right,' he whispered back. 'If it ever comes to it, I promise.' Vicente reached across, found Bernie's arm and clutched it with his thin hand.

'Thank you,' he said. 'You are a good friend. You will help me make my last defiance.'

Chapter Twenty-Two

IN MADRID November the first dawned cold and damp. Harry's flat was gloomy, despite the watercolours of English landscapes he had borrowed from the embassy to cover the blank walls.

Sometimes he thought of the vanished commissar. He wondered what sort of a commissar Bernie would have made if he had lived and his side had won. Harry's job had been to encourage Barbara to talk about Sandy when they met, and they had hardly mentioned Bernie's name; he felt oddly ashamed, as though they had written him out of their pasts. Bernie might have made an efficient commissar, he thought, he had had a hard angry streak along with the social compassion. But he couldn't see him becoming one of those he had heard about, who during the Civil War sentenced soldiers to be shot for grumbling.

He took his tea, Liptons supplied by the embassy, over to the window. He had lit the *brasero* and a welcome warmth stole from the little stove under the table. Rain dripped slowly from the balconies opposite. He had hated asking Barbara questions about Sandy, ferreting for information, and had been relieved when she didn't seem to know anything. He supposed that didn't make him much of a spy.

Harry had a session translating at an Interior Ministry function that morning, then another appointment with Sandy at the Café Rocinante. He had telephoned Sandy the day after his walk with Barbara. He said things were quiet at the embassy, did Sandy fancy meeting up again? He had accepted eagerly.

Harry went down to the street and set off for the cafe. He looked around him carefully, as usual, but there was no sign that Enrique had been replaced by another, more efficient spy.

SANDY WAS already at the Rocinante when Harry arrived, sitting at a table with his foot on a wooden block as a ragged ten-year-old boy cleaned his shoes. He waved an arm at Harry.

'Over here! Excuse me if I don't get up.'

Harry sat down. The cafe was quiet this afternoon; perhaps the rain and fog were keeping people indoors.

'Filthy weather, eh?' Sandy said cheerfully. 'Like being back home.'

'Sorry I'm late.'

'It's all right, I've only been here a few minutes myself. Winter's coming, I'm afraid.' The boy sat back on his haunches and Sandy inspected his shoes.

'OK, *niño*.' He passed a coin to the boy, who turned big sad eyes to Harry. 'I clean your shoes, *señor?*'

'*No, gracias*.'

'Oh go on, Harry, it's only ten centimos.'

Harry nodded and the boy placed the wooden block under his foot and began polishing the black shoes Harry himself had cleaned an hour before. Sandy beckoned the waiter and they ordered coffee. The boy finished with Harry's shoes; Harry passed him a coin and he moved on to other customers, whispering, '*¿Limpiabotas?*' in a sad wheedling tone.

'Poor little bastard,' Harry said.

'He tried to sell me some dirty postcards last week. Awful things, middle-aged whores lifting their knickers. He'd better watch out if the *civiles* catch him.'

The waiter brought their coffees. Sandy studied Harry thoughtfully. 'Tell me,' he asked, 'how did Barbara seem when you saw her?'

'Fine. We went for a walk in the Casa de Campo.' She hadn't seemed fine at all; there was something closed and reserved about her he'd never seen before but he wasn't going to talk to Sandy about that. It was one loyalty he could avoid betraying.

'She didn't seem preoccupied, worried?'

'Not really.'

'Hmm.' Sandy lit a cigar. 'There's something up with her, has been for a few weeks. She says it's nothing but I'm not so sure.' He smiled. 'Oh well, maybe this voluntary work will take her out of herself. Did she tell you about that?'

'Yes. It sounded like a good thing.'

'And you had an encounter with the Falange in the restaurant.' Sandy raised his eyebrows.

Harry nodded. 'Just a bit of rudeness.'

Sandy laughed. 'Hitler said once that Fascism can turn a worm into a dragon. It's done that to a good few worms here. Oh well, you just have to let them breathe their fire and smoke. It gets a bit wearing though.' He smiled with sudden affection. 'It's good to see a sober English face sometimes.'

'It must be odd, working with these people. The Ministry of Mines you work with mainly, isn't it? You were saying the other night.'

Sandy nodded, running a hand over his moustache. 'That's right. All my dinosaur hunting came in useful in the end, you know. More useful than that Latin they used to fill our heads with. I know a bit about geology – I met this mining engineer at a function a while back and we ended up going into business.'

'Really?' That's Otero, Harry thought. He tried to hide his interest.

'Franco's economic policy is to make Spain as self-sufficient as possible,' Sandy went on, 'relying on its own resources instead of being at the mercy of foreign powers. Classic fascist stuff. So if you're in mining exploration, the opportunities are limitless. They'll even subsidize exploration costs if you can supply the expertise.' He paused, studying Harry so keenly that for a moment Harry was afraid he knew.

'You remember the other night, when I said I could give you a few business tips?'

'Yes.'

'You can make a lot of money here if you know where to invest.'

Harry nodded encouragingly. 'I've saved quite a bit from my allowance over the years. Sometimes I've thought I'd like to do something with it rather than just have it sitting in the bank.'

Sandy leaned forward and clapped him on the arm. 'Then I'm your man. I'd enjoy helping you make some money. Especially in mining, as a reward for coming with me on all those fossil-hunting expeditions.' He inclined his head. 'They didn't bore you, did they?'

'No. I enjoyed them.'

'Still fascinates me. The things hidden in the earth.' He nodded judicially. 'Let me see what I can do. I'll have to be a bit careful; the Falangists at the ministry make an exception for me but they don't like Brits.' He smiled. 'I'll think of something. I'd like to show you I've made a success.' He paused, gave Harry one of his keen looks. 'You've been a bit dubious about that, haven't you?'

'Well . . .'

'I've seen it in your face, Harry. You've wondered what I'm doing mixing with these people. Barbara still wonders the same, I've seen it in her face too. But you can't be choosy in business.'

'It takes time to realize how – complicated everything is here.'

Sandy gave a quick ironic smile. 'It's complicated all right. Did you go to that party at General Maestre's?'

'Yes. I'm supposed to be taking his daughter to the Prado.' He would have to ring her tonight; he had been putting it off.

'Nice girl?'

'Very young. They were all Monarchists at the party. Didn't like the Falange at all.'

'They want an authoritarian monarchy, the aristocrats in charge like fifty years ago. But everything would just fall apart again.'

'They're pro-Allied.'

'Don't get them wrong, Harry. They're hard as stone. They all fought for Franco in the war; the Monarchists' pal Juan March financed the original army rebellion.'

'I've been hearing that name a lot lately.'

'The Falange reckon he's conspiring with the Monarchists and has links with the Allies. They say he's bribing the generals, buying their support for keeping Spain out of the war.'

And then Harry saw, it was like a light going on in his head. Bribery. That was what Hillgarth and Maestre had been talking about that day. The Knights of St George was a code for sovereigns, George slaying the dragon on the obverse. They would pay them in sovereigns. He took a deep breath.

'You all right?' Sandy asked him.

'Yes. I just – remembered something.' He took a drink of coffee and forced himself back to the present. 'Tell me,' he said for something to say, 'do you hear anything of your brother now?'

'Haven't heard from Peter in nine years. After I was sacked from

Rookwood Dad didn't want me near him. He said I belonged to the lost, he couldn't understand how anyone could do anything so wicked as what I did.' He gave a hollow laugh. 'Putting spiders in a master's room. God, if he could see some of the things that have gone on here. Anyway, after I left home I never heard any more from Dad, nor from Peter the perfect son either.' A bitter note came into his voice. 'I'm sure Pete's being heroic as an army padre somewhere.' He lit a cigar.

'Sorry, I didn't mean to—'

'It's all right. Look, about that other business, let me talk to one or two people, see what I can arrange.'

'That'd be good.' He hesitated. 'Can you tell me any more about it?'

Sandy smiled and shook his head. 'Not yet. Matter of business confidentiality. He looked at his watch. 'I'd better be going, I've a meeting of my Jewish Committee.'

'Barbara said you were doing some work with refugees.'

'Yes, they keep coming across the Pyrenees. They try and get to Portugal, in case Franco enters the war and hands them back to Hitler. Some of them are in a bad way when they arrive – we try to clean them up and help them with papers.' He gave a little smile, as though embarrassed at his charity. 'I like to help them; I suppose I've always felt a bit of a wandering Jew myself.' He sat up. 'Well, I must go. My treat. But we must do this again. I'm nearly always here at this time.'

Harry began walking home. It was still cold and dank. The conversation between Maestre and Hillgarth kept coming back to him, Hillgarth's terse order to forget Juan March and the Knights of St George. Could the embassy be involved in bribing ministers too? It seemed far-fetched once he thought about it; dangerous, too, if Franco found out.

He shook his head, there was a feeling of pressure in his bad ear, that faint annoying buzzing again. Perhaps it was the damp weather. He thought again about Miss Maxse saying they couldn't win this war by playing a straight bat. What else was it she had said – about people who got involved with extremist politics? 'Sometimes it's the excitement as much as the politics.' Sandy had always enjoyed taking risks – was that why he had ended up here? He wondered again about the Jews. Sandy had a good side. He would help people, if he was in charge: like educating him about fossils; like running Barbara's life, which is what he seemed to be doing.

He ought to go back to the embassy and report his progress. They would be delighted with the offer to involve him in one of Sandy's schemes. Of course it might be something else, nothing to do with the gold. But he kept thinking of the Knights of St George, what it all might mean. And what if they failed, if the Falangists won the struggle for Franco's ear and Spain entered the war? People like Maestre could be in danger; perhaps he wanted to get his daughter out of the country, if he could.

He realized he had wandered almost as far as the Puerta de Toledo. He stopped and stood momentarily, watching the carts and beat-up old cars passing by. Some of them looked as though they had been on the road for twenty years, as they probably had. A gasogene spluttered past. He had heard nothing from Sofia about a doctor for Enrique, it had been over a week now. What if Enrique developed rabies? Harry had heard the Chinese believed that if you saved someone's life you were bound to them for ever, but he knew it was Sofia that kept the family in his mind. He hesitated, then crossed the road and headed down towards Carabanchel.

Sofia's street, like all the others in the *barrio*, was silent and deserted. Dusk was starting to fall as he stopped in front of the tenement. Two children rolling an old cartwheel up and down like a hoop stopped and stared at him. Their bare feet were red with cold. Harry was conscious of his thick coat and wide-brimmed hat.

He went into the dank entrance, hesitated a moment, then mounted the damp stairs and knocked at their door. As he did so, the door of the neighbouring flat opened and an elderly woman came out. She had a round wrinkled face and cold sharp eyes. Harry raised his hat. '*Buenas tardes.*'

'*Buenas tardes,*' she replied suspiciously, just as Sofia opened her door. She looked at him in surprise, her large brown eyes widening.

'Oh. Señor Brett.'

Harry tipped his hat again. '*Buenas tardes*. I'm sorry to trouble you, I just wondered how Enrique was.'

Sofia glanced across at her neighbour, who was still peering at him nosily. '*Buenas tardes, Señora Avila*,' she said in a hard tone. '*Buen'dia*,' the old woman muttered. She closed her door and scuttled away down the stairs. Sofia looked after her a moment, then turned to Harry.

'Please come in, *señor*,' she said gravely. She did not smile.

Harry followed her into the cold damp *salón*. The old woman in the bed was using her good hand to play draughts with the little boy. At the sight of Harry he shrank back, shoulders twitching. She put her good arm round him.

'*Buenas tardes*,' Harry said to her. 'How are you?'

'Well enough, *señor*, thank you.'

Enrique was sitting at the table, his leg up on a cushion, swathed in bandages. His long thin face had a feverish look. It brightened at the sight of Harry.

'*Señor*. It is good to see you again.' He leaned across and shook Harry's hand.

'How's the leg?'

'Still bad. Sofia cleans it but it doesn't really get better.'

His sister looked embarrassed. 'It needs time,' she said.

There were some childish drawings on the table. Harry looked at them and then his eyes widened. Two Civil Guards, their green uniforms and yellow webbing coloured in exactly the right shade, were shooting a woman, little red jets coming out of her body. Alongside was a drawing of another *civil* being hanged from a lamppost, a little boy hauling him up on a rope. But the picture had been scored through with thick black lines.

'Paco did those,' Sofia said gently. 'He makes those drawings then crosses them out and gets upset. Only Mama can calm him. The noise he made this morning, I thought it would bring Señora Avila over.'

Harry looked at the little boy. He couldn't think of anything to say.

'Señor Brett,' Sofia said hesitantly. 'I wonder if I might talk to you in the kitchen.'

'Of course.'

Harry followed her into a concrete-floored room lined with cheap cabinets. The light was fading; she switched on the light, the low-watt bulb casting a dim yellow glow over the room. It was clean, though the sink was overflowing with dishes. Sofia followed his glance.

'I have to cook and wash up for them all now.'

'No – I didn't mean—'

'Please, sit down.' She motioned Harry to a chair by the kitchen table, then sat opposite, her small hands clasped in front of her. She looked at him thoughtfully.

'I did not expect you to come back,' she said.

He smiled. 'I never got that doctor's bill.'

'I hoped Enrique's leg would improve on its own.' She sighed. 'But the infection will not clear. I think yes, he needs a doctor.'

'My offer still stands.'

She frowned. 'You will forgive me, *señor*, but why should you help us? After Enrique spied on you?'

'I just felt I'd become involved. Please, it's only a doctor's bill; I can help you with that. I can afford it.'

'That old one in the flat next door, if she hears I am getting money from foreign diplomats I know what she will think.'

Harry reddened. Was that what Sofia thought too? 'I'm sorry. I didn't mean to embarrass you.' He half rose. 'I only wanted to help.'

'No, I see that. Please stay.' Sofia's tone became apologetic. She sat down and lit a cigarette. 'But it is a surprise, a foreigner offering to help us, after what Enrique did.' She bit her lip. 'I think my brother needs some of the new penicillin.'

'Then let me help. I can see things are – difficult.'

She smiled then, illuminating her face. 'Very well. Thank you.'

'Get the doctor, get any medicines your brother needs, then send me the bill. That's all you need to do.'

She looked uncomfortable. 'I am sorry, Señor Brett, you have saved my brother's life and I have not even thanked you properly.'

'It's all right.'

'Everyone is suspicious of everyone else these days.' She got up.

'Will you take coffee? It's not very good, it won't be what you're used to.'

'Thank you, yes.'

She filled a big black kettle at the sink. 'That old bitch you saw on the landing, now Enrique is ill she wants us to give Paquito to the church orphanage. But we won't. They are not good places.'

'No?' He was about to say he knew someone who was volunteering at one of them, but decided not to. Sofia handed him a cup of coffee. He looked at her. Where did she get such self-possession, such energy? Her hair was jet-black but where it caught the light it had a brown tinge.

'Have you worked at the embassy for long?' she asked.

'Only a few weeks, actually. I was invalided out of the army.'

'So you have fought?' There was a new respect in her voice.

'Yes. In France.'

'What happened to you?'

'A bit of ear damage when a shell went off. It's getting better.' He was aware of the pressure in his head, though, still there.

'You were lucky.'

'Yes. I suppose I was.' He hesitated. 'I had a bit of shell shock, too. Over that now.'

She hesitated, then said, 'So. You have fought the Fascists.'

'Yes. Yes, I have.' He looked at her. 'I'd do it again.'

'Yet many people admire the Generalísimo. I knew an English boy during the Civil War, a volunteer. He said many English people think Franco is a fine Spanish gentleman.'

'I don't, *señorita*.'

'He was from Leeds, this boy. Do you know Leeds?'

'No. It's in the north.'

'My father met him in the battles in the Casa de Campo. They both died there.'

'I'm sorry.' He wondered if the boy had been her lover.

'We have to make the best of things now.' She took out a cigarette and lit it.

'No chance for you to go back to medical school?'

She shook her head. 'With Mama and Paquito to look after? And Enrique now too?'

'With treatment perhaps he could work again.'

'Yes, and a different job this time.' She flicked ash angrily into a saucer. 'I told him he should not take that work.' She looked at him acutely again. 'How did you come to learn Spanish so well?'

'I'm a teacher, a lecturer, in England; at least, I was before the war came. Our war,' he added. 'I visited Spain in 1931, I told you, I suppose that's when my interest started.'

She smiled sadly. 'Our time of hope.'

'The friend I came here with in 1931, he came back to fight in the Civil War. He was killed at the Jarama.'

'Did you support the Republic too?'

'Bernie did. He was the idealist. I believed in neutrality.'

'And now?'

Harry didn't answer. Sofia smiled. 'You remind me of the boy from Leeds in a way, he had the same puzzlement in the face of Spain.' She rose. 'And now I should arrange for the doctor.'

Harry followed her back to the *salón*. 'Enrique,' she said. 'I have been talking to Señor Brett, I am going to get you a doctor. I will go now.'

Enrique gave a sigh of relief. 'Thank goodness. My leg is not a pretty sight. Thank you, *señor*. My sister is obstinate.'

The old woman tried to heave herself up. 'You are kind to us.'

'*De nada*,' Harry said awkwardly. The little boy stared at him with fearful eyes. Harry looked round the room again, taking in the musty smell, the stains of damp under the window. He felt ashamed of his own wealth and security.

'Señora Avila was hovering about again when Señor Brett arrived,' Sofia told her mother.

'That *beata*,' the old woman slurred. 'She thinks if she tells enough tales to the priests, God will make her a saint.'

Sofia reddened. 'Would you mind leaving first, Señor Brett? If we are seen leaving together there will be talk.'

'Of course,' Harry said, uncomfortably.

Enrique heaved himself up. 'Thank you again, *señor*.'

Harry said his goodbyes and walked slowly back to the tram stop in the Puerta de Toledo. He watched the ground for potholes and the coverless drains that sent a sickly stench up into the street. If you did not watch out, you could break a leg. He felt sad that now he might just get a doctor's bill, and that would be the end of it. They would not expect him to come back. But somehow, he decided, he would see Sofia again.

Chapter Twenty-Three

THE FOLLOWING MONDAY was a busy day at the embassy. Harry had arranged to meet Milagros Maestre at the Prado at four but a press release from the embassy about British victories in North Africa needed translating into Spanish and he was a quarter of an hour late.

He had rung her at the weekend. He hadn't wanted to but he couldn't just leave it, it would be rude; Tolhurst had said it might annoy Maestre and they couldn't afford that. Milagros sounded delighted and immediately accepted his invitation.

He had visited the Prado before, with Bernie one afternoon in 1931. It had been bustling with activity then but now the huge building was quiet. He bought his ticket and passed through into the main hall. There were hardly any visitors, fewer than the attendants who paced slowly round, keys clinking at their belts and footsteps echoing hollowly. The light was poor and in the dull winter afternoon the building had a gloomy, abandoned feel.

He half ran down the steps to the cafe where he had arranged to meet Milagros. She was sitting at the only occupied table, at the far end of the cafe. He was surprised to see a man sitting opposite her. The man turned and Harry recognized Maestre's companion from the ball, Lieutenant Gomez. There was a frown on his hard square face. Milagros smiled, looking relieved.

'Ah, Señor Brett,' Gomez said reprovingly. 'We were beginning to wonder if you were coming.'

'I'm so sorry, I was held up at the embassy.' He turned to Milagros. 'Please forgive me.'

'It is nothing,' she said. 'Please, Alfonso, it is nothing.' She was wearing an expensive fur coat and her brown hair was freshly set in a permanent wave. She was dressed as a grown woman but Harry thought again how child-like her plump face was.

Gomez grunted. He stubbed out a cigarette and rose. 'I will leave you. Milagros, I will see you in the entrance at half past five. Good afternoon, Señor Brett.' His look was cold as he shook hands. Harry remembered the basket of roses Maestre was supposed to have presented to the nuns, with the Moroccan heads in the middle. He wondered if Gomez had been there.

He sat opposite Milagros. 'I'm afraid I've offended him.'

She shook her head. 'Don Alfonso is too protective. He takes me everywhere, he is my chaperone. Do girls still have chaperones in England?'

'No. Not really.'

She pulled a packet of cigarettes from her pocket. Good cigarettes, Lucky Strike, not the poisonous things Sofia had been smoking. He had found himself thinking of Sofia all over the weekend.

'Would you like one, Señor Brett?'

He smiled. 'No thanks. And call me Harry.'

Milagros blew out a long draught of smoke. 'Ah, that is better. They don't like me smoking, they think I am too young.' She blushed. 'They think it is a sign of bad morals.'

'All the women I know smoke.'

'Would you like a coffee?'

'Not just now, thanks, maybe after we've seen the pictures?'

'That would be nice. I will finish this then.' She smiled nervously. 'It is a treat for me to smoke in public.' She blew out a blue cloud of smoke, angling her face away from him.

Harry didn't mind visiting art galleries if he didn't have to stay too long, but he wasn't really an enthusiast. The sense of the Prado's cavernous emptiness grew as they walked through the echoing galleries. Most of them were largely bare, empty spaces on the wall where the pictures had been lost or stolen during the Civil War. Black-uniformed guards sat on chairs in the corners, reading *Arriba.*

Milagros was even more ignorant of art than Harry. They would stop before one and he or she would make some stilted remark and move on.

In the Goya room the dark horror of the 'Pinturas Negras' seemed to make her uneasy. 'He paints cruel things,' she said quietly, looking at the 'Witches Sabbath'.

'He saw a lot of war. I think we've done nearly everything now – would you like a coffee?'

She smiled at him gratefully. 'Oh yes. Thank you.'

The galleries had been cold but the cafeteria was overheated. When he brought two cups of bad coffee over to their table she had taken off her coat, releasing an overpowering musk of expensive perfume. She had put on far too much. He felt suddenly sorry for her.

'I should like to see the galleries in London,' Milagros said. 'I should like to see all of London. My mother says it is a great city.'

'Has she been there?'

'No, but she knows all about it. My parents love England.'

Spaniards didn't like their daughters going out with foreigners, Harry knew, but in these times a place in England would be a desirable destination in the eyes of someone like Maestre. He looked into her plump earnest face.

'Every country looks better from a distance.'

'Perhaps.' Milagros looked downcast. 'But it must be better than Spain, here everything is so poor and dirty, so *inculto*.'

Harry thought of Sofia and her maimed family in that flat. 'Your father has a fine house.'

'But it is all so insecure. We had to flee Madrid during the war, you know. Now there is this new war hanging over us, what if we lose everything again?' She looked sad for a moment, then smiled again. 'Tell me more about England. I have heard the countryside is pretty.'

'Yes, it is very green.'

'Even in summer?'

'Especially then. Green grass, lots of big, broad trees.'

'Madrid used to be full of trees. When we came back the Reds had cut them all down for firewood.' She sighed. 'I was happier in Burgos.'

'Things are pretty insecure in England too now. It was different before the war.' He smiled. 'I remember at school, there was nothing nicer than a long game of cricket on a summer afternoon.' He had a vision of the green playing fields, the boys in cricket whites, the clop of bat and ball. It was like a dream, as far away as the world his parents' photograph had been taken in.

'I have heard of cricket.' Milagros laughed nervously, looking more like a plump schoolgirl than ever. 'But I do not know how it is played.' She lowered her eyes. 'I am sorry, this afternoon – I do not know anything about paintings, either.'

'Neither do I, really,' he replied awkwardly.

'It was just, I had to think of somewhere we might go. But if you like we could go out to the country some time, I could show you the Guadarrama mountains in winter. Alfonso could take us in the car.'

'Yes, yes perhaps.' She was blushing, there was no doubt about it, she was soft on him. Oh hell, Harry thought. He looked at the wall clock. 'It's time to go,' he said. 'Alfonso will be waiting. Mustn't annoy him again.'

Her mouth quivered slightly. 'Yes.'

The old soldier was standing on the steps of the Prado, smoking and staring across the road at the Ritz. It was starting to get dark. He turned and this time he smiled at Harry.

'Ah, right on time. *Bueno*. Did you have a good time, Milagros?'

'Yes, Alfonso.'

'You must tell your Mama all about the pictures you saw. The car is round the corner.' He took Harry's hand. 'Perhaps I shall see you again, Señor Brett.'

'Yes, Lieutenant Gomez.' Harry shook hands with Milagros. She looked at him expectantly but he said nothing about meeting again. Her face fell and he felt guilty but he wasn't going to string her along. He watched as they walked away. Why did she like him, they'd nothing in common at all. 'Oh, hell,' he said again, aloud.

Harry was meeting Tolhurst for a drink at the Café Gijón. He passed the closed Parliament building and then the ministry where he had met Maestre, the street patrolled by *civiles* with sub-machine guns. He pulled his coat collar up. It was cold again; after the baking summer and the failed harvest, it looked like a cold winter was coming.

Gran Vía had been renamed Avenida José Antonio for the dead founder of the Falange, but it was the same as Harry remembered from 1937, a long commercial street. The shops were reopening after the siesta, yellow light spilling on to the pavement. Even here the window displays were sparse. He had heard of the Gijón but never been there. Walking into the mirrored bar he saw people scattered about the tables. There were artistic types with beards and extravagant moustaches but no doubt they were regime supporters, like Dalí. 'Fascism is the dream made real,' a young man was saying enthusiastically to his companion; 'the surreal made real.' You can say that again, Harry thought.

Tolhurst was sitting with his bulk squeezed in behind a table against the wall. Harry raised a hand, then fetched a brandy from the bar and joined him.

'How was the date?' Tolhurst asked.

Harry took a slug of the brandy. 'That's better. Pretty awful actually. She's nice enough but she's – well – just a kid. She had a chaperone. Maestre's ex-batman or whatever he is.'

'They've got very old-fashioned ideas about women.' Tolhurst looked at him. 'Try and keep in with her if you can, it's a link to Maestre.'

'She wants to go for a drive in the Guadarrama.'

'Ah.' Tolhurst smiled. 'Get you on her own, eh?'

'With Gomez driving.'

'Ah well.' Tolhurst blew out his plump cheeks. 'Oh God, I wish I was back home sometimes. I get homesick.'

'Missing your family?'

Tolhurst lit a cigarette and watched the smoke curl up to the ceiling. 'Not really. My father's in the army, haven't seen him for ages.' He sighed. 'I've always wanted to live in London, enjoy the high life. Never managed to – first it was school and then the diplomatic service.' He sighed again. 'It's probably too late now. With the bombing and the blackout, all that sort of life must be over.' He shook his head. 'Have you seen the papers? They're still saying how well Franco got on with Hitler at Hendaye. And Sam's in appeasement mode; he's told Franco Britain would be happy to see Spain take Morocco and Algeria from the French.'

'What? As Spanish colonies?'

'Yes. He's playing up to Franco's dreams of empire. Can see his reasoning, I suppose. The French are finished as a power.'

Tolhurst spoke of what 'Sam' was doing as though he was the ambassador's confidant, as he often did, though Harry knew he was probably just repeating embassy gossip.

'We've got the blockade,' Harry said. 'We could turn off their food and oil supplies like a tap. Maybe it's time we did. Warn them off Hitler.'

'It's not that simple. If we left them with nothing to lose they could join the Germans, march in and take Gibraltar.'

Harry took another swig of brandy. 'D'you remember that night at the Ritz? I overheard Hoare saying there mustn't be any British support for special operations here. I remember a speech Churchill made just before I came out. Britain's survival kindling sparks of hope in occupied Europe. We could help the people here instead of sucking up to the leaders.'

'Steady on.' Tolhurst laughed nervously. 'The brandy's going to your head. The Reds would come back if Franco fell. They'd be even worse.'

'What does Captain Hillgarth think? He seemed to be agreeing with Sir Sam that night at the Ritz.'

Tolhurst shifted uncomfortably. 'Actually, Harry, he'd be a bit annoyed if he knew he'd been overheard.'

'It wasn't deliberate.'

'Anyway, I don't know anything,' he added wearily. 'I'm just the dogsbody. I arrange things, debrief sources and query their expenses.'

'Tell me,' Harry asked, 'have you ever heard the expression, "The Knights of St George"?'

Tolhurst's eyes narrowed. 'Where did you hear that?' he asked quietly.

'Maestre used the phrase when he was talking to Captain Hillgarth, the first day I went with Hillgarth to do some translating. It means sovereigns, Tolly, doesn't it?' Tolhurst didn't answer, just pursed his lips. Harry went on, not caring any more what protocols he might be breaking. 'Hillgarth talked about Juan March as well. Are we involved in bribing the Monarchists? Is that the horse we're backing to keep Spain out of the war? Is that why Hoare doesn't want anything to do with the opposition?'

'You know, Harry, it doesn't do to be too curious.' Tolhurst's voice was still quiet. 'It's not our job to think about – well – *policy*. And for fuck's sake, keep your voice down.'

'I'm right, aren't I? I can see it in your face.' Harry leaned forward, whispering intently. 'What if it comes unstuck and Franco finds out? We'd be in the shit then, and so would Maestre and his pals.'

'The captain knows what he's doing.'

'And what if it works? We're tied to these bastards for good. They'll rule Spain for ever.'

Tolhurst took a deep breath. His face reddened, his expression was angry. 'Christ, Harry, how long has this been going round in your noddle?'

'I only guessed what the Knights of St George might be the other day.' He leaned back in his chair. 'Don't worry, Tolly, I won't say anything.'

'You'd better not, if you don't want a charge of treason. This is what comes of recruiting academics,' he said. 'You're too bloody curious.' He laughed, trying to put matters back on a friendly footing. 'I can't tell you anything,' he continued. 'You must see that. But the captain and Sam know what they're doing. I'll have to tell the captain you've twigged this. You're sure you've told nobody else.'

'I swear, Tolly.'

'Then have another, and forget about it.'

'All right,' Harry said. He wouldn't forget, but there was no point in sailing into trouble. He wished he hadn't followed his impulse to ask Tolhurst.

Tolhurst heaved himself up, wincing as the corner of the table caught his belly. Harry stared into his glass. He felt a moment's panic, his beliefs about the world and his place in it shifting under him again, like sand.

Chapter Twenty-Four

THE MONEY ARRIVED on the fifth of November, the day before Barbara was due to meet Luis again. She was despairing of it ever coming and had prepared herself to plead with Luis to wait. As she grew more worried, Barbara knew she was becoming nervy and withdrawn. Sandy was clearly starting to wonder what was wrong with her. That morning she had pretended to be asleep while he dressed, though her eyes were open, staring down at the pillow, remembering it was Guy Fawkes Day. There would be no fireworks in England this year; they had enough real explosions every night. The BBC said there had been no more raids on the Midlands, but London was being bombed most nights. The Madrid papers said much of the city was reduced to rubble but she told herself that was propaganda.

After Sandy left she went down for the mail. There was one typed envelope on the mat with the King's head on the stamp instead of Franco and his cold stare. She tore it open. In coldly formal tones, the bank told her they had transferred her savings to the account she had opened in Madrid: over 5000 pesetas. She could sense their disapproval of her taking money abroad in wartime.

She went back to the bedroom and put the letter in her bureau. There were a couple of guides to Cuenca in there now, which she had bought and studied carefully. She locked it.

She dressed hurriedly; she was due at the orphanage at nine. It was her second morning there. Yesterday she had worn her usual clothes but Sister Inmaculada had said she should not dirty a good dress. Barbara found it a relief to revert to an old skirt and baggy jumper. She glanced at her watch. It was time she was off.

BARBARA HAD ARRANGED to come to the orphanage twice a week but already she was unsure if she could continue. She had been a nurse before but never in conditions like this.

She thought of the scrubbed, clinical corridors of the Birmingham Municipal Hospital with nostalgia as she approached the orphanage. A gasogene passed, the foul-smelling smoke belching from its little chimney making her cough. She knocked at the door and a nun let her in.

The grey nineteenth-century building was a former monastery, built round a central square with pillared cloisters. The cloister walls were covered with anti-communist posters: a snarling ogre wearing a cap with a red star looming over a young mother and her children; a hammer and sickle in a montage with a skull and the legend, 'This is Communism'. Yesterday she had asked Sister Inmaculada whether the posters might frighten the children. The tall nun had shaken her head sadly.

'Nearly all these children come from Red families. They have to be reminded they lived in the devil's shadow. Otherwise how can their little souls be saved?'

Sister Inmaculada was finishing roll-call in the central cloister as Barbara arrived, her clear high voice ringing round the yard, a cane tucked into the belt of her habit. Fifty boys and girls between six and twelve stood in lines on the concrete. She lowered her clipboard. 'Dismiss,' she called, then raised an arm in the Fascist salute. '*¡Viva Franco!*' The children replied in a ragged chorus, arms waving vaguely up and down. Barbara remembered the concert, Franco suppressing his yawn. She walked to the infirmary; 'Spain Reconquered for Christ!' was painted over the door.

Her first job of the day was to check the health of newly admitted children to see if any needed referring to the doctor. Inside the cold infirmary with its iron beds and steel instruments hanging from the walls her helper, Señora Blanco, was waiting. She was an elderly retired cook, a *beata*, a religious woman whose life revolved around the church. She had tight grey curls and wore a brown apron; her plump face was wrinkled and at first sight kindly.

'*Buenas tardes*, Señora Forsyth. I have hot water ready.'

'Thank you, *señora*. How many have we got today?'

'Only two. Brought by the *civiles*. A boy caught burgling a house and a little girl living wild.' She shook her head piously.

Barbara washed her hands. The children who came to the orphanage were mostly feral, living by begging and stealing. Their begging was a nuisance and when the police picked them up they handed them over to the nuns.

Señora Blanco rang a little bell and a nun led in a red-haired boy of about eight wearing a greasy brown coat too big for him. Sister Teresa was young, with a square peasant face. 'Caught stealing, the little beast,' she said admonishingly.

'What a bad child,' Señora Blanco said sorrowfully. 'Take off your clothes, child, let the nurse see you.' The boy disrobed sullenly and stood naked: ribs poking out, arms like matchsticks. He lowered his head as Barbara examined him. He smelled of stale sweat and urine; his skin as cold as a plucked chicken.

'He's very thin,' she said quietly. 'Nits, of course.' The boy had a long cut on his wrist, red and weeping. 'That's a nasty cut, *niño*,' she said gently. 'How did you get that?'

The boy looked up with big frightened eyes. 'A cat,' he muttered. 'It came into my cellar. I tried to pick it up and it scratched me.'

Barbara smiled. 'Bad cat. We'll put some ointment on it. Then we'll get you something to eat, would you like that?' He nodded. 'What's your name?'

'Ivan, *señora*.'

Señora Blanco compressed her lips. 'Who gave you that name?'

'My parents.'

'Where are your parents now?'

'The *civiles* took them.'

'Ivan is a bad name, a Russian name, do you not know that? The nuns will find you a better one.' The boy hung his head.

'I think that's all,' Barbara said. She wrote on a card and handed it to Señora Blanco, who led the boy away. Sister Teresa left by the other door to fetch the next child. The *beata* returned a few moments later, wiping her hands on her dark apron. 'Dear Lord, how he smelt.'

There was a commotion outside. Barbara heard high thin screams and the door was flung open. Sister Teresa dragged in a scrawny dark-haired girl of about eleven, struggling frantically. The nun was red-faced and her coif had been knocked askew, giving her a drunken look.

'*Madre de Dios*, she struggles worse than a pig.' Sister Teresa gripped the child's arms hard, forcing her to stand still. 'Stop that or you'll get the cane! The devil is in this one. She was living in an empty house in Carabanchel – the *civiles* had to chase her round the streets.'

Barbara bent down in front of the girl. She was breathing heavily, lips drawn back over bad teeth, eyes wide with terror. She wore a filthy blue dress and clutched a little woolly donkey, so dirty and torn it was hardly recognizable.

'What's your name?' Barbara asked gently.

The girl swallowed. 'Are you a nun?'

'No, I'm a nurse. I just want to examine you, see whether you need a doctor.'

The girl looked at her beseechingly. 'Please let me go. I don't want to be made into soup.'

'What?'

'The nuns make children into soup, feed it to Franco's soldiers. Please, please, make them let me go.'

Sister Teresa laughed. 'You can see who's brought this one up.'

Señora Blanco frowned at the girl. 'Those are wicked lies the Reds told. You're a bad child to say such things. Now get undressed for the nurse. And give me that!' She reached for the woolly donkey but the girl clutched it tighter. Señora Blanco's face flushed with anger.

'Give that to me. Don't defy me, you little Red!' She grabbed the toy and pulled sharply. It tore in two, white stuffing flying out. The *beata* was caught off balance and the girl jumped away, screaming. She ran under a bed and crouched there, holding the donkey's head, all that was left, to her face and howling. Señora Blanco threw the rest to the floor. 'Little bitch—'

'Be quiet!' Barbara snapped. The *beata* looked affronted. Sister Teresa folded her arms and looked on with interest as Barbara bent down to the girl.

'I'm sorry,' Barbara said gently. 'It was an accident. Perhaps I could mend your *burro*.'

The girl rubbed the head against her cheek. 'Fernandito, Fernandito – she killed him.'

'Give him to me. I'll sew him back together. I promise. What's your name?'

The girl studied her suspiciously, unused to a kind tone. 'Carmela,' she whispered. 'Carmela Mera Varela.'

Barbara felt a jolt in her stomach. Mera. The name of Bernie's friends. And they had lived in Carabanchel. She remembered her visits three years ago – the big amiable father, the overworked mother, the boy with TB. There had been a little girl too, about eight then.

'Do – do you have a family?'

The girl shook her head, biting her lip. 'There was a big shell,' she said. 'Afterwards I found an empty cellar for me and Fernandito.' She began to cry, quiet anguished sobs.

Barbara reached in but the girl wriggled away, still crying desperately. Barbara stood up.

'Dear God, she must have been living wild for years.' She knew she mustn't say she knew her, knew her family. A Red family.

'Might we perhaps get her out of there?' Señora Blanco asked coldly.

Barbara knelt again. 'Carmela, I promise the nuns won't hurt you. They'll feed you, give you warm clothes. You'll be all right if you do what they say but they'll be angry if you don't come out. If you do, I promise I'll mend your *burro*, sew him together. But you must come out.'

This time the child let Barbara pull her gently from under the bed. 'Good, Carmela. Now, stand still, take your dress off so I can look at you. Yes, that's right, give me Fernandito, I'll take care of him.'

The child's arms and legs were covered with eczema; Barbara wondered how she had survived. 'She's very undernourished. How did you get food to eat, Carmelcita?'

'I beg.' A look of defiance came into her eyes. 'I take things.'

'Come on,' Sister Teresa said brusquely. 'Get dressed and let's get you registered. And no more fun and games. You'll get some food if you behave. Otherwise it'll be the cane.'

The child put on her dress. Sister Teresa laid a plump red hand firmly on her shoulder. As she was led firmly away, Carmela turned and gave Barbara an anguished look. 'I'll bring Fernandito in a day or two,' Barbara called. 'I promise.' The door closed behind her.

Señora Blanco snorted. 'All this rubbish.' She bent down, picking up lumps of Fernandito's stuffing. Squeezing them into a tight ball, she threw it into a wastebasket together with the other half of the donkey's woolly skin. Barbara marched over and pulled it all out again, putting it in her pocket.

'I promised I'd mend it.'

The *beata* snorted. 'Filthy thing. They won't let her keep it, you know.' She stepped closer, her eyes narrowed. 'Señora Forsyth, in all charity I wonder if you are suited to the work here. We cannot afford sentimentality in Spain now. Perhaps you should discuss it with Sister Inmaculada.' With a toss of her tight curls, she walked out of the infirmary.

At home that afternoon Barbara tried to sew the donkey back together. It was dirty and greasy and she had to be careful putting the stuffing back or it would end up looking shapeless. She used her strongest thread but she wasn't sure it would withstand constant handling by a child. She couldn't stop thinking about Carmela. Had she come from that family, Bernie's friends? Were the others all dead?

Pilar came in to stoke the fire. She looked at Barbara oddly. Barbara supposed she must look strange, sitting there in her old clothes in the *salón*, sewing up a child's toy with frantic concentration.

When she had finished she stood the donkey on the hearth. She hadn't made a bad job. She poured herself a gin and tonic, lit a cigarette and sat looking at it. It had the meek enduring expression of a real *burro*.

At seven Sandy came in. He warmed his hands at the fire, smiling down at her. Barbara hadn't bothered to put the overhead light on and, apart from a pool of light from the reading lamp in which cigarette smoke swirled, the room was dark.

Sandy looked sleek and comfortable. 'It's cold out,' he said. He looked in surprise at the donkey. 'What on earth's that?'

'That's Fernandito.'

He frowned. 'Who?'

'It belongs to a child at the orphanage. It got torn when she was brought in.'

Sandy grunted. 'You don't want to get too involved with those children.'

'I thought it was useful to you, me working there. The *marquesa* connection.' She reached to the gin bottle on her sewing table and poured herself another. Sandy looked at her.

'How many of those have you had?'

'Only one. Want one?'

Sandy took a glass and sat opposite her. 'I'm seeing Harry Brett again the day after tomorrow. I think I'm going to be able to bring him in on something.'

Barbara sighed. 'Don't involve him in anything shady, for God's sake. He'd hate that. And he works for the embassy, they have to be careful.'

'It's just a business opportunity.' He frowned at her.

'If you say so.' She never usually talked to him like this, but she was depressed and exhausted.

'You don't seem awfully interested in Harry,' Sandy said. 'I thought he was so wonderful to you when Piper went west.'

She stared at him without replying. There was a nasty look in his eyes for a moment, something angry and cruel. With his heavy features lit by the firelight he looked middle-aged and dissipated. He shifted in his chair, then smiled.

'I told him you'd join us for coffee afterwards. Just the three of us.'

'All right.'

He smiled again. 'Funny chap, Harry,' he went on reflectively. 'Sometimes you don't know what he's thinking – he gets this quiet frowning look and you know he's turning something over.'

'I always found him very straightforward. D'you want the light on?'

His dark eyes fixed on her. 'What's the matter with you these days, Barbara? I thought doing some nursing might cheer you up but you're gloomier than ever.'

She studied him. He didn't look suspicious, just irritated. 'If you saw the things I see at the orphanage, you'd be gloomy.' She sighed. 'Or would you? Maybe not.'

'You'll have to snap out of it. I've a lot on at the moment.'

'I'm just tired, Sandy.'

'You're letting yourself go, look at that tatty old jumper.'

'I wear it for the orphanage.'

'Well, you're not at the orphanage now, are you?' He was annoyed, she could see. 'It reminds me of when I first met you. And you need your hair waved again. I can see why those girls used to call you frizzy-hair. And you keep wearing those glasses.'

The strength of the pain and anger that rose inside her surprised Barbara. Very occasionally, if she crossed him, Sandy would strike out like this. He knew how to wound. It was hard to keep a tremor from her voice. She got up. 'I'll go up and change,' she said.

Sandy gave his broad smile. 'That's more like it. I've got some papers to read – tell Pilar we'll have dinner at eight.'

She left the *salón*. On the way upstairs she thought, when I've got Bernie out I'll go back to England. Away from this terrible place, away from him.

Luis wasn't at the cafe when she arrived the next day. She looked in through the window and there were only a few workmen sitting at the bar. It was a cold grey afternoon.

She went to the counter and ordered a coffee. The fat old woman looked at her speculatively. 'Another assignment, *señora?*' she asked, then gave a wink. Barbara flushed and said nothing.

'Your *amigo* is quite handsome, *señora, sí*? Your coffee.'

An old couple were sitting at one of the tables, hunched over empty cups. They had been here last time, Barbara thought, as she took the usual table and lit a cigarette. She studied them. They didn't look like spies, just an old poor couple spending time in the cafe because it was warm. She sipped her coffee; it tasted like hot dirty water. She had been there ten minutes, getting more and more anxious, before Luis arrived. He was breathless and apologetic. He fetched a coffee and hurried over to her.

'*Señora*, I am sorry, *desculpeme*. I have been moving to new lodgings.'

'Never mind. Have you any news?'

He nodded and leaned forward, his face eager. 'Yes. We have made progress. Agustín has already got himself on the quarry rota as a guard. At the right time, he will arrange with your friend that he will ask to go to the toilet, say he has' – he coughed, embarrassed – 'diarrhoea. Then he will hit Agustín on the head, steal the key to his shackles, and run off.'

'They wear shackles?' It was one of the horrors she had imagined.

'He would be shackled to go to the toilet, yes.'

Barbara thought a few moments, then nodded. 'All right.' She lit another cigarette and passed him the packet. 'When? The longer we wait the riskier it is. Not just the political situation. I can't stand much more of this, my – husband – has noticed I'm not myself.'

Luis shifted in his seat. 'That is a problem, I am afraid. Agustín is due three weeks' leave, starting next week. He will not be back until early December. It will have to wait until then.'

'But that's a month away! Can't he change his leave?'

'*Señora*, please speak quietly. Think how suspicious it would be if Agustín suddenly cancelled the leave he booked months ago, and then he was on duty when there was an escape.'

'This is bad. What if Spain comes into the war, what if I have to leave?'

'They have been saying we will come in since June and nothing has happened, even after the Caudillo's meeting with Hitler. It will be done, *señora*, I promise, as soon as possible after Agustín gets back. And it will be easier when the days are shorter – the darkness will help your friend get away.'

'His name's Bernie – Bernie. Why can't you use his name?'

'Of course, Bernie, yes.'

She thought carefully. 'How will he get from the camp to Cuenca? He'll be in prison clothes.'

'It is all rough country till the gorge at Cuenca, plenty of cover. And there is a place in Cuenca where you can meet him. Agustín will arrange it all.'

'How far is the camp from Cuenca?'

'About eight kilometres. *Señora*, your Bernie is as strong as anyone in the camp. They are used to hard work and long walks in the winter. He will make it.'

'What does Bernie know? Does – does he know I'm trying to help him?'

'Nothing yet. It is safer that way. Agustín has told him only that there may be better times ahead for him. He keeps an eye on him.'

'He won't be able to keep an eye on him in Sevilla.'

'That is unavoidable. I am sorry, but we can do nothing.'

'All right.' She sighed and ran her hand over her face. How could she get through the next weeks?

'It is arranged now, *señora*.' Luis looked at her meaningfully. 'We agreed I would have half when it was arranged.'

Barbara shook her head. 'Not quite, Luis. I said I'd pay you half when we had a plan in place. That means, when I know how and *when* it will happen.'

She saw a glint of anger in his eyes. 'My brother will have to be struck hard on the head by your friend for them to believe his story. Then he will have to stay out in the Tierra Muerta, perhaps for hours, to give him a chance to escape. There is already snow on the tops of the sierras.'

Barbara stared him down. 'When I have a date, Luis. A date.'

'But—'

He broke off. Two *civiles* had entered the cafe, their bicorn hats and short capes glistening like insect carapaces. Guns were visible in the yellow holsters at their belts. They walked over to the bar.

'*¡Mierda!*' Luis muttered. He began to get up, but Barbara put a hand on his arm.

'Sit down. What will they think if we run off as soon as they appear?'

He sat down again. The old woman served the *civiles*, remarking how cold the weather was.

'Too cold to go straight home after duty, *señora*.' They took their coffees and sat down. One looked curiously at Barbara, then muttered something to his colleague. They laughed.

'Come on, *señora*, let us go now.' Luis was twitching with anxiety.

'All right. But slowly.' They rose and went out. Both exhaled with relief as the door shut behind them.

'I am disappointed about the money, *señora*,' Luis said sulkily. 'Some things are outside my control.'

Has he moved lodgings on the strength of the money, she wondered. Too bad. 'When I have a date, you'll have the money.'

Luis shrugged angrily. 'I will go to Cuenca again this weekend, see Agustín before he goes to Sevilla. We can meet again a week today.' Then to her surprise he shook her hand again with that stiff formality of his before turning and disappearing into the grey afternoon. Weeks more, Barbara thought, weeks more of this. She clenched her hands. As she walked away she avoided looking at the *civiles* through the window, but she saw the old couple looking down at their coffee cups, giving the *civiles* frightened glances. They were afraid of them, too; they weren't watchers.

Chapter Twenty-Five

ALREADY THE FIRST SNOW had fallen on the peaks of the Sierra Valdemeca far to the north-east. That morning for the first time there was a white crust of frost in the camp yard, a skin of ice on the little puddles. The early sun turned the snow on the distant mountains a gentle pink and Bernie thought it was beautiful even as he shivered in his thin boiler suit on the parade ground, waiting for Aranda to take the morning roll.

Beside him Vicente blew his nose on his sleeve, wincing as he looked at a streak of bright yellow snot. There was something wrong with his nose now; he had agonizing pains in his head and this ugly discharge that would not stop.

Aranda appeared from his hut in greatcoat and gloves. He strode towards the platform. He removed his gloves and blew on his hands, glaring at the prisoners. An icy breeze blew down from the sierras, ruffling the prisoners' hair with harsh fingers as Aranda called out the names in his ringing voice. There were half a dozen new men: Republicans who had fled to France when Franco won and been sent back by the Nazis. They surveyed their new prison without interest. One of them had said the Catalan leader, Companys, had been sent back to Madrid and shot.

At breakfast in the dining hut Bernie took a seat with some of the Communists. Pablo the ex-miner from Asturias moved along the bench for him. '*Buenos días, compañero. ¿Hoy hace frío, no?*'

'Very cold. It's come early this winter.'

Bernie spooned up the thin chickpea gruel. Down the table, Establo glanced at him. His scabies was getting worse, his face pitted with red streaks where he had been scratching. A patch of hard red skin on his wrist showed the disease was reaching the crusted stage, alive with eggs and mites underneath.

'*Compadre* Piper, you have decided to join us today.'

'You know I like to move around, *compadre*, you get more news that way.'

Establo fixed him with keen, hard grey eyes. 'And what news have you been gathering?'

'One of the guards told Guillermo the stone from the quarry is for a monument Franco's started in the Guadarrama. Apparently it's going to be his tomb; it'll take twenty years to build.'

'If it's in the Guadarrama,' Establo grunted, 'why do they want limestone from here?'

'Suitable for the monumental fittings, Guillermo said.'

Establo grunted. 'Sounds like propaganda to me. The guards sow these stories to make us believe Franco will be there for ever. You should analyse what you hear, *compadre*.'

'I always do, *compadre* Establo.' Bernie looked back at him steadily. With his domed bald head and the thin wattles on his neck, Establo reminded him of the lizards you saw in summer, scuttling over the rocks. Establo smiled coldly.

'I hope you analyse particularly what the bourgeois Vicente tells you.'

'I do. And he analyses what I tell him.'

'Still on the quarry detail?' Pablo asked, changing the subject.

'All this week. I'd rather be on the cookhouse with you.'

The guard blew his whistle. 'Come on, finish up. Time for work!'

Bernie spooned down a last mouthful and rose. Establo was scratching the crusted skin on his wrist, his mouth twisted with pain.

THE PRISONERS assembled in long lines in the yard. The sun was above the bare brown hills now and it was a little warmer, the ice in the puddles starting to melt. The gates were opened and Bernie's party stepped out, standing in a long file as guards with rifles took up positions every few yards. Sergeant Ramirez walked slowly down the length of the crocodile, his face sullen, staring at the prisoners. He was a fat man in his fifties with a straggling grey moustache, a red face and a drunk's bulbous nose. He looked decrepit but he was dangerous, a churning volcano of hatreds. He was an old professional soldier and they tended to be the cruel ones, the conscripts generally preferring a quiet life. Under his greatcoat the bulge where his whip was tucked into his belt was visible. He reached the head of the queue, blew his whistle, and the prisoners set off into the hills.

It was a three-mile walk. The Tierra Muerta was well named; it was bare and stony, a few fields sheltered by dwarf oaks scraped into hollows between the hills. They passed a peasant family labouring with an ox-plough at the stony soil. They did not look up as the crocodile passed; it was a convention that the prisoners were invisible.

A little further on they crested a hill and Ramirez blew his whistle for a five-minute rest. Vicente lowered himself on to a boulder. His face was pale and his breath came in jagged rasps. Bernie glanced at the nearest guard and was surprised to see it was Agustín, the man who had made that strange remark after his visit to the psychiatrist the week before.

'I am bad today, Bernardo,' Vicente said. 'My head feels as if it will explode.'

'Molina will be back next week – he'll let you have it easy.' He leaned closer. 'We'll work together, you can rest.'

'You're good to an old bourgeois,' the lawyer said with an effort at humour. He was sweating, moisture standing out on his wrinkled brow. 'I begin to wonder, what's the point of battling on? The Fascists will kill us all in the end. That's what they want, to work us to death.'

'They'll be beaten yet. We have to hold on.'

'They've won everywhere. Here, Poland, France. England will be next. And Stalin has made his non-aggression pact with Hitler because he is so afraid.'

'Comrade Stalin made his pact with Hitler to buy time.' It was what Establo had said when the guards told them of the Nazi–Soviet pact. Bernie couldn't swallow the idea that this war against fascism had now to be called a war between imperialist powers. That was when he had doubted the party line for the first time.

'Comrade Stalin.' Vicente laughed, a hollow laugh that turned into a cough.

Far away, where the Tierra Muerta sloped down into the hazy distance, Bernie saw an extraordinary thing. Above a layer of white mist was a cliff and set into its side were houses, sunlight sparkling on their windows. They seemed close, floating on the mist itself. It was a trick the light played here sometimes, like a mirage in the desert. Bernie nudged Vicente. 'Look there, *amigo*, is that not a sight worth staying alive for? You don't often get such a view as that.'

Vicente peered into the distance. 'I can't see, I haven't my glasses. Can you see Cuenca today?'

'You can see the hanging houses themselves; they look as if they're riding on the mist from the gorge.' Bernie sighed. 'It's like looking into another world.'

Ahead, Ramirez blew his whistle. 'Move it!' Agustín called. Bernie helped Vicente to his feet. As they moved on Agustín fell into step with them. Bernie saw the man was studying him, though pretending not to. He wondered if he was after his arse; such things happened in the camp.

The quarry was a great round gash carved into the side of the hill. For the last few weeks they had worked here every day, hacking out lumps of limestone and breaking them into smaller chunks that were taken away in lorries. Bernie wondered if the story about Franco's monument was true; sometimes, like Vicente, he wondered whether the quarrying was just an excuse to have them worked slowly to death in this wilderness.

Agustín and another guard built a fire outside the lean-to hut that had been erected at the front of the quarry but Ramirez didn't head for the warmth as Molina would have done. He went and stood on a pile of stones, watching with his hands behind his back as one of the guards set up the sub-machine gun. Other guards distributed picks and spades from the lean-to. There was no chance of the prisoners using the tools as weapons and charging them – the machine gun would have cut them down in a minute.

Bernie and Vicente found a heap of limestone blocks to work on, partly hidden by a projecting rock buttress. Bernie set to work with his pick, letting Vicente sort the broken rocks into smaller pieces at a snail's pace. They would work here, with only a short midday break for food and water, till sunset. At least now the days were getting shorter; in summer a work day lasted thirteen hours. The clang and crack of stone against metal sounded all around.

An hour later Vicente stumbled and sat down heavily. He blew his nose again, smearing his sleeve with a thin trail of the pus-like discharge, and groaned with pain. 'I can't go on,' he said. 'Call the guard.'

'Just rest for a bit.'

'It's too dangerous, Bernardo. You're supposed to call the guards if someone's ill.'

'Shut your bourgeois mouth.'

Vicente sat, his breath coming in gasps. Bernie worked on, listening for a footfall behind the buttress. His feet hurt in his cracked old boots and he had reached the first stage of the day's thirst, his tongue ceaselessly moving round his mouth in search of moisture.

The soldier appeared without warning, coming round the stone buttress too quickly for Bernie to call Vicente to his feet. It was Rodolfo, a grizzled veteran of the Moroccan wars.

'What are you doing?' he yelled. 'You! Get up!'

Vicente hauled himself shakily to his feet. Rodolfo rounded on Bernie.

'Why are you allowing this man to shirk? This is sabotage!'

'He was taken ill, *señor cabo*. I was about to call for you.'

Rodolfo pulled his whistle from his pocket and blew it fiercely. Vicente's shoulders slumped in despair.

There was a crunch of booted feet and Ramirez appeared. A moment later Agustín ran up behind him. Ramirez glowered at Vicente and Bernie.

'What the fuck is happening?'

Rodolfo's arm snapped out in the Fascist salute. 'I caught the *abogado* sitting doing nothing,' he said. 'The *inglés* stood by watching.'

'Please, *señor sargento*,' Vicente said. 'I felt unwell. Piper was about to call the guard.'

'You felt *unwell*, did you?' Ramirez's eyes bulged with anger. He slapped Vicente hard across the face with his gloved hand. The sound echoed across the quarry like a rifle shot, and the lawyer went down in a heap. Ramirez turned to Bernie.

'You were letting him slack, weren't you? Communist English bastard.' He stepped closer. 'You're one of those who's not beaten inside your head, aren't you? I think you need a day on the cross.' He turned to Rodolfo, who smiled and nodded grimly. Bernie set his lips. He thought of what a stretching would do to his old shoulder wound

– it ached badly enough after a day out here. He looked into Ramirez's eyes. Something in his look must have angered the captain. Faster than the eye could follow he pulled out his whip and lashed Bernie across the neck. Bernie cried out and staggered, blood welling up between his fingers.

Agustín stepped forward and nervously touched Ramirez's arm. '*Señor sargento*.' Ramirez looked round impatiently.

'What?'

Agustín swallowed. '*Señor*, the psychiatrist is studying this man. I – I do not think the *comandante* would want him harmed.'

Ramirez frowned. 'Are you sure? This one?'

'*Por cierto, sargento*.'

Ramirez pursed his lips like a child deprived of a treat. He nodded reluctantly.

'Very well.' He leaned over Bernie, hot breath rancid with garlic blasting into his face. 'Take that as a warning. And you – ' he gestured to Vicente – 'get back to work.'

He marched away, Rodolfo following. Agustín scurried after them; he did not look at Bernie.

THAT EVENING, as the men lay on their bunks waiting for lights out, Vicente turned to Bernie. The lawyer had slept most of the evening.

'Better?' Bernie asked.

Vicente sighed. 'I have rested at least.' His face was drawn and seamed in the dim candlelight. 'You?'

Bernie lightly touched the long cut on his neck. He had bathed it, he hoped it would not become infected. 'I'll be all right.'

'What happened this morning?' Vicente whispered. 'Why did they let you go?'

'I don't know, I've been trying to work it out all day.' Ramirez's leniency was the talk of the camp; at supper Establo had asked him about it suspiciously. 'Agustín said I was under the psychiatrist, but the psychiatrist wouldn't care what state I was in.'

'Maybe Agustín wants you in his bed.'

'I wondered that but I don't think so. He doesn't look at me in that way.'

'Someone looked at me as we came in,' Vicente said quietly. 'I saw him.'

'Father Eduardo? Yes, I saw too.'

Bernie had had to help the lawyer on the last part of the evening journey back from the quarry, supporting him as he walked. As they crossed the yard he had seen the young priest come out of the classroom hut. He had paused and followed them with his eyes as they hobbled to their hut.

'He has me marked down now,' Vicente said. 'For him I would be a good prize.'

Chapter Twenty-Six

Sandy's office was in a shabby square full of shops and little warehouses advertising bankrupt stock. It was raining, a cold thin rain. An old newspaper seller watched Harry lugubriously from the shelter of his kiosk as he crossed the square. On the other side some men unloading boxes from a cart looked at him curiously. So far as Harry knew no one was following him now, but he felt exposed nonetheless.

A line of electric bells was set into the lintel of a heavy, unpainted wooden door. A steel plaque beside the top one read 'Nuevas Iniciativas'. Harry rang and waited.

Sandy had telephoned him at the embassy. 'Sorry to have taken so long, but about this business opportunity – can we meet, at my office, not the cafe? I've got some things to show you. Barbara will be joining us afterwards for coffee.'

Harry had met with Tolhurst and Hillgarth in Tolhurst's office that morning for a briefing. Hillgarth was in a good mood, his saturnine face relaxed, self-satisfied.

'Could this be the gold?' he asked, his eyes dancing.

'He's been very cagey about that,' Harry replied cautiously.

Hillgarth ran a finger down the crease of his trousers, frowning thoughtfully. 'We hear Franco's trying to negotiate supplies of food from the Argentines. They'll want paying, eh, Tolly?'

'Yes, sir.'

Hillgarth nodded and leaned back in his chair. 'Whatever he's offering, I think you should take the bait.' He laughed softly. 'No, that's not quite right, you're the bait and he's the fish. OK, Tolly. The money.'

Tolhurst opened a folder and looked earnestly at Harry. 'You're authorized to offer to invest up to two thousand pounds in any relevant business proposal of Forsyth's. If he asks for more, you can come back to us. We'll provide the money, but you should show Forsyth your own bank book showing you've got funds.'

'I've got it here.' Harry passed over the little cardboard book. Hillgarth studied it carefully.

'It's a lot of money.'

'I got my parents' capital when I was twenty-one. I don't spend much.'

'You ought to live a little. When I was your age I was running a tin mine in Bolivia – what I wouldn't have given then for five thousand pounds.'

'Useful that Brett kept it,' Tolhurst said. 'London doesn't like fake bank books.'

Hillgarth's large brown eyes were still fixed on Harry. He shifted a little, remembering he hadn't told them about Enrique. It was stupid and stubborn but he hadn't. What harm could it do?

'Maestre tells me his daughter's heartbroken you haven't been in touch since you went to the Prado,' Hillgarth said.

Harry hesitated, then said, 'I'd rather not see her again, frankly.'

Hillgarth lit a Gold Flake, studying Harry over his lighter. 'Nice little *señorita*, I'm surprised at you.'

'She's hardly more than a child.'

'Pity. Could be useful diplomatically.'

Harry didn't reply. He was lying to Sandy and Barbara, wasn't that enough deception without adding Milagros?

'I suppose some would say you're an ideal agent, Brett,' Hillgarth said musingly. 'Incorruptible. You don't chase women, you're not interested in money. You don't even drink much, do you?'

'We had a few the other night,' Tolhurst said cheerfully.

'Only most agents *are* corruptible. They want something, even if it's only excitement. But you don't go for that either, do you?'

'I'm doing this for my country,' Harry said. He knew he sounded stiff and pompous but he didn't care. 'Because I was told it'd help the war effort. It's another form of soldiering.'

Hillgarth nodded slowly. 'All right, that's good. Loyalty.' He considered. 'How much would you do, for loyalty?'

Harry hesitated, but Hillgarth's contemptuous manner had

angered him and that made him bold. 'I don't know, sir, it would depend what I was asked.'

Hillgarth nodded. 'But there may be limits?'

'It would depend what I was asked,' he repeated.

'I doubt Forsyth has limits. What do you think?'

'Sandy only lets you see what he wants you to see. I don't really know what he could be capable of.' He paused. 'Probably just about anything.' Like you, he thought.

'Well, we'll see.' Hillgarth leaned back. 'As for today, see what he's offering, say you'll go in with him and then report back.'

'But don't jump at it, Harry,' Tolhurst added. 'Appear doubtful, worried about your money. Say you need to know everything before you commit yourself.'

'Yes,' Hillgarth agreed. 'That's the line to take. That way he'll show you more.'

A PLUMP WOMAN in her fifties with a lined face and grey hair tied in a bun answered the door. 'Yes?' she asked.

'I've an appointment with Señor Forsyth. Señor Brett.'

She led him up a narrow flight of stairs into a little office where a typewriter stood on a battered desk. She knocked on a door and Sandy emerged, smiling broadly. He wore a pinstripe business suit, a red handkerchief in his breast pocket.

'Harry! Welcome to Nuevas Iniciativas.' He smiled at the secretary, who blushed unexpectedly. 'I see you've met Maria, she brews the best tea in Madrid. Two teas and two coffees, Maria.' The secretary bustled away.

'Come in.' Sandy ushered Harry into a surprisingly large room. A big table cluttered with maps and papers took up one wall. Harry was surprised to see several gleaming metal canisters, like big thermos flasks, piled there too. Above the table was a reproduction of a nineteeth-century painting. A tropical sea teemed with savage life, giant reptiles seizing one another in bloody jaws as pterodactyls wheeled in the sky above. Opposite, behind a large oak desk, two men in suits sat smoking.

'Sebastian de Salas of course you know,' Sandy said.

'*Buenas tardes*.' De Salas rose and bowed, shaking Harry's hand.

The other man was small and sallow, dressed in an ill-fitting suit. In contrast to de Salas's sharp neatness, he looked like a dowdy clerk.

'Alberto Otero, the brains of our outfit.' Otero rose briefly, shaking Harry's hand with a moist grip. He didn't smile, studying him expressionlessly.

'I see you noticed my picture,' Sandy said. '"Ancient Dorsetshire" by Henry de la Beche. Painted in 1830, when people were first learning about dinosaurs.'

'It is all wrong, of course,' Otero said severely. 'The animals are grossly exaggerated.'

'Yes, Alberto. But imagine what people must have thought when they realized their nice English landscape had once been full of giant reptiles.' Forsyth smiled and sat down next to de Salas. Sitting facing them, Harry realized all three wore identical narrow moustaches, the badge of the Falange.

Sandy leaned back, folding his arms over his stomach. 'Now then, Harry, you've got some money to invest and we've got a project that could do with further capital. Alberto, though, he wants to know a bit more about the funds available.' He winked. 'Cautious, these Spaniards. Quite right too, of course.'

'I've a fair bit of money in the bank,' Harry said. 'Though I wouldn't want to put too much in one project.'

De Salas nodded but Otero's face remained expressionless. 'Might I ask where this has come from?' he asked. 'I do not want to seem impertinent, but we should know.'

'Certainly. It's the capital from my parents' estate. They died when I was a child.'

'Harry's an old sobersides,' Sandy said. 'Doesn't spend much.'

'Where is the money now?'

'In my bank in England.' Harry produced the bank book. 'Have a look, I don't mind. I thought you might want to see.'

Otero studied the book. 'What about currency restrictions?'

'Don't apply,' Sandy said. 'Embassy staff. Isn't that right, Harry?'

'I'm allowed to invest in a neutral country.'

De Salas smiled. 'And you would not mind investing here? I'm thinking of the political situation. We rather disagreed on that topic when last we met.'

'I support my country against Germany. I've no quarrel with Spain. It has to make its own future. As you said.'

'When there is money to be made, *eh, señor*?' Sebastian gave Harry a smile; conspiratorial but slightly contemptuous as well.

'What if Spain comes into the war?' Otero asked. 'If nothing else, that would freeze any British investments here.'

'They seem pretty confident at the embassy Franco won't come in,' Harry said. 'Confident enough for me to take the risk.'

Otero nodded slowly. 'How good is your information? Is this the ambassador's thinking?'

Knowledge like that really would be worth money, Harry knew. 'I just hear what the other translators say. Of course I've no access to any secret material.' He let a haughty note enter his voice. 'And I wouldn't dream of breathing a word of it if I did. I only know what people say generally; the Spanish messenger boys probably know as much.'

Sebastian raised a hand. 'Of course, Señor Brett. Forgive my curiosity.'

'Harry's loyal to the King,' Sandy said with a smile. Otero looked at him keenly.

'If we are to tell you about this venture of ours, you would have to keep it entirely confidential.'

'Of course.'

'We would not want it repeated anywhere else. Especially not at the embassy. They might be interested, perhaps?'

'I don't see why,' Harry said, looking naive. 'If it's just a business venture.' He put on a worried look. 'It's nothing illegal, is it?'

Otero smiled. 'Far from it. But it is a matter that could excite – considerable interest.'

'Of course I won't say anything to anyone.' He hesitated a moment. 'I promise.'

'Not even Barbara,' Sandy added. 'Honour bright, eh?'

'Of course.'

Sebastian de Salas smiled. 'Sandy has told us of the honour between public-school friends. It is a code, yes?'

'One Harry would never break,' Sandy added.

'A code of honour, like that among soldiers of the legion?'

'Yes,' Harry replied. 'Yes, that's right.'

Otero studied Harry a moment longer, then turned to Sandy. 'Very well. But on your responsibility, Forsyth.'

'I vouch for Harry,' Sandy said with a smile.

'How much would you consider investing?' Otero asked Harry.

'It depends. It depends what's on offer.'

There was a tap at the door and Maria brought in a tray. She poured tea and coffee for them. In the silence Harry felt an unexpected clutch of fear. He was conscious his armpits were soggy with sweat. It was hard with three of them all concentrating on him. The secretary left, closing the door quietly.

'OK.' Sandy opened a drawer in his desk. Everyone watched as he brought out a glass phial filled with yellow dust. He took a sheet of paper and carefully poured a little out.

'There. What d'you think that is? Go on, pick it up.'

Harry ran the dust between his fingers. He knew what it was but pretended innocence. 'It feels oily.'

Otero gave a barking laugh and shook his head. Sandy smiled broadly.

'It's gold, Harry. Spanish gold. It came out of a field some way from here. Alberto's been pottering about that neck of the woods for years, taking samples, and this spring he hit the jackpot. Spain has some small gold deposits but this one's big. Very big.'

Harry let the grains fall back on the paper. 'Is this how gold looks when it comes out of the ground?'

Otero rose and went over to the big table. He brought one of the canisters over to the desk and twisted off the top. It was full of a crumbly yellow-orange soil.

'This is the ore. You apply mercury and acid to separate the gold. Two canisters like this would produce about what's in that phial; the gold content is very high. Can you imagine how much a whole field of that ore would be worth? Twenty fields?'

Harry poked the crumbly earth gently. This is it, he thought. I've bloody done it.

'These canisters go to the Ministry of Mines for assay.' Sandy turned to de Salas. 'That's where Sebastian works, he's our contact there.'

De Salas nodded. 'Spain's economic policy is based on self-sufficiency, Señor Brett, as you know. Mineral exploitation is a priority. The Ministry of Mines grants licences to private companies to explore sites. Then if workable mineral deposits are found and the government laboratories are happy with the assay, the company receives a licence to develop.'

'And its shares go up,' Sandy added.

'And this is what Nuevas Iniciativas does?'

'That's right. We three are the principal shareholders. Sebastian shouldn't be a member, technically, as he's a Ministry of Mines official, but no one bothers about that sort of thing here. And he's got some colleagues to invest.'

'Are they happy with your ore?'

'There have been delays,' de Salas replied. 'Unfortunately politics are involved. Do you know about the Badajoz fiasco?'

'I heard something.'

Sandy nodded. 'Huge gold deposits were reported last year, but it turned out there was nothing there. After the Generalísimo told the country in his Christmas broadcast that Spain would soon have all the gold it needed.' Sandy smiled sadly. 'It was embarrassing – like that Austrian scientist Franco funded, who claimed to be able to manufacture petrol from grass. The Generalísimo was so desperate for these things that he became, shall we say, a little credulous. Now he's gone to the other extreme, become overcautious. There's a committee that studies all claims of substantial mineral deposits. The people on it are, well, not sympathetic politically to the Ministry of Mines. They see us as a Falange nest.'

'But if there are genuine resources, surely it's in everyone's interest to develop them?'

'So you'd think, Harry,' Sandy agreed. 'So you'd think.'

Otero shrugged. 'Certain people are dragging things out, ordering further assays, though enough tests have been carried out to satisfy any reasonable customer. Tests on samples taken from the site in front of government inspectors.'

'We may be able to show you those reports,' Sandy said. 'On a strictly confidential basis, of course.'

'I don't mind tests,' Otero continued. 'In fact, in the meantime I've been surveying neighbouring areas and they show even better potential. When we are past these bureaucratic hurdles and it is all public, everyone associated with this company is going to become very rich. But it all costs money, *señor*. Taking samples, making tests – and there is a neighbouring piece of land we want. The price is more than we can afford right now.'

'It's not just politics,' de Salas added. 'Those generals on the committee would like to run us out of money by demanding test after test, drive us to a position where we have to sell out to another exploration company. One controlled by them.'

'Always comes down to filthy lucre.' Sandy raised his eyebrows. 'A thousand pounds, say, could be *very* useful to us now. It could fund more drilling, sample preparation, and the purchase of rights on this new land. If they saw we'd got real financial resources I think the obstructiveness would fall away. Then we'd all be in for a packet.'

'Five hundred?' Harry said. 'That's a lot. It seems a bit – speculative.'

'It is not speculative,' Otero said frostily. 'I said, we have reports verifying the quality of our ore.'

Harry pretended to consider, pursing his lips. His heart was beating fast but he wasn't afraid any more, he scented success.

'These reports, are they in layman's language?'

'Of course.' De Salas laughed. 'They have to be understood by the committee.'

'You'd have to come here and read them,' Sandy said. 'We couldn't let them out of the office. But we'd take you through them.'

'You are privileged, Señor Brett,' Otero said seriously. 'Very few people know about this.'

Harry took a deep breath. In for a penny, in for a pound, he thought. 'I'd want to see the site. I wouldn't want to go in blind.'

Otero shook his head slowly. 'Its location is very confidential information, *señor*. I am not prepared to go that far, no.'

'The government must know where it is, surely?'

'Yes, Harry.' Sandy's voice was suddenly impatient. 'But only on the basis of guaranteed confidentiality.'

'It's just, if I'm to be part of this . . .' Harry spread his hands.

'We'll have to discuss that.' Sandy stroked his moustache, looking between de Salas and Otero. Both looked unhappy.

'All right,' Harry said. There was no point in pressing further now. He felt pleasure at having stirred them to obvious anxiety. That had knocked the complacent smile off Sandy's face. If they refused to show him he would go in with them anyway, but to see the site would be a real coup.

There was a tap on the door. Sandy looked up, still irritable, as Maria put her head through.

'What is it?'

'Señora Forsyth has arrived, sir. She's outside.'

Sandy ran a hand through his hair. 'She's early. Look, Harry, we'll need to discuss this. Why don't you take Barbara for that coffee on your own? We'll ring you later.'

'As you like.'

'OK. I'll come out with you, say hello.' Sandy rose; the Spaniards did too.

'Then, until we meet again.' Sebastian shook his hand, followed by Otero, who gave him another hard stare. Sandy ushered him out. Barbara was sitting by Maria's desk, in a patterned headscarf slick with rain. She looked pale and preoccupied.

'Hello, Harry.'

'You're early!' Sandy gestured impatiently at the scarf. 'And what are you wearing that for? You've enough hats.'

Harry stared at him, surprised by his tone. Catching his look, Sandy smiled and took Barbara's arm. 'Look, darling, change of plan. We've had a meeting, there's something I need to discuss with some friends. Why don't you and Harry go for a coffee on your own?'

'Yes, all right.' She gave Harry a quick smile.

'He'll take you home afterwards, won't you, Harry? Good man. I'll ring tomorrow.' He winked. 'I'll see what I can do with Otero.'

Outside the rain was still falling steadily, chill and dank. Barbara adjusted her headscarf.

'He doesn't like me wearing these,' she said. 'Thinks they're common.' She gave a tight cold smile, an expression Harry had never seen on her face before. 'What have you been up to – is he trying to rope you into one of his schemes?'

Harry laughed awkwardly. 'There is an investment possibility.'

'Look, d'you mind if we don't go for coffee? I'd rather get home, I think I've a cold coming.'

'Of course.' They walked on slowly. He looked at her pale set face. 'Are you all right, Barbara?'

'No, not really.' She sighed deeply. 'I went to a cinema after lunch, to pass the time till I met you. They had the newsreel, you know what they're like, pro-German propaganda.' She gave a shuddering sigh. 'There was an item about the bombing, "Britain on its Knees". They showed the centre of Birmingham.'

'I'm sorry. Was it bad?'

'Awful. Parts of the city were on fire. All those people killed in the last big raid and they were *gloating*.' She stopped suddenly. 'Oh God, I'm sorry, I feel faint.'

Harry looked around for a cafe but there were none in view, only one of the large city churches. He took her arm. 'Come on, let's go and sit down in there.' He led her up the steps.

The church interior was cold and gloomy, only the ornate gold-covered altar was lit. Along the shadowy benches a few dim figures sat huddled, some murmuring softly. Harry led Barbara to an empty bench. There were tears on her cheeks. She took off her glasses, pulling a handkerchief from her pocket.

'I'm sorry,' she whispered.

'I understand. I worry about my cousin Will.'

'He's the one whose wife's a bit of a dragon?'

'Yes. Though I saw another side to her just before I came out. We were caught in a raid, I had to get her to a shelter. She was terrified for her children. I didn't think she loved them, but she does.'

Barbara sighed. 'I saw raids here, of course, during the Civil War, but to see it in England—' She bit her lip. Things will never be the same after this, will they? Anywhere?'

Harry looked at her earnest face, pale in the gloom. 'No. I don't think they will.'

'I feel I should be there. England. I wanted security once, after

Bernie – ' she paused – 'after he went. Sandy gave me that, or I thought he did. But there's no security anywhere, not now.' She paused again. 'I'm not sure I even want it any more.'

Harry smiled sadly. 'I still do, I'm afraid. I'm not a hero. If I'm honest what I'd really like is to scuttle home and have a quiet life.'

'But you won't, will you?' She smiled at him. 'That would go against your sense of honour.'

'Funny, that word came up in the talk I've just been having with Sandy. Public-school honour. Of course, it never meant anything to him.'

They were silent a moment. Their eyes had adjusted to the gloom and Harry saw most of the people praying were poor women in black. Some had only scraps of black rag to cover their heads. Barbara looked at the figure of Jesus on the Cross in a side chapel, painted blood running from his wounds.

'What a religion,' she said bitterly. 'Blood and torture, no wonder the Spaniards ended up massacring one another. Religion's a curse, Sandy's right about that.'

'I used to think it held people's excesses in check.'

Barbara gave a bitter laugh. 'It does the opposite here, I think it always has.' She replaced her glasses. 'Do you remember that family Bernie was friendly with? The Meras?'

'Yes, I was with him when he first met Pedro Mera. In fact, I went – I went to see if I could find their flat.' He hesitated, he didn't want to tell Barbara what he had found in Carabanchel.

'Did you?'

'Yes. Why – have you seen them?' His face was eager.

Barbara bit her lip. 'You know I'm doing voluntary work at a church orphanage?' she said quietly.

'Yes.'

'It's a hell hole. They treat the children like animals. That little daughter of Pedro and Inés, Carmela, she was brought in two days ago. She'd been living wild. I think the others are all dead.'

'Oh God.' Harry remembered the little girl looking solemnly at him as he tried to teach her English words. Her brother Antonio who had watched the Communists chasing the Fascist with him and

Bernie; Pedro the big bluff father, Inés the tireless mother. 'All of them?'

'I think so.' Barbara reached into her bag and pulled out the ragged woollen donkey, sewn up round the middle. 'The old bitch who works with me pulled this out of the child's hand and tore it. I think it was the last possession Carmela had. I promised I'd mend it but when I took it back this morning they said she kept trying to escape so she'd been moved to a special home for recalcitrant children. You can imagine what that means. The nun in charge wouldn't tell me where it was, said it wasn't my concern. Sister Inmaculada.' There was a savage bitterness in her tone.

'Can't you find out?'

'How? How can I if they won't tell me?' Her voice rose, then she sighed. Her mouth set. 'I know, let's leave Fernandito the donkey as an offering to the Lord. Maybe then he'll take care of Carmela. Maybe.' She got up and took the toy to the rail of the side chapel. She thrust it angrily on top of the flowers in front of the Cross, then came back and sat beside Harry.

'I'm not going back to work at the convent. Sandy won't like it but he'll have to lump it.'

'Are you and Sandy – ' he hesitated – 'all right?'

She smiled sadly. 'Let's leave that one, Harry.' She shivered. 'Come on, let's get out of this mausoleum.'

He looked at her seriously. 'Barbara, if ever you need – well – any help, you can always come to me.'

She touched his hand. An old woman walking by clicked her tongue disapprovingly.

'Thanks, Harry. But I'm all right, I've just had a bad day.' Harry saw the old woman catch the sleeve of a priest and point to them. 'Come on,' Barbara said. 'We'll get arrested for immorality on sacred premises.'

OUTSIDE, BARBARA felt angry with herself for her momentary dizziness. She had to stay strong.

After leaving the church she let Harry take her to a coffee bar. She asked what the latest word was at the embassy about Franco entering the war. Harry told her they thought Franco's meeting with Hitler had gone badly. That was some comfort.

When she got home she made some tea and sat by herself in the kitchen, thinking and smoking. Pilar was out for the afternoon; Barbara was glad, she could never feel at ease around the girl. The weather forecast came on, the announcer promising more cold weather for Madrid and snow for the Guadarrama mountains. Barbara looked out at the rainswept garden and thought, that'll mean snow in Cuenca too. And nothing to do now but wait for Luis's brother to take his leave. She thought about Harry again. She wished she could have told him about Bernie, she hated letting him carry on thinking his old friend was dead and longed to tell him the truth, but he was Sandy's friend too, and what she was thinking of doing was illegal. It wasn't safe, it wasn't safe to tell a soul.

After a while she went into the *salón* and wrote a letter to Sister Inmaculada, telling her in coldly polite tones that domestic commitments meant she couldn't work at the orphanage any more. She was just finishing as Sandy came in. He looked tired. He smiled as he put down his briefcase. It made a chinking sound, as though it contained something metal. He came over and put a hand on her shoulder.

'How are you, darling? Listen, I'm sorry I was bad-tempered at the office. I've had a hard day. Been at the Jews' Committee for the last hour.' He leaned over and kissed her neck. Once that would have melted her, now she was conscious only of the tickling hairs of his moustache. She pulled away. He frowned.

'What's the matter? I've said I'm sorry.'

'I've had a bad day too.'

'Who are you writing to?'

'Sister Inmaculada. I've said I'm not going to the orphanage any more. I can't stand how those children are treated.'

'You haven't said that in the letter, have you?'

'No, Sandy, I've said domestic commitments. Don't worry, there won't be any trouble with the *marquesa*.'

He stepped away. 'No need to be so snappy.'

She took a deep breath. 'I'm sorry.'

'So what are you going to do with yourself now? You need something to do.'

I need a month till I can get Bernie away and escape, she thought. 'I don't know. Maybe I could help with your refugees? The Jews?'

Sandy took a sip of whisky. He shook his head. 'I've just been meeting some of them. They're very traditional. Don't like being told what to do by women.'

'I thought they were mostly professional people.'

'They're still very traditional.' He changed the subject. 'What did Harry have to say for himself?'

'We talked about the war. He doesn't think Franco will come in.'

'Yes, that's what he told me. You know, he's quite shrewd when it comes to business.' He smiled reflectively. 'More than I'd have expected.' He looked at her again. 'Look, lovey, I think you're making a mistake about the orphanage. You have to do things their way. When in Rome – I've said that often enough.'

'Yes, you have. But I'm not going back there, Sandy, I won't be part of how those children are treated.' Why did he always seem to provoke her to anger these days, just when she needed to keep things normal, on an even keel? Barbara knew he had noticed something was wrong. She even avoided love-making now, and when he persisted and she gave in, she couldn't fake pleasure.

'Those children are wild,' Sandy said. 'You've said so yourself. They need disciplining, not toy animals.'

'God, Sandy, sometimes I think you've got a stone instead of a heart.' The words came out before she could stop herself.

He flushed angrily and took a step towards her. His fists were clenched and Barbara flinched, heart thudding. She had always known he could be cruel, venomous when he was crossed, but until now she had never feared violence from him. She drew a sharp breath. Sandy checked himself and spoke coldly.

'I *made* you,' he said. 'Don't you forget it. You were nothing when I met you, a mess, because all you've ever cared about is what people think of you. All *you've* got for a heart is sentimental mush.' He glared at her furiously and she saw clearly, for the first time, what he had always wanted from her, what their relationship had been about from the start. Control. Power.

She got up and walked out of the room.

Chapter Twenty-Seven

When Harry returned home after leaving Barbara he found two letters waiting for him. One was a hand-delivered scribbled note from Sandy. It said he had persuaded Otero and de Salas to let him visit the mine, and that he would collect Harry early on Sunday, in three days' time, and drive him there. It was only a few hours' journey, he said.

He opened the other letter; the address was written in a small, neat hand he didn't recognize. It was from Sofia, and enclosed a bill for treatment and drugs from a doctor in the town centre, along with a letter in Spanish.

> Dear Señor Brett,
>
> I enclose the bill from the doctor. I know his charges are reasonable. Enrique is better already. Soon he will be able to work again and things will be easier for all of us. He sends his thanks, as does Mama. You saved Enrique's life and we will always remember what you did with gratitude.

Harry felt disappointed by the letter's formal tone, the hint of dismissal. He turned it over in his hands a couple of times, then sat down and wrote a reply.

> I am so glad Enrique is better and I shall pay the doctor's bill tomorrow morning. I would like to meet you to give you the receipt and also to buy you coffee. I enjoyed our talk and I meet few Spanish people informally. I hope you will feel able to come.

He suggested they meet in two days' time, at a cafe he knew near the Puerta del Sol, at six o'clock because he knew she began work early.

Harry sealed the letter. He would post it when he went out.

The receipt was an excuse, as she would realize. Well, either she would reply or she would not. He turned to the telephone table and dialled the embassy. He asked reception to tell Mr Tolhurst that he wished to come in to discuss the planned press release on the fruit imports. It was the code they had agreed for when he had news about Sandy. He had thought these codes were silly and melodramatic at first but realized they were necessary as the phones were tapped.

The receptionist came back and said Mr Tolhurst was available if he would like to call in now. He wasn't surprised: Tolly seemed to spend many of his evenings at the embassy. Harry fetched his coat and went out again.

Tolhurst was delighted when Harry told him what had happened. He said he would tell Hillgarth; he was in a meeting but he would want to know about this. He returned to his little office a few minutes later, beaming excitedly.

'The captain's really pleased,' he said. 'If there is a lot of gold my guess is the captain will go straight to Churchill and he'll order the blockade strengthened; let in fewer supplies to make up for any they can pay for with gold.' He rubbed his hands.

'What will Sir Sam say to that?'

'It's what the captain thinks that counts with Churchill.' Tolhurst's face flushed with pleasure as he rolled off the Prime Minister's name.

'They'll ask why the blockade's being tightened.'

'We'll probably tell them. Show them they can't keep anything from us. And one in the eye for the Falange faction. You said we should have a firmer policy, Harry. We might be going to get it.'

Harry nodded thoughtfully. 'That'll leave Sandy in the soup. I suppose he could end up in real trouble.' He realized he had been so focused on his mission, he had hardly thought about what might happen to Sandy. He felt a twinge of guilt.

Tolhurst winked. 'Not necessarily. The captain's got something up his sleeve there too.'

'What?' Harry thought a moment. 'You're not going to try and recruit him?'

Tolhurst shook his head. 'Can't say, not yet.' He smiled, a self-important smile that irritated Harry. 'By the way, that other business, the Knights of St George, you haven't told anyone else?'

'Of course not.'

'Important you don't.'

'I know.'

NEXT MORNING Harry accompanied one of the embassy secretaries to another interpreting session with Maestre, more certificates to be gone through. The young Falange interpreter was there again and they repeated the game of pretending Maestre spoke no English. The Spanish general's manner towards Harry was distinctly cool and he realized Hillgarth had been right; his failure to contact Milagros again had been taken as a slight. But he wouldn't pretend there might be something between him and the girl just to keep the spies happy. He was glad it was Friday, the end of the week. When he came home there was a reply from Sofia on the mat, just a couple of lines agreeing to meet him the next evening. He was surprised by the degree to which his heart soared.

The cafe was a small place, bright and modern. But for Franco's picture on the wall behind the counter it could have been anywhere in Europe. He was a little early but Sofia was there already, sitting at the back of the cafe nursing a cup of coffee. She wore the same long black coat she had had on the day he took Enrique back to the flat, a little threadbare he could see under the lights. Her elfin face, without make-up, was pale. She looked much younger, vulnerable. She looked up with a smile as he approached.

'I hope I haven't kept you waiting,' he said.

'I was early. You are on time.' There was something different in her smile. It was open and friendly but there was something knowing in it too.

'Let me get you a fresh coffee.'

He fetched the drinks.

'Enrique is much better,' she said as he sat down. 'He is going out to look for work next week.'

He smiled wryly. 'Different work.'

'Oh yes. Labouring if he can get it.'

'Did the – the ministry pay him while he was sick?'

Her smile became cynical for a moment. 'No.'

'I've got the receipt.' Harry had visited the surgery and paid the doctor's bill, as he said he would.

'Thank you.' Sofia folded it carefully and put it in her pocket.

'If he has any more problems, I'd be happy to help.'

'He will be all right now.'

'Good.'

'As I said in my letter, you saved his life. We will always be grateful.'

'That's all right.' Harry smiled, then dried up suddenly, he couldn't think of anything to say.

'Has he been – ' Sofia raised her eyebrows a little – 'replaced?'

'No, thank goodness. I'm being left alone. I'm not at all important, you know. Just a translator.'

She lit a cigarette, then leaned back, studying him. Her expression was enquiring but not hostile or suspicious. She was far more relaxed away from the flat.

'Will you be going home to England?' she asked. 'For Christmas?'

'Christmas.' He laughed. 'I hadn't thought about it.'

'It is only six weeks away. You make a lot of the celebration in England, I believe.'

'Yes. But I doubt I'll be going home. They need everyone at the embassy. You know, the way things are. Diplomatically.' He wondered how she knew about the English Christmas. That boy from Leeds she had met in the Civil War, perhaps. He wondered again if he had been her lover. How old was she? Twenty-five? Twenty-six?

'So you will not be able to spend it with your parents.'

'My parents are dead.'

'That is sad.'

'My father died in the First War. My mother died in the influenza epidemic just after.'

She nodded. 'Yes. Spain did not fight in the First War, though we suffered in the epidemic afterwards. It is sad to lose both parents.'

'I have aunts and an uncle, a cousin. He keeps me in touch with what's happening at home.'

'The air raids?'

'Yes. They're bad, but not quite as bad as the propaganda makes out here.' He saw her look quickly around at those words, and cursed himself for forgetting they were in a country full of spies, where you had to take care what you said. 'I'm sorry,' he said.

She gave that sardonic smile again. It was strangely attractive. 'There is no one in earshot. I deliberately chose a seat at the back of the restaurant.'

'I see.'

'And do you have anyone else back home?' she asked. 'A wife, perhaps?'

He was taken aback by her directness. 'No. Nobody. Nobody at all.'

'Forgive my question. It must seem bold. You will be thinking, it is not the sort of question Spanish women ask.'

'I don't mind directness,' he said. He looked into her large brown eyes. 'It makes a change from the embassy. I went to a party given by a government minister a couple of weeks ago, for his daughter's eighteenth. The formality was stifling. Poor girl,' he added.

Sofia blew out a cloud of smoke. 'I come from a different tradition.'

'Do you?'

'The Republican tradition. My father and his family before him were Republicans. Rich foreigners think of Spain in terms of ancient churches and bullfights and women in lacy mantillas, but there is a whole different tradition here. In my family we believed women should be equal. I was brought up to believe I was as good as any man. By my mother, at least – my father had old-fashioned notions. But he had the grace to be ashamed of them sometimes.'

'What did he do?'

'He worked in a warehouse. He worked long hours for little money, like me.'

'I think the family I met when I was here in 1931 were a part of that tradition as well. I didn't see it in those terms, though.' He thought of Barbara's story, Carmela and her donkey.

'You were fond of them,' Sofia said.

'Yes, they were good people.' He smiled. 'Your family, were they Socialists too?'

She shook her head. 'We had Socialist friends, and Anarchists, and Left Republicans. But not everyone joined a party. The parties talked of Communist and Anarchist utopias but all most people want is peace, bread on the table, self-respect. Is it not so?'

'Yes.'

She leaned forward, an intent look in her eyes. 'You don't know what it was like for people like us when the Republic came, what it meant. All of a sudden we *mattered*. I got a place in medical school. I had to work as well in a bar, but everyone was so hopeful, change was coming at last, the chance of a decent life.' She smiled suddenly. 'I am sorry, Señor Brett, my tongue runs away with me. I do not often get the chance to talk about those times.'

'Don't be sorry. It helps me understand.'

'Understand what?'

'Spain.' He hesitated. 'You.'

She dropped her eyes to the table, reached for her cigarettes and lit another. When she looked up there was uncertainty in her eyes.

'Perhaps you may have to leave Spain sooner than you planned. If Franco joins the war.'

'We're hoping he won't.'

'Everyone says England will give Franco anything he wants to stay out of this war. And what happens to us then?'

Harry sighed. 'I suppose my masters would say we have to do what we do to keep Spain out of the war, but – we haven't much to be proud of, I know.'

Unexpectedly Sofia smiled. 'Oh, I am sorry, you look so sad. You have done so much to help us and I argue with you, I am sorry.'

'Don't be. Look, can I get you another coffee?'

She shook her head. 'No, I am afraid I have to get back. Mother and Paco are expecting me. I have to buy some food. Try to find some olive oil.'

Harry hesitated. But he had seen an advertisement in the evening paper and had decided he would ask her, unless this evening went badly. 'Do you like the theatre?' he asked, suddenly, clumsily, so that Sofia looked at him in puzzlement for a moment. 'I'm sorry,' he continued hastily. 'Only *Macbeth* is on at the Zara theatre tomorrow night. I wondered if you'd like to go. I'd like to see it in Spanish.'

She hesitated, looking at him with those large brown eyes. 'Thank you, *señor*, but I think perhaps not.'

'That's a shame,' Harry said. 'I just meant – I'd like us to be friends. I haven't any Spanish friends.'

She smiled, but shook her head. '*Señor*, it has been good to talk to you, but we live in very different worlds.'

'Are we so different? Am I too bourgeois?'

'They will all be dressed up in their best for the Zara. I have no clothes like theirs.' She sighed, looked at him again. 'I would not have let that bother me a few years ago.'

Harry smiled. 'Well, then.'

'I have one dress that would do.'

'Please come.'

She smiled back. 'Very well, Señor Brett.' She blushed. 'But as friends, yes?'

Chapter Twenty-Eight

It had rained a lot during the last week, a cold rain that sometimes turned to sleet. On the path to the quarry the prisoners squelched through clinging red mud; each day the snowline on the distant mountains descended a little lower.

That morning it was raw and damp. The work detail stood in lines by the quarry, stamping their feet to keep warm as a pair of army sappers carefully placed sticks of dynamite in a long crack running the length of a twenty-foot rockface. Sergeant Molina, back from leave, stood talking to the driver of the army truck that had brought the explosives up from Cuenca.

Bernie thought about Agustín. A few days before he had gone on leave. He left during morning roll-call; Bernie saw him walking across the yard, kitbag over his shoulder. Agustín met his eye for a second before quickly turning his head away. The gate was opened and he disappeared up the road to Cuenca.

'That is a big charge,' Pablo muttered. Bernie's fellow-Communist was on the quarry detail with him now. He was an ex-miner from Asturias and knew about explosives. 'We should stand further back, there will be splinters flying all over the place.'

'They should have got you to set the charges, *amigo*.'

'They'd be afraid I'd set them under their truck, like we did in Oviedo in '36.'

'If we could get our hands on it, eh, Vicente?'

'Yes.' The lawyer sat slumped beside them on a rock. He had been helping Molina with paperwork that morning – the sergeant, a plump lazy man promoted beyond his abilities, could barely write and the lawyer was a godsend – but he had been sent to wait with the others while the charges were set. Vicente sat with his head in his hands. His nasal condition was worse; the discharge had stopped but now the poison seemed to be trapped inside his sinuses. He couldn't breathe through his nose and to sniff or swallow was painful.

'Stand back! Further away!' Molina called. The detail shuffled backwards as the sappers ran back to the truck; Molina and the driver joined them behind it.

There was a dull explosion and Bernie flinched but no chips of stone flew out. Instead the whole rock face collapsed, crumbling like a sandcastle hit by a wave. A cloud of dust fanned outwards, making them cough. A herd of the little deer that inhabited the Tierra Muerta ran down the hillside, bounding and leaping in terror.

As the dust subsided they saw the collapse had revealed a cave, four or five feet high, behind the rockface. The crevice evidently broadened out behind, running into the hillside. The sappers walked up to the cave. They produced torches and, crouching down, cautiously stepped in. There was a moment's silence, then a sudden yell and the two men reappeared, running back down to the truck with terrified expressions on their faces. Prisoners and guards alike watched astonished.

The sappers spoke to Molina in low urgent tones. The fat sergeant laughed.

'*¿Qué diceis? ¡No es posible! ¡Estáis loco!*'

'It's true! It's true! Go and see!'

Molina frowned, evidently nonplussed, then led the sappers over to where Bernie and the others stood. The sergeant nodded at Vicente and he stood up groggily.

'Ay, *abogado*, you are a man of learning, *no*? Perhaps you can make sense of this fool.' He gestured to the nearest sapper, a thin young man with acne. 'Tell him what you saw.'

The man swallowed. 'In that cave, there are *paintings*. Men chasing animals, deer and even elephants. It is mad but we saw it!'

A flicker of interest came into Vicente's face. 'Where?'

'On the wall, on the wall!'

'Something similar was found in France a few years ago. Cave paintings by prehistoric men.'

The young soldier crossed himself. 'It was like looking at the walls of Hell.'

Molina's eyes lit up. 'Could they be valuable?'

'Only to scientists I think, *sargento*.'

'May we see?' Bernie asked. 'I have a degree from Cambridge University,' he added untruthfully. Molina considered a moment, then nodded. Bernie and Vicente followed him back to the cave. The sappers hung back. Molina gestured brusquely to the man who had spoken. 'Show them.' The man swallowed, then took his colleague's torch and passed it to Bernie before reluctantly leading the way back to the entrance. The prisoners watched with interest.

The cave was narrow and thick with dust, making Vicente cough painfully. Ten feet in it broadened into a wide, circular cavern. Ahead, in the beams of the torches, they saw figures on the wall, stick-like men chasing huge animals, elephants with thick fur and high domed heads, rhinos, deer. Painted in bright reds and blacks, they seemed to leap and dance in the torchlight. One whole side of the cave wall was covered with them.

'Wow,' Bernie breathed.

'It's like in France,' Vicente said quietly. 'I saw pictures in a magazine. I had no idea the paintings could seem so – alive. You have made an important find, *señor*.'

'Who painted them?' the soldier asked nervously. 'Why paint pictures here in the darkness?'

'No one knows, *soldado*. Perhaps it was for their religious ceremonies.'

The sapper cast his torch uneasily round the cave, lighting stalagmites and bare rock. 'But there is no way in here,' he said uneasily.

Bernie gestured to a jumbled pile of rocks in a corner of the cave. 'See, perhaps there was an entrance there once, and it became blocked.'

'And these have been in darkness for thousands of years,' Vicente whispered. 'Older than the Catholic Church, older than Christ.'

Bernie studied the paintings. 'They're wonderful,' he said. 'It's as though they were painted yesterday. Look, a woolly mammoth. They're hunting mammoths.' He laughed at the wonder of it.

'I would like to go now.' The sapper turned, clattering back to the entrance. Bernie cast a last beam of light over a group of sticklike men running after an immense stag, then turned away.

Outside the sapper and Vicente went to talk to Molina. A guard gestured with his rifle for Bernie to return to the prisoners, still standing in ragged lines, many shivering now in the cold damp air.

'*¿Que pasó?*' Pablo asked Bernie.

'Cave paintings,' he said. 'By prehistoric men.'

'*¿De verdad?* What are they like?'

'Amazing. Thousands of years old.'

'The time of primitive communism,' Pablo said. 'Before social classes formed. They should be studied.'

Vicente rejoined them, his breath rasping like sandpaper as he crossed the uneven ground.

'What did Molina say?' Bernie asked.

'He's going to report to the *comandante*. They're moving us round the hill, they're going to blast somewhere else.' He coughed and more sweat stood out on his brow. 'Agh, I feel as if I'm on fire. If only I had some water.'

A soldier climbed to the cave mouth. He crossed himself, then stood at the entrance, guarding it.

THAT NIGHT at supper Vicente was worse. In the dim light of the oil lamps Bernie could see he was sweating heavily, shivering. He winced at every swallow of the chickpea gruel.

'Are you all right?'

Vicente didn't answer. He laid down his spoon and put his head in his hands.

The door of the mess hut opened. Aranda appeared, followed by Molina. The sergeant had a hangdog look. After them came Father Jaime, tall and stern in his *sotana*, thick iron-grey hair swept back from his high forehead. The men at the trestle tables shifted uneasily as Aranda faced them, his expression stern.

'Today at the quarry,' he said in a ringing voice, 'a discovery was made by Sergeant Molina's detail. Father Jaime wishes to address you about it.'

The priest nodded. 'These scribblings by cavemen on rock walls are pagan things, made before Christ's light shone on the world. They are to be shunned and avoided. Tomorrow fresh charges will be laid in that cave and the pictures destroyed. Anyone who even mentions them will be punished. That is all.' He nodded to Aranda, gave Molina a look of disfavour, and swept out again, followed by the officers.

Pablo leaned across to Bernie. 'The bastard. They're part of Spain's heritage.'

'These people are like the Goths and Vandals, eh, Vicente?' Bernie nudged the lawyer.

Vicente gave a groan then slid forward, his head striking the table. His tin plate crashed to the floor, bringing a guard rushing over. It was Arias, a carelessly brutal young conscript.

'*¿Que pasa aquí?*' He shook Vicente's shoulder. The lawyer groaned.

'He passed out,' Bernie said. 'He's ill, he needs attention.'

Arias grunted. 'Take him to his hut. Come on, bring him. I'll have to go out in the cold now.' He pulled his poncho over his head as he complained.

Bernie lifted Vicente. He was light, a bag of bones. The lawyer tried to stand but his legs were shaking too much. Bernie supported him out of the mess hut, the guard following. They went across the yard, stumbling through puddles where ice was forming, glinting in the spotlights from the watchtowers.

In the hut Bernie laid Vicente on his pallet. He lay semi-conscious, covered with sweat, breathing heavily. Arias studied the lawyer's face.

'I think it is time to call the priest for this one.'

'No. He's not that bad,' Bernie said. 'He's been like this before.'

'I have to call the priest if a man looks as though he is dying.'

'He's just ill. Call Father Jaime if you like, but you saw what mood he's in.'

Arias hesitated. 'All right. Leave him, come on. Back to the canteen.'

When they trooped back to the hut after the meal Vicente was awake again, though he looked worse than ever.

'What happened?' he asked. 'Did I faint?'

'Yes. You should rest now.'

'My head is on fire. It is full of poison.'

In the opposite bunk Establo lay watching them, his yellow

scabbed face monstrous in the light of a tallow candle. He called across. '¡*Ay*, *compadre!* You saw the paintings, the prehistoric men. What were they like? Fine men, eh? Primitive communists.'

'Yes, Establo, they were fine men. They were hunting furry elephants.'

Establo looked at him sharply. 'How could elephants be furry? Do not mock me, Piper.'

Next day was Sunday. There was a compulsory service in the hut that served as a church, a white cloth placed over a trestle table for an altar. The prisoners sat through it as usual, many dozing off. Father Jaime would have told the guard to jab them awake but Father Eduardo was taking the service and he let them sleep. Jaime's sermons were usually full of hell fire and vengeance but Eduardo spoke of Christ's light and the joys repentance could bring, with something almost pleading in his tone. Bernie studied him carefully.

After the services the priest was available for anyone who wanted to talk. Few ever did. Bernie hung back as the prisoners filed out, then muttered to the guard. The soldier looked at him in surprise, then led him to a little room at the back of the hut.

Bernie felt embarrassed going into the priest's room. Father Eduardo had removed his robes and was dressed once again in his black *sotana*. His plump face looked young, a scrubbed child's. He smiled nervously at Bernie, gesturing to a chair before his desk.

'*Buenos días*. Please sit. What is your name?'

'Bernie Piper. Hut eight.'

The priest consulted a list. 'Ah, yes, the Englishman. How can I help you, my son?'

'I have a friend in my hut who is very ill. Vicente Medina.'

'Yes, I know the man.'

'If he could have a doctor, something might be done for him.'

The priest shook his head sadly. 'The authorities will not allow a doctor here. I have tried, I am sorry.'

Bernie nodded. He had expected that. He went over the words he had rehearsed during the service.

'Sir, do you believe forced conversions are wrong?'

The priest hesitated a moment. 'Yes. The Church teaches that a conversion to Christianity that is not genuine, a form of words, has no validity.'

'Vicente is an old Left Republican. You know they are strong atheists.'

Father Eduardo's face set. 'I do. My church was burned by the mob in 1931. The police were ordered to do nothing; the Left Republican Azaña said all the churches in Spain were not worth one Republican life.'

'Vicente can do you no harm now.' Bernie took a deep breath. 'I want you to let him die in peace when the time comes. Don't try and give him the last rites. With his beliefs that could only be a mockery.'

Father Eduardo sighed. 'You think we press dying men into forced conversions?'

'Don't you?'

'How bad we must seem to you.' Father Eduardo looked at Bernie intently. His thick glasses enlarged his eyes so they seemed to be swimming behind the lenses. 'You were not brought up a Catholic, Piper?'

'No.'

'You are a Communist, I see.'

'Yes.' Bernie paused. 'Christians believe in forgiveness, don't they?'

'That is central to our faith.'

'Then why can't you forgive Vicente what his party may have done and leave him in peace?'

Father Eduardo raised a hand. 'You don't understand at all.' His voice had that pleading note again. 'Please try to understand. If a man dies having denied the Church he will go to Hell. But if he repents and asks forgiveness, even at the very end, after the worst life, God will forgive him. When a man is on his deathbed it is our last chance to save his soul. A man then is on the brink of eternity. Sometimes he can see his life and his sins truly for the first time, and reach out to God.'

'A man then is at his weakest point, terrified. And you know how to use that. What if a man takes the sacrament then through sheer fear?'

'Only God could know if he was truly contrite.'

Bernie realized he had lost. He had underestimated how deeply the priest was buried in his superstition. His natural compassion was just a flicker on the surface.

'You've an answer for everything, haven't you?' he asked heavily. 'Endless twisted logic?'

Father Jaime smiled sadly. 'I could say the same of your faith. The edifice Karl Marx built.'

'My beliefs are scientific.'

'Are they? I heard about the cave that was discovered in the hills, the prehistoric paintings. Figures of men chasing extinct animals, was it not?'

'Yes. They're probably priceless and you're going to destroy them.'

'That wasn't my decision. But you believe these people lived as Communists, don't you? Primitive communism, the first stage of the historical dialectic. You see, I know my Marx. But that is a *belief*, you cannot *know* how such people lived. You too live by faith; a false faith.'

It was like the psychiatrist again. Bernie wanted to hurt the priest, make him angry, as he had the doctor.

'This is not some intellectual game. We're in a place where sick men are denied doctors and worked to death by the government your church supports.'

The priest sighed. 'You are not a Spaniard, Piper, how can you really understand the Civil War? I had friends, priests, who were caught in the Republican zone. They were shot, thrown from precipices, tortured.'

'And so you take revenge on us. I thought Christians were supposed to be better than most men.' He laughed bitterly. 'What does the Bible say – by their fruits shall we know them.'

Father Eduardo didn't get angry, his face was sad and burdened. 'What do you think it is like for Father Jaime and me,' he asked quietly, 'working here among people who killed our friends? Why do you think we do it? For charity, to try and save those who hate us.'

'You know if it is Father Jaime who comes to Vicente he will enjoy what he does. His revenge.' He stood up. 'May I go now, please?'

Father Eduardo raised a hand, then dropped it wearily to the desk. 'Yes. Go.'

Bernie got up.

'I shall pray for your friend,' Father Eduardo said. 'For his recovery.'

THAT EVENING Establo ordered a cell meeting. The ten Communists gathered around Pablo's bed, at the farthest end of the hut.

'We need to strengthen our Marxist faith,' Establo said. Bernie looked into his face as he used that word. It was stern, severe. 'The discovery of these paintings has made me think. We should have classes on the Marxist understanding of history, the development of the class struggle through the ages. Something to bond us closer together again; we need that with another winter upon us.'

One or two of the men nodded but others looked weary. Miguel, an old tramworker from Valencia, spoke up.

'It's too cold to sit around talking in the dark.'

'And what if the guards find out?' Pablo said. 'Or someone tells?'

'Who's going to lead these classes?' Bernie asked. 'You?' He could sense the meeting was going against Establo; he should have made this suggestion before the cold nights sent the men shrinking back into themselves.

The scaly head turned in Bernie's direction, eyes bright with anger. 'Yes. I am the cell leader.'

'Comrade Establo is right,' said Pepino, a hollow-faced young farmworker. 'We need to remember what we are.'

'Well, I for one haven't the energy to listen to Comrade Establo lecturing us on historical materialism.'

'I have decided, comrade,' Establo said menacingly. 'I've been elected, I make the decisions. That's democratic centralism.'

'No, it isn't, I'll take your orders against the feeling of this group when a properly constituted Central Committee of the Spanish Communist Party tells me to. Not before.'

'There is no Central Committee any more,' Pepino said sadly. 'Not in Spain.'

'Exactly.'

'You should watch your mouth, *inglés*,' Establo said softly. 'I know your history. A worker's son who went to an aristocrat's school, an *arriviste*.'

'And you're a petit bourgeois drunk on power,' Bernie told him. 'You think you're still a factory foreman. I'm loyal to the party but you're not the party.'

'I can expel you from this cell.'

Bernie laughed softly. 'Some cell.' He knew at once it was the wrong thing to say, it would put them against him, but his head was spinning with exhaustion and anger. He got up and walked back to his bed. He lay down, listening to the mutterings from the other end of the room. Someone shouted to them to be quiet, people wanted to sleep. Shortly afterwards he heard the pallet creak as Establo lay down opposite him. He heard him scratch, felt his eyes on him.

'We are going to consider your case, *compadre*,' Establo said softly. Bernie didn't reply. He listened to Vicente's rasping gurgling breath and wanted to howl with sorrow and rage. He remembered Agustín's words that he had puzzled over. Better times. No, he thought. Whatever you meant there, you were wrong.

He couldn't sleep that night. He lay on his bunk in the cold, not tossing and turning but looking into the darkness. He remembered how, in London, the Communist Party's theories of the laws of class struggle had seemed to him like a revelation, the world explained at last. When he left Cambridge he had helped out in his parents' shop at first, but his father's depression and his mother's complaining disappointment that he had thrown Cambridge away stifled him and he left and took rooms nearby.

The contrast between the wealth of Cambridge and the bleak shabby poverty of the East End, where unemployed men lounged on street corners and there were stirrings of a home-grown fascism, angered him more than ever. Millions were unemployed and the Labour Party did nothing. He kept in touch with the Meras; the Republic was a disappointment, the government refusing to raise taxes to finance reforms for fear of angering the middle classes. A friend took him to a Communist meeting and at once he felt, this is the truth, this is exposing how it all really works.

He studied Marx and Lenin; their harsh prose was a struggle at first, different from anything he had read before, but when he understood their analyses he saw that here was the uncompromising reality of the class struggle: iron hard, as his party tutor said. Only Communists had the ruthlessness to destroy fascism, capitalism's last attempt to stave off its own destruction. Bernie slogged for the party, selling the *Daily Worker* outside factory gates in the rain, stewarding meetings in half-empty halls. Many of the local party members were middle-class, bohemian intellectuals and artists. He knew that for many of them communism was a fad, an act of rebellion, at the same time as he realized he felt more at home with them than the workers. With his public-school accent they took him for one of their own; it was one of them, a sculptor, who got Bernie his job as a model. Yet there was still a part of him that felt rootless, lonely, neither proletarian nor bourgeois, a disconnected hybrid.

IN JULY 1936 the Spanish army rose against the Popular Front government and the Civil War began. In the autumn the Communists started appealing for volunteers and he went to King Street and signed up.

He had to wait. The formation of the International Brigades, the routes and meeting points, was taking time. He became impatient. Then, after another fruitless visit to party headquarters, he disobeyed the party for the first and only time. He packed his bags and without a word to anybody he went to Victoria and caught the boat-train.

He arrived in Madrid in November; Franco had reached the Casa de Campo but so far he was being held, the citizenry of Madrid keeping back the Spanish army. The weather was cold and raw but the citizens, who five years before had appeared gloomy and listless, seemed to have sprung to life; there was revolutionary fervour and fierce enthusiasm everywhere. Trams and lorries full of workers in blue boiler suits and red kerchiefs passed by on the way to the front, *¡Abajo fascismo!* chalked on the sides.

He should have reported to party HQ but it was late in the day when his train arrived and he headed straight for Carabanchel. A group of women and children were building a barricade at one corner of the Meras' square, tearing up the cobbles. Seeing a foreigner, they lifted their hands in the clenched-fist salute. '*¡Salud, compadre!*'

'*¡Salud! ¡Unios hermanos proletarios!*' One day, Bernie thought, this will happen in England.

He had written to Pedro and they knew he was coming, though not when. Inés opened the door of the flat; she looked tired and weary, greying hair straggling round her face. Her face lit up when she saw him. 'Pedro! Antonio!' she called. 'He's here!'

There was a rifle in pieces on the *salón* table, an ancient-looking thing with an enormous muzzle. Pedro and Antonio stood turning parts over in their hands. They were dusty and unshaven, their boiler suits streaked with earth. Francisco, the consumptive son, sat watching in a chair, looking barely older after five years, thin and pale as ever. Little Carmela, eight now, sat on his knee.

Pedro wiped his hands on a piece of newspaper and rushed to embrace him. 'Bernardo! My God, what a day to arrive.' He took a deep breath. 'Antonio is going to the front tomorrow.'

'I'm trying to clean this old rifle they gave me,' Antonio said proudly.

Inés frowned. 'He doesn't know how to put it back together!'

'Maybe I can help.' Bernie had been in the OTC at Rookwood. He remembered annoying the other pupils by saying military knowledge might be useful when the revolution came. He helped them put the rifle together. Then they cleared the table and Inés brought a *cocido*.

'Have you come to help kill the Fascists?' Carmela asked. She was wide-eyed with excitement and curiosity.

'Yes,' Bernie said, putting a hand on her head. He turned to Pedro. 'I should report to Party HQ tomorrow.'

'The Communists?' Pedro shook his head. 'We are beholden to them now. If only the British and French had agreed to sell us arms.'

'Stalin knows how to fight a revolutionary war.'

'Father and I have been digging trenches all afternoon,' Antonio said seriously. 'Then they gave me this rifle and told me to get a night's sleep and report for action tomorrow.'

Bernie looked at Antonio's thin boyish face. He took a deep breath.

'Do you think there might be a rifle for me?'

Antonio looked at him seriously. 'Yes. They want as many fit men as can hold one.'

'When do you have to report?'

'At dawn.'

'I'll come with you.' Bernie experienced a strange leaping sensation, excitement and fear together. He gripped Antonio's hand, found himself laughing; they were both laughing hysterically.

BUT HE WAS frightened when he rose with Pedro and Antonio at dawn. When they went outside Bernie could hear shell-fire in the distance. He shivered in the cold grey morning. Antonio had given him a red scarf; he wore the jacket and slacks he had arrived in with the scarf round his neck.

In the Puerta del Sol officers in khaki called the men into lines, leading them into the trams that were lined up one behind the other. As they rattled out of the centre the men were tense, gripping their rifles between their knees. At first it was like a normal journey, but as they travelled east there were fewer people, more militiamen and army lorries. When the tram jangled to a halt at the gates of the Casa de Campo, Bernie could hear ragged gunfire. His heart was thumping wildly as the sergeant shouted to them to disembark.

Then Bernie saw the bodies, half a dozen dead men laid in a row on the pavement, still wearing their red kerchiefs. It wasn't the first time he had seen a body – his grandmother had been laid out in the room behind the shop before her funeral – but these men, whose faces were as still and grey as hers had been, were young. One boy had a round black hole in the middle of his forehead with a tiny drop of blood underneath, like a teardrop. His heart banged like a hammer and he felt a cold sweat on his brow as he followed Pedro and Antonio into a disorganized crowd of militiamen.

Pedro was led off to a digging detail and Bernie and Antonio and twenty others, some with rifles and others without, were ordered to follow a sergeant into a half-dug trench, men with spades pausing to let them by. Sandbags had been piled high on the side facing the Casa de Campo, from where sporadic gunfire was audible. Things were chaotic: men running to and fro, lorries sliding and slithering in the mud. The men leaned back uncertainly against the sandbags.

'Jesus,' Bernie said to Antonio. 'This isn't an army.'

'It's all we've got,' Antonio said. 'Here, hold this, I'm going to take a look.' There was a ladder next to Antonio and before Bernie could stop him he had started climbing up it.

'Stop it, you crazy bastard, you'll get hit.' Bernie remembered Pa saying that was how thousands of new recruits had died on the Western Front: taking a look over the top.

Antonio rested his arms on top of the sandbags. 'It's all right, they can't see me. Christ, they've got field-guns and everything out there. Nothing's moving—'

Bernie swore, put down the rifle and climbed up the ladder, grabbing at Antonio's waist. 'Get down!'

'It's all right.'

Bernie took another step up and grabbed Antonio's shoulder, and that was when the sniper fired. The bullet missed Antonio's head but hit Bernie's arm. He gave a cry and the two of them tumbled together down the ladder into the trench. Bernie saw the blood welling up through his jacket and passed out.

A Spanish commissar came to visit him in the field hospital.

'You're a fool,' he told him. 'You should have reported to Party HQ first; you'd have had some training.'

'My friends said they needed every man in the Casa de Campo. I'm sorry.'

The commissar grunted. 'You'll be out of it for weeks now. And we will have to billet you somewhere when you get out of here.'

'My friends in Carabanchel will look after me.'

The man looked at him askance. 'Are they party?'

'Socialists.'

The man grunted.

'How's the fighting?' asked Bernie.

'We're holding them. We're forming a Communist brigade, bringing in some discipline.'

BERNIE SHIFTED in his bunk, trying to warm his legs. In the next bed Vicente was making a horrible gurgling sound in his sleep. He remembered his weeks of convalescence in Carabanchel. His attempts to convert the Meras to communism were unsuccessful. They said the Russians were destroying the Republic, talking of cooperation with the progressive bourgeoisie while bringing in their secret police and spies. Bernie said the tales of Russian brutality were exaggerated, and you had to be hard in war. But it wasn't easy to argue with a veteran of thirty years of class struggle like Pedro. Sometimes he began to doubt whether what they said about the Russians could all be lies, but he put those thoughts from his mind; they were a distraction and in the midst of this struggle he must stay focused.

The doubts returned, though, in the cold night. They had needed hard men then but what if they had won, would people like Establo be in charge now? The priest Eduardo had said Marxism was a false faith. He had never understood dialectical materialism properly and he knew many Communists didn't, it was hard to understand. But communism wasn't a faith, it wasn't like Catholicism – it was rooted in an understanding of reality, of the material world.

He tossed and turned. He tried not to think of Barbara, it hurt too much, but her face still came back to him. Memories of her always brought guilt. He had abandoned her. He thought of her back in England, or perhaps in Switzerland, surrounded now by Fascist states. He used to say she didn't understand things; tonight he was starting to wonder how much he had understood himself. He made himself think of an old comforting image he sometimes brought to mind when he couldn't sleep, a scene from an old party newsreel he had seen in London. Tractors rolling through the endless Russian wheat-fields, followed by singing workers as they gathered in the plentiful grain.

Chapter Twenty-Nine

SANDY MET HARRY outside his flat early in the morning. It was a clear cold day, the sun low in a bright blue sky. Sandy stepped from his Packard and shook Harry's hand. He wore a heavy camelhair coat and a silk scarf; the sunlight glinted on his oiled hair. He looked happy, exhilarated to be out so early.

'What a fantastic morning!' he said, looking at the sky. 'We don't get many mornings like this in winter.'

They drove north-west out of Madrid, climbing into the Guadarrama mountains. 'Fancy coming round to dinner again soon?' Sandy asked. 'Just us and Barbara. She's still a bit out of sorts. I thought it might cheer her up.'

'That'd be good.' Harry took a deep breath. 'I'm grateful for your bringing me in on this.'

'That's all right,' Sandy replied quietly, patronizingly. He smiled.

They climbed to the top of the mountain road; above them, the highest peaks were already covered in snow. Then they descended back into the bare brown countryside, drove through Segovia and turned west, towards Santa Maria la Real. There was little traffic, the countryside was still and empty. It reminded Harry of the day he arrived, the drive into Madrid with Tolhurst.

After an hour Sandy turned into a dusty cart track that wound between low hills. 'We're in for a bit of a bone-shaking, I'm afraid. It's another half hour to the mine.'

On the track donkeys' hoofmarks were overlaid with deep ruts made by heavy vehicles. The car clattered and juddered over them. Sandy drove confidently.

'I find myself thinking about Rookwood since we met up again,' he said reflectively. 'Piper moved back into our study after I was sacked, didn't he? You said in a letter.'

'Yes.'

'Bet he felt he'd won.'

'I don't think so. He hardly mentioned your name again, as I remember.'

'I'm not surprised he turned to communism, he always had that fanatical streak. Used to look at me as though he'd like nothing better than to put me up against a wall to be shot.' He shook his head. 'The Communists are still the real danger to the world, you know. It's Russia England should be fighting, not Germany. I thought things were going to turn out that way after Munich.'

'Fascism and communism are as bad as each other.'

'Oh, come on. At least with right-wing dictatorships our sort of people are looked after so long as we toe the party line. There's hardly any income tax here. Though I admit dealing with the bureaucracy's a pain in the arse. Still, the government has to teach the people who's in charge. That's their thinking, make everyone follow all these procedures, teach Spaniards order and obedience.'

'But the bureaucracy's completely corrupt.'

'This is Spain, Harry.' He gave him a glance of affectionate irony. 'You're still a Rookwood man at heart, aren't you? Still believing all those codes of honour?'

'I used to be. I'm not sure I'm anything any more.'

'I admired you for it, you know, in the old days. But it's schoolboy stuff, Harry, it's not real life. I suppose the academic life's pretty sheltered as well.'

'Yes, you're right, it is. I've had my eyes opened to some things out here.'

'The real world, eh?'

'You could say that.'

'We all need security for the future now, Harry. I can help you get that if you let me.' There was something like an appeal for approval in Sandy's tone. 'And nothing's more secure than gold, especially these days. Look, here we are.'

Ahead a high barbed-wire fence ran round a wide stretch of rolling land. Large holes had been gouged in the yellow earth, some half filled with water. A couple of mechanical earth-movers sat nearby. The track ended at a gate with a wooden hut on the inner side. Two more huts, one large, stood at a little distance and there was a large stone blockhouse too. A board by the gate read: 'Nuevas Iniciativas S.A. Keep Out. Sponsored by the Ministry of Mines.'

Sandy sounded his horn and a thin elderly man ran from the hut and opened the gates. He saluted Sandy as the car tooled through and came to a halt. They got out. A cold wind was blowing; it stung Harry's cheeks. He pushed his hat down on his head.

Sandy turned to the gatekeeper. 'All well, Arturo?'

'*Sí*, Señor Forsyth. Señor Otero is here, he is in the office.' The gatekeeper's manner was deferential. What you'd expect from a junior staff member to the boss, Harry supposed. It was strange to think of Sandy as a boss, in charge of staff.

Sandy pointed into the distance. A sizeable farm, surrounded by poplars, was visible in a fold of the hills. Black cattle grazed in the fields around it.

'That's the place we want to buy. Alberto's been onto the land on the q.t., taken some samples. He's quite happy about your visit now, by the way. I talked him round. He was worried about trusting someone who worked at the embassy, but I told him your word was your bond, you wouldn't say anything.'

'Thanks.' Harry felt a stab of guilt. He concentrated on what Sandy was saying.

'The seam of gold runs right under that farm, gets richer there too. The owner breeds bulls for the *corrida*. He's none too bright, he hasn't twigged what we're doing here. I think we could get him to sell.' He laughed suddenly, gazing over the fields. 'Isn't it wonderful? All just lying there. Can't believe it myself sometimes. And we'll get that farm, don't worry. I've told the farmer I'll pay him cash, he can go and live with his daughter in Segovia.' He turned to Harry. 'I can usually persuade people to see things my way, sniff out something they want and dangle it before them.' He smiled again.

Harry bent and scooped up some of the yellow soil. It was similar to the earth in the canister in Sandy's office. It felt friable, cold. Sandy clapped him on the arm.

'Let's go and get a cup of coffee in the office. To warm us up.' He led Harry towards the nearest hut. 'No one's here today, just the security people.'

The office was spartan: a desk and a few folding chairs. There was a picture of a flamenco dancer on one wall, and a photograph of Franco above a desk where Otero sat, reading a report. He rose when Harry and Sandy entered and shook Harry's hand. He smiled, his manner much friendlier than a few days ago.

'Señor Brett, welcome, thank you for coming all this way. Would you both like a coffee?'

'Thanks, Alberto,' Sandy replied. 'We've been freezing our *cojones* off. Sit down, Harry.'

The geologist fussed with a kettle and gas stove that stood in a corner. Sandy sat on a corner of the desk and lit a cigarette. He picked up the document Otero had been reading.

'This the report on the latest samples?'

'Yes. The results are good. That section by the stream is one of the best. We only have powdered milk I am afraid, Señor Brett.'

'That's OK. It's a big site.'

'Yes. But the land we have has been comprehensively surveyed.' He looked round at Harry. 'The new samples are from the farm nearby.'

Otero handed round mugs of coffee and sat down again. 'It is so frustrating. We cannot start intensive work until we have ministry clearance. Under Spanish law minerals under the soil belong to the government and it is a matter of agreeing our mining rights, our commission. The ministry keep demanding more samples, which cost more money, and we need funds if we are to buy the farm. We have the Generalísimo's support in principle, but the ministry keep telling him to be cautious and he follows their advice after the Badajoz fiasco last year.'

'If Madrid agreed and you got the farm, how much could you make? Over a year, say?'

Sandy laughed. 'The big question.'

Otero nodded. 'One cannot say exactly, but I would say twenty million pesetas. Once we bring the farm to full production, who knows – thirty, forty?'

'That's over a million pounds the first year,' Sandy said. 'If you bought a three per cent share, that'd be fifteen thousand sterling for a five hundred pounds investment. Thirty thousand if you put in a thousand.'

Harry sipped his coffee. It was bitter, globules of powdered milk floating on the surface. Sandy and Otero sat looking at him, smoke curling from their cigarettes.

'That's a lot of money,' Harry said at length.

Otero laughed. 'You English, always you understate everything.'

'Especially Harry.' Sandy laughed and stood up. 'Come on, we'll show you the diggings.'

They walked him over the site, showed him how slightly different colours in the earth indicated different gold content. The ground was dotted with little circular holes; Otero explained that was where samples had been taken. Clouds appeared, chasing each other across the sky.

'Let's look at the labs,' Sandy said. 'How's your hearing these days? It seems OK.'

'Yes, it's pretty much back to normal now.'

'Harry injured his ear at Dunkirk, Alberto. The Battle of France.'

'Really?' The geologist inclined his head in sympathy. They came to the laboratory hut and went in. There was a harsh chemical tang in the air. Long benches were covered with glass filters, big metal pans and trays full of clear liquid and the yellow earth.

'Sulphuric acid,' Sandy said. 'Remember that from stinks lessons at school? Don't touch any of those jars.' They led him round, Otero explaining the processes for extracting gold from the ore. It didn't mean much to Harry. As they left he looked again at the blockhouse, noticing the little windows were barred.

'What's that?'

'We keep the ore for the second stage of the refining process there. It's too valuable to leave lying around. The key's back in the office, but have a look through the window if you like.'

The interior was dim but Harry made out more laboratory equipment. There were a number of large bins as well, mostly full to the brim with yellow soil, ground down to a fine tilth.

They went back to the office where Otero, still friendly, made more coffee.

'I have experience on the South African goldfields,' Otero said. 'It was the place for a geologist to go when I was young. I learned some English there but I have forgotten it now.' He smiled apologetically.

'How does this place compare?'

Otero sat down. 'Much smaller, of course. The Witwatersrand deposits are the biggest in the world. But there the quality of the ore is poor and the seams run deep underground. Here the quality is high and it is on or near the surface.'

'Enough to give Spain serious gold deposits?'

'Enough to make a significant difference to the country? Yes.'

Sandy looked at Harry over the rim of his cup. 'What d'you say, then?'

'I'm interested. But I'd like to consult my bank manager in London, write to him. Just in very general terms, about investing in a gold mine with proven reserves, I won't say where, comparison with other investments and so forth.'

'We'd need to see the letter,' Sandy said. 'Seriously, this is a confidential project.'

Otero looked at him with the sharpness Harry remembered. 'As we said, no one at the embassy must know. A letter to England may be opened by the censor.'

'Not if I send it via the diplomatic bag. But I don't mind you seeing it before it goes, if you like.'

'A bank manager will say it's a risky investment,' Sandy warned.

Harry smiled. 'I won't necessarily *take* his advice.' He shook his head. 'Three per cent of a million.'

'In the first year.' Sandy paused to let this sink in. Harry thought, perhaps that could have been mine if I wasn't spying on them. He had a sudden urge to laugh.

Sandy rose and clapped his hands on his knees. 'OK! I should be getting back. Dinner with Sebastian tonight.'

Otero smiled again as he shook Harry's hand. 'I hope you will come in with us, *señor*. It is the right time for you to invest. A thousand pounds would be useful to us now, prevent the ministry from grinding us down. And for you – ' he waved a hand – 'the possibilities . . .' He raised his eyebrows.

As Harry and Sandy crossed to the car the gatehouse door opened. A different man emerged, small and thin. To his astonishment Harry recognized Maestre's ex-batman, Milagros's chaperone.

'Lieutenant Gomez,' he said without thinking. '*Buenos días*.'

'*Buen'día*,' Gomez muttered. His face wore an impassive soldier's expression but an agonized beseeching look in his eyes brought Harry up short. His heart sank as he realized he had made a mistake, a serious one.

'You know each other?' Sandy's voice was sharp.

'Yes, we met at a – a function a while ago, didn't we?'

'*Sí señor*, a function, that was it.' Gomez turned and opened the gate, keeping his head averted as the car passed through. Sandy watched him in his mirror as he went back into his hut.

'He's our new gatekeeper,' he said. 'Just come on duty.' He spoke quietly, conversationally. 'How did you come to meet him?'

'Oh, at a function, a party.'

'You met a doorkeeper at a party?'

'As a servant, a servant. Family retainer or something. Perhaps he got caught pinching the spoons.' Harry laughed.

Sandy was silent for a moment, frowning. 'General Maestre's party that you told me about? For his daughter?'

Hell, Harry thought, hell. Sandy was so bloody quick; Maestre's party was the only one he had mentioned and Sandy would have remembered, Maestre being an enemy. Sandy was still looking at the gatekeeper in the driving mirror.

'Yes. When I took Maestre's daughter to the Prado later, he picked her up. As I say, he must have been sacked.'

'Perhaps.' Sandy paused. 'He came recommended, said he was an unemployed veteran.'

'If he was sacked, he'd need to explain not having references.'

Sandy's voice became casual. 'Seen any more of the daughter?'

'No. I told you, she's not my type. I've met someone else,' he added, to distract Sandy's interest. But Sandy only nodded. He was frowning now, thinking. Harry thought, Maestre's put Gomez in here as a spy and I've just betrayed him. Hell. Hell.

They passed through a village. Sandy stopped at a bar. Outside, two donkeys stood tied to a rail.

'Can you wait just a minute, Harry?' he asked. 'Got to make a quick phone call, something I forgot.'

Harry waited while he went into the bar. The donkeys at the rail made him think of the Wild West. Gunfights at dawn. What would they do to Gomez? The stakes were very big. He swallowed. *Had* Maestre sent him here as a spy? A couple of ragged children stood looking at the big American car. He waved and they turned and ran away, bare feet slithering in the mud.

Sandy emerged. His face was set and cold in a way that reminded Harry of the day he had been caned in class, the day he began planning his revenge on Taylor. He opened the car door and his face relaxed, he smiled. He got in. 'Tell me more about this girl,' he said as he started the engine.

Harry told a story of rescuing a stranger from some dogs and meeting his sister. The best lies are closest to the truth. Sandy smiled and nodded but that chilling look on his face as he returned to the car stayed in Harry's mind. He had been phoning Otero, he must have been. He realized that he had been wrong about Sandy, wrong to think he didn't really know about the terrible things that could happen, like Dunkirk. He knew about them and he could do terrible things himself. It was like at school, he didn't care.

Chapter Thirty

It had been arranged that when Harry returned from the mine he would go straight to the embassy for a debriefing. He asked Sandy to drop him at his flat, saying he had a document to translate. As soon as the car disappeared round the corner he left again, catching a tram to Calle Fernando el Santo.

Tolhurst was in his office, reading a four-day-old *Times*. There was a power cut, and he was wearing a chunky pullover with a garish design against the cold. It made him look younger, like a plump schoolboy. He waved Harry in.

'How'd it go?' he asked eagerly.

'There's a mine all right.' Harry sat down. He took a long deep breath. 'But something's gone wrong.'

Tolhurst's round face seemed to narrow. 'What? He's not on to you?'

'No. He took me round the mine. It's out beyond Segovia; covers a big area, though production seems to be at an early stage. Otero was there, very friendly this time.'

'And?'

'As we were leaving, the watchman came out to open the gate and I recognized him. It was a man called Gomez. He works for Maestre; remember, we met him at the party?'

'Yes, his old batman, or something.'

'I didn't think, I said hello. He acknowledged me but I could see he was terrified.'

'Hell. How did Forsyth respond?'

'He was on to it straight away, asked me where I'd met Gomez.'

'Did you tell him?'

'Yes. I'm sorry, Simon, I – I was on the spot, I couldn't think of a lie. I said he'd worked for Maestre, I said perhaps he'd been sacked. It was all I could think of.'

'Damn.' Tolhurst picked up a pencil, and turned it over and over in his hands. Harry felt furious with himself, horrified by the thought of what the consequences of his slip might be for Gomez. 'I could see Sandy was worried. He stopped in a village, said he had to make a phone call. He looked grim when he came out. I think he was ringing Otero. Simon, how is Maestre mixed up in all this?'

Tolhurst bit his lip. 'I don't know, but he's mixed up in most of the Monarchist-Falange battles. We knew he was on the committee dealing with the gold mine but the captain hasn't been able to get anything out of him. He's close-mouthed where what he sees as Spain's national interests are concerned.'

So the Knights of St George will only take you so far, Harry thought.

'You shouldn't have blurted out hello to someone you knew worked for him,' Tolhurst said sharply. 'You should have guessed he might be undercover.'

'I haven't had to think fast on my feet like that before. I'm sorry. I was concentrating so much on the site, trying to seem like a bona fide investor.'

Tolhurst put the pencil down. 'Forsyth will realize Maestre wouldn't just sack an ex-batman he allowed to be a chaperone for his daughter. Christ, Harry, this is a balls-up.' He put both hands on the table and lifted himself up reluctantly. 'I'm going to have to tell the captain. He's with Sir Sam, there's a diplomatic bag going tonight. You wait here.'

He left, leaving Harry staring miserably out of the window. A pedlar rode a little donkey down the street, his feet almost touching the ground on either side. Heavy bundles of wood were strapped to its back. Harry wondered at the load the small beasts were made to carry; you would think its spine would break.

Rapid footsteps sounded outside. Harry stood up as Tolhurst held the door open for Hillgarth to enter, his face grim. He was followed by the ambassador. Hoare's thin face was red with anger. He threw himself into Tolhurst's chair, glowering.

'You bloody fool, Brett,' Hillgarth began. 'What possessed you?'

'I'm sorry, sir, I didn't know that Maestre—'

Hoare addressed Hillgarth in tones that cut like a knife. 'Alan,

I warned you this operation was risky. I've always said, no covert operations, we should be gathering intelligence, nothing else. We're not the bloody SOE. But oh no, you and Winston had to have your adventures! Now we could have compromised relations with the whole Monarchist faction thanks to this idiot.' He waved at Harry as though flicking away a troublesome insect.

'Come on, Sam, Maestre should have told us if he was running his own show.'

'Why should he? Why? It's his bloody country. Why shouldn't he put a spy into a Falange-controlled project?' Hoare put a hand, shaking with fury, to his brow. 'Maestre's one of our best sources. I've sweated blood this last five months to convince the Monarchists we have common interests, England's not a threat to them. I've tried to persuade Winston to make friendly noises about Gibraltar and expel Negrín's rabble. You know what else I've done too. And now they'll find out we're running a covert operation, one that clashes with one of theirs, despite all my promises of support.'

'If something happens to this Gomez,' Hillgarth said, 'there's no connection to us.'

'Don't be a fool! If Maestre's had a man on site he'll have been nosing about their papers. That's the first thing he'd do. And what if there's a note about a potential investor in this project called H. Brett Esquire, translator in His Majesty's Diplomatic Service.' Hoare's thin face sagged, he looked exhausted. 'I suppose I'd better ring Maestre and warn him, try to limit the damage.'

'I'm sorry, sir,' Harry ventured. 'If I'd known—'

Hoare glared at Harry, his top lip curling over little white teeth. 'If you'd known? It's not your bloody business to know, it's your job to stay sharp and field the balls.' He turned back to Hillgarth. 'You'd better abort the project. Send this bloody fool home, he can go and fight the Italians in North Africa. I said if we had to do this we'd have been better to approach Forsyth directly and try to buy him, without all this cloak and dagger stuff.'

Hillgarth spoke quietly, though his voice had an undertone of suppressed anger. 'Ambassador, we agreed that course was too risky unless we knew what the project was worth to him. We know that now, we know how important it is. And Brett's cover isn't blown; if he told Forsyth he knew Maestre's man that could even strengthen his credibility.'

'I must phone Maestre. We'll talk later.' Hoare rose. Tolhurst ran to open the door for him. The ambassador glared at him as he passed through. 'You should have known better, Tolhurst. Hillgarth, I want you with me for this call.'

Tolhurst closed the door slowly behind them. 'You'd better go home, Harry. They'll be arguing about this all evening.'

'I'm supposed to be going to the theatre tonight. *Macbeth*. Will that be all right?'

'I suppose so.'

'Tolly, what did Hoare mean there, you should have known better?'

Tolhurst smiled wryly. 'I'm your watcher, Harry. I keep a close eye on how you're doing, report to Captain Hillgarth. Every inexperienced spy has a watcher and I'm yours.'

'Oh.' Harry had wondered, but the realization still gave him a sinking, disappointed feeling.

'I've always said you were doing well; Hillgarth's been a bit impatient but I've told him you were playing Forsyth carefully. You've done very well, up to now. But you can't afford any mistakes, not in this job.'

'Oh.'

'I didn't think you'd drop a bollock like this. That's the trouble, if you like a fellow, it biases you in his favour.' Tolhurst gave Harry a resentful look. 'You'd better go. Stay out of Hillgarth's sight. I'll ring you when we need you.'

HARRY ARRIVED LATE at the theatre. He had spent hours pacing round the flat, thinking about his mistake, Hoare's and Hillgarth's anger, Tolhurst's revelation that he had been, in a way, spying on Harry. I'm not cut out for this, Harry thought; I never wanted it. If they sent him home he wouldn't be sorry, even if it was in disgrace. He'd be glad never to see Sandy again. But he couldn't get rid of the thought of Gomez, the sudden terror in the old soldier's eyes.

He told himself this wasn't doing any good. He looked at his watch and was startled to realize how late it was. After thinking about

Sofia for so long, he had hardly thought of her at all that day. He changed hurriedly, grabbed his coat and hat and hurried out.

Sofia was already waiting when he arrived at the theatre, a little figure in a beret and her old black coat, standing in the shadow of the doors as well-dressed couples went up the theatre steps. She wasn't carrying a handbag; perhaps she couldn't afford one. The sight of her, small and vulnerable, made his heart lurch. As he approached he saw that a beggar, an old man in a homemade wheelchair, was wheedling her.

'I've given you all I can spare,' she said.

'Please, just a little more. To eat tomorrow.'

Harry ran up. 'Sofia,' he said breathlessly, 'I'm so sorry I am late.' She looked at him with relief. He passed fifty centimos to the beggar and he wheeled himself away.

'There was a – a bit of a crisis at work. Have you been waiting long?'

'No. But because I am here that man thought I had money.'

'Oh dear, what can I say?' He smiled. 'It's good to see you.'

'And you.'

'How's Enrique?'

She smiled again. 'Almost healed.'

'Right.' He coughed. 'Shall we go in?' He offered her his arm diffidently. She took it. Her body against his warmed him.

Sofia had made a big effort: her long hair was curled fashionably at the ends and she wore powder and lipstick. She looked beautiful. The rest of the audience milling in the vestibule were well-dressed bourgeois, the women with pearl earrings and necklaces. Sofia surveyed them with a look of amused contempt.

Harry had got seats in the middle of the theatre. It was full. Someone at the embassy had said cultural life was flickering back into life, and those who could afford it were evidently hungry for a night out.

Sofia removed her coat. Underneath she wore a long, well-cut white dress that set off her dark skin, her neckline lower than was strictly proper now. Harry turned his eyes away hastily. She smiled at him.

'Ah, it is so warm in here, how do they do it?'

'Central heating.'

At the interval they went for a drink to the bar. Sofia seemed ill at ease in the crush and coughed at her first sip of wine.

'Are you all right?'

She laughed, a nervous laugh, a change from her usual confidence.

'I am sorry. Only I am not used to such a crowd. When I am not at home I am in the dairy.' She smiled wryly. 'I am more used to cows than people.' A woman stared at her with raised eyebrows.

'What's it like there?' Harry knew the back streets of Madrid were full of little dairies, cramped, unhygienic places.

'Hard work. But at least I get milk for the family.'

'You must get tired of it.'

'It keeps us going. The men from the government agency come every day to take their hundred litres. By the time they have watered it down for the ration it is two hundred litres.'

'Terrible.' Harry shook his head.

'You are a strange man,' she said.

'Why?'

'Your interest in my life. A smelly dairy is far from what you are used to, I think.' She leaned forward. 'Listen to these people talking of the things they have bought on the black market and their troubles with servants: are those not the things your class usually discuss?' The faint mocking smile was on her face again.

'Yes. But I'm tired of it.'

A bell rang and they returned to the play.

During the second half Harry turned to look at her a couple of times, but Sofia was absorbed in the performance; she didn't turn and smile as he hoped. They reached the point where Lady MacBeth sleepwalks, tortured with guilt for the murder she has urged her husband to commit. 'What, will these hands never be clean.' Harry felt a sudden wave of panic at the thought that he might have brought death to Gomez, might have blood on his hands. He gasped and gripped the arms of the chair; Sofia turned and looked at him. When the play ended, the national anthem sounded through loud-speakers. Harry and Sofia stood but did not join the many in the audience who raised their arms in the Fascist salute.

Outside in the cold, Harry felt strange again, stranger than he had in months. The buzzing in his ears was back, his heart was beating fast and his legs, he realized, were shaking. He supposed it was a delayed reaction to all that had happened that day. As they walked to the tram stop he tried to make conversation, aware there was a tremble in his voice. He did not take Sofia's arm; he didn't want her to feel his trembling.

'Did you enjoy the play?'

'Yes.' Sofia smiled. 'I had not realized Shakespeare could be so passionate. The murderers all got their just reward, did they not?'

'Yes.'

'That is not how it is in the real world.'

He hadn't heard her properly. She had to repeat herself. 'No, it isn't,' he agreed.

They had reached the tram stop. Harry was trembling all over now, he longed desperately to get out of the cold damp air. There were no trams waiting at the stop. There was nobody else waiting, either, which probably meant one had just gone. He needed to sit down as well. He cursed his panic; if it had to come, why couldn't it have been at the flat, when he was alone?

'Are you all right?' he heard Sofia ask.

There was no point in pretending, he could feel his face covered with a cold sweat now. 'I don't feel too good. I'm sorry, I get these little attacks sometimes, since I was in the fighting in France. I'll be all right, I'm sorry, it's stupid.'

'It is not stupid.' She looked at him with concern. 'It happens to men in war, I saw it here. You should get a taxi, I will take you home. You should not wait here in the cold.'

'I'll be all right, honestly.' He hated showing weakness like this, hated it.

'No, I will get a taxi.' Suddenly she was the one in charge, as she had been at the flat. 'Will you be all right for a moment while I go to the junction, I saw some waiting there.'

'Yes, but—'

'I will only be a minute.' She touched his arm, smiled and was gone. Harry leaned against the cold tram stop, taking deep breaths, in through his nose and out through his mouth as they had told him at the hospital. A few moments later a taxi drew up.

He felt better at once, sitting down in the warmth. He smiled sadly at Sofia. 'What an end to the evening, eh? Drop me off and I'll pay the taxi to get you home.'

'No, I want to make sure you are all right. You are very pale.' She studied him with a professional gaze.

The taxi dropped them off. Harry was afraid he would need her help to get up the stairs but he was much better now; he walked up unaided. He let them in and they went into the *salón*.

'Sit down on the settee, there,' she said. 'Have you any spirits?'

'There's some whisky in that cupboard.'

She fetched a glass from the kitchen and made him drink. The whisky gave him a little jolt. She smiled. 'There. The colour is coming back to your cheeks.' She lit the *brasero* then sat on the other end of the settee, looking at him.

'Have one yourself,' he said.

'No thank you. I do not like it much.' She looked at his parents' photograph.

'That's my mother and father.'

'It is a nice photograph.'

'Your mother showed me her wedding photograph, that day I brought Enrique back.'

'Yes. Her and Papa and Uncle Ernesto.'

'Your uncle was a priest, wasn't he?'

'Yes. In Cuenca. We haven't heard from him since the Civil War started. He may be dead; Cuenca was in the Republican zone. Do you mind, Harry, may I smoke?'

'Of course.' He took an ashtray from the coffee table and passed it to her. His hand trembled slightly, he saw.

'Was it bad?' she asked. 'The war in France?'

'Yes. A shell landed right beside me, killed the man I was with. I was deaf for a while and had these wretched panic attacks. It's been much better recently. I fought it, I thought I'd beaten it, but it came back tonight.'

'I wonder if you take enough care of yourself.'

'I'm all right. I can't complain, I get good rations and live in this big flat.'

'Yes, it is nice.' She looked around the room. 'But it has a gloomy atmosphere somehow.'

'It's too big for me really. I rattle about a bit. It used to belong to a Communist official.'

'Those people did themselves well.' She sighed.

'Sometimes I seem to feel his presence.' Harry laughed self-consciously.

'Madrid is full of ghosts now.'

All the lights went out, plunging them into total darkness except for the glow of the *brasero*. They both exclaimed, then Sofia said, 'It is only another power cut.'

'God, what a moment for that to happen.'

They both laughed.

'I've got some candles in the kitchen,' Harry said. 'Give me a match to see by and I'll fetch them. Unless you'd rather go home now?'

'No,' she said. 'It is good to talk.'

Harry lit candles and set them in saucers. They cast a flickering yellow light over the room. Where it caught the candlelight Harry noticed again how her hair wasn't quite black, there were elusive shades of brown there too. Her face was sad.

'We are always getting cuts,' she said. 'We get used to it.'

Harry was silent a moment, then said, 'I've seen more hardship here than I ever thought possible.'

'Yes.' Sofia sighed again. 'Remember our *beata*, Señora Avila? She visited us yesterday. She says the priest is concerned we cannot afford to look after Paco properly; he wants us to let him go to the orphanage. The priest would not come himself as we do not go to church. That of course is the real reason they want Paco away from us. But they will not get him.' Her mouth went hard for a moment. 'Enrique will soon be able to work again. There may be a place for him at the dairy.'

'I have a friend, an Englishwoman, she worked for a while in one of the orphanages. She said it was a bad place. She left.'

'I have heard of children who kill themselves. That is what I fear for Paco. He is always so frightened. He hardly ever speaks, and only to us.'

'Is there nobody who could – I don't know – help him?'

She laughed bitterly. 'Who? There is only us.'

'I'm sorry.'

She leaned forward, her large eyes glinting in the candlelight. 'You have no reason to be sorry. You have been kind. You care. The foreigners, and those who have money here, they shut their eyes to how people live. And those who have nothing are beaten down, apathetic. It is good to meet someone who cares.' She gave a little smile. 'Even if it makes you sad. You are a good man.'

Harry thought of Gomez, his terrified eyes. He shook his head. 'No, I'm not. I'd like to be but I'm not.' He put his head in his hands. He sighed deeply, then looked up at her. She smiled. Then he slowly put out his hand and took hers. 'You are the good one,' he said.

She did not move her hand. Her eyes softened. He leaned slowly towards her and put his lips to hers. Her dress made a rustling sound as she leaned forward and kissed him back, a long deep kiss with a sharp exciting tang of smoke. He pulled away.

'I'm sorry,' he said. 'You're alone in my flat, I didn't mean—'

She smiled and shook her head. 'No. I am glad. It was not hard to see how you felt. And I have been thinking of you since the first time you came, sitting in our *salón* looking so lost but wanting to help us.' She lowered her head. 'I did not want to feel this, our lives are complicated enough. That is why I did not get the doctor at first.' She smiled. 'Poor Enrique. You see, I *am* selfish really.'

He leaned forward and took her hand. It was small, warm, pulsing with life.

'You're the least selfish person I've ever met.' Something in him still hesitated, he couldn't quite believe this was happening.

'Harry,' she said.

'You pronounce my name like no one else,' he said with a little choking laugh.

'It is easier to pronounce than the way the English say David.'

'The boy from Leeds?'

'Yes. We were together for a while. In war you have to take chances while you can. Perhaps I shock you. The Catholics would say I am an immoral woman.'

'Never.' He hesitated, then leaned forward and kissed her again.

Chapter Thirty-One

BARBARA HAD HEARD that if you loved a person and then stopped loving them, sometimes it turned into hate. She hadn't believed it but it was true. Sandy had said her heart was full of sentimental mush, but it wasn't, it was full of loathing now.

She had to hide her feelings. It was Wednesday, and she had met Luis again; Agustín would be back from leave in three weeks' time, on the fourth of December. As soon as he came back, Luis would go to Cuenca and finalize everything. The date for the escape would depend on the guards' timetables but they should be able to do it before Christmas. During that time she had to make sure Sandy suspected nothing.

The house with its big rooms and expensive, immaculately clean furniture felt increasingly oppressive. Sometimes Barbara wanted to pull down the highly polished mirrors and smash them on the waxed tables. As she moved restlessly through the house or looked out at the wintry garden, she began wondering if she was going a little mad.

After their argument over the orphanage Barbara had once again made herself as agreeable and submissive as she could. The Sunday after their row Sandy went out for the morning in the car; business, he said. Barbara went for a walk and bought some Andalusian roses in an exclusive flower shop; they were expensive but they were Sandy's favourites. She brought them in to dinner in a vase. He picked one up and sniffed it.

'Very nice,' he said flatly. 'You're out of the sulks, then?' He was still in an angry mood.

She said quietly, 'There's no point in quarrelling.'

'Your letter to Sister Inmaculada's raised a few eyebrows. One or two people have asked if I'm harbouring a subversive.'

'Look, Sandy, I don't want to cause problems with your business friends. Why don't I volunteer for something else, work at one of the veterans' hospitals perhaps?'

He grunted. 'They're mostly run by the Falange. I don't want you rowing with them next.'

'So long as I don't have to see children mistreated, that's all.'

He looked at her, his eyes bleak and cold.

'Most children are mistreated. It's the way of the world. Unless you're lucky, like my brother. You were mistreated, so was I.'

'Not like that.'

'It's all mistreatment.' He shrugged. 'I'll talk to Sebastian about the veterans.'

'Thanks.' She tried to sound grateful. Sandy grunted and bent his head to his plate.

He hadn't approached her for sex since their row. The next afternoon, Barbara had gone down to the kitchen to speak to Pilar and on the stairs she had heard a laugh. Sandy was there, leaning on the table, smoking a cigarette and smiling, a lubricious smile. Pilar stood washing dishes at the sink, laughing too; when she caught sight of Barbara she blushed scarlet and bowed her head.

'I've brought the shopping list, Pilar,' Barbara said coldly. 'I'll leave it on the table.'

Afterwards she said nothing but he did. They were sitting in the *salón* and he sat back, twirling his whisky glass. He smiled. 'Nice girl, Pilar. She can be quite cheeky sometimes.'

Barbara continued threading a needle. He's doing this to punish me, she thought, as though I cared now. 'How you men like to flirt with servants,' she said lightly. 'I suppose it's a fantasy, a public-school thing.'

'If you knew what some of my fantasies are,' he said, 'you wouldn't like them.' Something in his tone made her look at him sharply. He looked at her coldly and took another swig of whisky.

'I must get that pattern Mum sent,' she said. She went out and stood in the hall, taking deep breaths. Sometimes she just had to get away from him. She would think, I'll sit with him for an hour, then get out for a few minutes. And that'll be another hour nearer getting away for good.

She went up to their bedroom. She didn't need the pattern but supposed she had better take it. While she was there she unlocked the drawer in her bureau and fingered her bank book. She was glad the bureau had a good strong lock; she always kept the key in her pocket.

She took a deep breath. She would have to go back downstairs, try to calm things. She could ask him how things were going with Harry, whether Harry was joining this project, whatever it was. But if he insisted on using Pilar to mock her, let him. She would pretend to be hurt and that would be another excuse to avoid making love if he came near her again.

TO HER RELIEF Sandy didn't mention Pilar again that evening. When she asked him about Harry he said he had invited him to dinner again on Thursday week. He got up, saying there was some paperwork he needed to sort out in his study. She sighed with relief as the door closed behind him.

Shortly afterwards she heard the telephone ring twice then suddenly stop; Sandy must have answered it on the study extension. It made her jump slightly; she started again a moment later as the doorbell rang loudly. Who on earth's this, she thought, it's getting late. She put down her sewing.

She heard Pilar come up from the kitchen, her heels clacking on the tiles. A minute later she knocked and entered the *salón*. Little as she cared what Sandy did now, Barbara felt a spurt of anger. 'Who is it?' she asked.

Pilar wouldn't meet her eyes. 'If you please, *señora*, it is a man to see Señor Forsyth. He looks a little – ' she hesitated – 'foreign. I know Señor Forsyth does not like to be disturbed in his study.'

'I'll see who it is.' She got up and walked past the girl. A blast of cold air came from the hall; Pilar had left the front door ajar. A small elderly man in a stained coat and a battered Homburg hat stood on the doorstep. He wore spectacles held together over the bridge of his nose with tape. He lifted his hat.

'*¿Perdon, señora, esta el señor Forsyth en casa?*' He spoke Spanish slowly and with effort, in a strong French accent. Barbara replied in French.

'Yes. How can we help you?'

The old man's face creased with relief. 'Ah, you speak French. My Spanish is poor. I am sorry to disturb you. My name is Blanc, Henri Blanc, I have something I must give Señor Forsyth.' He felt inside his coat, producing a little canvas bag. It made a chinking sound. Barbara stared in puzzlement.

'I am sorry,' he said. 'I should explain. I am one of the refugees Señor Forsyth has been assisting.'

'Oh, I see.' That explained the down-at-heel clothes, the French accent. He was one of the Jews. She held the door open. 'Please come in.'

The old man shook his head. 'No, no, please. I do not wish to disturb you so late. Only I heard today I have my pass to go to Lisbon.' He smiled, unable to conceal his delight. 'I leave with my family early tomorrow. I could not go without bringing what I had promised.' He proffered the bag again. 'Please, take it. Tell him it is pure quality as I said. These have been in our family a long time but it is worth it to get to Lisbon.'

'All right.' Barbara took the package. 'You must have had a long walk – are you sure you won't come in for a minute?' She looked at his shoes, the heels were almost worn away, he had probably walked from France in them.

'No, thank you. I must get back.' He smiled. 'But I had to keep my promise. Thank Señor Forsyth for me. We have been so worried; we hear the Germans are sending Republican refugees back from France and worry they may demand us in return. But now we will be safe, thanks to your husband.' He reached out and shook her hand, then replaced his hat and turned, limping slowly down the drive.

Barbara closed the door. She saw a shadow at the top of the basement stairs and realized Pilar had been standing there listening. Was this how it was going to be with her from now on?

'Pilar,' she called sharply, 'could you make me a chocolate please.' The shadow jumped and the girl called, '*Sí, señora.*' Her footsteps clumped rapidly down the steps to the kitchen. Barbara stood in the hall, weighing the bag in her hands. It wasn't coins, it was something lighter. She went back into the salon and opened the drawstring. She tipped the contents into her palm.

There were rings and necklaces, a couple of brooches and some strangely shaped items that looked as though they might have a religious function. They were all gold, bright shiny gold. She frowned, puzzled.

She supposed she had better take the bag up to Sandy. She mounted the stairs slowly. The central heating hissed and gurgled in the quiet hallway. A light shone under the study door. She could hear him talking, he must still be on the telephone. She was about to knock but something in his tone stopped her. It reminded her of when he had mentioned his fantasies earlier.

'He should be talking by now. You've had him all day. What have you done to him?' There was silence, then Sandy's voice again. 'Those old Moroccan sweats are tough. He still says Gomez is his real name? Well, I suppose it makes sense, they'd have had to run up forged papers for a false name and that's Gestapo territory.' There was more silence, a couple of grunts acknowledging what the man at the other end was saying, then Sandy's voice again, a harsh, angry edge to it. 'I'll leave it in your capable hands.' He paused, then added, 'There're enough places around Santa Maria. Look, I've got to go. I've Brett's paperwork here. No, he trusts me. Yes. *Adíos*.' There was a tinkle as he replaced the receiver.

The phrases rang in Barbara's head. What have you done to him? Gestapo territory. And Harry was involved somehow. She stood there, heart thumping. She heard Sandy opening a drawer in his desk, a grunt. She swallowed and stepped quietly from the door, holding the canvas bag tightly. She would give it to him later.

In the *salón* Pilar had left a cup of chocolate on the sewing table. She sat down heavily, the bag in her lap. Just what the hell was Sandy involved in? She thought again of his taunt about his fantasies. He could be capable of anything, she thought; I've never really known him at all. She swallowed again and placed the bag on the sewing table. She stared at it, her body tensed, ears alert for his footstep outside.

Chapter Thirty-Two

SOFIA AND HARRY walked slowly through the Rastro crowds. It was Sunday, a cool cloudy day, and Madrid's main street market was packed. The rickety wooden stalls with their awnings spilled into the narrow streets around Plaza de Cascorro. They were covered with junk of every imaginable variety – cheap ornaments, pieces of broken down machinery, canaries in wooden cages. Harry would have liked to take Sofia's hand but that was now forbidden as immoral unless the couple were married. Pairs of *guardias* stood in doorways here and there, looking at the crowd with cold hard eyes.

It was exactly a week since they had made love in Harry's flat. Since then they had managed to see each other most days. Harry had time on his hands; he had had no further instructions from the spies. Sofia would come round to his flat in the evenings, leaving early because of her early shifts at the dairy.

He was happy to be in love for the first time, happy that his orderly world had been turned upside down. When the latest letter from Will arrived he read of their problems with getting a cleaner for their house in the country, the children's schooling, and felt unimaginably distant from his cousin's world at the same time as he felt a warm rush of love for him.

There were secrets, though. Harry wanted nothing more than to tell Sofia about his work as a spy and how he hated it, how his only friend at the embassy had turned out to be his watcher: but he couldn't and mustn't. Sofia, meanwhile, had not told her family of their relationship. She said it wasn't the right time. When she left Enrique to look after their mother and Paco in the early evenings she told him she went visiting one of the girls from the dairy. She didn't seem to mind lying to her brother; Harry wondered whether perhaps families as close as theirs could only cope with that closeness by having secrets.

Today was Sofia's weekly day off from the dairy. She had arranged for Enrique to stay at home to look after their mother and Paco.

They had made love at Harry's flat and then Sofia suggested the Rastro. As they threaded their way through the crowds, Harry whispered to her. 'You never smell of milk. Why don't you smell of milk?'

She laughed. 'What do I smell of?'

'Just you. A clean smell.'

'When I went to work there I promised myself I wouldn't end up smelling like the others. There is a shower there; it is freezing cold and has a concrete floor with a broken metal drain you must be careful not to fall into, but I shower every day.'

'No one will ever keep you down, will they?'

'No.' She smiled at him. 'I hope not.'

They walked deeper into the crowds, laughing at some of the bizarre things up for sale, and passed into the part of the market that sold food. Most of the stalls were nearly empty, only a few dried-up vegetables here and there. A meat stall sold offal that Harry could smell six feet away but there was a queue waiting to buy it. Sofia saw his disgusted look.

'People will buy anything now,' she said. 'The ration wouldn't feed a dog.'

'I know.'

'Everyone is desperate. That's why Enrique took that job, you know. He is a good man at heart, he didn't want to be a spy.'

'I wonder whether not being good at spying makes you a better man?'

'Perhaps it does. People who are good at deceiving cannot be good people, can they? He is happier as a street cleaner.'

'How is his leg?'

'All right. He is still tired in the evenings, but that will get better. Señora Avila is disappointed. Now there is more income coming into the family she has lost one excuse to run to the priest with, that we cannot afford to care for Paco.'

He looked at her. 'What was your uncle the priest like?' he asked.

Sofia smiled sadly. 'Mama and Papa moved from Tarancón to Madrid to find work when I was small and Uncle Ernesto went to a parish in Cuenca. Although my parents were Republicans they kept in touch, family is everything in Spain. We used to go and stay with Uncle Ernesto for a few days every summer when I was small. I remember being amazed by his *sotana*.' She laughed. 'I remember I asked my mother why Uncle wore a dress. But he was kind. He let me clean the candlesticks in the church. I would leave great fingermarks all over them, but he said it didn't matter. He must have got one of his *beatas* to polish them again afterwards.' She looked at Harry. 'Since the war ended Mama has said one of us should go to Cuenca and see if he is still alive. But even if we could afford it I do not think it is a good idea. I heard bad stories of what happened to the priests and nuns there.'

'I'm sorry.'

She grasped his hand for a moment, hidden by the press of the crowd. 'At least I had a family to look after me. I wasn't sent away to some school like you.'

Ahead of them the street broadened out. It was particularly busy here and Harry saw an unusual number of well-dressed customers crowded round a stall, their faces intent, frowning. A pair of *civiles* stood in a doorway, watching.

'What's going on?' Harry asked.

'This is where all the things that were taken from the houses of the rich in 1936 end up,' Sofia said. 'The people who took them need the money for food so they sell them to the stallholders. Rich Madrileños come here to try to find their family heirlooms.'

They walked past the stalls. There were expensive-looking vases and dinner services, porcelain figures and even an old record-player with a silver horn. Harry read the inscription on it. 'To Don Juan Ramirez Dávila from his colleagues at the Banco de Santander, 12.7.19.' An elderly woman picked through a heap of brooches and mother-of-pearl necklaces. 'We'll never find it, Dolores,' her husband murmured wearily. 'You have to forget about it.'

Harry picked up a porcelain figure of a woman in eighteenth-century dress, her nose chipped. 'Some of these probably meant a lot to someone once.'

'They were bought with money stolen from the people,' Sofia replied, a harshness in her voice.

They passed on to a table with a huge pile of photographs. People were crowded around sorting through them, and here the faces were sad, stricken, some looking frantic as they delved through the piles.

'Where did all these come from?' Harry asked.

'Photographs would be taken from the frames when they were sold. People come here looking for photographs of their families.'

Some of the photos were recent, some half a century old. Wedding photographs, family portraits, black and white and sepia. A young man in a military uniform, smiling into the camera; a young couple sitting outside a taverna hand in hand. Harry realized many of them must be dead now. No wonder these people were looking so intently; here they might find the only image left of a lost son or brother.

'So many gone,' he muttered. 'So many.'

Sofia leaned in to him. 'Harry, do you know that man over there? He is looking at us.'

Harry turned and drew in his breath sharply. General Maestre was standing by the porcelain stall with his wife and Milagros. He wore civilian clothes, a heavy coat and a trilby. Out of uniform his weatherbeaten features looked harsher, older. Señora Maestre was examining a silver candleholder but the general was frowning in Harry's direction. Milagros was looking at him too, her eyes sad in her plump face. He met her eye and she blushed and lowered her head. Harry nodded at the general. He raised his eyebrows slightly before nodding briefly in return, a jerk of the head.

'It's a government minister, General Maestre,' Harry whispered.

'How do you know him?' Sofia's voice was suddenly sharp, her eyes wide.

'I had to translate for him. It's embarrassing, I went out with his daughter once, I was pushed into it. Come on, let's go.'

But the crowd round the pile of photographs was so thick they had to turn the other way, towards Maestre. The general stepped forward into Harry's path and greeted him unsmilingly.

'Señor Brett, good morning. Milagros was wondering if you had vanished from the earth.'

'I'm sorry, general, I've been very busy, I—'

He glanced at Sofia. She gave him a cold, angry look. 'Milagros was hoping you would ring her,' the general went on. 'Though she has given up now.' He glanced back at his family. 'My wife likes to come here, try to find some of our looted family treasures. I tell her she will catch something, mixing with these whores from the slums.' He raised his eyebrows at Sofia, running his eyes up and down her old black coat, then turned and walked back to his wife and Milagros, who was pretending to be absorbed with a Dresden shepherdess. Sofia stared after him, her hands clenched, breathing hard. Harry touched her shoulder.

'Sofia, I'm so sorry—'

She thrust his hand away and turned into the crowd. The press of people stopped her from walking faster than a shuffle and Harry quickly caught her up.

'Sofia, Sofia, I'm sorry.' Gently he turned her round to face him. 'He's a pig, a brute, insulting you like that.'

To his surprise she laughed, harshly and bitterly. 'Do you think people like me aren't used to insults from people like him? Do you think I care what that old shit says?'

'Then what?'

She shook her head. 'Oh, you don't understand, we talk of these things but you don't understand.'

He fumbled for her hands, clutched at them. People were staring but he didn't care. 'I *want* to understand.'

She took a deep breath. She pulled away from his grip. 'We'd better walk on, we're offending public morals.'

'All right.' He fell into step beside her. She looked up at him.

'I have heard of that man. General Maestre. His was one of the names we feared during the Siege. They say in one village he ordered all the Socialist councillors' wives brought into the town square and got the Moors to tie them up and cut off their breasts in front of their men. I know there was a lot of propaganda but I nursed a man from that village, he said it was true. And when they occupied Madrid last year, Maestre had a big part in rounding up subversives. Not just Communists; people who only ever wanted a secure peaceful life, a share of their country.' Harry saw she was crying, tears running down her face. 'The cleansing, they called it. Night after night you could hear the shots from the east cemetery. You still can sometimes. They took this city like an occupying army and that's how they still hold it. And the Falange strutting and rampaging over *our* city—'

They had reached a quieter area. Sofia came to a sudden halt. She took a deep breath and wiped her face with a handkerchief. Harry stood looking at her. There was nothing he could say. She touched his arm. 'I know you try to understand,' she said. 'But then I see you talking to that creature. You have come to visit this – this hell – from another world, Harry. You will stay a while and then go back.' She bent her head. 'Take me back to your flat, Harry, let's make love. At least we can make love. I don't want to talk more now.'

They walked on without talking, back to Plaza de Cascorro where the market began. As they threaded their way through the square Harry thought, what if I could get her out, get her to England. But how? She'd never leave her mother and Enrique and Paco and how could I get them out too? She walked ahead of him, shoving her way through the crowds, strong and indomitable but so small, so vulnerable in this city ruled by the generals that Hoare and Hillgarth plied with the Knights of St George.

Chapter Thirty-Three

In the Tierra Muerta the weather had turned bad. One morning the camp woke to find everything covered in snow, even the steep roofs of the watchtowers. The snow was thick on the mountain path to the quarry, soaking through the prisoners' cracked old boots. Bernie remembered his mother, when he was a child, saying he must be sure never to get his feet wet in the winter, it was a sure way to catch a cold. He laughed aloud and Pablo turned and gave him an odd look.

The men stopped for their brief rest at the fold in the hills from which, if conditions were right, Cuenca appeared in the distance. You couldn't see anything today, only a glimpse of the brown cliff of the gorge between the white hills and the cold milky sky.

'Come on, you lazy bastards!' the guard called. The men stamped their feet to restore the circulation and got back into line.

Vicente was dying. The authorities had seen enough deaths to know when someone was on the way out and had stopped trying to make him work. For the last two days he had lain on his pallet in the hut, drifting in and out of consciousness. Whenever he woke he begged for water, saying his head and throat were on fire.

That night a strong wind came in from the west, bringing a heavy sleety rain that melted the snow. It was still raining heavily next morning, the wind driving it across the yard in vertical sheets. The men were told there would be no work parties that day: the guards don't fancy a day out in this, Bernie thought. The storm continued; the men stayed in their huts and played cards or sewed or read the Catholic tracts and copies of *Arriba* that were all they were allowed.

Bernie knew the Communist group had held a meeting to discuss him a couple of days before. Since then they had avoided him, even Pablo, but they didn't say what they had decided. Bernie guessed they were waiting till Vicente died, giving him a short period of grace.

The lawyer slept most of the morning but woke towards noon. He made a croaking sound. Bernie had been lying on his pallet but got up and leaned over him. Vicente was very thin now, his eyes sunk deep inside black circles. 'Water,' he croaked.

'I'll get some, wait a minute.' Bernie put on his old patched army greatcoat and went out into the rain, wincing as pellets of sleet blew into his face. There was no water supply to the huts and he had carefully cleaned out his piss-bucket, leaving it out overnight to catch the rain. It was almost full. He carried it in, scooped some water into a tin cup, then gently lifted the lawyer's head so he could drink. Establo, lying on the opposite bed, laughed throatily. 'Ay, *inglés*, do you make the poor man drink your piss?'

Vicente leaned back; even the effort of drinking exhausted him. 'Thanks.'

'How are you?'

'A lot of pain. I wish it was over. I think, no more quarry, no more Sunday services. I'm so tired. Ready for the endless silence.' Bernie didn't reply. Vicente smiled tiredly. 'Just now I was dreaming about when we first came here. Do you remember, that lorry? How it jolted?'

'Yes.'

After Bernie's capture he had spent many months at the San Pedro de Cardena prison, where the first psychiatric tests had been done. By then most of the English prisoners had been repatriated through diplomatic channels, but not him. Then in late 1937 he had been transferred, along with a mixture of Spanish and foreign prisoners considered politically dangerous, to the Tierra Muerta camp. Bernie wondered whether his party membership was the reason the embassy hadn't petitioned for his release; surely his mother would have tried to get him out when she learned he was a prisoner.

They were driven to the Tierra Muerta in old army lorries and Vicente was shackled next to him on the bench. He asked Bernie where he was from and soon they were engaged in an argument about communism. Bernie liked Vicente's wry sense of humour, and he had always had that soft spot for bourgeois intellectuals.

A few days after their arrival at the Tierra Muerta, Vicente sought him out. The lawyer had been delegated to help the administration with the mountain of forms involved in inducting prisoners into the new camp. Bernie was sitting on a bench in the yard. Vicente sat beside him and lowered his voice.

'You remember you told me how the other English prisoners have gone home; you thought your embassy were not troubling themselves with you because you are a Communist?'

'Yes.'

'That is not the reason. I had a look at your dossier today. The English think you are dead.'

Bernie was astonished. 'What?'

'When you were captured on the Jarama, what happened exactly?'

Bernie frowned. 'I was unconscious for a while. Then I was taken by a Fascist patrol.'

'They asked you the usual things? Name, nationality, political affiliation?'

'Yes, the sergeant who captured me took some notes. He was a bastard. He was going to shoot me but his corporal persuaded him not to, he said there could be trouble since I was a foreigner.'

Vicente nodded slowly. 'I think he was more of a bastard than you realized. Embassies of foreign prisoners of war should always be informed of their capture. But according to your dossier, you were put down as a Spaniard. You were given a twenty-five-year sentence by a military court under that Spanish name, with a batch of others. The authorities didn't find out the error till later; they decided to leave things as they were.'

Bernie stared into the distance. 'Then my parents think I'm dead?'

'You would have been reported as missing believed killed by your own side. I would guess the sergeant who captured you gave false details precisely so your embassy wouldn't be told you had been captured. Out of malice.'

'Why was it never put right?'

Vicente spread his hands. 'Probably just bureaucratic inertia. The longer it was left before they were notified, the more fuss your embassy might make. I suspect you became a nuisance, an anomaly. So they have buried you away here.'

'What if I said something now?'

Vicente shook his head. 'It would do no good.' He looked at him seriously. 'They might shoot you to get rid of the anomaly. We have no rights here, we are nothing.'

Vicente slept for the rest of the day, occasionally waking and asking for water. Then, that evening, Father Eduardo came. Bernie saw him crossing the yard through the wind and rain, clutching his heavy black cloak around him. He entered the hut, dripping water on to the bare boards.

Father Jaime would have crossed straight to the bed of the sick man, ignoring the others, but Father Eduardo always sought to make contact with the prisoners. He looked round the hut with a nervous smile. 'Ay, what a storm,' he said. Some men stared at him coldly, others went back to their reading or sewing. Then the priest walked towards Vicente's pallet. Bernie got up and stood barring his way.

'He does not want to see you, father,' he said quietly.

'I have to talk to him. It is my duty.' The priest leaned closer. 'Listen, Piper. Father Jaime wanted to come but I said I felt this man was my responsibility. Would you rather I fetched him? I do not want to but if you bar my way I must report it, he is the senior priest.'

Wordlessly Bernie stepped aside. He wondered if it might be better to have Father Jaime here, that brutal man might be easier for Vicente to resist.

The noise had woken the lawyer. He stared up as the priest leaned over him. Drops of water fell from the priest's cloak on to the sack-cloth sheet.

'Is that the holy water, father?'

'How are you?'

'Not dead yet. Bernardo, *amigo*, will you give me more water?'

Bernie dipped the cup in the pail and passed it to Vicente. He drank greedily. The priest glanced at the piss-pail with distaste. '*Señor*, you are very ill,' he said. 'You should make confession.'

There was complete silence in the hut. All the prisoners were watching and listening, their faces dim white circles in the weak candlelight. Everyone knew Vicente hated the priests, had known this moment was coming.

'No.' Vicente managed to raise himself a little. The light glinted on the grey stubble on his cheeks and his weary, angry eyes. 'No.'

'If you die unconfessed, your soul will go to Hell.' Father Eduardo was uneasy, twisting a button on his *sotana*. His spectacles reflected the candlelight, turning his sad eyes into two little fires.

Vicente ran his tongue over dry lips. 'No hell,' he gasped. 'Only – silence.' He coughed, then began to make a gurgling noise in his throat. He lay back, exhausted. Father Eduardo sighed and turned away. He whispered to Bernie, bending close. He gave off a faint smell of incense and oil.

'I think this man has only a day or two. I will again come tomorrow. But listen, is that piss-pail all you have to give him water?'

'I cleaned it out.'

'All the same, to have to use that. And where did you get the water?'

'It's rainwater.'

'The rain won't go on for ever. Listen, I have a tap in the church, and a bucket. Come tomorrow and I'll give you some water.'

'You won't worm your way into his confidence that way.'

'I do not want to see him suffer more than he should!' Father Eduardo said with sudden anger. 'Come or not as you please, but there is water if you want it.' He turned on his heel and marched out of the hut, back into the storm. Bernie turned back to Vicente.

'He's gone.'

The lawyer smiled bitterly. 'I was strong, Bernardo, wasn't I?'

'Yes, yes you were. I'm sorry I couldn't stop him.'

'You helped distract him. I know there is only nothingness ahead. I embrace it.' Vicente took a gasping breath. 'I was trying to work up enough phlegm to spit at him. If he comes again I shall.'

That night the wind veered round to the east and it snowed again. The following morning was bitterly cold. The wind had dropped; the snow lay thick and noises in the camp were muffled, the men's feet making a creaking sound as they lined up for roll-call. Aranda didn't like the cold weather; he went round muffled in a balaclava helmet that looked odd with his immaculate uniform.

It was Sunday and there was no labour detail. After roll-call some of the prisoners were set clearing the snow from the yard, sweeping it into great piles against the huts. Vicente had woken with a raging thirst. Bernie had set the pail outside before going to bed and it was full of snow. He looked at it. It would take ages to melt in the cold hut and even then it would only be a quarter full. He stood a moment, shivering in the icy morning, the old wounds in his shoulder and thigh aching. He looked across to the hut housing the church, a cross painted on its side. He hesitated, then walked towards it.

Aranda stood in the doorway of his hut, watching the snow-clearing detail. He stared at Bernie as he passed. Bernie walked through the church and knocked at the office door. Inside a large stove was burning, the warm air was like a balm. Father Jaime stood beside it warming his hands while Father Eduardo worked at the desk. The older priest looked at Bernie suspiciously.

'What do you want?'

'This man and I are having some discussions,' Father Eduardo said. Father Jaime raised his bushy eyebrows.

'This one? He's a Communist. Has he taken confession?'

'Not yet.'

Father Jaime wrinkled his nose with distaste. 'I left my missal in my room. I must fetch it. The air in here is not what it was.' He rustled past, closing the door with a snap. Bernie looked at Father Eduardo with raised eyebrows.

'Telling a lie to your superior, isn't that a venial sin or something?'

'It was not a lie. We have talked, haven't we?' Father Eduardo sighed. 'You're quite implacable, Piper, aren't you?'

'I've come for the water.'

'Over there.' The priest nodded to a tap in the corner. A clean steel bucket lay underneath. Bernie filled it, then turned back to Father Eduardo.

'I wouldn't put it past you to have put a drop of holy water in the bottom of the bucket this morning and then blessed it.'

Father Eduardo shook his head. 'You know so little of what we believe. You know how to fashion shafts that bite, but one does not need to see deeply to do that.'

'At least I don't plague people's last hours, father. *Adíos*.' Bernie turned and left.

The yard was almost clear of snow now; the men were piling their shovels against the wall of the *comandante*'s hut. Halfway across Bernie heard a shout.

'You there! *¡Inglés!*'

Aranda descended the steps of his hut and walked towards him. Bernie put down the bucket and stood to attention. The *comandante* halted in front of him, frowning angrily.

'What is in that bucket?'

'Water, *señor comandante*. There is a man ill in my hut. Father Eduardo said I could take some water from the church tap.'

'That stupid pansy. The sooner the *abogado* dies the better.'

Bernie sensed Aranda was bored and trying to provoke a reaction. He looked at the ground.

'I do not believe in softness.' Aranda kicked the bucket over with his booted foot, the water splashing out over the earth. He smiled. 'I say, *¡Viva la Muerte!* Take that pail back to the pansy priest. I will have a word with Father Jaime about this. Go on!'

Bernie picked up the bucket and walked slowly back to the hut. He felt anger but also relief. He had got off lightly. Aranda was in a mood to persecute someone.

He told the priest what Aranda had said. 'He says he's going to report you to Father Jaime.'

'He is a hard man.' Father Eduardo shrugged.

Bernie turned to go. 'Wait,' the priest said. He was still looking out of the window. 'He is going back inside his hut.' He turned to Bernie. 'Listen, I know him, he will go and warm himself at the stove now. It is at the back of his hut. Fill the bucket again and go quickly, he won't see you.'

Bernie's eyes narrowed. 'Why are you doing this?'

'I saw your friend desperate for water and I wanted to help. That is all.'

'Then leave him in peace. Don't trouble his last hours for the million to one chance he'll repent.'

The priest did not reply. Bernie refilled the bucket and left the hut without another word. His heart pounded as he crossed the yard. He and the priest were both mad. If Aranda saw he'd been disobeyed he'd go berserk.

He reached the hut safely, shutting the door behind him. He went up to Vicente's bed. 'Water, *amigo*,' he said. 'Courtesy of the church.'

The priest came again that afternoon. Most of the men who were fit, tired of being cooped up, had gone outside and were playing a desultory game of football in the yard. Vicente was delirious, he seemed to imagine himself back in his office in Madrid, and kept muttering to someone to bring him a file and open the window, he was too hot. He was covered in sweat although the hut was freezing cold. Bernie sat beside him, wiping his face now and then with a corner of the sheet. On the bed opposite Establo lay smoking, watching them. He seldom went outside now.

Bernie heard a rustle at his elbow and turned. Father Eduardo was there; he must have come in quietly.

'He's in a dream, father,' Bernie whispered. 'Leave him, he's far away from this place.'

The priest put a box on the bed, a box of oils Bernie supposed. His heart thumped; the moment had come. Father Eduardo leaned over and touched Vicente's brow. The lawyer grimaced and flinched away, then slowly opened his eyes. He took a deep rattling breath.

'*Mierda*. You again.'

Father Eduardo took a deep breath. 'I think your hour is close. You have been slipping into dreams and next time you may not return. Even now, Señor Vicente, God will receive you into eternal life.'

'Don't listen to him,' Bernie said.

Vicente gave a ghastly rictus of a smile, exposing pale gums. 'Don't worry, *compadre*. Give me some water.'

Bernie helped Vicente to drink. He took long slow sips, his eyes never leaving the priest, then lay back gasping.

'Please.' There was a pleading note in Father Eduardo's voice. 'You have a chance of eternal life. Don't throw it away.'

Vicente began to make a gurgling noise in his throat. The priest spoke again.

'If you do not take this last chance, you must go to Hell. That is what is written.'

Vicente's throat was working, he gurgled and spluttered. Bernie knew what he was trying to do. The priest leaned forward and Vicente took a deep breath but the phlegm he had been working slipped down his throat. He coughed, then started choking, gasping frantically for breath. He sat up, his face red, heaving for air. Bernie reached over and slapped him on the back. Vicente's eyes bulged as he gagged and retched. Then a spasm ran through his wasted body and he fell back on the pallet. A long gurgling sigh came from his throat, a sound of terrible weariness. Bernie saw the expression leach out of his eyes. He was dead. The priest sank to his knees and began to pray.

Bernie sat on the bed. His legs were shaking. After a minute Father Eduardo rose and crossed himself. Bernie looked at him coldly.

'He was trying to spit at you, father, did you realize?'

The priest shook his head.

'You threatened him with Hell and he tried to spit at you and choked on it. You gave him his death.'

The priest looked at Vicente's body then shook his head and turned away, walking down the hut. Bernie shouted after him.

'Don't worry, father, he's not in Hell. He's out of it!'

VICENTE WAS buried the next day. As he had not received the last rites there could be no church ceremony. Vicente would have been pleased. Bernie trudged through the snow behind the digging detail that carried the body, sewn into an old sheet, to the hillside where the graves were. He watched as it was lowered into a shallow grave that had been dug that morning. '*Adíos, compadre,*' he muttered quietly. He felt very alone.

The guard accompanying them crossed himself and signalled with his rifle for Bernie to return to the camp. The digging detail began filling in the grave, struggling with the frozen earth. It began to snow again, white heavy flakes. Bernie thought, Father Eduardo will be thinking you're in the eternal fire, but really you're going to be encased in ice. The joke would have amused Vicente.

THAT AFTERNOON Bernie was leaning against the wall of the hut, smoking a cigarette one of the digging party had given him out of kindness, when Pablo came up to him. He looked uncomfortable.

'I've been detailed to speak to you, on behalf of the party cell,' he said.

Because you were my friend, Bernie thought, to show me Establo's brought everyone into line.

'You have been found guilty of incorrigible bourgeois individualism and resistance to authority,' Pablo said woodenly. 'You are expelled from the party, and warned if you make any attempts to sabotage our cell, measures will be taken.' Bernie knew what that meant; a knife thrust in the dark; it had happened before among the prisoners.

'I'm a loyal Communist and I always have been,' he said. 'I don't accept Establo's authority to lead us. One day I shall take my case to the Central Committee.'

Pablo lowered his voice. 'Why do you make trouble? Why be so obstinate? You are obstinate, Bernardo. People say you only became friends with the lawyer to annoy us.'

Bernie smiled bitterly. 'Vicente was an honest man. I admired him.'

'What was the point of making all that trouble with the priest? These things cause trouble. There's no point arguing with the priests. Establo's right, it's just bourgeois individualism.'

'Then what do we do? How do we resist?'

'We keep strong, united. One day fascism will fall.' Pablo winced and scratched at his wrist. Perhaps he had scabies – that was a risk if you were round Establo too much.

'One thing more, Establo wants you out of the hut. He wants you to apply for a transfer, say being in the hut is hard after your friend's death.'

Bernie shrugged. 'They may not let me move.'

'Establo said you must.'

'I'll ask, *comrade*.' Bernie put a bitter emphasis on the last word.

Pablo turned away. Bernie watched him go. And if I don't get a transfer, he thought, which I probably won't, Establo will say I'm making more trouble by staying. He's got it all worked out. He looked through the wire at the hill where Vicente was buried, a brown slash in the snow. He thought he wouldn't mind joining him under the earth. Then he set his lips. While he lived he would fight. That was what a real Communist did.

Chapter Thirty-Four

THERE WAS AN uneasy atmosphere round the dinner table. Sandy and Barbara were both smoking constantly, lighting up between courses. Sandy was unusually quiet, withdrawing into little silences, while Barbara's attempts at conversation seemed nervous and brittle, and once or twice she looked at Sandy strangely. They seemed to Harry to be distant from each other, oddly disconnected. The atmosphere made Harry feel nervous, uneasy. He couldn't stop looking at Sandy's preoccupied, slightly surly face and thinking, what happened to Gomez? What have you done to him?

The spies knew he had been invited for dinner at Sandy's again and he had had an interview with Hillgarth that afternoon. He hadn't seen him for over a week. The captain's office was at the rear of the embassy, an area Harry had never visited. A business-like female secretary led him into a large room with high coved ceilings. Framed photographs of battleships lined the walls; on a shelf, beside *Whitaker's Almanac* and *Jane's Fighting Ships*, were bound copies of Hillgarth's novels. Harry remembered one or two titles he had seen Sandy reading at school: *The Princess and the Perjurer*, *The War Maker*.

Hillgarth sat behind a big oak desk. His face wore a heavy, frowning expression; there was anger in the large expressive eyes although his tone was quiet. 'We're in trouble with Maestre,' he began. 'He's bloody furious. He and some of his Monarchist chums *were* spying at that bloody mine and Gomez was working for them. It's a pity you were the one who gave his man away. Maestre wasn't too pleased with you anyway for leaving his daughter in the lurch. It's the end of their operation.'

'Can I ask what's happened to Gomez, sir? Is he—'

'Maestre doesn't know. But he doesn't expect to see him again. Gomez worked for him for years.'

'I see.' Harry felt his stomach sink.

'At least Forsyth doesn't seem to be on to you.' Hillgarth stared at him. 'So keep stringing him along, agree to invest, and tell me about these reports they talked about when you get them. It's them I want to see.'

'Yes, sir.'

'Sir Sam's lobbying in London. They may pull the plug on this operation. If they do, or if anything goes wrong, I've got a contingency plan for Forsyth.' He paused. 'We'll try to recruit him. We can't offer him what he's hoping to make from that mine, but we could maybe bring other pressures to bear. He's still estranged from his family?'

'Completely.'

Hillgarth grunted. 'Nothing we can use there, then. Oh well, we'll have to see.' He looked at Harry sharply. 'You look worried. Don't like the idea of us putting the squeeze on Forsyth? I'd got the impression you despised him.'

Harry said nothing. Hillgarth went on looking at him. 'You're not really cut out for this sort of work, are you, Brett?'

'No, sir,' Harry said heavily. 'I just did what I was asked to do. I'm sorry for what happened to Lieutenant Gomez.'

'So you should be. But we need you to carry on doing what you're doing, for now. Afterwards we'll send you home. Probably quite soon.' He gave a half smile. 'I expect that will be a relief, eh?'

PILAR BROUGHT IN the main course: a paella, mussels and prawns and anchovies on a bed of rice. She set the dish on the table and withdrew, avoiding everyone's eye. Barbara scooped portions onto their plates.

'It's a treat getting fresh fish,' Sandy said, seeming to come to life at the smell of food. He smiled at Harry. 'There's less of it around than ever.'

'Why's that?'

'The fishermen get a petrol allowance to run their boats, but the black-market price of petrol's so astronomical they just sell it on for a huge profit and don't bother going to sea. That's what our blockade's doing, you see.'

'Can't the government make them use the petrol for fishing?'

Sandy laughed. 'No. Even when they do make laws they can't enforce them. Half the ministers have their noses deep in the trough anyway.'

'How's this project going that you're investing in?' said Barbara. She gave Harry another strange look.

'Well—'

Sandy interrupted. 'Slowly. Nothing happening just now.'

She looked between them for a moment.

'I had a letter from Will yesterday,' Harry said. 'He's enjoying being in the countryside now.'

'His wife'll be pleased to be away from the raids,' Barbara said.

'Yes, it's been too much for her.' He looked at her seriously. 'Have you heard about Coventry?'

She took a long drag of her cigarette. Behind her glasses her eyes were tired, little rings around them Harry hadn't noticed before. 'Yes. Five hundred killed, the reports said. The city centre flattened.'

'Those reports in *Arriba* are exaggerated,' Sandy said. 'They always make the bombing sound worse than it is – the Germans tell them what to write.'

'It was on the BBC.'

'It's true all right,' Harry agreed.

'Coventry's only fifteen miles from Birmingham,' Barbara said. 'Every time I listen to the BBC I'm frightened of hearing about more raids there. I think my mother's feeling the strain, from her letters.' She sighed and smiled at Harry sadly. 'It's strange when your parents suddenly seem like frightened old people.'

'You should go and visit them,' Sandy said.

She looked up at him in surprise.

'Why not? You haven't been home for years. Christmas is coming up. It'd make a nice surprise for them.'

Barbara bit her lip. 'I just – I don't think it's the right time,' she said.

'Why ever not? I could get you a place on a plane.'

'I'll think about it.'

'Please yourself.'

Harry looked at Barbara. He wondered why she didn't want to go.

She turned to him. 'What about you, Harry, will you be getting any Christmas leave?'

'I shouldn't think so. They like to keep the translators on tap in case there's an emergency.'

'I expect you'd like to see your aunt and uncle.'

'Yes.'

'Sandy says you've got a girlfriend,' she said with an effort at brightness. 'What does she do?'

Harry wished again he hadn't told Sandy that in the car the day they'd visited the mine. 'She – she works in the dairy sector.'

'How long have you been seeing her?'

'Not long.' Harry thought back to the previous evening, which he had spent at the Carabanchel flat. Sofia had revealed, quite unexpectedly, that she had told her family they were going out together. Harry had wondered how they would react. Sofia's mother and Enrique had welcomed him effusively though Harry guessed they were pleased Sofia had found someone rich, even though he was a foreigner. Paco had seemed more at ease and had spoken to Harry for the first time. He had felt strangely privileged.

'You'll have to bring her round to dinner,' Barbara said brightly. 'Make a foursome.'

'That's why you're not going home for Christmas.' Sandy pointed a finger at Harry. 'You sly dog.' He wiped his mouth with his napkin. 'Where's the pepper? Pilar's forgotten it.'

'I'll go and get it,' Barbara said. 'Excuse me.'

She left the room. Sandy looked at Harry seriously. 'Wanted to get rid of her for a minute,' he said. 'I'm afraid there's a problem with the mine.'

Harry's heart began thumping. 'What is it?'

'Sebastian's got cold feet about a foreigner investing. I'm afraid it's no go.' He looked downcast.

'That's a shame.' So there would be no reports for Hillgarth after all. 'I'm surprised, I thought it was Otero that was suspicious.'

Sandy toyed with his crystal wineglass. 'He's afraid this supervision committee won't like the idea of an English investor. They're putting us – ' he paused – 'under pressure.'

'General Maestre's committee?'

'Yes. They've a closer eye on us than we thought. They know about you, we think.'

Harry wanted to ask about Gomez but he dared not. 'You'll still have problems with funding, then?'

Sandy nodded. 'The committee are talking about more or less taking the project over. Then bang go our profits. The people on the committee will make a mint of course.'

'I'm sorry.'

'Oh, we'll make something out of it, I suppose. I'm sorry to let you down.' He looked at Harry, his brown eyes sad and liquid like a dog's. How quickly their expression could change.

'It's all right. Maybe I'm better off out of it. I'm not sure it was my type of thing.'

'Good of you to take it like that. Pity, I wanted to do something for you, for – you know, old times' sake.'

The telephone rang in the hall, making Harry jump. He heard footsteps and Barbara's voice speaking English. A moment later she returned, her face anxious.

'Harry, the embassy want to speak to you. They say it's urgent.' She looked at him with concern. 'I hope it's not bad news from home.'

'You gave them our number?' Sandy looked at him sharply.

'I had to, I'm on call tonight. I have to go in if there's something needs translating urgently. Excuse me.'

He stepped out into the hall. A little *brasero* set under the telephone table warmed his feet, casting a yellow glow over the floor. He picked up the phone.

'Hello. Harry Brett.'

A cultured female voice answered. 'Oh, Mr Brett, I'm so glad we were able to reach you. I've got a caller holding, a Miss Sofia Roque Casas.' The woman hesitated. 'She says it's urgent.'

'Sofia?'

'She's holding now. Do you want to take the call?'

'Yes. Please, put her on.'

There was a click and for a moment Harry thought he had lost the connection, then Sofia came on. It seemed strange, hearing her voice there in Sandy's hall.

'Harry, Harry is that you?' There was panic in her voice, normally so composed.

'Yes. Sofia, what is it?'

'It's Mama. I think she has had another stroke. Enrique's gone out, I'm alone. Paco is in a terrible state, he saw it. Harry, can you come?' He heard tears in her voice.

'A stroke?'

'I think so. She is unconscious.'

'I'll come at once. Where are you?'

'I walked two blocks to find a telephone. I'm sorry, I couldn't think what else to do. Oh, Harry, she is bad.'

He thought a moment. 'OK. Go back to the flat, I'll get there as soon as I can. When's Enrique back?'

'Not till late. He has gone out with some friends.'

'Listen, I'm in Vigo district. I'll try and find a cab and get there as soon as I can. Get back to your mother and Paco.'

'Please hurry, please hurry.' It was frightening to hear the panic in her voice. 'I knew you'd come,' she added quickly, then there was a click as she replaced the receiver.

The *salón* door opened and Barbara put her head out. 'What is it? Did you say someone's had a stroke? Is it your uncle?'

He took a deep breath. 'No, it's Sofia's mother, my – my girlfriend.' He followed Barbara back into the dining room. 'She rang the embassy and they put the call through here. She's alone with her mother and a little boy they look after. I have to go there now.'

Sandy looked at him curiously. 'Can't they get a doctor?'

'They can't afford one.' He must have sounded snappy because Sandy raised his hand.

'All right, old boy, all right.'

'Can I call a cab from here?' Harry had taken a tram to the house.

'It'll take ages at this time of night. Where do they live?'

He hesitated. 'Carabanchel.'

'Carabanchel?' Sandy raised his eyebrows.

'Yes.'

Barbara's voice was suddenly decisive. 'I'll drive you. If this poor woman's had a stroke, I might be able to help.'

'Sofia was a medical student once. But you could help. Do you mind?'

'It's not safe taking the car down there,' Sandy said. 'We can call a cab.'

'I'll be all right.' Barbara stepped to the door. 'Come on, I'll get the keys.'

Harry followed her. In the doorway he turned back. Sandy was still sitting at the table. His expression was angry, petulant. He had always hated being ignored.

THE NIGHT WAS cold and clear. Barbara drove fast and well, through the city centre and into the dark narrow streets of the working-class districts. She seemed relieved to be out of the house. She looked at him curiously. 'I didn't realize Sofia was from Carabanchel.'

'You were expecting someone middle class?'

'I suppose I was, subconsciously.' Barbara smiled sadly. 'I should know it's unpredictable who we fall in love with.' She gave him another searching look. 'Is she special?'

'Yes.' Harry hesitated. 'I wondered for a while if it was – oh, I don't know, guilt or something, wanting to experience how ordinary Spaniards live.' He gave an embarrassed laugh.

'Going native?'

'Something like that. But it's just – it's just love. You know?'

'I know.' She hesitated. 'What do the embassy think?'

'I haven't told them. I want some part of my life to myself. It's here, the next street.'

They parked the car outside Sofia's block and hurried inside, running up the dark staircase. Sofia had heard them coming and stood in her doorway, weak yellow light shining into the hall. The sound of a child's hysterical crying came from inside. Sofia looked pale and her hair was lank and uncombed. She stared at Barbara. 'Who is this?'

'Barbara, she's the wife of a friend of mine. We were all having dinner together. She's a nurse, perhaps she can help.'

Sofia's shoulders slumped. 'It is too late. Mama has gone. She was dead when I got back from telephoning you.'

She led them in. The old woman lay on the bed. Her eyes had been closed and her white face looked still and peaceful. Paco lay on top of the body, clinging to it tightly, sobbing, a wild keening noise. He looked up as the three of them came into the room, eyeing Barbara with fear. Sofia went over and stroked his hair.

'It's all right, Paco, this lady is a friend of Harry's. She's come to help us. She is not from the Church. Please, come away now.' She lifted him gently from the body and held him to her. They sat on the bed, both crying now. Harry sat beside them, putting his arm round Sofia.

Paco stood up. He looked at Barbara, still afraid. She went over and very gently took his small dirty hand in hers.

'Hello, Paco,' she said in Spanish. 'May I call you Paco?' He nodded dumbly. 'Listen, Paco, Sofia is very upset. You must try to be a big boy if you can. I know it's difficult. Here, come and sit by me.' Paco let her lead him gently away from the bed. She sat him on one of the spindly chairs and pulled up another to sit next to him.

Sofia, still holding Harry tightly, looked at her mother's body. 'I thought this might happen and that it would be best for her but it is hard. I should call an ambulance, we cannot leave her here.'

'Won't Enrique want to see her?' Harry asked.

'I think maybe it is better he does not.' She got up and went to get her coat from behind the door.

'Let me go,' Harry said.

Barbara stood up. 'No, stay with Sofia. I saw a phone box nearby, on the way. I'll go.'

'You should not go alone,' Sofia said.

'I've been in tougher places than this. Please let me go.' She sounded brisk, business-like, wanting to be of service. 'I won't be a minute.' Before they could argue further she was gone, her footsteps clattering down the steps. Sofia took Paco's hand and led him back to sit on the bed with them. She looked at Elena's still face.

'She had been very tired recently,' Sofia whispered. 'Then this evening after dinner she cried out, a horrible groaning noise. When I went over to her she was unconscious. Then after I came back from telephoning you she had gone. I left poor Paco alone with her.' She kissed the boy's head. 'I should not have; I should have been here.'

'You did all you could.'

'It is better this way,' she said again, dully. 'Sometimes she used to wet the bed. It upset her terribly, she would cry.' She shook her head. 'You should have known Mama before she was ill, she was so strong, she took care of us all. Papa did not want me to go to university but Mama always supported me.' She looked over at the photograph, her mother in her wedding dress, standing between her husband and her brother the priest, all of them smiling into the camera.

Harry held her tightly. 'Poor Sofia. I don't know how you've endured it all.' She held him tightly. At length there were footsteps on the stairs. 'Here's Barbara,' Harry said. 'She'll have sorted something out.'

She looked at him. 'You know her well?'

He kissed her forehead. 'For a long time. But only as a friend.'

Barbara came in, her face red from the cold. 'I got through to the hospital. They're sending an ambulance, but it may be some time.' She produced a paper bag from her coat. 'I stopped at a *bodega*, got us some brandy. I thought we could all do with some.'

'Oh, well done,' Harry said.

Sofia fetched some tumblers and Barbara poured them each a stiff measure. Paco, curious, asked for some, and they gave him a little mixed with water. He screwed up his face. 'Ugh,' he said. '*¡Es horroroso!*' It broke the tension and they all laughed, a little hysterically.

'It is not respectful we should laugh,' Sofia said guiltily.

'Sometimes you just have to, ' Barbara said. She looked round the flat, taking in the damp-stained walls and the broken-down furniture, then lowering her eyes guiltily as she saw Sofia studying her.

'You are a nurse, *señora*?' Sofia added. 'Do you work as a nurse here?'

'No, not now. I'm – I'm married to a British businessman. He went to school with Harry.'

'Barbara did some voluntary work at one of the church orphanages,' Harry said. 'She couldn't stand it.'

'No, it was an awful place.' Barbara smiled at Sofia. 'Harry said you trained as a medical student.'

'Yes, until the Civil War came. Do you have women doctors in England?'

'Some. Not many.'

'There were three of us in my year at university. Sometimes the teachers did not know what to make of us. You could see they were embarrassed at the things they had to show us.'

Barbara smiled. 'Not ladylike?'

'Yes. Though in the war everyone saw such things.'

'I know. I was in Madrid for a while, working for the Red Cross.' She turned to Paco. 'How old are you, *niño?*'

'Ten.'

'Do you go to school?'

He shook his head.

'He couldn't cope,' Sofia said. 'Besides, the new schools are useless, full of Nationalist veterans without teaching experience. I try to teach him at home.'

There were footsteps on the stairs, heavy male footsteps. Sofia drew her breath in sharply. 'That will be Enrique.' She got up. 'Let me speak to him alone. Would you take Paco into the kitchen, please.'

'Come on, young man.' Barbara took the boy's hand and Harry followed her. He lit the stove; Barbara pointed to a book on the table to distract Paco as a murmur of voices came from outside. The book had a green cover, a picture of a boy and girl walking together to school.

'What is that book?'

Paco bit his lip, listening to the voices outside. Harry heard Enrique's voice, a sudden anguished cry.

'What is it?' Barbara went on, trying to distract him.

'My old schoolbook. From when I went to school before Mama and Papa were taken. I liked it.'

Barbara opened it and pushed it towards him. They could hear crying outside, a man crying. Paco looked at the door again. 'Show me,' Barbara said gently. 'Just for a few minutes. It is good to leave Sofia and Enrique together for a little.'

'I remember that book,' she added. 'The Meras showed it to me once. Carmel had a copy.' Her eyes filled with tears. Harry realized that behind the forced brightness she was at the end of her tether. She turned to Paco. 'Look at all the sections. History, geography, arithmetic.'

'I used to like geography,' Paco said. 'Look at the pictures, all the countries in the world.'

It was quiet again outside. Harry got up. 'I'll see how they are. Stay with Paco.' He squeezed Barbara's shoulder and went back into the main room. Enrique was sitting on the bed with Sofia. He looked up at Harry, a bitter expression Harry had never seen before on his pale tear-stained face, making it ugly.

'You see all our family dramas, *inglés*.'

'I'm sorry, Enrique.'

'It's not Harry's fault,' Sofia said.

'If only he could see us with some dignity. We had dignity once, *señor*, you know that?'

There was a knock at the door. Sofia sighed. 'That must be the ambulance.' But as she approached the door it opened and Señora Avila's thin face peered in. She wore a black shawl round her head, the ends held tightly in her hand.

'Pardon me, but I heard crying, is something wrong – oh.' She saw the body on the bed and crossed herself. 'Oh, poor Señora Roque. Poor lady. But she is at peace now, with God.' She looked curiously at Harry.

Sofia stood up. 'Señora Avila, we would rather be alone, please. We are waiting for them to take our mother away.'

The *beata* looked round the room. 'Where is Paco? The *pobrecito*.'

'In the kitchen. With another friend.'

'You should have a priest at this time,' the old woman said wheedlingly. 'Let me fetch Padre Fernando.'

Something seemed to snap inside Sofia. Harry felt it almost physically, as though a crack had sounded in the room. She stood up and marched up to Señora Avila. The older woman was taller but she flinched back.

'Listen to me, you old vulture, we do not want Padre Fernando here!' Sofia's voice rose to a shout. 'However long you try to sneak him into our house, however long you try to get hold of Paco, you will never succeed! You are not welcome here, do you understand? Now go!'

Señora Avila drew herself up to her full height, her pale face reddening.

'This is how you greet a neighbour who comes to help you, this is how you greet Christian charity? Padre Fernando is right, you are enemies of the church—'

Enrique got up from the bed. He crossed to Señora Avila, his hands clenched into fists. The *beata* backed away.

'Go and denounce us to the priest then, you dried-up old bitch! You who got a whole flat to yourself because your priest is friends with the block leader!'

'My father was killed by the Communists,' the *beata* replied shakily. 'I had nowhere.'

'I spit on your father! Get out!' Enrique raised a fist. Señora Avila gave a cry and ran out of the flat, slamming the door. Enrique sat down on the foot of the bed, breathing in great gasps. Sofia sat wearily next to him. Barbara came out and stood in the kitchen doorway.

'I'm sorry,' Enrique said. 'I shouldn't have shouted at her.'

'It doesn't matter. If she reports us we can say you were overcome with grief.'

Enrique bowed his head, clasping his bony hands together on his knees. From somewhere outside Harry heard a faint howling sound. It grew louder, seeming to come from a dozen places at once.

'What on earth is that?' Barbara asked, her voice shaky.

Sofia looked up. 'The dogs. The wild dogs. At this time of year they sometimes howl with cold. It is a sign winter is truly here.'

Part Three

☆

DEEP COLD

Chapter Thirty-Five

THE SNOW HAD LAIN THICK in the Tierra Muerta for nearly a month. It had come early and stayed; the guards said people in Cuenca were calling it the hardest winter for years. Clear icy days alternated with heavy snow, the wind always from the north-east. Sometimes at night the little deer from the hills, smelling food, came and stood at a little distance from the camp. If they came too close the guards in the watchtowers shot them and there was venison in their mess.

Now, early in December, there was a well-worn path through the drifts between the camp and the quarry. Each morning the work detail shuffled into the hills where the endless white vista was broken only by the thin bare branches of the mountain oaks.

Bernie was lonely. He missed Vicente and none of the Communists would speak to him now. In the evenings he lay on his pallet in silence. Even at Rookwood there had always been someone to talk to. He thought of Harry Brett; Vicente had reminded him of Harry sometimes, good-natured and principled, if hopelessly middle-class.

The prisoners were finding the hard weather difficult. Everyone had colds or coughs; already there had been deaths, more processions to the unmarked graveyard. Bernie found his old arm wound troubling him; by mid-afternoon wielding his pick in the quarry was agonizingly painful. His leg injury from the Jarama, which had healed quickly and never really troubled him again, had started to ache too.

He hadn't managed to move huts as Establo had ordered. He had made a request weeks ago, but nothing had happened. Then one evening when he returned from the quarry, he was told Aranda wanted to see him.

Bernie stood before the *comandante* in his warm hut. Aranda sat in his leather chair, his riding crop propped against the side. To

Bernie's surprise he smiled and invited him to sit. He picked up a folder and glanced through it.

'I have Dr Lorenzo's report,' he said jovially. 'He says you are an antisocial psychopath. For him, all educated leftists suffer from a form of inborn antisocial madness.'

'Yes, *comandante*?'

'Myself, I think it is bullshit. In the war your side fought for your interests and we fought for ours. We hold Spain now by right of conquest.' He raised his eyebrows. 'What do you say, eh?'

'I agree with you, *comandante*.'

'Good. We are *de acuerdo*.' Aranda took a cigarette from a silver box and lit it. 'Would you like one of these?' Bernie hesitated. Aranda waved the box at him. 'Go on, take one. I order you.'

Bernie lifted out a cigarette and Aranda held up a gold lighter. The *comandante* leaned back in his chair, the leather squeaking.

'Now, what is this about your wishing a change of hut?'

'Since my friend died last month I have found it hard to be there.'

'Also I hear you have fallen out with your Communist friends. With Establo Cabo specifically. He is a strong man, I admire him in a way.' He smiled. 'Do not look so surprised, Piper. I have my ears among the prisoners.'

Bernie was silent. He knew there were informers in most huts. In his own they had been suspicious of a little Basque, a Catholic who attended the services. He had died from pneumonia two weeks before.

'It is not easy to be a prisoner and unpopular with the men as well. Your Communist friends have abandoned you, why not have some revenge?' He raised his eyebrows. 'You could have as many cigarettes as you wanted, and other privileges. I could take you off the quarry detail. It must be cold up there, I feel frozen even going out in the yard these mornings. If you were to become one of my friends among the prisoners I would not ask for much, just some information now and again. Whether anyone is breaking any rules, that sort of thing. Having friends in the enemy camp makes life much easier.'

Bernie bit his lip. He guessed if he refused there would be trouble. He replied quietly, making his voice as respectful as possible.

'It would not work, *comandante*. Establo already believes I am disloyal. He watches me.'

Aranda considered. 'Yes, I can see that, but perhaps your trouble with the Communists would be a good excuse for you to seek other friends. You could find out things that way.'

Bernie hesitated. '*Comandante*, you spoke of the battle between our two sides earlier—'

'You are going to tell me you cannot change your loyalties,' Aranda said. He was still smiling but his eyes narrowed.

Bernie was silent.

'I thought you might say that, Piper. You ideologues, you do make trouble for yourselves.' He shook his head. 'All right, you can go, I am busy now.'

Bernie got up. He was surprised to get off so lightly. But sometimes Aranda waited and got you later. His cigarette had burned down and he leaned across to stub it out in the ashtray. He half expected the *comandante* to lift his riding crop and slash it across his face, but he didn't move. He smiled cynically, enjoying Bernie's fear, then raised his arm in the Fascist salute. '*¡Arriba España!*'

'*¡Grieve España!*' Bernie left the hut and closed the door. His legs were shaking.

ESTABLO WAS ILL. His scabies was worse than ever and now he had developed a stomach illness; he had diarrhoea most days. He was wasting away, he was skin and bone now and had to walk with a stick, yet the weaker his body grew the more brutally authoritarian he became.

Pablo had taken Vicente's bunk but was under orders to ignore Bernie. He turned his head away as Bernie came in from seeing Aranda and flopped down on his pallet. Establo had been talking with the other Communists at the bottom of the hut but now he approached Bernie out of the candlelit gloom, his stick tapping on the wooden floor. He stood at the foot of the bed.

'What did Aranda want with you? His voice was a throaty wheeze. Bernie looked up at the yellow scabbed face.

'It was about my request to move huts. He said no.'

Establo looked at him suspiciously. 'He treats you very lightly. As he does all informers.' He spoke loudly and some of the other men turned to stare at them.

Bernie raised his voice. 'He asked me to inform, Establo. He said he would move me if I did. Did you guess he might do that, now you've got me isolated? I told him a Communist does not inform.'

'You are no Communist,' Establo wheezed. 'Be careful, Piper, we are watching you.' He limped off to his bed.

NEXT DAY Bernie was working with a group clearing the area where the cave had stood. A huge charge of dynamite had been detonated inside, completely demolishing it and leaving a gigantic pile of rubble. The group was ordered to sort them into chunks of different sizes, breaking up those that were too big to handle. A lorry would be coming that evening to take them away: to Franco's monument, it was still rumoured.

Pablo was working next to Bernie. Suddenly he put his pick aside and picked something up. 'Ay, look here!' he exclaimed.

Bernie turned, wondering what could have made Pablo break the prohibition on speaking to him. Glancing at the nearest guard to make sure he was unobserved, he bent to where Pablo held a flat piece of stone in his chapped hands. Its surface was dark red; the head of a black mammoth was painted on it, confronted by two of the stick-like men who held spears poised to strike.

'See,' Pablo whispered. 'Something has survived.'

Bernie ran his finger lightly over the surface. It felt just like ordinary stone, the paint baked hard thousands of years before. 'It's beautiful,' he whispered.

Pablo nodded. He slipped the stone into the pocket of the old oilskin poncho he wore. 'I shall keep it hidden. One day I will show people what they destroyed here.'

'Be careful,' Bernie whispered. 'They'll be angry if they find out.' Prison life, Bernie knew, was made more bearable by tiny victories against their captors, but such victories could be costly.

AT LEAST in winter the days at the quarry were short. The whistle blew at half past four, as dusk began to fall. It had been another clear cold day. A big red sun that gave no heat was sinking to the horizon, casting a pink glow over the distant mountains. The pile of rubble was almost gone, leaving a jagged gap in the hillside. As the lorry sent to fetch the load of stone lurched away down a mountain road, the men handed in their tools and began the weary trudge back to camp.

You couldn't see Cuenca today; there was too much haze. They had been able to see it most mornings recently. Bernie wondered if the guards stopped the column to rest there deliberately, to torment the men with a glimpse of freedom. Sometimes he thought about the hanging houses. What must it be like to live in one of them, have a view across the gorge from your window? Did it give you a sense of vertigo? With so few people to talk to his mind seemed to turn more and more to fantasy these days. Even the non-Communists were avoiding him; Bernie guessed Establo had told them he was an informer.

In the yard the men stepped wearily into line for roll-call. The sun was almost touching the horizon, casting a red glow over the yard, the huts and watchtowers. Aranda stepped on to the dais and began calling names.

Halfway through Bernie heard a sudden 'chink' from the row in front of him, as something hit the ground. He saw Pablo clap a hand to his trousers and look down. The piece of stone had worked through the frayed old material and lay on the earth. One of the guards walked swiftly over to him. Aranda, on his dais, looked up sharply.

'What's happening there?'

The guard bent and picked up the stone. He looked at it, stared at Pablo, then marched up to the dais. He and Aranda bent their heads over the stone. Pablo watched them, his face white.

At a nod from Aranda the guard jumped down. He and another guard pulled Pablo out of line, jerking his arms behind his back. Aranda held up the stone.

'We have a souvenir collector amongst us!' he shouted. 'This man has found a fragment from those blasphemous paintings at the quarry and brought it back. Has anyone else brought any nice little paintings for their hut?' He looked out across the silent rows of prisoners. 'No?' Well, you will all be searched tonight, as will the huts.' He shook his head sorrowfully. 'Why will you not learn to do as we tell you? I shall have to make an example of this man. Put him in solitary confinement for tonight. You'll all see him again tomorrow.'

The guards frogmarched Pablo away. 'That means the cross,' someone muttered.

Aranda went back to the roll, calling out the names in his clear harsh voice.

THAT EVENING in the hut, after the search, Establo came up to Bernie's bed. He was flanked by four of the other Communists. He sat on Pablo's empty pallet. Establo crossed his hands on the top of his cane. You could see the tendons working over the bones beneath the dry skin.

'I'm told you were talking to Pablo at the quarry today. Did you tell the guards he had that piece of stone? *¿Eh, hombre?*'

Bernie sat up, looked Establo in the eye. 'You know I didn't, Establo. Everyone saw what happened – it fell out of his pocket.'

'What were you saying to him? He is forbidden to talk to you.'

'He showed me the piece of stone he'd found. I told him to be careful. Ask him yourself.'

'I think you informed on him.'

'It fell from his pocket,' Miguel the old tramworker said. 'Come, *compadre*, we all saw.'

Establo gave Miguel an evil look. Bernie laughed. 'See, people are coming to see you for what you are, *hijo de puta*. A man who would make capital out of what is to be done to Pablo.'

'Leave him, Establo,' Miguel said. The old man turned and walked away. Hesitantly, the other three followed. Bernie smiled at Establo.

'As your body withers, Establo, your heart shows through.'

Establo rose painfully to his feet, clutching his stick. 'I will finish you, *cabrón*,' he whispered.

'If you don't die first,' Bernie called after him as he limped away.

NEXT MORNING after roll-call the prisoners were ordered to remain standing in their rows. Bernie noticed Agustín was back on duty. He looked cold standing there – this would be a change after Sevilla. The man met his eyes for a moment and looked away; he seemed to be studying him. Bernie wondered again if he was after his arse, if that was why he had helped him, that morning on the hill. 'Better times,' Agustín had said. Bernie almost laughed aloud.

Two guards brought Pablo from the solitary hut and manhandled him over to the cross that stood beside the mess hut. Bernie saw Agustín sigh, as though with weariness. They stood Pablo beside the thing, their breath making a fog in the air. Aranda marched towards them, tapping his riding crop against his thigh. Father Jaime and Father Eduardo were with him, huddled inside their heavy black cloaks. They had stood with Aranda on the dais during roll-call: Father Jaime cold and grim, Father Eduardo with bowed head. They stopped in front of Pablo. Aranda turned and addressed the prisoners.

'Your comrade Pablo Jimenez is to have a day on the cross as punishment for his piece of smuggling. First, though, you should see this.' The *comandante* took the piece of painted stone from his pocket and laid it on the ground. Father Jaime stepped forward. He took a little hammer from his pocket, bent down and smashed it on the piece of stone. It shattered, chips flying in all directions. Father Jaime nodded to Father Eduardo and he picked up the pieces. Father Jaime pocketed the hammer and looked over the men, satisfaction on his grim face.

'This is how the Church Militant has dealt with paganism since its earliest days,' he called out. 'With hammer blows! Remember that – if anything can penetrate your thick irreligious skulls.' He marched off, Father Eduardo following with the pieces of stone cupped in his hands.

The guards took Pablo's arms and tied them to the crosspiece with ropes. They tied him so only the tips of his feet touched the ground, then stepped back. Pablo sagged for a second then lifted himself up by his toes. The torture of the cross depended on a man's inability to breathe with his arms stretched out above him unless he could lift himself up. After a few hours in that position every movement was an agony, but it was the only way to breathe: pulling agonizingly up and down, up and down.

Aranda studied Pablo's position and nodded with satisfaction. He smiled grimly at the prisoners, then called 'Dismiss' and marched back to his hut. The guards ordered the men into their labour gangs. Agustín was on Bernie's detail. As they marched through the gate he stepped close.

'I want to talk to you,' he whispered. 'It is important. Leave your hut tonight after supper, as though you were going to piss. I will be waiting at the back.'

'What do you want?' Bernie whispered fiercely. From the anxious expression on his face it didn't look like the man wanted to fuck him.

'Later. I have something to tell you.' Agustín stepped away.

IN THE LATE afternoon it began to snow heavily and the guards ordered the men to stop work early. On the walk back Agustín stayed at the other end of the crocodile, avoiding Bernie's eye. Back at the camp Pablo was still tied to the cross, snow whirling round his head. '*Mierda*,' the man next to Bernie muttered. 'He's still there.' Pablo was pale and still and for a moment Bernie thought he was dead but then he lifted himself up, his toes pressing into the ground. He took a deep breath and expelled it with a long rattling moan. The guards locked the gates and walked away, leaving the prisoners to make their way to their huts. Bernie and some of the others went over to Pablo.

'Water,' he croaked. 'Water, please.'

The men bent and started gathering handfuls of snow, holding it up to him to drink. It was a slow process. Then the door of Aranda's hut opened, yellow light stabbing through the thick snowflakes. The men tensed, expecting the *comandante* to come and order them away, but it was Father Eduardo who emerged. He saw the crowd round the cross, hesitated a moment, then walked towards them. The prisoners stood aside to let him pass. 'I thought it was the Romans who crucified innocents,' someone said loudly. Father Eduardo paused for a second, then moved on and lifted his head to Pablo.

'I have spoken to the *comandante*,' he said. 'You will be taken down soon.' Pablo's only answer was another rattling breath as he heaved himself agonizingly up once more. The priest bit his lip and turned away.

Bernie stepped into his path. Father Eduardo looked at him, blinking, his glasses covered with a film of melting snow.

'Is this what you mean, *cura*, by Christians sharing Christ's sufferings on the Cross?'

Father Eduardo turned and walked slowly away, head bowed. As he struggled through the snow that swirled round him, someone called out, '*¡Hijo de puta!*'

A slap on the back made Bernie jump. He turned to see Miguel.

'Well done, Bernardo,' he said. 'I think you shamed the bastard.' But as he watched Father Eduardo's retreating back, Bernie felt shame too. He would never have dared to insult Father Jaime like that, none of them would. He had picked on their weakest representative, the one he could hurt most easily, and where was the courage in that?

BERNIE LEFT the hut after supper, saying he needed to piss and his bucket was full. They were allowed to do that until lights out. Agustín made him uneasy but he needed to know what he wanted. He left Pablo lying on the next pallet, covered in a thick pile of blankets donated by the other men, for he was frozen, his shoulders an agony. Bernie had laid his blanket on the pile. Pablo's face was white. Miguel whispered to Bernie, 'He is young and strong, with luck he will come through.' Evidently he had chosen to ignore Establo's orders to snub him; perhaps others would follow.

Outside the snow had stopped. Bernie went round to the back of the hut, where the moonlight cast a long shadow. Within the shadow Bernie saw the red glow of a cigarette butt. He walked up to Agustín. The guard trampled his cigarette underfoot.

'What the hell do you want?' Bernie asked bluntly. 'You've been giving me shifty looks for ages.'

Agustín stared back at him. 'I have a brother in Madrid, who was a guard, do you remember? A tall thin man like me, Luis?'

Bernie frowned. 'He left months ago, didn't he? What's he got to do with me?'

'He went to Madrid to seek work; there is none in Sevilla. There he met an English journalist who knows a friend of yours.' Agustín hesitated, looking at Bernie, then went on. 'They have been planning an escape for you.'

'What?' Bernie stared at him. 'Who is this friend?'

'An Englishwoman. Señora Forsyth.'

Bernie shook his head. 'Who? I don't know a Señora Forsyth. I knew a boy at school called Forsyth, but he wasn't a friend.'

Agustín raised his hand. 'Quietly, *señor*, for the love of God. This woman has married the man from your school. You knew her in Madrid during the war. Her name then was Barbara Clare.'

Bernie's mouth fell open. 'Barbara's still in Spain? She's married *Sandy Forsyth?*'

'*Sí.* He is a businessman in Madrid. He knows nothing, she has kept it from him. She is paying us. *Señor*, my own term is nearly up, I do not want to have to sign up again. I hate this place. The cold and the isolation.'

'Christ.' Bernie stared at Agustín. 'How long have you been planning this?'

'For many weeks. It has not been easy. *Señor*, I have been watching you since I returned. You should take care, you have been making enemies. Winter is not a good time in the camp, everyone is cold and stuck indoors and their minds turn to mischief.'

Bernie ran his hand over his scrappy beard. 'Barbara. Oh God, Barbara.' He felt suddenly faint, he leaned against the wall of the hut. 'Barbara.' He spoke the name softly. His eyes were wet with tears. Then he took a deep breath and stepped close to Agustín, who flinched slightly away. 'Is this true? Is this really true?'

'It is.'

'She married Forsyth?' He laughed unbelievingly. 'Does he know about this?'

'No, only her.'

He took a deep breath. 'How is it to be done? What's the plan?'

Agustín leaned closer. 'I will tell you.'

Chapter Thirty-Six

SINCE EARLY DECEMBER it had been bitterly cold in Madrid, and on the sixth Harry woke to find the city covered in a thick mantle of snow. It was strange seeing snow here. It buried some of the ugliness and the scars of war but as he walked to the embassy, watching the pinched red faces of the passers-by, he wondered how the half-starved populace would cope if this went on.

The snowfall had been so heavy the trams weren't running; Harry walked through a strangely quiet city, every sound muffled, under a slate-grey sky that promised more snow. Crossing the Castellana he saw a gasogene stuck in the middle of the road, belching out clouds of thick smoke as the driver tried frantically to get it going. An old man walked slowly past, leading a donkey laden with cans of olive oil. The old man's cracked ancient boots were soaking.

'*Hace mal tiempo*,' Harry said.

'*Sí, muy mal.*'

He was due to see Hillgarth at ten; he hadn't been looking forward to the meeting and now he was going to be late. During the fortnight since the dinner party had been interrupted by Sofia's call, Harry had continued with his 'watching brief' on Sandy, met him twice in the cafe and been round to the house again for dinner, but he had learned nothing more. Sandy hadn't mentioned the gold mine again and when Harry asked him how things were going there he said 'difficult' and changed the subject. He seemed preoccupied, keeping up his customary bonhomie only with an effort. At their most recent meeting in the cafe he had asked Harry how things were in England, how big the black market was and what sort of money the spivs were making. Harry had asked him if he was thinking of coming home after all, but he only shrugged. Harry wished it were all over, he was sick of the deception and lies. The thought that Gomez had probably been murdered was never far from his thoughts.

Barbara still seemed troubled too, and distant with him. But as she showed him out after his visit earlier that week she had asked how Sofia was. Sofia had said she would like to see Barbara again and Harry had suggested that the three of them meet for lunch. Barbara had seemed to hesitate, but then agreed.

THE SPIES had not been pleased to learn about Sofia. Tolhurst had quizzed him about her telephone call to the embassy; Harry guessed any calls concerning him were reported to Tolhurst automatically.

'You should have told us if you've found a Spanish floozy,' he said. 'How did you meet?'

Harry told him the tale of rescuing her brother from the dogs, missing out who Enrique was.

'She could be a spy,' Tolhurst said. 'You can't be too careful with women here. You said you weren't being followed any more. Still, if you met by chance—'

'Completely by chance. And Sofia hates the regime.'

'Yes, Carabanchel was a Red district. But they're no friends of ours down there. Be careful, Harry, that's all I'm saying.'

'I've told her I'm a translator. She doesn't ask about my work.'

'Is she pretty? Got her between the sheets yet?'

'Oh bloody hell, Tolly, she's not one of your tarts,' Harry said with sudden exasperation.

A hurt offended look came over Tolhurst's face. He brushed a lick of hair back from his face and adjusted his Eton tie. 'Steady on, old man.' He raised his eyebrows. 'Don't get too involved.'

THE SNOW had been cleared from the front of the embassy. There was no wind and the Union Jack hung lifeless from its pole. Harry passed the two *civiles* outside, huddled in their capes. The meeting was in Tolhurst's office again. Hillgarth was already there, in naval uniform today, sitting behind the desk smoking Players. Tolhurst stood studying papers. From the wall, the King's thin sombre face looked down from his portrait.

'Morning, Harry,' Tolhurst said.

'Morning. Sorry I'm late, the trams aren't running with this snow.'

'OK.' Hillgarth said. 'I want to review the position with Forsyth. I've been looking at the reports of your recent meetings. He's not saying any more about the gold mine, but you say he seems worried.'

'Yes, sir, he does.'

Hillgarth drummed his fingers on the desk. 'We can't get any information out of Maestre on the mine. We know he's on that oversight committee now, but he won't say anything. No matter what we offer him.' Hillgarth raised his eyebrows at Harry. 'There's still no sign of his man Gomez. For which he blames us. Particularly you, Harry.' Hillgarth lit a fresh cigarette, exhaling in a rush of breath. 'You'd better steer clear of him from now on.'

'I saw him in the Rastro a couple of weeks ago. He wasn't very friendly.'

'I imagine not.' Hillgarth thought a moment. 'Tell me, d'you think Forsyth is someone who could get actively involved in foul play?'

'I think he could,' Harry said slowly. 'If he felt his interests were threatened.'

Hillgarth nodded. 'We need to know about that mine, what gold resources the regime's banking on. The only avenue we've got left now is Forsyth.' Hillgarth looked at him speculatively. 'I'd like to give you a chance to redeem yourself. We're thinking of trying to recruit him. Since Maestre won't be bribed. Tell him, Tolly.'

Tolhurst looked at him with owlish seriousness. 'This is classified information, Harry. You remember you asked about the Knights of St George.'

Harry nodded.

'Our government has set aside large sums to bribe people here in Spain. High-up Monarchists in the regime and anyone else who has a voice with the government and can argue for Spain staying out of the war.'

'Most embassies have funds for bribery,' Hillgarth went on. 'But this is on a different scale. It's not just dislike of the Fascists that makes Maestre feed us information. Him and a good few other senior figures. If Forsyth were to come over to us we could make funds available to him. And diplomatic protection if necessary. I've decided it's the only way to find out about the gold. The shares in that company of his are falling fast. I guess Maestre and his committee are putting the squeeze on him. They want to wrest control of the gold from the Falange.'

'That would fit, sir.'

'London wants to know if there *is* gold, and how much. They're putting pressure on Sam but he can't even get an appointment with Franco at the moment. He's going out of his way to treat us with disdain to please the Germans. And what we've learned about Forsyth's personality makes me think he'd be willing to jump into our ship if his project's in trouble.' He leaned forward. 'What d'you think, Harry?'

Harry thought a moment. 'If he's in trouble my guess would be he'd do it.' He had come to despise Sandy, but found that the prospect of Hillgarth throwing him a lifeline made him feel relieved.

'If he needs an escape route he'd be happy with less money,' Tolhurst added. 'We don't want to strain the budget.'

Harry looked at Hillgarth seriously. 'I don't know how far you could trust Sandy though. He always plays his own game.'

Hillgarth smiled. 'Oh, I can see that. Actually, I think Forsyth could make a very good spy. Someone who likes having secrets, perhaps enjoys the frisson of danger. Does that sound about right?'

'I'd say so long as the danger doesn't come too close. I think perhaps he's scared now.' Harry added, looking Hillgarth in the eye, 'You could be taking on someone who's been involved in murder.'

He inclined his head. 'He wouldn't be the first, we can't be choosy.'

There was silence for a moment. Tolhurst broke it. 'Has Forsyth any politics?'

'I think he'd support any system that allowed him free rein to make money. That's why he likes Franco. He hates the Communists of course.' Harry paused. 'But he's no loyalty to Britain, none at all.'

'Father's a bishop, isn't he?' Hillgarth asked. 'Clergy's sons often go wonky.'

'Sandy thinks the church and all the old traditions are out to stifle people like him.'

'He's got a point.' Hillgarth nodded, then steepled his hands in front of him. 'OK, this is what we'll do. See Forsyth again. Just tell him there's someone at the embassy who's got a proposition for him. Don't give too much away, just encourage him to come. You can say you've got contacts on the intelligence side if you think that'd be useful. If you can pull this off you can wipe the slate clean, go home with a bit of a feather in your cap.'

Harry nodded. 'I'll do what I can. I'm meeting Barbara for lunch today. I can try to arrange something then.' Thank God it's the last thing they want, he thought.

'Good. How is Forsyth's wife?'

'I don't think they're very happy.'

'She still doesn't know anything about his business?'

'No. I'm pretty sure he tells her nothing.'

'We were worried you might be forming an attachment there till you hooked up with this dairymaid,' Hillgarth said. He gave Harry a sudden and unwelcome wink.

AS HARRY WALKED to the town centre at lunchtime he thought about his interview. Hillgarth's casual dismissal of Gomez and what Sandy might have done chilled him. Didn't they know what it was like for a normal person, having to do this work? Little gangs of men were out, desultorily sweeping the snow from the pavements with brooms and spades. Harry looked out for Enrique among them but did not see him.

Barbara had suggested meeting him and Sofia at the Café Gijón. Harry thought it a strange choice; he knew Barbara used to go there with Bernie during the Civil War. She had still hardly mentioned his name. Poor Bernie, he thought, at least he never saw what Spain had turned into.

The bar was full of wealthy Madrileños taking coffee and complaining about the snow. There was a wet oily smell. Harry took a *café con leche* to an empty corner. He realized he was very early.

Sandy and the spies would suit each other, he thought. Well, he would leave them to it and go home. But, he thought, home to what? Back to Cambridge, alone. He looked at his face in the mirrors. He had lost weight since coming here, it suited him. Could he get Sofia out? he wondered. Was there any way? He would have to take Paco, too; she would never leave him. To be able to get them away, get them to England. And what if it didn't work out? Part of his mind said, too, that he was mad, he'd only met her six weeks ago.

The barman had put his change in the saucer. One of the new five-peseta coins with Franco's head on. He thought again of Hillgarth talking calmly of recruiting someone who might be a murderer, telling him how they bribed the Monarchists. Hoare had said he'd sweated blood trying to convince the Monarchists he and they spoke a common language. He's sweated gold, too, Harry thought. People like Maestre talking about Spanish honour, the traditions they were protecting, and all the time taking bribes from a potential enemy. And Britain was interested in Spain only for its strategic value – even if they won the war Spain would probably be left to Franco, forgotten again.

He hunched over his cup. He thought, perhaps it would be better if Hitler did invade Spain. Even Sandy said the regime was weak; perhaps the people would rise up against the Germans as they had against Napoleon. But then Gibraltar would go and Britain would be weakened even further. He remembered the picture he had seen on his first day, the German and Spanish soldiers greeting each other at the border. The Führer and the Caudillo in eternal friendship, victorious in Europe. It was a horrible thought. He looked at his set face in the mirror. He would do this last thing: he would try to recruit Sandy for them.

He jumped at a hand on his shoulder. Sofia was standing there, wrapped in her old black coat. Her face was flushed; with the pleasure of seeing him, he realized with a warm glow. She smiled. 'What were you thinking about?'

'Nothing. Just some problems at work. Here, sit down.'

'Is Barbara not here yet?'

'No.' He looked at his watch, surprised to see it was nearly one o'clock. 'She's late. Let me get you a coffee.'

She hesitated for a second. 'OK.'

There had been arguments about Harry paying for everything and buying her presents as well. He had said, 'I've got money, maybe I don't deserve it, but I have. Why shouldn't I spend some of it on you?'

'People will say I am a kept woman,' she had replied, blushing.

Harry had realized Sofia wasn't as free of what she called 'bourgeois sensibilities' as she liked to think.

'You know it's not true, that's what matters.'

But she wouldn't let him give the family money; she said they could manage. Harry wished she would let him do more at the same time as he loved her pride. He fetched her coffee.

'How's Paco?'

'Very quiet. Enrique is with him today; it is his day off too.' With Elena dead and Sofia and Enrique both working, the little boy had to be left alone in the flat most days now. He refused to go out unless one of the adults came with him.

"He liked the crayons you brought him. He wants to know when the red-haired lady will come again. She made an impression on him. He calls her "the kind lady".'

'We could ask her if she'd like to visit.'

'That would be good.' Sofia frowned. 'I am afraid one day Paco will let Señora Avila in. I know she comes knocking. I have told him not to answer. The knocking scares him, it reminds him of when his parents were taken. But I am frightened one day he will open the door and she will take him because he is on his own.'

'He won't open the door if he's scared of her.'

'We cannot carry on like this for ever, just leaving him at home on his own.'

'No.' Harry agreed.

'I will not lose him.' Sofia sighed. 'Do you think we are silly, burdening ourselves like this? Enrique thinks so sometimes, I know, but he has also come to love Paco.'

He thought, she's lost her mother, now she's frightened of losing the boy, and if they send me back home she'll lose me. He frowned.

'What is it, Harry?'

'Nothing.' He looked up to see Barbara approaching, her headscarf and glasses dotted with snowflakes, and waved her over.

'Sorry I'm late. It's started up again outside.'

'I have never seen anything like it,' Sofia said. 'The drought in the summer and now this.'

Harry got up and took Barbara's coat. 'Shall we get the lunch menu?'

She raised a hand. 'No, listen. I'm awfully sorry, but I can't stay. I've an appointment on the other side of town at two and the trams aren't running, I'll have to walk. Just get me a coffee, could you?'

'All right.' Harry studied Barbara. There was something serious, determined in her manner. He fetched another coffee. When he returned Barbara and Sofia were talking earnestly.

'Barbara says Paco needs to see a doctor,' Sofia told him.

'Well, a doctor might have some ideas how to help. I could help pay—' He bit his lip as Sofia frowned. He shouldn't have spoken about giving her money in front of Barbara.

'If it could help the poor little scrap,' Barbara said. 'But I realize it's difficult.'

'Have you started at the veterans' hospital?' Harry asked her, changing the subject.

'Yes, it's better than that orphanage at least. But war wounds, awful injuries. All the things the Red Cross tried to prevent.' She sighed. 'Oh well, it's too late to think like that now.' She looked at Harry. 'I may be going home for Christmas after all.'

'To England?'

'Yes, you remember, Sandy suggested it, and I thought, why not? At least I'll get to see how things really are there.'

'Will they let you back into Spain?' Sofia asked. 'I suppose so, as your husband is working here.'

Barbara hesitated. 'I should think so.'

But Sandy's not her husband, Harry thought. Something occurred to him. 'It's the same the other way round, isn't it? I mean, if an Englishman had, say, a Spanish fiancée, he might have problems taking her into England. But if you're married they'll let you both in.'

'Yes,' Barbara said. 'At least that's how it was before the war. I remember all those rules from the Red Cross. Getting refugees from one country to another.' She looked blank for a moment. 'Less than five years ago. It seems a lifetime.'

Sofia lowered her voice. 'There is still the risk Franco could declare war.'

Barbara took off her glasses, which had steamed up, and cleaned them on her handkerchief. Without them, her face looked more attractive but vulnerable as well. She stirred her coffee carefully, then looked up at them.

'I probably won't come back,' she said flatly. 'I don't think Sandy and I can go on.'

'I'm sorry,' Harry said. 'I could see you weren't happy.'

Barbara drew on her cigarette. 'I owe him a lot. He put me back together again after – after Bernie. But I don't think I like the shape he put me back into any more.' She laughed awkwardly. 'Sorry to blurt all this out. Only I've had no one to talk to, you see. Does it make sense?'

'There comes a time when you have to face things,' Harry said. 'Take the blinkers off.' He shook his head. He looked at Sofia. 'Spain's done that for me. Made me see the world's more complicated than I realized.'

Barbara looked at him, stared at him in that odd, keen way. 'It certainly is.'

There was silence for a few moments. 'Have you told him that you will not be coming back?' Sofia asked Barbara.

'No. He doesn't care any more anyway. I've got a – a bit of business to see to, then I'll go over for Christmas. I hope.'

'I think Sandy might have business problems,' Harry ventured.

'Do you know something?' Barbara asked.

Harry hesitated. 'He was going to get me involved in – in one of his companies. But it fell through.'

'What company?'

'I don't know. I know very little.'

Barbara nodded. 'I'm sorry if I seem disloyal,' she said, 'but I've watched you with him. You don't really like him now, do you? You just keep up with him because of the old school thing?'

'Well – something like that.'

'It's strange, he wants your approval.' She turned to Sofia. 'The bonds between men who went to these English public schools, there's nothing like it in Spain.' She laughed a little hysterically. Sofia looked embarrassed. Harry thought, she's close to the edge.

Barbara bit her lip. 'You will both keep this quiet, won't you? I'm sorry.'

'Of course.'

Sofia smiled. 'Paco keeps asking after you. Perhaps you could come and see him again, before you go back to England.'

Barbara smiled too. 'I'd like to. Thanks. Maybe we could take him out somewhere. A treat.'

Harry took a deep breath. 'I do need to talk to Sandy about something. To do with that business deal. Do you know if he's in his office today?'

'He should be.' Barbara glanced at her watch. 'Oh God, I must go. I'm sorry, I've kept you from your lunch, telling you all my woes. I am sorry.'

'It's all right. Listen, ring me, we'll arrange for you to come and see Paco.'

'I will. Good to see you both.' She leaned across and kissed Sofia's cheek in the Spanish way, then got up and walked to the door, pausing to tie on her headscarf. Harry watched her, but he was thinking, marriage. Could he dare take that leap? And would Sofia have him? He could find out more at the embassy, but first he must try to recruit Sandy; get Hillgarth's feather in his cap.

Barbara opened the door. She turned and gave them a quick wave, then disappeared into the whirling snowflakes.

Chapter Thirty-Seven

BARBARA CURSED HERSELF inwardly as she walked away. She hadn't meant to spill everything out like that. It had been seeing them sitting together; they looked so domestic, so *safe* somehow.

She had been afraid for a while, after overhearing that telephone call, that Harry was involved in whatever awful things Sandy was mixed up in. But watching him later, she had realized he couldn't be; he was being used as some sort of pawn. Thank God the deal was off, whatever it had been. She felt guilty every time she saw Harry because he still thought Bernie was dead. Her appointment was with Luis; today she hoped to discuss the actual plans for Bernie's escape. Agustín, she knew, was back from his leave. She had suggested meeting Harry in the Café Gijón because now the possibility of seeing Bernie was so close, Barbara wanted to revisit all the places they had been together, places she had avoided for so long. Three years in prison camps, she thought. What will he be like? How will he react to me? She told herself she mustn't hope for anything, they would both have changed beyond recognition. She must just hope to get him out.

The snow was still coming down heavily, covering cars and the coats of the people moving through the storm like white wraiths. It was melting through her headscarf; she should have brought a hat. The wind blew it against her glasses and she had to wipe them with her gloved hands.

She passed two *civiles* on guard outside a government office; with their heavy capes and bicorn hats covered in snow they looked like snowmen with grim masks painted on. It was the first time the sight of a *civil* had made her want to laugh.

She knew she was often close to hysteria these days; it was getting harder to keep everything inside. But it might only be a short time now before she could leave. Ever since the night two weeks ago when she overheard the telephone conversation she had been trying to analyse his words. 'Those old Moroccan sweats are tough? He still says his name is Gomez?' She had tried a dozen different interpretations but always came back to the same thing: someone was being tortured. And she had begun to think: if he found out what I'm doing I could be in danger too.

When he had come down from the study after that call she had given him the bag the old Jew had left, but he hadn't seemed much interested. He put it on the floor by his chair and sat staring into the fire, ignoring Barbara. He looked more worried than she had ever seen him: sweat was glistening on his black moustache. Since that night he had been increasingly withdrawn. He hardly seemed to notice her now; not that she minded. If only she could get through till they had got Bernie out, then escape to England. Perhaps Sandy would never find out what she had done.

Two nights ago he had come home late. Though he drank a lot, Sandy hardly ever got drunk. He had remarkable control. That night, though, he was staggering a little as he entered the *salón*, looking round blearily as though seeing it for the first time.

'What you starin' at?' he asked Barbara in a thick voice.

Her heart began to pound. 'Nothing, darling. Are you all right?' Still the peacemaker, her instinctive gambit. She put down her knitting. She spent most evenings knitting now, the regular movements soothed her.

'You're like an old woman, always bloody knitting,' he said. 'Where's Pilar?'

'It's her evening off, remember?' He probably wanted to go to her; that'd be nice for Pilar, having him paw her in this state.

'Oh, yes, so it is.' He smiled lubriciously then went to the drinks cabinet and poured himself a whisky. He sat opposite her and took a long swig of his drink. 'Bloody cold again tonight.'

'The frost's killed off a lot of plants in the garden.'

'Plants,' he repeated in a mocking tone. 'Plants. I've had a bloody awful day. Something big I had on, it's up the spout, finished.' He turned to her and gave his old, wide grin. 'Fancy being poor, Barbara?'

'Things aren't that bad, are they?'

'Not that bad? Poor Barbara.' He laughed to himself. 'Poor Barbara, that's how I used to think of you when we first met.'

Her smile trembled. If only he would fall asleep. If only he would fall into the fire. He looked at her again, his face serious now. 'We won't be poor,' he said. 'I won't allow that to happen. Understand?'

'All right, Sandy.'

'I'll bounce back. I always do. We'll stay in this house. You and me and Pilar.' A glint came into his eyes. 'Come to bed. Come on, I'll show you what I'm still made of.'

She took a deep breath. She remembered her plan to confront him with the relationship with Pilar to keep him off but she was too frightened.

'Sandy, you've had a lot to drink.'

'That doesn't stop *me*. C'mon.' He got up, lurched over to her and planted a wet beery kiss on her mouth. She suppressed her instinct to shrink away and allowed him to lift her up, put his arm round her, lead her up the stairs. When they got to the bedroom she hoped he would collapse on the bed but he seemed more in control of himself now. He began undressing, and she took off her dress feeling sick inside. His shirt came off, exposing the heavy muscular body that had excited her once but now made her think of some strong vicious animal. Somehow she managed to control her shrinking as he took her, making strange little grunts of what sounded like desperation. Afterwards he rolled off her and a minute later began to snore. Barbara wondered how she had managed it, managed not to cry out and beat him off. Fear, she supposed. Fear can crush you but it can give you strength and control as well. She padded quietly to the bathroom, closed the door and was violently, heavingly sick.

THE LITTLE CAFE was full of people who had come in to escape the snow; every seat was taken and people stood two deep at the bar. There was a wet musty smell. The old woman ran between the counter and the coffee urn with cups of coffee. The windows were steamed up; even Franco's portrait had a wet film on it. Barbara's glasses steamed over at once. She rubbed them on her coat sleeve and looked around for Luis. Their usual table was taken but she could make him out in the far corner where he had squeezed behind a table for two, his coat draped over the other chair. He was sitting staring into his coffee cup, a weary, tired look on his face. He looked up and changed his expression to a smile as Barbara made her way through the crowd to join him. She sat and took off her sopping headscarf, running a hand over her wet hair.

'This snow is terrible,' she said.

Luis leaned across the table. 'Do you mind not having a coffee? There is such a crush at the bar.'

'Could we go somewhere else? Somewhere quieter?'

'Everywhere will be the same today.' There was an unaccustomed sharpness in his manner.

'What's wrong?' she whispered anxiously.

'Nothing is wrong. All these people make me nervous.' He lowered his voice. 'Everything is ready. Have you brought the money?'

'Yes. Seven hundred pesetas when you tell me when and where. The rest after he's out.'

He nodded, looking relieved. She took out her cigarettes and offered him a Gold Flake.

'Thank you. Now, please listen carefully.' He leaned close to her, his voice a hoarse whisper. 'I have just come back from Cuenca. I saw Agustín yesterday. He has told your friend about the escape. He has told him it is you that is arranging it.'

'How did he react?' Barbara asked eagerly. 'What did he say?'

Luis nodded seriously. 'He was very pleased, *señora*. Very glad.'

Barbara hesitated. 'Does he know I'm – I'm with someone else?'

'Agustín did not say.'

She bit her lip. 'So what's the plan?'

'The escape will take place on December the fourteenth. A Saturday.'

Eight days, Barbara thought, another eight days. 'Can't we do it sooner?'

'That will be a good day. Christmas celebrations will be beginning; things will be getting lax at the camp and in the town. Agustín does not want it to happen too soon after his return, and I agree that might look suspicious. And with luck the snow will be gone by then. A man running would stand out against the snow.'

'Surely it will be gone by then. Heavy snow's not usual this early.'

'We must hope so.'

'Is it going to be how you said? An escape from a working party?'

'Yes. Señor Piper will pretend to have diarrhoea, Agustín will go into the bushes with him, he will hit him on the head, hard enough to cause a bruise, and Señor Piper will take Agustín's keys and free himself. Then he will run downhill towards Cuenca. Your friend will get some distance away, hide in the bushes and trees among the hills until it is quite dark, then make his way to the town.'

'Won't they look for him in Cuenca? Won't they know that's where he'll go?'

'Yes. In fact, it is the only place he can go; in the other direction it is all wilderness and mountains. So yes, they will be looking for him in the town.' Luis smiled. 'But we have a place there for him to hide.'

'Where?'

'There are some bushes and trees on the road by the gorge, near the bridge, on the other side from the town. He will hide there until you arrive with some clothes for him to change into.

Barbara took a deep breath. 'All right.'

'You must drive to Cuenca on the fourteenth, be there by three in the afternoon. It is important you arrive there before it is dark – a woman walking alone in the town might be questioned. There is a place outside the town, a secluded place, where you can leave your car.' He looked at her seriously. 'Agustín has spent all his days off tramping the streets in and around Cuenca, to make sure everything is right.'

'So I wait in the town until it is dark?'

Luis shook his head. 'No. We have a place where you can wait, a place you can say you have come to visit if anyone asks questions. The cathedral. It is there you should take your friend afterwards. Once he has changed in the bushes, you walk across the bridge, a pair of English tourists who have come to see the cathedral. In there he can shave – he has a beard – and clean himself up.'

'What if someone is there?'

Luis shook his head. 'There will be no visitors to the cathedral on a Saturday in winter. And there will be someone there to help you.'

'Agustín? Will he be there?'

'No.' Luis smiled wryly. 'But he sometimes goes to the services in Cuenca Cathedral on Sundays. It is his excuse for going into town – they think he has become religious. There is a watchman there, employed by the church to keep an eye on things. He has offered to help us.'

'A church employee?' Barbara asked sharply. 'Why would he help?'

'For money, *señora*.' Impatient anger flashed in Luis's face for a moment. 'He has a sick old wife and no money to pay for a doctor. So he will help you for the same reason that we are helping. He wants three hundred pesetas.'

She took a deep breath. 'All right.'

'So, you drive to Cuenca on the fourteenth, get there by three. Leave the car where I will tell you and go to the cathedral. The old man, Francisco, will be expecting you. Wait there until dark and then go to the hanging houses. You know where they are?'

'Yes. I've been studying a map and guidebook. I could probably find my way around blindfold.'

'Good. Bring some clothes for your friend, a suit if you can get one.'

'All right. I'll get a large size. Bernie's tall, quite a strong build too.'

Luis shook his head. 'Not after three years in the camp. A suit for a thin man will do. And shaving materials.'

'What about a hat? With a wide brim to hide his face and his fair hair?'

'Yes. That would be good.'

'I can get the clothes,' Barbara said. 'I can pretend I'm doing Christmas shopping. The car might be difficult, my – my husband might be using it.'

Luis frowned tensely. 'You must deal with that, *señora*.'

'Yes, yes, I will. Somehow. What do I do when I get to the hanging houses?'

'At the foot of the Tierra Muerta is a river gorge. It is very deep, you cannot scale it. On the other side of the gorge is the old town, which leads to the road to Madrid. There is a big iron bridge across the gorge, for pedestrians. On the town side are the hanging houses, and on the opposite side a road. A little way along the road is the clump of trees where your friend will be waiting.'

'What if they've put guards on the bridge? If they know a prisoner's escaped?'

'That is possible. The camp will have rung the town. If that happens, wait in the cathedral. Señor Piper will cross the gorge further down and make his way there. Then go back to your car, pretend to be an English couple who have driven out to Cuenca for the day. And remember they will be looking for a prisoner, not a clean-shaven man in a suit. With luck there won't be roadblocks, they won't be expecting him to leave in a car.' Luis looked at Barbara with his deep, hard olive eyes. 'Your wealth will be your best disguise, *señora*.'

'How far is Cuenca from the camp again? Eight kilometres?'

'Yes.'

'Will he be fit to walk that far?' Barbara asked, a tremor in her voice.

'He should be. With the cold a lot of people are ill in the camp but so far your friend is well. And it is all downhill.'

'What if they find him on the way down?'

'Let us just hope they don't,' Luis said flatly. He took another cigarette from the packet on the table. 'We must hope for no snow and no moon.' He lit up and took a deep drag. 'He will know to move carefully, keep to the shadows.'

Barbara was suddenly overcome with doubt. 'If he's caught—'

Luis looked into her eyes. 'This is what he wants, *señora*.'

'Yes.' She bit her lip. 'Yes, he'd take the chance, I know. I have to do this for him.'

Luis looked at her curiously. 'When you have him, what will you do?'

Her face set. 'I'll take him to the British Embassy. He's a British citizen; they'll have to take him in. They sent all the other International Brigaders home.'

'And you?'

'We'll see.' She wasn't going to tell him her plans.

'I trust you to pay me the rest of the money when you return.'

'I'll meet you on the sixteenth,' Barbara said. 'Here, at noon.

What if there has to be a change of plan, if Agustín's rota is changed or Bernie's ill or something?'

'Agustín will get a message to me and I will telephone you at home. I will need your number.'

'That's risky.' She thought a moment. 'If I'm out, say you're the baker phoning about my cake for Christmas and will ring again. Then I'll come straight here. All right?' She wrote the number on the packet of cigarettes and passed it to him. He smiled, always delighted to have the cigarettes, then looked suddenly weary.

'You have planned this well,' she said. 'You and your brother.'

He avoided her eyes. 'Do not thank us,' he said. 'Please do not thank us.'

'Why not?'

'We have done this for money. We must have money for Mama.' That look of weariness again in his face. They were silent a moment.

'Tell me,' she asked, 'do you ever hear from that journalist? Markby?'

Luis shook his head. 'No. He contacted me through a friend, he was going to do an article on the camps but I heard no more. I think he has returned to England.'

'I tried to ring him several times but he was always away somewhere.'

'Journalists. They are rootless people.' Luis looked round the cafe, then coughed. '*Señora . . .*'

'Of course.' Barbara opened her handbag and passed him a thick envelope under the table. He took it, sat very still for a moment, then nodded. Barbara noticed that the shoulders of his threadbare jacket were wet; she realized he had no coat.

'Gracias,' he said. 'Now, I suggest we meet here next Wednesday, the eleventh, to discuss the final preparations. Just to make sure everything is going smoothly.'

'All right.' She felt elated. It was happening, it was going to happen.

Luis stuffed the envelope into his pocket, his eyes flickering round the customers to check he was unobserved. Barbara suddenly felt crowded, pressed in. She wanted to get away. She stood up. 'Shall we go?'

'I will stay a while, till the snow stops. Until next week, *señora.*' He looked up at her, then added unexpectedly, 'You are a good woman.'

Barbara laughed. 'Me? I don't think so. I just bring trouble.'

Luis shook his head. 'No. That is not true. *Adios, señora.*'

'*Hasta luego.*'

She fought her way to the door. It was a relief to stand out in the cold air again. The snow was lessening. She lit a cigarette and headed back to the Centro. There were few people around now; everyone who could, had gone indoors. People wouldn't want to risk their shoes; even if they could find replacements, prices were astronomical.

She passed through the Plaza Mayor. Its palm trees looked strange covered with snow. Beside one of the fountains a newspaper seller stood by his kiosk. A headline scrawled on a billboard caught her eye. 'Veteran Tortured and Murdered in Alcalá: Red Terror Gang Suspected.'

She bought a copy of *Ya*, the Catholic newspaper. She went into the doorway of a closed shop and looked at the front page. Below a picture of a thin man in army uniform, standing stiffly to attention, she read:

> The body of Lieutenant Alfredo Gomez Romero, aged 59, was found yesterday in a drainage ditch near the village of Paloblanco, outside Santa Maria de Real. Major Gomez, a veteran of the Moroccan wars who took part in the relief of Toledo in 1936, had been horribly tortured, his hands and feet burned and his face disfigured. It is believed one of the gangs of Red bandits active in parts of the sierras was responsible. Major Gomez's employer and former commanding officer, Junior Trade Minister Colonel Santiago Maestre Miranda, said that Major Gomez had been a friend and comrade for thirty years and he would personally ensure that his killers were hunted down. 'There is no safety or refuge for the enemies of Spain,' he said.

Barbara's knees felt weak and she thought she would faint. She crumpled the newspaper in her hand. A priest passing the doorway gave her a curious look. So now she knew. Sandy had mentioned the name Gomez on the telephone, and she had heard Maestre's name mentioned as an opponent by Sandy's Falange friends. He had been involved in torturing and killing this old man. Sandy had said they would have to deal with it and he had meant murder. And this was the man she was deceiving to rescue his boyhood enemy. She gripped the handle of the closed door, taking deep breaths to prevent herself from fainting.

Chapter Thirty-Eight

After seeing Barbara and Sofia, Harry returned to the embassy. He telephoned Sandy's office from the little room where there was a private phone for the spies. The secretary put him through. 'Sandy? Harry here. Look, I wonder if we could meet. There's something I'd like to discuss.'

He caught an undertone of impatience in Sandy's voice. 'I'm really busy, Harry. What about after the weekend?'

'It's rather urgent.'

'All right. It's Saturday tomorrow, but I'm coming into the office. I'll meet you in the cafe.' Harry caught a quickly suppressed sigh. 'Three o'clock?'

'Thanks.'

Next Harry went to the registry, to make enquiries about entry visas for Britain. When he returned to his office Tolhurst was waiting for him, leaning against his desk reading a copy of *Ya*. He nodded.

'Hello there, Harry.' His voice was flat, preoccupied.

'I've phoned Forsyth,' Harry told him. 'We're meeting at the cafe tomorrow.'

'Good.' He passed over the paper. 'You should see this.'

Harry read the article about Gomez. He laid the paper on the desk. 'So they killed him,' he said bleakly.

Tolhurst nodded. 'Seems so. It's what we suspected. It doesn't make any difference to recruiting Forsyth.' His voice was cool and even. Harry remembered their first meeting, Tolhurst as the friendly fat boy. He was seeing another side now.

'Even after you know he's involved in this?' he asked.

'Suspected of involvement, Harry, suspected. And we're not the police.'

'No.' Harry put the paper on the desk. 'It's all right, Tolly, I'll still try to get him for you.'

Tolhurst smiled. 'Good man,' he said, with a touch of the old friendliness. 'How's the ear, by the way?'

'Fine. I think part of it was psychological, like the panics.' He hadn't had another since that night outside the theatre. Being with Sofia seemed to have cured him.

'Jolly good,' Tolhurst said. 'Well, must fly. Good luck.'

After he left Harry sat looking at the article, read the things they had done to Gomez. The poor bastard. Had Sandy been there? No, Harry thought bitterly. He'd leave that to others.

Sofia looked tired when she arrived at his flat that evening: there were black shadows under her eyes.

'Are you all right?' Harry asked as he took her coat.

She smiled, a brave child's smile. Sometimes she looked so young. 'I do not want to go back to work tomorrow. I am fed up of cows,' she said. 'It is so boring. How I hate the smell of milk.'

'Sit down, I'll bring the dinner in. I've done a *cocido*.'

He had the record player on, Vera Lynn singing 'When the lights go on again all over the world' in longing tones, but Sofia followed him into the kitchen and leaned against the wall, watching as he mixed the contents of the pans he had been boiling on the stove.

'You are the first man I have met who can cook.'

'You learn when you're on your own. You have to.'

She inclined her head. 'You look worried. Is there trouble at work?'

He took a deep breath. 'No. Listen, I've something to tell you.'

'What is it?' She sounded apprehensive at once. He realized that for a long time, news for her had meant bad news.

'Wait till we're sitting down.'

He had bought a good red wine and when they were seated he poured her a glass. The dim electric light cast a glow of light over the table, leaving the rest of the room in shadow.

'Sofia,' he said. 'The embassy want to send me back home.'

She seemed to shrink into herself, her face paled a little. 'But why? Surely they need you here, nothing has changed, unless—' She drew in her breath sharply. 'Unless Franco is about to declare war. Oh God, they are evacuating you all—'

He raised a hand. 'No, no, it's not that. It's me, they – they think I'd be better deployed at home.'

'Harry,' she asked softly. 'Are you in trouble?'

'No, honestly. It's just – I've been doing other work, not just translating, and it's nearly finished.'

She frowned. 'What sort of work?'

He hesitated, then said, 'Intelligence.' He bit his lip. 'Please, I can't tell you any more. I shouldn't tell you at all. But it's nearly finished. I'm pleased, I hate it.'

'Intelligence against this regime?'

'Yes.'

'Good. I am glad.' She took a deep breath. 'When will you go?'

'I'm not sure. Perhaps before the end of the year.' He looked into her eyes. 'Sofia, will you come with me? You don't have to answer now, but listen, I've been thinking all afternoon. You remember what Barbara said, about foreigners being allowed into England if they're married to an Englishman?'

She stared at him with a set face. Her voice trembled. 'Harry, do not ask. I couldn't leave Paco. Enrique can look after himself but not Paco too. The *beata* would get him.' She reached out and took Harry's hand. 'Don't ask me to make such a choice—'

'I've been thinking about that too. If somehow you could adopt Paco—'

She shook her head wearily. 'I can't. The Church is in charge of those things now and they would never allow it.'

'No, not in Spain, in England. If we say you've been looking after him since his parents died and we could get him to England, then *we* could adopt him. I think there are ways. This job, you see, there's this last little thing I need to do and if I succeed I'll be in their good graces, the people at the embassy. They might help us.'

She looked at him steadily. 'Is what you are doing dangerous?'

'No, no.' He laughed. 'Honestly it isn't, I swear. It's just trying to get information out of businessmen. There's no danger. Forget about that. Sofia, what do you say?'

'How would Paco find England? A strange language, the bombs. I have to think of Paco.'

He couldn't help feeling hurt that the boy seemed to be more important than him. 'We could go to Cambridge,' he said. 'There aren't any bombs there. We could have a good life; you can still get most things in England if you have money. I've enough. And Paco would be safe, no more knocks at the door. I'd try and get Enrique out too later but that might be more difficult.'

'Yes, Paco would have a better chance in England. Unless the Germans come, but they may come here too. They say this is the worst time but Spain will take years, decades, to recover from what Franco has done to it. If it ever can.' She looked at him with wonder. 'You would take on Paco, take that responsibility?'

'Yes. I don't want to leave him either. I'm sure if he got some proper medical attention that could help him.'

She nodded. 'There must be many doctors in Cambridge.'

'Loads. Sofia, if we can bring Paco out, will you – will you marry me? You – you haven't said what you feel about that. If – if you don't want to . . .'

She studied him. 'You would settle for a life with me and Paco? Knowing how Paco is?'

'Yes, yes. It's the only responsibility I want now. Sofia, will you marry me?'

She got up from her seat and came over to him. She knelt down and kissed him, then lifted her mouth from his and smiled.

'Yes. Yes, I will. Though I wonder if you are mad.'

He laughed aloud with relief and joy.

'Perhaps I am, a little, but I want to be. I've been thinking what to do all day, ever since they told me I'd be going back—'

She leaned over and put a finger to his lips. 'You will sort something out. I know. Yes, Harry, I will marry you.'

'I know we've only known each other a few weeks. But in these times you have to seize the good things while you can.'

'The best few weeks of my life.' She knelt beside him on the floor and he bent over and held her.

'I had to think of Paco,' she said. 'I could not abandon him, you see that.' Her voice sunk to a whisper. 'He has been the only thing I have been able to rescue, from all the hopes we once had.'

'I understand. Sofia, perhaps in England you could study again, be a doctor.'

'I must learn English first. That will be hard. But anything, if it is with you. And to think we wouldn't have met but for Enrique.' She shook her head. 'Such a strange fragile chance.'

THE PROSTITUTE Harry had once mistaken for a spy was in the Café Rocinante when he arrived next afternoon. Sandy wasn't there yet. The woman sat at her table at the back of the room; a fat middle-aged businessman was with her, talking Spanish with a strong German accent. He was boasting about how much money he had made since he came to Spain, the deals he had done. The woman smiled and nodded but there was a distant look on her face. She sat at an angle to the table, displaying shapely legs for her age. She had a line painted down the back of them, Harry saw; she was pretending to be wearing the new nylon stockings but you could see from the way the light reflected from her legs that they were bare. She must be frozen, walking through the snow like that.

The German saw Harry staring and raised shaggy eyebrows. Harry took a seat as far away from them as possible. There was a breath of cold air as the door opened and Sandy came in. He wore a heavy black coat and Homburg hat, the hat and his shoulders covered with a dusting of snow for it had started up again. Waiting there, knowing what Sandy had done, Harry had wondered if he might feel fear when he saw him now, but there was only disgust and anger.

Sandy made his way to Harry's table, pausing to exchange remarks about the weather with an acquaintance. Harry raised an arm to attract the elderly waiter who was standing in a corner, talking to the shoeshine boy. The boy was new; perhaps the last one had gone away or died of cold in a doorway somewhere.

'Hello, Harry.' Sandy extended a hand. His fingers were icy.

'Hello. Coffee?'

'Chocolate, I think, on a day like today.' Sandy looked up at the waiter who had hurried over. '*Un café con leche y un chocolate, Alfredo.*'

Harry studied Sandy's face. He was smiling his broad smile but he had a tired, strained look. He lit a cigarette.

'How are things?' Harry asked.

'They've been better. What's this urgent business? I'm intrigued.'

Harry took a deep breath. 'Sandy, I mentioned at the embassy that I had an English friend who's been having some business problems. There are a couple of people there who'd like to talk to you. You might be able to do some work with them.'

Sandy looked at him, a long hard look. You could almost hear the cogs turning. He took out his cigarette case and lit up. 'That sounds like intelligence work,' he said crisply.

God, he was quick. Harry didn't reply. Sandy's eyes narrowed.

'Are they spies?' He stopped and gave a little gasp of surprise. 'Are you a spy, Harry?' he asked softly. He hesitated a moment. 'By God. You are, aren't you? Translating's a good cover, I suppose. Have you been rifling through Franco's wastebaskets?' He laughed incredulously, looked at Harry, then laughed again.

'I can't say any more now, Sandy, I'm sorry. It's just – I've seen things haven't been going well for you, I'd like to help.' How easily the lies were coming. 'Just an exploratory meeting with a couple of people at the embassy, no strings.'

'I suppose they want to recruit me?' Sandy went on in the same quiet tone. The waiter reappeared and Sandy took the tray from him. 'Ah. Alfredo, *muy bien*. Sugar, Harry?' He made a fuss of organizing the drinks; giving himself time to think. He leaned back and blew out a cloud of smoke, then kicked Harry's shin playfully. 'Sure you can't tell me any more, old chap?'

'I'm sorry.'

A spasm, a stricken look, suddenly crossed Sandy's face. He looked at Harry with wide eyes. 'Jesus, this wouldn't have anything to do with the gold, would it?'

For the first time Harry did feel a twitch of fear. 'I can't say any more.'

Sandy leaned back in his chair. He made his face expressionless but he still had the stricken look in his eyes.

'They say the British Embassy's full of spies,' he said. 'More spies there than any other embassy except the Germans. Not that I've been to the German embassy, though I know people who have. I hear Hoare's furious because Franco keeps saying he's too busy to see him while von Stohrer's in and out of El Pardo.'

Harry didn't reply. Sandy took a long deep breath.

'Oh well, it seems to be a time of change. My brother's dead, you know.'

Harry looked up. 'Is he? I'm sorry.'

'Had a letter a week ago. He was in Egypt, an Italian shell hit his tent.' He smiled wryly. 'Probably aiming for Wavell – it'd be like the wops to get the padre by mistake.'

'I'm sorry, Sandy. That's bad news.'

He shrugged again. 'I hadn't seen him for years. Never got on with Peter, you know that.'

'Did your father write?'

'No, an old acquaintance in London saw it in the paper and sent me a letter. The dear old pater wouldn't write even if he knew where I was. He's written me off, I'm destined for the flames. Peter'll be in heaven though, safe in the arms of Jesus.' He laughed harshly. 'You look uncomfortable, Harry. You don't believe all that religious stuff, do you?'

'No. Even less after what I've seen here.'

Sandy sat back, drawing reflectively on his cigarette, then laughed, a harsh bitter sound. 'Sometimes it all just seems so funny.'

'What?'

'Life. Death. The whole bloody thing. Look at that tart over there with her pencilled nylons. Thousands of years of evolution and it's led to that. I often think the dinosaurs were more impressive. A hundred and sixty million years they lasted.' He drained his chocolate. 'You were spying on me, Harry, all the time, weren't you?'

'I told you, I can't say any more now.'

Sandy shook his head. 'I wanted your approval, you know. I did at Rookwood too. I don't know why. It felt so strange when you came back. So strange . . .' Sandy looked into the middle distance for a moment, then turned his gaze back to Harry, his eyes hard. 'I wanted to help you make some money, you know that. My old friend Harry. More fool me, eh?'

Harry didn't reply; there was nothing to say. Sandy nodded.

'I'll come and see your intelligence people. Got a number?' He shoved his cigarette packet towards Harry. He wrote down the number that would take him through to Tolhurst. Sandy put it in his pocket, then gave an odd half-smile, the corners of his mouth twisting. 'Might have some information that would surprise them.'

'What?'

Sandy inclined his head. 'Wait and see. By the way, I haven't told Barbara about my brother. Don't want her getting all weepy. Don't say anything if you see her.'

'I won't.'

'Does she know you're a spy?'

'No. She doesn't know anything, Sandy.'

He nodded. 'I wondered for a moment there if that might be what's up with her.' He smiled that strange half-smile again. 'Funny, when I was a little boy I wanted to be good. But I could never seem to manage it somehow. And if you're not good, the good people will throw you to the wolves. So you might as well just be bad.' He looked into his empty cup for a moment, then reached for his coat.

'All right. Let's go.'

They headed for the door. Sandy waved the cigarette boy aside. They stood in the doorway – the snow was still falling; drifts were banked high against the buildings. Across the street people were leaving a church service, huddling into their coats as they descended the steps, the priest shaking hands in the doorway.

Sandy put on his hat. 'Oh well, out into it all again.'

'Yes.'

'Don't get found nosing in those wastepaper baskets. See you, Harry.' Sandy turned abruptly away, hunching down into his coat. Harry took a deep breath then headed out into the snow, to tell Tolhurst he had landed his quarry.

Chapter Thirty-Nine

THE TAXI WOUND ITS WAY slowly through Carabanchel. There had been a power cut and the streets were pitch-black except for faint glows of candlelight at the windows of the tall blocks. The taxi lurched over the uneven, snow-covered streets. A cart parked by the kerb appeared in the twin globes of the headlights and the driver skidded as he swerved to avoid it. '*Mierda!*' he muttered. 'This is like a drive to hell, *señor*.'

When Harry hailed him in the Puerta del Sol the driver hadn't wanted to drive him out to Carabanchel, not in the middle of a power cut. The snow had stopped as darkness fell and the moon had come out; with the power off, no streetlights and only feeble glows of candlelight from the windows, it was like driving through a crumbling dead city that had been abandoned to the elements.

THAT MORNING Harry had been called round to Tolhurst's office. The power cut had affected the central heating and Tolhurst's chubby form was again wreathed in thick pullovers.

'Forsyth's rung already,' he said. 'He must be keen.'

'Good.' It's done, Harry thought, that's that.

'We'd like you present when we interview him.'

'What?' Harry frowned. 'Is that necessary?'

'We think it would help. In fact, we'd like to have the meeting at your flat.'

'I thought this was the end of it so far as I was concerned.'

'It will be. This is the last thing. I know you're keen to be off.' Tolhurst's tone became disapproving, almost hurt. 'The captain says you can go home after this, there should be a place for you on the plane taking people home for Christmas. But he thinks Forsyth might be more amenable on your territory. These little things can make a difference, you know. And if he denies he told you something, you'll be there to contradict him.'

Harry felt angry, his stomach clenched into a tight knot. 'It'll be humiliating. For him and me. At least do it in the office, don't rub our noses in it.'

Tolhurst shook his head. 'Captain's orders, I'm afraid.'

Harry was silent. Tolhurst looked at him sadly. 'I'm sorry it hasn't worked out as well as we'd hoped. That's the trouble with this line of work; one word out of place and you're sunk.'

'I know.' Harry studied him. 'Listen, Tolly, you know I've been seeing this girl?'

'Yes.'

'I want to marry her. Take her back to England.'

Tolhurst raised his eyebrows. 'The little dairymaid?'

Anger welled up in Harry. But he had to try and get Tolhurst on his side. He made his voice calm. 'She's agreed to marry me.'

Tolhurst frowned. 'I say, are you sure about this? If you take her to England you'll be stuck with her for good.' He rubbed his chin. 'You haven't got her into trouble, have you?'

'No. Though there is a child she and her brother have been looking after, a war orphan. We'd like to take him as well.'

Tolhurst eyed Harry owlishly. 'Look, I know things haven't been easy for you, is it the right time to be taking decisions like that? If you don't mind me saying?'

'Look, Tolly, it's what I want. Can you help? With the immigration people?'

'I don't know. I'd have to speak to the captain.'

'Would you? Please, Simon, I know it would be a big responsibility but it's what I want, you see.'

Tolhurst stroked his chin. 'Have the girl or her brother any political affiliations?'

'No. They're anti-regime but that's hardly unusual.'

'Not for that class of people, no.' Tolhurst tapped his fingers on the desk.

'If you could do what you can, Tolly, I'd be really in your debt.'

He looked pleased. 'All right. I'll try.'

HARRY AND SOFIA had agreed he would come over to Carabanchel for dinner and they would tell Enrique and Paco their plans. When at last the taxi dropped him at Sofia's block, Harry opened the door with the key she had given him. He made his way carefully up the dark staircase; he couldn't see his hand in front of his face and had to light a match. That had been one of Tolhurst's tips, always carry matches in case of power cuts.

He knocked and Sofia answered, pale light spilling out on to the landing as she opened the door. She wore the dress she had the night they went to the play. Behind her the room was full of candles; their soft light hid the damp on the walls, the battered scruffiness of the furniture. Her mother's bed still stood against the wall. He leaned forward and kissed her. She looked tired.

'*Hola*,' she said softly.

'Where are Enrique and Paco?'

'They have gone out to get some coffee. They should be back soon.'

'Do they know something's up?'

'Paco's guessed there's something. Come on, take your coat off.'

There was a clean patchwork quilt on the bed that had been her mother's, a white cloth on the table. The *brasero* had been on for some time and the room was warm. They sat side by side on the bed. He told her he'd spoken to a colleague about visas.

'I think he'll do what he can. It could be before Christmas.'

'As soon as that?'

He nodded.

She shook her head. 'It will be hard for Enrique.'

'We can send him money. Then at least he could keep the flat.' He took her hand. 'Are you still sure about this?'

'Yes.' She looked at him. 'What about this work of yours? Is it nearly finished?'

'Yes. Listen, are you sure we shouldn't wait until it's certain we can do this, before we tell them?'

Sofia shook her head decisively. 'No. We do not want to leave it until we are about to go. They should know what we plan, now.'

'I am glad.'

Footsteps sounded on the stairs. Enrique came in with Paco. He looked tired but Paco, at his side, had an unaccustomed colour in his cheeks. Enrique shook hands with Harry. '*Buenas tardes. Madre de Dios*, it is colder than ever.' He turned to Sofia. 'See, we have found some coffee. This stuff, anyway.' Paco pulled a bottle of chicory essence from under his coat and held it up like a trophy, with a rare smile.

Sofia prepared the dinner, chickpeas with some small pieces of *chorizo*. They ate together at the table, Enrique talking about his work snow-clearing, the rich women who still wore high-heeled shoes and kept falling over. When they had eaten Sofia pushed away her plate and took Harry's hand.

'We have something to tell you.'

Enrique stared at them, puzzled. Paco, his head only a little above the level of the table, frowned worriedly.

'I've asked Sofia to marry me,' Harry said. 'I'm going back to England soon and Sofia has said she'll come back with me so long as we can take Paco with us.'

Enrique's face fell. He looked at Sofia. 'I will be left here alone?' Then he shrugged and forced a smile. 'Well, what would I do in England? I can hardly read and write. It was always you who was the clever one.'

Paco had been looking between the three of them. At Enrique's words his face stiffened. 'No! No! I won't leave Enrique, no!' He threw his arms round him, burying his face in his shoulder, making desperate squealing noises. Enrique lifted him up.

'I will take him to the kitchen,' he said. He lifted Paco up and went out. As the kitchen door closed, Sofia sighed. 'Enrique is being brave. This, so soon after Mama.'

Harry took one of her hands, pulled it away from her face. 'When we're settled, we can try to get him over—'

He broke off as a loud knocking sounded at the door. Sofia got up, her face weary. 'If that is Señora Avila again—'

She marched to the door and threw it open. Barbara stood there. Her face was pale and she had been crying.

'What is it?' Harry asked sharply. 'What's happened?'

'Can I come in? Please? I went to your flat and then I thought you might be here. I'm sorry, I'd nowhere else to turn.' She looked desperate, frightened.

Sofia looked at her for a moment, then took her arm. 'Come in.' She led her to a chair. Barbara sat down heavily.

'Have some wine,' Harry said. 'You look frozen.'

'Thanks. I'm sorry, were you eating?'

'We've finished,' Sofia said. 'Paco was upset, Enrique has taken him into the kitchen for a moment.'

Barbara bit her lip. 'He'd better not hear why I've come.' She pulled a packet of cigarettes from her handbag, offered one to Sofia and lit up. She sighed with relief.

'It's good to be with friends. You've no idea.'

'What is it?' Harry asked. 'What's got you into this state?'

She clasped her hands tightly on the table and took a deep breath. 'You know Sandy and I haven't been getting on. You know I've talked about going home.'

'Yes.'

She swallowed. 'A while ago I overheard a telephone conversation he was having in his study. It was an accident, I wasn't eavesdropping, but what he was saying was so strange. He was talking to someone about your investments, then he asked about what the person on the other end had done to some man – ' she shivered – 'saying he was tough. It kept going round in my mind. They mentioned a name. Gomez.'

Harry's eyes widened as Barbara pulled the copy of *Ya* from her handbag. 'Then the evening before last I saw this.'

Sofia leaned forward to read the article. Harry sat back, staring at Barbara, his mind whirling.

Sofia looked up. 'You are saying there is a connection?' she asked urgently.

The kitchen door opened and Enrique looked out enquiringly. Sofia rose and went into the kitchen with him. Barbara remained slumped in her chair. Harry looked at her. Sofia came back.

'I have asked them to stay in the kitchen.' She sat down again. '*Señora* Barbara, are you sure of this? You are – forgive me – overwrought.'

Barbara shook her head vigorously. 'It all fits.' Her voice rose. 'Sandy's been involved in torturing and murdering a man. After I read the paper I didn't want to go home. I made myself. I told him I'd a bad headache and had to go to bed. Now I can hardly bear to talk to him.' Her whole body shook for a moment. 'I heard him laughing in the hall with the maid, he's having an affair with her. I felt so scared, lying there in bed, I've never felt so afraid. Then today I went out early, to the veterans' hospital. Afterwards I – I just couldn't go home. I should, I must, but I just couldn't face it.'

'Barbara,' Harry said quietly. He coughed, for a moment he couldn't find his voice. 'I know about this.'

'What?' She looked at him blankly. Sofia stared at him.

He laid his hands on the table. 'I'm with intelligence. I'm a spy. It was my fault that man died.'

Barbara's expression was shocked, aghast.

'You told me what you did was not dangerous,' Sofia said, her voice sharp as a whip.

'I never wanted to do this. Never.'

He told the two women everything: his recruitment in London, his meetings with Sandy, his trip to the mine, his slip that had cost Gomez his life. They listened in horrified silence. From the kitchen they heard occasional sobs from Paco, soothing noises from Enrique.

'A gold mine?' Barbara said when he had finished. She looked Harry in the eye. 'You bastard, Harry.' She didn't shout, she spoke in low sorrowful tones. 'These last two months you've been coming to dinner and meeting me for lunch and all the time you were spying on Sandy. On me as well, presumably!'

'No! No, when I came over to Spain I'd no idea you were with him. I've hated deceiving you, I've hated the whole bloody business if you want to know. Hated it!' he said, so loudly and bitterly Sofia looked at him in surprise.

'And what about the danger I was in?' Barbara continued. 'You knew about Gomez and you didn't warn me!'

'I didn't know for certain till Friday. Though I said you should go home.'

'Oh, thanks, Harry, thanks so bloody much!' Barbara took off her glasses and ran her hands across her face. 'Your name was mentioned when I overheard Sandy on the phone. I couldn't believe you could be involved in murder. And yet you were a spy all the bloody time.'

Harry looked at Sofia. She had turned her face away.

'It's over, please believe me. Listen, they're kicking me out because of Gomez. I'm glad.' He took a deep breath. 'They're trying to recruit Sandy now.' Looking at the two women's shocked faces he thought, oh God, what have I done to them?

Sofia turned back to him. 'That man Gomez was at Toledo. Where the streets ran red with Republican blood and the Moors took heads as trophies. You need not mourn a man like that.'

Barbara turned to her. She looked shocked. Sofia met her eye. 'You should go back to England, *Señora*, away from here. You could stay in a hotel till you can get a boat or an aeroplane.' She gave Harry a firm look. 'We will help you, won't we, Harry?'

'Yes, yes.' He nodded eagerly, grateful for the 'we'. 'Sofia's right, Barbara, you should go home as soon as you can.'

'Do you think I don't know that?' To his surprise she laughed, a hard bitter laugh. 'I can't go home yet. My God. You don't know the half of it.'

Something in her voice chilled Harry. 'What do you mean?'

She took a deep breath, squared her shoulders. 'You don't know about Bernie. Bernie's alive. He's being held in a labour camp near Cuenca and I'm involved in a plan with an ex-guard in Madrid to get him out. To rescue him. On Saturday, in six days' time.' She stopped, looked at him. 'There, it's your turn to be shocked, isn't it?'

Harry's mouth had fallen open. Barbara laughed again; shrilly, with that hysterical edge he'd heard before. Harry had a mental picture of Bernie, laughing as they walked down a Madrid street, green eyes full of excitement and mischief.

Sofia looked puzzled. 'Who is Bernie? You mean your friend who came to fight here?'

'Yes.' Harry looked into Barbara's eyes. 'God, this is true, isn't it?'

'Oh, yes.'

Sofia was looking at him, her large dark eyes shining with emotion. Hell, Harry thought, I've ruined everything. She won't forgive me for the way I've treated Barbara.

'So that's it,' Barbara concluded. 'I have to stay here till this Saturday.'

'You could still leave that man,' Sofia said.

'No. He'd come after me, he wouldn't just let me go. There'd be a terrible hue and cry. He mustn't know.' Her mouth set hard. 'If he found out he might get his friends to do something to Bernie out of spite.'

'You could get someone else to go to Cuenca.' Sofia gave Harry a searching look. 'Us, perhaps?'

Barbara looked at her in surprise. 'Why should you put yourself in danger?'

'Because it would be helping someone who fought for us. And something against these bastards who rule us now.' She looked at Harry. 'I keep my loyalties. They are important.'

'It wouldn't work,' Barbara said. 'If a stranger turned up to meet Luis, the ex-guard, he'd run off, he's nervous enough already.' She told them of her plan, from the first meeting with the journalist in October. They listened in silence. At the end she said quietly, 'No, I'll have to go back to Sandy. I'll pretend I'm ill, say I've got the flu and ask for a separate room. He won't mind, he'll probably take that girl into our bed.'

'It'll be a bloody hard week,' Harry said. 'Pretending to Sandy all the time.'

'Well, you'd know!' she replied angrily. 'I can almost feel sorry for him knowing how you've treated him.' She sighed and put her head in her hands. 'No, that's wrong,' she said more quietly. 'He let himself in for all this.' She looked up. 'I think I can do it, if it means getting Bernie out.' She looked at the newspaper again. 'It was just the shock of finding out about that man, it's been going round in my head.'

Sofia was looking at the photographs on the wall, her mother and father and her uncle the priest. 'You should not go to Cuenca by yourself,' she said. 'As a foreign woman on your own you will stand out. It is a remote town.'

'You know it?'

'I visited it often as a child. We come from Tarancón, which is the other side of the province, but I had an uncle there. You should not go alone,' she repeated.

Barbara sighed. 'I haven't even got a car to go in unless I can take Sandy's. That's the other problem.'

'I could help there,' Harry said. 'I could take out an embassy car and let you have it.'

'Wouldn't that be against the rules?'

Harry shrugged. He didn't care. If Bernie was alive—

Sofia leaned forward. 'We could take you, me and Harry. Yes, it would work. Harry could be a diplomat taking two friends on a day out. A car with diplomatic plates.'

Sofia looked at him. Harry's heart pounded. He thought, this was mad, if they were caught it would be the end of Sofia's chances of getting out of Spain. He and Barbara might be expelled but Sofia— He looked at her. He sensed she wanted him to say yes, to redeem himself. And if Bernie was alive, if they could get him out— He turned to Barbara. 'Are you sure this Luis knows what he's doing?'

'Of course I am,' she answered impatiently. 'Do you think I haven't questioned everything, these last weeks? Luis is no fool, he and his brother have thought this out carefully.'

'All right,' he said. 'I'll come with you. But not you, Sofia, you've got too much to lose.'

Barbara looked surprised. 'What if the embassy found out? You could get into trouble, couldn't you, especially with – what you've been doing?'

He took a deep breath. 'To hell with them. You're right, Sofia, about loyalty. You've helped me lose a lot of my old loyalties, did you know that?'

Anger flashed in her eyes. 'You *should* lose them.'

'I suppose my loyalty to Bernie's the oldest of all.' He shook his head. 'I've heard rumours about these secret camps.'

Barbara was frowning with concentration. 'We could bring Bernie back in the car and leave him at a phone box near the embassy. They'd send someone to fetch him, wouldn't they?'

Harry thought a moment. 'Yes. Yes, they would.'

'He could say he'd hitched a lift from Cuenca, no one need ever know you were involved in the rescue.'

'Yes. Yes, that could work.' He sighed. He faced losing everything over this, but he had to do it. For Sofia. And for Bernie. Bernie, alive—

'I will come too,' Sofia said determinedly. 'I will guide you.'

'No,' Harry said. He laid a hand on her arm. 'No, you mustn't come.'

'Listen, Harry. It will be far less risky for all of us together. I tell you, I know the town. We can go directly where we need to, without looking at maps and attracting attention.'

'Sofia, think—'

She sat up. Her voice was quiet but there was a light in her eyes now. 'I have felt so guilty, at the thought of running away from my country. I did not tell you but I have. But now I have a chance to do something. Something against *them*.'

Chapter Forty

FROM TIME TO TIME the men were dragooned into spending an evening in the church watching propaganda films. Last year they had watched Franco's victory parade, a hundred thousand men marching past the Caudillo as the German Condor Legion flew overhead. There had been films about the rebirth of Spain, battalions of Falange Youth helping in the fields, a bishop blessing the reopening of factories in Barcelona. More recently, they had seen film from the Hendaye meeting, Franco walking past a guard of honour with Hitler, his face aglow.

The freezing weather had continued unabated. The deer, desperate for food, continued to be drawn to the camp by the smell of cooking. The guards had more venison than they needed; they shot the deer now just to relieve their boredom.

The prisoners shuffled into the church hall, glad at least of the warmth from the stove. They sat on the hard wooden chairs, shuffling and coughing as a pair of guards manhandled the ancient projector into position. A screen had been set up against the wall and Aranda stood before it, his uniform immaculately pressed, twirling a swagger stick in his hands as he looked impatiently at the projectionist.

Bernie sat huddled in his coat, massaging his shoulder. It was the ninth of December now; five days until the escape. He was careful not to look at Agustín, who was on duty by the door.

At a nod from the projectionist, Aranda stepped forward, smiling. 'Many of you foreign prisoners will be keen for a glimpse of the outside world. Our own Noticiario Español is therefore proud to present a film about events in Europe.' He waved his stick at the screen. 'I give you – Germany Victorious.' He's an actor, Bernie thought, all the things he does, from this to torturing people, it's all about him being centre stage. He was careful not to catch

Aranda's eye, as he had been ever since his refusal to become an informer.

The film began with newsreel of German troops marching into Warsaw, shifted to tanks smashing through the French countryside, then Hitler looking out over Paris. Bernie had never seen any of it before; the scale of what had happened was terrifying. Then a bombed and smoking London appeared on the screen. 'Only Britain has not surrendered. She ran away from the field of battle in France and now Churchill sulks in London, refusing either to give battle or surrender honourably, believing he is safe because Britain is an island. But revenge comes from the skies, destroying Britain's cities. If only Churchill had followed the example of Stalin and made a peace that would benefit both him and Germany.'

The images shifted from a burning London to a room where Soviet Foreign Minister Molotov sat at a desk signing a paper, while Ribbentrop stood laughing as Stalin patted him on the back. Seeing it was a shock to Bernie. So often he had wondered why Stalin had made his pact with Hitler last year instead of joining the Allies, it had seemed crazy. The Communists said that only Stalin knew the concrete realities, you had to trust his judgement, but seeing him celebrating with Ribbentrop sent a shiver down Bernie's spine.

'Through its pact with Germany, Russia now not only occupies half of Poland but has a booming trade with Germany, receiving foreign exchange in return for its raw materials.'

There was a shot of a huge goods train being checked at a border, German soldiers in coal-scuttle helmets looking through manifests with greatcoated Russians. The film went on to laud German achievements in the occupied countries; Bernie's attention drifted away as Vidkun Quisling welcomed a German opera company to Oslo.

At the quarry that afternoon, he had complained to Agustín of diarrhoea. It was a trial run to establish Bernie had a problem. 'You'd better go behind the bushes then,' Agustín said loudly. He shackled Bernie's feet and led him round the side of the hill. From there the land sloped downhill, there was a vista of white rolling hills. It was a cloudy day; the light starting to fade.

Bernie looked at Agustín. His narrow face was set in its customary gloomy, worried expression but his eyes scanned the landscape with keen intelligence. 'Go to that fold in the hills first,' Agustín said quietly, pointing. 'There's a path, you can just make it out through the snow. I have been down there on my days off. There are some trees – hide among them until it's dark. Then just keep going straight downhill, follow the shepherds' tracks. Eventually you come to the road alongside the gorge.'

Bernie looked across the unbroken expanse of snow. 'They'll see my footprints.'

'Perhaps the snow will have gone. But even if it hasn't, if you go late in the afternoon they will not be able to start a proper search before dark. Your tracks will be harder to follow then. The guards will send someone down to the camp to raise the alarm but by the time Aranda has sent a search party out you should be almost in Cuenca.'

Bernie bit his lip. He had a vision of running downhill, the sound of a shot, crashing down to the earth. The end of everything. 'Let's see how the weather is on Saturday.'

Agustín shrugged. 'You may only have this one chance.' He looked at his watch, then glanced round nervously. 'We should go back. Study the landscape, Piper. If we come back here a second time before the day someone may think it odd.' He hitched his rifle over his shoulder, giving Bernie an uneasy, unhappy look. Bernie gave a wicked grin.

'Perhaps they'll think we are making a marriage, Agustín.'

Agustín frowned, indicating with a sharp gesture with his rifle for Bernie to walk back to the quarry.

The film droned on, showing German engineers modernizing Polish factories. A damp unwashed smell rose from the prisoners. Some had fallen asleep in the unaccustomed warmth, others sat staring sullenly ahead. It was always like this during propaganda films and church services: miserable, resentful sullenness. Could even Father Eduardo believe those services had any value? They were like the films, just another type of revenge, punishment. Bernie glanced at Pablo, sitting further along the row. Since the crucifixion he had been withdrawn, hollow-eyed, his arms gave him much pain. Sometimes he had the look of one who had given up – Vicente had had an expression like that towards the end. Establo treated Pablo with surprising kindliness. His strength was failing and he got Pablo to help him with things; Bernie suspected to give Pablo something to do, stop him sinking into depression.

Father Eduardo, too, had been affected by the crucifixion. Bernie had seen him watching Pablo as he shuffled uncomfortably across the snowy yard. The priest seemed withdrawn, preoccupied, his face full of pain as his eyes followed Pablo. Bernie avoided Father Eduardo now, he still felt ashamed of his part in tormenting him. But the previous day the priest had come up to him in the yard after roll-call.

'How is Pablo Jimenez?' he asked. 'He is in your hut.'

'Not good.'

The priest looked Bernie in the face. 'I am sorry for it.'

'You should tell *him*.'

'I did. Or I tried to, he ignored me. I wanted you to know too.' Father Eduardo shuffled away, his head sunk between his shoulders like an old man's.

There was a whirr and a click and the screen went black. A guard lit the oil lamps and Aranda stepped in front of them. He folded his hands behind his back, smiling. He enjoys our humiliation, Bernie thought.

'Well, gentlemen, did the film impress you?' he asked. 'It showed what shivering, frightened cowards the Communists are. They would rather sign a treaty with their enemy Germany than fight. They are not real fighting men, any more than the skulking British.' He waved the swagger stick. 'Come on, let me hear what you think, who has something to say?'

Responding to these verbal challenges was a dangerous game. Aranda could label a reply that displeased him as insolence and punish the man who made it. Next to Pablo, though, Establo dragged himself painfully to his feet with the aid of his stick. His face was yellow and jaundiced now, making a terrible contrast with the red streaks of his scabies. But Establo would never give up.

'Comrade Stalin is wiser than you think, *señor comandante*.' His voice was a wheeze; he had to pause for breath. 'He waits. For the imperialist powers to wear themselves out with their war. Then, when the British Empire and Germany have fought each other into the ground, the workers of both countries will rise, and the Soviet Union will help them.'

Aranda was delighted. He smiled at Establo's ravaged face. 'But Britain stands on the verge of defeat, while Germany is mightier than ever. There will be no fighting to a standstill, just a German victory.' He waved his stick at Bernie. 'What does our English Communist think?'

Everything depended on keeping out of trouble now. Bernie stood up. 'I don't know, *comandante*.'

'You saw from the film that Britain will not come out and give Germany a clean fight. Do you not hope they will fight, so that Britain and Germany's ruling classes can destroy each other as your comrade said?'

Establo stared round at him challengingly. Bernie said nothing. Aranda smiled. Then, to Bernie's relief he indicated he should sit down again.

'The British know they will be defeated, that is why they stay at home. But next spring, Chancellor Hitler will invade and then all will be over.' He smiled round at the prisoners. 'Then, who knows, he may turn his attention to Russia.'

AFTERWARDS in the hut, Bernie was lying on his bunk, thinking. Thick snow on the ground for weeks now, surely it couldn't go on for much longer. But only five days left. He heard the tap of a stick and looked up. Establo couldn't walk unaided now and Pablo was supporting his other arm. He stood at the foot of his pallet and contemplated Bernie, his eyes as alive and intense as ever in the candlelight, the only part of him that wasn't shrinking, being eaten away.

'You did not have much to say to the *comandante* tonight, Piper.'

'There is no point in arguing with madmen.'

'Britain still fights on the sea. It remains a formidable foe to Germany.'

'I hope so.'

'Because then Britain and Germany can so weaken each other that the workers feel safe to rise, no? You saw how Comrade Stalin fooled the Germans into thinking they are his friends.'

'If he'd joined Britain and France last year, perhaps Germany might have been beaten.'

'So you agree with Aranda then, Comrade Stalin is a coward?'

'I don't know why he made the pact. No more than you do.'

'He is right. This is an imperialist war.'

'It's a war against fascism. That's what I fought for in 1936. Go away, Establo, I would not argue with a sick man.' Bernie glanced at Pablo. His face was drawn with pain, one hand on the bedrail to support himself even as his other hand supported Establo.

'One day,' Establo said quietly, 'when the Soviets have won, you will wish you had kept your faith. I will not be here to denounce you as an enemy of the working class, but others will.' He jerked his head at Pablo. 'These people will be my memory.'

'Yes, comrade.' Bernie rose from the bed. He had to bring this to a halt. 'I have to piss, if you will excuse me.' He walked to the door then went round the side of the hut and relieved himself. He looked through the barbed wire at the white landscape beyond. Let there be no moon that night, he thought. Then he jumped, almost cried out, at a hand on his shoulder. He whirled round. Agustín was standing there.

'What the fuck are you doing?' he whispered angrily.

'I have been waiting an hour, waiting to see if you would come out.' Agustín took a deep breath. 'The shifts have been changed. I am being made to take Saturday off. We cannot go.'

Chapter Forty-One

HILLGARTH AND TOLHURST were due at Harry's flat at seven, Sandy at half past. When Tolhurst told Harry he would be accompanying Hillgarth, his face had flushed with pride. 'The captain's asked me to come and help this time as I know all about it,' he said self-importantly, as though Harry cared.

When Harry got home from the embassy late that afternoon the flat was bitterly cold. It hadn't snowed again but there was a heavy frost, thick fingers of ice on the window. He lit the *brasero* and went into the kitchen and he put his keys in the little saucer where he kept them. They had been in his overcoat and the metal was cold. He remembered a line from *Richard III* – he had helped produce the play at school: Gloucester seeking assurance the Duke of Clarence was dead and being told he was 'key-cold'.

He went into the *salón* and straightened one of the watercolours. Waiting was the worst part. There would be a lot of it between now and Saturday when they went to Cuenca.

The room held the faint tang of Sofia's scent. Strange how scent smelt musky in warm air, tangy in cold. The two of them had sat up most of last night, talking about the rescue. What they were doing was a serious offence. If they were caught there would be diplomatic immunity for him and protection for Barbara, but Sofia was Spanish and it could mean a long prison sentence. Harry had spent half the evening trying to dissuade her from coming, but she was adamant.

'I faced enough danger during the Siege,' she said. 'If I'm going to leave my country at least I can do one good thing, rescue one person.'

'Bernie's important to me – I wouldn't do it otherwise. But you don't owe him anything.'

'I owe all the people who came out here to help the Republic.

I want to do something before I leave.' She smiled sadly. 'Does that sound very romantic and Spanish and stupid?'

'No, no. It's something clean.' He wondered for a moment if she wanted to see if he too was capable of something clean, after the murk he had been involved in, the betrayals. He had told Barbara he would help, partly because his heart had leapt at the news Bernie was alive, partly to make up for his lies, but also to show Sofia he could do something good. Something had changed between them; a slight withdrawing on her part, a tiny hesitation only a lover would have noticed.

She hadn't hesitated though when Harry told her he had arranged for them to be married at the embassy. It would be a civil ceremony as he wasn't a Catholic, but the embassy could do that, perform a marriage according to English laws. Tolhurst had had a word in certain quarters, smoothed the wheels.

'The only thing that worries me,' he said, 'is whether Barbara is strong enough for this.'

'I think she is. She's brought it this far alone. This Bernie, he must be very special. Most of the Spanish Communists were bad people.'

'He was my best friend. Bernie would never let you down, he was like a rock.' Not like me, he thought. 'And how he stuck to his socialism.' He laughed softly. 'It didn't go down well at Rookwood, I can tell you.' He smiled wryly. 'Paco must never go to one of those public schools. Either you rebel, or they send you sleepwalking through life.'

THE DOORBELL rang shrilly, bringing Harry out of his reverie. He took a deep breath and went to open it. Hillgarth and Tolhurst stood together in trilbies and thick overcoats. He invited them in and took their coats and hats. Underneath they wore smart suits. Hillgarth rubbed his hands.

'God, Brett, it's cold in here.'

'It takes a while to warm up. Would you like a drink?'

He poured whisky for Hillgarth, brandy for Tolhurst and himself. He looked at his watch: a quarter to seven. Tolhurst sat down on the sofa, looking nervous. Hillgarth walked round the room, examining the pictures. 'These from the embassy?'

'Yes, the walls were bare when I came.'

'Find any souvenirs of that Communist who had it before?' He smiled. 'Any directives from Moscow down the backs of the chairs?'

'No, nothing at all.'

'Franco's people would have picked the place clean. By the way, you're still not being followed, are you?'

'No. Not for weeks now.'

'They must have decided you're too junior.'

God, Harry thought, the things he was keeping from them; and that was nothing to what he was going to do on Saturday. He mustn't think about that, he must stay cool. Key-cold.

'By the way,' Tolhurst said, 'your fiancée needs to come for an interview at the embassy tomorrow. Just for political vetting, to make sure she's not a Franco agent. I can brief you on what she should say.'

'OK. Thanks.'

'The little boy should be OK,' Tolhurst continued, 'but she'll need to prove she's been looking after him.' He looked at Harry with that serious, owlish expression of his.

'She collects his rations, has done for a year and a half.'

He nodded. 'That should do.'

Hillgarth looked between them, nursing his drink. 'You should be grateful to Tolly, Brett. He was over in immigration half yesterday afternoon.'

The doorbell rang again, a sharp peal. For a second all three stood silent, as though gathering their resources. Then Hillgarth said, 'Let him in, Brett.'

Sandy was outside, slouching, smiling. 'Hello, Harry.' He looked over Harry's shoulder. 'They here?'

'Yes. Come on through.'

He led him into the *salón*. Sandy nodded at Hillgarth and Tolhurst, then looked round the room. 'Nice flat. See you've got some English pictures.'

Hillgarth stepped forward, extending a hand. 'Captain Alan Hillgarth. This is Simon Tolhurst.'

'Pleased to meet you.'

'Drink, Sandy?' Harry asked.

'Whisky, please.' He looked at the bottle on the sideboard. 'Oh, you've got Glenfiddich. I wonder if your supplier's the same as mine. Little black-market place behind the Rastro?'

'Embassy supplies, actually,' Hillgarth said. 'Straight from England. Perk of the job.'

'Home comforts, eh?' Sandy gave Harry his broad smile as he took his drink. Harry squirmed inwardly.

'Shall we sit down?' Hillgarth asked.

'Of course.' Sandy took a seat, offering his silver cigarette case to Hillgarth. 'Smoke?'

'Thanks.' Sandy offered one to Tolhurst. 'I know Harry doesn't,' he said, snapping the case shut. He leaned back in his chair. 'So. What can I do for you?'

'We've been keeping an eye on you, Forsyth,' Hillgarth said smoothly. 'We know about your involvement in the mine out beyond Segovia, we know it's a big project and you've been having trouble with Colonel Maestre's committee. We believe his Monarchist faction want to wrest control of a major resource from the Falangists at the Ministry of Mines.'

Sandy's face went blank, expressionless. He stared at Hillgarth. Harry thought, Sandy will realize the only way you could know all this is through me. Hillgarth could have warned him they were going to dive straight in like this.

'The shares in your company, Nuevas Iniciativas,' Hillgarth went on, looking Sandy in the eye. 'They're going down.'

Sandy leaned forward, tapped the ash from his cigarette carefully into the ashtray, then sat back, raised an eyebrow. 'That's the stock market for you.'

'And of course things must be getting very difficult now Lieutenant Gomez's body has been discovered.'

Sandy's face remained expressionless. He said nothing. It was only a few seconds but it seemed to stretch out for ever. Then he glanced at Tolhurst before returning his gaze to Hillgarth's face.

'You seem very well informed,' he said quietly. 'So Harry has been spying on me? Not my old pal?' He turned slowly and looked at Harry. The large brown eyes were full of sorrow. 'You've been into everything, haven't you?'

'The information's accurate, isn't it?' Hillgarth prompted.

Sandy turned back to him. 'Some of it might be.'

Hillgarth leaned forward. 'Don't play games with me, Forsyth. You're going to need a bolt-hole soon. If the state takes over exploiting the mine you'd be seriously out of pocket. Someone could even decide to prosecute you for Gomez's murder.'

Sandy inclined his head. 'Not my fault if some of the people I work with got carried away.'

'Our information is you set them on to him.'

Sandy didn't reply, he took a long swig of his whisky. Hillgarth leaned back. All the time Tolhurst stared owlishly at Sandy. If it was meant to make him uneasy, it failed – he didn't seem to notice.

'All that's beyond our jurisdiction,' Hillgarth went on, waving a hand. 'We're not really interested. The point is, if you are in difficulties, you might consider a change of job. Working for us.'

'What sort of work might that be?'

'Intelligence. We'd get you back to England. But first you'd have to tell us all about the mine. That's what we sent Brett to find out about. How big is it, how near to starting production? Will it give Spain the gold reserves to buy food abroad? At the moment they're dependent on loans from us and the Americans, which gives us a lever.'

Sandy nodded slowly. 'So, if I tell you everything about the mine, you'd get me out?'

'Yes. We'd send you to England, and if you like we'll train you up and get you work somewhere else where your talents might come in useful. Perhaps Latin America. We think it might suit you. It'd be good pay.' Hillgarth leaned forward a little. 'If you're happy to carry on as you are, fine. But if you want to get out, we need to know everything about the mine. Everything.'

'That's a promise?'

'A promise.'

Sandy put his head on one side, swirling the whisky in his glass. Hillgarth went on, his voice steady and slow. 'It's up to you. You can come in with us, or go back to your gold mine. But that's a dangerous game, however profitable it might have looked once.'

To Harry's astonishment, Sandy threw back his head and laughed.

'You've actually been spying on me and you haven't realized. Oh, Jesus. You never twigged.'

'What?' Harry asked, puzzled.

'What?' Sandy mimicked. 'Still a bit deaf, or was that just a cover story?'

'No,' Harry said. 'But what do you mean? Twigged what?'

'There isn't any gold mine,' Sandy said then, quietly but with withering contempt. 'There never was.'

Harry jerked upright. 'But I saw it.'

Sandy looked at Hillgarth, not Harry, as he answered. 'He saw a stretch of land, some equipment and huts. Oh, the land's the type that might bear gold deposits, only there aren't any.' He laughed again and shook his head. 'Have any of you heard of salting?'

'I have,' Hillgarth said. 'You take a sample of the right type of soil and put fine grains of gold in it, to make it look like ore.' His jaw dropped. 'Jesus Christ, is that what you've been doing?'

Sandy nodded. 'That's right.' He took out another cigarette. 'Christ, it's almost worth being betrayed by Brett to see your faces.'

'I've worked in mining myself,' Hillgarth said. 'Salting's a difficult job, you'd need to be a skilled geologist.'

'Quite right. Like my friend Alberto Otero. He worked in South Africa, he told me some of the stunts that have been pulled out there. I suggested it might work in Spain, the government's desperate for gold and the Ministry of Mines is full of Falangists seeking to increase their influence. He scouted out a suitable spot and we bought the land. I already had some useful contacts in the ministry.'

'The man de Salas?' Tolhurst asked.

'Yes, de Salas. He's had a difficult time keeping Maestre at bay. He thinks the mine's real too. He thinks it's going to help Spain be a great Fascist nation.' He turned back to Hillgarth with a smile. 'We use our labs to distribute fine gold dust within the ore, the breccia, then we send it off to the government labs. We've been doing it for six months. They keep demanding more samples and we supply them.'

Hillgarth's eyes narrowed. 'You'd need a fair bit of gold to do that. The black-market price is fantastic. Any sizeable purchases would get talked about.'

'Not if you're on a committee that helps poor benighted Jews escaping from France. They're only able to bring what they can carry and most bring gold. We relieve them of it in return for visas for Lisbon, then Alberto melts it down, turns it into tiny grains. We have as much gold as we need and nobody's any the wiser. The Jews were my idea actually.' He exhaled a cloud of smoke. 'When I heard that French Jews were turning up in Madrid fleeing from the Nazis, I thought I might help them. Harry might not believe it but I felt sorry for them, people who can never seem to do anything right, always sent wandering. But to get visas for them I needed money and all they had was gold. That set me talking to Otero about how gold is always valuable, always makes men's eyes light up. That's where the idea came from.' He smiled at Hillgarth; still he seemed reluctant to look at Harry.

So it was all a trick, Harry thought. All this, the work and the betrayals and Gomez's death, it was all for nothing. Smoke and mirrors.

Hillgarth looked at Sandy for a long moment. Then he laughed, a loud guffaw.

'By Christ, Forsyth, you've been bloody clever. You had everyone fooled.'

Sandy inclined his head.

'What were you going to do, wait till the company shares rose enough, then offload them and disappear?'

'That was the idea. But someone in the Ministry of Mines has been putting the word about that the company's likely to be taken over. Their latest tactic to get control. Crafty bunch of bastards.' He laughed again. 'Only they don't know it'll be control of nothing, just a couple of useless farms. But then Maestre put his spy in down there. He had keys to the offices – if he had anything about him he'd have found out the truth.'

'So you could find yourself penniless.' Hillgarth's eyes were cold as stones. 'Maybe with a price on your head.'

'At any moment. Or stabbed down a dark alley. I don't like having to watch my back all the time.'

'You've been playing a very risky game.'

'Yes. I thought Harry could be an asset.' Still he wouldn't look at him. 'I knew he had money and if we put more capital in and bought more land it would make us look stronger, harder to buy out. Harry would have made a big profit, too. I'd have seen to that, told him when to sell. Then when we learned about Gomez we were terrified he'd found out the whole thing was a fake, but he can't have because nothing more happened. Gomez wasn't very bright. But Maestre's still scheming to get hold of the gold. It's time to get out now.'

Then Sandy did turn to look at Harry. His face was expressionless, but his eyes were full of pain and anger. 'I trusted you, Harry, you were the last person in the world I still trusted.' He smiled thinly. 'Never mind, eh? It's all turned out for the best.' He sat back for a moment, reflecting. Harry noticed a tiny twitch above his left eye. He felt ashamed, too ashamed to reply despite what Sandy had done. Sandy turned back to Hillgarth. 'You're the Alan Hillgarth who used to write adventure novels, aren't you?'

'That's right.'

'And now you're doing it for real, eh? I used to read your books at school. Harry didn't like them but I did. Adventures. You're like me, you like adventures.'

Hillgarth didn't reply.

'Though you romanticized things. Remember that one set in Spanish Morocco? You didn't show what the colonial wars were really like. The savagery.'

Hillgarth smiled. 'What it was really like wouldn't have got past the censor.'

Sandy nodded. 'I dare say you're right. There are censors everywhere, aren't there, making us believe the world's better and safer than it really is.'

'Let's get back to business, Forsyth. I think you could still be useful to us. Someone who could pull off a stunt like that, Jesus. But if we rescue you from this mess, it'll be on our terms. To start with, you'll need to tell this to people in London. We'll escort you back on a plane. Understand?'

Sandy hesitated a moment, then inclined his head. 'Perfectly.'

'Right. Come to the embassy at ten tomorrow. You're living with an Englishwoman, aren't you?'

'Yes.'

'How much does she know about the mine?'

He gave a cynical half-smile. 'Nothing. Nothing at all.' He looked at Harry again. 'Barbara's as innocent as a babe in the woods, isn't she, Harry?'

Hillgarth grunted. 'You'll have to tell her something about why you're going back to England.'

'Oh, I think she'll just be pleased to be going home. Besides, I doubt we'll be together much longer. She's not a factor.'

'Good.' Hillgarth rose and looked down at Sandy. 'That'll do for now. I think you've the makings of a good agent, Forsyth.' He smiled at him. 'But don't piss us around.'

Sandy nodded. He stood up, extending a hand to Hillgarth. He shook it.

'What about your house?' Tolhurst asked.

'Rented from one of the ministries. Rent free, actually.' Sandy extended his hand to Tolhurst, who hesitated a moment, then rose and shook it. Harry got up too. Sandy looked at him for a second, then turned away and walked to the door. Tolhurst followed him out.

Hillgarth stared at Harry. 'Christ, he's a cool customer. That mine, Jesus, the work we've put into it. I suppose he couldn't've been lying?'

'I think he was telling the truth,' Harry said quietly.

'Yes. If the bloody thing was real it would've been a big bargaining counter and he'd have used it. I suppose that's why he confessed it was all faked straight away. He'd guess it was probably only a matter of time before the truth came out.' Hillgarth thought a moment.

Tolhurst came back and sat down. 'Sir Sam will go mad, sir. All these resources, Maestre alienated, all for a mine that never existed. My God.'

'Yes, I'll have to pick the right moment to tell him.' Hillgarth shook his head and laughed. 'Screwing Franco himself. Well, Forsyth's got balls, you have to give him that.' For the first time he looked at Harry sympathetically. 'Sorry your role had to come out, but there was no alternative if we were to discuss the mine.'

Harry hesitated. Then he said, 'It's all right, sir, nothing surprises me any more. I'm not even surprised any more at the Knights of St George, the government going in for mass bribery of the Monarchists.'

'Harry,' Tolhurst said uncomfortably. Hillgarth raised his eyebrows. Harry went on, it was all over and he didn't care any more.

'Only I wonder why it was necessary to bribe them,' he added bitterly. 'They don't want to go to war against us, they know we don't mind what they do to the people here.'

Harry expected Hillgarth to lose his temper, part of him wanted him to, but he only gave a little contemptuous smile.

'Go away, Brett. Get yourself sorted out with your girly, then you can go home. Leave Spain to people who understand what needs to be done.'

Chapter Forty-Two

THAT EVENING BARBARA sat at home, nursing a cold. She really did have one – it had come on the day before, and with her running nose and red eyes it had been easy to exaggerate the symptoms and pretend it was flu. She had suggested sleeping in one of the spare bedrooms to reduce the risk of Sandy catching it and he had agreed. He seemed more preoccupied than ever, he hardly seemed to notice what she said now.

He had told her he wouldn't be back until late. She had spent the afternoon in her bedroom, keeping up for Pilar the pretence of having flu. She listened to the radio, trying to get the BBC, but reception was bad. Then she sat by the window, looking out over the snowy street. After a while she became conscious of a dripping sound somewhere. She opened the window. The air was distinctly warmer and meltwater was dripping from the trees. Already a green patch had appeared under the elm in the front garden. She felt a surge of relief. If the snow was going, that would make Bernie's rescue easier.

Tomorrow she was taking Harry and Sofia to her final meeting with Luis. They had agreed she would meet him alone first; Barbara feared if she came in with two other people Luis might take fright and flee. After she had explained matters to Luis, the others would arrive. She didn't see how he could object. Sofia was right: having her and Harry there could only help their chances. She was grateful to them but still felt betrayed by Harry; what complexities there had turned out to be under that quiet surface.

Her reflections were interrupted by a knock at the bedroom door. She jumped up and closed the window. As she crossed to the door she blew her nose loudly and tried to settle her features into the tired look of an invalid. Pilar stood outside, her face surly, her hair under the little cap frizzier than ever.

'May I have a word, *señora?*'

'All right. Come in.' Barbara's tone was curt. The girl could hardly expect otherwise; she and Sandy had hardly bothered to hide what they had been doing. She stood in the centre of the room and faced Pilar.

'What is it?'

Pilar crossed her hands over her white apron. There was sullen anger in her eyes. People always hate those they've injured, Barbara thought. She supposed it kept guilt at bay.

'I would like to give my notice, *señora*.'

That was a surprise. 'Oh, yes?'

'I would like to leave at the end of next week if that is convenient.'

It wasn't much time to find someone else but Barbara would be glad to see the back of her. The daily would cope. She wondered what had happened. Had Pilar and Sandy had a row?

'This is very sudden, Pilar.'

'Yes, *señora*. My mother in Zaragoza is ill, I have to go to her.'

It was an obvious lie: Barbara knew her parents came from Madrid. She couldn't resist a dig.

'I hope you haven't become unhappy, working for my husband and me.'

'No, *señora*,' Pilar replied, still looking at her with angry half-closed eyes. 'My mother in Zaragoza is ill,' she repeated.

'Then you must go to her. Go tonight if you like, I'll pay you till the end of the week.'

Pilar looked relieved. 'Thank you, *señora*, that would be good.'

'You'd better go and pack. I'll sort your money out.'

'Thank you.' Pilar curtsied and walked quickly out of the room. Barbara took the key to the bureau where she kept her money. Good riddance, she thought.

PILAR WAS PACKED and gone within an hour. From her window, Barbara watched her walk away up the path with her heavy battered suitcase, her shoes leaving deep footprints in the fast-melting snow. She wondered where the girl would go to. She went down to the kitchen. It was a mess, dishes piled in the sink and the floor unswept.

Barbara supposed she ought to do something about it but she couldn't be bothered. She sat there, smoking and watching the dusk fall. Then, to pass the time, she made a *cocido* for dinner.

It was past nine when she heard Sandy's footsteps. He went into the *salón*. Barbara walked quietly up the basement steps, hoping to get to her room without him hearing, but he called out from the partially open *salón* door. 'Barbara, is that you?'

She paused on the steps. 'Yes.'

'Come in a minute.'

He was standing by the unlit fire, smoking, still in his hat and coat. 'How are you feeling?' he asked. He sounded a little drunk. There was a dull, sad look in his eyes she had never seen before.

'Still pretty bunged up.'

'This room's cold. Why hasn't Pilar made up the fire?'

Barbara took a deep breath. 'Pilar's gone, Sandy. She came to see me this afternoon and handed in her notice. Her mother's ill in Zaragoza, so she says.'

Sandy shrugged. 'Oh well.' He looked at her. 'I've been with some people from the British Embassy. Then I went for a drink.'

'What was that about?' She knew, of course. Harry had said they wanted to recruit him.

'Sit down,' Sandy said. She sat on the edge of the sofa. He lit another cigarette. 'Tell me, when you and Brett met did he ever ask questions about me? About my work?'

Oh God, she thought, he knows about Harry. That's why he's calling him Brett. 'A few times, when he first came. There wasn't much I could tell him.'

Sandy nodded reflectively, then he said, 'Harry's not an interpreter at all, he's a spy. He's been spying on my business ventures for the fucking secret service.'

She pretended surprise. 'What? Are you sure you've got this right? Why should they spy on you?'

'I've been involved in a big project.' He shook his head angrily. 'That's done for now. I'm finished here.'

'What? Why?'

'It had too many enemies. Brett's people are offering a lifeline, but – Harry, he took me in. I should have realized,' he said, more to himself than her. 'I should have stayed alert. But I trusted him. They probably knew I would.'

'Who? Who did?'

'Eh? His bosses, the sneaky little beakies.' He shook his head again. 'I should have seen. I should have seen. Never let your guard down,' he muttered, 'never trust anybody.' His eyes were unfocused; she thought she saw tears forming.

'Are you sure this is right?' Barbara asked. 'Why – why would he spy on you?'

'He told me himself.' Sandy spoke in a flat unemotional voice. 'Or rather his bosses did, while he sat there. You could see he didn't want it to come out. They've been interested in my business activities. They want me to work for them now. Back in England.' He shook his head again. 'England. The drizzle and the regulations and the sniffling hypocrisy. And the bombs. That's if they don't shove me in jail or knock me on the head once I'm back. Under escort.' He looked at her keenly. 'You want to go back, don't you?'

'Yes.' She hesitated. 'What about your business?'

'I told you, that's done for.' His mouth worked for a second. 'All over. The biggest thing I ever did.'

She had a sudden mad urge to blurt it all out, tell him about Bernie and the rescue. It was the tension, she couldn't stand the tension another moment. But Sandy said abruptly, 'I'm going upstairs. I've some things to sort out. Then I'm going out for a bit.'

'At this time of night?'

'Yes.' He turned and left the room.

She went to the drinks cabinet and poured herself a stiff whisky, then sat down and lit a cigarette. So Harry had been unmasked. He would have hated that. But perhaps he deserved it.

The telephone rang shrilly in the hall. 'Hell,' she breathed, 'what now?' She waited for Pilar to answer it then remembered the girl was gone. The ringing went on. Why didn't Sandy answer it on his extension? She went into the hall and picked up the receiver.

'Señora Brett?' She recognized Luis's voice at once, hoarse and breathless. She stared round the hall frantically, terrified Sandy might appear from upstairs and ask who it was.

'Yes,' she whispered. 'What is it? Why are you ringing here?'

'Forgive me, *señora*, I had to.' He paused. 'Is it safe to talk?'

'Yes. But if you hear a click that'll be him on the extension, stop speaking.' She spoke in a frantic whisper. 'What is it? Be quick.'

'I have just heard from Agustín. We have an arrangement he can telephone me at a bar I go to in the evenings—'

'Yes, yes, please be *quick*.'

'The staff rota has been changed. Agustín will not be with Piper at the prison quarry on Saturday.'

'What, oh God—'

'It will have to be Friday, can you come to Cuenca the day before? The same arrangement, meeting Piper in the bushes by the bridge at seven? Agustín has gone into Cuenca, to see the old man at the cathedral.'

'Yes, yes, all right, yes.' She frowned. Would Harry be able to get Friday off from the embassy?

'I know we are meeting tomorrow, but I wanted to let you know, *señora*, as soon as possible. In case there were arrangements you had to change.'

'All right, yes, all right. I'll see you tomorrow.'

'Goodbye.' There was a click and the phone went dead, the whirr of the dialling tone filling her ear. She replaced the receiver. She went back into the *salón* but she couldn't settle. She went out again and mounted the stairs. The hallway was dim and she remembered when she was a child going up to bed, her fear of the dark at the top of the stairs. She thought suddenly of Carmela, the woolly donkey she had left in the church.

There was a strip of light under their bedroom door. He had gone in there, he was opening and closing drawers. What was he doing?

She went back into the *salón* and sat smoking and drinking. After a while she heard his footsteps on the stairs. She tensed, expecting him to come to the *salón*, but then heard the front door close, followed by the car starting up. It drove away. Barbara ran upstairs to her bedroom. He had taken some clothes, a suit and a shirt. She looked out of the window. A fog had descended, the weak streetlamps showing through as a faint yellow haze. Where was he going? What was he doing? It wasn't safe weather for driving.

She sat at the window for hours, smoking, alone in the house.

Chapter Forty-Three

IT WAS QUIET in the restaurant by the Royal Palace. Barbara ordered a coffee from the plump little owner; she could tell he remembered her from the day she was here with Harry. Only a few weeks ago, though it seemed like a lifetime.

It was just after two o'clock. Harry and Sofia were not due for another hour, but Barbara had had to get out of the empty house. Sandy had still not returned. The daily had arrived at nine and Barbara set her to clearing the kitchen. Then she walked through the silent rooms, no sound apart from her own footsteps and the ceaseless dripping from outside. The snow was almost gone. She went into Sandy's study. Everything appeared normal, all the pictures and ornaments still in place. She opened the drawer in his desk where he kept his bank books. It was empty. He's gone for good, she thought, he's left me. She felt strangely downcast, discarded. She shrugged off the feeling, telling herself not to be silly, it was what she had wanted. She reflected with a strange detachment that not so long ago Sandy having an affair with the maid, let alone leaving her, would have left her prostrate, all her worst feelings about herself confirmed.

The restaurant was filling up with lunchtime customers by the time Harry and Sofia arrived. They both looked serious.

'Is everything all right?' she asked them.

'Yes.' Harry sat down. 'Except Sandy was supposed to turn up for a meeting at the embassy this morning, and he never arrived.'

She sighed. 'I think he's gone. Cleared out.' She told them what had happened the night before. 'Some of the funny things he said make sense now. I think he's gone off with Pilar.'

'But where would they go?' Sofia asked.

'Lisbon, perhaps,' Harry said. 'He told us last night about some committee to help Jewish emigrants from France; they took gold in return for visas to Portugal.'

'So that was it,' Barbara said. 'So that was why he helped them.'

'They crushed the heirlooms up to make gold to doctor their samples with.' Harry told her what he had learned the night before: that the gold mine was a fake.

Barbara sat staring at him for a second, then sighed. 'Everything was a fake, then,' she said. 'Absolutely everything.'

'I expect Sandy's gone off with a false passport.'

'My God.'

'Hillgarth said he half expected it, he thought Sandy wasn't someone who'd buckle down and take orders.'

'No,' said Barbara, 'that's true.' She sighed. 'So that's that. I wonder what he'll do now.'

Harry shrugged. 'Set up in business somewhere, I expect. America perhaps. I wonder why he didn't take the chance to get back to England.'

'He said something about it stifling him. And he was afraid he'd be locked up.'

'I don't think he would have been. They wanted to use his – talents.' Harry grimaced. 'And yet – he said it all started off because he really wanted to help the Jews. Oddly enough, I believe him.'

Barbara was silent.

'What will happen to your house?' Sofia asked.

'Sandy got it rent free from one of the ministries. I expect they'll want it back. I'll camp out there for the meantime. It won't be for long.' The waiter appeared and Harry and Sofia ordered coffees. They still had nearly an hour before she was due to meet Luis; the café was a fifteen-minute walk away. Sofia looked at her closely.

'How do you feel, about his leaving?'

Barbara lit a cigarette. 'I would have left him in a few days anyway. I wonder how long Pilar will last. They must have been cooking this up for a while.' She blew out a cloud of smoke.

'It makes things easier for us,' Sofia said hesitantly.

'Yes.' She took a deep breath. 'Listen, there's another problem. Luis rang last night. His brother's rota's been changed, it'll have to be brought forward a day. It's going to have to be Friday.'

Sofia frowned. 'Why have they changed his shift at the last minute?'

'They've changed rotas at the camp. I didn't go into that. I was standing in the hall terrified Sandy would come down any minute,' she added with irritation, 'We can ask Luis when we meet him.'

Harry stroked his chin. 'I'll have to change my car booking. I've got one for Saturday – one of the little Fords the junior staff are allowed – said I wanted a run out to the country at the weekend. But it shouldn't be a problem, I'll say the arrangements have changed. I'm on duty tomorrow – there's a Christmas bash for the translators at the Spanish Academy and I don't want to go, I've put my name down to cover the office. But Friday's free.'

'And I will go sick at the dairy on Friday instead of Saturday,' Sofia said.

Barbara looked at her. 'I'm sorry I snapped just then. I suppose we're all getting edgy.'

Sofia nodded, then smiled back. 'It's all right.'

They were silent for a few moments. Harry smiled and took Sofia's hand. 'We've got our special licence. We're getting married on the nineteenth. A week tomorrow. Then we're off to England by plane on the twenty-third. We've got a visa for Paco.'

'That's wonderful.' She smiled. 'I'm so glad.'

'Paco has taken our family name on the form,' Sofia said. 'It is strange to see it. Francisco Roque Casas.'

'Thank God one child can be got out of here. How is he?'

'He does not really understand what going away means.' A shadow crossed her face. 'He is still sad Enrique is not coming.'

'You couldn't get him over?'

'No.' Harry shook his head. 'We're going to try again from England. But I think it'll be impossible while the war lasts. We were lucky to get places on the plane.'

'I'm so pleased for you.'

'Have you booked anything?'

'No. I'll trust to luck, I'm not planning anything till Bernie's inside the British Embassy and it's settled he's going home. I'm worried there might be problems because he's a Communist. From what you've said about Hoare I wouldn't put it past him to give Bernie back to the Spaniards.'

Harry shook his head firmly. 'No, Barbara, the embassy has to take him in. Whatever Hoare might like to do he was a prisoner of war, he was held illegally under international law. And my guess is the Spanish authorities won't make a fuss. It'd look bad for them. But you must keep out of it.' He thought a moment. 'But don't take him in at the front. If he's escaped, the *civiles* on the door might have been told to watch out for him and they could seize him; he won't be on British soil until he's actually inside the embassy.'

'I'll take him to a phone box in the centre of Madrid. He can phone the embassy from there and get them to fetch him. He can say he stole the clothes and hitched a lift to Madrid, like we agreed. They can't disprove it.'

Harry laughed. Barbara thought it was the first laugh of genuine pleasure she had heard from him since they met again. 'It'll be the talk of the embassy the next day; I can say I knew him at school. Then I can help him get back to England.' He shook his head in wonderment. 'He may even come on the same plane as us.'

'It sounds as neat as clockwork,' Sofia said. 'But remember things may go wrong, we may have to improvise.' She looked at Barbara sharply again. 'Are you all right? Do you have a cold?'

'It's nothing. It's better today,' Barbara said. She was surprised at how Sofia seemed to be taking charge now.'

'I have a gun,' Sofia said. 'Just in case.'

Harry leaned forward. 'A *gun*? Where did you get it?'

'It was my father's, during the Civil War. It has been in the flat since then.' She shrugged. 'There are many guns in Madrid, Harry.'

Barbara looked horrified. 'But why do you want to bring a gun?'

'In case we have to run. As I said, we may have to improvise.'

Barbara shook her head vehemently. 'Guns just make things worse, make more danger—'

'It is only for an emergency. I do not want to use it.'

'Have you bullets?' Harry asked hesitantly.

'Yes, and I know how to fire it. Women were trained to shoot during the war.'

'Will you let me take it?' Harry asked. 'I know how to fire a gun too.'

Sofia hesitated, then said, 'All right.' She turned to Barbara. 'This is not a peaceful thing we are involved with, you know.'

'All right. All right, I know.' Barbara ran a hand over her brow.

Bearing arms went against her every instinct but Sofia was right, she was the one who knew life here.

'I still don't think you should come,' Harry told Sofia. 'There's more danger for you than for either of us.'

'It will make things easier,' she said firmly. 'Cuenca is an old medieval town; it is not easy to find your way around.' She turned to Barbara. 'Should you not go and meet the guard now?'

'Yes. Give me a quarter of an hour, then follow.' When she got up her legs were shaking.

The afternoon was damp and raw, the streets wet with melting slush. There was still a trace of last night's fog and some shops already had their lights on. The first Christmas displays had appeared in the windows, the three wise men standing round the crib with their gifts. Barbara wondered what sort of Christmas Sandy would give Pilar in Lisbon.

Real Madrid were playing a football match and there was a little crowd round the counter at the cafe, listening to a radio. Luis sat at his usual table. His nervous air irritated her today.

'You gave me a fright last night,' she said brusquely as she sat down.

'I had to let you know.'

'Why did the shift change?'

He shrugged. 'It happens. One of the guards was ill and everything had to be adjusted. It will be exactly the same arrangement, only on Friday instead of Saturday.'

'Friday the thirteenth,' she said with a brittle laugh. Luis looked at her uncomprehendingly.

'It's supposed to be an unlucky day in England.'

'I had never heard that.' He ventured a smile. 'It is Tuesday the thirteenth that is unlucky in Spain, *señora*, so do not worry about that.'

'It doesn't matter. Listen, will the snow be melting in Cuenca too?'

'I should think so. The radio said the thaw is happening all over the country.' Luis looked round, then leant forward. 'The escape will be at four, as we said. Your friend should reach the bridge by seven. If there is heavy snow and he is not there by nine, or in the cathedral if the bridge is guarded, you will know they have decided to call it off because of the weather.'

'Or he's been caught.'

'In either case there is nothing you can do. If he does not come you should drive back to Madrid. Do not stay the night in Cuenca – details of all hotel visitors go to the *civiles* and an Englishwoman staying alone would be noticed. Do you understand?'

'Yes, of course I understand.' She gave him a cigarette and left the packet of Gold Flake on the table.

'I think you may be lucky. Despite this Friday the thirteenth. The snow will stay on the high mountains but in the lower part of the Tierra Muerta it should be gone.'

'I've been lucky in another way,' she said, looking him in the eye. 'There's an old English friend of Bernie's here in Madrid, he's going to get me a car. He's going to drive me there with his Spanish fiancée. She knows Cuenca.'

'What?' Luis looked horrified. '*Señora*, this was supposed to be secret. How many people have you told?'

'Only them. They can be trusted. I've known Harry for years.'

'*Señora*, you were going to go alone, that was the agreement. This complicates things.'

'No it doesn't,' Barbara replied calmly. 'It makes them easier. Three of us on a day out won't be as noticeable as a woman alone. And anyway, I couldn't get a car without Harry. What are you so scared of?'

Luis looked utterly disconcerted. Through the window Barbara saw Harry and Sofia crossing the road. 'There's no point arguing, they'll be here in a minute.'

'*¡Mierda!*' Luis gave her a trapped, angry look. 'You should have told me.'

'I didn't tell them until two days ago.'

'You should have spoken to me first! On your own heads be it, *señora*.' He glowered at Harry and Sofia as they entered the cafe. There was a shout from the crowd as someone scored a goal.

Sofia and Harry came over. Luis shook their hands unsmilingly.

'Luis isn't very happy,' Barbara explained. 'But I've told him it's all settled.'

Luis leaned forward. 'This is a dangerous venture,' he said angrily.

'We know,' Harry replied, his manner reasonable, authoritative. 'Why don't we go over things and see if there being three of us makes matters more difficult in any way. Now, we drive to Cuenca, get there by four, and leave the car somewhere, yes?'

Luis nodded. 'Agustín spent an afternoon tramping the lanes to look for the best place. There is an abandoned collective farm just outside the town, and there is a field screened from the road by some trees just beyond the sign saying you are about to enter Cuenca. You should leave the car in the field, it will not be seen.' He leaned forward. 'It is important you leave the car there, it is the nearest hidden place to the town. Few people have cars in Cuenca; yours could attract attention from the *civiles* if it's just left parked in a street.'

Harry nodded. 'Yes, that makes sense.'

Luis looked at Barbara through narrowed eyes. 'Agustín put a lot of work into this. And if it fails he could be shot.'

'We know, Luis,' Barbara said gently.

'And then we walk up to the old town, to the cathedral?' Harry continued.

'Yes. It will be dark by the time you get there. You wait in the cathedral until seven, then cross the gorge by the bridge, to the stand of trees. There will be few people around, if any, at that time on a winter night. But the old man, Francisco, is expecting only Señora Forsyth.'

'Then we can explain,' Harry said. 'I think I should be the one to fetch Bernie. You two can wait in the cathedral.'

'No,' Barbara replied quickly. 'It should be me, he'll be expecting me alone.'

Luis threw up his hands. 'This is what I mean. You cannot agree even on this.'

'We can sort that out later,' Harry said. 'Barbara, you've got the clothes?'

'All packed up. He changes behind the bushes, we cross the bridge to the cathedral, then we all walk back to the car.'

Harry nodded. 'Like two couples on a day out. It's very plausible.'

'Can this old man in the cathedral be trusted?' Sofia asked.

'He needs money desperately. He has a sick wife.'

'The cathedral.' Sofia hesitated. 'I expect like most cathedrals in the Republican zone they will have the names of priests killed during the Republic listed there.'

Luis gave her a puzzled look. 'I expect so. Why?'

'I had an uncle who was a priest there.'

'I am sorry, *señorita*.' Luis looked at Harry. 'Why are you in Spain, *señor*? Are you a businessman like Señora Forsyth's husband?'

'Yes, yes I am.' Harry lied with a straight face. You do it easily, Barbara thought.

'Your husband still knows nothing?' Luis asked her.

'Nothing.'

He looked between them, then shrugged. 'Well, it is on your heads, as I say. And I will meet you the day after, *señora*?'

'Yes. As arranged.'

'And your brother?' Harry asked. 'He will let himself be hit on the head, stick to his story after?'

'Of course he will! I told you, he could be shot for aiding an escape!'

'All right.' Harry nodded. 'That's it, then. It's settled. I don't see any problems.'

'And then you and your brother will go back to Sevilla,' Sofia said.

Luis blew out a cloud of smoke. 'Yes. Forget the army and the war and danger.'

'You were conscripted when the Fascists took Sevilla at the beginning of the war?' she asked.

'Yes.' He stared at her. 'We had no choice. If you refused you were shot.'

'Then you were on Franco's march to Madrid in 1936. With the Moors.'

Luis's voice hardened. 'I told you, *señorita*, we had no choice. I was at the Siege that winter, on the other side of the lines to you no doubt. But there is hardly a street in Spain that did not have people on opposite sides.'

'That's true, Sofia,' Harry said. 'Look at you and your uncle.'

There was a disappointed shout from the crowd. The football match was over; Real Madrid had lost. The men round the bar started drifting over to the tables.

'If you have no more questions I should go,' Luis said.

'I think we've covered everything.' Harry looked enquiringly at the women, who nodded.

Luis got up. 'Then I wish you good luck.'

'I do not like that man,' Sofia said after he had gone.

Harry took her hand. 'What he said about the war was true. People often had no choice about which side they fought on.'

'He never pretended to be doing this for any other reason than money,' Barbara said. 'If he was tricking me he could have taken the money I've given him already – quite a lot – and disappeared.'

'All right.'

Two men at the next table started talking loudly. 'That's Real down again.'

'Ay, it is bad luck,' his friend replied. 'And have you heard, there's another freeze on the way. It is going to get colder again. Perhaps more snow.'

Barbara bit her lip. She thought, Friday the thirteenth. Even the best plans needed luck in the end.

Chapter Forty-Four

THE NEXT MORNING Harry and Sofia walked down the Castellana, towards the embassy. Harry would have liked to put his arm in hers but there was a pair of *civiles* nearby.

Overnight the weather had turned colder again; there were patches of black ice on the pavements, frozen slush in the gutters. People going to work were huddled into their coats. But there had been no snow and the morning sky was a clear electric blue.

'You'll be all right?' Harry asked.

'Yes.' Sofia smiled at him. 'It is just a matter of filling in forms and Spaniards are used to that. I got through the political questions yesterday.' There were some documents to prepare for the marriage ceremony; this morning she had an interview with the embassy lawyer. The man wanted to see her on her own but she would come to Harry's office afterwards.

'This time tomorrow we'll be on our way to Cuenca,' he said.

'Are you quite sure the ambassador will send Bernie back to England?'

'He has to. He can't act illegally.'

'They would here. They do it all the time.'

'England's different,' Harry said. 'It's not perfect but it is different that way.'

'I hope so.'

'Get reception to call me when they've finished with you. I'll show you my office. The hours are going to go pretty slowly today. When are you due at the dairy?'

'Twelve. I'm on the afternoon shift.'

'I've had a letter from Will. He's rented a house for us. It's on the outskirts of Cambridge, it's got four bedrooms.'

Sofia laughed, shaking her head at the idea of such luxury.

'We can move in when we like. Then I'll see about a teaching job and getting a doctor for Paco.'

'And I will take English lessons.'

He smiled at her. 'And see you behave yourself. Don't cheek the teacher.'

'I will try.' She looked around her, at the tall buildings of the Castellana, the high blue Madrid sky. 'It seems so strange, in a couple of weeks we shall be so far away.'

'You'll find England odd at first. You'll have to get used to how formal we are, how we don't speak our minds.'

'You do.'

'I do to you. Well, there's the embassy. See the flag?'

He signed her in and waited with her till the lawyer appeared. A bluff friendly man, he introduced himself and shook their hands before leading Sofia away. As Harry watched them go another door opened and Weaver appeared.

'Hello, Brett, not coming to the Spanish Academy do? Better buck up or we'll be late.'

'I'm on standby.'

'Oh yes, I forgot. So many parties this time of year. You've got tomorrow off, haven't you?'

'Yes. I've booked a car, going for a spin in the country.'

'Bit cold for that, isn't it? Oh well, have a good time. See you next week.'

Tolhurst was at his desk, a pile of files beside him. Sheets of paper were covered in calculations in his neat round hand.

'Agents' expenses?'

'Yes, have to get these all done before Christmas. Are you coming to the American embassy reception tomorrow? Should be a good do.'

'No, I've got the day off. Taking Sofia out for a ride in the country.' Harry felt a spark of the old affection for him. 'Listen, Tolly, about the wedding. I'm grateful for your help.'

'Oh, that's all right.'

'I'm sorry things didn't work out with Forsyth.'

Tolhurst folded his hands over his plump stomach. He was getting fatter.

'Oh well, at least we know they've no gold.'

'Any more news on that?' Harry asked diffidently.

'According to the captain, Sam was thinking of telling Maestre the mine was a fake. He'll know how far we've been involved, but at least he'll have been given some information he could use. Let the Falangists make fools of themselves.'

'I see.' Harry didn't care any more.

He smiled at Harry. 'You're off soon, I hear.'

'Yes, after the wedding.'

Tolhurst looked at him for a moment. 'Got a best man?' he asked.

'We're asking Sofia's brother.' Harry realized Tolhurst had been hoping to be asked. Tolhurst, his watcher. Harry was grateful for what he had done over the wedding but he hadn't even considered that.

'Are you going back to England for Christmas?' he asked to change the subject.

'No,' Tolhurst replied huffily. 'Staying on duty. Sitting around in case any problems come up with our agents.' The telephone rang. Tolhurst picked it up and nodded. 'That's reception. They've finished with your girly. She says everything's OK and she's waiting for you downstairs.'

'I'll get off then.'

He looked at Harry. 'By the way, have you seen anything of Miss Clare? Forsyth's girl?'

'I met her for coffee yesterday,' Harry said carefully.

'Forsyth seems to have cleared out properly. I suppose the woman will go back to England now.'

There was a knock at the door and an elderly, frockcoated secretary came in. He looked anxious. He peered at Harry though gold pince-nez. 'Are you Brett?'

'Yes.'

'The ambassador would like to see you in his office.'

'What? What about?'

'If you could just come with me, sir. It is urgent.'

Harry glanced at Tolhurst but he only shrugged, looking puzzled.

Harry turned and followed the secretary down the corridor. He was on the verge of panic. Had they somehow found out about Cuenca?

The secretary ushered Harry into Hoare's office. He had not been inside the luxurious room since the day he arrived. The ambassador was standing behind his desk, dressed in a morning suit, his thin face pink with anger. He frowned at Harry.

'Is he the only one here?' he snapped at the secretary.

'Yes, ambassador.'

'I cannot *believe* all the translators were allowed to go to that reception.'

'Mr Weaver's just left, sir, he was the last. I've tried phoning the Spanish Academy but their phones are down.'

Hoare gave Harry an icy look. 'Well, you'll have to do, Brett. Why aren't you at the reception?'

'My fiancée's here, getting the documentation for our wedding.'

Hoare grunted. He waved the secretary irritably away. 'Where's your morning suit?' he snapped at Harry.

'At home.'

'Then you'll have to borrow one from here. Now listen. I've been trying to get an interview with the Generalísimo for weeks. He keeps me waiting, refuses to see me, while von Stohrer and the Italians are in and out of there every five minutes.' Hoare's voice was full of petulant anger. 'Then out of the blue I get a message he'll see me this morning. I must go, there are important matters to raise and I need to make my presence felt.' He paused. 'I read Spanish of course, but I'm not quite fluent.'

Harry wanted to laugh, with relief that it wasn't trouble and at Hoare's posturing; everyone knew he spoke barely a word of the language.

'Yes, sir.'

'So I'll need a translator. I'd like you ready in half an hour, please. We're driving out to El Pardo. You've translated for junior ministers, haven't you?'

'Yes, sir. And some of Franco's speeches.'

Hoare shook his head irritably. 'Don't refer to him like that. You mean *Generalísimo* Franco. He's the head of state.' He shook his head.

'This is why I needed an experienced man. Go and get ready.' He shooed Harry away, like a troublesome insect.

IT WAS A LONG drive out to the palace in the north of the city that Franco had appropriated as his residence. The car drove out into the countryside, the road following the Manzanares river as it flowed cold and grey between high wooded banks of skeletal trees. Sitting in the back with Hoare, Harry glanced up at the sky; it was still cloudless, icy blue. He hoped desperately there would be no more snow before tomorrow.

Harry had borrowed one of the spare morning suits they kept at the embassy and returned to Hoare's office, then walked with the ambassador to reception. Sofia, sitting waiting, looked at them with astonishment. He went over and explained quickly where he was going while Hoare glared at him impatiently. When he mentioned Franco's name, Sofia's mouth tightened. As they left the embassy he felt her eyes on them.

The ambassador sat riffling through a file, making notes with a black fountain pen. At length he turned to Harry.

'When you're translating make sure you convey the *exact sense* of my words. And don't look the Generalísimo in the eye, it's considered impertinent.'

'Yes, sir.'

Hoare grunted. 'There are photographs of Hitler and Mussolini on his desk. Don't stare, just ignore them.' Hoare ran a hand through his thin hair. 'I'm going to have to sound quite harsh about all the pro-Axis propaganda in the press. But you keep your voice formal, unemotional, like a butler. Understand?'

'Yes, sir.'

'If the Generalísimo was a reasonable man he'd be thanking me for the extra wheat I've persuaded Winston to let them have. But reasonable's the last thing he is. All this is sudden, very sudden.' Hoare produced a comb and smoothed down his hair.

Pictures passed through Harry's head: the woman foraging through dustbins, arrested when her dress blew over her head, the wild dogs attacking Enrique, Paco clinging to the old woman's corpse. Now he was actually going to meet the man who had created this new Spain.

The car came to a little village. It had been turned into a barracks, there were troops everywhere; the soldiers peered into the car as it ran alongside a high wall. The driver pulled up at a pair of tall iron gates guarded by soldiers with machine guns. He handed over their papers to be checked, then the gates were opened and they drove slowly through. The guards gave the car the Fascist salute.

El Pardo was a three-storey building of yellow stone surrounded by wide lawns, white with frost. Moroccan guards with lances stood by the flight of steps leading up to the entrance; one came down and opened the car door for them. From somewhere Harry heard the sad howling cry of a peacock. He shivered; it seemed even colder out here.

An aide in civilian clothes met them on the steps and led them through a series of rooms full of eighteenth-century furniture, opulent but dusty. Harry's heart began to beat faster. They came to a large door flanked by more Moorish guards, their brown faces impassive. One knocked on the door and the aide ushered them in.

Franco's office was large, full of dark heavy furniture that made it gloomy despite the sunlight coming through the tall windows. The walls were lined with heavy ancient tapestries showing medieval battle scenes. The Generalísimo stood in front of a large desk, the photographs of Hitler and Mussolini prominent alongside, to Harry's surprise, one of the Pope. Franco wore a general's uniform with a broad red sash round his plump middle. His sallow face had a haughty expression. Harry had been expecting presence but Franco had none; with his balding head, double chin and little greying moustache, he reminded Harry of what Sandy had said that first day in the Café Rocinante: he looked like a bank manager. And he was short, tiny. Lowering his eyes as instructed, Harry saw the Generalísimo wore built-up shoes.

'Generalísimo, *buenos dias*.' Hoare said. He knew that much Spanish at least.

'*Excelencia*.' Franco's voice was high pitched and squeaky. He shook Hoare's hand, ignoring Harry. The aide took up a position beside Franco.

'You requested a meeting, *excelencia*,' Franco said softly.

'I am glad to be able to see you at last,' Hoare said reprovingly. He wasn't intimidated, you had to give him that. 'His Majesty's Government has been very concerned by the support for the Axis in the newspapers. They are virtually inciting the Spanish people to war.'

Harry translated, concentrating on keeping his voice even and unemotional. Franco turned and stared at him then. His brown eyes were large and liquid but somehow blank. The Generalísimo turned back to Hoare with a shrug.

'I am not responsible for the press, your excellency. Surely you would not wish me to interfere with it?' He gave Hoare a wintry smile. 'Is that not the sort of thing the liberal powers criticize us for?'

'The press is controlled by state censorship, Generalísimo, as you well know. And a good deal of the copy comes from the German embassy.'

'I do not concern myself with the press. You should speak to the interior minister.'

'I certainly shall.' Hoare's sharp voice cut like a file. 'It is a matter my government regards most seriously.'

The Generalísimo shook his head, the wintry smile back again. 'Ah, excellency, it saddens me, these impediments to the friendship of our countries. If only you would make peace with Germany. Chancellor Hitler does not wish to see the destruction of the British Empire.'

'We shall never allow the Germans to dominate Europe,' Hoare replied abruptly.

'But they do, ambassador, they already do.' A big antique world globe stood nearby. Franco reached out a small, surprisingly delicate hand and turned it gently. 'The English are a proud people, I know, like we Spaniards. But realities have to be faced.' He shook his head again. 'Only two years ago, when he signed the Munich agreement, I thought your old friend Mr Chamberlain would join the Germans and turn against the real enemy, the Bolsheviks.' He sighed. 'But now it is too late.'

As Harry translated Hoare stiffened with anger. 'There is no point in discussing this further,' he snapped. 'Britain will *never* surrender.'

Franco drew himself up, his cold look reminding Harry of his expression on the coins. 'Then I fear you will be defeated,' he said.

'I wished to discuss the wheat imports,' Hoare said. 'Your government will need to apply for certificates to bring them through the blockade. We still control the seas,' he added waspishly. 'We need assurances none of the wheat will be re-exported to Germany, and that it will be paid for entirely by the Spanish government.'

Franco smiled again, a smile with genuine amusement. 'It will be. The Argentines have agreed to accept credit terms. After all, we have no gold reserves, and we are not a gold-producing country.' He turned slowly and looked at Harry, and though he smiled there was something in his eyes now that frightened Harry. 'I was talking about that only yesterday, with General Maestre,' the Generalísimo continued smoothly.

Oh God, Harry thought, he knows. Hoare told Maestre and Maestre's told him.

Hoare gave the Generalísimo a startled look.

'I do hope everything can proceed smoothly,' Franco went on. 'Otherwise – ' he shrugged again – 'we would not want to look on England as an enemy, but it is always a question of how a power *acts* in its relations with us. In its open dealings and its secret ones.' He raised his eyebrows at Hoare. The ambassador reddened. Harry wondered what Franco would have said if he had known about the Knights of St George. He gripped a table behind him for support.

In the car going back to Madrid, Hoare was furious. The meeting had gone on for another half hour. Hoare had discussed trade agreements and the rumours of lorry-loads of food being sent to France for the German army, but he had lost the initiative. Franco's manner had been that of an injured party dealing with an importunate negotiator.

'Wait till I see Hillgarth,' he snapped, glaring at Harry. 'I was humiliated in there, humiliated! That was why he called me in, to throw that bloody mine in my face. Just my bloody luck you were the only translator available. These adventures have got to stop! I've been made to look a fool!' Hoare was almost hissing, his thin features a mask of fury. Harry felt a drop of spittle land on his face.

'I'm sorry, sir.'

'Maestre must have told Franco everything, after Hillgarth told him it was all a racket. Maestre's made the Falange look stupid but he's made us look a damn sight worse.' Hoare took a deep breath. 'Just as well you're leaving soon. We must make sure the Generalísimo knows you've gone. Marrying some lower-class Spanish girl – I don't know how you think that'll help your future career, Brett. In fact, I should say *that* was pretty well finished,' the ambassador added spitefully. He turned away and opened his briefcase with a snap, pulling out a file. Harry stared out of the window as the first suburbs of Madrid flashed by. This time tomorrow they would be almost in Cuenca and a few days after that they would be away from here. To hell with you, Harry thought, to hell with you all.

Chapter Forty-Five

THERE WAS STILL SNOW high in the Tierra Muerta, but below the quarry most of it had melted during the brief spell of warmer weather that had turned the camp yard into a sea of mud.

Yesterday when they paused for their rest on the way to work, Agustín had sidled up to Bernie as he looked downhill towards Cuenca. 'Are you ready for tomorrow?' he whispered.

Bernie nodded.

'Pick up a sharp stone tomorrow morning, put it in your pocket.'

Bernie looked at him in surprise. 'Why?'

Agustín took a deep breath. He looked afraid. 'To hit me with. You should make a cut, draw blood, it will look more realistic.' Bernie nodded and bit his lip.

Lying his pallet in the hut that evening, Bernie massaged his shoulder, which was afire with pain after the day's work. His leg was stiff too; he hoped it didn't give way going down the mountain tomorrow. Down the mountain. It sounded incredible yet it was real. He looked at the bed opposite. Establo had died two nights before, in great pain, and the other prisoners had shared out his blankets. The Communists in the hut were sad, subdued.

When morning came he felt groggy. He got up and looked out of the window. It felt colder than ever but there was still no snow. His heart began thudding. He would do it. Carefully he exercised his stiff leg.

At breakfast he avoided the Communists' eyes. He felt shame again at leaving the other prisoners. But there was nothing he could do for them. If he got away he wondered whether they would cheer him or condemn him. If he got to England he would tell the world about the conditions here, he would shout it from the rooftops.

He lined up with the others in the muddy yard for roll-call. The undulating mud had frozen and was covered with white frost, like a frozen sea. Aranda took the roll. Sometimes since Bernie had refused to be an informer, Aranda's eye lighted on him at roll-call: he would pause for a moment and smile, as though he had something nasty in store. One day he would pick him out for something, but today wasn't the day; Aranda passed on to the next name. Bernie exhaled with relief. You've missed your chance, you bastard, he thought.

Father Eduardo emerged from the church, looking tired and miserable as he usually did these days. It struck Bernie that his dark red hair was almost the same shade as Barbara's. He had never noticed that before, but he had thought of her so much since he learned she was behind his escape plans. The priest went to the gate, raising his arm in response to the guard's Fascist salute as he let him through. He must be going into Cuenca. Neither of the priests had come for Establo. Perhaps they hadn't dared; Establo, unlike poor Vicente, had been a feared man.

Roll-call over, the quarry detail gathered in front of the gate. Agustín didn't look at Bernie. The gates opened and the crocodile made its way into the hills. At first the path climbed through brown grass, then fingers of snow appeared in the gullies and finally they rose above the snowline, the world white again. Agustín was walking some way ahead of Bernie; he wouldn't want anyone to remember them being together before the escape.

Bernie was put with a group breaking up large boulders. He had hoped to give himself an easy day to conserve his energy but it was so cold that if he stopped work he began shivering at once. Late in the morning he found a suitable stone to hit Agustín with; flat and round, with a jagged edge that would draw blood and make the blow look worse than it was. He slipped it in his pocket, pushing away a memory of Pablo on the cross.

At the short break for lunch he took as much of the chickpeas and rice as he could from the pot. In the afternoon as he worked he watched the sky. It remained cloudless. The sun began to set, casting a pink glow over the bare hillsides and the high white mountains to the east. Bernie's heart began pounding with anticipation. One way or another, this was the last time he would see that view.

At last he spotted Agustín, who had ensured he was guarding his section, moving closer. It was their signal that the time had arrived. Bernie took a deep breath and counted to three, preparing himself. Then he dropped his pick and clutched his stomach, crying out as though in pain. He bent double and cried out again, louder. The men he was working with stared at him. There were no other guards in sight. They were in luck.

'What is it, Bernardo?' Miguel asked.

Agustín unslung his rifle and approached.

'*¿Que pasa aquí?*' he demanded roughly.

'I've got diarrhoea. Agh, I can't hold it.'

'Don't do it here. I'll take you behind the bushes.' Agustín raised his voice. '*Dios mío*, why are you men so much trouble. Stand still so I can chain you.'

He can act, Bernie thought. Agustín put down his rifle and produced the shackles, a long thin chain with cuffs at the end, from the pouch at his belt. He secured Bernie's legs.

'Please, quickly!' Bernie held his face in an agonized rictus.

'Come on then!' Agustín picked up his rifle and waved him to walk ahead. They went quickly up the little track that wound around the hill. In a minute they were out of sight, by the bushes. Bernie panted with relief.

'We've done it,' he breathed. Agustín bent quickly and unlocked the shackles with trembling fingers. He threw the key to the ground. Then he put down his rifle and knelt in the snow. He looked up at Bernie, his eyes full of terrified appeal now he was at his mercy.

'You will not kill me, will you?' He swallowed. 'I have made no confession, I have sins on my conscience—'

'No. Just a knock on the head.' Bernie took the stone from his pocket and hefted it.

'Do it now,' Agustín said quickly. 'Now! Just not too hard.' He clenched his teeth and closed his eyes. For a second Bernie was irresolute, it was difficult to judge how hard to strike. Then he hit Agustín on the temple with the stone. Without a sound the guard rolled over and lay still. Bernie looked at him in surprise, he hadn't meant to knock him right out. A thin trickle of blood ran from a cut where the stone had struck. He knelt over the guard. He was still breathing.

He stood up and looked back along the path, then down the hillside. He considered taking Agustín's rifle but it would encumber him. He took a deep breath and began running downhill through the melting snow, terribly conscious of how his tattered brown coat and green boiler suit stood out. His back twitched, waiting for a bullet. It was like the Jarama, the same helpless fear.

He passed below the snowline and paused, looking back at the line of footprints he had left above. He had veered to the right and now he ran to the left, hoping the change of direction might fool the guards. There were folds in the hills both ways. It was frightening to be alone, running through this bare wilderness; unexpectedly Bernie had a frantic longing for the enclosing walls of the hut. Then he slipped on a patch of frosty grass and found himself rolling over and over, gasping and grunting. He bumped his shoulder and had to stifle a cry of pain.

He came to a stop at the bottom of the first fold in the hills and sat up, gasping for breath. He looked upwards. Nothing. Nobody. He smiled. He had got where he wanted much faster than he had intended. He got up and ran round the lee of the hill. As Agustín had said, a stand of the little holm oaks grew in a sheltered spot. He ran into the middle of the copse and lay down against a tree trunk, breathing in gasps. Well done, he thought. So far so good.

He sat listening but there were no sounds, nothing, just a silence that seemed to hum in his ears. It unsettled him, he hadn't experienced complete silence for over three years. He was tempted to run on, but Agustín was right, he should wait till dark before going any further. Molina would soon notice that Agustín and he were missing. He leaned back, wriggling his frozen toes. A little later he thought he heard a faint shout, far off, but it was not repeated.

A half moon rose and stars appeared. Bernie was surprised to see the stars really did come out one by one. When the sky was quite black, Bernie lifted himself up. Time to go. Then he froze. He had heard a rustling sound, a few yards away at the entrance to the clump of trees. Oh God, he thought, oh God. It came again, from the same spot. Gently, his teeth gritted, he parted the branches of a bush and peered out. A little deer stood cropping the coarse grass, a few feet away. It was very young; perhaps its mother had been shot by the guards. Now the snow had gone the deer would be climbing the mountain again to forage. Bernie felt suddenly moved; tears welled up in his eyes and he reached up to brush them away. The deer heard him; it jerked up its head, turned and shot away, crashing down the hill. Bernie held his breath, listening. If they were hunting him and were anywhere nearby, that sound would draw them. But the silence remained unbroken. He crept out of the bushes again. A cold wind was blowing. He crouched down, feeling terribly exposed again. Then he forced himself up and began loping down the hill once more. Seven kilometres to go. Four miles.

He was surprised how much he could see in the moonlight once his eyes became accustomed to it. He kept to the shadows, following the little trackways the shepherds had made, moving steadily downhill. He guessed it was nearly two hours since he had left Agustín but he had no way of telling. Down and down, pausing every so often to catch his breath and listen behind one of the little oaks that grew more frequently now. His shoulder hurt and his feet began to ache. It felt as though he had been running downhill forever, but his weak leg held out.

Then, cresting a little rise, he saw the lights of Cuenca straight ahead of him, startlingly close: yellow points from lit windows. One little group of lights was lower than the others: the hanging houses set into the cliff itself. He took a deep breath. He had been lucky to come out right opposite the town.

He moved more slowly now, hugging every piece of shadow. Clouds had appeared, scudding across the face of the moon, and he was grateful for the minutes of extra darkness they gave. He could make out the gorge now and the black struts of the iron bridge across it. It looked surprisingly fragile, the wooden walkway barely wide enough to take three people walking abreast. He saw there were actually only a few houses built into the cliff on the other side. They were much smaller than he had imagined.

The road that ran parallel to the gorge was visible a hundred yards below him. Bernie ducked behind a bush. No sign of anyone. The camp would already have phoned the *civiles*; perhaps they would be sending someone to guard the bridge. But it wasn't the only bridge, he remembered Agustín telling him, there were others further along, other ways into the town. If the main bridge was guarded Barbara would wait for him in the cathedral.

He heard voices and froze. Female voices. A group of four shawled, black-clad women appeared, accompanied by two donkeys laden with firewood. He watched as they passed beneath him; he couldn't make out their faces but the harsh voices sounded old. He hadn't seen a woman in three years. He remembered Barbara lying in his bed waiting for him and his heart pounded and warm saliva rose in his mouth. He swallowed it and took a deep breath.

The women and their donkeys passed on. They crossed the bridge and disappeared. Bernie left his shelter and looked down the road. Some way past the bridge he saw a large clump of trees beside the road. That must be the place. There was little cover; he would have to walk along the exposed hillside now, facing the town across the gorge. He left his shelter and began edging his way along, stopping at each little oak.

As he came out from behind a tree he heard a sound somewhere above him, like the chink of metal. He threw himself down, waiting for a shot. Nothing happened. He opened his eyes: there was only the bare hillside. A little way above him he made out another, larger oak, standing on its own. He thought the sound had come from there, but if it were a *civil* or a guard surely there would have been a shot by now. He went on, glancing constantly back at the tree, but heard nothing more. Perhaps it had been another deer or a goat.

He reached the trees and plunged in among them. There were thick bushes here too, stiff branches whipped at his legs.

He couldn't see the road from here but he must stay concealed. He would hear Barbara coming. She would know he was here. Barbara. He shivered, conscious of how cold he was now that he had stopped moving. And tired, his arms and legs were trembling. He rubbed his hands together and blew on them. He would have to put up with it. There was nothing to do now but wait; wait until Barbara came to save him.

Chapter Forty-Six

HARRY HAD WOKEN early that morning. The old humming was back in his ears for the first time in weeks, but as he lay there it faded away. Opening the curtains he saw the street was white and his heart sank for a moment. Damn, he thought, more snow. Then he realized it was only frost, thick white hoar frost on the pavements and roads. He blew out his cheeks with relief.

Sofia arrived at nine as arranged. He made breakfast for her. They were both subdued now the moment was here.

'Sleep well?' she asked.

'Not very. I've got the car, one of the old Fords. It's outside. You?'

'Good.'

'Did you get away all right?'

'Enrique is cross at having to stay home with Paco. I told him we were having a day out and he wanted to bring him.' She shook her head. 'I hate lying to them.'

He took her hand. 'No more lies after today. Come on, we should eat.' He carried plates of scrambled egg through to the *salón*.

'How is Barbara?' Sofia asked as they ate.

'All right.' The previous evening, after collecting the car from the embassy, Harry had driven round to Barbara's house. He had told her the news of the fake gold mine had reached Franco himself; it was likely the authorities would be hunting Sandy now.

There were footsteps on the stairs. They both tensed. 'I think it's her,' Harry said.

Barbara was carrying a large rucksack and her face was strained and pale.

'Sorry I'm a bit late,' she said breathlessly. 'Some people came at six, I was still in bed. A couple of *civiles* and someone from the government. I was terrified they'd found out about this. They wanted to know all about Sandy. I played the little woman, said I didn't know anything.' She sat down and lit a cigarette. 'Told them he'd walked out a couple of days ago. It was easy to take them in. They don't think women are capable of anything. They took everything away from his study, even his fossil collection. I almost felt sorry for him.'

Harry took a deep breath. 'He brought it all on himself, Barbara.' He found he felt nothing for Sandy any longer. He was just a blank.

'Yes.' Barbara nodded. 'Yes, he did.'

'We should go now if we have everything,' Sofia said. She went to her coat and pulled out a heavy German pistol, a Mauser. She held it out to Harry. 'You take it.'

'OK.' He checked it. It had been cleaned and oiled and the chambers were full. He slipped it in his pocket. Barbara shuddered slightly and looked at Sofia, who met her gaze evenly. Harry stood up. 'All right,' he said. 'Let's check over everything, then go.'

Outside it was so cold it hurt to breathe at first. They had to scrape frost from the windscreen of the Ford. Harry worried the engine wouldn't start but it leapt into life at once; the British embassy maintained their cars well. Barbara and Sofia got in the back and they set off along the Valencia road. They were quiet; the issue of the gun seemed still to be a barrier between them. After a while Sofia spoke.

'I have been thinking about what we should say if anyone asks why we have come to a remote town like Cuenca. We could tell them you are bringing me to find out about my uncle. That would be a reason for going to the cathedral too, to look at the list of priests killed during the war.'

'Do you think your uncle's name might be there?' Barbara asked.

'Yes, if he was killed.' Sofia turned her head away and in the mirror Harry saw her blink back tears. Yet she was still willing to use her family's tragedy to help them. He felt a choking sensation of love and admiration.

They drove all morning. In many places the road was in poor condition, slowing their progress. There was very little traffic and few towns; this was the dry heart of Castile. In the early afternoon the ground began to rise, steep hills breaking up the brown landscape. Frozen streams ran down the sides, thin slashes of white against the brown landscape. Key-cold, Harry thought, key-cold.

Towards three they saw a line of low mountains with rounded summits on the horizon. The countryside began to change; there were more cultivated areas, patches of bright green where the land was irrigated. A large town came into view in the distance, a jumble of grey-white buildings climbing a hillside so steep they seemed to be built one on top of another, up and up to the sky. They came to a sign telling them they were about to enter Cuenca and Barbara leaned over and touched Harry's arm. She pointed to a track leading from the road into an uncultivated field, winding behind a clump of trees that would screen the car from the road.

'That must be the place.'

Harry nodded and turned on to the track, the car bumping over frozen ruts. He halted behind the clump of trees. On the other side the meadow rose gently up to the horizon.

'What d'you think?' he asked.

'It'll be a long walk back,' Barbara said.

'We ought to follow Luis's advice. He said it was the nearest concealed spot.'

'All right.'

They opened the doors. Outside Harry felt suddenly vulnerable, exposed. A bitterly cold breeze ruffled their hair as they walked out to the road. Harry slung the rucksack with the clothes and food over his back. Sofia stood at the side of the road, looking towards Cuenca.

'I can't see the cathedral,' Harry said.

'It is at the very top of the hill. The gorge is behind it.'

'And the Tierra Muerta is on the other side of the gorge?' Barbara asked.

'Yes.' Sofia took a long breath, then began walking towards the town. The others followed her down the long empty road.

Only a couple of carts and a car passed them before they reached a bridge over a swirling grey-green river. By then the winter sun was low on the horizon. They walked through the poor shabby houses of the new town, past the railway station. There were few people around and no one paid them much heed. They kept an eye out for *civiles* patrolling the barrios but only a couple of mangy dogs challenged them, barking angrily but scurrying away at their approach. Their barking reminded Harry of the feral pack and he put his hand on the Mauser in his pocket for comfort.

Then they were climbing over worn cobbles into a soaring wilderness of stone, higher and higher as dusk began to fall. The narrow streets wound up and up: endless four- and five-storey tenements, centuries old, unpainted and with crumbling plaster. Each tenement block loomed over them, then they would climb to the next street and be looking down on the roofs. Weeds grew between cracked tiles, the only green things among all the stone. Thin wisps of smoke rose from the chimneys; there was a smell of woodsmoke and animal dung, stronger than in Madrid. Most windows were shuttered but occasionally they glimpsed faces peering at them, quickly withdrawn.

'How old are these buildings?' Harry asked Sofia.

'I don't know. Five hundred years, six. No one knows who built the hanging houses.'

In a little square halfway up the hillside they paused to let an old man lead his donkey past, the *burro* almost buried under a load of wood.

'*Gracias*.' He looked at them curiously. They paused for a moment to recover their breath.

'I remember all this,' Sofia said. 'I worried I might have forgotten the way.'

'It's very bleak,' Barbara said. The setting sun cast a cold glow on the street, turning the little piles of frozen snow in the gutters pink.

'Not for a child.' Sofia smiled sadly. 'It was exciting, all the steep streets.' She took Harry's arm and they climbed on.

The old Plaza Mayor crowned the summit of the hill, municipal buildings lining two sides. The third side was a sheer drop over a parapet to the street below, left unbuilt on to give a clear view of the cathedral that dominated the fourth side, its huge square facade solid and intimidating. A wide flight of steps rose to where a group of beggars sat huddled in the deep porch of an immense doorway. There was a bar next to the cathedral but it was closed; apart from the beggars the *plaza* was deserted.

They stood in the doorway of the bar, their eyes darting over the shuttered windows surrounding them. An old woman carrying an immense bundle of clothes on her head passed across the square, her receding footsteps echoing through the frosty dusk.

'Why is it so quiet?' Harry asked.

'This was always a quiet town. On a day like this people will be indoors, trying to keep warm.' Sofia looked at the sky. Clouds were spreading across the sky from the north.

'I think we should go into the cathedral.' Barbara looked at the door, brown and studded with nails, the beggars crouched beside it eyeing them silently. 'Get out of sight.'

Sofia nodded. 'You are right. We should try to find the watchman.' She led the way up the steps, shoulders hunched and hands thrust deep into the pockets of her old coat, past the beggars who stretched out their hands. She pushed the huge door and it slid open slowly.

The cathedral was vast, empty, lit with a cold yellowish light filtering through the stained-glass windows. Harry's breath made a fog in the air in front of him. Barbara stood by his side. 'There doesn't seem to be anyone here,' she whispered.

Sofia walked slowly on between the soaring pillars, towards the chancel where a huge altar screen, decorated in bright gold, stood behind high gates. She stood frowning up at the screen, a tiny figure in her old black coat. Harry went and put his arm round her.

'So much gold,' she whispered. 'The church has never had any shortage of gold.'

'Where's the watchman?' asked Barbara, who had walked up to them.

'Let's find him.' Sofia pulled away from Harry's side and continued down the nave. The others followed. The heavy rucksack dug into Harry's shoulders.

To the right a large stained-glass window let in the fading light. Underneath stood a confessional box, a tall narrow thing of dark wood. As they progressed up the cathedral the light grew dimmer. Harry started violently at the sight of a figure standing in a side chapel. Barbara clutched his arm.

'What is it?'

Looking closer, Harry saw it was a life-size tableau of the Last Supper. It was Judas that had made him start, a startlingly realistic Judas carved in the act of rising from the table. His face, turned slightly to the master he was about to betray, was brutally cold and calculating, his mouth half-open in a grim snarl. Beside him Christ in a white robe sat with his back to the nave.

'Hideous, isn't it?' Barbara whispered.

'Yes.' Harry looked at Sofia, a little ahead, her hands still driven so deeply into her pockets the shoulder seams of her coat threatened to part. She stopped, and as they drew level with her she turned and whispered to Harry. 'See, there he is, on that bench.'

A man was sitting beside a shrine to the Virgin, indistinct in the gloom. They approached him slowly. Then Harry heard a sharp gulp of indrawn breath from Sofia. She was looking at a large new plaque set into the wall. Candles were lit in niches beside it and a bunch of winter roses had been laid underneath. The inscription 'Fallen for the Church' stood out above a list of names.

'He is there,' Sofia said. 'My uncle.' Her shoulders sagged. Harry put his arm round her. She felt so small, so delicate.

She pulled away again. 'We must go to the watchman,' she said quietly.

The man rose from the bench as they approached. He was old, short and stocky, wearing an ancient greasy suit and threadbare shirt. He studied them with sharp blue eyes, his seamed face hostile and distrustful.

'You are from Luis, the brother of Agustín?' he asked Barbara.

'Yes. You are Francisco?'

'I was told to expect only one Englishwoman. Why are there three of you?'

'The arrangement changed. Luis knows.'

'Agustín said one.' His eyes darted anxiously between them.

'I have the money,' Harry said. 'So. Is it safe to wait, to bring our friend here?'

'It should be. There is no evening service today. It is cold, no one has been in this afternoon except Father Belmonte's sister.' He nodded briefly at the memorial. 'With flowers. He was one of those martyred for Spain,' he added pointedly. 'When priests were murdered and nuns raped for the pleasure of the Reds.'

So he's a Nationalist, Harry thought. 'We have the three hundred pesetas,' he said.

The old man held out a hand. 'Then give it to me.'

'When the man we came for is here.' Harry made his voice clipped, authoritative, an officer's voice. 'That was the arrangement.' He reached into his coat pocket and showed the old man the billfold, angling his body so he caught a glimpse of the gun as well. His eyes widened and he nodded.

'*Sí. Sí.*'

Harry looked at his watch. 'We are early. We will have to wait a little.'

'Wait then.' The watchman turned and shuffled back to his bench. He sat watching them.

'Can we trust him?' Barbara whispered. 'He's very hostile.'

'Of course he is,' Sofia replied sharply. 'He supports *them*. Do you think the church recruits Republicans?'

'Luis's brother must trust him,' Harry said. 'And he could be shot if this goes wrong.'

They went and sat on a bench that gave a view of both the watchman and the door. 'It's six ten,' Harry said. 'Sofia, how long does it take to get to the bridge from here?'

'Not long. Fifteen minutes. We should wait another quarter of an hour. I will take you – we go round the back of the cathedral and then we are at the gorge and the bridge.'

Barbara took a deep breath. 'Leave me there and come back, Sofia. He's expecting me to come alone.'

'I know.' Sofia leaned forward and squeezed Barbara's hand. 'It will be all right, everything will be all right.'

Barbara reddened at the unexpected gesture. 'Thanks. I'm sorry about your uncle, Sofia.'

She nodded sadly.

Harry thought of the old priest put up against a wall and shot. He wondered if similar pictures were going through Sofia's mind. He put his arm round her again.

'Sofia,' Barbara said quietly. 'I wanted to say – I'm so grateful to you, for coming here. Neither of you needed to do this.'

'I did,' Harry said. 'For Bernie.'

'I wish I could do more,' Sofia said with sudden fierceness. 'I wish there were barricades again, I would take a gun this time. They should not have won. Even my uncle would not have died if they had not started the war.' She turned to Barbara. 'Do I seem hard to you?'

Barbara sighed. 'No. It's difficult for someone like me sometimes, to realize all you've been through.'

Harry squeezed Sofia's hand. 'You try your best to be hard but you don't want to be, not really.'

'I have had no choice.'

'It will be different in England.'

They sat without speaking for a little while. Then Sofia slid Harry's sleeve up to see his watch. 'Six thirty,' she said. 'We should go.' She glanced at the watchman. 'You stay here, Harry, keep an eye on him. Give Barbara the rucksack.'

He didn't want to leave her. 'We should all go.'

'No. One of us should stay here.'

Harry released her hand and the two women stood up. Then, with his back to the watchman, he took out the gun.

'I think you should take it. In case of trouble. Not to shoot, just to threaten.' He held it out by the barrel but Sofia hesitated; she seemed reluctant to take it now. Barbara reached out and grasped it gingerly.

'I'll take it,' she said. She put it carefully in her pocket. Harry passed her the rucksack. She smiled wryly. 'Funny, it does give you a sense of security.' She took a deep breath. 'Come on, Sofia.'

The two women walked to the door. It creaked open and closed again behind them. Harry felt the separation from Sofia like a physical pain. He looked at the old man. He could feel his hostile eyes.

Chapter Forty-Seven

Outside it was almost dark. Barbara shifted the rucksack with the clothes and food inside to the centre of her back. It was heavy. The beggars had gone from the steps. Clouds hid the moon but the weak streetlights had come on. Sofia led the way into a narrow alley running along the side of the cathedral. It led to a broad street with the back of the cathedral on one side. On the other, beyond a stone parapet, the street fell away into a broad, deep canyon. Barbara looked across the chasm. She could just make out the outlines of hills against the sky, a white line of road running along the bottom. A little way ahead a footbridge supported on iron struts spanned the gorge.

'So that's it,' Barbara said.

'Yes. The bridge of San Pablo. There is nobody guarding it,' Sofia said eagerly. 'The authorities cannot know he has escaped yet.'

'If he has.'

Sofia pointed at the hills. 'See, that is the Tierra Muerta. He will come down from there.'

To her right Barbara saw lights shining from houses built right on the cliff edge, balconied windows hanging out over the yawning drop.

'The hanging houses,' Sofia said.

'Extraordinary.' Barbara tensed suddenly at the sound of heavy footsteps approaching from a side road. A man in a long black cloak appeared, a slash of white at the throat. A priest. He was young, about thirty, with glasses and a round gentle face under red hair almost the same shade as hers. His expression was preoccupied but he smiled when he saw them.

'*Buenas tardes, señoras*. It is late for a walk abroad.' Hell, Barbara thought. She knew priests could question women out in the streets, order them home. Sofia dropped her eyes demurely.

'We were just returning, *señor*.'

The priest looked at Barbara curiously. 'Forgive me, *señora*, but are you from abroad?'

Barbara put on a cheerful tone. 'I'm English, sir. My husband works in Madrid.' She was conscious of the heavy weight of the gun against her side.

'*¿Inglesa?*' He looked at her intently.

'Yes, *señor*. Have you been to England?'

'No.' He seemed about to say something more, then checked himself. 'It is getting dark,' he said gently, as though to a child. 'I think perhaps you should both be getting home.'

'We were about to go back.'

He turned to Sofia. 'Are you from Cuenca?'

'No.' She took a deep breath. 'I came to see the memorial in the cathedral. My friend brought me from Madrid. I had an uncle here, a priest.'

'Ah. He was martyred in 1936?'

'Yes.'

The priest nodded sadly. 'So many dead. My daughter, I can see from your face you feel bitter, but I think we must begin to forgive if Spain is to be renewed. There has been too much cruelty.'

'That is not a sentiment one hears much,' Sofia said.

The priest smiled sadly. 'No,' he agreed. There was a short silence, then he asked, conversationally, 'Where are you staying?'

Sofia hesitated. 'The convent of San Miguel.'

'Ah. So am I. Just for tonight. Perhaps I shall see you at dinner later. I am Father Eduardo Alierta.' He nodded to them and turned into the street leading to the cathedral. His footsteps died slowly away. The women looked at each other.

'We were lucky,' Sofia said. 'Some priests would have insisted on walking us back to the convent.'

'If he's going back there, he'll find they've never heard of us.'

Sofia shrugged. 'We will be gone by dinner-time.'

'He seemed sad. Most priests look stern to me, but he looked sad.'

'The whole of Spain is sad,' Sofia said. 'Come on.'

As they walked up to the bridge Barbara's heart began pounding. Her mouth was dry. Images of Bernie filled her mind, Bernie as he had been. What would he be like now? She took hold of the metal strut at the end of the bridge and looked down at the walkway; wooden boards laid across iron meshwork. The far end of the bridge was a vague outline in the darkness.

'You get back to Harry,' she said to Sofia. 'I'll be back inside an hour, I hope.'

'All right.' Sofia hugged her quickly. 'It will go well, you'll see. Tell the *brigadista* a friendly Spaniard is waiting to meet him.'

'I will.'

Sofia kissed her quickly on the cheek, then turned and walked back along the path. She glanced back once, then disappeared down the alleyway the priest had taken.

Barbara stood alone in the silent empty street. A pulse of excitement juddered at her throat. She stepped forward and took the handrail. The metal was cold. With her other hand she gripped the gun in her pocket. Be careful, she told herself. Don't press the bloody trigger and shoot yourself in the leg. Not now. She stepped on to the bridge, moving slowly in case there was ice on the planks. Still she could not see the other side, only the bulk of the hill, a shade darker than the sky. She started walking. A light breeze, bitterly cold, ran down the river valley. Everything was silent, there was no sound from the river far below; looking down she could see only blackness, blackness underneath and all around the narrow iron bridge. For a moment her head spun with vertigo.

Pull yourself together! She took a couple of deep breaths and pressed on. She felt something cold on her cheek and realized it had started to snow lightly.

Then she heard footsteps, crossing the bridge from the other direction. She caught her breath. Could it be Bernie? Could he have seen her and Sofia from the other side and decided to cross and meet her? No, surely he would stay hidden till he could get rid of his prison clothes; it must be someone from the town.

The footsteps came closer; she could feel little reverberations through the wooden planks now. She walked on, gripping the rail hard, trying to force her face into a relaxed expression.

A tall male figure appeared, dressed in a heavy coat. He was walking down the centre of the bridge, not touching the handrail.

Gradually she made out his face, saw the eyes staring fixedly at her. Her heart stopped for a second before thumping back into life.

Sandy stopped ten feet from her, in the middle of the walkway, one hand in his coat pocket and the other clenched in a fist at his side. He had shaved off his moustache and his face looked different, puffy and yellowish. He smiled, his old broad smile.

'Hello, lovey,' he said. 'Surprised to see me? Expecting someone else?'

INSIDE THE CATHEDRAL the old man stood up and shuffled over to a switch on the wall. A loud click made Harry jump as an electric light came on above the altar, the white sodium glow bleaching the screen of its gold colour. He watched the old man trail back to his seat. He wished he had the gun, he had got used to its comforting feel. Like in the war. A picture of the beach at Dunkirk appeared in his mind, a vivid flash.

He stood and paced up and down to warm himself a little. If only Sofia would hurry, surely she should be back by now. It had been hard for her, finding her uncle's name on the memorial.

He spun round at a creak from the door. It wasn't Sofia, it was a tall red-haired priest who stood there. Harry dropped to the nearest bench, clasping his hands together and lowering his head as though praying. Between his fingers he watched as the priest walked over to the altar and knelt before it. He crossed himself then walked over to Francisco. The old man rose from his bench, looking flustered. Harry clenched his hands together. What if the old man panicked, betrayed them?

'*Buenas tardes, señor*,' the priest said quietly. 'I am visiting the town, staying at the convent for two nights. I would like to pray here for a little while.'

'Of course, *señor*.'

'It is quiet tonight.'

'There are few visitors in this weather.'

'Ay, it is cold. But not too cold to pray.'

The priest walked over to the seats and took one a few rows ahead of Harry. He seemed preoccupied and appeared not to have noticed the other penitent in the gloom. Francisco sat down again.

His eyes darted between Harry and the priest, who had got down on his knees, burying his face in his hands.

The door opened again. Harry shot a glance at the priest but he went on praying as Sofia came in. Harry leaned round and pointed at the priest. To his surprise Sofia slipped quickly over to the ugly confessional box under the window and flattened herself against its side, concealing herself. Harry stood up, puzzled. His knee banged against the bench and he set his teeth at the noise and the sharp pain. He crossed to the confessional, trying to keep his echoing footsteps to a slow measured pace: the priest would surely look up if he heard anyone running in here. But still the priest knelt, praying.

'What is it?' he whispered anxiously. 'Is Barbara safe?'

'Yes. I left her at the bridge. But that red-haired priest, we met him. I told him we were staying at the convent, going straight back there. He mustn't see me here with you. And when Barbara comes with Bernie—'

'I'll have to get the old man to get rid of him.'

Sofia shook her head rapidly, a frightened gesture. 'He won't tell a priest to leave the cathedral.'

'He must.' Harry squeezed her arm and walked steadily down the nave to where Francisco stood.

Barbara stood stock still, clutching the cold rail.

'Cat got your tongue?' Sandy jeered. He smiled again, enjoying her astonishment. 'Remember that call you had from the prison guard? I was listening in; I picked up the phone at the same time.' His tone was mild, conversational. 'Afterwards I opened that bureau of yours, saw all the details you had in there. The map with the bushes by the bridge marked.'

'But how did you open it?'

'I kept a key to the bureau when I bought it.' He smiled. 'I always keep a duplicate key for everything I buy with a lock. Especially if it's for someone else. Old habit.'

Barbara said nothing, just stood looking at him, her breath coming in sharp stabs.

'How long have you known Piper was alive?' he asked. 'How long have you been planning this?'

'A couple of months,' she replied quietly. She studied his face. What was he going to do? His eyes were furious. Despite the cold there was sweat on his brow.

A muscle twitched in his cheek. 'Was Brett in this too?'

'No.' Bernie didn't know Harry was here. She looked at the hand Sandy kept in his pocket. There was a bulge there. Did he have a gun too?

'They've been to the house for you,' she said. Her heart was pounding; it was hard to keep her voice steady, but she must. 'The police. They took everything from your office.'

'Yes, I thought they would have by now. I've got a passport that'll see me onto a ship at Valencia. Belonged to one of the French Jews but it's got my face on it now. I thought I'd just stop off here on the way.'

She gripped the gun, working her fingers so they held the trigger. 'Where's Pilar?' she asked. Her voice was steadier now.

'Gone. I paid her off. She was just a little diversion. Nothing important, like the way you *betrayed* me.' He hissed the word with sudden fury, then took a deep breath and continued in his bantering tone. 'Well, the worm turned into a dragon all right. And to think I made you. I should have left you to rot in Burgos.'

She didn't reply, just stood looking at him. He glanced back along the bridge.

'He's over there,' he said, 'waiting in some trees up the road. I saw him. I've been behind a tree up there, waiting. I was going to kill him. I wanted you to find him dead. But he heard me lighting a ciggy behind a tree and that put him on the alert, so I came here instead. After all, nothing's more dangerous than a cornered man. I shouldn't think he can see us at this end of the bridge.' Sandy inclined his head towards his pocket. 'I've got a gun, by the way.'

Barbara could just make out the clump of trees a few hundred yards up the road. Was Bernie really there? 'Why, Sandy?' she asked. 'I mean, what's – what's the point now? It's all over.'

Sandy's voice was still low but it had turned cold. 'He used to treat me like a piece of dirt at school, like my bloody father. He tried to keep Harry from me. And now he's got you to betray me and get him out of prison. Well, I'll have my revenge.' He smiled again; a strange smile, almost childish. 'I like revenge; it's real.'

She stepped back involuntarily. There was something wild now, deranged, in his voice.

'Don't bloody look like that,' he said. 'Have I done anything worse than what Piper and all the other ideologues did to Spain? Eh? Have I?'

'Bernie didn't get me to do this, Sandy, it was my idea. He didn't even know until a little while ago.'

'I've still been betrayed,' he said. 'But I won't let it happen again. I won't be just cast out, discarded. If that's my fate, I'll fight it to the end. I will.' His dark eyes were wild, bulging. She didn't reply. They stood facing each other for a moment, the occasional snowflake drifting down. Sandy took a deep breath, closed his eyes for a second, and when he spoke his tone was conversational again.

'How did you get here? Train?'

'Yes.' He didn't know Harry and Sofia were here, he thought she was alone. But they couldn't help her in the cathedral.

'I suppose you've got a change of clothes for him in that rucksack.'

'Yes.'

'Well, I'll tell you what you can do. You can turn round and go back the way you came. Go back to England. Then I'll deal with him.' He nodded at his pocket. 'I'd like to kill you too but a shot from here might be heard.' He leaned forward then, his face working. 'Just don't ever forget, for the rest of the life I'm letting you have, don't forget *I won*.' He almost hissed the words; he sounded silly, like a child. He gestured with the thing in his pocket. 'Now, turn round and start walking.'

She released her hold on the rail, took a deep breath.

'Go on.' His voice rose. 'Now. Or I will shoot you, damn it. Three years I spent building you up from nothing so you could betray me. Bitch. Turn round, start walking.'

Barbara put her hand in her pocket and drew out the Mauser. She took it in both hands and thrust out her arms, slipping the safety catch as she levelled it at his chest.

'Throw your gun over the bridge, Sandy.' She was surprised how clear her voice was. She spread her legs, concentrating on her balance. 'Do it. Do it now or I'll kill you.' As she spoke she knew she could if she had to.

Sandy stepped back a pace. He looked astonished. 'You – you've a gun?'

'Take yours out of your pocket, Sandy. Slowly.'

He clenched his fists. 'Bitch.'

'Throw your gun off the bridge!'

Sandy looked into her eyes, then pulled his hand slowly from his pocket. She thought, what if he whips it out and shoots me. But she would get her shot in first. He wouldn't get Bernie, he wouldn't.

Sandy pulled out a large stone. He looked at it, then smiled at her and shrugged. 'There wasn't time to get a gun. I was going to brain Piper with this.' He dropped the stone on to the bridge. It bounced and went over the side, disappearing into the void. There was no sound of it hitting the water, it was too far.

Barbara ran her eyes quickly over his other pockets. 'Put your hands on your head,' she said.

Sandy's face darkened again, but he did as she ordered. 'What are you going to do?' he asked. There was fear in his voice now, something she had never heard before. She was glad; he realized she meant it. She thought quickly.

'We're going back across the bridge. To Bernie.'

'No.' His face seemed to crumple. 'Not like this.'

She jerked the gun up, towards his face. 'Turn round.'

He flinched. 'All right.' He turned and began slowly walking back the way he had come. Barbara followed, an arm's length away in case he made a sudden grab for her. They walked to the end of the bridge and stepped on to the grass verge by the road. The snow had stopped and the moon appeared from behind the clouds.

'Stop,' she said. Sandy halted. He looked ridiculous standing there with his hands on his head. She had to think what to do now. She turned to stare at the clump of trees. Can Bernie see us? she thought. What are we going to do with Sandy? She knew she couldn't shoot him in cold blood, but Bernie might.

Then she heard a patter of feet. She turned and saw Sandy running across the road. He had moved like lightning, the moment she had looked away.

'Stop!'

He began zigzagging from side to side. She tried to aim but it was impossible. She remembered what he had said earlier, a shot would echo all over the place. She lowered the gun as Sandy reached the other side of the road and began running up the hill, still twisting and turning. He disappeared among the trees. She heard the creak and rustle of branches.

She lowered the gun. Let him go, she thought, don't risk a shot. He hadn't a weapon and he wasn't in a position to go into town and tell the authorities about her – they were looking for him too.

She walked quickly up the road, glancing continually up at the hillside, feeling alone and exposed. She looked across the gorge at the lights of the town, making out the dark bulk of the cathedral where Harry and Sofia would be waiting.

She found the clump of trees. It was dark and silent. Had Sandy been lying, was Bernie really there? She stood looking up at the bank for a moment, then began to climb. She realized she was still carrying the gun and slipped it into her pocket. Her feet slipped on the frosty grass. She looked back at the road and the bridge, both still deserted. She wondered how she had known to say those things, hands up and hands on your head? A decade of talkies, she supposed, everybody knew such things now.

'Bernie,' she called into the trees in a loud whisper. There was no reply.

'Bernie,' she called again, louder.

There was a sound of branches moving from inside the copse. She tensed and took hold of the gun again as a man appeared. Barbara saw a gaunt shape in a ragged old coat, a beard and an old man's limp. She thought it was some tramp and reached for the gun again.

'Barbara.' She heard him cry out, heard his voice for the first time in more than three years. He stepped forward. She opened her arms and he fell into them.

THE OLD MAN Francisco had taken out a rosary and was turning it over and over in fretful hands. Harry bent over him, putting his lips to the old man's hairy ear.

'You must get the priest to leave. He saw my friends outside. They said they were going to the convent. If they come back and he sees them, there will be questions.'

'I cannot ask a priest praying to Our Lord to leave the cathedral,' Francisco whispered furiously.

'You must.' Harry stared into his eyes. 'Or there will be danger for us all. And no money.'

Francisco ran a callused hand over the stubble on his cheeks. '*Mierda*,' he breathed. 'Why did I agree to this?'

The priest's muttering had stopped. He had lifted his face from his hands and knelt looking at them. He couldn't have heard their whispered words but the urgency in Harry's tone might have carried. Hell, he thought, bloody hell. He whispered again.

'He's not praying now. Tell him there's a family emergency and you have to lock the cathedral up for a while.'

The priest rose and came over to them, black cloak swishing round his legs. Francisco stood up. The priest smiled gently at him.

'Are you all right, *viejo*?'

'I am afraid his wife has been taken ill,' Harry said. He tried to make his accent sound more Spanish. 'I am a doctor. It would be a great favour, sir, if he could close the cathedral and go home to her. I can fetch the other watchman.'

The priest gave him a keen look. Harry wondered how easy it would be to overpower him. He was young but flabby-looking.

'Where are you from, *doctor*? I do not recognize your accent.'

'Catalunya, *señor*. I fetched up here after the war.'

Francisco gestured at Harry. 'Father, he has, he has—' But he couldn't continue. He bowed his head.

'If you like I can stay while you fetch the other man,' the priest said.

Francisco swallowed. 'Please, *señor*, the rules say the cathedral must be closed if there is no watchman here.'

'It is best if we close the cathedral,' Harry said. 'I will take Francisco home; the dean's house is on the way and I can fetch the other man.'

The priest nodded. 'Very well. I should be back at the convent anyway. What is your wife's name?'

'Maria, *señor*.'

'Very well.' He turned away. 'I will pray to the Virgin for her recovery.'

'Yes. Pray for us.' The old man broke down then, dissolving into floods of tears and burying his face in his hands. Harry nodded to the priest.

'I'll take care of him, *señor*.'

'*Vaya con Dios, viejo*.'

'*Vaya con Dios, señor*.' The watchman's reply was a shamed mumble. The priest touched his shoulder. Then at last he walked away, down the nave and out of the church.

Francisco wiped his face but did not look at Harry. 'You have shamed me. *Cabrón rojo*. You have shamed me in this holy place.'

Bernie and Barbara held each other tightly. She felt the rough material of his coat, like sacking, smelt his sickly odour, but the warm body underneath was his, his. 'Bernie, Bernie,' she said.

He pulled away, looked at her. His face was thin, seamed with dirt, his beard unkempt.

'My God,' he said. 'How did you do this?'

'I had to, I had to find you.' She took a deep breath. 'But listen, we have to go.' She looked up at the hill. 'Sandy was here earlier.'

'*Forsyth?* He knows?'

'Yes.' Quickly she explained what had happened. His eyes widened when she told him Harry was in the cathedral with his Spanish fiancée.

'Harry and Sandy.' He laughed incredulously, shook his head. 'And Sandy's out there somewhere.' He looked up at the hill. 'He sounds mad.'

'He's gone. He won't come back while I've got a gun.'

'You with a gun.' He shook his head. 'Oh, Barbara, what you've done for me.' His voice broke with emotion. Barbara took a deep breath. She had to be practical now, practical. Sandy was gone but there were so many other dangers.

'I've got some clothes here. You should change and shave off your beard. No, there's not enough light for that, we'll have to do that at the cathedral. But change.'

'Yes.' He took her hands. 'God, you've thought of everything.' He studied her in the gloom. 'How different you look.'

'So do you.'

'The clothes. And you're wearing perfume. You never used to do that. It smells so strange.'

She bent and started unpacking the rucksack. It was hard to see among the trees, she should have brought a torch. 'I've got a warm coat in here.'

'Did you come through the town?'

'Yes. It was very quiet.'

'The camp should have radioed to the *civiles* by now.'

'We didn't see any.'

'Have you a car?'

'Yes. One with diplomatic number plates. Harry's car. It's hidden outside the town, we're going to drive you back to the embassy. They'll have to take you in.'

'Won't Harry get into trouble?'

'They won't know he was involved. We'll leave you outside and you can say you stole the clothes, broke into a house or something, then hitch-hiked.'

Bernie looked at her, then suddenly burst into tears. 'Oh, Barbara, I thought I was finished, then I heard you were going to save me. And I abandoned you to go back to the war. Barbara, I'm so sorry—'

'No. No. Look, darling, come on. Someone might come. You have to change.'

'All right.'

Bernie began undressing, grunting painfully as he took off the shirt he had worn for days, stuck to his body with dirt. In the gloom Barbara caught glimpses of scars, of the physique she had loved reduced to skin and bone.

A few minutes later he stood before her dressed in Sandy's suit, coat and trilby that she'd brought from home, crushed from the rucksack but making him look plausibly normal except for his dirty tramp's face and beard. She pulled at a couple of creases. 'There,' she said softly. She had a sudden wild desire to laugh. 'You'll do.'

THE HALF HOUR after the priest left was the longest in Harry's life. He and Sofia paced about uneasily, looking between the door and the old man. They had had a narrow escape with the priest. And they were on the verge of happiness, he and Sofia and perhaps Paco too.

Let nothing else go wrong, he prayed to the God he didn't believe in, nothing else.

At last the door opened again. Harry and Sofia tensed. The old man stared too, fearfully, as Bernie and Barbara came slowly in, Barbara supporting Bernie who was limping with exhaustion. At first Harry didn't recognize the gaunt, bearded figure, then he ran over to them, Sofia following behind.

'Bernie,' he said quietly. 'Christ, you look as if you've been through it.'

Bernie laughed incredulously. 'Harry. It is you.' He kept blinking rapidly, as though this new world where he found himself was too much to take in. 'Jesus, I couldn't bloody believe it.'

Harry felt his face working with emotion at the sight of the scarecrow face. 'What the hell have you been up to? Look at the state of you. Rookwood would have something to say.'

Bernie bit his lip. Harry could see he was close to tears. 'Been fighting a war, Harry.' He leaned forward and hugged him in the Spanish way. Harry allowed himself to relax into the embrace and they held each other tightly for a moment before Harry pulled apart, embarrassed. Bernie swayed a little.

'Are you all right?' Sofia asked anxiously.

'I'd better sit down.' Bernie smiled at her. 'You must be Sofia.'

'Yes.'

'*Viva la República*,' he said softly.

'*Viva la República*.'

'Are you a Communist?' he asked her.

'No.' She looked at him seriously. 'I did not like the things the Communists did.'

'We thought they were necessary.' He sighed.

Barbara took his arm. 'Come on, you have to shave. Go to the font. Go on.' She handed Bernie a shaving bag and he limped down to the font. Harry went over to the old man. Francisco glared up at him, his face smeared from his tears. Harry handed him the roll of notes. 'Your money, *señor*.'

Francisco crushed them in his fist in an angry gesture. Harry thought he was going to throw them to the floor but he slipped them in his pocket and slumped against the wall. Bernie reappeared, his face still a little stubbly, older and much thinner and marked with deep lines but now recognizably Bernie.

'I must sit down,' he said. 'I'm bloody shattered.'

'Yes, of course.' Barbara turned to the others. 'He's very tired, but we have to get away as soon as possible.'

'Did something happen?' Sofia asked, the sharpness in her voice making Harry look up. Barbara told them about Sandy.

'Jesus Christ,' Harry said. 'He's gone over the edge. Mad.'

'Half mad anyway, with anger.'

'We should go as soon as we can,' Sofia said. 'I am worried about the priest telling them at the convent that the cathedral is closed, them sending someone to the old man's house.'

'Yes.' Harry glanced over to where Francisco sat looking at them stonily, then put his hand on Bernie's shoulder. 'The car's a few miles away. Outside the town. D'you think you can make it? It's all downhill.'

He nodded. 'I'll try. Yes. If we go slowly.'

'You look human again.'

'Thanks.' He looked up. 'Is it true England's still holding out?'

'Yes. The bombing's bad but we're holding on. Bernie, we ought to go,' Barbara said.

'All right.' Bernie stood, wincing as he rose. He's completely exhausted, Harry thought, burnt out.

'What were you saying about a priest?' Bernie asked.

'Sofia and Barbara met him on their way to the bridge. Then he came into the church to pray, but I managed to get the watchman to get rid of him. It was a nasty moment; I'll see him kneeling there praying for the rest of my life I think, his black *sotana* and red hair.'

'Red hair?' Bernie thought a moment. 'What was he like?'

'Young, tall. Fattish.'

He took a deep breath. 'God, that sounds like Father Eduardo. He's one of the priests at the camp.'

'Yes, that was his name,' Barbara said. 'Good lord. He didn't seem the type.'

'He isn't, he's a sort of holy innocent or something.' Bernie set his lips. 'But if he finds us here we're done for. He'd still report us.' He took a deep breath. 'Come on. Let's go.'

Harry took the empty rucksack and they headed for the door. He felt an overwhelming relief at leaving the building. He looked back at the old man; he still sat on his bench, his head in his hands, a tiny figure among all the gigantic monuments to faith.

Chapter Forty-Eight

THEIR PROGRESS back down the steep, badly lit streets was slow. Bernie felt exhausted. The few people they passed turned to look at them; Bernie wondered whether with his unsteady gait they thought he was drunk. He felt drunk, intoxicated with amazement and happiness.

He had wondered how he would feel seeing Barbara after so long. It was a tougher, more sophisticated woman who had appeared on the cold hillside but it was still Barbara, he could see that all the things he had loved were still there. It felt as though it was only yesterday he had last seen her, that the Jarama and the last three years were all a dream. But the pain in his shoulder was all too real, while his feet, which had swollen into every crevice of his cracked broken boots, were an agony.

Halfway down the long hill they came to a little square with a stone bench under a statue of a general. 'Can I sit down?' Bernie whispered to Barbara. 'Just for a minute?'

Sofia turned and looked at them seriously. 'Can you not go on?' She glanced nervously at a bar on one side of the square. The windows were lit and voices came from within.

'Just five minutes?' Barbara pleaded.

Bernie slumped on to the bench. Barbara sat beside him and the other two stood a few paces off. Like guardian angels, Bernie thought. 'I'm sorry,' he said quietly. 'I just feel a bit dizzy. I'll be all right in a minute.'

Barbara put her hand on his forehead. 'You're a bit feverish,' she said. She took out her cigarettes and offered him one.

He laughed. 'A proper cigarette. Gold Flake.'

'Sandy used to get them.'

He held her hand, looked into her face. 'I tried to forget you,' he said. 'In the camp.'

'Did you manage it?' she asked with forced lightness.

'No. You have to try and forget the good things or they just torment you. But they keep coming back. Like the glimpses of the hanging houses. We used to see them sometimes on the way to the quarry. Hanging above the mist. It was a sort of mirage. They looked so small when we passed them earlier.'

'I'm sorry about Sandy,' she said. 'Only – when I thought you were dead I was so broken up. And he was kind at first, he seemed kind.'

'I should never have left you.' He gripped her hand tight. 'When Agustín told me it was you arranging the escape, when he said your name, that was the best moment, the best.' He felt a rush of emotion. 'I'll never leave you again.'

The bar door opened, letting out a smell of stale wine and cigarette smoke. Two labourers came out and walked up the hill, glancing in surprise at the quartet by the fountain. Harry and Sofia came over.

'We mustn't stay here,' Harry said. 'Can you go on?'

Bernie nodded. When he stood up it was as though he put his feet in fire; but he made himself ignore it, they were nearly there.

They walked slowly on, saying little. Bernie found that despite the pain from his feet he seemed to notice everything with newly heightened senses: the sound of a dog barking, the sight of a tall tree looming up in the darkness, the smell of Barbara's perfume; all the thousand and one things that had been kept from him since 1937.

They cleared the town, crossed the river, then walked down the long empty road to the field where the car was. It began to snow again, not heavily, little flakes that made a tiny pit-pit noise in the silence as they landed on the grass. His new clothes kept Bernie warm, their unfamiliar softness another new sensation.

'We're nearly there,' Barbara whispered at length. 'The car's behind those trees.'

They turned through the gateway and on to the rutted track, Bernie gritting his teeth as his boots slipped on the uneven surface. Harry and Sofia walked a little ahead, Barbara was still at Bernie's side. He saw the dim shape of a car ahead.

'I'll drive,' Barbara told Harry.

'Are you sure?'

'Yes. You drove us out. Bernie, if you go in the back you can stretch your legs out.'

'All right.' He leaned against the cold metal of the Ford as Barbara opened the driver's door. She threw in the rucksack and slid into the passenger seat, pulling the catches that unlocked the other doors. Harry opened a rear door, smiling the old solid reassuring smile. 'Your car, sir,' he said. Bernie squeezed his arm.

Then Sofia raised a hand. 'I heard something,' she whispered. 'In the trees.'

'It'll be a deer,' Bernie said, remembering the one that had disturbed him in his hiding place.

'Wait.' Sofia stepped away from the car and walked slowly over to the stand of holm oaks. They sent long black shadows over the grass. The others watched her. She stopped and squinted into the branches.

'I can't hear anything,' Bernie whispered. He glanced into the car. Barbara was looking over her shoulder at them questioningly.

'Come on,' Harry called out.

'Yes, all right.' Then Sofia turned away.

A searchlight beam lanced from the trees. The crashing rattle of a machine gun spat from the copse and Bernie saw little branches flying into the air as Sofia, caught in the searchlight, jumped and jerked as bullets tore into her. Gouts of blood flew from her small form as it crashed over and hit the ground.

Harry began running to her but Bernie grabbed his arm and with a strength he didn't know he had left threw him against the side of the car. Harry struggled for a second, then froze as two *civiles* stepped from the trees, their black bicorn hats glinting in the searchlight. One, an older man with a hard-bitten face, pointed a heavy sub-machine gun at them with a cold, unemotional expression. The other, who was young and scared-looking, held a revolver.

Bernie found himself unable to breathe. He gasped as he tried to suck in air, still holding Harry by the shoulders. The older *civil* went and prodded Sofia's head with his foot, grunting with satisfaction as it lolled back lifeless. Harry tried to move again but still Bernie held him, though it hurt his shoulder.

'It's too late,' he said.

He turned to look into the car. Barbara was still leaning over the seat watching, her expression terrified. The *civiles* stood at a little distance, covering them, as two men in army uniform stepped into the open. One was Aranda, a smile on his handsome face. The other was thinner, older, thin strands of black hair combed across his bald head, grim satisfaction on his craggy face.

'Maestre,' Harry said. 'Dear God, it's General Maestre. Oh God, Sofia.' His voice lurched and he began to sob helplessly.

The officers marched purposefully to them. Maestre flicked a look of contempt at Harry.

'All of you stay where you are.' He raised his voice. 'Señorita Clare, get out of the car.'

Barbara stepped out. She seemed on the point of collapse; she leaned against the open door, her face stricken as she looked at Sofia's body. Aranda smiled happily at Bernie.

'Well, we have caught our little bird again.'

Harry stared at Maestre. 'How did you know about this? Was it Forsyth?'

'No.' The minister stared at him coldly. 'This rescue was set up by us, Señor Brett. Colonel Aranda and I are old friends, we served in Morocco together. One night at a reunion he told me of an Englishman being held at the Tierra Muerta camp, with an English girlfriend who was now in Madrid. The name rang a bell.' He put his hands in his pockets. 'We have files on anyone who was involved with the Republic and when I saw Miss Clare was passing herself off as Forsyth's wife, my friend and I decided we could embarrass him. Today would have been a good day to bring it all to a head – there is an important meeting to do with the gold mine tomorrow.'

'Oh, no,' Barbara groaned.

Maestre took out a cigarette and lit it. He blew a cloud of smoke at the sky then looked at Harry again with hard concentration, as though he hated him, Bernie thought. But his voice was still quiet, urbane.

'Although there was no gold mine in the end, was there? We know that now.'

Harry made no reply. He hardly seemed to be listening any more.

He tried again to jerk away from Bernie's grip but Bernie held him fast, though he winced with the effort. If he tried to run they might shoot him. Maestre went on.

'We bribed the English journalist Markby to start things off – oh, do not look so surprised, Señorita Clare, the English can be bribed too – and then Colonel Aranda arranged for one of our former guards who was unemployed in Madrid to develop things. He knew that he and his brother needed money for their mother.'

'Luis?' Barbara asked. 'Luis was working for you? Oh, Christ.'

'He and Agustín *will* be getting money to help their mother, but from us. Though we are also letting them keep the money you gave them.' He shook his head. 'Luis tried to get out of it a couple of times. I think deceiving you troubled both him and his brother. But we have to be hard if we are to rebuild Spain.'

Maestre began walking to and fro, his tall slim form moving in and out of the searchlight beam where more and more snowflakes whirled, a soldier reflecting on a successful campaign. The light twinkled on his polished buttons. Aranda watched him with a smile. A little way off the snow was settling on Sofia's black coat and in her hair. Harry had stopped sobbing, he stood slumped in Bernie's arms now.

'We always planned to arrest you here. Forsyth doesn't matter now and we thought of preventing the escape. But we knew you would make trouble at the embassy about the camp, Miss Clare, perhaps involve your Red Cross friends. And Señor Brett is involved too. That would embarrass Ambassador Hoare, who has already annoyed the Generalísimo because of his spying, and because the Englishman Forsyth tried to deceive him over the gold. We will catch Forsyth by the way, all the ports and borders are being watched. And we need Hoare, we need his help to keep Spain out of the war, so that the people who have always ruled Spain can take control from that Falange rabble.'

'What are you going to do with us?' Bernie heard a tremble in Barbara's voice.

Maestre shrugged. 'Keep you locked away for now. It might be most convenient for all if Piper was shot trying to escape, and you and Señor Brett were reported dead, in a car accident perhaps.'

Aranda stepped up to Maestre, his smile gone. 'We should kill them all now,' he said.

Maestre shook his head. 'No. We'll keep them locked away for now. I need to think. We have the big meeting tomorrow. But thank you, Manuel, for bringing the escape forward a day. I wanted to see them for myself.' Maestre smiled again.

They all turned as Barbara gave a little moan and slumped to the ground. Aranda laughed. 'The stupid whore has fainted.' He nodded to the young *civil*. 'Wake her up.'

The man knelt beside her. He shook her shoulder and she groaned. 'What—'

'You fainted, *señorita*,' he said, surprisingly gently.

'Oh. Oh God.' Barbara sat up, put her hands between her knees. Bernie moved to go to her but the *civil* motioned him back with his pistol. Harry, freed from Bernie's grasp, tottered away. He walked slowly over to Sofia's body, bent like an old man, passing unheedingly through the searchlight beam. The *civil* with the machine gun swivelled towards him but Maestre raised a hand, watching as Harry knelt beside her. He stroked her snow-spotted hair, then looked at Maestre.

'Why did you kill her? Why?'

'She broke the law.' Maestre waved a finger in a minatory way. 'That will not be tolerated now. This disorderly people needs keeping in order and we know how to do it. Now get back to the car.'

'Murderers,' Harry said, stroking Sofia's hair. 'Murderers.'

'And to think my daughter wanted to walk out with you,' Maestre said. 'You little prick. It was because of you Alfonso died.'

Barbara stood up. She leaned on the open car door, her face white. 'Please,' she said weakly. 'May I sit in the car? I can't stop shaking.'

'She looks ill, *mi general*,' the young *civil* said.

Maestre nodded, looking disdainfully at Barbara as she climbed inside. The young *civil* closed the door. Aranda smiled at Bernie. 'Englishwomen, they have no guts, eh?'

Maestre grunted. 'They are an effete, decayed people. If they could win the war we could get rid of the Falange but I wonder if they are capable of it.'

Bernie glanced round. He could see the back of Barbara's head, trembling slightly. Harry was crouched over Sofia, sobbing, the snow settling on him too now.

'It is time to leave,' Maestre said. 'You!' he called to Harry. 'Back to the car!'

Harry got up and walked slowly back to Bernie. Bernie took his arm and looked at him. He looked awful, his face sagging with shock.

Maestre waved to the *civil* with the pistol. 'Go to our car. Radio your office we are coming in.'

The man saluted. 'I will be back in a quarter of an hour, *mi general*.' He ran off towards the road. His colleague stood motionless, the other *civil* still covering Harry and Bernie with the machine gun.

Aranda waved a finger at Bernie, his good humour restored. 'General Maestre made a special trip from Madrid to join me here. We knew you were at the cathedral, of course; the watchman and the church authorities were in on this too. I have seen you these last weeks, Piper, waiting for your punishment for not informing for me. That was a game I played with you. Well, here is your punishment.' He laughed. 'Do you know, the *civiles* have had Father Eduardo pestering them, saying two women were missing, they had not arrived at the convent where they were staying. What a simpleton he is.'

BARBARA HADN'T really fainted, although when the general talked of them being killed she almost had. That was what had given her the idea to pretend to collapse in order to get back in the car. The two officers were standing directly behind it. She guessed they wouldn't know she could drive, few Spanish women drove. She watched the scene behind her in the mirror, trying to keep her eyes from Sofia's body, calculating. When she saw the young *civil* go back to the trees she thought, it's now or never. It would be a risk but she had to try. They were probably all going to be killed anyway, and she hadn't come this far not to be able to take Bernie back with her, to share her life with him. She wouldn't leave him to them again.

Slowly, checking in the mirror that she was unobserved, she grasped the key in the ignition. It all depended on the engine catching first time but it was a good car; it had started that morning after a whole night outside. If she reversed fast then Bernie and Harry, leaning against the side of the car, would be pushed away; the officers would be hit, and if the *civil* with the machine gun gave her time she could swerve and get him too. She looked at the *civil*. His eyes were fixed on Harry and Bernie, his face still hard and expressionless.

She took a deep breath and quietly turned the key. The engine roared into life and she threw the car into reverse. She felt Bernie and Harry fall away, Bernie shouting 'No!' The older officer, the one who had taunted Harry, managed to jump aside but fell over backwards. For a split second, in the mirror, she saw an expression of outraged surprise on the face of the other officer, the colonel from the camp. Then he fell beneath the car; she heard a scream and felt a crunch as the wheels went over him.

The *civil* stood with an astonished look on his face, then he turned, raising the heavy machine gun to point at the car. But those seconds gave Barbara time to slew round; the rear corner hit the man hard and the sub-machine gun flew into the air, bouncing off the car roof with a bang as the man went down. Barbara hauled the handbrake up and jumped out, pulling the gun from her coat pocket. The engine was still running.

Harry and Bernie were picking themselves up from the grass. Harry looked stunned but Bernie was alert. 'Look out!' he shouted.

The *civil* was pulling himself groggily to his feet, reaching for his pistol. Barbara didn't stop to think, she just pulled the Mauser up and fired. There was a roar and a flash and a spout of blood from the man's chest. He pitched over backwards and lay still. She stood, shocked by what she had done. She turned to where Aranda lay under the car. He too was dead; his eyes stared unbelievingly upwards, his mouth open, white teeth bared in a final snarl of rage. A sliver of blood trickled down his chin.

'Oh God,' she said.

Maestre sat up groggily; he looked stunned, the rats' tails of black hair that had been combed over his head falling absurdly down one side of his face. 'Don't shoot me,' he cried out in a new voice, hoarse and terrified. He held up his arm as though it could ward off bullets. 'Please, please.'

Barbara felt Bernie take her arm, pull the gun from her hand.

He pointed it at Maestre. 'Get in the car,' he said urgently over his shoulder to Barbara. 'Get Harry in. Can you drive?'

'Yes.'

'We haven't much time,' he said, 'the other one will be back.'

Maestre was lying on his back on the grass, supporting himself on his elbows. Barbara watched as Bernie walked slowly towards him, aiming the gun at his head. The general blinked snow out of his eyes. It was coming down faster, settling on his uniform. Near him Sofia's body was a white mound now.

Barbara couldn't face hearing another shot, seeing someone else die. 'Bernie,' she said. 'Bernie, don't kill him.'

Bernie turned to her and she saw Maestre's hand move to his pocket, quick as a striking snake. 'Look out!' she called as the general pulled out a gun. Bernie turned and fired at the same time as Maestre. The general and Bernie each jerked backwards. Barbara saw the side of Maestre's head fly off, blood and brains spurting out as Bernie tottered and slumped against the side of the car. She heard a wild animal scream and realized it was her own voice.

'Bernie!'

'Hell!' he shouted. 'Barbara, get me in the car.' He gritted his teeth with pain. He grasped his thigh. Blood welled through his fingers.

Harry had stood staring at the scene, a confused expression on his face, but now he seemed to come back to life. He looked at Bernie. 'Oh Christ, no,' he groaned.

'Help me get him in,' Barbara said to him. Harry stepped forward and the two of them managed to manoeuvre Bernie into the back seat.

'Harry, please drive,' Barbara said. 'I need to help him. We have to get away now, before the other *civil* comes back. Harry, can you do it?'

Harry looked past her, at Sofia. 'She's dead, isn't she? There's nothing we can do for her.'

'Yes. Harry, *can you do it?*' She took his head between her hands and stared into his eyes. She was terrified the engine would stop again.

He took a deep breath, focused on her. 'Yes. Yes. I'll do it.'

Bernie felt a heavy throbbing pain in his thigh. He couldn't move his leg and he could feel blood welling up through his fingers, a lot of blood. Barbara had taken off her coat and was ripping out the heavy lining. In front of him he could see the back of Harry's head and his hands, steady on the wheel. In the headlights the snow was whirling relentlessly down.

'Where are we going?' he asked.

'Back to Madrid, the embassy's our only hope.'

'Won't they put calls out when that *civil* gets back, try to stop us?'

'We have to try for Madrid. Don't talk, darling.' She was calling him darling, just like the old days. Bernie smiled up at her, then winced as she took a pair of nail scissors and cut his trouser leg open.

'It's smashed your leg, Bernie. I think the bullet's lodged in the bone. I'm going to bandage you up. We'll get you to a doctor in Madrid. Try to sit up now.' She began winding the strips of lining round his body with cool, practised hands.

When she had finished he fell back against the seat. He found it hard not to close his eyes. He felt for her hand and squeezed it. He passed out for a while; when he came to Barbara was still holding his hand. The snow was still whirling in the headlights. His leg felt numb. Barbara smiled at him.

'Remember something for me, Barbara,' he said. 'Will you remember something?'

'You'll be all right. I promise.'

'If I'm not. Remember something.'

'Anything.'

'The people, the ordinary people, it looks like they've lost but one day, one day people won't be manipulated and hounded by bosses and priests and soldiers any more; one day they *will* free themselves, live with freedom and dignity as people were meant to.'

'You're going to be all right.'

'Please.'

'I will. Yes. I will.'

He closed his eyes and slept again.

Chapter Forty-Nine

HARRY DROVE FAST and steadily, like an automaton. He tried to concentrate only on the patch of light created by the car's headlights. Everything beyond their white glow was pitch black. After a while the snow stopped but it was still difficult, driving along the uneven road in the dark. And all the time there was a feeling like a terrible dark hole in his stomach, as though he had been shot as well. The picture of Sofia's body raked by bullets would stab into his brain and make him want to cry out but he forced himself to push it aside, concentrate on the road, the road, the road. In the mirror he could see Barbara's anxious face as she leaned over Bernie. He was asleep or unconscious, but at least the sound of his breathing, heavy and laboured, meant he was still alive.

At every village or town he feared the *civiles* would appear and flag the car down, but they saw hardly a soul on the whole journey. A little after eleven they reached the outskirts of Madrid and Harry slowed down as he headed through the still white streets towards the embassy.

'How is he?' he asked Barbara.

'Still unconscious,' she replied quietly. 'I was worried. He was in a weak condition anyway, and he's lost a lot of blood.' She lifted a blood-smeared hand and looked at her watch. 'You've made good time.'

'Why haven't we been stopped?' he asked anxiously.

'I don't know. Maybe that *civil* took a long time to get back.'

'He had a radio. And the police force is the one thing that's efficient here.' A thought that had been in the back of his mind throughout the journey came to the surface. 'They may be waiting to catch us here, in Madrid. He looked at her face in the mirror, pale and exhausted. 'Where's the gun?'

'In Bernie's pocket. I don't want to disturb him. Movement could start the bleeding again.'

Harry watched the tall buildings flashing by; they were approaching the city centre now. 'We might have to shoot our way through,' he said. 'Let me have it.' She hesitated a moment, then felt in Bernie's pocket. She passed the gun, black with dried blood, to Harry. He cradled it in his lap. He had a sudden memory of he and Sofia in the cathedral, sitting together, and jumped, then swerved to avoid a passing gasogene that was creeping and sputtering along the snowy road. The driver hooted angrily.

At last the embassy came into view. Harry drove past the entrance, drawing a stare from the single *civil* on duty, then round the corner to the car park. It was almost empty. Harry drew to a halt beside the back door. They were on British territory now. On the first floor he saw a light at a single curtained window; the duty officer. He sounded the horn. The curtain twitched and a head looked out.

Harry turned to Barbara. There was a smear of blood on her white face. 'Someone will be down in a minute. Let's get Bernie out. Oh, God, he looks awful.' Bernie's eyes were closed. His breathing seemed shallow and his cheeks more sunken than ever. Broad strips of Barbara's coat lining were wound tightly round his trousers.

'Can you wake him up?' he asked.

'I'm not sure we should move him.'

'We have to get him inside. Try.'

Barbara squeezed Bernie's shoulder, lightly then harder. He groaned, but did not stir. 'You'll have to help me with him,' she said.

Harry stepped out of the car. He opened the rear door and took Bernie's shoulders. He was surprised how light he was. Barbara helped him pull him into a sitting position. Blood was seeping from under the makeshift bandage. It was all over the back seat, all over Barbara.

There was a sound of bolts being drawn back. A door opened and footsteps crunched on the snow. They turned to meet the gaze of Chalmers, a tall thin man in his thirties with a prominent Adam's apple. Even at this time of night he wore a formal suit. He shone a torch into their faces. His eyes widened at their bloodstained clothes. 'Good God, what's this? Who are you?'

'I'm Brett, one of the translators. We've got an injured man here, he needs medical attention.'

Chalmers turned the beam on to Bernie. 'Jesus Christ!' He shone the torch into the car, staring in horror at the blood on the back seats. 'Christ, what's happened? This is one of our cars!'

Harry helped Barbara drag Bernie towards the open door. Thank God he was still breathing. He moaned again. Chalmers hurried after them.

'What happened? Who is he? Has there been an accident?'

'He's been shot,' Harry said. 'He's British. For Christ's sake, man, will you stop dithering and ring for a doctor?' Harry pushed the door open and they staggered inside. They were in a long corridor; Harry threw open the door of the nearest office and went in. He and Barbara laid Bernie carefully on the floor while Chalmers went to the desk and picked up the telephone.

'Dr Pagall,' he said. 'Get Dr Pagall.'

'How long will he be?' Harry asked tersely as Chalmers put the phone down.

'Not long. Listen, Brett, for Christ's sake, what's happened?'

The picture of Sofia's body jerking backwards appeared in his mind again. He winced and took a deep breath. Chalmers was looking at him curiously.

'Listen, phone Simon Tolhurst, Special Operations, his number's in the book. Let me speak to him.'

'Special Operations? Jesus.' Chalmers frowned; the regular staff disliked the spies. He rang another number and passed the receiver to Harry. A sleepy voice answered. 'Hello, yes?'

'It's Harry. It's an emergency. I'm at the embassy with Barbara Clare and an Englishman who's been shot. No, not Forsyth. A prisoner of war. Yes, the Civil War. He's badly injured. There's been an – an incident. General Maestre's been shot dead.'

Tolhurst was surprisingly quick and decisive. He told Harry he would be there at once, he would phone Hillgarth and the ambassador. 'Stay where you are,' he concluded. As though there was anywhere else they could go, Harry thought as he put the phone down. He remembered Enrique and Paco; at home, waiting. They would be wondering where he and Sofia were. This would be the end for Paco. 'I told her not to come,' he whispered aloud.

The doctor and Tolhurst arrived at the same time. The doctor was a middle-aged Spaniard, still blinking sleep from his eyes. He went over to Barbara and she explained what had happened. Tolhurst took in the sight of Bernie lying on the floor, his and Barbara's clothes spattered with blood, with surprising calmness.

'Is that Miss Clare?' he asked Harry quietly.

'Yes.'

'Who's the man?'

Harry took a deep breath. 'He's an International Brigader who's been held illegally in a labour camp for three years. He's an old friend of ours. We had a plan to rescue him; it went wrong.'

'Christ, I'll say.' Tolhurst glanced at Barbara. 'The two of you had better come to my office.'

Barbara looked up. 'No, I'm a nurse, I can help.'

The doctor looked at her. He spoke quietly and his eyes were kind. 'No, *señorita*, I will be better alone.' He had begun unwinding the bandages. Harry glimpsed red pulp and white bone underneath. Barbara looked at the wound and swallowed.

'Can you – can you help him?'

The doctor raised his hands. 'I will do better if you will all leave me. Please.'

'Come on, Barbara.' Harry took her elbow and helped her stand. They followed Tolhurst out of the room and up a dark staircase. Around the building lights were clicking on and voices muttering as the night staff prepared to deal with the crisis.

Tolhurst switched on his office light and ushered them to seats. Harry thought, I was here yesterday, only yesterday. In another time, another world. Sofia was alive. Tolhurst sat behind his desk, his plump features composed into a stiff alertness.

'All right, Harry. Tell me exactly what's happened. What the hell's this about Maestre being shot?'

Harry told him the story, from Barbara coming to Sofia's flat and telling them of her plan, to the rescue that afternoon. Tolhurst kept glancing at Barbara. She had sunk into her chair and was staring into space with a glassy-eyed look.

'You did all this without telling Forsyth?' Tolhurst asked her sharply at one point.

She replied indifferently, 'Yes.'

Harry told him about the ambush in the clearing. 'They shot Sofia,' he said and for the first time his voice broke. 'I asked Maestre why and he said because Spaniards need keeping in order.'

Tolhurst let out a deep breath. Help us, Tolly, Harry thought, help us. As he went on to describe how they had escaped, Tolhurst's eyes widened and he stared at Barbara again.

'You ran over one man and shot another dead?'

'Yes.' She met his gaze. 'They left me no choice.'

'Have you the gun now?' he asked.

'No. Harry's got it.'

Tolhurst stretched out a hand. 'Give it to me please, old chap.'

Harry reached into his pocket and passed it over. Tolhurst placed it in his desk drawer, grimacing with distaste at the blood on it. He wiped his fingers carefully on a handkerchief, then leaned forward.

'This is *bad*,' he said. 'A government minister killed and an embassy official involved. And after what Franco said to Hoare yesterday – hell.' He shook his head.

'It wasn't murder,' Barbara said flatly. 'It was self-defence. Sofia was the only one who was murdered.'

Tolhurst frowned at her as though she was someone stupid who couldn't understand what was important. Harry felt a weight of disappointment settle on top of the dull heavy grief. He had thought Tolly might help them somehow, speak for them. But what could he have done?'

Tolhurst's head jerked round as the telephone on his desk rang. He picked it up. 'Right,' he said. He took a deep breath. 'The captain and the ambassador are here. I'll have to brief them.' He got up and left.

Barbara looked at Harry. 'I want to see Bernie,' she said flatly. He noticed there was a smear of blood on her glasses.

'That doctor seemed to know what he was doing.'

'I want to see him.'

Harry felt sudden anger. Why had she survived while Sofia was dead? It was strange, they should be comforting each other, but he felt only this terrible anger. When he had knelt over Sofia, her blank eyes had been half open and her mouth too, showing a glimpse of her white teeth that she had clenched as the life was ripped out of her. He blinked, trying to clear the picture from his mind. They sat in silence. They seemed to wait a very long time. Occasionally they heard sharp voices and footsteps outside. The whining noise began again in his bad ear.

Voices sounded in the corridor. He heard Hillgarth's deep tones and the ambassador's shrill jabber. Harry tensed as the door opened. Hillgarth was in a suit and looked as fresh as ever, black hair slicked back, the large brown eyes keen. Hoare was a mess, his suit pulled on untidily, eyes red and his wispy white hair standing on end. He glanced furiously at Harry, then blenched at the sight of Barbara covered with blood. He sat behind Tolhurst's desk, Tolhurst and Hillgarth on either side of him. The little room seemed very crowded.

Hillgarth looked at Barbara. 'Are you injured?' he asked, surprisingly gently.

'No, I'm all right. Please, how's Bernie?'

Hillgarth didn't reply. He turned slowly to Harry. 'Brett, Simon says your fiancée's dead.'

'Yes, sir. The *civiles* shot her with a machine gun.'

'I'm very sorry. But you've betrayed us. Why did you do this?'

'They shot her with a machine gun,' Harry repeated. 'She broke the law. You have to keep people in order.'

Hoare leaned forward, his face a mask of outraged fury. 'And they want you too, Brett, for murder!' He turned and pointed at Barbara. 'And you!' She blinked at him in surprise. The ambassador's voice rose. 'I've phoned one of our friends in the government. They know all about it, that *civil* came back to the glade and found a bloodbath. His superiors went to El Pardo. They've had to wake the Generalísimo! Hell!' he shouted. 'I should let them have the pair of you, let them put you up against a wall and shoot you!' His voice trembled. 'A government minister shot dead!'

'It was the man Piper who did that,' Hillgarth said quietly. 'They don't really want Brett and Miss Clare, Sam, Franco doesn't want a major diplomatic incident now. Think about it, they could have picked them up on the way but they let them come here.'

Hoare turned back to Harry, a tic in his cheek making one eye blink spasmodically. 'I could have you charged with treason, young man, I could have you sent home to jail!' He ran a hand though his hair. 'I should have been Viceroy of India, Winston all but promised me! I should have been Viceroy, not dealing with this madness, this rubbish, these fools! This is a fine thing for this new man on the Madrid desk in London – what's his name—'

'Philby,' Hillgarth said. 'Kim Philby.'

'A fine thing for Philby to have to deal with! And Winston will blame me!'

'All right, Sam,' Hillgarth said soothingly.

'It is *not* all right!'

Barbara asked in a quiet voice, 'Please, can you tell me how Bernie is? Please. This is his blood, we brought him from Cuenca, please tell me.'

Hoare made an impatient gesture. 'The doctor's having him removed to hospital, he needs a blood transfusion. Let's hope they've got the equipment, I'm damned if I'm sending him to a private clinic. If he comes through he may not be able to use his left leg again, nerve damage or something.' The ambassador frowned at her. 'And if he doesn't make it, so far as I'm concerned it'd be good riddance! A major diplomatic incident over a bloody Red terrorist! At least we don't have to worry about the other one, the Spanish woman they killed.'

Barbara jerked back in her chair, as though struck. A momentary look of satisfaction crossed the ambassador's face and that did something final to Harry, all the pain and grief and anger welled up in him and he cried out and launched himself across the room at Hoare and fixed his hands round the ambassador's scrawny neck. Squeezing that dry skin, feeling the tendons give under his grip, filled him with a tremendous sense of release. Hoare's face reddened and his mouth opened. Harry could see right down the throat of His Britannic

Majesty's Ambassador on Special Mission to the Court of Generalísimo Francisco Franco. Hoare's arms fluttered weakly as he tried to grip Harry's shoulders.

Then he heard Barbara cry 'Look out!' and felt a terrific blow on his neck. It stunned him and made him relax his grip. He looked round dazedly and saw it was Tolhurst who had hit him, Tolhurst who was dragging him off the ambassador with surprising strength, his face horrified. Hoare had fallen back in his chair, retching and gagging, two angry red weals standing out on his throat.

Harry felt dizzy. His legs buckled. As he fell to the floor he caught a strange expression on Hillgarth's face, something almost admiring. Perhaps he thinks it's all an adventure, Harry thought, just before he blacked out.

Epilogue

Croydon, May 1947

THE SCHOOL WAS in a leafy suburb of mock-Tudor houses. Barbara walked from the station down a succession of tree-lined streets, through the spring sunshine. The briefcase with her papers for the meeting was slung over her shoulder. The stockbroker belt, she thought. Even here there were scars: bombsites overgrown with grass and weeds.

She heard the school before she saw it, a cacophony of boyish voices growing stronger. She walked along the side of a high brick wall until she came to a gateway with a big sign outside, the name Haverstock School in black letters under a coat of arms. In the asphalt playground in front of the imposing Victorian building, dozens of boys were talking, running, shouting. They wore black-and-white-striped blazers and caps with the school crest. She remembered Bernie telling her once that school coats of arms were fake, only aristocrats were allowed real coats of arms.

She walked through the throng to the main door. The boys ignored her; she had to step aside to avoid a game of football that came a little too close. 'Give us the ball, Chivers,' someone called. They all had upper-class accents, drawing out their vowels. Barbara wondered what they were like to teach. In a far corner a fight was going on, two boys rolling over and punching each other while a crowd egged them on. She averted her eyes.

She stepped into a wide oak-beamed entrance hall with a stage at one end. It was empty; everyone seemed to be outside enjoying the sun. It was a grand setting, very different to the narrow painted corridors of her old grammar school, although the faint pervasive tang of disinfectant was the same. A new war memorial had been put up on one side of the stage, the brass shining, the inscription 1939–45 above a list of names. The list was shorter than that on the 1914–18 memorial on the other side; but long enough.

Harry had told her the way to his classroom in his letter. She found the corridor and followed the numbered doors until she came to 14A. She could see him through a window, sitting at his desk marking papers. She knocked and went in.

He stood up and smiled. 'Barbara, how nice to see you.' He was dressed in a tweed jacket with patches at the elbows, like a caricature schoolmaster, and he had put on a lot of weight; he had a double chin now. There were flecks of grey in his black hair now; like her he was approaching forty.

She shook his hand. 'Hello, Harry. Gosh, it's been quite a while, hasn't it?'

'Nearly a year,' he said. 'Too long.'

She looked round the classroom: posters of the Eiffel Tower, tables of French irregular verbs, rows of scuffed desks. 'So this is where you teach.'

'Yes, this is where the French master lives. French masters have a reputation for being easy targets, you know.'

'Do they?'

'Yes.' Harry gestured at the cane lying across his desk. 'I have to use that sometimes to remind them who's boss, unfortunately. Come on, let's go and get some lunch. There's a nice little pub not far from here.'

They left the building and walked back to the town centre. The trees were in blossom. As they passed a cherry tree the warm breeze shook off a cloud of white petals that drifted around them, making Barbara think of snow.

'D'you teach any Spanish?' she asked.

'There's no call for it. Just French. They learn just about enough for a few phrases to stick.' He gestured at her briefcase with a smile. 'You're the Spanish expert these days. Who is it you're meeting at Croydon airport?'

'Oh, a crowd of businessmen from Argentina. They've come over with Eva Perón's European tour and they're flying here from Paris to look at trade opportunities. Tinned beef and meat products, not very exciting.'

When they had returned to England in 1940 Barbara had taken work interpreting and translating in Spanish. The money had helped during the long period of nursing Bernie back to health. They had said he would never walk properly again but with endless determination he had proved them wrong. When they married at the end of 1941 he had been able to walk down the aisle unaided, without a limp despite the bullet lodged in his femur. That eased her guilt, for she knew that if she hadn't called out to Bernie in the field, Maestre would never have had time to reach for his gun.

'Still working with the refugees?' Harry asked her.

'Yes. It's mostly academics now, the resistance is pretty well beaten. I'm teaching a writer from Madrid English at the moment.' She glanced at him. 'Any news of Enrique and Paco?'

Harry's face softened into a smile. 'I had a letter last month, I don't hear so often now. Paco's starting work labouring for a local farmer.'

'How old is he now?'

'Sixteen. I never thought he'd make it but he has. Enrique says he still doesn't talk much, but he enjoys working.'

'Enrique saved him.'

'Yes.'

After the massacre Barbara and Bernie and Harry had been bundled out of Spain on the first plane. As soon as they were back in England Harry had written to Enrique; he did not even know if Sofia's brother had been told what had happened to her. A few weeks later a reply came from Asturias, in the north of Spain: the *guardias* had come to tell Enrique Sofia was dead and that night Enrique had packed a couple of suitcases, taken Paco to the station and caught a train to the north. He had thrown himself on the mercy of distant relatives who kept a small farm near Palencia. They had taken them in and Enrique and Paco had been there ever since. Harry sent them money every so often. They barely scratched a living but Enrique said the countryside was peaceful and quiet and that was what Paco had needed. He was better, though Enrique thought he would never leave the village. He had escaped the orphanage, unlike Carmela Mera.

Carmela would be in her late teens now, Barbara thought. If she had lived. It was one of the things she tried not to think about. She shook her head to clear it.

'It's a shame to let the language go,' she told Harry. 'You should get some practice.'

'Oh, I'm happy enough just doing French.' He gave her a sad tight smile. 'I had to let a lot of things go when they wouldn't take me back at Cambridge.'

'That was so unfair.'

'Hoare's revenge,' Harry said flatly. 'They were crying out for Fellows back then.'

'Yes. And they didn't like Bernie trying to get the papers to publish the truth about the Spanish camps.'

'He was naive. He should have known they'd put a D-notice on the story.'

'Have you thought of trying again? I mean, it's been nearly seven years.' Barbara hesitated. 'I don't think they're keeping tabs on me any more.' For years after she returned she noticed her mail had been opened, the flaps stuck down crudely, and sometimes there were strange noises on her telephone. Harry had experienced the same things.

'Will says once you're on a blacklist you stay on it.' He paused. 'Besides, I'm happy enough at Haverstock.'

'I sometimes wonder,' she said, and then paused.

'What?'

'Seeing the new war memorial there reminded me. I wonder if Bernie's name is on the memorial at Rookwood.'

Bernie had been called up in 1943, after he was certified fit. With all his injuries he could probably have got out of it but he didn't try, he wanted to fight fascism again. He had died on D-Day, the sixth of June 1944, shot down as he struggled ashore on Juno beach. In the car on the way to Madrid he had told Barbara he would never leave her again, but he had. She saw now that a man like him, in the times they lived in, would always go to fight. But she still longed for him, and for the child they had never had.

'Did you see Hoare's published his memoirs?' Harry asked.

'Has he?'

'Viscount Templewood now, of course.' Harry laughed bitterly. 'Ambassador on Special Mission. He says Franco stayed out of the war entirely because of his own firm diplomacy. No mention of Hillgarth, of course. Memoirs of the pink rat.'

They reached the pub, a large place that served lunches. It was full of salesmen. As he led Barbara to a table Harry nodded to a couple of people at the bar.

'The food's not bad. When do you have to be at the airport?'

'Not until four. Oodles of time.'

They ordered steak and kidney pudding. It was overcooked and gristly but Harry didn't seem to mind.

'So work's keeping you busy?' he asked.

'Yes, work and the refugees.'

She studied him; he had a nasty shaving cut on his chin. 'What do you do these days, apart from teaching? What happened with that woman teacher you got friendly with?'

He shrugged. 'Oh, that fizzled out. I don't do much really, apart from teach.'

'Work's my life too, I suppose. And the refugees. I thought I might do a part-time degree in Spanish.'

Harry nodded. 'Good idea. You'd probably find it easy.'

'I'd have to cut back on the refugee work.' She laughed. 'I've ended up one of those do-gooding single women. I always thought I would.'

'I suppose at least we've got memories,' Harry said, but his eyes were bleak. He smiled tightly again. 'I'm thinking of giving up my digs and living in at Haverstock. Will's son's at Haverstock now, you know. Ronnie. Bright lad. Coming up to the sixth form. Looks like his dad. They couldn't afford the Rookwood fees in the end.'

'Are Will and Muriel still in Italy?'

'Yes. I miss Will, especially since Uncle James died.' That tight smile again. 'Muriel hates it. Rome's too hot and dusty for her, she wants a Paris posting.'

Barbara pushed the horrible food around her plate. 'Wouldn't moving in make you a bit – well – cut off from the world?'

'What's so marvellous about the world? Anyway, teaching's what I do now. Might as well go the whole hog. It gets boring sometimes but I'm used to it. And you can help a boy now and again, that makes it worthwhile.'

'Bernie used to say public school was a closed world. A privileged world.'

He looked up sharply. 'I know. Sofia wouldn't have approved either.'

She took a deep breath. 'No, they wouldn't, but that's not what I meant. You were angry when we came back from Spain, you wanted to *do* things. You seem to have – well – turned in on yourself.'

'What is there to do?' The bitter smile again. 'What have either of us done?'

'At least I help the refugees. After I came back I thought I might do something political, there was something – something Bernie said in the car.' She heard the words again in her head, and sighed. 'He let his Communist Party membership lapse. He'd become disillusioned with them, but he still had the principles he'd always had. But – it's not as if we can change things in Spain. I suppose at least things are better here, with Labour in.'

Harry grimaced. 'Are they? Who owned everything before the war? The people who went to schools like Haverstock. And who owns everything now? It's the same.'

'Then why do you stay there?' she asked. She felt angry with him, sitting there stoically eating the revolting food, already looking like some dusty old bachelor.

'Because you can't really change anything,' he said wearily. 'They're all too strong, they beat you down in the end.'

'I don't believe that. You have to fight.'

'I lost,' he said simply.

They spoke little during the rest of the meal. Harry apologized for not walking her to the bus, but he had a class. They shook hands and promised to meet again but Barbara knew somehow that they wouldn't, this was the last time. When they were together it was probably the only time they spoke of Bernie and Sofia and that seemed to cause more pain, not less, as the years passed. On the bus she found tears pricking at her eyes but she blinked them away. She opened her briefcase and forced herself to read the details about the people she was meeting, their names and the companies they represented. Señor Gomez, Señor Barrancas, Señor Grazziani. A lot of Argentines had Italian names; immigrants, she supposed.

At the airport she was met by a representative from the London Chamber of Commerce, a tall urbane man with a Guards tie who introduced himself as Gore-Brown. There were half a dozen businessmen with him. 'Gosh,' she said. 'I didn't know there would be so many in your group. There are only four Argentines. You'll have to take turns, I'm afraid.'

'I'm told one or two of them speak English. A lot of Argentines do, I believe.'

'Oh well, we'll see how we get on.' Barbara adopted the jolly, confident-spinster manner she used with men like these. She hoped she would be all right with the difficult, lisping Argentine accent.

'The plane's just about to land, I believe,' Gore-Brown said. 'We could go up to the departure lounge and watch.'

'Oh, that'd be good,' one of the businessmen said. 'I've never seen a plane land before.'

'You can tell you weren't in the RAF,' a red-faced man with a handlebar moustache said.

'Five years on the battleships, old boy. Shot down a few, but I've never seen one land.'

Laughing, the group mounted the stairs to the observation deck. A large window gave on to the tarmac. A couple of planes stood there, passengers disembarking.

'Here she comes,' the navy man said, and Barbara looked as a twin-engined plane, surprisingly small, slid on to the runway and taxied slowly towards them. She took the papers from her briefcase. Gore-Brown leaned over her. 'Which one's the Fray Bentos man?' he asked.

'Barrancas.'

'Jolly good. Make sure you put me next to him. There could be some good business in this for me. I'm in distribution. You can make a lot off the meat ration.' He winked.

The plane had halted. A couple of overalled men slid steps on wheels up to the door. It opened and a little group of men descended the steps. They all had sunburned faces and wore hats and heavy overcoats; England must seem very cold, Barbara thought.

She squinted, adjusting her glasses. There was something familiar about the last man in the group. He hung back a little, looking round as though fascinated by his surroundings. She stepped to the glass and peered out.

Gore-Brown joined her. 'That last man, that's Barrancas. They sent me a photo. He's one of the English speakers, I think.'

But his name wasn't really Barrancas, Barbara knew. She knew that stocky form, bulkier now and with a stoop, that hard heavy-featured face, the Clark Gable moustache. She watched as Sandy Forsyth walked across the tarmac towards them, smiling like an eager curious schoolboy as he lifted his face to the sunny English afternoon.

Historical Note

Nearly three quarters of a century after its end, the Spanish Civil War remains controversial.

In the early years of the twentieth century, Spain's oligarchic monarchist regime faced increasing resistance from middle-class Republican reformers, Catalan and Basque regionalists and above all from the impoverished working classes, rural and urban. A cycle of resistance and oppression fed a class struggle and polarization unique in Europe outside Russia.

In 1931 King Alfonso XIII abdicated and the Second Republic was proclaimed. A succession of unsuccessful governments, first liberal-socialist and then conservative, followed until in 1936 a radical left-wing coalition was elected to power. Working people began taking matters into their own hands, seizing control of estates and local institutions.

Whether the Popular Front government could have succeeded will never be known, for in 1936 the long-feared military rising, supported by conservative forces and with major financial support from Juan March, took place. The initial coup failed, however: many officers remained loyal to the elected government and in the largest cities the rising was defeated. The insurgents were left in control of only a little over a third of mainland Spain, and none of its industrial regions.

It is possible that without foreign intervention the rising might have been entirely defeated, but Hitler and Mussolini immediately sent planes to General Franco, enabling him to airlift crack troops from Spain's Moroccan colony to the mainland and begin his march on Madrid. Meanwhile the Conservative-dominated British government pressured France into denying aid to the Republic and closing the border. As a result the Republic was forced to turn to the only power willing to help them, the Soviet Union. The Republican zone became dependent on

Stalin and his 'advisers', who exported his apparatus of terror as well as weapons. There is still a myth in Spain, fostered by the Franco regime, that the army rose to forestall a communist coup, but the Spanish Communist Party before 1936 was tiny and the tradition among Republicans, Socialists and Anarchists was strongly anti-authoritarian. The Communists' rise to power was a direct consequence of Britain's pressure on France to stay clear of involvement in the conflict.

The bloody civil war that followed lasted for three years and ravaged Spain. Perhaps 250,000 died in combat and another 200,000 in the campaign of terror waged by both sides, many of them apolitical people with 'suspect loyalties' who happened to end up on the wrong side of the lines.

When the war ended with Franco's victory in April 1939, there was no reconciliation, only continued executions and disappearances as Franco sought to 'cleanse' Spain. The 1940s, for most Spaniards, were scarcely less of a nightmare than the Civil War years as the effects of drought were worsened by the ruin of much of the infrastructure in the war, Franco's fascist economic policy of self-sufficiency, and the chaotic, corrupt distribution system. Franco himself fantasized about solutions such as giant gold reserves and manufacturing oil from grass.

The Franco regime itself was divided from the start between the Fascists of the Falange, whose armed bands Franco had co-opted during the Civil War and who became Spain's only political party, and the Monarchists, traditional Spanish conservatives. The Monarchists were often pro-English and anti-German, but the England they admired was that of the aristocratic country house; they despised the Falangists as 'common' and had, if anything, even less sympathy with the sufferings of ordinary Spaniards than the Falange. In the Civil War they were no less violent. Franco himself stood somewhere in the middle; a skilful political tactician, his ability to balance the factions that made up his regime helped keep him in power for nearly forty years. After the defeat of Hitler, however, the Falange were always a junior partner in his coalition.

In 1939–40 the main question before Franco was whether to enter the war on Hitler's side, as the Falange wanted. Franco himself had dreams of carving out an expanded Spanish African empire from the colonies of defeated France, but the Monarchists wanted to stay neutral, regarding entry into the war as a risky venture as well as one that would consolidate Falange power. In the end, as usual, Franco's position was pragmatic. The son of a naval officer, he knew the power of the British navy, which was blockading Spain and could turn off supplies easily. Therefore he would only join the war if and when Britain was almost defeated. When this seemed to have happened in June 1940 he made overtures to Hitler, but the Führer's reply was cautious. By autumn 1940, when Hitler wanted Franco in mainly so that Gibraltar could be taken, the Battle of Britain had ended in German defeat and Franco realized that Britain was far from finished.

The meeting between Hitler and Franco on the French–Spanish border in October 1940 remains a focus for argument. Franco's apologists contend that his skilful diplomacy kept Spain neutral; his opponents argue he would have entered the war if the terms were right. I think the latter view is correct; but by the autumn of 1940, the amount of German aid Franco would have needed to prevent a British blockade driving Spain into starvation and perhaps renewed revolution was impossible for Hitler to provide. Franco's persistent demands resulted in the Führer leaving the Hendaye meeting in disgust. Thereafter negotiations between Franco and the Axis continued but any real prospect of Spain's entering the war receded, thanks to the Royal Navy's continued control of the seas.

In May 1940 Churchill, Prime Minister of Britain's new wartime coalition, sacked Sir Samuel Hoare from the Cabinet and sent him to Spain as Ambassador on Special Mission with a brief to keep Franco out of the war. Hoare had been a Conservative minister since 1931 and a leading appeaser. Vain, effete and arrogant, but a skilful administrator and politician, Hoare's abilities, status and history of soothing dictators made him a shrewd choice, though he was disappointed not to achieve his long-held ambition of becoming Viceroy of India. Churchill neither liked nor trusted Hoare, and may have chosen his friend Alan Hillgarth as officer in charge of covert operations in Spain (including the bribery of potentially sympathetic Monarchists) partly to keep an eye on Hoare. Certainly Hillgarth reported directly to Churchill.

As ambassador, during the autumn and winter of 1940–1, Hoare followed a predictable path. Franco and his chief minister, the pro-Falange Serrano Suñer, treated him with disdain but he managed to build links with the Monarchists and to obtain important information from them. He was insistent that (apart from bribery) covert activities in Spain be limited to intelligence gathering; there were to be no SOE men 'setting Europe ablaze' and he rebuffed approaches from the underground left-wing opposition, arguing that Franco's was the established government and all Britain's efforts should be concentrated there. That seems to me a poor argument: the threat of support for the opposition would surely have added another string to Britain's bow. But Hoare's outlook, like that of many British conservatives, was emotionally sympathetic to the aristocratic, anti-revolutionary Monarchists. Hoare argued successfully for a policy of having no truck with the Spanish left, thus sowing the seeds of the postwar Allied policy of leaving the Franco regime in place.

Hoare's views, however, changed as the war progressed and by the time his ambassadorship ended in 1944 he had become a vigorous opponent of leaving the Franco regime in place after the war, arguing for a programme of propaganda and economic sanctions. The thinking of Churchill, however, had evolved in the opposite direction. He had come to believe that Fanco was a bulwark against Communism and should be left in place. Hoare was unable to shake Churchill's view, which in the end was decisive.

My interpretation of Hoare's and Hillgarth's characters is my own; it may seem harsh but is, I think, in accord with the known facts. All the other British and Spanish characters are fictional, except for some of the major figures of Spanish history in those years who make brief appearances: Azaña, the bizarre Millán Astray, and of course Franco himself.

The picture I have painted of Spain in 1940 is a grim one, but it is based largely on accounts by contemporary observers. The camp outside Cuenca is fictitious, but there were many real ones. I do not think my picture of the Spanish Church at the period is unfair; they were involved root and branch with the policy of a violent regime in its most brutal phase and those like Father Eduardo who found it hard to square their consciences seem to have been few and far between.

General Franco's archaic vision of an authoritarian, Catholic Spain died with him in 1975. Spaniards immediately turned their backs on his legacy and embraced democracy. The past was forgotten in the '*pacto de olvido*' – the pact of forgetting. Perhaps that was the price of a peaceful transition to democracy. Only now, as the 1940s generation passes away, is that changing and Spanish historians are looking at the early years of the Franco regime once more, uncovering many new stories of horror that will be of little comfort to the regime's apologists but remind us of what ordinary Spaniards endured, not only during the Civil War, but after it was won.

I have tried to be scrupulous in tying the pattern of events in the novel in with historical dates. Twice, however, I have altered these slightly to meet the demands of the plot: I have postdated Himmler's visit to Madrid by a couple of days, and antedated the founding of *La Barraca* by a year to 1931. I have also invented Franco's attendance at the first performance of Rodrigo's *Concierto de Aranjuez*, which was actually in Barcelona.

Acknowledgements

I am very grateful indeed to a number of friends who read the manuscript of *Winter in Madrid*, and who grappled with me over the thorny issues of political, historical and cultural perspective which the book raised from a refreshingly wide variety of viewpoints. My thanks to Roz Brody, Emily Furman, Mike Holmes, Caroline Hume, Jan King, Tony Macaulay, Charles Penny, Mari Roberts for her copy-editing, and William Shaw; and to my agent Antony Topping and my editor Maria Rejt at Macmillan. Thanks also to Will Stone for his help with research at a crucial juncture. As ever, I am grateful to Frankie Lawrence for her typing and for spotting the occasional howler.

Select Bibliography

There are many books in English on the Spanish Civil War and its origins. After more than sixty years I think Gerald Brenan's *The Spanish Labyrinth* (Cambridge 1943) is still the best on the origins of the war. Antony Beever's *The Spanish Civil War* (Cassell 1982) is the most accessible introduction to the war itself.

Denis Smyth's *Diplomacy and the Strategy of Survival: British policy and Franco's Spain 1940–41* (Cambridge UP 1986) is the main academic account of the period, though I think it underestimates the importance of the cultural affinities between the Spanish Monarchists and the British ruling classes. Paul Preston's monumental biography *Franco* (Harper-Collins 1993) is also very useful on the regime's wartime foreign policy, although discussion of domestic conditions in those years is curiously absent. Hoare's account of his ambassadorship, written after he became Viscount Templewood, *Ambassador on Special Mission* (London 1947), is self-serving and unreliable in its account of events in 1940–1 (although many aspects, such as the bribery of ministers, could not be revealed when it was written), but shows the evolution of his thought to a strongly anti-Franco position by the war's end. Richard Wigg's *Churchill and Spain* (Routledge 2005) throws interesting new light on the evolution of both Churchill's and Hoare's perspectives on Spain as the war progressed. Phillip Knightley's *Philby, KGB Masterspy* (London 1978) opened the world of wartime espionage for me. Miss Maxse was real; she interviewed Philby for the SIS in St Ermin's Hotel. Caroline Moorhead's *Dunant's Dream* (HarperCollins 1998) is a history of the Red Cross that manages to be both vivid and fair. The article by J. Bandrés and R. Llavona, 'Psychology in Franco's Concentration Camps' (*Psychology in Spain*, 1997, vol. 1, no. 1, pp. 3–9) is a chilling account of the abuse of psychiatry. For details of the goldmine fraud I have drawn on the story of an even more remarkable modern fraud told in V. Danielson and J. White's *Bre-X: Gold Today, Gone Tomorrow* (Canada 1997).

For contemporary accounts of the Battle of the Jarama, Tom Wintringham's *English Captain* (London 1939) tells the story from the icy viewpoint of an upper-class Stalinist; Jason Gurney's *Crusade in Spain* (London 1974) from that of a committed, and later disillusioned, volunteer.

For details of life in Madrid during the early Franco years I have relied mainly on works by British and American journalists and diplomats who were there at the time. Even allowing for their mainly anti-Franco viewpoints, the picture they paint is a horrifying one. T. Hamilton, *Appeasement's Child* (London 1943), E. J. Hughes, *Report from Spain* (New York 1948) and C. Foltz, *Masquerade in Spain* (London 1948) were particularly useful. The letters of David Eccles, economic attaché at the British Embassy in 1940, *By Safe Hand, Letters of Sybil and David Eccles, 1939–42* (London, Bodley Head, 1983), provide a vivid and enthralling account of diplomacy and everyday life by a man who, however odd some of his political ideas may seem today, was clearly moved by the condition of the Spanish people. The story of the woman arrested when her dress blew over her head is based on an incident he recounts, as is the story of Hoare hiding under a table to avoid a bat. The Café Rocinante owes a debt to Doña Rosa's café in Camilo José Cela's *The Hive* (USA 1953).

SOVEREIGN

The third novel in C. J. Sansom's spectacular Shardlake series is now available in Macmillan hardback. The first chapter follows here.

Chapter One

It was dark under the trees, only a little moonlight penetrating the half-bare branches. The ground was thick with fallen leaves; the horses' hooves made little sound and it was hard to tell whether we were still on the road. A wretched track, Barak had called it earlier, grumbling yet again about the wildness of this barbarian land I had brought him to. I had not replied for I was bone-tired, my poor back sore and my legs in their heavy riding boots as stiff as boards. I was worried, too, for the strange mission that now lay close ahead was weighing on my mind. I lifted a hand from the reins and felt in my coat pocket for the Archbishop's seal, fingering it like a talisman and remembering Cranmer's promise: 'This will be safe enough, there will be no danger.'

I had left much care behind me as well, for six days before I had buried my father in Lichfield. Barak and I had had five days' hard riding northwards since then, the roads in a bad state after that wet summer of 1541. We rode into wild country where many villages still consisted of the old longhouses, people and cattle crammed together in hovels of thatch and sod. We left the Great North Road that afternoon at Flaxby. Barak wanted to rest the night at an inn, but I insisted we ride on, even if it took all night. I reminded him we were late, tomorrow would be the twelfth of September and we must reach our destination well before the King arrived.

The road, though, had soon turned to mud, and as night fell we had left it for a drier track that veered to the north-east, through thick woodland and bare fields where pigs rooted among the patches of yellow stubble.

The woodland turned to forest and for hours now we had been picking our way through it. We lost the main track once and it was the Devil's own job to find it again in the dark. All was silent save for the whisper of fallen leaves and an occasional clatter of brushwood as a boar or wildcat fled from us. The horses, laden with panniers containing our clothes and other necessities, were as exhausted as Barak and I. I could feel Genesis' tiredness and Sukey, Barak's normally energetic mare, was content to follow his slow pace.

'We're lost,' he grumbled.

'They said at the inn to follow the main path south through the forest. Anyway, it must be daylight soon,' I said. 'Then we'll see where we are.'

Barak grunted wearily. 'Feels like we've ridden to Scotland. I wouldn't be surprised if we get taken for ransom.' I did not reply, tired at his complaining, and we plodded on silently.

My mind went back to my father's funeral the week before. The little group of people round the grave, the coffin lowered into the earth. My cousin Bess, who had found him dead in his bed when she brought him a parcel of food.

'I wish I had known how ill he was,' I told her when we returned to the farm afterwards. 'It should have been me that looked after him.'

She shook her head wearily. 'You were far away in London and we'd not seen you for over a year.' Her eyes had an accusing look.

'I have had difficult times of my own, Bess. But I would have come.'

She sighed. 'It was old William Poer dying last autumn undid him. They'd wrestled to get a profit from the farm these last few years and he seemed to give up.' She paused. 'I said he should contact you, but he wouldn't. God sends us hard trials. The droughts last summer, now the floods this year. I think he was ashamed of the money troubles he'd got into. Then the fever took him.'

I nodded. It had been a shock to learn that the farm where I had grown up, and which now was mine, was deep in debt. My father had been near seventy, his steward William not much younger. Their care of the land had not been all it should and the last few harvests had been poor. To get by he had taken a mortgage on the farm with a rich landowner in Lichfield. The first I knew of it was when the mortgagee wrote to me, immediately after Father's death, to say he doubted the value of the land would clear the debt. Like many gentry in those days he was seeking to increase his acreage for sheep, and granting mortgages to elderly farmers at exorbitant interest was one way of doing it.

'That bloodsucker Sir Henry,' I said bitterly to Bess.

'What will you do? Let the estate go insolvent?'

'No,' I said. 'I won't disgrace Father's name. I'll pay it.' I thought, God knows I owe him that.

'That is good.'

I came to with a start at the sound of a protesting whicker behind me. Barak had pulled on Sukey's reins, bringing her to a stop. I halted too and turned uncomfortably in the saddle. His outline and that of the trees were sharper now, it was beginning to get light. He pointed in front of him. 'Look there!'

Ahead the trees were thinning. In the distance I saw a red point of light, low in the sky.

'There!' I said triumphantly. 'The lamp we were told to look out for, that's set atop a church steeple to guide travellers. This is the Galtres Forest, like I said!'

We rode out of the trees. A cold wind blew up from the river as the sky lightened. We wrapped our coats tighter round us and rode down, towards York.

✠

The main road into the city was already filled with packhorses and carts loaded with food of every kind. There were enormous foresters' carts too, whole tree-trunks dangling dangerously over their tails. Ahead the high city walls came into view, black with the smoke of hundreds of years, and beyond were the steeples of innumerable churches, all dominated by the soaring twin towers of York Minster. 'It's busy as Cheapside on a market day,' I observed.

'All for the King's great retinue.'

We rode slowly on, the throng so dense we scarce managed a walking pace. I cast sidelong glances at my companion. It was over a year now since I had taken Jack Barak on as assistant in my barrister's practice after his old master's execution. A former child of the London streets who had ended up working on dubious missions for Thomas Cromwell, he was an unlikely choice, even though he was clever and had the good fortune to be literate. Yet I had not regretted it. He had adjusted well to working for me, doggedly learning the law. No one was better at keeping witnesses to the point while preparing affidavits, or ferreting out obscure facts, and his cynical, slantwise view of the system was a useful corrective to my own enthusiasm.

These last few months, however, Barak had often seemed downcast, and sometimes would forget his place and become as oafish and mocking as when I had first met him. I feared he might be getting bored, and thought bringing him to York might rouse him out of himself. He was, though, full of a Londoner's prejudices against the north and northerners, and had complained and griped almost the whole way. Now he was looking dubiously around him, suspicious of everything.

Houses appeared straggling along the road and then, to our right, a high old crenellated wall over which an enormous steeple was visible. Soldiers patrolled the top of the wall, wearing iron helmets and the white tunics with a red cross of royal longbowmen. Instead of bows and arrows, though, they carried swords and fearsome pikes, and some even bore long matchlock guns. A great sound of banging and hammering came from within.

'That must be the old St Mary's Abbey, where we'll be staying,' I said. 'Sounds like there's a lot of work going on to make it ready for the King.'

'Shall we go there now, leave our bags?'

'No, we should see Brother Wrenne first, then go to the castle.'

'To see the prisoner?' he asked quietly.

'Ay.'

Barak looked up at the walls. 'St Mary's is guarded well.'

'The King will be none too sure of his welcome, after all that's happened up here.'

I had spoken softly, but the man in front of us, walking beside a packhorse laden with grain, turned and gave us a sharp look. Barak raised his eyebrows and he looked away. I wondered if he was one of the Council of the North's informers; they would be working overtime in York now.

'Perhaps you should put on your lawyer's robe,' Barak suggested, nodding ahead. The carts and packmen were turning into the abbey through a large gate in the wall. Just past the gate the abbey wall met the city wall at right angles, hard by a fortress-like gatehouse decorated with the York coat of arms, five white lions against a red background. More guards were posted there, holding pikes and wearing steel helmets and breastplates. Beyond the wall, the Minster towers were huge now against the grey sky.

'I'm not fetching it out of my pack, I'm too tired.' I patted my coat pocket. 'I've got the Chamberlain's authority here.' Archbishop Cranmer's seal was there too; but that was only to be shown to one person. I stared ahead, at something I had been told to expect yet which still made me shudder: four heads fixed to tall poles, boiled and black and half eaten by crows. I knew that twelve of the rebel conspirators arrested that spring had been executed in York, their heads and quarters set on all the city gates as a warning to others.

We halted at the end of a little queue, the horses' heads drooping with tiredness. The guards had stopped a poorly dressed man and were questioning him roughly about his business in the city.

'I wish he'd hurry up,' Barak whispered. 'I'm starving.'

'I know. Come on, it's us next.'

One of the guards grabbed Genesis' reins while another asked my business. He had a southern accent and a hard, lined face. I showed him my letter of authority. 'King's lawyer?' he asked.

'Ay. And my assistant. Here to help with the pleas before His Majesty.'

'It's a firm hand they need up here,' he said. He rolled the paper up and waved us on. As we rode under the barbican I recoiled from the sight of a great hank of flesh nailed to the gate, buzzing with flies.

'Rebel's meat,' Barak said with a grimace.

'Ay.' I shook my head at the tangles of fate. But for the conspiracy that spring I should not be here, and nor would the King be making his Progress to the North, the largest and most splendid ever seen in England. We rode under the gate, the horses' hooves making a sudden clatter inside the enclosed barbican, and through into the city.

✝

BEYOND THE GATE was a narrow street of three-storey houses with overhanging eaves, full of shops with stalls set out in front, the traders sitting on their wooden blocks calling their wares. York struck me as a poor place. Some of the houses were in serious disrepair, black timbers showing through where plaster had fallen off, and the street was little more than a muddy lane. The jostling crowds made riding difficult, but I knew Master Wrenne, like all the city's senior lawyers, lived in the Minster Close and it was easy to find, for the Minster dominated the whole city.

'I'm hungry,' Barak observed. 'Let's get some breakfast.'

Another high wall appeared ahead of us; York seemed a city of walls. Behind it the Minster loomed. Ahead was a large open space crowded with market stalls under brightly striped awnings that flapped in the cool damp breeze. Heavy-skirted goodwives argued with stallholders while artisans in the bright livery of their guilds looked down their noses at the stalls' contents, and dogs and ragged children dived for scraps. I saw most of the people had patched clothes and worn-looking clogs. Watchmen in livery bearing the city arms stood about, observing the crowds.

A group of tall, yellow-haired men with dogs led a flock of odd-looking sheep with black faces round the edge of the market. I looked curiously at their weather-beaten faces and heavy woollen coats; these must be the legendary Dalesmen who had formed the backbone of the rebellion five years before. In contrast, black-robed clerics and chantry priests in their brown hoods were passing in and out of a gate in the wall that led into the Minster precinct.

Barak had ridden to a pie stall a few paces off. He leaned from his horse and asked how much for two mutton pies. The stallholder stared at him, not understanding his London accent.

'Southrons?' he grunted.

'Ay. We're hungry. How much – for – two – mutton pies?' Barak spoke loudly and slowly, as though to an idiot.

The stallholder glared at him. 'Is't my blame tha gabblest like a duck?' he asked.

''Tis you that grates your words like a knife scrating a pan.'

Two big Dalesmen passing along the stalls paused and looked round. 'This southron dog giving thee trouble?' one asked the trader. The other reached out a big horny hand to Sukey's reins.

'Let go, churl,' Barak said threateningly.

I was surprised by the anger that came into the man's face. 'Cocky southron knave. Tha thinkest since fat Harry is coming tha can insult us as tha likest.'

'Kiss my arse,' Barak said, looking at the man steadily.

The Dalesman reached a hand to his sword; Barak's hand darted to his own scabbard. I forced a way through the crowd.

'Excuse us, sir,' I said soothingly, though my heart beat fast. 'My man meant no harm. We've had a hard ride—'

The man gave me a look of disgust. 'A crookback lord, eh? Come here on tha fine hoss to cozen us out of what little money we have left up here?' He began to draw his sword, then stopped as a pike was jabbed into his chest. Two of the city guards, scenting trouble, had hurried over.

'Swords away!' one snapped, his pike held over the Dalesman's heart, while the other did the same to Barak. A crowd began to gather.

'What's this hubbleshoo?' the guard snapped.

'That southron insulted the stallholder,' someone called.

The guard nodded. He was stocky, middle-aged, with sharp eyes. 'They've no manners, the southrons,' he said loudly. 'Got to expect that, maister.' There was a laugh from the crowd; a bystander clapped.

'We only want a couple of bleeding pies,' Barak said.

The guard nodded at the stallholder. 'Gi'e him two pies.'

The man handed two mutton pies up to Barak. 'A tanner,' he said.

'A what?'

The stallholder raised his eyes to heaven. 'Sixpence.'

'For two pies?' Barak asked incredulously.

'Pay him,' the guard snapped. Barak hesitated and I hastily passed over the coins. The stallholder bit them ostentatiously before slipping them in his purse. The guard leaned close to me. 'Now, sir, shift. And tell thy man to watch his manners. Tha doesn't want trouble for't King's visit, hey?' He raised his eyebrows, and watched as Barak and I rode back to the gates to the precinct. We dismounted stiffly at a bench set against the wall, tied up the horses and sat down.

'God's nails, my legs are sore,' Barak said.

'Mine too.' They felt as though they did not belong to me, and my back ached horribly.

Barak bit into the pie. 'This is good,' he said in tones of surprise.

I lowered my voice. 'You must watch what you say. You know they don't like us up here.'

'The feeling's mutual. Arseholes.' He glared threateningly in the direction of the stallholder.

'Listen,' I said quietly. 'They're trying to keep everything calm. If you treat people like you did those folk you don't just risk a sword in the guts for both of us, but trouble for the Progress. Is that what you want?'

He did not reply, frowning at his feet.

'What's the matter with you these days?' I asked. 'You've been Tom Touchy for weeks. You used to be able to keep that sharp tongue of yours in check. You got me in trouble last month, calling Judge Jackson a blear-eyed old caterpillar within his hearing.'

He gave me one of his sudden wicked grins. 'You know he is.'

I was not to be laughed off. 'What's amiss, Jack?'

He shrugged. 'Nothing. I just don't like being up here among these barbarian wantwits.' He looked at me directly. 'I'm sorry I made trouble. I'll take care.'

Apologies did not come easily to Barak, and I nodded in acknowledgement. But there was more to his mood than dislike of the north, I was sure. I turned thoughtfully to my pie. Barak looked over the marketplace with his sharp dark eyes. 'They're a poor-looking lot,' he observed.

'Trade's been bad here for years. And the dissolution of the monasteries has made things worse. There was a lot of monkish property here. Three or four years ago there would have been many monks' and friars' robes among that crowd.'

'Well, that's all done with.' Barak finished his pie, rubbing a hand across his mouth.

I rose stiffly. 'Let's find Wrenne. Get our instructions.'

'D'you think we'll get to see the King when he comes?' Barak asked. 'Close to?'

'It's possible.'

He blew out his cheeks. I was glad to see I was not the only one intimidated by that prospect. 'And there is an old enemy in his train,' I added, 'that we'd better avoid.'

He turned sharply. 'Who?'

'Sir Richard Rich. He'll be arriving with the King and the Privy Council. Cranmer told me. So, like I said, take care. Don't draw attention to us. We should try to escape notice, so far as we can.'

We untied the horses and led them to the gate, where another guard with a pike barred our way. I produced my letter again, and he raised the weapon to let us pass through. The great Minster reared up before us.

9910

9070

9150